Late Arrival

A Novel

By Christopher Ross

Notice:
This work is completely fictional. The characters, names, incidents, companies, products, and plot are products of the author's imagination or are used fictitiously. Any resemblance to actual persons, companies, products, or events is purely coincidental.

Reader discretion advised.
Late Arrival contains coarse language, mature subject matter, graphic depictions of gore, and a ridiculous amount of violence. This work may not be suitable for those with delicate sensibilities.

Chapter 1

Susan Brewbaker slammed her bedroom door closed, throwing the weight of her body against it to make sure it could not be opened behind her. She reached a trembling, sweat-glazed hand to the door handle, twisting the flimsy tab in the center of the knob to engage the lock. The latch clicked into place just as something crashed into the door, splintering the top section of the frame. One thunderous strike sounded at first. It was followed by the briefest of pauses and then a flurry of thumps and bangs from the hallway just outside the bedroom.

It was a struggle to control her breathing. Susan fought to be silent as she leaned into the door; her shoulder firmly planted against the glossy oak finish. She expected the door to break apart, or for the hinges to snap off, or for the frame itself to tear away from the wall. The barrier that protected her would only last for so long. And then what? She tried not to think about it as her body was rocked by another crashing blow to the door.

Every bit of her, right down to her bones, wished that she could let go and collapse to the floor in a heap. Tears had begun to form but it wouldn't be enough to cry. She wanted to scream until her lungs bled, to ball her fists and swing her arms and push out all of the pain and fear and anguish. And there would be time for this. But it wouldn't be now and Susan knew that. What came next wouldn't be easy. Nothing was going to be easy for her ever again. Susan was going to have to be tough, tougher than she had ever been. She would eventually have the opportunity to mourn, but only if she pulled herself together and survived the rest of the day.

A cramp formed in her hands. She had been holding onto the doorknob to keep it in place in case someone tried to turn it. No one did but the banging on the door persisted. Susan cautiously removed her hand from the knob but kept it outstretched, prepared to grab it again should the need arise. Her body stayed pressed on the door, which shook again as it was smashed once again from outside the bedroom. The top right and bottom right corners of the door bowed slightly from the impact, causing the door to split and form cracks.

The corners of the door continued to lurch inward with every hit. The door, frame, and screws keeping the hinges in place all seemed to be holding strong, stronger than one might expect, given the age of the house. It looked like the door would remain intact, at least for a little longer. Susan slowly, tentatively removed herself from the entryway. She held her hands out in front of her, as if willing the door to stay closed.

Walking barefoot to the other side of the room, Susan stopped to stand next to the head of the bed, right in front of the second-floor window. She looked out to examine the roof over the garage on the side of her home. It wasn't a flat roof, but it probably wasn't too steep to walk on. She gripped the handle on the lower portion of the window.

Susan tried to slide the bottom pane up and open, only to discover the window refused to budge. The August humidity must have caused the wooden sections of the window frame to swell and stick together. The white paint along the trim was soft and had the texture of a gooey plastic. Susan tugged with both hands, but as a woman approaching her sixty-eighth birthday, she lacked the strength to force the window open.

Susan turned back to the bed. It was neatly made and covered with a heavy lavender comforter embroidered with a floral pattern and topped with a total of seven pillows. And lying at the center of the bed was a bolt action hunting rifle.

It had a rather plain look to it. Made mostly of metal and wood, the weapon didn't look anything like those newfangled all-black military types of guns you see in sporting goods stores nowadays. There was no laser sight or flashlight, no vertical grip or adjustable stock. The rifle's accessories consisted only of a magnified scope and a tan leather sling with the word *Ruger* etched into it. Susan picked up the gun and stepped back toward the window, catching a glimpse of herself in the mirror as she went. She couldn't help but spare a brief pause to look herself over.

She was wearing tan pants and a plain purple sweater. Susan adjusted her glasses, the lenses of which had grown thick over the past four decades. Her hair, now a mess, was thin and gray and the wrinkles around her eyes were more pronounced than ever. It was foolish to pay any mind to vanity, given the circumstances but it was difficult not to. She looked tired and felt old. Where had all the years gone? And would there be any left, or was this it? If this was the end, what comes next? What happens to you when you die?

Yeah, yeah- your heart stops and so does your breathing. Your body temperature drops. Calcium builds up in your muscles and makes them grow rigid for a while. Your skin dries out and you start to stink as your organs begin to digest themselves and you soon become food for bacteria and bugs. But that's not what the question is asking.

Everybody knows what happens to your body when it dies. Your soul, your spirit or essence, whatever you want to call it, is something different and intangible. It's separate from your body, something more. It's that thing that makes you *you*. So maybe there's a better way to ask the question. What happens to you when your body dies? Susan had little doubt that she would soon find out.

Her focus shifted to the weapon in her hands, the barrel aimed at the floor with the carrying strap dangling loosely below. Susan was uncomfortable and looked out of place holding the firearm. Before she woke up that morning, she had only ever held a gun one time. She had never fired one, and certainly had never shot at a person. Trying to muster up some confidence, some courage, she tightened her grip on the rifle. The weapon was heavy in her hands, but it felt solid. It made her feel just a little bit safer.

Lifting the gun to her shoulder, she leveled it toward the bedroom door and tried to imitate how she'd seen her husband hold and aim it. Susan looked down the barrel and focused on the front sight as much as her eyes would permit. She caressed her index finger along the trigger and imagined what it might feel like to squeeze. She wondered if there would be a strong kickback. How loud would it sound? Would it hurt?

Another crash rang out, rattling the door, followed by what sounded like the scraping of nails digging into the oak finish. The noises were accompanied by a moan, deep and guttural, like it was coming from somewhere in the guts rather than from the lungs. There were no words, only noise- a noise that would tear the throat to ribbons on its way out. It was rage and agony made audible; a beast angry at the pain and to have been so unlucky to be in its grasp.

The groaning continued but Susan could hardly hear it over the smashing of wood, which had now increased in frequency and intensity. She moved closer to the doorway with the rifle leading the way. Glancing down to the gun, Susan slid the safety off and pressed the barrel against the door at chest height.

Her tears flowed freely now and despite her efforts to be quiet, several audible whimpers escaped her mouth. Now was the time to exercise that toughness. She squeezed her eyes shut and tried to slow her breathing, trying to calm herself and ignore the reality of what she planned to do. Susan wrapped her hand around the grip of the gun and placed her finger against the trigger. She would squeeze on three.

"One," she whispered to herself. Several moments passed. The banging on the door continued, along with the scraping and moans. She couldn't possibly go through with this. It just wasn't who she was. Who was she to take a life?

"Two," she said louder this time. Susan blocked out the churning in her guts and the aching in her chest. She should be able to defend herself, right? Everyone has the right to preserve their own life. But what if this was just her time to go? Was she trying to stick around past her allotted time? Who did she think she was? She should accept her fate.

"Three," came out so low not even Susan could hear. *Here we go,* she thought and shifted her grip on the rifle. Her eyes were closed as her countdown concluded and she kept them shut now. Susan was not willing to see what came next.

There was no explosive blast from the rifle. The painful jolt of the butt against her shoulder never came. Her finger had refused to pull the trigger. She just couldn't do it. It really was no surprise, not to Susan. She had been a fool for trying to trick herself into thinking she was stronger than she really was. And now there was no time left to reflect on this.

Sections of the door finally started to break apart. With all the punching, pounding, and kicking, there had been no doubt that the door would be penetrated sooner rather than later. Several inches along the door's bottom had already been kicked free and the hallway carpet could be seen through the opening.

Susan stepped back as a foot kicked through the hole, spraying scraps of wood into the room. Along with the debris, a full yellowed corn chip toenail sailed two feet through the air before it landed on the hardwood, spinning and skidding across the floor until it came to a stop just in front of Susan's feet. She couldn't stand it anymore. Her stomach rebelled. The petrified woman bent forward and coughed up a mouthful. Vomit rolled over her lips and down the front of her sweater. It splattered onto the bedroom floor and all over the severed toenail.

Bile torched the back of her throat. Susan ran her tongue between her teeth and gums, freeing bits of partially digested hot dog and potato salad. She spit up a wad of orange paste that hadn't quite made its way out on its own. The front of her sweater was crusted with dried regurgitation. Susan ran a sleeve over her mouth to clean off her lips. She tried to keep herself from heaving again as a whiff of stomach acid and old food caught in her nose.

Susan couldn't take her eyes off the foot in the hallway, the same one that was destroying her bedroom door, the bare and unprotected foot. It was still being swung and kicked into the door, darting into the room for a second and then retreating to gain more momentum and do it again. Each time it did this, more damage appeared on the door and the foot itself.

The little skin that remained was stretched and twisted, looking like a purple and black dish rag that was rung out and stuck to the bottom of a bleeding ankle. Surely all of the toes had been broken. The pinkie toe was nowhere to be found. The big toe had become twisted and pressed into the base of the foot, which was now little more than shredded tendons, raw meat, and exposed bones. Remarkably, this did not slow the attacker at all. It was like he hadn't even noticed. He just kept slamming his fists and kicking his ruined foot into the door.

Susan couldn't believe it. He was still trying to get into the room. The time for hesitation had run out and since she hadn't killed the maniac in the hall, she was going to have to get that damned window open as soon as possible. Holding the rifle with both hands, she readied herself to slam the

4

butt of the gun through the glass. She drew the weapon back, but immediately thought better of it.

Instead, she placed the gun on the floor, leaning it upright against a night stand. Smashing the window would be loud and could draw unwanted attention. Plus, climbing out the window would be difficult enough without having to maneuver around shards of broken glass.

With a flat palm, Susan struck the top and bottom edges of the window frame, hoping to jar it loose with four solid whacks. Once more, she grabbed the handle on the bottom of the window and pulled as hard as she could. This time, the lower section of the window slid upward a couple of inches. It was a nice start, but not enough room for an adult to fit through.

Maybe it was the adrenaline. Perhaps it was the panic and sense of urgency that had been growing. Enough was enough and there would be no more pussyfooting around. Susan balled her digits into a fist and punched the window frame as hard as she could. The first blow sent waves of pain through her hand and wrist, but she kept swinging over and over again until the window frame became free and dropped all the way back down.

The woman grasped the bottom of the window once more. It was a struggle but she managed to push it all the way to the top, as far open as the window would go. Susan grabbed the barrel of the rifle and stuck it butt-first out the window, placing it on the surface of the roof.

"Oh shoot," she said to no one. As soon as she let go, the gun began to slide down the slope of the roof, stopping only a few inches from the edge.

Relieved to see the rifle had not slid all the way off and fallen to the ground, Susan began moving herself outside. Using the window sill and the edge of the night table for leverage, the older woman lowered herself and began crawling through the opening. It was a slow process. She planted her hands on the surface of the roof and moved herself on all fours through the window into the afternoon sun.

Susan landed face down on the roof of the garage. She rolled over, resting her bottom on the shingles. After a moment to catch her breath, Susan used the exterior wall of the house for support as she carefully raised herself to her feet. She faced the house and looked back in through the window. The bedroom door was still mostly intact. She slid the window down to close it, leaving an opening of about an inch and a half. She could pull it open again if she needed to get back in, even though a small part of her knew she would never be back inside her home.

With unsteady footing, the woman walked in a half crouch with one hand out for balance as she went to retrieve the rifle. She moved little by little, dragging her feet, afraid she may fall and tumble off the roof if she went too fast. Susan wished she had grabbed a pair of shoes before locking herself in the bedroom. Her feet scraped against the hot asphalt shingles and each step burned even more than the last.

Susan made her way to the edge of the roof and slowly lowered her entire frame to grab the weapon. She picked up the gun and examined it. She didn't really know what she was looking for but couldn't find anything that was obviously broken. Deciding the gun was fine, she walked back up the way she had come, all the way to the white aluminum siding. She followed the exterior wall as far as it would go and gradually made her way to the far edge.

Pausing for a few breaths, she looked out and surveyed the suburban neighborhood. In the distance, there was a thick trail of black smoke rising from ground level into the sky. It was impossible to make out the source of the smoke as her view was obscured by houses and trees. Several cars were stopped in the streets, some still running and with doors left open. Susan could make out the faint sound of sirens. Were they from the police? Maybe they came from a fire truck or ambulance. She could never tell the difference.

The roar of a low-flying jet caught Susan off guard. She turned and instinctively ducked as the airplane passed overhead. There's no way it was a passenger or cargo plane. She was by no means an expert in aviation, but Susan thought it looked like a fighter jet. She knew a military aircraft when she saw it. Feeling silly for ducking when the plane was obviously much too high to hit her, Susan rose back to her feet and straightened her sweater with her left hand; the rifle still clutched in her right. She watched as the plane continued into the distance.

In the corner of her eye, Susan noticed a man slowly walking across the lawn on the other side of the street. The man, about six feet tall and wiry, wore blue jeans and a red flannel shirt with a faded red baseball cap. Thinking the man might be lost- or drunk by the way he was stumbling about, she feared he may not be fully aware of what was happening around him. She tried calling out to him.

"Young man," she shouted, "Are you okay?"

He didn't respond, at least not out loud. He turned to face her general direction and then took a few slow steps toward the street. The man was at least 40 yards away. Susan had to squint to make him out, and even then, she still couldn't see the man clearly. Despite her limited vision, she knew that something was off about him.

Remembering the rifle she was holding, Susan raised it high enough to look through the scope. It took her a moment to work out the details of how to position the rifle and how close to hold the lens to her eye. When the image became clear, she found she was looking at the grass of the lawn across the street. Scanning back and forth, she eventually managed to set her sights on the tall thin man, starting at his feet. Moving up his frame, she found his shirt was stained with dark red that had previously been camouflaged by the flannel pattern. Moving up and examining the man further, she was finally able to see his face.

"Dear Jesus," she said aloud.

The man's features were drenched in red. The tuft of black hair that stuck out from under his hat was matted to his forehead. There was a gaping hole where his left eye used to be, a crust of dead flesh and congealed blood framed the vacant socket. The man's lower jaw hung open. A dark liquid oozed out of his mouth and down the front of his shirt. His left arm bent at an unnatural angle, like there was another joint between his elbow and wrist.

Susan, though numb from her experience inside the house, couldn't stand the sight for more than a glance. Shuddering, she lowered the scope from her eye but still watched as the man took a few staggering steps in her direction. She heard what may have been a scream from the man, but it was muffled and wet sounding, like shouting underwater. The man had definitely seen her with his remaining eye and Susan couldn't be certain, but he looked like he was staring right at her.

"Just stay where you are," she begged. "If you can hear me, don't come any closer."

The man kept moving, now with a little more purpose. Taking one deliberate step after another, he was heading in the direction of the woman on the roof. Across the street, Susan watched the man, knowing he was coming for her. The woman was relatively safe while she was on the roof. Although she doubted he would be able to climb up to where she stood, Susan knew that allowing him to hang around on the ground below her was a lousy idea. What if she had to climb down? What if he attracted more people like him?

Susan once again raised the rifle and peered through the scope. She found the man in the sights

6

almost instantly. Cross hairs centered on the man's chest. The older woman had heard that people often survived a gunshot wound to the torso, assuming the bullet missed the heart and major arteries. Unfortunately, Susan was not a proficient shooter. She adjusted the gun to aim for the center of his face, just above the nose. How often did people live through a shot to the head? Less often, she imagined.

Still lacking confidence with the weapon and wanting to make sure one shot would be sufficient, she planned to wait until he got close enough for accuracy to be guaranteed. Susan tracked the man through the scope as he approached. She watched as he took his first step off the opposite curb and into the street. As soon as he stepped on the curb in front of her house, she would take the shot.

"Come on you bastard," she whispered through gritted teeth.

He was still coming, closer and faster now. The one-eyed man in the red flannel shirt was halfway across the street. Susan's body stiffened, preparing for the kick of the gun and the roar of the shot. The stock of the weapon was pulled firmly into her frail shoulder. She would not waver this time. She traced her finger along the grip of the rifle and onto the trigger, ready to squeeze. A gasp passed her lips as her concentration was broken by the sound of a horn and a blue colored blur streaking before her eyes.

"Son of a bitch," Jim shouted as he cut the steering wheel hard to the left. He'd avoided running the man over, but failed to keep from hitting him at all. Jim looked to the passenger side mirror to check if the man was still standing, but found the mirror was gone. There was no going back for it.

"Asshole," Jim muttered to himself. That guy had just walked right out in front of the car. Who does that? He hadn't even flinched at the sound of the horn. Jim looked over his shoulder and out the back window. The man was still up and moving. Was he okay? Was he aware that he'd just been struck by a vehicle? And holy shit- is that woman on her roof holding a gun?

Jim pivoted in his seat; his focus back on the road. The faint report of a gunshot sounded in the distance behind him but he didn't look back. His foot pressed down harder on the accelerator, the engine whined and then complied. The blue coupe continued its trek through the suburbs, weaving around the occasional stopped car and barely slowing as it approached the next intersection where it turned right. Luckily, no one else was running the stop sign.

He had been driving in silence. He was sweating- he was always sweating but the summer months produced an obscene amount of perspiration. A salty mist had formed between his palms and the steering wheel. The pale skin of his forehead glistened below a thicket of auburn hair. He ran the back of his wrist across his brow and dried his hands on the front of his black polo shirt, right on the small pocket of pudge just above his waist.

Jim rolled down the driver's side window and switched on the radio. Static poured from the speakers. Keeping his finger on the scan button, the young man tried to find a station that was still broadcasting on the AM band. There came one station after another of crackling, distortion, and prerecorded emergency messages. He had nearly reached the end of the dial before a clear, live channel came through.

"...we have been following this story the best we can," came a woman's voice, halfway through a sentence.

"According to police, the violence that broke out in downtown Buffalo this morning has expanded into the surrounding neighborhoods. There have been reports of sporadic violence, including

7

random attacks in Amherst, Niagara Falls, the Twin Cities, and other suburban areas. Officials are urging residents to stay inside and to keep the doors locked..." the voice faded into the background. Jim had already stopped listening.

The blue Pontiac slowed to a crawl, about ten miles per hour. Jim spun the volume knob and reduced the stereo to barely a hum. His head swiveled back and forth, scanning out the driver's side window, then out the passenger's window and back again. Rows of houses passed by on each side. He made a mental note of each home with an open front door. One in particular was a two-story cottage style home with clapboard siding, a cedar shake roof, and a large flagpole in the front yard. There was a picture window on the lower level with a thin lace curtain on the inside.

Some sort of commotion was taking place on the other side of the glass, in what Jim presumed to be the living room. All he could see was a pair of shadows moving from left to right; the curtain being tussled as one of them passed by. For an instant, the drapery was pressed against the window and yanked hard to the right before falling back into place. Everything remained still.

There were no people outside. The yards were clear and no one was visible from between the houses. There was enough time to get out. The car came to a stop several feet past a driveway. Using his right arm for leverage, Jim leaned as far as he could into the passenger's side of the car and pressed his face to the window. He looked up to see a modest Colonial with redwood siding and a single car garage attached on the left side.

The steering wheel cut all the way to the right and the car jumped backwards, Jim giving it a little too much gas as he backed into the driveway. The Pontiac rested with its rear bumper pressed against the wooden garage door. Leaving the window down and the car running, he got out of the vehicle and walked towards the house, gently closing the door behind him.

He walked about ten steps and stopped. Turning back, he jogged to the car and opened the door as wide as it would go. Jim figured he would probably be leaving in a hurry. The time it takes to open a car door may not seem like much, but the ability to skip this seemingly insignificant task could mean all the difference in the world.

Eight stairs led to the front porch of the house. Taking them two at a time, Jim made his way to the top and across the bare wood floor. He reached the front door and tried the knob. It was unlocked. Before opening, he pressed his ear to the door, straining to make out any sounds from the inside. Not hearing any noise, and not knowing if he should have expected to hear anything through two inches of solid wood, Jim twisted the knob and opened the door. His foot raised to take the first step inside, but froze before landing again. He was losing his nerve.

"Don't be a pussy," he scolded himself.

Jim pushed the door the rest of the way open and walked into the front hallway. Though it was still bright outside, little sunlight made its way into the house. The curtains were all down, completely blocking the windows. All of the lights were off. The stairs to the second floor were at the opposite wall on the right side. Straight ahead was the living room. The glow from a TV could be seen from within.

"Hello?" Jim called into the house. No one answered.

In the living room, a woman sat on the couch. She had a heavy green blanket wrapped all around her, clutching the edges and pulling it tight to her body. The woman was maybe in her late forties but looked to be much older from the way the skin on her face seemed to droop. Her brown hair, now mostly grayed, clung to her forehead, which was shimmering with sweat. She wore a blue hooded sweatshirt and faded jeans that were covered in mud.

8

She faced the TV but didn't seem to be watching. For one thing, her eyes were aimed at the floor in front of her. For another, the TV showed only the colored bars of a test pattern. She didn't react when Jim entered the room. The woman didn't even look up. Neither person spoke.

Jim couldn't decide if he should try to talk to her. Careful to avoid getting too close, he took a half step in the woman's direction. He leaned down, trying to look up at the woman in an effort to establish eye contact. Getting no reaction from her, Jim slowly waved his hand in front of his body. She still refused to acknowledge that there was anyone in the room with her.

This was preferable. Jim stood upright and strode across the living room, heading for the door to the basement. Once on the basement stairs, he closed the door and tried to do it as quietly as possible. The steps were unpainted wood planks that should have been replaced years earlier. Each one creaked and settled as he made his way to the uncovered cement floor at the bottom.

The basement was lit by a pair of naked bulbs hanging from the ceiling. The space was completely unfinished. It housed the furnace and water heater but not much else. Adjacent to the stairway was a small collection of cardboard boxes stacked neatly on top of each other and a solid wood gun cabinet with clear sliding Plexiglas doors. Jim was not surprised to find the cabinet had been left unlocked. He was, however, let down to see that of the 10 slots inside the case, only one actually held a gun.

There was a lone double barrel shotgun resting inside the case. It was an Ithaca Model 600 with stacked barrels and a gold trigger. Jim reached in, grabbing the gun by its cool iron barrels. Turning away from the case, Jim held the gun by the grip and forearm. He pulled the stock in to his shoulder and closed one eye as he looked down the top barrel and focused on the front sight bead. Jim felt like an ass and realized that all people must do this when they first pick up a gun. He lowered it to his side, struck with a bit of private embarrassment.

There's not a person alive who doesn't immediately mock-aim a gun as soon as they hold it. Whether it was real life or in the movies, he always noticed this and it always stuck out to him as being odd. Stupid Jim probably would have spent the rest of the afternoon contemplating this if he hadn't been pulled back to reality by the sound of footsteps on the floor above him. The boards that lined the basement ceiling jostled slightly, releasing a thin cloud of dirt that floated to the ground in slow motion. The dust made a haze around the bare bulbs and reminded Jim that he really didn't have time to stand around pondering his banal observations.

Jim turned and moved toward the stairs after giving the gun cabinet one last look-over. There was nothing else inside. He looked up to the ceiling, back to the gun case, and then down to the gun in his hand. He pressed his thumb against the top lever. The front end of the weapon dipped forward as the breach clicked open. Looking down into the yawning barrels, Jim saw two vacant holes and realized he was forgetting something: ammunition.

"Balls."

He dropped the shotgun at his feet and raced back to the stacked containers along the wall. He grabbed the box on top of the pile and pulled the lid open. Of course none of the boxes were labeled. The first was empty and he tossed it aside. One by one, boxes were pulled from their places. The tops were yanked open so Jim could look inside. Most held gloves, small tools, and outdoorsy stuff. Each of the boxes fell to the floor, spilling their contents onto the cold cement.

"Come on dammit," Jim said out loud, reaching the last box.

He knelt down to look inside. *Finally*, he thought to himself. There was gun oil with cleaning cloths, safety glasses, and yes- ammo. There were two yellow and green boxes of Remington twenty-gauge shotgun shells. One was sealed and the other was about half empty. He stuffed the full box of twenty-five into one of the over-sized cargo pockets in his shorts.

There were fourteen shells left in the already-open box. Grabbing three or four at a time, Jim put all but two into his right front pocket, discarding the empty container before he retrieved the gun from the floor. Shells were loaded into both of the open barrels and Jim slammed the gun closed. He began to climb the stairs, but not before making sure the safety was off.

Jim flung the door open and slowly entered the living room. He kept a tight grasp on the gun and hoped he wouldn't be shooting it. He could feel moisture collecting between the grip and the palm of his hand. Looking further into the room, he saw the woman was still on the couch. She hadn't moved. Jim thought the woman was the only other person in the house, but if she wasn't up and walking around, who was?

His question was soon answered. As Jim began to walk toward the front hall, he passed the doorway into the kitchen and knew that he'd detected something in his peripheral vision. He stopped short, despite his better judgment begging him to keep moving.

The best thing for him to do was to walk right through the room and out the front door. There would be absolutely no problem in just exiting the house, not stopping, not turning around, and not investigating what he thought he may have seen. That was the smart thing to do. But instead of doing what was smart, Jim took a half step backwards and turned to peer through the passage that led into the kitchen.

The girl stared at the floor, not moving. She was about Jim's age, early twenties, and about five and a half feet tall. Her gaunt figure stood hunched over just a bit, causing her greasy blonde hair to hang forward and cover her face. She was wearing a white tank top and jeans. Both looked too big on her small frame and both were smeared with red and brown stains. Her head raised and her mouth hung open. A thick stream of saliva poured over her lips and down her chin as her eyes met Jim's.

Jim stepped backwards, calmly and silently so as not to startle the girl. He gradually shifted the gun to his hip, moving it up and closer to his shoulder as he tried to make his way across the room to the front door. He kept his index finger on the trigger, but applied no pressure. Jim was able to put about eight feet between himself and the girl.

She let out a shriek, loud and ferocious. Muscles wriggled below her jaw, twisting tendons into cords that pressed against the inside of her neck. Her hands formed gnarled fists and the blue veins in her forearms stood out in defiant contrast through her near-translucent skin. The pitch of her voice deepened as she clenched her jaw with enough force to crack teeth. Her eyes burned a hole through Jim, as if watching something only she could see, something she needed to tear out of him.

He couldn't believe it; she was actually growling at him like some kind of animal. Jim moved quicker now, but kept facing her. The girl lunged forward and ran at him; arms in front of her and mouth opened, baring teeth. She covered the distance to Jim almost instantly but he reacted in time. There was no thinking about it. No hesitation.

Thunder filled the room, echoing off walls that only served to intensify the roar of the blast. The stock slammed into Jim's shoulder. Pellets exploded from the top barrel, moving eleven-hundred feet per second through the air and slicing into the girl's shirt. Holes appeared immediately as the buckshot tore into her abdomen, kicking out bits of torn cloth and wet flesh. Mid-stride, the girl crumpled to the floor, landing face-down as a red mist settled around her body.

The woman on the sofa seemed as though she hadn't noticed the commotion. She was still sitting in the same spot, still looking straight ahead. The TV remained on, showing the same test

10

pattern and playing a low constant ringing sound. The room looked just as it had when Jim arrived, aside from the addition of a corpse.

Jim reached into his pocket for his keys before remembering that the car was still running. He meant to take his first step toward the front door but found himself unable to move his left leg. It must have been caught on something. Or perhaps more accurately, his leg was caught by something.

As it turns out, the girl wasn't dead after all. If she had been killed, she wouldn't have been able to grab the heel of Jim's shoe with her left hand. If deceased, the girl would not be reaching for his ankle with her other arm. And again, if she was in fact dead, she sure as Hell would not be opening her mouth and preparing to take a bite out of his exposed calf. Dead people just don't do that type of shit.

The young man stumbled backwards and almost fell on his ass but he managed to pull his foot free, barely managing to stay upright in the process. The girl screamed as he freed himself from her grasp. She placed her hands on the carpet and pressed to raise herself but ended up not making it any further. Before she could even look up, Jim pressed the barrel of the gun against the top of her head and squeezed the trigger again. The second blast didn't seem quite so loud as the first.

Jim was confident the girl would not be getting up again. Blood soaked into the carpet, forming a burgundy lake around the upper half of her body. A broken pasta bowl of bone, hair, and brain lie where her head should have been. Her neck just sort of ended, leaving a cavernous tube of flesh that spewed red gristle out onto the floor.

Again, the woman on the couch refused to look up, still mesmerized by the test pattern on the television. Bright red specks dotted her face. The blanket and sofa were now littered with clumps of scalp, strings of blonde hair and pink colored mush.

If Jim didn't get out of there soon, he knew he was going to be sick. Or worse, maybe he would find someone else who was inside the house and waiting to be discovered. He pressed the top lever of the gun, causing the barrels to open and eject the spent casings. He walked toward the door, careful not to step in any of the red fluid as he went.

Jim loaded two more shells into the shotgun once he was back outside. He made his way down the front steps and climbed into his car. The gun went onto the passenger's side with the business end pointed at the floor. He pulled the door shut and put the car in drive. Jim pulled out of the driveway going left, back the way he had come. He mashed the accelerator into the floor, racing down the road and out of the neighborhood.

Chapter 2

Jim sank into a padded black cushion and tried to somehow get comfortable on the rickety secondhand futon. Realizing that he was about as cozy as he was going to be able to get, Jim tried to relax as he stared ahead into an empty blue screen. The room was otherwise devoid of light. There was only one window and someone had used thumbtacks to hang a blanket over the glass and block out the orange glow of a slowly setting sun.

Okay, so you might be wondering what happened to Susan. You've probably got a few other questions, like, where was Jim going with that shotgun? Who was that blonde girl he killed? Why would anyone own a futon? Just what in the Hell is going on here? Relax. You're going to find out. But in order for you to properly understand, it's best to start at the beginning, a few days before everyone went a little nutty and everything fell apart.

It was Saturday- date night. Well, it was sort of date night. Jim's rent was going to be due soon and Beth never had any cash so the couple was going to have an evening in at Beth's house, that is to say, Beth's mother's house.

Beth slid a disc into the DVD player and sat down beside him. She smiled and held his hand, squeezing gently. Now they both stared into a blue screen on the TV. Beth grabbed the remote control and began pressing buttons before opening the battery door. There were batteries inside and the player was on, but nothing showed on the screen. Beth stood back up and marched over to the television where she fumbled with the cords that ran behind the set to the DVD player.

Her hair, dyed glossy black, was pulled back into a pony tail. She wore a pair of stretchy black yoga pants and a white tank top. It wasn't what you'd call a fancy outfit, but Jim liked the way the fabric clung to the skin of her toned body. Beth could never be described as full figured. She was one of those girls who looked like she would benefit from a few extra meals here and there, but what little there was of her, Jim enjoyed. He sat on the futon, his eyes scanning up her legs and pausing to enjoy the view of her ass.

"My sister's been messing with my stuff again," Beth announced, pulling Jim from his trance. She was still half crouched, unplugging cables and then plugging them back in. She continued, raising the tone of her voice, "I told her to stay out of my room and stop touching my things."

"Let me take a look at it," Jim told her. "I bet I can fix it."

"This is bullshit," said Beth, ignoring Jim's offer to help.

"I can't keep dealing with this crap all the time," she punctuated her statement by pounding her fist on the top cover of the DVD player.

That's going to fix it, Jim thought and rolled his eyes at Beth, whose back was still turned. He didn't see what the big deal was. Her sister used the DVD player and when returning it, had set it up incorrectly. Jim didn't think this was the end of the world, but what did he know?

"What crap?" Jim asked. He held in a sigh and did his best to sound concerned rather than annoyed. "Has she been doing something else? Other than borrowing the DVD player, I mean."

"Ugh, you don't get it," she groaned, "And I don't know why you ask. I'm sure you don't care."

"No, I care," Jim replied with sincerity. "What's going on?"

"Just forget it."

"No, I-" Jim was cut off.

"I said just forget it!" Beth shrieked as she swiped the DVD player off the TV stand.

Without another word, she walked out of the room, stomping her feet as she went and almost tripping on the piles of laundry strewn across the floor. She passed the empty laundry basket and walked out of the bedroom. Jim could hear her feet thumping through the hallway and down the steps to the first floor of the house. He sat in place for a few moments, debating whether to follow her or stay in the bedroom and fix the TV.

Jim grunted as he pulled himself off the futon. He shut off the television and followed Beth's path to the ground floor, past the bare walls of the upstairs hall and down the carpeted steps. He found Beth in the sparsely finished kitchen, leaning against the counter with her arms crossed and looking at her feet.

"Okay, baby doll. What's wrong?" he asked when she looked up to acknowledge he had entered the room.

"I can't stand living here, my sister's always coming in my room and taking my stuff. She's always starting fights with me and my mom. Plus, I have to listen to my parents bitching at each other whenever my dad feels like showing up." The sink beside her was piled high with dirty dishes. She grabbed a foggy-looking glass and filled it halfway with tap water. She continued on about how her mother treated her sister like the favorite child, cussing her mother between sips.

"You know where they are now?" Beth asked. Not waiting for an answer, she said, "They're out having mother-daughter time, dinner and ice cream. Of course, I wasn't asked to go."

"That's because they knew you were having me over," Jim explained. "I'm sure they figured you wouldn't be able to go if I was coming over. It's not like they intentionally excluded you. I could take you for ice cream if you want."

"They planned this two days ago," Beth said. "They didn't know what my plans were. They could have at least asked."

"Well, have you tried sitting down with your mother and sister and talking with them? Maybe the three of you should get together and see if there's some way to cut down on the fighting and whatnot. It might be a way for you to explain how you feel about everything and maybe they wouldn't give you such a hard time." Jim hoped his low-quality advice would calm her down, but it didn't.

"I've tried to talk to them but they don't listen. All they do is bitch all the time and no one wants to hear my side." Beth slammed the glass onto the laminate counter top. "My mom isn't interested, my sister's a pain in the ass, and even when my dad does show up, he doesn't come to see me. He asks my sister about school and her boyfriend, then he gives my mother some excuse about why he's so busy, and then he leaves."

She sniffled and rubbed back tears before continuing. "Last time he was over, he didn't even say hello. I was on the couch and he walked right by."

Jim handed her a napkin from the stack on the kitchen table. Beth took it without saying a word. She wiped at her eyes again, blew her nose, and tossed the napkin in the direction of the already overfilled garbage can in the corner of the room. The soiled napkin bounced off the top of the heap and fell to the floor. Neither Jim nor Beth could be bothered to pick it up.

Beth returned to her original position and folded her arms across her chest. Jim, now feeling sorry for her, went to her and put his arm around her. She didn't react; it was like trying to hug a statue. He took a step back, getting the hint that she didn't want to be touched.

"I uh, I'm sorry you're having a rough time lately," Jim stammered. "I wish there was something I could do to help."

"Yeah right," Beth scoffed.

"I'm serious," Jim said defensively. "*Is* there something I can do?"

"Not unless you can find me another place to live," she answered. "And I know you don't want me to move in with you."

Beth's comment was more of a question than a statement.

"I guess I hadn't really thought of it." Jim didn't realize he had taken a step back from her. "We've been together six months, you don't think that's a little soon to move in together?"

"It's been almost seven months," she corrected him. "And so what, you don't think we're going to stay together?"

"No, it's not that. It's just, my apartment is sort of small for two people and since you aren't working right now, I mean, not that I would expect you to pay all the bills or anything, but I'm not sure I can afford to support both of us right now. I guess maybe we could talk about it, but," Jim let his words trail off, he was rambling and Beth's expression had changed from inquisitive to stern. "Hey, do you want to try to watch the movie and relax, ya know, get your mind off of this stuff?"

"No," Beth answered, absent of tone and expression.

"Are you sure? I bet we can get the TV fixed and-" Jim was cut off again.

"No," Beth sharply repeated herself.

"Okay, is there something else you want to do?"

"No, I just want to be alone," Beth said quietly.

"Did I do something wrong?" Jim asked, sounding a little sheepish.

"Just leave me alone," she answered.

"But-" Jim began to protest.

"Leave me alone!" Beth shouted. She stormed out of the kitchen, going around the corner and into the bathroom, closing herself inside. Jim could hear something crash against a wall from the other side of the door.

"Fine," Jim said to no one as he left the kitchen. He walked through the living room to the front door and began to put on his sneakers. He grabbed the door's handle to leave and then stopped. Jim patted the pockets of his shorts but didn't hear the jingling of keys. He reached into his pockets to confirm they were empty. Jim kicked off his shoes and turned around to go back upstairs.

What a mess, Jim thought as he walked into the bedroom. Assuming the keys must have fallen out of his pocket when he was sitting down, he started with the futon. He grabbed all three pillows off the big cushion one at a time, looking under them and tossing them away. When the keys didn't turn up under the pillows, he grabbed the comforter off the seat with both hands and shook it out.

It looked like the blanket held nothing but dust, and quite a lot of it. But given a good shake, the blanket revealed itself to have been hiding something else between its folds. Fluttering end over end, it fell to land in front of Jim's feet on the stained and worn-out carpet. He looked down to find the red and white foil of an empty condom wrapper. It was not his preferred brand.

He just looked at it. Jim didn't move for what felt like an hour, but really couldn't have been more than thirty seconds or so. He was frozen in place, paralyzed by that kicked-in-the-balls feeling that was spreading and making his entire abdomen ache.

She thought they were going to move in together and she's sleeping around? How exactly did she expect that to work? Unemployment would leave you with plenty of time to get humped by strangers. Or maybe that's why she couldn't work. Who's got time for a job when there's neighborhood men to jump on? You can fill your free time by filling your- okay, you get the point.

Pushover Jim immediately began to invent excuses on her behalf. *You're jumping to conclusions*, he told himself. She's dated and had boyfriends before Jim came along. There was no way to know how long that wrapper had been sitting there. The room wasn't exactly tidy. It had probably been years since its last thorough cleaning. A spent condom wrapper could have easily been hiding in the mess of scrambled bedding for seven months. And it's probably not the only one in the bedroom. Jim cringed as he considered this.

Sure, he didn't know what she did most of the time when he wasn't with her. That's not a big deal though, is it? The used condom wrapper wasn't necessarily proof of infidelity. And Beth hadn't given any solid indication that she was sleeping around. But maybe he was wrong to trust her. On the other hand, maybe he never actually trusted her in the first place.

So what was he to do? March downstairs and demand an explanation? He couldn't do that. He wouldn't. The best thing to do was to forget about it. Beth was a good girl, wasn't she? Of course she was. *You're crazy, she's not cheating,* he thought. Jim had to forget about the wrapper and all his panicky thoughts. He just needed to find his keys and get moving. He could evaluate this on the drive home, think things through before taking any action.

Jim scanned the rest of the room, sifting through clothing, jewelry, magazines, and whatever else was lying wherever it happened to fall out of Beth's hands. Then he remembered the chest of drawers along the wall adjacent to the door.

His keys were on top of the dresser, next to some pens, a pair of panties, and two prescription pill bottles. Jim picked them up and examined the labels. Along with Beth's full name, the first label read *Valproic Acid* and the second bottle was labeled *Xanax*. The prescriptions had been filled over a month earlier and both bottles were still filled almost to the top. Beth's recent mood swing now began to make sense.

Jim gave a quick look over his shoulder to confirm he was still alone in the room. He shrugged to himself, opening the Xanax bottle and isolating one of the tiny white pills. There was nothing he could use to wash it down, so Jim popped the tablet into his mouth and swallowed it dry. It was bitter and chalky going down, sort of like chewing an aspirin. Jim replaced the cap and put the bottle back where he'd found it, not that anyone would notice anything out of place in this hog parlor of a bedroom. Then he grabbed his keys from the top of the dresser and hurried back downstairs.

Beth was sitting on the sofa in the living room watching TV, or at least looking at the TV. She was facing the direction of the set, purposely ignoring Jim and avoiding eye contact. Jim crossed the room and sat down next to her on the couch.

"Are you okay?" Jim placed his hand on Beth's. She tensed but otherwise didn't react; not even a look in his direction.

15

"I really wish you would talk to me," Jim added, "You know I hate it when you get like this."

"Well, get used to it." Her response was cold. She narrowed her eyes, still forcing herself to look straight ahead.

"Fine," Jim said as he stood back up.

He walked in silence to the front door and slipped into his sneakers. Beth wasn't going to talk to him and there was no point in trying. He'd been through this with her a number of times, enough to know that she couldn't be reasoned with once she was in one of her moods.

All he could do was give her space and time to let her sort things out on her own. He'd try calling her later. Hopefully she'd be feeling better by then. That was the best plan. That was what he should have done. And even though he knew better, Jim couldn't stop himself from trying one last time to get through to her.

"I know you haven't been taking your medicine," Jim said softly. He was careful to make it sound more like an observation and not an accusation.

"Yes I have," Beth spat her response. "I take it every day."

"No," Jim sighed, "You haven't."

"Oh?" Beth asked raising her eyebrows and finally looking in Jim's direction. "And how would you know?"

"I saw the bottles in your room," he admitted. "They're both full."

"Well, it really isn't any of your damn business, is it?"

This was not the response Jim had hoped for but it was the one he'd expected. Beth quickly went back to pretending he wasn't there. She picked up the remote control and continued flipping through channels.

"I'm not trying to give you a hard time, I just worry-" Jim was interrupted.

"Just leave," Beth demanded.

"But-"

"Just leave! Get the hell out of my house," she yelled; her voice cracking with anger halfway through her statement.

The TV remote sailed across the room. Jim was the intended target but it slammed into the wall about 2 feet from where he was standing, losing two of its rubber buttons as it fell to the floor. Not another word was said by either of them. Beth shifted in her seat, now looking away from Jim and no longer facing the television. Was she crying again? Jim couldn't tell.

He let himself out and walked to the blue coupe parked in the driveway. Jim climbed in and started the engine. Looking through the windshield, he strained to see in through the front window of the house. He hoped to see Beth looking back at him, calling for him to come back inside, eager to apologize for how she'd been acting and ready to make everything good again. What he saw instead was the glow of the TV reflecting off the glass and a pair of curtains left partially open. No Beth.

The transmission caught and jerked as Jim shifted into reverse and backed out of the driveway. Beth lived in one of Lockport's less desirable neighborhoods. Jim had been making the thirty-minute drive to see her on a regular basis for six, make that seven, months at this point. Even after all this time, the neighborhood still made him nervous.

About half of the homes on her street were vacant. Most had at least one boarded door or window, including those that were still occupied. There was still enough sunlight to see the glaring signs of neglect. Block after block, there were houses with peeling trim, rotted siding, shingle roofs that were bowed and deteriorating, overgrown lawns, and with driveways where weeds victoriously pushed through a multitude of cracks and towered over the concrete.

Jim switched on the radio as he pulled onto South Transit Road. He lit a cigarette and forced himself to stop clenching his jaw. Heading home angry and alone in the afternoon; this was not how the day was supposed to turn out. He'd planned to spend the evening relaxing, watch a movie and maybe wrap things up with an intimate encounter. From the looks of things, Beth had been having some encounters without him and Unlucky Jim was only around for the Bipolar mood swings.

He decided to treat himself to a few beers along the way. If he couldn't get laid, at least he could still get drunk. Jim had never been big on going to bars or clubs, so he'd pick up a six pack to drink at home. He'd be drinking alone but that suited him just fine. Jim would be spending another boring evening watching reruns on cable in the world's loneliest apartment but he didn't have to be sober for it.

Chapter 3

You've heard of Louis Pasteur. Most people know him as that old French dude who figured out how to keep you from getting diarrhea from a glass of milk. What you may not know is he also developed some of the world's first vaccines, including one for the rabies virus. Pasteur began studying the disease in 1880 and over the next four years, he would identify the infectious agent and find a way to slow it down.

By 1884, an early version of the rabies vaccine had proven effective in dogs. The first human subject would be treated the following year. News of the vaccine's success spread quickly and soon, people from all over were traveling to France for treatment after having been bit by a rabid animal.

Pasteur had created what is known as a live attenuated vaccine. It consisted of desiccated nervous tissue which contained a weakened, though still active virus. The theory was that if you introduced a less aggressive strain of a virus to an organism, the organism's immune system would identify the infection and strengthen its own defenses against it.

Work to improve the rabies immunization would continue over the years and decades to come. The next incarnations of the vaccine would still be derived from infected nervous tissue, but they would begin using inactive strains of the virus. That is, until 1946 when Hilary Koprowski decided to get in on the rabies action.

Hilary Koprowski is a name that might not sound so familiar. He, yes *he*, was a Polish virologist who moved to the United States and is best known for inventing the world's first effective live polio vaccine in 1948. Koprowski used a rat brain to cultivate the virus. He then used a regular kitchen blender to liquefy the brain before drinking the horrible concoction. It was gross, but it worked. Koprowski had successfully inoculated himself against polio.

This seemingly overshadowed his work on the rabies vaccine from two years earlier. Until that time, rabies vaccines were still using virus taken from nervous tissue. It was effective in combating rabies, but it came with the risk of unwanted side effects, including infections and encephalitis. Koprowski had discovered a way to adapt the rabies virus to non-nervous tissue, resulting in fewer complications. His new live virus vaccine was tested in 1961 with promising results.

A decade later, Koprowski and his team of scientists had produced a new and improved version of his rabies vaccination. It was originally accomplished using a living version of the virus but the medical community at the time was strongly opposed to using a live rabies vaccine. The team then developed a version using an inactive strain and progress continued from there.

By the end of the 1980's, an oral inoculation method had been created to immunize wildlife and limit the threat of rabies. This was made using live vaccine virus that had been genetically altered to create a concentration of a material that stimulates immunity to the disease. The essential compound within the vaccine enters the animal's cells while in the animal's mouth. The cells then produce a chemical called rabies virus glycoprotein, which causes the immune system to produce disease-fighting antibodies.

Pellets were then made to distribute the oral vaccine. The pellets were a couple of inches long and an inch or so tall and wide. Each tablet was filled with a clear paste that contained the vaccine itself. The outer shells were a yellow-brown film made of fish meal. Raccoons apparently find this delicious and irresistible.

The idea was that the small bars would be distributed in areas where they would be found by wild animals. The critters would eat the pellet, their natural disease defense systems would learn how to fight the infection, and they would become immune to rabies. Even if that critter was then bit by an infected predator, they would not develop the illness. They'd probably still die, there's no inoculation for that quite yet.

In 1990, the United States Department of Agriculture began a trial program in which thousands of the vaccine pellets were dropped from airplanes over rural neighborhoods and wooded areas in Virginia. The same test was performed in Pennsylvania the following year. A variety of agencies in a number of states would then go on to develop their own versions of the program, including the New York Department of Health.

The practice would continue periodically for years to come. The problem with this strategy was getting the animals to actually eat the vaccine. Many pellets would remain in the spots where they landed for long periods of time. Seasons of rain and snow would pass and the elements would eventually cause the pellets to dissolve and soak into the ground, but this process could take years.

Keep an eye out on your next hike through the woods. You might be able to find some of these pellets on the ground, untouched and uneaten. Your new pal Chester would have spotted one if he'd been paying attention. One of these vaccine bars was lying half-covered in grass about three feet from where he was resting.

Chester woke bit by bit, slowly regaining consciousness after spending close to an hour in that stage between deep sleep and wakeful grogginess. His brain knew he was awake, but the rest of his body refused to play along. Sunlight warmed his body and glowed through his closed eyelids. The faintest hint of a breeze caressed the length of his naked body. A breeze? That couldn't be right.

Opening his eyes, Chester looked up to see a cloudless sky; the sun's rays partially obscured by tree branches overhead. He detected the scraping of claws on wood. An Eastern Gray Squirrel made its way up the trunk of the tree, freezing in place when it heard Chester stirring below. The squirrel looked back at Chester and almost seemed to make eye contact. The salt and pepper fur on the rodent's face looked wet and clumped together. It sniffed the air; its nose twitching and head bobbing. The squirrel then scurried higher up the tree where it disappeared amongst the foliage, leaving only wet footprints behind.

His waking stupor had left him temporarily transfixed by the filthy rodent. Now fully alert, Chester forced himself to snap out of it and return to reality. He must have fallen asleep outside, but how could he have slept so soundly on the ground? Normally he wouldn't be able to sleep unless he was in his own bed. Chester rolled to his side and looked up to inspect his surroundings.

The sun's position in the sky indicated that it was some time in the afternoon. How could he have slept so late and why on Earth was he waking up in his yard? Wait- scratch that. He woke in *a* yard, but it wasn't *his* yard. Chester quickly became aware of a throbbing in his chest as he struggled to make sense of his predicament.

He could hear people nearby, but he didn't see anyone. They probably hadn't seen him either. Or had they? Of course they hadn't. There definitely would have been a reaction if someone had seen him. They would have at least approached him, right? Chester pulled himself to his feet. He did one of those full-body stretches and shook free the blades of grass that clung to his back.

His stomach bellowed an audible demand for food. He was starving. It felt like he hadn't eaten in days, but there's no way he could have been lying in the yard for that long. The aroma of meat invaded Chester's olfactory system. He couldn't place the meat exactly, nor could he see if someone was barbecuing, but damn that smelled appetizing. A stream of drool ran over his lips and trickled to the ground as he continued sniffing the air. His nostrils would lead him to his next meal.

Chester knew he should try to get home but could he figure out how to get there? None of his surroundings looked familiar. He was in someone's back yard and facing the rear of the house. There would presumably be a street on the other side. There was a wooded area behind him. The vegetation was too dense to make out anything past the initial tree line. He turned back, looking forward again and facing the yard leading up to the back of a two-story home. There was no fence around the yard. This was good. Chester would make his way to the street and try to gain his bearings.

He took his first steps toward the house, moving quickly at first and then slowing. Something didn't feel right. There was an odd sensation on his left side that he hadn't noticed until he started moving. It wasn't painful but there was sort of a fuzzy numb feeling along his left ribs. Chester stopped moving and examined himself. Thick mounds of congealed blood matted to the skin and clung to his hair, creating a rust colored-plaster over where the skin had broken and making it impossible to see the wound itself.

On one hand, it didn't hurt. There probably would have been pain if he'd sustained any real damage. That made sense. Pain is the body's way of letting you know something is wrong. Receptors throughout the body send a pain signal through the central nervous system to tell the brain, "Hey buddy, we've got a problem here."

So, it stands to reason that if you've got no pain, you probably haven't got a serious injury. But what if the nerves themselves had been damaged? If you've got pierced skin, shattered bones, and dead tissue, those pain receptors might not be working the way they used to. Based on the volume of blood and the rotten stench that wafted up from the lesion on his chest, Chester absolutely should have been concerned, whether it hurt or not.

For the time being, it was a blessing to feel no pain. Any further unpleasantness would slow him down and at that moment, his top priority was getting out of there. The fuzzy feeling and the blood on his side could be ignored until he got home. He needed to get out of this yard, away from this strange neighborhood. And he needed to eat.

Chester not only failed to remember what had caused the hole in his chest, he had no idea what had gotten in through that same hole. He had no way of knowing what sickness had invaded his body, or that it used the flow of his own blood as an express route to his brain; that it had settled in and made itself at home. Oblivious to the symptoms that lie just ahead, he pushed any thought of this injury to the back of his mind. Chester was on a mission and nothing else mattered, only home and getting fed.

Trotting across the grass, Chester continued toward the house. He could still hear people nearby; the voices growing louder and seeming to come from all directions. There was no one in sight, but his ears told him there was definitely someone close to him, someone behind him. He immediately came to a stop and spun around to look. There was no one there, just the open space of a vacant yard. They were hiding, waiting for him to let his guard down. They were going to sneak up on him. They were going to kill him.

Well, we'll just see about that. You think you're going to sneak up on Chester? You want to try and take him out? Good luck, you son of a bitch. You go ahead and try. Every muscle fiber tensed as his adrenal glands pumped epinephrine into his veins, preparing for fight-or-flight. No, his body prepared only for a fight. He would not run from his attackers.

Chester had never been violent or aggressive, not to anyone. He had never been in a position where he needed to defend himself. He'd never faced a physical threat but he somehow knew that was about to change. His lungs sucked in oxygen through fast, deep breaths. His upper lip curled to reveal grinding teeth. The echo of his pulse hammered in his head. The world seemed to slow around him as Chester readied himself for the inevitable confrontation. And just as his fury reached its peak, the threat seemed to vanish.

There were no signs of movement in the back yard. Whoever was there had gone. The sounds of talking and shouting had begun to fade. He could still hear them, but instead of sounding from all around him, the only commotion now came from in front of the house. No longer were they hiding from him, they were waiting for him right out in the open. They knew he would have to come around the side of the home, there was nowhere else for him to go.

Chester could either walk to the front of the house and face them or he could stay in the back and try to wait them out. Staying put meant he would not be getting home any time soon. He could forget about eating as well. That just wouldn't do. He had never felt such hunger. Or such anger. His decision was made. Chester knew exactly what he had to do.

"Puppy!" he heard one of them shout as his head popped out from the side of the house. Chester's silky coat of white fur with brown spots shimmered in the sunlight. His floppy ears bobbed up and down ever-so slightly as the three-year-old Brittany Spaniel rounded the corner of the home and entered the front yard.

There were three humans standing on the far side of the lawn. One of them was much larger than the other two but it was the smaller ones that made the first move. They weren't running fast, but they were coming right for him. Chester growled at them, so loud and ferocious it scratched his throat. His hackles raised and his ears pulled back to lie flat against his scalp. Chester started to run. His nails dug into the Earth with each stride, gaining traction and picking up speed as he sprinted to meet the humans head-on.

The distance shortened in an instant. The smaller humans stopped moving and the bigger one was yelling something at them. The large human moved in front of the smaller ones. He used his hands to direct them behind his body and shielded them with his arms. The little humans turned to run away but the big one stood right in Chester's path. The snarling dog did not slow down.

Chester sprang into the air; saliva spilling out of his gaping mouth and streaking down both sides of his face. The human took a defensive posture, holding his arms in front of his face and chest. It almost seemed like he was more concerned with stopping Chester from getting to the smaller humans than he was with fighting back or running away. This was so stupid.

The dog's canines and premolars bit down on the man's left forearm. His teeth slid easily through the skin, finding little resistance until they reached bone. Even before he fell to the ground, Chester could taste the blood jetting onto his tongue and along his gums. The coppery liquid filled his mouth and sprayed his face.

The human stumbled backwards and began to fall. He landed with his back on the ground and the dog on his chest. The man fought to free his left arm but the dog's jaws were firmly locked in place. He screamed as skin was twisted and torn. Chester jerked his head from side to side in a bid to pull tissue away from the limb. Hell, he would have pulled the whole damn arm off if he had the strength to do so.

The man struck the dog. His vision was obscured by a blur of white and brown fur but he punched the animal anywhere he could land a blow. Closed fists from the man's right hand slammed into the dog's neck and side. The crunch of broken ribs could not be heard over the screaming and

21

growling, but with each thrust, the man's knuckles could feel the shifting of shattered bones.

Chester felt the sensation of impact against his body. Even with this punishment, it was a sensation only. No pain, no reason to slow down. The muscles in his jaw strained to hold on and dig deeper. Tendons pulled loose and slid between his teeth like floss before dropping loosely into the dog's mouth. Chester wanted to swallow the sweet nourishment, but he couldn't afford to let go.

The next fist smashed into the animal's snout, causing a reflexive wince. Chester's hind legs slid off the human's body and gained purchase on the ground. The writhing dog pulled harder, separating more meat and dousing himself with blood. The man's white tee shirt absorbed the red and clear fluids that rained down from the dog's mouth and his own arm.

With the shift in positions, the man was able to partially role onto his left side and line up another shot. The next desperate punch sank into the dog's ribs. A fragment of crushed bone slid from its place and pierced the outer wall of the dogs' left lung. Chester let go. The dog struggled for air and drew back, offering his victim a slight reprieve. It wasn't long, but it was enough time for the man to reclaim his limb.

He pulled his left arm into his chest, instinctively covering the gaping holes with his right hand in an effort to suppress the flow. Blood pushed its way out of the arm and between the man's fingers. Still on his back, he pushed his heels into the ground to put some space between himself and the wheezing dog.

Chester was furious. No one had ever hit him before. Even though his brain didn't register any pain, it was evident that his body had sustained some pretty serious damage. This would not go unpunished. His narrowing eyes aimed at the heaving Adam's apple in the man's neck. Chester's jaw dropped open and he lunged for the man's throat.

But his attack was interrupted, cut short by something cold and wet and terrible splashing into the dog's face. Chester recoiled with a shrill yelp. The cowering dog dropped his tail and backed away from the stream of water, afraid he'd be splashed again. He looked up to find one of the smaller humans holding a hose. The stream began to form a puddle on the ground in front of him. Chester barked at the one with the hose. Then he flashed his teeth one last time before turning around and running as fast as he could in the opposite direction.

Chapter 4

His car sat alone, stopped at a red light waiting to turn left onto Shawnee Road. To the right was a large open field that looked like it was once used as a crop farm, but its soil had not grown anything substantial in quite some time. To the left was a steep ditch that ran along the side of the road, followed by a small patch of woods.

Twenty minutes had passed since Jim left Beth's house and he was barely halfway home. Once beyond the Lockport City Limits, he'd cruised a length of Route 31 to cut through the rural zones of Sanborn and Wheatfield on his way back to the suburbs.

The sun hung a bit lower in the sky when Jim arrived at Bennett's Supermarket. A faint orange glow illuminated the parking lot as Jim pulled in and searched for a place to park. The lot was less than half full and there was a vacant space in the first row just past the handicap spots. Jim pulled in and after rolling the windows all the way up, then double-checking to make sure the doors were locked, he walked inside the store.

Through the automatic sliding doors, Jim went in and moved along the front of the building. The walls to his right were lined with displays of soda, potato chips, and cereals. Hand-drawn cardboard signs announced that prices had been slashed and there were fantastic deals to be had. To Jim's left were the back sides of the clerk stations and check-out aisles. He pretended not to be checking out the cashiers as he passed behind them.

The first two looked like college girls. Petite and bubbly, they must have been about nineteen or twenty years old. They were wearing those black tight-fitting work pants. Nice. Jim admired one firm youthful buttock after another before finding something a little less appealing, the third cashier. She was a woman of advanced age and size, and wearing the same outfit. Jim winced inwardly and quickly found himself thankful that he himself was not on display.

With his ultra-pale skin, freckles, and horrible puffy hair, Jim wasn't in a position to criticize anyone's appearance. An ever-present luster of perspiration and his well-worn clothing certainly didn't help matters either. He felt his belly and checked to see how much flub he could pinch between his thumb and index finger. Disgusted with himself, Jim kept walking. He found the next register was closed and cut through the empty aisle; faded white sneakers shuffling with every step.

There were fewer people in the store than he'd expected. Only a handful of people stood in line for each cashier and Jim passed no more than three other shoppers as he sauntered deeper into the store. He turned down the center aisle, both sides of which were lined by open refrigerated cases of beer, wine coolers, and the ever-so-classy bottles of malt liquor. A six-pack of Newcastle Brown Ale waited for him on the lowest shelf in the case to his left. Both knees cracked and popped as he knelt to retrieve the beer.

When he stood back up, his guts rumbled a complaint to remind him that he hadn't eaten since breakfast. Maybe he should grab dinner as long as he was already at the supermarket. There was a small deli counter in the back of the store, next to the butcher's station. That would have to do.

Having made his way to the sandwich shop, Jim placed his six-pack on the counter and found no one standing on the other side. The small deli nook looked like it was still open. Two illuminated neon signs above the deli case indicated where to place an order and where to pick it up. Through the

Plexiglas sneeze guard, several open containers of meats and cheeses could be seen. A single ceiling fan spun on the slowest setting above the counter.

"Sir, is someone helping you?" a female voice asked from behind him.

"Um, no actually," answered Jim, turning to face the person.

"Jim, I thought that was you!" the girl exclaimed through a smile of perfect teeth. "How are you?"

Jim turned to see a thin, attractive and athletic-looking blonde standing about a yard away from him. She wore glasses, a yellow tank top with a green polo shirt thrown over her shoulder, and yes-those same tight black pants.

"Hey Lindsey. I'm- well, ya know. Pretty much the same," Jim said. "How are you?"

"I'm okay," Lindsey answered, "I'm working here and that kinda sucks but I'm pretty good other than that."

"Not working at that store in the mall anymore?" Jim asked.

"I'm still there," she said, "But I'm here too. It sucks being broke."

"Yeah, I know wha-" Jim began to say.

"Can I help you?" a male voice interrupted from behind the deli counter. A younger guy, about eighteen years old, wore the store uniform- a green polo shirt and black slacks with a black baseball cap. He was holding a spatula and looking to Jim and Lindsey expectantly.

Jim asked Lindsey if she was hungry and if he could get her anything. Lindsey thanked him but her lunch break was almost over and she didn't have time to eat. Jim was secretly relieved, knowing how little he had left to spend before the next payday. However, he would stretch his budget a little further if it meant being able to do something thoughtful for a pretty young lady and an old friend. Instead, Jim ordered a single hot chicken sub to go.

"Cheese on that?" asked the male employee.

"No cheese, Lance," he answered, reading the clerk's name tag. Jim patted his stomach and added a one-word explanation, "Lactose."

"So, are you seeing anyone?" Lindsey asked Jim as the kid behind the counter threw a handful of chicken clumps onto the grill.

"Yeah, sort of," Jim said with more than a touch of hesitation.

"Sort of?" she asked lightheartedly. "How are you sort of seeing someone?"

"I am seeing someone. But it's not that serious and it's only been for a little while," Jim lied. He swallowed down his momentary guilt and continued, trying to imitate how he thought a happy boyfriend would sound. "Her name's Beth. She's a really cool chick."

"That's good to hear," said Lindsey.

"And what about you? Seeing anyone?" Jim inquired, trying to push the conversation along.

Before she could answer, the deli worker cut in and asked, "Sorry, but did you say you wanted cheese or didn't want cheese?"

"No cheese."

"Oh, I already put cheese on it," said Lance, "Sorry about that, but I won't charge you for it."

"Okay, no problem," Jim replied, privately preparing himself for an upset stomach.

"And besides, everyone likes cheese," the kid said, using a much-too-large knife to cut into a sub roll. He tore off the top section and began piling dairy-glazed chicken morsels onto the bottom half. Lance finished making the sandwich and added, "Cheese makes everything better."

"It doesn't make my trips to the bathroom any better," Jim said, trying not to smile. He noticed Lindsey trying to keep herself from giggling.

"Gross," said the worker from behind the counter as he finished wrapping up the sub. He slid the food into a thin plastic bag, along with a small pile of napkins.

Jim paid for his meal and then followed Lindsey through the aisles to the front of the store. He was a half-step behind her and at some point, he caught himself staring. It was hard not to. Lindsey's firm heart-shaped ass was covered in the same paper-thin fabric that squeezed against her perfectly toned calf and thigh muscles. While these things had certainly drawn Jim's attention, it was Lindsey's radiant blonde locks that made him unable to look away.

She wore her hair down and it hung just past her shoulders. It looked soft and smooth and had just a little bit of a wave to it. The bright color stood out against her creamy tanned skin. Jim thought she looked like she belonged in a commercial for makeup and skin cream instead of stocking shelves at a dumpy supermarket. From her neck, across her shoulders and upper back, and down the length of her arms, there wasn't a single blemish to be found.

Realizing that neither of them had spoken in several minutes, Jim struggled for something to say. He wanted to be clever and charming but he'd settle for anything if he could just bring himself to speak before he ran out of time and missed his opportunity. But before he could spit something out, they had already reached the exit at the front of the building.

"Are you in a hurry?" she asked.

"Not exactly," Jim replied. He'd have stayed there all night if she wanted. "Why, what's up?"

"I still have a few minutes left on my break if you want to talk for a bit."

"Sure," Jim said, hoping he didn't sound too eager.

The pair walked out of the store and over to Jim's car, again mostly in silence. He opened the passenger's side door and placed his beer and sandwich on the floor in front of the seat. Then Jim remembered that Lindsey hadn't answered his question from earlier.

"So, you said you're seeing someone?" he asked.

"Yeah, I'm still seeing Chad," she told him.

"Chad?" Jim crinkled his nose. "Chad from high school? Still?"

"Yep, still with Chad." Her answer was matter-of-fact with a touch of resignation.

"Oh. That's good I suppose," Jim said not too convincingly.

Lindsey was eager to change the subject. She adjusted her glasses and asked, "So how are your parents?"

"They're good," Jim started. "They're on their yearly trip to Tampa and won't be back for another ten days."

25

"Oh, that sounds like fun," Lindsey said. "Are you house-sitting?"

"No, they have my aunt and uncle keeping an eye on things. They live a little closer, so it's easier for them to pop in here and there."

"That's right!" Lindsey perked up, "I forgot they're so close. I haven't seen them in such a long time. How are they? Is Ted already planning his big hunting trip for the fall?"

"Not sure," Jim shrugged. "I haven't gone with them in years. Uncle Ted would never let me shoot or even hold a gun. He said I was too little."

"Okay, but how long ago was that? How old were you then?"

"About twelve, I guess."

Lindsey smirked. "And you don't think that twelve is too young to be shooting rifles in the middle of the woods with no hospitals or doctors nearby?"

Jim put on his most grown-up expression, the one he had used to argue this same point with his uncle more than a decade earlier. "I'm sure I would've handled it just fine."

"That's right," she said. Then as if making a joke, "Jim always knows better."

"Okay, okay." Jim impishly put his hands up in mock-defeat. "Maybe you and Uncle Ted were both right. Either way, me and my cousin found it annoying."

"I forgot to ask about your cousin," Lindsey told him with mild embarrassment. "How is Mark? What has he been up to?"

"He's fine. Ya know, same old. He's been dating this new girl he met, Christina or Kristen or something. I can't remember her name. She's sort of a lump, bitchy and rude. I'm not a big fan. Not bad looking though, maybe a bit on the skinny side."

"Ah," said Lindsey. "But maybe she's just bitchy and rude to you."

"Well, why would that be?" His tone was almost defensive.

"Oh, I don't know." She smirked and suggested, "Maybe she'd be nicer if you did something thoughtful for her, you know, like remembering her name."

"I suppose it's possible," Jim replied with a grin.

"Yeah," Lindsey said softly.

"Yep."

Lindsey exhaled audibly, long and slow.

"So," Jim's single-syllable response trailed off.

And there it was again. Jim's pulse quickened, nervously observing that they had slipped into the uncomfortable silence he was expecting and trying to avoid. He looked to his feet, avoiding eye contact. Lindsey looked over her shoulder, back toward the front of the store and then surveyed the expanse of the parking lot to where it met Division Street.

"We had the cops in here a couple of nights ago." Lindsey finally spoke.

"The cops? What for?"

"Customers said some crazy guy was screaming his head off in the parking lot. He was running around the side of the building near where we take the garbage out. The night manager called the police, but he was gone before they got here. It was probably just some homeless guy," she speculated. "But there was trash thrown all over and blood on the ground near the dumpsters."

"Homeless? Out here?" Jim asked. "I've only seen homeless people downtown. I didn't know they were making their way out here."

"I guess so," said Lindsey.

"Well, be careful if you're out here at night," Jim told her.

"Thanks grandma, I'll be real careful," she mocked playfully. Lindsey then pulled her cell phone from her pocket to check the time. "Oh, it's almost eight o'clock. I'm going to have to get back inside."

"Okay," Jim replied. With great hesitation, he continued and said, "Hey, so, I'm not sure if it's weird or not, but let me give you my number. If you ever have some free time and want to catch up or whatever, give me a call."

Lindsey agreed and Jim watched as she tapped away on the buttons of her phone, entering the digits as Jim sounded them off. She saved the number in her phone, but did not offer to give Jim hers in exchange. Jim knew better than to ask.

Lindsey stuck the cell phone back into her pocket and said, "So, I guess I'll see ya later."

"Alright," said Jim.

Lindsey held her arms in front of her, inviting Jim in for a hug. He carefully moved in and gently put his arms around her. Lindsey reciprocated and they held each other for a split second. Jim began to release and Lindsey held on for just a moment longer.

She looked up at him and said, "It was really nice to see you, Jim."

"Yeah," he agreed. "It was nice to see you too."

Jim climbed into his car and watched through the window as Lindsey walked back to the store. He waited until she was out of sight before lighting a cigarette. The window rolled down and the engine started. Jim paused, taking a moment to himself before leaving.

It was nice to see Lindsey. She looked terrific. She was nice to him, or at least she was friendly. And *she* approached *him*. She could have just as easily turned down an aisle or walked by without saying a word. Jim gazed out the windshield and considered going back inside the store. He could ask her to hang out. They could grab dinner or a drink some night and just talk.

On the other hand, there was probably a reason she didn't offer her number. If she wanted to spend time with him, she would have at least given him her phone number. Maybe she would call him. But the more he thought about it, the less likely it seemed.

He correctly decided not to go back inside. Also, Jim figured Lindsey wouldn't be too happy to find him still sitting out in the parking lot alone like some kind of creep. She probably wouldn't want to see him at all. Plus, she was still dating Chad. That could be why she didn't want him calling her. But seriously, how could she *still* be with Chad? Jim rolled his eyes and put the car in reverse. It was time to go home.

Less than ten minutes later, Jim turned onto his street. Kenney Field passed on his right, a wide open park with three soccer fields. The next block had a couple of small stores and office buildings on both sides. There was the video shop on his left and the coffee shop to his right. He could see the parking lot that led to the two-story brick apartment building coming up just past the next intersection.

His headlights reflected off the parked cars. There were other lights shining in the distance as well, red and blue colored lights. Jim switched on the blinker and slowed to make the sharp right turn into the lot. He pulled up and parked in his usual spot, between a red Ford Ranger pickup truck and a small blue Honda sedan.

There were a pair of police cars parked up near the walkway in front of the building. The sidewalk itself was littered with trash and debris and something wet glistened on the concrete. Two uniformed officers were standing under the building's security lights. Six of the building's occupants, four men and two women, were outside speaking to them.

Jim watched them in the mirror. He couldn't hear what they were saying, but the women seemed upset, one was crying. One of the men was flailing his arms around and looked to be raising his voice. Jim's stomach rolled over. Something rotten had happened. He dried his sweaty palms on the edges of the car seat and opened the door.

Chapter 5

Punch yourself in the face as hard as you can. Can't do it, can you? Instead of doing that, try holding your breath until you pass out. Are you finding this difficult as well? Can't do that either, huh? Okay, there's one final experiment you can try. Fill up your kitchen sink and hold your head underwater until you drown. Impossible, you say? Ever wonder why that is? It's simple. Self-preservation.

It's biologically coded into every living creature on the planet. The mechanism that keeps you from smashing in your own nose is the same thing that makes you breathe if you hold your breath for too long. The survival instinct is the driving force of life itself and it is so powerful that, outside of extreme circumstances, it's what prevents creatures from harming themselves.

Sure, you can tie a couple of cinder blocks to your feet and jump in a lake. But before you reach the bottom and run out of air, your whole body will react. You'll spend your last few moments of life in a panic as you try to swim back to the surface. Your flailing hands will claw at water until you lose consciousness and let water fill your lungs. This last-ditch effort to save one's self is powered by the same mechanism that forces living things to fight for life and to multiply.

Everyone has heard the phrase, *survival of the fittest*. This is often misinterpreted to mean that whatever organism is the biggest or strongest is the one that will be around for a long time. What this expression actually means is that prosperity is reserved for the organism that is best fitted and adapted to its specific environment. The more suited an organism is to its surroundings, the better chance it has for longevity.

People who buy into the theory of evolution think of it as a long, slow process that can take thousands of years before any significant modifications can be observed. This may be true for larger and more complex animals, but is not necessarily the case for smaller things. Viruses, for example, have been known to evolve and change very quickly. This is often necessary for a particular disease to avoid total annihilation.

When is the last time you heard of someone dying from diphtheria? Odds are you haven't. People generally don't get it any more. Diphtheria is a great example of a virus that did not adapt and has been virtually eradicated thanks to modern medicine.

But have you ever gotten a flu shot one winter, stayed healthy all year, and then wound up getting sick with the flu the following season? You bet your ass you have. Influenza is a very adaptive virus. It's been able to remain a perennial health concern thanks to its remarkable ability to conform to an ever-changing environment.

Part of what makes influenza capable of such change is the fact that it crosses species. It infects birds, pigs, and human beings alike. As the virus is transmitted from one animal to the next, the strain changes slightly, taking small genetic pieces from each animal and adjusting its coding little by little. If not for its ability to alter its makeup, influenza could be eradicated through the use of vaccines.

Rabies also affects multiple animals but it's only effective in mammals. But despite being one of the world's oldest infectious diseases, rabies cannot evolve as quickly as the flu and has therefore struggled to persevere against humanity's efforts to destroy it. The rabies virus has experienced a number of disadvantages that have kept it from reaching its full potential.

First, if the virus is untreated, the host invariably dies. And when the host dies, the infection dies. Second, transmission of the disease requires an infected creature to bite an uninfected creature. It's not airborne and you cannot catch it from a sneeze or cough. Rabies, in its original form, could not be detected in blood, urine, or stool. It couldn't infiltrate the digestive or renal systems and it was not yet capable of employing the circulatory system. The only way for the infection to take hold was for infected saliva to get deep into the victim's body.

Once inside the brain, the virus causes a fever, pain, and delirium before traveling down the jaw and into the salivary gland. This is where the virus multiplies. Production of saliva is increased and the infected animal's spit is laced with the disease.

The third problem for rabies might be the most difficult to overcome. Once a person or animal had been bitten, symptoms usually wouldn't appear for about a month. When the virus entered the body, it would attach to peripheral nerves and begin making its way toward the central nervous system, up the spinal cord and toward the brain. This was the only way it could travel. The whole process took too long and made it difficult for a rabies infection to be successful, particularly in humans.

A newly infected person would have had plenty of time to get to the hospital or doctor's office and receive a vaccination. They could stop the virus long before it had time to reach the brain and do any real harm. The slowly-but-surely approach just didn't hold up against new medicine. Fresh vaccines made for fewer and fewer infections because the virus just didn't move fast enough.

The time had come for rabies to adapt to the changing times. It would need to follow the example set by influenza and begin mutating at a higher rate. A rabies infection can only be successful if it reaches the brain and traveling along the nervous system was too slow and took too much time. The circulatory system would be a much more efficient means of travel.

If the virus used the host's circulatory system, it could get from one part of the body to anywhere else in the body in about a minute. Regardless of where the virus enters, the host's own pulse and blood flow could deliver the infection to the brain in almost no time at all. The onset of symptoms would not be far behind.

Greg had not yet begun to experience these symptoms. Right after that dog attacked him, he had ushered his daughters off to the neighbor's house. The woman next door, Ginger Anne, said she had seen the ordeal through her kitchen window. When Greg showed up at her door, shaking and bloody with his girls in tow, she had agreed to look after them while Greg drove to the hospital to get his rabies shots.

He now stood in the master bedroom on the second floor of his home with a yellow terrycloth towel around his left arm. With his right hand, the man pulled a pair of scissors from his front jeans pocket. Greg pulled back the towel to examine his wounds and found the bleeding had barely slowed. He pulled free the clean and not-yet-stained half of the towel and cut it free from the rest. The soiled end fell to the floor and the clean section was wrapped around the bleeding forearm as tight as Greg could make it using only one hand to do the work. He tucked the last few inches under the bottom layer of cloth to hold it in place.

The scissors were tossed to the floor and Greg reached his right hand over his shoulder to pull off his white shirt. It was covered in red stains and there's no way he could walk around like that. He pulled the shirt over his head and then slid his right arm out of the sleeve to expose his thin pail torso and a small patch of hair in the center of his chest. Careful not to undo the makeshift bandage, Greg slowly moved the shirt's fabric around his left arm before letting it fall to the floor with the scissors and saturated towel.

Greg crossed the room to the corner where a laundry basket sat with no lid. He reached in and grabbed a black tee shirt which went on with the same level of care as the white one had come off. Turning toward the adjacent wall, he opened the sliding wood doors to his closet and pulled out a red flannel shirt with buttons down the front. This went on easier than the tee shirt; the open buttons eliminating the need to pull it over his head while minding the bandage.

His arm throbbed and he could already feel the wetness of blood soaking into the towel. A trickle of red dripped into the palm of his left hand, causing Greg to wonder how much blood he'd already lost. He might need stitches in addition to the rabies shots. No problem- the drive to the hospital wouldn't take too long and they could have him fixed up in no time.

He'd needed stitches after a bicycle accident when he was a kid, so that part didn't bother him. The shots were another story. Greg had heard stories from people who had been bit by an animal and their accounts had him dreading the experience. The vaccination allegedly came in the form of five injections; each from an extra-large syringe. The shots reportedly went into various places on the body, through the belly and into various large muscle groups. The fluid in the needles was said to be so thick, the patients could literally feel the muscles separating and being forced apart as the medication was pushed into their bodies.

Come to think of it, those vaccination stories had come from people who'd been bitten by a wild animal. Sometimes it was a raccoon or maybe a bat, but he'd never actually heard of someone being attacked by a rabid dog, and certainly not a Brittany Spaniel.

Sure, Greg was only speculating that the dog had been rabid but it seemed like a pretty safe guess. If it wasn't rabies, then what the Hell was it? What makes an otherwise docile breed of dog turn so aggressive, so ferocious? And what had happened to it after it ran away? Greg only pondered this for a moment before deciding he didn't give a shit. The man secretly hoped he would see the dog on his way to the hospital so he could run it over.

Greg snatched the scissors from the floor and stuck them back in his pocket. He then scooped up the soiled linen from the floor and carried it with him downstairs where he tossed it into the garbage pail in the kitchen. The scissors were placed on the kitchen table in exchange for a red baseball cap. He pulled the hat on over his greasy dark hair and walked to the front door.

Climbing into the driver's seat of a slightly older, slightly rusted white pickup truck, Greg reached for the door and slammed it shut. He did this out of habit, having temporarily forgotten about his injuries. Greg drew back from the door, expecting the impact to cause a surge of pain through his leaking arm. But for some reason, it didn't hurt. The pain had mostly gone away. Greg grinned in relief as he switched the headlights on and backed out of the driveway. If the pain was already fading, he was confident that he would be just fine.

A fifteen-minute drive, mostly down an out-of-the-way country road, was all that stood between Greg and proper medical treatment. There were no stop signs and very little traffic. He could probably even shave a few minutes off the ride. Greg was going about sixty miles per hour and praying the emergency room wouldn't be too busy when his stomach groaned. He was famished.

How could he be hungry at a time like this? His boxing match with the pooch must have worked up an appetite. He wasn't sure if Ginger Anne would offer the girls something to eat, but Greg decided he would hit up a drive-thru as soon as he left the hospital. Maybe McDonald's, maybe Taco Bell; he could stuff his face on the drive home. And if the girls hadn't eaten yet, they would all go out to dinner together. Greg could eat twice.

Something dripped onto the front of his shirt, causing him to look down. A thick rope of saliva descended from his lower lip. He was so hungry he was drooling. Laughing to himself, he wiped his mouth with the sleeve of his right arm. As he did so, he realized there was more drool than he initially thought. Most of his chest and abdomen were moist with his own slobber.

Attempting to dab out some of the wetness with his sleeve again, he glanced down at his stomach for just a moment to see how visible the wet spots had become. When he looked back up, Greg could have sworn he saw the white and brown fur of a Brittany Spaniel by the side of the road, only half visible in the tall grass. He considered stopping the truck to go after the dog, but immediately decided against it.

It was impossible to know if it was the same dog. With the blood loss and possible infection, there was no way Greg could turn the truck around and go chasing after some dog he thought he saw out in the middle of nowhere. When he checked his mirrors and saw nothing but an empty field, he wondered if he'd actually seen a dog at all. Maybe it was an illusion brought on by some kind of delirium. The thought of that rotten canine made him forget all about being hungry. Now Greg was furious, even if it was just a hallucination.

He began taking deep breaths in through his nostrils and out through clenched teeth. His foot pressed harder on the gas pedal and the needle of the speedometer moved rapidly across the face of the gauge; seventy, seventy-five, eighty miles per hour and still climbing. Street signs, lamp posts, and trees all raced by in a blur of silver and green. Exhaust and burnt oil spewed from the truck's tailpipe as it raced down the road.

Greg was lucky there were no other cars in sight. He was beginning to have a hard time focusing on the street and keeping the vehicle between the lines. He understood he was driving fast but he wasn't driving *that* fast, not so fast the street itself should be blurry. His foot eased off the gas. He was going to let the vehicle naturally slow back down to about fifty-five miles per hour. The needle on the dash board started to move in the opposite direction but the street remained out of focus.

It looked to be swaying from side to side. Greg reflexively tried to correct this by steering the truck from left to right, and then back to left again. Tires chirped against the cement with each jerk of the wheel. Greg found himself struggling to control the truck and keep it on the road. Something was seriously wrong with him.

Had he lost even more blood than he initially thought? A dangerous amount? Was this the rabies virus already affecting him? Or had he contracted something else from that crazy animal? He couldn't say. The only thing he knew for certain was he had that damn dog to blame. That stupid mutt was going to pay.

Greg pulled the truck to the shoulder of the road, barely applying the brakes before turning the wheel all the way to the left and stomping the accelerator to the floor. The rear tires screeched and lost traction. The back of the truck spun around so the entire vehicle was now facing the opposite direction. He straightened the wheel and drove as fast as he could. Greg was heading back the way he had come, back toward where he knew he had seen that dog.

A rage washed over him. The man was gripped by a seething madness. There was no rationalizing, no calming down. He was going to find the dog. Then he was going to beat the dog with his bare hands until it was nothing more than a lifeless husk of brown and white fur with its teeth scattered across the pavement. The crazed man envisioned himself standing triumphantly over the dead dog. The thought made Greg's lips curl up into a half sneer, half smile.

He was still unable to see the street clearly. The double yellow lines on the concrete appeared wavy and uneven. To make matters worse, the sun was beginning to set. The low light made it even harder to judge the street from the shoulder. In the glow of the headlights, the darkening sky and the sparsely-lit ground ahead blended into one another. It also didn't help that Greg had now accelerated past one hundred miles per hour.

Greg screamed. There were no discernible words, just a primitive yell; a beastly outpouring of emotion. He pulled on the wheel as if he were trying to yank it free from the steering column, groaning all the while. When the wheel didn't come off, Greg slammed his right fist into the center, causing the horn to sound. His left hand, now feeling like brand new, was mashed against the glass of the window, pounding over and over.

Distracted by his tantrum, Greg didn't realize that he was approaching a curve to the right in the road just ahead. By the time he noticed, it was too late to maintain control of the vehicle. Greg overcompensated by turning the wheel all the way to the right and instead of hitting the brake pedal, he pressed down harder on the gas.

The back of the truck swung out to the left, then back to center, and then all the way to the right. The old pickup was already halfway off the road before Greg was able to stomp on the brakes, causing them to lock up. The truck skidded on the gravel shoulder and into the grass. It bounced as it passed over bumps and divots in the ground.

Greg lost his grip on the steering wheel and his head ricocheted off the window. In a move of desperation, he grabbed the gear selector on the column and moved it into the park position. A terrible grinding sound bellowed from beneath his feet but the truck had too much momentum and it kept moving forward.

The vehicle finally came to a stop when it crashed into the thick base of an elm tree. Greg was thrown forward and out of his seat. His head struck the windshield with a deafening blow. The glass held strong but Greg began to break apart. A considerable gash had opened across his forehead. His poison blood painted over the gauge cluster and drained into the defroster vent.

The engine was no longer running. The truck fell silent except for the hiss of steamed coolant escaping through a hole in the radiator. Greg didn't make a sound either. His limbs were twisted into positions they'd never before achieved. The right side of his face rested on the vinyl ledge above the glove box on the passenger's side of the cab. A nearly imperceptible patch of condensation formed on the dash board under his nose with each shallow breath.

Chapter 6

The sun had dipped below the horizon just moments before Jim arrived home. A haze of humidity and cloud cover blocked the moon's gleam in the night's sky. The darkness should have signified the end of the day; a welcomed break from the stress and bullshit that had gone on in the daylight hours. Not tonight.

Jim's evening of drinking and feeling sorry for himself would have to wait just a bit longer. First he'd have to find out what all the fuss was about. He gathered his beer and food and walked over to join the small crowd of people gathered outside the tenement.

The building itself had two full stories over a basement. It was a daylight basement, or maybe you'd call it a garden level, so the first floor was actually about four feet off the ground. Eight small balconies overlooked a scenic four-lane roadway beyond the crumbling parking lot. Faded orange and red veneer brickwork wrapped the exterior walls. The roof was covered by standard three-tab asphalt shingles, most of which were badly stained and if you looked closely, you could see that many had begun to curl.

If you saw the place from the outside, you'd think it was a dump. A quick tour of the interior would confirm your suspicion. The carpets were worn flat and had become loose in several areas. Window and door frames were littered with scuffs and nicks. Ceilings showed places where someone had been painting, missed a spot, and then never bothered to go back over and touch it up.

There were four apartments on the first floor, four on the second, and two in the basement for a total of ten. The basement units were on opposite ends of the lower level. The middle portion of the basement was used for the mechanical systems, tenants' storage spaces, and a laundry area with a coin-operated washing machine and dryer.

"Hey guys, what's going on?" Jim asked as he approached the group. Getting closer to them, he was able to make out several faces illuminated by the outdoor security lights. He intentionally looked to the other tenants and not at the officers. No one seemed to notice him as Danny was mid-sentence explaining to the cops what had happened.

"...it was totally crazy, man. I mean, I'm minding my own business, taking some trash to the bins, and this dude just comes at me." Danny, who was about the same age as Jim, was wearing dark jeans that were ripped at the knees and a black tee shirt with the sleeves cut off. His thin pale arms flailed around as he told his story.

"So, this dude was standing at the end of the parking lot, near the sidewalk," Danny pointed toward the street. "I barely even noticed him. So I threw my garbage out and when I was heading back inside, he starts yelling at me."

"What was he saying?" asked the taller of the two officers. He was in full cop uniform with that ridiculous hat that they wear and a pair of sunglasses hanging from his left shirt pocket. His shoulders were fairly broad and despite his protruding beer belly, he looked physically strong.

"I don't know, man," Danny answered. "Didn't seem like he was saying anything, just making noise. I call over to him and ask him what's up, like why is he just standing out there yelling 'n shit? He looks right at me and starts running for me- right for me! I mean, what did I ever do to him? That dude was just crazy."

"Okay, so then what did you do?" asked the same cop, looking down to scribble something on a notepad that looked tiny in his thick hands.

"Man, I ran my butt inside as fast as I could go." Danny pumped his fists in a mock running motion; his long black hair falling to cover most of his face.

"I think that's when I came outside," said one of the others. "Daniel must have been inside by then, but I heard the commotion and came out to see what was happening."

"Comin' out to save me?" Danny asked through a big smile. He laughed, snapping his fingers and pointing to the other man. "You're my hero, Chucky!"

"It's Charles," the man answered. He adjusted his glasses and folded his arms across his chest. "I was investigating a disturbance. I wasn't looking for a fight or anything like that. I just heard something and thought I'd better check it out, that's all."

Charles was older than Jim, probably thirty-three or thirty-four. He was taller too, standing at about six feet. He had on a pair of tan khakis and a powder blue oxford shirt that had been stained with spots of something near the collar and top buttons. His hair was short and styled with an uneven part on the left side. He had a beard that was trimmed to form some definition between his chin and neck. Charles wasn't what you'd call a fat guy, he just wasn't what you'd call thin either.

Speaking of not being thin, a rather hefty gal stood next to him. She was holding a box of tissues in one hand and dabbing her eyes with the other. Jim assumed this woman was Charles' girlfriend, but the two had never been properly introduced and Jim didn't care enough to ask.

When Charles finished speaking, she leaned in with a fresh tissue to wipe moisture from his face and neck. Assuming it was just perspiration, Jim had to look twice to see the tissues come away red. The woman balled up the used paper and tossed it to the ground.

"Did this man attack you as well?" the same officer asked Charles.

"Well sort of," Charles began to explain. "I ducked back inside when I saw him, but we had a little bit of a struggle. He was trying to pull the door open. This fella was certainly stronger than he looked, I could barely keep it shut. You can see there are no latches on these front doors, anyone could just walk right in."

Charles turned to point over his shoulder toward the building's entrance. There were two sets of double doors at the front of the structure. Each had a metal frame and the rest was all glass, roughly a half an inch thick. There were handles on the interior and exterior sides of each one, but there was no way to actually secure the doors or to keep them closed. Charles indicated a door on the right side of the front wall, which was streaked with red liquid.

"So how did that happen?" asked the officer, glancing at what he obviously knew to be blood.

"The man chased me into the building," Charles explained. "Didn't even slow down when he got to the doors. It was like he didn't see them. Or maybe he thought he could go through them."

"He smashed his face pretty hard on the edge of the door frame, busted up his lip pretty good. I think this guy must have been messed up on drugs or something because it didn't seem to faze him at all. When he was trying to get the door open, he was pulling the handle and screaming at me and spewing blood all over. I ended up getting some on me." Charles lifted both arms to show just how much blood and other fluids had splattered onto his shirt.

Jim had been standing back listening to Charles and Danny explain the evening's events. He looked over the small crowd that partially blocked his way into the building. He found Jenna, who was also standing back and taking everything in.

She had on scuffed sneakers, tight faded jeans, and an oversized tee shirt. There was a baseball cap on her head with a pony tail pulled through the opening in the back. You got the impression she was constantly going to or coming from a softball game. She was definitely into sports, more than most guys were at her age, which was an early twenty-something. She never shut up about it either, quoting scores and stats and critiquing coaches, especially when the Sabres were playing.

Naturally, Jim observed that she could easily be one of the hottest girls around if she didn't dress like such a tomboy. She never seemed to wear any makeup, which Jim didn't care about one way or another, but the summer humidity made for a greasy and displeasing complexion. A bath and a sundress would do her a world of good in Jim's opinion.

"What about you?" Jim asked, realizing Jenna was looking back at him. "Are you okay?"

"Who are you?" asked an unfamiliar voice. It was the other police officer speaking to Jim.

It wasn't until that moment Jim realized the second officer was a woman. Sure, it was dark out, but her squat build and buzz-cut hairdo didn't exactly radiate femininity.

"Me?" Jim asked. "I'm Jim. Jim Flanagan, I live here."

The female officer didn't say anything else. She made a sort of grunting noise and turned back to face the other cop, who was listening to Charles as he continued to describe his attacker.

Jenna walked behind the group and stepped beside Jim. She said, "I'm fine. I just came out to see what was happening after the police got here. I heard something going on, but I was in the shower at the time."

"In the shower, eh?" Jim asked with a sly grin. "Go on."

"You're so bad," Jenna said with a giggle. She playfully punched Jim's shoulder and said, "Seriously though, this sounds kinda messed up. Chuck's got that crazy guy's blood all over him."

"Charles," Jim corrected her with a knowing expression. "I'm sorry I missed all the excitement. I'm sure Charles is going to be fine though. Looks like whoever it was is gone."

"True. Looks like we're safe for now. Anyway, I have work in the morning so I'm heading in. Have a good night." She walked back the way she had come. Jim watched, thinking maybe those jeans weren't so bad on her after all.

Jenna passed by Albert and Adam on the other side of the group, patted Albert's shoulder and said goodnight. Albert was an older guy, somewhere in his seventies. He walked with a cane and stood with a slight hunch. The man, clad in beige slacks and a cardigan, removed his hat. It was one of those plaid, floppy looking hats that taxi drivers used to wear. He held it in his cane hand and used his free hand to comb fingers through his gray hair before replacing the cap. He positioned the cane in front of him and leaned into it for balance.

Jim knew Albert as the grandfatherly old man who lived at the other end of the building on the first floor. The man spent most of each summer day sitting on the balcony and smoking tobacco out of an old wooden pipe. Albert would always greet the other tenants when they arrived home. Whenever possible, he would get them to pause and chat before letting them go into their apartments.

Because of this, Jim was grateful he lived on the opposite side. He didn't mind a wave here and there, but he didn't have the patience for daily timeworn conversations about the weather, traffic, and whatever had come in the mail that day.

Albert's proudest achievement was being Polish. No matter the topic, he would always steer the discussion back to how he was born in Poland, how he grew up in Poland, how things had been so nice- so much better in Poland. Weeks earlier, Jim was hearing for the tenth or eleventh time about how Poland was the greatest place on Earth. Jim asked why he had moved to The States and why he didn't move back if he preferred living in Poland. Albert had politely excused himself and went inside from the balcony without answering.

On his left side, gently leaning into Albert's leg, sat a German Shepherd. Black and brown fur was spotty with patches of gray which dulled the coat of the aging dog. There was a black nylon collar around the dog's neck. Affixed to the collar were several pristine tags that shimmered in the glow of the outside lights. He did not wear a leash. Droopy, bloodshot eyes looked up at his master as though he knew the man was about to speak.

"So, what are you going to do about this?" Albert interrupted the officer. "I'm not going to sit back and let these crazies run amok in my neighborhood. I've got a gun, ya know." His chest seemed to inflate with that last statement.

The cops, who were finishing up their report with Charles and Danny, gave a polite nod. The policewoman said, "I'm confident he's gone. Keep the lights on out here and keep an eye out, especially at night. If you see this man again or anyone who looks out of place, call us and we'll look into it."

Albert's son Adam stood to his right, a half step behind him. He had not said a word the whole time, like he was being careful not to draw attention to himself. Adam was about thirty-five years old. But dressed in baggy black jean shorts and a Buffalo Bills jersey, he looked like a much younger man. The sideways hat was a fitting addition. Jim for the first time noticed the top edge of a tattoo peaking over the neckline of Adam's shirt.

Adam and Albert lived together. They were both pleasant enough and Jim didn't think anything of a father and son cohabiting. He did often wonder about the sleeping arrangements for two grown men in a one-bedroom apartment. Were there two beds in the bedroom? Did one of them sleep on the couch? If so, it was probably Adam. Was the sofa a pull-out?

"I think we're all set here," said the male officer. "I would get checked out by a doctor or at the urgent care center. You don't know what that guy may have had, diseases or whatever. Just a suggestion."

"I plan to, sir. Just going to jump in the shower and grab some fresh clothes first," Charles told him. A little spaced out, Charles stared through the police, like the officers weren't standing there anymore. Then he added, "And maybe something to eat."

The woman standing with him, Charles' apparent girlfriend, agreed. "Let's go for burgers on the way," she suggested with a note of glee, seeming to have forgotten all about the recent attack at the mere mention of food.

"Yeah," Charles muttered vacantly. "Or maybe we could get a meatball sub."

The police packed up and left shortly after. The crowd didn't linger much longer. Charles and his lady went inside, down the half flight of stairs and into Charles' garden level apartment. Albert and his dog slowly wandered to the far end of the building and disappeared inside with Adam following close behind. Danny hung around outside. Jim noticed him staring at the six pack he was holding.

"You want one?" Jim asked.

"Sure, thanks man." Danny grabbed a brew and popped the top with a bottle opener on his key ring. He looked to Jim and asked with a thoughtful tone, "Wow man, could you believe that?"

"Uh-" Jim didn't have a chance to reply.

"A lady cop!" Danny exclaimed. "How ridiculous. Chick cops! Who are they fooling?"

"Beats me," Jim sighed. "Going in?"

"Yep."

Danny opened the door using only his thumb and middle finger on the handle, careful not to touch the blood that no one had wiped up.

"Nobody's going to clean this?" Jim asked.

"I don't know, man. I guess the maintenance guy will have to take care of it." Danny opened the door wide and tilted his head to indicate Jim should go in first.

Jim nodded thanks but hesitated before going in. Something in the light caught his attention when the door had been opened all the way.

"What is that?" he asked.

"What's what?" Danny tried to follow Jim's gaze.

"This. On the door frame," Jim said. He leaned in to get a closer look.

"Oh shit," Danny said raising his voice a little, but he did not elaborate. He waited for Jim to reach the same conclusion.

A lump of something stuck to the inner part of the frame just below eye level. There was blood all around it, which was probably why no one else had seen it. The item was roughly the same size as the tip of Jim's pinky finger. The part facing outward had a tan color, which turned to a darker red and purple along the edges.

"That dude's lip is on the door," Danny stated. "That shit is so gross."

Jim scrunched his face but didn't have anything to add. Danny held the door open with his foot and bent down to the ground. He sprung up, holding something in front of his face between his thumb and index finger.

"And this is his tooth!" he added, clearly excited by this discovery.

"Oh," Jim drew back. "You're not worried about picking it up?"

"Nah," Danny answered.

He studied the fallen front tooth in his hand. It wasn't a whole tooth, maybe about two-thirds of what would have stuck out past the gums. There was no root, but most of the top looked intact. The enamel was stained yellow with specks of red. Danny rolled the tooth between his fingers, flicking his thumb along the jagged edge where it had broken away from the bottom, which was presumably still in the crazy man's mouth.

"It stinks," Jim observed. He waved his hand in front of his face to waft away the stench of rotten gums. "Get rid of it."

"Shouldn't the cops have taken this?" he asked. "You know, like for the CSI team or whatever. It's evidence. Maybe they can do whatever it is they do with DNA and find the guy."

"CSI team?" Jim laughed. "And when are they going to show up?"

38

"Should I call and ask them to come back and take it?" Danny asked. Jim realized he was being serious.

"Come on," Jim started, "What do you think they're going to do with that? They only evaluate DNA evidence for serious crimes like murders and rapes, stuff like that. Some guy shows up at an apartment building, runs into a door, knocks his own tooth out, and then goes away; as far as the police are concerned, case closed. It sounds like he did more damage to himself than anyone else."

"He ruined Chucky's shirt," Danny countered.

"You're worried about Charles?" Jim asked with mock sincerity.

"Nope." Danny didn't hesitate on that one. He thought for a moment and then tossed the dead tooth behind him, not looking to see where it landed. "I guess you're right. No way is that dude coming back around here, not if he saw the cops show up."

They both walked inside then, into the front hallway and over to the steps. After wordlessly going up the eight risers that led to the main floor, Jim reached into his pocket for his keys when he noticed Danny had turned and was heading up the stairs to the second floor.

"Hey, you wanna hang out for a little bit?" Jim called after him.

"Can't tonight man, thanks for the beer though," Danny's voice echoed down the stairwell.

Balancing the bag of food and six- make that five pack of beer in one hand, Jim unlocked the door and walked into his apartment. He was home at last, ready to finally put his feet up and take it easy. The door opened into the living room. The floor was covered by a cream-colored carpet with the odd stain here and there, none of which were visible in the dim light.

The door was closed tightly behind him. He locked the deadbolt out of habit, but also secured the chain lock. This was for peace of mind more than anything else. Anyone who could get past the deadbolt would absolutely get by the chain as well. But it made Jim feel better, safer. Now that he was alone and in silence, it dawned on him that he'd gotten a bit skittish from listening to Charles and Danny. Seeing the spilled blood and severed lip only added to the tension.

The room measured about fourteen feet by sixteen feet. To the right of the entrance stood a tall, thin lamp with a black metal frame and then a TV in the corner. On the adjacent wall hung a set of vertical blinds that hid the sliding glass door leading out to the balcony. A tan secondhand sofa and matching love seat lined the other two walls. There was an old wood coffee table in not-too-bad condition sitting in front of the couch.

A large opening made for only a partial border between the living room and a fairly basic kitchen, which was roughly half the size of the main room. Jim kicked off his shoes and walked across the blue and white linoleum floor tiles to the counter top next to the sink. He set down the pack of beers and the plastic bag holding the sub. He could feel that the beer was getting warm and the sandwich had cooled to room temperature.

Reaching over the sink, Jim slid the window to the left, opening it as far as it would go. He was lucky to be able to do this. Only four of the ten units in the building had the extra kitchen window, the outer units on the first and second floors. The rest of the apartments only had windows at the back wall, one in the bedroom and one in the bathroom. The windows in the bathroom were located at head level in the shower. Jim had always assumed no one could see in.

When he moved in, the maintenance man had explained that if he opened the front sliding door and the back windows, there would be a cross breeze that would keep the whole place cool all summer long. It was good enough for the spring, but not so much through the summer months. When the temperatures soared, Jim needed to employ the air conditioning unit mounted through the front wall of the living room. The electric bill doubled when it was hot out, but he would rather pay extra than spend all of July and August sitting in a puddle of ass sweat and ball soup.

His apartment was in better condition than the building's common areas but it was still by no means a fancy place. The green paint on the walls was covered in smudges. The furnishings and appliances were run down and outdated. The ceilings were somehow done in four different shades of white. But the apartment was close to work and the rent was cheap. Jim could afford to live here without a roommate.

And for his part, he kept the place spotless. Jim was meticulous with his cleaning and organization. You could try, but you wouldn't find a speck of dust on any surface. The dishes were always promptly washed and put away. Any item could be found in its rightful place. For example, Jim didn't need to search for a bottle opener. He could have found it in the dark. He fetched it from the center kitchen drawer, on the right side, resting next to a corkscrew and an unopened book of matches.

Sliding a bottle out of the carrier, Jim popped the cap off and placed the other four in the fridge as he rounded the corner into the bedroom. In a single fluid motion, he reached one hand over his head and pulled off his shirt without spilling a drop. The shirt was tossed into a hamper in the corner of the room, next to a wooden night table and a double size bed.

He paused for a moment, sipping the Newcastle and considering whether he should shower or put on a clean shirt and eat first. The internal debate was over when he knelt down to pull his socks off and caught a whiff of himself. It was definitely shower time.

From where he stood, there was a closet to his right and a short, long dresser behind him and to the left. The closet ran the length of the short wall. Jim went to it and grabbed a plain black tee shirt from a hanger and a pair of gym shorts from the shelf above. Boxer shorts were pulled from the dresser and he passed through the minuscule hallway into the bathroom.

The clothes were situated on the lid of the toilet and the beer was placed on top of the medicine cabinet over the sink. Jim examined his reflection in the mirror. He had gotten some sun. The usual pallor had been replaced with a pinkish hue. A dew of perspiration clung to his skin. Patches of stubble scolded him for not having shaved in days. Jim ran fingers through his short chestnut hair and turned away.

Two sips later and Jim was reaching into the tub to turn on the water. It rushed out of the spigot, splashing cool drops up to his face and neck. He twisted the center dial to direct its flow to the shower head and began to unbuckle his belt. Something made him freeze in place.

His left ear twitched, pulling his attention away from the shower and back into the apartment. He could have sworn he heard someone moving around, footsteps maybe. After waiting a few heartbeats and not hearing anything more, Jim shrugged and decided it must have been Danny walking across the floor in the unit upstairs.

Jim pulled off his belt and hung it over the doorknob. He was undoing the button on his cargo shorts when the dissonance returned. His ears were not playing tricks, he was sure of it. Leaning back into the shower, the water was turned off and Jim tilted his head in the direction of the noise, straining to hear.

He listened and tiptoed into the kitchen. Somebody was just outside the apartment. The floor creaked from shifting weight in the hallway. The sounds resembled whispering or murmurs but Jim was not able to make out any distinct words. Okay, he had to be over-thinking. Maybe one of the neighbors had visitors. Maybe Jim was a panicky little bitch who was about to freak out over something as innocent as Danny or Charles having company. He was being silly and overreacting.

All the commotion with the police and the crazy guy was messing with his head. It had to be someone just walking by or waiting for the tenant in the next apartment. Jim felt foolish. It was ridiculous to think that someone was going to be sneaking around his apartment late at night after the police had just left. What was he thinking? Did he expect the lunatic would come back?

That was doubtful. And why should he feel like he has to hide out in his own home? It probably shouldn't matter who was out there but it had still piqued his curiosity. Jim decided to have a look through the peephole. He was halfway through the kitchen when the thuds began; a roar of explosive fists against the door. The force was so intense, the brass chain lock swung back and forth, clanging against the door frame.

Chapter 7

Methane. Ammonia. Hydrogen Sulfide. This combination of gases is what creates the stench of death. It's the smell of rot that spews out of a corpse during decomposition. The process starts when the heart stops beating and oxygen is no longer being delivered to the cells. Bacteria in the respiratory system and gastrointestinal tract start to break down the cells and tissue inside the fresh cadaver. The pancreas releases enzymes that cause the organ to begin digesting itself, a process that then spreads throughout the rest of the body.

This particular body was small, covered in black fur with a white stripe down its back. And it happened to be flattened against pavement by the side of a dimly-lit country road. Portions of the digestive system had been squeezed out through opposite ends of the creature. The tell-tale imprint of a tread pattern across the matted fur and broken skin suggested this animal had met with a gruesome and painful end.

A squirming carpet covered more than half of the dead skunk. A pair of paws pressed into either side of the body to hold it in place. Chester leaned down and chomped into the critter decaying before him. His teeth made quick work of the first mouthful, which consisted mostly of hair and squished maggots. Stomach roiling and hungry for more, most of the writhing mass was swallowed whole and still wriggling about. The paste of half-chewed larvae slid over his lips and down his chin as Chester again buried his snout into the spoiled food.

Incisors hooked into muscle, which now only weakly clung to crushed bones. The meat was rubbery, stretching and tearing in irregular patterns as it was pulled from the torso. Chester barely came up for air between bites. Each morsel slid easily down his throat. It was the most delicious and satisfying meal he had ever had.

Chester, same as most dogs, had a sense of smell more than ten thousand times stronger than that of humans; not that this was necessary for his nose to lead him to the precise location of his dinner. The stench of sun-roasted road-kill is enough to make most people wretch but for Chester, it was a pleasurable and alluring aroma. If this sounds strange to you, you're not alone and there's a theory that might help you understand.

So, you know how when two dogs meet each other, they immediately sniff each other's asses? They don't do this because they like the scent of dog shit. Some folks think dogs don't actually smell the lingering traces of excrement. Instead of the waste itself, they are able to detect individual pieces of food that were eaten by the other dog. Similarly, Chester could enjoy what remained of the healthy meat, rather than having to endure the taste and smell of putrefaction.

His ears perked up mid-bite. Sense of smell is not the only area where dogs outperform human beings. They also have incredibly sensitive hearing. The hum of tires against concrete and the growl of an eight-cylinder internal combustion engine could be heard from miles away. Chester's attention was drawn to the vehicle long before it passed by. The pup knew something was coming his way even before the headlights became visible in the distant dark.

Chester pushed out a growl. It was the kind usually reserved for when someone tried to take away his biscuit. He kept eating though, looking up at routine intervals and waiting for whatever it was that was coming for him. The car noise had grown louder now. It was getting close. He could hear music playing from the stereo. Chester's head lifted all the way up, aiming his nose at the sky to let the last of his supper slither down into his gut.

The car finally passed by. It was a large black four-door model. Headlamps raced by in a flash. Exhaust and burnt oil poured from the tailpipe. In about two seconds, all that could be seen was a pair of taillights fading into the night. Chester chased behind in a valiant, yet failing effort to catch the two glowing amber beads. Leg muscles tensed and pushed, the pads on the bottoms of his feet scuffed against the street and toenails chipped and broke as they failed to penetrate the hard surface. This new prey was too fast, but it might lead him to his next meal.

Moments later and a few miles down the road, nervous knuckles tapped on the driver's side window of a rusted white pickup. Whoever had been driving apparently lost control and slid off the road. The truck's front end was wrapped around the base of a tree. Segments of the hood and fenders were bent completely out of place and the front bumper had crumbled to bits.

Owen, a pudgy fellow of average height and twenty-five years of age, stood on the gravel shoulder of the road, wearing sweat pants and a white tank top. He had seen the crashed truck, but not until he had driven past the scene. The young man had put his sedan in reverse and backed up far enough to confirm what he thought he had seen. Planning to call in the accident, he got out to check the cab before doing so; no point in calling emergency services for an unoccupied vehicle and no immediate signs of trouble. To Owen's surprise, not only was the bloodied driver inside, but he seemed to still be breathing.

"You okay, buddy? I'm going to call for help," he shouted through the glass. Owen pulled a cellular phone from his pants pocket. He held the phone up to his face and with his thumb, dialed nine-one. He paused, noticing that the body in the truck had begun to stir.

The tapping was muffled, but loud enough to hear inside the cab. Someone was out there but the words were disjointed. It was simply noise; a series of sounds with no value. Greg's body was jerked into consciousness. His sleep was being disrupted and anger was building. This was the first part of the man to become fully awake, his rage. Someone had come for him while he slept, they'd found him. It was a good thing he was up now so he could show the bastard that this sort of intrusion would not be tolerated.

Eyes opened with a shot, wide and piercing. Greg jerked upright, pulling his head away from where it had been wedged between the dashboard and windshield. A sticky red rope stretched from the cracked glass to his blood-saturated hat. Flopping back into the seat, he struggled to gain his bearings. More tapping sounded against the window, accompanied by more vocal dissonance.

"Oh man, I thought you were dead," called Owen from outside the truck. "Look at your arm! I'm calling an ambulance."

A pair of bleach-white bones stuck through the soft hairless skin on the underside of Greg's left arm, halfway between his elbow and wrist. He flung himself at the window, furious and desperate to get at the enemy outside the truck. His right hand balled to a fist and drove into the glass, leaving knuckle skin smeared at the points of impact. As he punched away with his right, the back of his useless left hand bounced off the forearm and let the exposed broken bones absorb the blows. A dark viscous fluid streaked the clear barrier, obstructing Greg's view of his target.

"Okay, okay. Just take it easy, I'm going to help you out of there," said Owen; his voice soothing to emphasize his good intention. He popped his phone back into his pocket and gripped the handle to open the truck door. It was at this exact moment the young man sealed his fate. He was doomed. What came next should serve to remind you that you should never help anyone.

The lever pulled, the latch clicked and released, the door flung open. The Good Samaritan lost his grip on the handle; the door swinging hard with the weight of Greg's body pressed into the other side. Owen stood back, avoiding contact with the door as it whizzed by. He knew he was being rude, but Owen couldn't bring himself to do anything more than stare at the other man as he flailed his limbs in all directions and sprayed blood all over the vehicle.

A ravaged shell of his former self, Greg had sustained countless bruises, a skull-rattling concussion, and three broken ribs in addition to the compound fracture to his arm. But the man paid no mind to his injuries as he worked to free himself from the confines of the pickup. The goal was achieved, but with little grace. Greg tried to plant his left foot on the loose ground and the gravel shifted beneath him. He fell face down; the full weight of his body landing on his left arm. Fresh blood burst from the wounds to form red rivulets in the dirt.

The man in sweatpants felt a swell of shame and embarrassment. This guy in front of him was badly hurt and obviously in a state of shock. He could no longer just stand aside while the man suffered. Kneeling down to Greg's left side, Owen reached over his back to help him to his feet.

"Here, can you stand?" Owen hadn't gotten a single verbal response from the man, but he kept trying anyway. "See if you can sit upright."

Greg felt the pressure of the man's hands as they squeezed below his armpits and attempted to roll him over. The aggressor was upon him. Greg, knowing he had to act, to defend himself, rolled to his right side and found the face of his attacker was only inches from his own. He had to strike back, swiftly and relentlessly. With his only useful hand, he gripped the other man's arm. This sonofabitch was going to get slaughtered.

"Relax man, I'm going to help you get up," Owen insisted.

Despite the hand wrenched around his arm and fingernails digging into skin, he managed to get the battered man back on his feet. Owen stood him up and positioned him so his back could lean on the outside wall of the truck bed. He let go, confident the mangled mess of a man could stand on his own. As he removed his hands, Owen found the other man did not loosen his grip.

"Take it easy. You're going to be fine, just let me call-" Owen was cut off mid-sentence.

He was yanked forward by the elbow. Owen put a hand up and tried to resist but it was no use. He was already within biting distance. The bleeding maniac lurched forward and chomped down on Owen's forearm, just above the wrist. Teeth cut into skin, tearing through muscle and tendon. Both men pulled away at the same time and Owen spotted the damage right away. His bones were just as sparkling white as Greg's until blood poured in and flooded the hole.

Owen cried out, but there was no one who could help him. He was on his own with little he could do to defend himself. In his panicked state, Owen turned to run back to his car, slipping and almost falling on the silty ground.

Greg swallowed the slimy wad of flesh, not bothering to wipe the saliva and blood from his chin and cheeks. His taste buds were alive with delight. He'd enjoyed the first bite so much, Greg hardly noticed that his meal was trying to get away. His left hand swung lifelessly as he pumped his arms and sprinted to close the distance between himself and his retreating foe.

A strong right hand locked onto Owen's right shoulder, spinning him around mid-stride and gripping tight onto his cotton tank top. He now understood the danger he faced, so as he turned to face the crazy man, Owen used his own momentum and mashed a left hook into the man's right cheek.

Stunned for a split second, Greg's head ricocheted to the left and a broken bicuspid shook loose from his jaw. He swallowed the tooth and tugged even harder on the man's shirt. The fabric stretched and began to rip apart. Greg opened his mouth and lunged for the man. His teeth sunk into the top of Owen's meaty right shoulder. The muscle was firm and the flesh did not come away easy. Blood rolled out of evenly-spaced tooth holes, dumping more red onto the man's shirt and exposed skin.

Owen howled in agony, screaming and crying, pleading for the attack to end. His assailant would not relent. Greg charged into Owen's shoulder, causing Owen to lose his footing and both men tumbled to the ground. Owen felt tendons twisting and separating as the madman bit harder and deeper. Owen did what he could to fight back; his left fist delivering multiple blows to Greg's head but the bastard refused to let go.

Crack! Another crashing fist rocketed through the air and into the lunatic's face. Crunch! This one was into his nose. The man's head twitched, but the teeth stayed locked in place. The punches were beginning to affect the madman, slowing him down and weakening his hold, even if just a little. Owen, determined to survive the encounter, had now found some hope that he could do just that.

He swung harder, right into Greg's nose. Over and over again, hitting the same spot until his hand hurt as much as his shoulder. Each punch crushed and flattened the nose, pressing it deeper into the nasal cavity. The cartilage inside had been ground to dust and the center of the man's face was caving inward. It took dozens of thrusts to force this maniac into taking some defensive action.

Instead of letting go and backing off, Greg moved his right hand from the ground where he'd been using it for balance and placed it on Owen's throat. Fingers clenched like a vise, pinning Owen to the ground and cutting off his air supply.

Greg's grip tightened. Owen's right hand tried and failed to pry fingers from under his chin. Vessels, deprived of blood flow and oxygen, swelled and protruded from Owen's neck. Blackness promptly filled his periphery as life was literally being squeezed out of him. Feet kicked at air. His back arched, lifting the center of his spine off the ground as barren lungs begged for breath. Owen's movements were restricted. No longer could he punch his attacker but he could still reach his face. In a last-ditch effort for survival, he felt around on the man's face until his right thumb found an eye.

It had the texture of a grape and it popped like one too. Owen's thumb nail split through the front of the eyeball. Squishing and shifting, it filled the space around the invasive digit. Clumpy wet goo spilled from the opening, streaming down his hand and wrist. The thumb hooked in, twisting and turning, making mush of the eye and the muscles behind it.

Greg growled; the rumble of a tortured animal. His head wriggled back and forth, eventually tearing free a chunk of bloodied trapezius muscle. The thumb fell out of his face. His victim's limp hand landed on his chest. Owen let out an obstructed cough; burgundy spittle dotting the faces of both men. And then he was gone.

At long last, Greg's prey had stopped struggling. It was finally time to eat. The victor bit into a spot on the abdomen, just below the sternum. The skin gave some resistance, but nothing he couldn't handle. Once a hole was established, he reached in with his right hand to pull out a strand of glistening innards. He eagerly shoveled them into his mouth. Like a magician with an endless scarf up his sleeve, Greg dragged lustrous lengths of sausage-like small intestine from Owen's gaping torso.

Half of each mouthful fell back out while Greg hurriedly chewed, swallowed, and reached down for more. Every bit was pure ecstasy but his joy would be short-lived as his meal would soon be interrupted. He slowed chewing and listened to the sound of light footsteps approaching.

The canine had been trotting along the road, following the path of the red lights that had passed him earlier. In the dark of the night, he could barely make out the street, but he could easily hear the two men fighting in the distance. Chester knew he was getting close to the food and that was all that mattered. The rotten hole in his side, the shattered bones, and the broken toenails were all irrelevant. He'd tracked down another meal and the damage to his body was well worth it.

He was almost there. Chester could see the car now. It was stopped but the engine was still running and the radio remained on. And there was another vehicle near it. He could make out the faint outline of shapes moving in the darkness between the pair of autos. Something was out there, but he could not yet see what it was. Chester crouched as he moved, keeping his body as close to the ground as possible and trying to stay hidden for as long as he could.

A sweet and hearty odor wafted through the air and into Chester's nostrils. It grew stronger as he stepped close enough to see what was moving in the dark. One of the humans was on top of the other. The one on the bottom was not moving but the one on top looked like he was sitting up, leaning down, and then sitting back up. He did this over and over again.

The human on top was eating the other, stopping only when he discovered Chester watching him. The dog walked forward another couple of steps, waiting for his eyes to adjust to the point where he could make out the upright figure. It was a familiar face. Chester registered some recognition in the man's expression as well.

Greg shot to his feet, startled by the presence of a dog. However, when their eyes met, he could tell that the pup was not a threat. The two of them maintained eye contact, neither looked away and neither felt the urge to attack or to flee. Greg looked to the partially consumed corpse at his feet and then back at Chester. He slowly lowered himself back to the body.

Again, he looked to the Brittany Spaniel, then back to the cadaver, and then back at the pup. It was an invitation. Chester's ears perked up. He trotted over to the man, close enough so that only Owen occupied the space between them. Greg knelt all the way down and Chester leaned in, following his lead. The two infected animals shared a feast.

In thirty minutes, all that remained of their meal was a flimsy stalk of bone, skin, and tattered sweat pants. Now that the food was gone, there was little to do but hunt for more. After all, they would be hungry again soon enough. Chester and Greg moved a lot slower now that their bellies were full. The two new friends strolled out to the street, guided by the moon's glow and drawn toward the faint lights of Niagara Falls Boulevard.

Chapter 8

Four large carrots with leafy green tops lie on a wooden cutting board with three plump potatoes and six fresh celery stalks. About a dozen pearly onions were scattered across the counter top. Jars of cumin, paprika, and garlic powder were lined up next to an expensive-looking butcher's block. Charles lurched over the counter and examined the cutlery set.

Stubby fingers danced along the rounded edges of thermo-resin handles. After a breath of indecision, a sweat-glistened hand pulled out the largest knife available. The high-carbon stain-resistant steel caught the light perfectly, reflecting the length of the flat metal. The word *CUTCO* was etched into the shoulder of the blade in black lettering.

The potatoes were picked first and Charles was eager to begin slicing. The largest of the three was grabbed from the others and placed in the center of the chopping board. First, he cut it in half the long way. It was so easy; no resistance, a smooth clean cut. But when you pay over a thousand dollars for a set of kitchen knives, they sure as Hell better be able to slice through a potato. At that price, you should be able to cut through a cinder block.

Next, Charles spun the potato ninety degrees and began rapidly pressing the knife through each half simultaneously; the blade firmly striking the bamboo board with each hurried pass. The first few slices were as thin as he could get them but less than halfway through, patience was lost and the pieces grew larger and thicker as the knife reached the end of the spud.

With the first tater fully chopped, Charles scooped up the pieces and dropped them into a boiling pot on the stove. Beef broth sloshed inside the black ceramic saucepan, running over and down the side. The fluid dripped onto the electric stove coil, where it hissed sharply and released a small cloud of steam. Charles had already finished cutting up the next potato before the vapor dissipated.

When he had come inside after the police left, he immediately busied himself with the task of preparing the evening meal. He'd wanted to get his mind off of that junkie who'd tried to force his way into the building. Hopefully the rest of the night would be uneventful. But if that nut case did come back for another showdown, Charles would be happy to show him who's boss. And he wouldn't be quite as restrained as he had been the first time.

Of course, it would be up to him to deal with the fool if he returned. It's not like anyone else in the building was willing to step up and defend themselves. Pussies. They really should show him a little more appreciation. But if he did have to defend his home and neighbors again, Charles hoped it could wait until after dinner.

He placed the knife on the counter and opened the cupboard overhead. Not finding what he needed, he moved to the next cupboard, and the next, not bothering to close the cabinet doors as he moved. How could he have forgotten where the snacks were stored? The bright yellow bag was in the fourth cabinet on the bottom shelf, Lays Classic potato chips. Charles tore open the bag and stuffed an entire handful into his mouth.

"What are you doing in there?" a woman's voice sounded from the living room.

All of the units in the building had the same basic layout. The living room was situated toward the front of the building, with the kitchen in the middle and the bathroom and bedroom at the rear. Charles lived in the garden level apartment, so the front living room wall had a window near the ceiling instead of a sliding glass door with a balcony.

The rotund young lady, who had earlier helped clean blood spatter from Charles' face, sat on a black leather couch in the front room, wearing a white blouse and tan capri pants. She absently flipped through magazine pages and waited for a response.

"Charles?" she called again. The woman turned to look over her shoulder but didn't go so far as to get up and walk to the next room.

"What do you think I'm doing?" Charles barked at her. "If you had to guess, what would you assume I'm doing in the kitchen at dinner time with the stove on? You think it over and let me know when you've reached a conclusion."

"Okay," the woman answered, not reacting to Charles' nasty tone. "But aren't we going to go see the doctor?"

"The urgent care place is open twenty-four hours. We can go after I eat," Charles called to her; portions of half-chewed potato chips tumbling out of his mouth as he spoke.

"Alright, but if you're cooking, could you at least change shirts?" she urged, "I don't want you to ruin that one. It looks nice on you. Plus, it was expensive."

"This shirt?" Charles asked, sliding the chip bag onto the counter. "You mean this shirt that's got blood stains all over it? I might as well use it as a damn napkin at this point, see?"

Charles rubbed both hands along either side of his belly, leaving trails of grease from each finger. Then he giggled. There was a short pause before a few more titters escaped his lips, which grew into a booming guffaw. This went on for about a minute, Charles chortling to himself and then finally busting out and filling the apartment with laughter.

It was like someone told the most hilarious joke anyone had ever heard. Sure, it was a little funny. He was wearing a napkin shirt. You'd find it at least mildly amusing. But the good cheer had less to do with his great sense of humor, and more to do with the remarkably high level of serotonin collecting in his brain.

Serotonin is a neurotransmitter that is created in neurons that lie deep within the brain stem. This chemical plays an important role in regulating mood, aggression, and appetite. In an effort to keep the host away from medical help, the virus triggered a mechanism in the brain causing it to produce loads of the stuff. The infection, which entered Charles' body when it was coughed onto the mucosal surfaces of his eyes, nose, and mouth, had infiltrated his brain within minutes.

The result was hunger, mood instability, and then symptoms resembling mania- a state of hyper-arousal and feelings of invincibility. This is why Charles could go from snapping at his girlfriend one moment, to doubling over with laughter the next.

Once the serotonin was in full effect, the pathogen activated the hypothalamus, the part of the brain responsible for regulating the sympathetic nervous system. Two signals were sent out. The first traveled down the nervous system to the adrenal medulla, a pair of glands situated on top of the kidneys. This caused the production and release of epinephrine, also known as adrenaline. The second message caused neurons throughout the body to secrete norepinephrine, also known as- you guessed it, noradrenaline.

This is an important reaction that occurs when the brain is alerted to something in the environment that requires immediate attention and prompt action. When an individual's safety is threatened, the body can be ready to respond almost instantly. They call this the Fight or Flight response because it usually happens when you've got to battle some type of threat or run away fast enough to avoid the danger.

Epinephrine and norepinephrine act as hormones and neurotransmitters. When released in the body, these substances have very potent effects. The heart rate increases, a faster pulse allows for more nutrients and energy stores to be sent throughout the body. Pupils dilate and the eyes process input at triple their resting rate, going from about twenty frames per second to almost sixty. This makes it easier to spot and track the source of danger. Breaths become deeper and quicker to get as much oxygen into the system as possible.

Adrenaline binds to receptors in the liver, causing it to release glucose- blood sugar that can be used as a source of emergency fuel for the body. Blood vessels expand so the fuel can get to where it needs to be, the muscles.

In order for the body to focus on increasing strength and improving reaction time, epinephrine suppresses the immune system. For the contagion, this was a win on all sides. The host grows powerful enough to defend itself and the virus won't be destroyed by the immune system.

You know how you get a fever when you're sick? This is an immune response. The rise in temperature is the body's way of trying to kill the pathogen by making its environment too hot to survive. Other symptoms of an infection are also caused by an immune response. A runny nose is your body's way of trying to wash infectious materials from your sinuses. Coughing is your body's way of ridding your throat and airway of germs and irritants.

Without an immune response, people like Charles wouldn't experience these symptoms and might not know they're sick. They may become agitated or hostile, but they won't feel physically ill. Noradrenaline, like serotonin, is psychoactive. When it binds to receptors in the brain, it has been known to cause drastic changes in a person's mood and a distorted perception of reality.

Charles was usually sort of a mopey prick but the infection was making him particularly irritable. The incessant chatter from his girlfriend only made things worse. She just wouldn't shut up about doctors and blood and getting checked out. Didn't she understand he was cooking? What was so difficult to understand about that? Was it too much to ask for her to keep her mouth shut for a few minutes so he could get the food ready? Or was she in some way compelled to keep opening her jaw to let audible idiocy spill out?

"I don't get why you've got to do that now," she complained from a well-worn spot on the sofa. "I thought we were gonna hit the drive-through."

"I'm cooking now because I'm hungry now and there's food here now," Charles hissed. "Is that okay with you, Dana? Is it okay if I make myself some God damn dinner before you drag me to see some doctor that I don't need?"

He stood in the center of the kitchen, glaring through the opening into the living room waiting for an answer; his mood worsening.

"I guess so," Dana relented. Her gaze drifted from Charles and back to the tabloid magazine in her lap. She added sheepishly, "I'm just worried, that's all."

Charles pushed out an exaggerated sigh and then returned to the cutting board. He didn't know what he was making exactly. There wasn't a recipe to follow or anything like that. When he had returned to the apartment after the police left, Charles decided to make stew but he wasn't sure how. So he just started boiling a bunch of ingredients that he thought should probably be in a stew.

While the work continued in the kitchen, work also progressed on a microscopic level. The newly evolved rabies was still shaking things up. In fact, it was just getting warmed up. As the infection continued to spread throughout the brain, it made a few more adjustments. Next up was the mid-brain region, home to the two areas where dopamine is made.

Everyone has heard of dopamine, especially if you know someone with Parkinson's Disease. The Substantia Nigra is one portion of the brain that produces dopamine. The dopamine created here plays a role in changing and regulating physical movements. This is the part of the brain that breaks down and causes the symptoms associated with Parkinson's. The Substantia Nigra was essentially given a pass and was not affected. Interfering with the body's ability to control its movements would be counter-productive.

Dopamine is also created in the Ventral Tegmental Area, VTA for short. The dopamine produced here plays a role in rewarding certain behaviors such as drug use, satisfying appetite, and generally anything that feels good- even if it isn't good for you. Irregular dopamine levels in the VTA can lead to a syndrome that looks like Attention Deficit Hyperactivity Disorder, schizophrenia, and obsessive-compulsive disorder. This is where the viral intruder applied itself, forcing the VTA to pump out dopamine at a rate it would never have done on its own.

So far, so good. But inside the brain, not all of these interactions were beneficial to the viral interloper. The first significant shortcoming was in how the infectious agent affected the Prefrontal Cortex. To put it plainly, this section of the brain was turned off.

The Prefrontal Cortex is the part of the brain that aids in organizing thoughts, regulating aggression, controlling impulsive behavior, and making responsible decisions. Without a properly functioning Prefrontal Cortex, anger is not suppressed. Unchecked rage maturates and takes over. Violent behavior and primitive reactions to stimulus are expressed freely with no concern for the outcome or consequences.

Charles was about to illustrate this. The potatoes had all been diced and added to the boiling concoction on the stove. He pulled a carrot from the pile and slid it onto the cutting board. While he was lining up the knife in his right hand to begin cutting, he lost his salty, moist grip on the vegetable. It rolled away from his left hand and fell to the floor.

Now the average person would simply bend down and pick it up, wash it off, and try again. Charles had a different approach. He grabbed the edge of the cutting board and flung it across the room. It banged into the wall, leaving a dent and removing some paint chips before landing on the linoleum floor. Drywall dust formed a small cloud and gave the kitchen a sort of foggy ambiance.

"What was that?" asked Dana. The commotion had her curious but she wasn't concerned enough to get off of the couch or look away from her reading.

"Carrots," Charles grumbled.

"What? I can't hear you," she called.

Charles didn't answer. He reached for the knife and turned back to the counter where he pulled a new carrot from the group. Since the chopping board was still on the floor, Charles just used the surface of the counter top. A moment later, he was back in the zone.

The remaining carrots were cut up in no time at all. Their green tops were thrown at, but not into, the garbage can. Next it was time for the celery. Charles lined up three stalks next to each other and quickly began cutting. He kept the blade in the same place, working the knife up and down while pushing the celery beneath. It was hypnotic. The first three pieces were fully cut and pushed aside to make room for more.

It was on to the next three. Up, down. Up, down. The rhythm grew faster; light reflecting off the razor-sharp and fast-moving stainless steel. As the cutting speed increased, the celery was pushed through quicker and quicker until Charles noticed that at some point, the counter top surface had turned from yellow to red. Glossy pink smears had appeared on the knife as well. A half inch of fingertip sat alongside the freshly cut vegetables.

When the blade cut into the skin, and then bone, and then severed a piece of the digit, neurons called nociceptors sensed there was damage to the tissue. They immediately fired off a signal through the peripheral nerves toward the spinal cord. The message was carried by the spine up to the thalamus, which is made up of two small lobes in the low brain.

The thalamus acts as a relay center. Nerve signals come in and it is the job of the thalamus to redirect the messages to where they can be interpreted. A pain signal, let's say from a severed fingertip, should be sent to the parietal lobe, which sits at the top and toward the back part of the brain. The message reaches this region of the brain almost instantly and that's when you feel the pain.

There are other parts of the brain that react to a pain signal, especially as it pertains to understanding why the pain is being experienced, an emotional reaction to the injury, developing a strategy to avoid being harmed in the future, and so on. But none of this mattered for Charles. When the pain signal reached his thalamus, it went nowhere. It just stopped. There was no bodily response, no reflex, no sensation of pain; another side effect of the recent cranial modifications.

Charles picked up the detached portion of his finger with his right hand. He studied it as if having just discovered some bizarre artifact. His mind struggled to interpret what was happening. He understood he was holding something. He also understood his left hand had one finger that was a lot shorter than the rest. And that was about it.

Panic should have set in. Charles should have been packing the digit in ice. He should have been wrapping a bandage around his bleeding stump. He should have been running out the door and heading for the hospital to have his finger reattached. Charles did none of these things. He just stood there, transfixed by the stubby clump of flesh.

He popped the fingertip into his mouth and bit down with his molars. It was salty and tough to chew. The texture was rubbery and foreign. Charles could feel the nail crack between his teeth. The muscles in his jaw strained to break down the small bits of bone and tissue. Coarse bits of broken nail scraped the inside of his cheeks and gums. It lacked flavor and with the exception of a trickle of something metallic, it was unpleasantly dry. Charles rolled the tenderized wad across his tongue and swallowed.

"How much longer until we eat?" a voice called from somewhere in the apartment. No answer was given.

Charles walked to the refrigerator and opened the door, paying no mind to the bright red fluid that oozed down the handle. It was a few shades lighter than the spots on his trousers and shirt. Inside the fridge, sitting uncovered on a large plate was a thick slab of chuck roast. He reached in and grabbed the meat with both hands. Blood squirted from the shortened left index finger, mixing with the beef's natural juices.

The door hung open and Charles stood in the center of the kitchen. He looked down at the meat and then up to the ceiling. How long had he been standing there? It felt like a week or more. Charles struggled to remember what he had been doing and what it was that he was supposed to do. He was cutting vegetables. Wait, was that right? Yes, that was it. Charles spotted the celery and bloody knife on the counter. His hands quivered. The roast slid free and hit the floor with a heavy wet plop.

While Charles had been preparing dinner, hormones and neurotransmitters had continued to flood his brain, blood, and nervous system. In less than a half hour, each had climbed to unnaturally high levels. Charles' systems were overwhelmed. The mind and body had grown severely altered. His drool-soaked shirt was evidence that the virus had expanded into the salivary gland, the final stage and ultimate goal of the infection.

"Are you okay?" The voice sounded like it had been whispered in a tunnel.

Charles turned to see Dana standing in the doorway between the living room and kitchen. He heard the sound of her speaking but he couldn't make sense of it. Her words came as indecipherable white noise.

"Oh my God, what happened?" cried a wide-eyed Dana. She walked toward Charles and grabbed for his hand to take a closer look. Charles shuddered and pulled back. She was coming at him. She wanted him dead.

"What is going on with you?" Dana pleaded.

It was a perfectly reasonable question. Charles was covered in blood, as was the counter top and refrigerator. There were vegetables all over the place. The chopping board was on the floor and so was a big slab of meat. Dana had overlooked his curt tone earlier. And against her better judgment, she let him delay the trip to the medical center. But this couldn't go on any longer. Something was obviously wrong with Charles.

Muscles throughout the body store a chemical called adenosine triphosphate, or ATP. The substance is found in every living cell. ATP is an energy molecule that can instantly fuel muscles by immediately burning sugars and fats stored in the tissue. Using ATP is another part of the Fight or Flight response.

It kicks in when you need to act now- not in a few moments when adrenaline kicks in. Now. This reaction is so powerful, it generates an instant burst of superhuman power. You know that old story about the mother who lifted an overturned car to free her child that was pinned under it? That's ATP in action. And okay, sure, this isn't really fighting or fleeing, but you understand how the moniker came to be. That instant strength helps prepare you for combat or for fleeing a conflict.

Charles wasn't the fleeing type and there was nowhere to run even if he wanted to. The threat was right in front of him. His attacker was getting in his face and grabbing at him, trying to get to his injured hand. He was going to defend himself. What else was he supposed to do? Dana would try once more to tend to her boyfriend's wound. She would find out too late that he was already gone and there was nothing she could do about it.

Chapter 9

"Who is it?" Jim shouted. His attempts to sound menacing were a total failure. What a surprise. Too much hesitation and concern came through in his voice. He pulled the soiled shirt back over his head to once again cover his pale and mostly hairless torso.

No one answered from outside the apartment and the pounding continued, loud and hurried. Jim walked to the entryway to confront the offender. He moved slowly to give himself enough time to consider his actions before opening the door. As he reached for the knob, Jim tried to picture who or what might be on the other side. What first came to mind was the lunatic that had gone after the neighbors earlier that night. Could it be the same guy? Had he returned?

That wouldn't have been very bright. But when the other tenants gave their statements to the police, it didn't sound like they were describing a genius. After all, this is the same idiot who ran at full speed head-first into a glass door. The man would have had to be exceptionally stupid or incredibly deranged. Maybe both. But even so, why come back? To pick up where he left off? To carry out an all-night attack on innocent people in their homes? The more he thought about it, he only grew more convinced that this is exactly what was happening.

"Hold on a second," Jim called through the wall as he turned away from the door and bolted toward the bedroom.

He slid open the closet door and reached inside. There was a baseball bat in there somewhere but Jim hadn't seen it or used it for as long as he could remember. Behind the hanging shirts, buried under a pile of sparsely-used athletic gear and a pair of duffel bags, Jim made out engraved black letters that spelled the words *Louisville Slugger*.

Jim had to crawl halfway into the closet to reach it. He was able to get a grip on the handle and after a few firm tugs, the bat slid free. It must have been how King Arthur had felt when he freed Excalibur from the stone. Although King Arthur probably hadn't had to endure the stink of his own ball sweat when he'd freed the sword. Jim tested his grip on the wood handle and briskly walked back to the apartment's main door.

"Who is it?" he tried again. There was no response apart from another loud knock. Holding the baseball bat with both hands around the grip, Jim sighed and whispered, "Okay, here goes."

If he opened the door and was greeted by a maniac coughing blood on himself and posturing for a fight, Jim would simply smash his head with the bat, shove him into the hall, and close the door. This was the fantasy, anyway. In reality, he'd have been much more likely to run away like Danny had. But there wasn't really anywhere to run to. He'd end up having a doorway tug-o-war like Charles had. Eventually one of them would tire, probably Jim, and then what would he do? With the bat in his right hand, Jim twisted the knob with his left and flung open the door.

She jumped back a step, alarmed by the quickness with which the door had been pulled away from her pounding fist. If the girl noticed the bat, she didn't say as much. Jim bent to his right side, just out of site of the young woman. He leaned his would-be melee weapon upright in the corner next to the kitchen table before she had the chance to spot it.

Beth stood in the doorway as if waiting to be invited inside. She twirled a lanyard with a bunch of keys on the end. The orange cord whirled through the air, coiling around her finger and then back the opposite direction as she spun her hand the other way.

Jim was more surprised than relieved to see her. He looked her over before speaking. She wore the same clothes as she'd had on earlier, though her tight yoga pants didn't have the same appeal as they had that afternoon. There was an addition to the outfit, an over-sized dark blue hoodie. Her dark hair was pulled back into a loose pony tail with several floating strands hanging loose. Her skin nearly glowed and a trace of perspiration outlined the top of her forehead. She hadn't said a word either. In fact, her chest raised and fell like she was out of breath.

"What are you doing here?" Jim asked; his voice shaky as the adrenaline had yet to subside.

"Am I not supposed to visit my boyfriend?" Beth answered Jim's question with one of her own. She shifted her weight, leaning her right shoulder into the door frame. "Were you in the middle of something?"

"No, not really," he answered. "I was just about to get a shower."

"Oof, good thing," said Beth, humorlessly adding, "You smell like a dead bird."

"Right," Jim said, ignoring the jab while sneaking a sniff from the pit of his shirt. "I guess I asked the wrong question. How'd you get here?"

"I got a ride from a friend," she explained casually. No longer waiting to be invited, she walked into the apartment, leaving the door wide open behind her.

Jim thought he caught a whiff of something as she moved in front of him. He wasn't the only one who reeked. Did she smell of sex? No, he was being paranoid again. Beth's skin was flushed and dotted with moisture. That must have been sweat he was smelling. Yuck. But if Jim had to choose, he'd rather be grossed out by some BO than devastated by the scent of infidelity.

"I thought none of your friends had cars," said Jim. "Who finally got some wheels?"

"My friend Jeremy," she told him; her voice betraying a subtle air of defiance.

"Your friend Jeremy, huh?" Jim's eyes narrowed.

"Yep." Beth's eyes widened.

"That's interesting."

"If you say so."

"So why have I not heard of this friend before?" Jim asked, finally closing the door. He walked to the front of the living room and pulled the blinds away from the sliding glass door to look out at the parking lot.

Sitting in front of the building with its parking lights on, was a white sedan. It was one of those smaller Mazda models, about fifteen years old. The windows were tinted, making it impossible to see anyone who might be in the car at that time of night. Jim observed there was a patch of rust along the passenger's side fender. The wheels were covered by plain gray hubcaps.

"You can now, he's outside. Would you like to meet him?" Beth offered, crossing the room to stand in front of the couch.

"No," Jim stated flatly.

Taking advantage of the short silence, he contemplated whether there would be any benefit in trying to explain to her why it might be inappropriate for a young lady to unexpectedly show up at her boyfriend's house in the later hours of the evening, being driven around by some strange guy he had never heard of, and looking as if she'd just concluded some sort of rigorous physical activity.

Deciding the effort would be wasted, he turned to face her and asked, "Okay, so what's up?"

"I thought you might want to talk," Beth said, letting her body drop onto the sofa's tan cushions.

"You could have called and we could've talked on the phone," Jim said.

"I could have, but I wanted to stop by instead," Beth explained. "What's the problem with me coming over?"

"There's no problem with you coming over, but what about your buddy out there?" asked Jim, pointing to the front wall.

"What about him?"

"What is he doing out there?" Jim pressed.

"I told him to wait for me," Beth answered as though this wasn't at all out of the ordinary.

"So you don't plan to stay long, I take it," Jim's gaze focused on her.

"I don't know," Beth answered with a shrug. "I didn't really think about it."

"Seems a little inconsiderate," Jim pointed out. "To keep him sitting out there by himself, I mean."

"Didn't realize you were so concerned."

"Oh, I'm not," Jim corrected her. "Frankly, I don't give a shit about whoever he is. He can sit out there all night for all I care."

"Nice attitude," Beth frowned. She looked down to a cell phone in her hands.

Jim was still standing at the edge of the living room. He sighed. "Alright, so what is it you would like to talk about?"

"I don't know. Whatever, anything." She didn't look up at him.

"You didn't seem to want to talk earlier," Jim stated plainly. "You kicked me out of your house. I got the impression you wanted to be alone but I must have been mistaken."

"Oh. Yeah. I was in a bad mood earlier."

"You don't say." Jim's statement was loaded with sarcasm. "A bad mood for me, but a good mood for Jeremy."

"It's not like that," Beth objected but her voice lacked the exuberance to make it convincing.

"Okay, so what is it like then?" Jim's voice took a sharper tone than before and he subconsciously took a wider stance, letting his hands hang at his waist.

"He took me to get a new phone, see?" She held up the shiny new device, proudly presenting its large, bright touch screen display. "It's got a ton of stuff on it, it's going to take me forever to get used to the features and all the extra junk it has."

"Okay, that's great," Jim said, refusing to feign interest.

"Really?" Beth asked in a manner unclear as to whether it was rhetorical. "You're really going to act like that? Do you not want me here?"

"I didn't say that, but do you really not understand why I might be a tiny bit upset with you?"

Jim continued before Beth had a chance to reply, "You kicked me out, you refused to talk to me, and then a few hours later you show up with some guy driving you around? It really didn't occur to you that I might be less than happy with this series of events? And obviously this isn't a friend you actually want me to meet. That's why he's waiting out in the car."

"So what are you saying? You don't trust me?" Beth accused.

"Your actions don't exactly warrant trust, but that's beside the point." Jim was about to elaborate. He debated whether he should mention the condom wrapper he discovered in her room earlier that day but decided to keep it to himself. If he brought it up, she'd lie and he'd be too spineless to pursue the matter any further. "I'm really just too tired to argue with you."

"Right," answered Beth. "Because you've got something else to do, is that it?"

"I've got anything else to do!" Jim raised his voice louder than he'd intended. "Anything would be better than constantly fighting with you. I can't keep up with the odd behavior and nasty mood swings. I don't know what you expect me to do."

"Ya know what- do whatever you want." Beth stood and crossed the room to the door. "I'll just have Jeremy give me a ride home then."

She let herself out before Jim could intervene, slamming the door behind her.

"Yeah, let Jeremy ride you all the way home!" Jim snapped, but it was too late. She was already gone. He thought about opening the door to shout it at her, but that would have been too childish, even for him.

Jim shut out the light in the living room so he wouldn't be seen when he went to watch her leave. He walked back to the front door and peeked through the blinds to see Beth walk out the front door of the building. She passed around the front of the rusted white car and got in the driver's seat. The headlights turned on and Jim closed the blinds. He stopped watching before the sedan had left the parking lot.

"Bitch," he muttered to himself.

Jim turned the deadbolt to lock the main door as he passed by on his way into the kitchen. He grabbed the room-temperature Newcastle from the kitchen counter and carried it with him into the bathroom. Jim twisted the shower knobs to get the water going and he began to undress, taking pulls from the bottle between each article of clothing. The garments fell to the floor in a heap which got kicked into the corner of the tiny bathroom.

Small or not, the room had a full-size bath with a shower head, not the compact shower-only setup you sometimes see in apartments. Jim stepped into the tub and pulled the curtain closed. It was one of those cheap disposable shower curtains. The dark speckles of mold along the bottom were becoming harder and harder to ignore. Jim made a mental note to replace it next time he was running errands. He then placed the bottle of Newcastle next to the shampoo on the small rack at the rear of the bath.

The water was as hot as he could stand. It had been running for less than a minute and steam was already collecting at the ceiling. Jim stood directly below the head of the shower, so it rained down on him, soaking his hair, running over his shoulders and down his back. He stood motionless for several long moments, letting the water rush over his body. If he waited long enough and scrubbed thoroughly, maybe the whole day could be washed away; tension and bad memories rinsing off of his raw skin and disappearing down the drain.

Jim closed his eyes and let the water splash him straight in the face. He combed fingers through his hair so the near-scalding water could roll over his scalp. Turning so his back was to the stream, he wiped drops from his face and snatched the beer from where it sat on the rack. Careful to shield the bottle from the shower's flow, he enjoyed two sizable gulps before setting it down on the edge of the tub. He faced the water and stepped back into it.

When his eyes closed again, he didn't see blackness. In flashes, there were images of Beth. They weren't like photographs, there was motion to them. Fingers rubbed Jim's face and gently massaged his temples. He took another gulp of beer and tried to get on with his bathing. Once again, it was Beth he saw when his eyes squeezed shut.

He looked at her from behind. Her black hair hung loose, flowing over uncovered shoulders. Fingers ran through wavy locks. Beth's head cocked slightly to one side. There was the outline of another person in front of her, they were facing each other. The view was obscured. Jim was only permitted a glimpse of dark hair, styled short with a man's haircut. Beth's shoulders rolled, shifting as she raised her arms, wrapping them around his frame. Her breath was heavy. They were kissing.

Jim opened his eyes. His dopey imagination was starting to get the better of him. He groaned, inwardly scolding himself for being so insecure and irrational. Jim once again closed his eyes and leaned into the jetting water.

Beth appeared again. She was topless this time, writhing atop a faceless lover. Jim's ears rang from her pleasure-induced moaning and pleas for more. A pair of hands reached up to caress her bare breasts. Fingers darted over her flawless bare skin, brushing erect nipples before gliding across her ribs and down to her waist where they gripped firmly, pulling her in closer. Beth's back arched and her breasts aimed at the sky.

At her sides, Beth's hands tightened to fists. Her entire body tensed in a futile effort to delay climax and prolong the ecstasy that had overtaken her. Veins bulged in her wrists and neck while the ability to breathe temporarily escaped her. Beth's tan and glistening body froze in position as every muscle seemed to contract simultaneously. The girl's mouth freed a cry of satisfaction as the orgasm ran through her, transporting her to a place somewhere between reality and paradise before releasing her from its clutches.

Beth sucked in a deep breath. Every part of her relaxed at once, save for a spasmodic pulsating in her loins. Collapsing into his embrace, Beth reached around and dug her fingernails into the man's back, scratching his skin and leaving behind several scarlet welts. In response, his pelvis thrust harder, forcing himself even deeper inside of her.

Both eyes shot open. The moaning had faded, replaced by the sound of water splashing against the tile walls and porcelain tub. It was Jim who now struggled for breath. With his hands on his knees, he doubled over and pulled in oxygen. A sharpness ran down from his chest, turning to nausea in his guts. Paranoid Jim finished rinsing and turned the water off. He stepped, with beer in hand, out of the shower and onto the black memory foam bath mat. The bottle was placed on the toilet lid so Jim's hands were free to grab a towel and dry off.

He collected the bundle of dirty clothes from the floor, walking naked out of the steam-clouded bathroom and into the bedroom, where it was several degrees cooler. The soiled linen was dumped into the laundry basket with the lid promptly replaced. Plain white socks, boxers, and black gym shorts were removed from the dresser and tossed on the bed. The closet door was still open. Jim pulled a tee shirt from a hanger, paying no mind to style or color. It too was thrown on top of the bed as Jim left the room, retrieved his beer, and then returned.

Jim threw on his clothes in a hurry. Once fully dressed, he walked to the front of the living room, pulling back the blinds and opening the sliding glass door. In his socks, he stepped onto the balcony, cigarette and lighter in hand. He made sure to slide the door closed so no smoke would make its way indoors. He took a seat on one of two white plastic lawn chairs and lit up. Jim produced his cell phone from his shorts pocket and called Beth.

"Hello?" she answered. Her voice came out even, calm. She was not panting. There were no blissful emissions to indicate that her ringing phone had interrupted some carnal exultation.

"Hey!" Jim blurted into the phone with an unplanned tone of aggression. "Uh, I mean- hi. I just, I don't know, thought we should talk, ya know, clear the air from earlier."

"Everything's fine," she said.

"Are you sure?" Jim asked. "Are you- what are you doing? Are you at home?"

"Yes, I'm at home. I told you I was going home." She answered his questions, but she sounded distant and distracted.

"Okay, and Jeremy?" Jim asked with hesitation in his voice.

"I don't know if he's home," Beth answered. Jim couldn't tell if she was trying to make a joke or if she was just being dumb.

"You know what I mean," Jim pushed. "He isn't there with you?"

"Would you shut up? I'm on the phone!" she shouted at someone, not covering the mic portion of the receiver. Her yelling wasn't intended for Jim, but it blasted his ear nevertheless. "Sorry about that, my sister and mom are yelling at each other over the TV. They're so loud. What did you say?"

Jim could hear indistinct female voices yipping at each other in the background. He pretended not to notice and said, "No problem. I asked if your friend Jeremy was over there with you."

"What?" Beth stifled a laugh. "Why would he be here?"

"I don't know," Jim said, "Why was he *here*?"

"To give me a ride," she explained.

"Just to drive you here?"

"Actually, I was driving. He let me drive his car." Her answer again made Jim wonder whether she was a bad comedian or an average dullard.

"But it was just to get over here?" he asked. "That's all?"

"Yes, it was just so I could stop over and see you," she told him. "That's all, I promise."

"Okay," Jim exhaled a breath of relief. "I was just getting a little..."

"Jealous?" Beth cut him off.

"Yeah, I suppose so." Jim sounded ashamed.

"There's no reason to be jealous. I'm home. There's no guys here. I love you and we're fine." Beth's reassuring words forced a hint of a smile to pull at the edges of Jim's lips.

"I'm glad to hear that," he began, "I love you t-"

Beth interrupted, "Hang on, that's my other line, I'll be right back."

Before Jim could say anything, he heard the rustling noise of Beth fumbling with her cell phone. Her fingers scraped against the receiver, sending muffled distortion over the air. The connection never went silent, the way it should have when the person on the other end takes another incoming call.

"Hey, you there?" she asked. "Sorry about that, I'm still getting used to this phone and figuring out where the buttons are."

Jim opened his mouth to reply, but before words could pass through his lips, another voice answered for him. It was a male voice.

"Not a problem," said the guy on the other end. "What are you doing? You busy?"

Jim was stupefied. Who the Hell was calling his girlfriend at this late hour? Still in his seat on the balcony, Jim stared vacantly out across the parking lot. His intestines suddenly felt like they were squirming around and trying to escape. It was that kicked-in-the-balls feeling. Whether the kicking is literal or figurative, the pain in the stomach is quite real.

"I'm not doing anything tonight, not that I know of," Beth answered his question.

Jim continued listening, careful not to make a peep. Beth, in her limited wisdom, must have selected the option for a three-way call, rather than to simply answer the new call, placing the original caller on hold. How's that fancy new phone working out for you, Beth? How much are you going to regret not reading the owner's manual?

"You wanna grab something to eat, maybe come hang out for a bit?"

"Sure," Beth said. "You gonna pick me up?"

"I just gotta grab some cash," said the caller. "But I'll be there soon."

"I'll be ready," she replied. "And if you hurry, I may have a surprise for you."

"A surprise, huh?" the caller asked, sounding intrigued. "I like that. What sort of surprise?"

"I got a little outfit I think you'll like," Beth teased.

"Go on," he urged, "Do I get a description?"

"You'll have to wait and see." You could hear her seductive smile as she spoke.

Jim hung up.

He raced to the bathroom and applied deodorant. Jim considered opening a tube of gel and combing his hair but for time's sake, he pulled on a hat instead. His feet slid into a pair of sneakers; the laces were always tied. They were set loose enough to get the shoes on and off without having to re-tie them, while still being tight enough so that they would stay on when walking around. The empty beer bottle dropped into the kitchen garbage can as Jim walked out the door.

His cell phone buzzed in his pocket as he settled into the car seat. The caller ID said it was Beth. With the call ignored, the phone landed on the passenger's seat and Jim started the engine. He applied the brake to shift the car into gear and could already hear the phone vibrating against the seat cushion, another call from his girlfriend. Reluctantly, Jim answered instead of driving.

"Hello?" He couldn't tell if he sounded natural. Did his voice falter? He didn't want to let on that he had just heard most of her conversation.

"Sorry about that, I must have lost you," she said.

"It's okay," Jim replied. His lower jaw hurt from grinding his teeth. "Who was that?"

He did his best to sound as though everything was totally normal, like he hadn't just heard her flirting with some dude on the phone. Flirting. That was a polite way to put it. This wasn't like the condom wrapper. Jim couldn't lie to himself this time. It was impossible to misinterpret the meaning of that discussion.

"My aunt," Beth responded. Her lie came so easily. The voice held no tremor, no change in pitch. It made Jim wonder what else she might have lied about.

"Your aunt, huh?" He was growing increasingly furious. "What did she want? It's awfully late for her to be calling. Is everything okay?"

How far was she going to go with this? Jim was determined to throw her for a loop with his follow-up questions. Most people can pull off the initial fib but their manufactured stories will fall apart when pressed for more detailed information. He wanted to see whether she would cave in and admit the truth, or let herself get tripped up by failing to provide believable answers.

"She's fine. She was just calling to catch up."

"This late at night?" Jim asked, trying to distract himself by shifting the transmission from park to reverse, to drive, and back to park. "And you were only on the phone with her for like two minutes. That's pretty short for catching up. Unless she's, like, the world's fastest talker."

"I told her I couldn't talk because I'm getting ready for bed," Beth explained. "Since it is so late, ya know. But I think I am going to get to bed, so I'll give you a call in the morning, okay?"

She was going to bed. That much was true. But she obviously wasn't going to be sleeping and she wasn't going to be alone.

"You can't be tired already," Jim argued. "I thought we were going to talk for a bit."

"Yeah, I know. But I really am worn out," Beth asserted. "We'll talk tomorrow."

"I think we should talk now," Jim insisted. "Do you not want to talk to me?"

"Jim, I have to go," she said firmly.

"But-"

"Goodbye." Beth hung up the phone.

Jim's phone went silent and he immediately called back. The line rang and rang until the call was ultimately transferred to voice mail. His thumb pressed the redial button. Again, the line rang multiple times with no answer. Jim tried for a third time and the call went immediately to voice mail.

About ten minutes later, Jim was running a red light to cross through the intersection at Niagara Falls Boulevard. Since driving out of the parking lot, he had tried calling Beth four more times but never got an answer. He hung up each time the prerecorded voice mail greeting picked up.

"Hey y'all, it's Beth. I'm out and about doin' my thing. Leave one at the beep and I'll call ya back soon." The greeting was bubbly, cheery. What a piece of whorish crap she was. Jim hung up when the tone played.

Like a robot programmed with a single specific task, he drove in the direction of Beth's home. Jim focused on nothing but his destination. It probably would have done the angry young man some good to take a step back and think things through. You could usually rely on Jim to think things through over and over until he reached the point of obsession. Now when it would have saved him the drive time, the stress, and another wasted evening, he'd abandoned the thinking part of his brain.

60

What exactly did he intend to do upon arrival? Plead with her not to go out with whoever it was who had called? Catch her in the act, doing something unsavory with some strange fellow? Demand she stay in? Beg her to be faithful? Confront this guy when he showed up to take her out? All of these were shit ideas. If Jim had paused to consider his options, he might have realized that the best thing he could do was to go home and forget about her forever.

Whether he could convince her to stay home that night was irrelevant. His ability, or inability, to scare away her mystery suitor also mattered very little. What did matter was that his girlfriend was betraying him, heading out for a tawdry encounter with an unknown male caller. Speeding to her house to catch her in the act wasn't going to transform her into the loyal, trustworthy girl he wished he was dating. Plus, the drive from his apartment took almost thirty minutes. Would she even still be there when he arrived? He would soon find out.

Several broken speed limits and some very reddish looking yellow lights later, Jim's car idled in the street in front of Beth's mother's house. The porch light was off and the house looked dark throughout. He turned his headlights off and pulled into the driveway. Jim considered knocking on the door but how could he explain himself? Rational thought was starting to return. It was a lousy and tactless approach.

Maybe if he sat in the driveway with the engine running, someone would come out to see what he was up to. But so what? What could he possibly say if someone came outside to check on things?

"Sorry to bother you in the middle of the night, ma'am. But it appears as though Beth, you know- my girlfriend and your daughter, it seems as though she's an indiscriminate slut and I was hoping I could catch her before she went out to bang some random guy. You see, I was planning to beg and cry like a fool in hopes that my pathetic behavior would make her be a good girl from now on."

This promised to be humiliating and ineffective. Jim backed the car out of the driveway, aiming in the direction from which he had come, back toward South Transit Road. As he rolled up to the first stop sign, Jim recalled pieces of Beth's conversation with the stranger. They said they were going to get something to eat, didn't they? Jim couldn't recall if either had suggested a specific place, but there weren't too many restaurants open late.

The twenty-four-hour diner was only a mile or so down South Transit. Jim pulled into the parking lot, which was filled with more cars than he expected to find. The blue coupe crept past the front of the building; its image reflecting in the glass wall exterior. Jim leaned out the window, straining to recognize any of the many faces inside. The diner was packed, which he supposed would account for the high number of cars parked outside.

The car reached the far side of the building and there, around the corner of the front wall, sat two people. One was a guy who was about Jim's age and build, wearing a hat and a Buffalo Bills jersey. His back was towards Jim. The other person faced Jim's direction. It was a girl, a dark-haired girl to be specific, and she had the hood of a dark blue sweatshirt pulled over her head.

Jim shifted into park without waiting for the car to come to a complete stop. With gears grinding beneath the driver's seat, the front end bounded up and down for a few quick seconds before the suspension leveled out. Jim left the car there, not in a proper parking spot, but inside the space used for entering and exiting the lot. He sprang out of the car and entered the restaurant.

An older blonde woman who looked like she could be somebody's grandmother approached Jim as he stepped into the lobby. She held up a stack of menus and asked, "Hi, how many for tonight?"

Jim ignored her and pushed past a group of three youths who were waiting to be seated. It was about this time when he realized he had neglected to think of something to say or do if given the opportunity to confront his deceptive girlfriend. It looked like he was just going to sort of, ya know, wing it. Incensed as he was, Jim felt confident in his ability to improvise.

With a full head of steam, Jim marched through the crowded seating area and up to the table where the couple was sitting. Sneering, he planted his fists on the tabletop and leaned in toward the girl and declared, "I've got to talk to you. Right now."

The girl had been looking down, picking tomatoes out of her salad. She raised her eyes to meet Jim's. Her befuddled expression told Jim that he had caught her completely off guard. The girl looked at Jim and said, "Excuse me?"

"Uh..." The girl's comrade stirred, setting his utensils on the table next to a plate of half-eaten meatloaf. Perplexed, he struggled to understand what was happening and why someone was glowering at his date. His single syllable trailed off into silence.

"What do you want?" the girl asked with a mix of irritation and shock.

"Oh, um. Never mind."

It wasn't Beth. Jim felt like an asshole. The girl and her companion probably would have agreed. He slunk away from the table, his shoulders drooped and his eyes fixed on the floor. Jim noticed the hostess looking at him and whispering something to the cashier. He waved and offered an embarrassed half smile before turning toward the exit and seeing himself out.

Walking to his car, Jim made a point not to look back. He'd have expected to see several faces staring in his direction and wondering what was wrong with him. He and his embarrassment flopped into the driver's seat to determine his next move. The answer was simple and came to him quickly. It was time to go home.

Is this what he wanted for himself? To be driving around at all hours, twitchy with panic, obsessing about what his girlfriend was doing? Of course not. He should have stayed home in the first place; enjoyed a night to himself as a recently single young man. As soon as Beth screwed up the controls on her phone, that should have been it. He should have just let her go.

The drive home took longer than the initial drive to Beth's house since Jim was now stopping for traffic lights and observing the posted speed limits. And it was a good thing too. Jim was forced to swerve at a point along Town Line Road. A man was walking his dog right down the middle of the street. There were no streetlights and the dark made it impossible to spot them until he had nearly run them over. Jim maneuvered around them and shouted something unpleasant out the window.

He was home about twenty minutes later. Back inside the apartment, Jim locked the door and cracked open another beer. He didn't eat anything. Supper time had come and gone, as had his appetite. The chicken sandwich was tossed into the trash, along with each emptied bottle of Newcastle. Jim swallowed the final sip of the last beer just before stretching out on the sofa, letting the bottle drop to the carpet. He slept poorly, alone, tossing and turning at irregular intervals in the glow of a muted television.

Chapter 10

Greg lazily trudged across an overgrown lawn; his feet scraping the ground with every step. His shoulders slumped and his arms dangled at his sides. The evening's exertions had left him fatigued and without the energy to even keep his head upright. The man's one-eyed and blood-caked noggin lulled from side to side, making it difficult to see where he was going. That was alright. He just needed to keep moving.

Chester was with him, walking right by his side and traversing the yard just as slowly. The dog was totally burned out but he forced himself to keep going. He had to. Even in his exhausted state, Chester's hackles remained raised and his lips curled into a permanent half-sneer. His wobbly and unnatural gait accentuated the movement of his shoulder blades, visibly raising up and down below a haggard coat of blood-stained fur. Chester's snout dipped to the ground; nose grazing blades of grass and sniffing around for the next thing he could eat.

There was something approaching the diseased duo and naturally, Chester was the first to hear it. His ears perked up, the hair along his neck and spine stood upright and tingled in anticipation. A large metal body cutting through air, rubber rumbling along pavement; the Brittany Spaniel knew the car was coming in his direction and it was moving at a considerable speed.

Greg stopped when he realized the canine was no longer moving forward and had turned to face the opposite direction. This confused the man. He looked to Chester as if to demand an explanation for the holdup. Of course none was forthcoming but through the silence, Greg could also hear the vehicle driving in the distance. He too turned to look down the road.

With the same slackened pace, the man and his dog began to trek across the field back toward their original path. As their feet met the dirt and loose stones along the shoulder, they could see a pair of headlights reflecting against a thin layer of fog. The car was only about a hundred yards away.

Neither could muster the strength to run toward it. Chester and Greg could barely keep themselves upright. It had been less than an hour since they'd devoured that pudgy fellow and their bellies were still hard at work trying to digest him. They had both depleted their ATP stores and their adrenal glands had nothing left to give. The Pathogen Pals were totally wiped out but neither wanted to let a potential meal get away.

A ball of white grew larger, brighter. The brilliance intensified, blossoming into a blinding wall of projected light. Greg felt the warmth of the bulbs on his cheeks. A breeze ruffled his red plaid shirt. Something was yelled out a window as the coupe passed by but the words were indecipherable in the churning wind. Chester barked at it. Greg's mouth opened with a raspy groan. Both tried to sprint after the car but it was no use.

Chester, to his credit, made the more valiant attempt to capture his stealthy prey. The plan, which had certainly worked previously, was to leap at the object and tackle it to the ground. Fortunately for him, the jump was feeble and came much too late. The dog's feet barely left the ground and he clumsily landed in the spot where the car had been several seconds earlier.

Greg's efforts were even more pathetic. He had only the strength to weakly grab for the car. His unusable left hand flopped against the inside of his elbow and spilled more blood on the ground. The man turned his stiff frame toward the coupe. He reached out with his right hand, clenching at air and coming up empty.

So, the companions were left alone to watch the car dissolve into a pair of radiant red dots and then disappear completely from view. With what little fuel remained, the man and his new best friend followed slowly behind, sluggish and dragging their feet as they went. They would eventually become rested. Their bodies would restore the lost ATP and regain their ability to make adrenaline. But until then, they were physically useless.

The road was dark and quiet, practically deserted at this time of night. It was as good a time as any for the pair to recover. Most of the houses along the route were too far back from the road and too poorly lit to arouse any interest. Every so often, Chester would stop to lap the blood from his fur and pick at his wound. A few times, he strayed off the road to sniff through patches of brush, trying to find some small animal he thought he'd seen.

Greg didn't notice the same things Chester apparently did. His eye was fixed on the trail in front of him. He paid no mind to his own injuries. The man didn't even notice the things his body had experienced; not the damage to his arm, not the sore muscles from walking and fighting, not the fact that his bladder had stretched to its capacity. After hours of holding it in, Greg's detrusor muscle finally contracted back into place, forcing urine to flow out. Piss soaked into the front of his pants, streamed down his legs and into his socks.

The infected creatures continued down Shawnee Road, along the double yellow lines at first, and then gradually drifting to the right side of the street. The passing car had long been forgotten. Now they just moved, not knowing anything but to keep going forward. They behaved like shambling lost idiots and a snail would have mocked their speed. But with no need for a snack break or bathroom stop, Chester and Greg eventually covered enough ground to find themselves at an intersection.

When the pair arrived at Klemer Road, they found it to be the path with the least resistance thanks to a slight downhill slope. So it was down Klemer they went, around the bend and past a small patch of woods, following the route to its end. Greg and Chester had regained some of their energy by the time they emerged from the shadowy side street to look out across Niagara Falls Boulevard.

There wasn't a great deal of traffic but to their left, the monsters could see a handful of cars lined up at a red light. No words needed to be spoken. There was no eye contact and there were no clever glances; no outward sign of their mutual understanding. The connection they shared was the same as you might have with your best friend or favorite child. They both knew what to do and started running at the same time.

The power of a Fight or Flight response still escaped them but Greg and Chester still managed to get a respectable hustle going. All six feet slapped the boulevard as the two creeps raced for the waiting cars. Unfortunately for them, they weren't quick enough. The traffic light turned green before they made it to the turning lane and the would-be predators were already running out of juice. Once more, they would watch in defeat as their intended victims got away. Lucky for them- just as they couldn't feel pain, they could also no longer feel shame.

Happily though, there was a convenience store with gas pumps on the other side of the boulevard. Parked beside one of the pumps, was a large white cargo van. Apart from the windshield, the van had only two windows, one each for the driver and front passenger. Across the length of each side were the words, *Silly Bits Vending*.

A rotund man was pumping gas. An obese belly was barely restrained by a large white tee shirt that was tucked into a pair of thick blue work pants. From a belt loop on the man's trousers, hung a novelty-size key ring, the kind you always see janitors walking around with. Though the heat had drastically subsided since sundown, the fat man was sweating profusely. Beads collected and rolled down his scalp, dribbling through a horseshoe-shaped patch of gray hair on an otherwise bald head. Dampness stained the front of his shirt, accumulating in the crevasse between his breasts and outlining the top of his gut.

It couldn't be so easy, could it? A man of such girth would never stand a chance. Even if he noticed Greg and Chester coming at him, it would be impossible for the man to get away. He definitely wasn't going to outrun them. Could he fight back? Doubtful. He didn't have what you might call a fighter's physique. He was practically wheezing just from getting out of the van and walking ten paces to the fuel pump.

In they went. Sneakers and paws thumped against the pavement as Greg and Chester advanced to secure their next meal. The portly man had finished gassing up and replaced the nozzle in its receptacle. He popped the fuel cap back in place and began a slow sort of waddle-walk back to the driver's side door. The movement was more side-to-side than forward motion.

For the pair of inbound attackers, seizing this prey would be completely without challenge. Not that either required a challenge, but there is something to be said for the thrill of the hunt; gratification in taking down a formidable opponent. A worthy foe, this man was not. He might as well have been sitting on a platter and shaped like a juicy three-hundred-pound steak, obviously not a lean cut.

There must have been some part of Greg's former self poking through as he crossed the remaining two lanes of the boulevard. Before reaching the curb, he got a little distracted. A woman- a young, attractive, athletic blonde woman, was out for her evening run. She had on a pink Lycra sports bra, black spandex shorts, white sneakers, and a pair of headphones. It wasn't the way her C cups struggled to escape the confines of the bra, it wasn't how her toned legs flexed and stretched with each stride, and it wasn't how her tight ass moved with a hint of a wiggle, but something told Greg he had to have her.

The virus controlling his brain must not have affected his testosterone. As any man would, Greg forgot all about the slob at the gas station and chose instead to pursue the hot chick. He didn't realize this at first, but Greg wasn't quite as smooth as he used to be. He made no attempt to conceal just how eager he was to get to her. And okay, this may be a little misleading. Of course, Greg didn't want sex from her, but she was still much more attractive than the alternative.

Despite her headphones, the woman heard him coming almost instantly. When she had jogged along Niagara Falls Boulevard, she noticed someone walking through traffic. She only saw him in passing but that brief glance was enough. She could tell he wasn't right. But it's rude to stare so she made a point to not look directly at him. It would mean cutting the workout short, but she decided to modify her route and turn down Ruie Road to head home a little early. As long as she could avoid getting too close to that man, she wouldn't mind making it up the next night. She could do an extra-long run, maybe in another neighborhood.

An unwavering doubt nagged at her, making her suspicious she hadn't avoided him at all. The young lady heard the trace of someone's footsteps behind her and it wasn't long before they increased in volume. Hoping to be subtle, the young woman turned down the volume on her music player to listen more closely. The earphones went silent just in time for her to feel hot breath on the back of her neck.

She looked over her shoulder to see a one-eyed drooling man covered in blood with a badly broken arm only several feet away. He was running behind her, running at her. The other arm, red-smeared but unimpaired, was outstretched. A filthy hand clutched for her smooth blonde hair, narrowly missing. The woman screamed a single violent shriek. She switched from a jog, now sprinting down the tree-lined suburban street with Greg keeping pace behind her.

Chester slowed to a leisurely trot, still well within the line of traffic. He looked up to find that Greg had run off to chase some other potential meal along an adjacent street. He gave one final look in his friend's direction, able to make out only the silhouette of a body drifting out of focus below the worn-out street lights. Seconds later, his ally was gone forever.

Chester had only paused for an instant before once again setting his sights on the pot-bellied man under the fuel canopy. He and his paunch were still outside the van. There was enough time for the dog to take two more steps toward the gas station before he was nearly deafened.

A horn blared. Tires spun to the right. Brakes locked and rubber screeched over cement. The grille of an SUV grew bigger and bigger, so large that Chester couldn't see anything else. The front bumper slammed into Chester, catching him broadside. The impact shattered both right legs and every rib on the right side of his body. Chester was thrown to his left, rolling over twice and then sliding for close to fifteen feet before coming to a halt in the center of the right lane. The pavement's abrasive texture grated the left side of his torso, leaving a streak of blood and fur to show where he had been. More than a dozen pea-size clumps of shredded raw skin stood above the liquid.

The sick dog lay in an expanding pool of red, struggling for air. With each breath, Chester sucked more saliva back into his mouth, causing most to trickle into his lungs. The remaining fluid bubbled into a froth at his lips. He wanted to get up. He tried to get up. But his legs refused to cooperate. The signal to move simply wasn't making it to his limbs. A break somewhere in the spine had severed the brain's connection to the nerves that controlled muscle movement. With desperation, his front left paw clawed at the ground. The dog even tried planting his chin on the cement for leverage, but it was no use. His twisted, ruined body was failing him.

A door could be heard opening and rotating on a squeaky hinge. Then a second door opened and both slammed shut. Chester could hear voices. There were people coming up behind him, but he couldn't roll over to see them. The talking got louder and he detected strong emotions in their words. They were coming for him.

Chester knew he had to take them out. And it wasn't just about eating. If he let them, they would kill him. He would have to be the aggressor. But no matter how hard he tried, he just couldn't make himself rise. So Chester did what scared injured dogs do, he growled and whimpered and fought back tears. What he didn't do though, is hurt. Pain eluded him, even in this awful state.

"Shit!" It was a male voice. "Shit, shit, shit."

"Oh my God," a woman chimed in.

"I didn't even see him," came the man's voice again. "He just ran out in front of me."

Chester could see the edges of their faces. They were coming closer to him and all he could do was wait. He was completely at their mercy. The man walked up first and leaned over the broken dog. He rubbed his face and ran his hands through his hair, clasping his fingers together behind his head.

"He's still alive," he reported to the woman without a trace of optimism.

"Oh, I can't look at him," she said, turning to face the sidewalk. The woman unzipped the main compartment of her purse and pulled out a ball of tissues. She sniffled and dabbed her eyes. "What are we going to do?"

"Um, I'm not sure. What can we do?"

"Isn't there someone we can call?" she asked, still averting her gaze. When she didn't hear an answer, she shouted to him. "Brandon!"

"Huh, what?"

"Shouldn't we call someone?"

"Oh. Sorry, just trying to think about this. I'm not sure," said the man, "I guess we could call the police."

"The police? And what? Have him lay here suffering until whenever they show up?" She sounded agitated.

"I don't know." Brandon turned away from Chester to face the woman. "I thought I saw someone with him, like walking him."

"Well, where did he go? I don't see anyone walking around, do you?"

"I thought I saw some guy run down the road but I don't see him now. Maybe I'm wrong."

"Who would just leave their dog out here?" asked the woman, as though she expected a reasonable answer.

"I don't know," the man called to her, frustration now obvious in his voice. "Maybe he just got loose from somewhere, ran out of somebody's yard."

Chester barked and waved his head from side to side, trying to generate some momentum to pull himself upright. His tail and legs, with the exception of his front left paw, remained motionless. The Brittany Spaniel lie on his left side; his remaining fur now heavy, saturated with coagulating blood.

"Okay boy, okay," said Brandon in the most soothing tone he could muster. "You're going to be alright."

"But he isn't going to be alright, is he?" demanded the woman.

"No," came the definitive response after a moment's pause. The man looked the Spaniel over more closely, observing the hole in his side, the legs with joints where they didn't belong, the multitude of open, oozing wounds. "I can't imagine he's going to last much longer."

"I told you to slow down, didn't I?" She didn't allow for an answer, "I'm always having to tell you to watch your speed."

"It was an accident," the man spat defensively.

"But do you ever listen to me? No. Of course not, because you always know better."

"I told you it was an accident," he repeated. "What was I supposed to do?"

"You're supposed to be careful. You're supposed to watch where you're going and not drive like an asshole who thinks he owns the whole fucking road. Well, what now? Are you happy now?"

"Of course I'm not happy, Sandra," the man shouted. Pointing to the scene in front of his SUV, he added, "You think I wanted this?"

The woman didn't say anything. She rolled her teary eyes and shook her head softly. Cursing under her breath when she noticed several sad drops had fallen onto the front of her soft pink top, Sandra retrieved a fresh tissue from her purse. The woman feverishly rubbed the fabric, making the wet spots a little less noticeable and then stuffed the wad of used tissues into the pocket of her tan-colored shorts.

"No, I-" the man lowered his voice, noticing another vehicle was coming to a stop behind his. Several people had gathered just outside the convenience store, trying to observe while keeping their distance. "I obviously didn't mean for this to happen. But it did happen, so you can help me take care of it or you can sit and wait for me in the car."

Brandon walked closer to Chester, kneeling down beside him. Blood rolled up the sole of his tall tan hiking boots and seeped into the fabric of his jeans. He reached his hand out to stroke the dog's fur, quickly withdrawing as the dog snapped at him. Chester bit down in hopes of catching some meat between his teeth, but to no avail.

The dog heard another door open; this one didn't have the creak of a rusted hinge. This new door closed and a third voice could be heard, another female.

"Is everyone okay?" a younger woman called. Chester heard her shoes clap against the street as she came up to join the couple in front of the SUV.

"We're okay, but we've had an accident," the man pointed at the crumpled dog.

"I can't look at him, I'm going to wait in the truck," said Sandra before walking back to the green Jeep Cherokee and closing herself inside. Mounted to the top of the SUV, was a black metal roof rack with four round light fixtures bolted to the front. When Sandra shut the door, the second bulb from the left flickered, offering an anemic pulse of yellow light before fading out completely and going permanently dark.

"I tried to stop. I tried so hard not to hit him but he ran out in front of me. There's nothing I could do," the man explained.

"Do you know where he came from?" asked woman number two.

"No. I thought I saw some guy walking him, but I must have been mistaken. The guy took off down the road and I haven't seen anyone else around. I'm thinking he may have gotten loose from a yard close by, but I have no idea." Brandon was still kneeling beside the dog.

Only the man was close enough for Chester to see. The woman stood too far away and out of his line of vision. He would have needed to be able to get up or at least roll over in order to see her.

"I don't think he's going to make it," the man continued.

"How awful," said the young woman.

"Yeah, but like I said, it was an accident."

"I know, I know. It's not like someone would hit a dog on purpose. I'm sure you did what you could to avoid him. Sometimes these things just happen." Her voice was soothing, understanding. "I'll check this house and see if anyone knows where he came from."

"Thank you. That's a good idea. I'm going to grab a blanket from my truck to cover him, try to keep him warm," the man said. "Could you do me a favor?"

"Sure," she said.

"Could you ask my wife to go with you? She's really upset and I think if she had something to do, something to focus on, it'd make her feel a lot better."

The woman nodded and jogged to the passenger's side of the Jeep, which still had its headlights shining on the Brittany Spaniel and reflecting in a pond of spilled blood. The two women talked through an open window and then they both left the truck, walking toward the first house situated at the corner of Ruie Road and Niagara Falls Boulevard. The home sat on the opposite side of the street from the gas station. The man stayed with the dog until they were out of sight. He didn't try to touch him again, for fear of being bitten.

Chester had, for all intents and purposes, given up. His paw stayed still and his head rested on the ground, no longer trying to eat the man who was so close to him. Brandon, thinking the dog might have passed, leaned in to look Chester in the eye and tried to discern whether he was still breathing. He was, and when the man's bearded face was only inches from Chester's snout, he barked and shot his face forward, baring his teeth and curling his lip.

Brandon let out a gasp and fell backwards, landing on his ass. Toxic red fluid quickly soaked into the seat of his pants. As before, Chester's bite failed to connect. The endeavor wasn't totally fruitless however. The breath exhaled towards the man was strong enough to propel saliva onto his face, into his eyes, and past his lips. If the blood contact hadn't been enough to infect the man, the spittle sure would be. Regardless of Chester's ultimate fate, his legacy would carry on. A small part of him would go home with Brandon and Sandra, if they could make it that far.

The man cussed, got himself to his feet, and used a sleeve from his blue and white striped tee shirt to wipe the drool from his face. Brandon turned and walked out of sight. Chester, still gripped by paralysis, could do nothing but lie on the pavement, bleed, and wait.

The man stopped at the rear of his Cherokee and opened the hatch. Stored behind the back seat was a folded wool blanket, several quarts of oil, a tool box, flashlight, and tire iron. The man popped open the lid of the tool box. There should have been a hammer inside, but the closest thing to it was a small mallet with a wood handle and rubber head. The top of the box was slammed shut, loud enough to muffle Brandon's mumbled swearing. Moments later, the truck's hatch was closed and the man headed back to the dog. He carried the wool blanket with him, concealing the tire iron.

Chester didn't hear the man return. He was static, not moving and not blinking. The blanket fell in a heap on the ground, beyond the reach of the wide red puddle. Brandon bent once more to kneel in front of the pup. The fingers of his right hand wrapped tightly around the stem of the tire iron. He raised it overhead and prepared to swing. But instead of driving the metal instrument down, crushing the back of the dog's skull as he'd intended, the man let it fall gently to his side.

The three-year old Brittany Spaniel with a once-beautiful silky coat of white fur and brown spots, the puppy with the playful bobbing ears, had stopped breathing. It may have been the overwhelming trauma from the collision with the truck. Perhaps it was the extensive blood loss. There's also a chance that too much fluid had collected in his lungs. And it's possible that it was the combination of all these things, but the result was the same. Chester was gone.

Chapter 11

There were no markings on the vial. The small glass container had no etchings and held no labels. It looked like a miniature test tube with a cork plug. At maximum capacity, it would have held up to fifteen milliliters, but it was only about two-thirds of the way full. A fine electric powder rolled from the bottom to the brim as the bottle shifted inside the driver's pocket.

The rusted Mazda bounded down Cottage Street and without signaling or slowing, made a sharp right turn into an empty parking lot adjacent to Altro Park. So, calling it a park was an exercise in politeness. It was little more than an empty grass field the size of a small city block. At the far end, stood the derelict remains of a chain-link backstop. The baseball field, like the rest of the park, had long been overtaken by tall grass and weeds. Even in the weak glow of the car's headlamps, dandelions made the ground of Altro Park look more yellow than green. Every three or four weeks in the summer, city workers would show up and mow the lawn with one of those novelty-size lawn tractors. Evidence would suggest they'd been neglecting their duties.

No lines were painted on the cement of the lot so the sedan parked wherever it happened to stop. The man in the driver's seat released the clasp for the safety belt and reached to the floor on the passenger's side. There was no floor mat, but there was a pair of dirty socks, an empty Pepsi bottle, three empty beer cans, a spent lighter; nothing useful.

"Shit," he blurted. The young man cursed again moments later when he discovered the glove box only held a lapsed insurance card, a flashlight with a dead battery, and a handful of pens. He slammed the compartment shut.

Slumped back in his seat, the driver scooped the small glass tube from his pocket. He flicked on the car's dome light, illuminating every inch of the plain gray interior. Dust caked the dashboard. The windows were cloudy with greasy smudges. A pair of cigarette burn holes marred the upholstery on the passenger's seat. A frayed red wire hung loosely from the space between the aftermarket stereo and the HVAC controls, yet the unit still worked.

The young man held the glass bottle up toward the ceiling, shaking it gently to assess its contents. There would definitely be enough for him, but no way was he sharing. He turned the engine off and pulled the key from the ignition. Using his teeth to remove the cork stopper, the driver tapped out a small measure of cocaine into the groove of his key. Careful not to spill, Jeremy directed the end of the key into his right nostril and snorted with all his might.

The dust ripped through the sinus cavity, tearing into mucus membranes and quickly absorbing into a series of capillaries. Seconds later, the stimulant reached the heart, where it caused the organ to beat harder and faster. It would soon arrive in the brain and precipitate a furious euphoria, thanks to a rapid release of dopamine and adrenaline. Jeremy's blood pressure increased. Pores on his forehead began leaking droplets of perspiration.

He flipped down the sun visor to check his reflection in the vanity mirror, angling his head back to get a clear view up his nostrils. Both holes were clean of white residue but his nose hair could use a good trimming. Jeremy's pale skin looked almost gray. Pupils of sunken eyes dilated in response to the drug. He was clenching his jaw, grinding his teeth. A skeletal hand combed through his short blond hair. Jeremy flipped the visor back up and reached for his cell phone. Beth picked up in the middle of the second ring.

"Hey, you there?" she answered. "Sorry about that, I'm still getting used to this phone and figuring out where the buttons are."

"Not a problem," Jeremy replied as he wedged the cork back in place to seal the vial. "What are you doing? You busy?"

"I'm not doing anything tonight, not that I know of," Beth told him.

"You wanna grab something to eat, maybe come hang out for a bit?" he asked, only half listening for an answer as he slid the key back in the ignition.

"Sure," came her response. "You gonna pick me up?"

"I just gotta grab some cash," Jeremy told her. "But I'll be there soon."

"I'll be ready. If you hurry, I may have a surprise for you."

"A surprise, huh?" Jeremy grinned and began rubbing his crotch through his loose-fitting jean shorts. "I like that. What sort of surprise?"

"I got a little outfit I think you'll like," Beth teased.

"Go on," he urged. His member was stirring in anticipation. "Do I get a description?"

"You'll have to wait and see," replied the seductress before she was momentarily startled by a click that sounded over the line. "Hello?"

"I'm here," said Jeremy.

"Oh, okay. It sounded like you hung up."

"Nope."

"Alright. So, when will you be here?"

"Um," Jeremy glanced at the digital green clock display on the car's stereo. "Ten, fifteen minutes I guess."

"Okay. Be quick."

Jeremy hung up. He started the car and wheeled out of the parking lot, twisting the volume knob as he absently maneuvered back onto Cottage Street. An amplified subwoofer rattled the trunk lid as the car rolled ahead and made a right turn onto Willow Street. The thunderous bass was loud enough to drown out the earsplitting moans of a worn-out muffler. Jeremy actually liked the sound of the exhaust. It reminded him of a race car.

Okay, so the Mazda could barely produce a hundred horsepower and it had a top speed of about sixty miles per hour. But this didn't stop Jeremy from revving the engine whenever he was lined up next to someone at a traffic light. He'd slip the gear shifter into neutral and stomp the gas pedal before slamming the transmission back into drive with the engine turning over at five thousand revolutions per minute. The passenger's side front tire would emit an effeminate chirp of rubber on cement and the car would doggedly gain speed. The driver of the car next to him would easily win a race he hadn't known was taking place.

Jeremy continued down Willow. A fenced-in tennis court and derelict playground passed by on the right; a series of shabbily-maintained homes on the left. The sedan crossed the intersection at South Transit road and continued on past five more dwellings before Jeremy executed a three-point turn and stopped in front of an abandoned two-story house.

The car eased to the side of the road. There was no paved curb, the lawn just sort of blended into cement. Headlights turned off and the stereo was silenced. Jeremy left the engine running as he climbed out of his seat and gently closed the door. A streetlight directly overhead shined down a deep orange beam. The streetlamps behind him and in front of him were out, either due to a lack of power or burned-out bulbs. Jeremy hadn't noticed, but it had apparently gotten dark out some time ago. And though the sun had gone, it had not taken all of the day's heat with it.

Even in shorts and a thin white tank top, his skin radiated warmth. Xylophone ribs pressed into cotton, which was nearing its saturation point. Salted droplets slithered down his pock-marked face, across his frail chest, and from out of his armpits. He patted his pockets, simultaneously checking to make sure he hadn't lost his phone, wallet, or drugs and drying his palms on the denim.

On foot, Jeremy began to make his way back in the direction from which he had come. Of course driving would have been quicker than walking, but it was important that no one see his car. To be more exact, no one could see his license plate. He told Beth he needed to get cash. That *was* the truth, but he was in no way obligated to tell her *all* of the truth. It didn't concern her. To be frank, it was none of her business. She didn't need to know how he got his money. She was going to be mad about having to wait longer for him to arrive, but that's just the way it was going to be. He considered grabbing her some beer to sooth her mood; maybe some of those sissy alcoholic fruit drinks, whichever was cheaper.

After about two minutes of walking, Jeremy found the intersection to be lit up brighter than he would have liked. On his right, was a one-story house with white aluminum siding. It was the last home before the Kwik Fill gas station at the corner of Willow and South Transit. Keeping to the sidewalk, he turned right and marched forward thirty feet to face the front of the fuel pumps and canopy. Twenty feet past the pumps was the convenience store and cashier's station.

There was only one car in the lot. A brand new Cadillac sedan sat at the front right pump, facing away from the store. The shimmering white paint was totally free of blemishes. A hood ornament sparkled as if it were made of diamonds. No one was pumping gas and the car looked empty. Perfect. Jeremy started moving closer to the vehicle. A smile formed as he neared the car, spotting an unattended purse through the open passenger's window.

Kneeling so the car's trunk would shield his body, he looked toward the store and through the window. Jeremy could see an older woman chatting up the much-younger gas station attendant working the register. She must have been asking for assistance in trying to locate a particular product. The clerk pointed to something on the far wall and the woman followed his gaze.

The sweating tweaker squatted back down and shuffled up to the front passenger's side door. He lifted the handle and the door softly popped open. Making just enough room for him to squeeze his thin frame inside, Jeremy slid half of his ass onto the tan leather seat, sure to keep his right foot on the pavement. He wasted no time in grabbing the purse and perusing its contents.

The bag itself was made of dark red leather. Maybe it was imitation leather. Jeremy could never tell the difference. If not for the old-timey smell of moth balls and medicine, he would have just snatched the purse along with everything inside. It would have made a nice gift for Beth. Or he could try to sell it. Maybe he could sell it *to* Beth. Probably not. This operation was risky enough. He wouldn't want to have to explain where it came from and he definitely didn't want to be spotted carrying a large red purse down the street as he went back to his own car.

Inside the bag was everything you'd expect to find in a woman's purse. Everything except money, that is. There were two combs, a packet of gum, lipstick, some sort of cream in an unmarked jar, a bundle of receipts, three gloves- not three pairs of gloves, but three individual gloves that did not match each other, and one of those eyelash brush things. A small pocket sewn into the lining of the purse held two credit cards. Jeremy slid those into his back pocket.

He chanced a glance through the driver's side window and into the store. The woman had made her way back to the counter and was waving her hands around over her head. He couldn't tell if she looked angry or was just being animated. She did look like she was wrapping up though.

"Shit," Jeremy muttered. "Oh, to Hell with this."

He flipped the purse upside-down and let all of the woman's possessions spill out onto the floor.

"Ah ha!" he exclaimed.

A small wad of cash sat on top of the pile. It must have been buried under all the rest of her junk. He grabbed it; no time to count the bills before stuffing them into his shorts pocket. Another brief glance toward the store revealed that the front door was opening.

The woman was coming back and she was moments away from finding a drug-addled punk rifling through her belongings. She pressed her back into the tinted glass of the door, still facing inside and shouting something to the clerk. Had she spotted him? Was she asking him to call the police? No. Jeremy could hear her laughing and then saw her wave goodbye to the attendant like she was passing him by at a parade.

Jeremy used both hands to scoop up the batch of papers, pens, and makeup and hastily shoveled them back into the purse. It was a disorganized mess when he found it, so the woman wasn't likely to notice that she'd been robbed until she looked for the cash or a credit card. With a bit of luck, she'd be miles down the road by then. The purse fell back to its original place on the seat as Jeremy slowly backed out of the car and closed the door as quietly as possible.

The gaunt criminal pulled himself to his feet in time to see the glass door of the convenience store swing shut behind the woman. She was carrying two plastic bags and heading right for the sedan. Jeremy wanted to run, to get away from the car as fast as he could but it would have drawn way too much attention.

So instead, he bent to the ground and made pretend he had to tie his shoes. Why he needed to do this so close to a stranger's brand new luxury car that probably cost more than fifty thousand dollars, was something he hoped no one would question. He probably wouldn't have been clever enough to explain himself.

As luck would have it, Jeremy didn't need to be fast with his feet or his wit. The old woman was humming to herself and if she saw the young thief at all, she didn't let on. She opened the back door to her sedan and placed the overflowing plastic bags on the rear seat. She then reached through the driver's window to a panel inside the car and pressed a button to release the cover for the fuel door. The woman removed a hose from its place on the gas pump.

Jeremy crossed the parking lot and walked past the masonry building that housed the convenience store. He cut a sharp turn and ducked into the darkened alley behind the structure. Shielded on one side by a hedge and a brick wall on the other, this would be as good a place as any for Jeremy to wait and listen. He wanted to make sure the woman was out of there before he went inside to spend her money. Plus, it gave him a few private moments to do another bump of cocaine.

The stimulant freak tapped some cocaine out onto a knuckle and snorted, careful not to spill any in the process. Jeremy wiggled his toes inside his sneakers. The webbing was getting cheesy and his digits were slick from sweat. Socks folded and bunched beneath the balls of his feet. His molars pressed into one another. He waited, forming his hands into fists and then relaxing them over and over.

By the time Jeremy saw the white Cadillac pull onto the street and disappear, he had gotten himself even more wired than before. So much so, that he hadn't noticed someone sneaking up behind him. It took him a moment to realize why his right foot wasn't moving when he tried to take a step. After three unsuccessful attempts to drag his foot forward, Jeremy finally looked down to see what was holding him back.

What appeared to be a hobo had his claw of a hand wrapped around the heel of his shoe. Right, so *hobo* isn't a very polite term. To rephrase, a filthy bum in a tattered tan overcoat, badly soiled brown trousers, and a too-tight wool hat was face down on the ground with his left hand firmly locked around the back of Jeremy's foot. The man's legs were bent in ways that seemed both unnatural and extremely painful. There looked to be as many as four knee joints between the pair of limbs. His left foot was twisted all the way around so that his toes aimed at the sky.

How did Jeremy not hear the vagrant approaching? For that matter, how could he not smell the man as he had gotten close? Disgusting. You could almost see the stench cloud around the bum. What you couldn't see in the darkness of the alley was a trail of blood left behind as the older man crawled toward an unsuspecting victim to-be. The tramp craned his neck to look up to reveal a wild gray beard and meeting Jeremy's bewildered stare.

The shifty drifter opened his mouth. A cascade of virus-rich saliva spilled through gaps of missing teeth. The teeth that remained had been stained a bright shade of burgundy. The creature, which Jeremy still believed to be some sort of delirious homeless person, let out a threatening hiss. Spittle dotted the younger man's ankles.

"What the shit!" Jeremy wailed. With a great deal of force, he yanked his foot free from the vagrant's hand. "Hey, what's your problem, man?"

Of course, the tramp didn't answer. He raised his right arm over his head and let it slam elbow-first into the pavement, then repeating the motion with his left. The older man was dragging himself toward Jeremy, still hissing and snapping his teeth in the air. His throat produced a wet growl.

"Do you need some help or something?" Thinking the man was merely struggling to get up, Jeremy leaned down and offered a hand in assistance. He jumped back immediately, seeing the man's elbows had both been rubbed completely raw. The joints of his arms had worn through the coat sleeves and the firm ground had made quick work of removing the skin. Both elbows were nothing but glossy, slippery bones which gained no purchase on the cement.

Not wanting the younger man to escape, the vagrant desperately reached out. He pressed his hands into the ground, slithering closer to the scrawny snack that stood just a foot away. The bum pulled his body forward; two of his fingers snapping from strain as he tried to claw into the pavement. The nail on his right ring finger broke and cracked backwards. His newly-exposed nail bed oozed a poison viscous fluid.

Jeremy fought to comprehend the sight. He rubbed his eyes before opening them as wide as they'd go. Was this for real or was he tripping out? He must have lost his mind. Was there something else in that vial besides cocaine? That had to be it.

That twisted sonofabitch dealer of his had dosed his cocaine with a hallucinogen as some kind of sick joke. Not that Jeremy minded, he just wished he had known what to expect. Wow. This drug, whatever it was, packed an incredible punch. It was way more realistic than magic mushrooms. And it couldn't have been LSD. He'd had enough acid trips in his life to tell the difference. He would have to remember and ask next time he went to score.

He chuckled and mumbled to himself, "That's pretty good shit," before he turned from the hobo and walked to the entrance of the convenience store.

Pie-sized pupils let in far too much light as Jeremy entered the shop. He was forced to squint in order to make his way around. It sounded like the clerk had offered some sort of greeting, but Jeremy ignored him. He did the same to the racks of cookies, chips, and sodas he passed. Counting the cash, he strode down the center aisle of the store. He had made forty-seven dollars; not bad for less than a half hour worth of work.

The air conditioning inside must have been stuck on full-blast. Even in his heightened state, Jeremy found it distracting. The drying perspiration was making his skin itch. The stimulants may have been helping that along. He reached the beer cooler at the rear of the store. Jeremy looked back toward the cash register to see if he was being watched right before he reached down the front of his shorts and scratched angrily at his balls. When fifteen or so seconds had elapsed and he finished tending to himself, the tweaker smeared fungal sweat and flecks of crusted skin onto the glass. He winced, catching a whiff of his own putrid genital stink.

The walk from the store to the Mazda was a little blurry. He purchased a six-pack of hard lemonade for Beth and a twenty-four ounce can of high gravity lager for himself. His can was empty before he climbed back into the driver's seat of his car. The six-pack of bottles was placed on the passenger's seat and the lager can was pitched out the window, but not before Jeremy double checked to make sure he had consumed every last drop.

Beth's house was less than a five-minute drive from where he had parked. He ran the red light, making a left onto South Transit and then making a right a block and a half later. As he got closer, Jeremy made a point to turn the stereo down low so the overly loud pounding of subwoofers would not create a disturbance for people who may have gone to bed already.

Don't misinterpret this as an act of decency or consideration for others. Beth had already scolded him a number of times for playing his music too loud when he came to pick her up. She didn't care, but her mother had registered a complaint or two with Beth and she had to pass along the message. The girl actually liked the thudding bass, but she would rather not have to hear about it from her mom. If her mother was unhappy, Beth was unhappy. Jeremy wanted to make sure she was in a good mood, particularly for what he had planned for the night.

The white Mazda swung into the short driveway of a smaller two-story home with light blue vinyl siding. Out of dumb habit, he punched the center of the steering wheel to honk the horn. He realized his mistake right away and hoped Beth wouldn't think anything of the noise. In the front window of the first floor, a heavy curtain jostled and Beth looked out to see him waiting.

In less than a minute, she was outside and coming down the steps of the front stoop. She had on a pair of dark jeans and a hooded sweatshirt with a backpack strapped around her. She looked good. She always looked good, but Jeremy was a little let down. Jeans and a hoodie wasn't exactly a special sexy outfit. Jeremy got out of the car and went to greet her.

The couple embraced and kissed with more tongue than genuine affection. Still wrapped in each other's arms, Jeremy slid his right hand down the small of Beth's back and gave her tight ass a firm squeeze.

"Stop that," Beth laughed, playing as though she was trying to pull away.

She made no attempt to remove Jeremy's hand. Taking this as encouragement, he ran his left hand up the front of her shirt, helping himself to a handful of tit.

"You're so bad," Beth giggled and leaned in for another kiss; her hands planted firmly on

Jeremy's lower back.

"So, I thought you said you had a surprise for me," Jeremy questioned. "Some sort of sexy outfit type of surprise."

"I do, it's in the backpack," she explained. She glanced behind her as if to add meaning to the statement.

"Oh, cool," Jeremy said dryly with a roll of his eyes. "It's doing me so much good in there."

"Well, silly. It's the type of outfit I can't really wear in public." Beth shot an obvious glance downward to the front of Jeremy's pants.

"Oh, I like that." Jeremy tried to shove a hand down the back of her jeans, but they were too tight against her body. He tickled her hips, moving his fingers to the front of her waistline in an effort to unbutton her pants. Beth stopped him.

"I thought we were going for food first?" she asked.

"I was thinking we could just head to my place, maybe have a couple of drinks and ya know..." Jeremy let his words trail off.

Beth frowned. "I'm not that type of girl," her features taking on an austere appearance.

"Since when?" Jeremy asked completely seriously.

Beth sighed and her shoulders fell. She released herself from Jeremy's arms and murmured, "Okay, let's go."

"Nice!" Jeremy proclaimed. "Yes, let's definitely go."

He turned and walked back to the driver's door of his car, which was still idling. The wiry tweaker flopped into the seat.

"But we're going for food right after," Beth fairly demanded as she leaned in through the open passenger's window.

"Uh huh." Jeremy wasn't really listening. He was lost in thought, planning a primitive sexual assault that would take place in just a few short minutes. "Come on, get in."

Beth did what she was told and got into the passenger's seat. She threw her bag into the back of the sedan. No more than four seconds after the Mazda backed out of its spot, Jeremy cranked the stereo volume. The echo of bass could be heard several streets over.

Chapter 12

Jim slept until noon. When his lazy ass finally woke up, the first thing he did was check his cell phone. Don't roll your eyes- you know you do the same thing. Apparently, Jim had missed two calls from Beth while he was sleeping. He would not be returning her calls. Jim shut the phone off and let it drop to the coffee table. Then he got up and paced the apartment for an hour before plopping down on the couch with his laptop computer.

He checked his email, no new messages. Jim opened the web browser and perused several porn sites before boredom caused him to lose his drive. By two o'clock that afternoon, Jim had fallen back asleep for a five hour nap. A full Sunday morning and afternoon had been thoroughly pissed away.

The sun was starting to go down when Jim awoke for the second time that day. His belly growled, reminding him that he hadn't eaten in over twenty-four hours. There was nothing in the refrigerator besides a half empty tub of sour cream that had likely turned brown inside, a stick of butter, a bottle of water, and an unopened can of Del Monte sliced peaches that Jim knew he would never eat but kept anyway. He was going to have to go out if he wanted proper food.

Jim changed out of the clothes that he'd been wearing since the previous night and, without showering, replaced them with a pair of tan khaki shorts, a plain cream-colored tee shirt, and fresh white socks that weren't yet stained from foot sweat and shoe filth. He topped off the outfit with a faded hat that showed the Buffalo Blizzard soccer team logo over the brim. Sharply dressed, Jim grabbed his keys and wallet from the kitchen counter and left the house.

A Burger King, a McDonald's, and a Taco Bell were all just a short drive from the apartment building. Jim drove past each one. He had to eat something but the thought of fast food made his stomach turn. Jim would have to go to the supermarket. He made a point to go to a different store from where Lindsey worked. Aside from looking like a slob, it would have been a little too obvious and uncomfortable to show up at her place of employment twice in two days.

There was a grocery store on Young Street, Lowell's Food Emporium, which was right next to Eppard's Outdoor Living, a sporting goods shop. That would have to do. Jim parked at the side of the building, pulling right up to the massive block wall. He turned the car off and went in, moving quickly and with purpose.

The idea was to be in and out as fast as he could; grab the first thing that looked halfway appetizing, pay, and get back home with as little human contact as possible. He did pretty well with this. Jim was ready to leave the store in under seven minutes, having already collected a package of meat, a bag of six wheat rolls, and a two-liter bottle of cola without having said a single word to anyone. He even managed to communicate with the cashier using nothing more than a series of nods and facial expressions.

Jim returned home to find Danny waiting for him at the top of the steps. He had on a ratty-looking pair of black jeans with a dark blue sleeveless shirt. His black hair ran over a white bandanna that was tied around his head like a headband. There was a hand-rolled cigarette behind his left ear. Danny looked up when Jim came through the door.

"Jimmy, did you see? The door's been cleaned off."

"Oh. Um, yeah, I guess it has." Jim hadn't noticed and he didn't turn around to confirm.

"Hey man, do you got a lighter I can borrow?"

"Sure," Jim said. He tossed his yellow Bic to Danny and began climbing the stairs.

Danny lit up, it wasn't tobacco. He drew in hard and held his breath for ten seconds before releasing a thick cloud of skunky smoke, coughing as the last of it escaped his lungs. Danny handed the lighter back to Jim, who was unlocking the door to his apartment.

"You probably shouldn't smoke that in the hallway," Jim commented.

"Good point," Danny said and followed Jim inside, closing the door behind him.

"Oh, that wasn't what I meant." Jim glared at the burning joint.

"Huh?"

"I don't want it to smell like pot in here," Jim told him. He placed the bag of groceries on the kitchen counter, pulling out the soda bottle to put in the fridge.

"Oh. Sorry, man." Danny walked to the counter at the far end of the kitchen and tapped ash into the sink. He snuffed the joint out against the metal lining at the top part of the drain, but not before taking another long hit and filling the room with marijuana smoke. "So, what was up with you last night?"

"What do you mean?" Jim asked. He knelt to get a frying pan from the lower cabinet next to the stove.

"Didn't I hear you racing outta here last night? Heard your tires chirp out in the parking lot."

"Oh, that. It's kind of a long story," Jim said.

Danny looked back at Jim; his glossy eyes open wide in anticipation.

"Alright." Jim realized he was going to have to try to explain himself. "I found out Beth was screwing around. Some guy was coming to pick her up and I tried to get out there to, I don't know, stop her or fight the guy or something."

"So what happened? Did you go out there and kick the guy's ass or what?" Danny made his hands into fists and boxed the air.

"Not exactly. She was gone by the time I got to her house so I ended up just coming home." Jim omitted the part about how he had made an asshole out of himself by confronting a pair of strangers at the restaurant.

"That's bad times," Danny stated as a matter of fact. "Really shitty."

"Yeah." Jim leaned against the counter top. He didn't want to start cooking while Danny was still there and it felt good talking about what had gone on, even if he wasn't completely forthcoming.

Danny sat at the kitchen table. He kicked his feet up without taking off his sneakers and asked, "So, what are you going to do now?"

"I don't know. Nothing, I guess." Jim tried to hide his disappointment and resignation.

"Nothing?" Danny sounded appalled. "You gotta do something. You can't do nothing."

"There's really nothing to do," Jim argued. "I wanted to yell about it, but I don't have the energy. She even called me a couple times today but I didn't answer."

"What a bitch," Danny said. "Call her back and tell her she's a bitch."

Jim smiled. "She is a bitch. But calling her mean names over the phone isn't really going to accomplish anything."

"It might make you feel better," Danny suggested. "That'd be something."

"It probably won't," Jim countered. "Any contact with her is just going to make me feel worse. Plus, she'll claim that I'm wrong. She'll say that whoever it was is just a friend. I'm overreacting and I don't know what I'm talking about."

"Any chance it could be just a friend?"

"No," Jim answered flatly. He turned from Danny, opening the center drawer and taking out a spatula. Turning back around, he tried to change the subject. "Hey, do you have any beer?"

"Nope. Sorry buddy."

"That's okay." Jim replied. "I just want to be able to sleep later, but I'm sure I'll manage."

"Cool. If you want, you can have some of this," Danny held out what remained of the joint.

"I'm okay, but thanks."

"So, you're not going to talk to her. What *are* you going to do? You gotta get on top of this Beth situation."

"I'm sure she's got plenty of people on top of her..." Jim paused and hopped up to sit on the kitchen counter, "Situation."

Danny laughed, "Ya know what I mean."

"Yeah," Jim agreed. "Actually, there's this girl I knew from high school-"

"Daniel!" A woman's voice interrupted Jim mid-sentence. Danny's eyes opened wide and Jim frowned.

"You've got company?" Jim asked.

"Balls," Danny moaned. "I forgot she was upstairs. Guess she got tired of waiting."

"She sounds upset," Jim noted.

"Yeah... I guess I should head back." Danny got up from the chair and walked to the apartment door. "I'll catch ya later, Jimmy."

"Alright." Jim slid off the counter and watched Danny walk into the hall without pulling the door shut. Once he was gone, Jim walked to the entryway, pushed it closed and applied the chain lock and deadbolt.

Alone again, he returned to his groceries in the kitchen. Jim grabbed the bottom of the plastic bag and let its contents spill out; the package of sub rolls and a thin white box with the words, *Sirloin Philly Steak*, written on it.

A picture on the box showed a Philly style sandwich with plump, juicy pieces of beef, melted Swiss cheese, and sautéed peppers and onions. It was that delicious-looking image which had tricked Jim into making the purchase. The meat inside the package didn't look anything like the picture on the label. Not even close.

There were four individual slabs of beef. The instructions indicated that the product was to be kept frozen until cooked. Jim had assumed the meat would have started to warm up on the drive home and during the time Danny had been giving his relationship advice. However, the meat looked like it was thawed out a long time ago, if it had ever actually been frozen in the first place.

The plan was to have two sandwiches, so Jim needed two of the four sections of beef. They had, probably from being at room temperature for a prolonged period of time, melded together into a single large gelatinous glob. It slithered out of the box's plastic lining and fell into the Teflon frying pan with a dense splat. Upon impact, blood and beef juices squirted out. Rivulets ran down over each fold to form a puddle around the brownish wad.

There was more fat than Jim expected to see. Some sort of thin film covered the meat, giving it a slight purple hue in the light of the weak bulb over the stove. The scent of something pungent worked its way up and into Jim's nostrils. The funk made his head snap back. It smelled like how he assumed a dead body would, if left untreated for a week. He half expected to find hairs growing out of the so-called steak.

Jim looked in the container at the remaining pieces and shrugged. He had already paid for it, so not only was he going to eat the ball of questionable meat in the pan, but he would also keep whatever was left to have at a later date. He placed the box in the freezer and began cooking. Fifteen minutes later, Jim sat on the couch and ate his dinner from the coffee table in front of the television.

He spent more nights on the sofa than in his bed and this evening would be no exception. Jim choked down his pair of purple meat subs, with no cheese of course. When the plate held nothing but crumbs, he pushed it to the edge of the table, content to neglect his dish-washing duties until the following morning. And soon after, Jim passed out.

Chapter 13

Jim sat up and sucked in a mouthful of air. A sweltering heat had filled the apartment while he slept. A hand dragged across his forehead; the pale rind slick and cool with sweat. His tee shirt was matted to his back and chest. Jim rotated in his seat on the sofa and leaned forward to plant his elbows on his knees. He scratched a salty crust from his scalp before grabbing the remote control from the coffee table.

The TV switched off and blanketed the living room in darkness. Jim got up and walked to the bathroom. He turned the lights on and ran the tap over the sink. Both hands reached into the stream of cold water and splashed his face. Wet fingers ran over his head until his hair was soaked, the excess splattered on the floor and absorbed into his socks. Jim pulled his shirt off and used it as a towel. Going into the bedroom, he balled up the shirt and tossed it in the hamper. Jim opened the bottom drawer of his dresser to find a replacement.

In the kitchen, Jim took a cigarette from the pack on the counter. He didn't like smoking in the apartment and would normally take the ash tray out to the balcony. There was something dirty about blowing smoke all over the walls and furniture, letting it stick to the fabric and carpet fibers. He would have to light some candles the next day, or maybe pick up a bottle of that liquid air freshener stuff.

He walked back to the living room, placing a glass of water on the coffee table and his ass on the couch. Jim lit up, tossing the lighter to the table and turning the television back on. Tendrils of smoke floated up from the cigarette to congregate at the ceiling. Jim drew in another lungful and held it for a second before exhaling. The cloud glowed white and blue, reflecting the light from the TV.

Jim completed a full lap, flipping from one channel to the next. There was never anything on that was worth watching in the middle of the night. It was mostly reruns of old sitcoms and paid programming. Jim eventually settled on one of the twenty-four-hour news networks. There was something happening in Detroit, but he wasn't paying attention. The remote fell to the floor and Jim pulled his cell phone up to his face.

The clock on his phone read 3:08am. Also on the screen was the icon indicating that he had missed a call and had a new voice mail message. The call was from Beth and had come in about a half hour earlier. Jim stared at the phone, debating whether he should bother listening or just erase the message- as if his curiosity would let him ignore it. He sighed and dialed the voice mail service. The message played. It was brief.

"Hey, it's me. I was just calling because," the voice became distant. She sounded tired, maybe drunk or worn out from some physical exertion. Jim could hear her giggling and talking to someone in the background, but the sound was too muffled to make anything out. Then her voice came back, "I saw you called me the other night and I was calling you back. So, call me back 'cause I'm calling you back. Okay? Alright, bye."

She stretched out the word, "Bye," like she was trying to be cute. It didn't work. It made her sound ditsy and annoying; not like anyone you'd want to be around. Did she think she was being playful? Flirty? What a dolt.

When the message concluded, Jim selected the option to delete it. He wouldn't be listening to it again and there was no way in Hell he was calling her back. More than a full day had passed since he'd last spoke with her and she calls back now? Not to mention her recent whorish antics; she runs off in the middle of the night with some guy and then expects she can just give him an early-morning ring and chat like everything is fine and normal? No way.

Jim stubbed out his cigarette. He was too annoyed to fall back asleep right away so he grabbed the remote control. Just as he was about to change the channel, Jim saw something on screen that caught his attention. The broadcasters had done their best to pixelate and obscure the image but it was obviously that of a bloody severed arm.

"Authorities are not treating this as a terrorist event," said a female reporter off screen. The view changed to overhead footage from a news helicopter. It showed an aerial view of a three-story parking structure with a white Ford Mustang convertible crashed into one of the outer walls. At least a dozen blurred-out bodies lie motionless around the scene.

The broadcast then showed B-roll of people crossing the street, heading away from a large stadium. Children carried baseball gloves, some supporters had on replica jerseys and others wore shirts and hats emblazoned with cartoon tigers.

After a short pause, the reporter continued. "It was a sold-out crowd at Detroit's Comerica Park this evening. Over forty-one thousand satisfied fans were celebrating the Tigers' win over the Cleveland Indians by a score of eight runs to two. As the spectators were leaving the ball park, a car traveling down East Montcalm Street ran a red light at the Brush Street intersection and struck a group of pedestrians. Six people were hit directly and one of them was pulled under the vehicle and dragged for seventeen feet before the vehicle collided with this concrete wall."

That's terrible, Jim thought. *But why is a car accident national news?*

As if she was reading his mind and speaking directly to Jim, the reporter said, "The driver of the Mustang convertible crawled out of the wrecked automobile and attacked members of the crowd who had gathered to assist the wounded. This has led authorities to believe this was a deliberate act, not just the subsequent attack, but the initial collision as well."

Jim leaned forward in his seat. The view changed again. Now the camera showed the reporter standing in the street with the wrecked car behind her, sure to capture all the gory bits on film. Most of the bodies were still blurred-out but the production crew wasn't able to block out everything. Just a few feet from the car's rear tire, Jim saw a single Nike sneaker sitting upright with an ankle sticking out of it and a bright red streak down one side.

With police and EMS working in the background, the woman continued her story. "Officers who tried to subdue the man were then attacked themselves. A spokesman for the Police Department has confirmed that the suspect was killed at the scene, bringing the total death toll to seven. Witnesses say the man looked like he was under the influence of some kind of hallucinogenic drug, and that the man was shot as many as eleven times before going down. The Medical Examiner's office is expected to release a statement some time tomorrow morning and we'll be sure to bring you all the latest updates."

The channel went to commercials and Jim leaned back in his seat. Drowsiness had once again set in. He stretched his legs out on the couch and rolled onto his right side. His shoulder dug into the well-worn cushion and he closed his eyes. He planned to listen to the TV but he fell back asleep before the news program returned.

The alarm went off too early, just like every morning. Jim had gotten used to sleeping in the living room and relied on his cell phone to wake him up. The phone allowed up to ten alarms and the first alert went off at 5:30am. Nine additional alarms were set to go off every ten minutes thereafter.

He always slept through the first few.

Sometime after six o'clock, the alarms had finally annoyed the sleepy boy enough to force him from his slumber. A full bladder offered some additional encouragement. With half-lidded peepers, he shuffled through the kitchen and into the bathroom. Having done the needful, Jim brushed his teeth and looked at himself in the mirror. He badly needed a shower.

A fog of body odor seemed to roll off of him. His thick chestnut hair was plastered against the left side of his head, the rest stood up in all directions. Purple circles sat below each bloodshot eye and three days' worth of stubble had grown scratchy and unattractive. The door to the medicine cabinet slid open and Jim found a bottle of Visine and a can of shaving cream. He proceeded to sleepwalk through the rest of his morning routine and about thirty minutes later, Jim was clean, dressed, and ready to leave the apartment.

He walked down the steps and out the front door. Jim noticed something peculiar as he approached his car. Two large green garbage bins were out of place. It was a pair of those chest-high refuse containers provided by the city. They were moved to the middle of the parking lot where they'd been overturned.

The lids were open and several bags had been pulled out. Trash was spilled all over the place. The biting odor of old vegetables and spoiled meat caused Jim to gag. That stench was just going to get worse as it grew hotter throughout the day.

Pick-up day wasn't until Wednesday. So on a Monday morning, the garbage bins should have been lined up on the far side of the building. Jim wondered why someone had moved them. And who would leave such a mess? It was unacceptable... but not exactly Jim's responsibility. He looked back at the building. No one was outside and he didn't see anyone watching. Of course, nobody was on their way out to help clean up. Jim shrugged. He got in his car and left.

Jim worked in a four-story office building located at the corner of Broad Street and Main Street, about two blocks from the Erie Canal. The structure was at the end of a series of attached solid brick row style buildings. The neighboring units were mostly occupied as storefronts, including a furniture store, a tanning salon, two bars, and a beauty supply shop. There was a city-owned parking lot behind the building, which served as the main parking area for Jim's office.

The lot itself was a dump. Crumbling pavement stretched to about one hundred yards behind the buildings. There were loose rocks everywhere and too many potholes to count. Yellow lines on the concrete had faded in most areas; the painted cement cracked and chipped away. And there was litter all over the place. You couldn't walk ten feet without seeing a discarded paper bag, empty beer cans, or old burger wrappers.

It was especially bad after a rainstorm. Potholes made it impossible to tell if you were about to step into a shallow puddle or if your foot was going to sink ankle-deep into brown water. Most people found these to be only minor inconveniences. The lot was close to work and more importantly, the parking was free.

Jim carried a bottled water in one hand as he left his vehicle and started for the office. As he walked, he wedged the bottle under his left arm so he could change the ringer on his phone to silent. Normally he would use the vibrate setting but he wanted to make sure there would be no distractions. Specifically, he didn't want to have to deal with Beth while he was supposed to be focusing on work. He let the muted cell phone drop back into his front pocket and from the opposite pocket, he removed his pack of cigarettes and lit one as he neared the rear entrance to the building.

"Hey Jim. You're here early. You got an extra one for me?"

It was Jim's boss, the day shift supervisor. It felt like he had been waiting for Jim to arrive. The man, somewhere in his later thirties, was leaning against the masonry wall next to the door. Almost six feet tall and wiry thin, he was bald except for a stubbly horseshoe of dark brown hair. He wore dress slacks and had sunglasses hanging over the collar of his white button-up shirt. He placed his leather briefcase on the ground and reached a hand out in expectation.

"Sure, Paul. Here ya go," Jim offered the man a cigarette from his pack, along with a lighter.

"Jim," Paul began, pausing to suck in a mouthful of smoke. "I know this isn't exactly work-appropriate..."

"Yeah?" Jim answered nonplussed.

"You wouldn't happen to have any single female friends, would you?"

"Um, none that come to mind." Jim told him.

"Shit." Paul's shoulders slumped.

"Shit?"

"I've been single for over a year," the gaunt man professed. "I haven't dated anyone since my whore of an ex-wife, not really anyway."

"Ah. Bad times," Jim observed. He flicked a length of ash to the cement.

"So anyway," Paul went on, "I was hoping I could find someone to help me out. Ya know, set me up on a date or something. I realize it's not something I should be asking employees about, but I'm not great at meeting girls and well, ya know, it'd be nice to get back out there."

"Right," Jim said softly. "I'm not sure if I'm the one to ask though. My own relationship hasn't been going so great and if I had any single lady friends, I'd be trying to bang them myself."

Paul laughed and said, "Hey man, I hear that."

"Okay." Jim wasn't sure what to say next.

"Hey what about that girl- the secretary from the third floor?" asked Paul.

"Who?"

"You know- that one secretary broad who just lost all that weight?"

Jim shrugged; a vacuous expression on his face.

Paul persisted, "I think her name is Vanessa or Vicki or something."

Jim's features brightened with understanding. "The LC?"

Paul furled his brow. "LC? No, her name definitely starts with a V."

"Her name is Veronica," Jim clarified.

"Right, Veronica." Paul took another puff. "Saucy."

"But, she's not a secretary," said Jim. "She's an import specialist. That's why she's always dealing with shippers and carriers and Customs."

Paul rolled his eyes. "Jim, let me tell you something."

"Oh boy," Jim smirked.

The older man went on, "In my day, women were only allowed to be secretaries. Or nurses, they could be nurses too. Or I guess they could have been stewardesses. And yes, they were stewardesses. No one would have ever called them *flight attendants*. If anything, they woulda called them air waitresses."

"Aren't you only like forty?" Jim inquired.

Ignoring the question, Paul added, "Women were something pretty to look at while the men did the work. Now they want to do all the work? I'll never understand the whole *feminist* thing. Don't get me started on this, I could go on for hours."

"That's why you're the boss," Jim observed sardonically.

Paul snapped his fingers and pointed at Jim. "You got it."

"Keep 'em barefoot, pregnant, and in the kitchen, eh Paul?" Jim chided.

Paul's face took on a serious expression. He leaned forward and placed a hand on Jim's shoulder. With a solemn tone he stated, "I never said they had to be pregnant."

Jim had to crane his neck to avoid blowing smoke in his boss' face. "Well, I don't think the LC has any kids."

"Perfect," Paul grinned. "But why do you call her LC?"

"Well, it's short for a nickname she's got around here," Jim said apprehensively. "And she's not exactly aware she's got a nickname."

"What is it?" Paul asked eagerly. He stood completely upright and looked Jim in the eye.

"The Lagoon Creature."

Paul boomed with laughter, which quickly turned into a fit of coughing through his smoke. "Why do you call her that?" he asked through a smile.

"Just to be clear, I don't," Jim explained. "I actually think it's pretty mean, so I don't call her that. Not to anyone who would repeat it, anyway. But a few people do because she maybe looks a little bit like a fish. You ever see that show, Swamp Thing?"

"Oh, come on. She isn't that bad," Paul insisted.

"I know I'm not the most attractive person ever," Jim started. "So, I'm not in a position where I should be critical of other people's appearance, but yeah. She is that bad."

"Well anyhow, do you talk to her at all? Do you know if she's single?"

"You're really interested in the Lagoon Creature? Come on, Paul, I thought you were better than that." Jim dropped his spent cigarette to the ground and stepped on it to snuff it out.

"I don't care if she does look like a fish. Have you seen her ass in those jeans she always wears?" Paul asked. "You know, the ones with no pockets in the back? Delicious."

"Fair enough," Jim said after taking a second to really consider the point. "But you can't have a relationship with just her butt."

"We'll see about that," Paul said defiantly and tossed his smoke into the street.

"Lovely conversation!" sounded a familiar voice. Jim and Paul both turned to find Renee, one of the administrative assistants.

They silently wondered how much of their discussion she had heard. Renee was a smaller girl, maybe twenty-one or twenty-two years old and very cute. She was one of those understated, girl-next-door types with straight brunette hair to her shoulders and a slightly prominent nose. Her soft brown eyes had a way of making you feel like when she looked at you, no one else existed.

Her thin, five and a half foot tall body always had a hint of a tan. She never wore anything too revealing and never looked like she spent too much time applying makeup. This only added to her subtle appeal. Despite her modest dress, there was no denying her intense beauty and physical perfection. The way her jeans set off the figure of her legs to show just a hint of a curve, how her shirts always seemed to highlight flawless proportions. Most guys had a hard time not staring.

For most men in the office, she was the frequent focus of their pornographic fantasies. The giant diamond on her left hand was an ever-present reminder that daydreaming was as close as any of them would ever get. The two men blushed and looked at their feet to hide their embarrassment.

Renee smiled and said, "Please, don't mind me. So, who wants to bang who? I wanna hear all about it."

"Paul is back on the market," Jim explained. "He'd like to start dating and find himself a lady friend."

With her fingers, Renee combed the hair out of her face and tucked it behind her ear. Her face took on a playful and artificially thoughtful expression. She took a moment before speaking, as if truly considering whether she had any advice to offer. Holding back a laugh, she announced, "I don't know any single girls, but I'll keep my eyes peeled for a woman with limited vision and a hit-or-miss relationship with her father."

Jim buried his face in his hands to hide a broadening smile.

"You guys are jerks," said Paul, struggling to hold back a grin of his own. He looked to his wrist, which didn't have a watch on it, and announced, "Alright people, it's time to go to work. So, let's get to it."

Jim shrugged and Renee rolled her eyes. They followed Paul inside the building, where the three of them separated, each to their own work spaces.

It was a typical Monday, somehow busy and boring at the same time. Jim sat at his desk and watched the clock slowly move from 8am to 4pm while he performed a series of mindless, unskilled data entry tasks. When quitting time rolled around, Jim clocked out and shut down his computer. He got up from his workstation and slid the chair under the desk before gathering his belongings and walking directly to the exit.

Jim had managed to avoid looking at his phone all day. But now that work was over, he couldn't help but check it. He pulled the phone out of his pocket as he walked to his car. The screen flickered to life and said that he had twenty-seven missed calls. They were all from Beth and she had apparently left three voice messages. With a shake of his head, Jim connected to the voice mail system and listened.

In the first message, she came across as though everything was fine. It was like they hadn't gone two days without any contact. She was letting him know her plans for the day, which involved cleaning her bedroom, making lunch, and a possible trip to the hair salon. In her second message, Beth apologized for what had happened Saturday night.

She said that she went out with a friend, insisting the guy was nothing more than a buddy she knew from high school, and that nothing bad had happened. She was sorry for the way it must have seemed, but promised it would never happen again and asked him to call her as soon as he could.

Jim could feel his willpower starting to wane. Beth sounded sincere, like she was truly regretful. Maybe she was telling the truth. Probably not, but she was trying to make amends. Didn't she deserve another chance? It was a tough decision. A firm ass, flat stomach, and plump tits could inspire a man to be exceptionally forgiving. Jim was actually considering calling her back. That is, until he listened to the third and final voice mail. This one had a much different tone and it began with Beth shouting into the phone.

"So what, you're not going to call me back? You're such an asshole. What is your problem anyway? You think you're too good to talk to me? You really couldn't take one minute-" Jim disconnected before the message ended.

He got into his car and instead of driving home, he headed for Bennett's Supermarket, the store where Lindsey worked. The trip lasted about twenty minutes and took him past Lowell's Food Emporium and two convenience stores along the way. When he pulled into a parking space outside the store, a nervous belly reminded him that he hadn't really thought this out yet.

There was no fooling himself. He had a boyish little crush on Lindsey and he wanted to find out if she might be feeling something too. Jim had obviously selected this store because he wanted to run into her, but what if Lindsey wasn't as happy to see him as he would be to see her? She was pleasant the last time but that didn't give him a pass to show up and bother her whenever he felt like it. Plus, didn't she say she was seeing someone?

It didn't matter. Even if she was involved with somebody, Jim still liked talking to her. It was a nice change to have a regular conversation with someone without getting stressed out and having it turn into a fight. Jim would be happy just to rebuild his friendship with Lindsey. Plus, maybe she would be single soon. It's not like she was married, so how serious could it be?

Chapter 14

"I went for a run Saturday night," Lindsey said. She pressed her glasses up the bridge of her nose and bent down to collect four cans of tomato soup from a plastic rack. Arranging them on the shelf, Lindsey was sure to turn each one so that the labels faced forward. "And this guy, I don't know if he was crazy or on drugs or what, he just started chasing me down the street."

"You went for a run? What do you wear when you go running?" The question was posed by a pudgy fellow wearing the black pants and green polo shirt that made up the staff uniform at the supermarket. Poorly groomed designer stubble covered his chin and cheeks. His greasy dark hair was long and uncombed; it covered most of his forehead down to his eyebrows. Each earlobe held a large cubic zirconia earring. He ate from a bag of potato chips and spoke as he chewed.

"I wear a running outfit," Lindsey answered; a hint of annoyance in her voice.

"A running outfit, huh? What makes up a running outfit? Is there spandex involved?" Lindsey's coworker smirked and shoveled another handful of chips into his mouth.

"Are you listening to me?" Lindsey asked, still stocking the shelves as she tried to tell her story.

"Yeah, I'm listening. Some druggy chased you down the street. And?"

"And I guess that's it. Thanks for showing such concern." Lindsey turned her back to him and made as though she was too busy with her work to continue the discussion.

"No, come on," her friend implored. "I'm listening. He chased you and you were scared. So then what?"

"Then I ran away- I had to sprint for more than a block. I guess he ran out of steam at some point along the way. It really freaked me out though. At first, I thought he was just some creep but there was something really off about him. His clothes were covered in blood and he was sort of yelling and groaning. It was so weird."

"What did he say?" Lindsey's companion asked.

"Nothing, he was just making noise. I thought about calling the cops when I got home but he was long gone by then. I figured there wasn't much point." Lindsey placed the last can on the shelf and picked up the rack from the floor. She was about to speak again when she heard somebody calling her name.

"Hey Lindsey, I um, I just saw you down here and thought I'd, ya know, pop over to say hi."

"Oh- Jim, hi. What brings you in today?" She sounded pleasant, but not really what you'd call welcoming. It was the niceness of an employee greeting a customer. The tone indicated she was being polite, but not inviting him in for a long conversation.

"Oh, uh, I need a..." Jim's eyes looked up as he searched for an answer that wouldn't make him sound like a stalker. He blurted, "I need a new shower curtain. You sell those here, right?"

"Yes, we sell those." Lindsey's eyes narrowed at him. He seemed like he was lying but what a silly thing to lie about. Her expression softened and she said, "I thought maybe you enjoyed that chicken sub so much that you had to come back for another one tonight."

"Oh, yeah. That was good," Jim said without conviction. His mind wandered to his kitchen where the spoiled meat and cheese was probably starting to stink. "But, no. My shower curtain is getting kinda gross. I meant to grab one last time but I guess I forgot."

Jim's voice trailed off and he looked down at his feet, where he noticed a new shadow move across the floor. He looked up to find that some chunky store worker had lumbered up behind Lindsey, standing a little closer to her than Jim would have liked. Who the Hell was this nosing his way into their chat? Is this the guy she's dating? This? This out of shape loser with the greasy hair and beer gut stuffing salty treats into his face? Or was this just some frump she happened to work with?

"Well, I won't hold you up," Jim said. He was disgusted with himself. This guy hadn't said a word yet and Jim was ready to turn and leave at the mere sight of what might potentially be a rival for Lindsey's affection. It was despicable but he couldn't stop himself. Feeling like he was watching a movie starring an even sadder version of himself, he took a step back from Lindsey and told her, "I guess I'll see ya later."

"Hang on, I'll show you where you need to go," Lindsey said as she began to lead the way. She only made it a couple of steps before stopping and turning to face the lingering snack fanatic. "Don't you have something to do? You don't need to follow me around all day."

The guy with the ridiculous fake earrings huffed, "Whatever."

He crumpled the now-empty bag in his hands and while looking Lindsey directly in the eye, stuffed his garbage onto the shelf between two rows of chicken noodle. Before he walked away, the male clerk eyed Jim, looking him from head to toe. Snorting, he walked to the end of the aisle and disappeared toward the rear of the store.

This encounter had gone from uncomfortable to disastrous in a matter of seconds. And things weren't looking up. Jim and Lindsey walked awkwardly, not speaking for a few moments. He didn't know what to say to her or if he should even try at that point. Maybe he should just go; run out of the store, never to return. He would have to make a point to avoid this supermarket from now on, or at least until he knew she had quit. Lindsey finally broke the quiet.

"So, what are you up to today?" It wasn't much, but it was better than silence.

"Just work," Jim answered plainly.

"What do you do again?" Lindsey asked.

Jim couldn't tell if she was genuinely interested. He doubted it, but answered anyway. "I work for Sigler Global Logistics, it's a customs broker."

"That sounds exciting."

"It isn't. It's actually pretty boring."

"So, what does a customs broker do?" Lindsey looked at Jim, ready to listen.

"Well," he began, "When trucks full of cargo come into the States from Canada, the government charges a tax on the goods being imported. The company sending the product is usually not the same as the trucking company who's actually carrying the goods over the border. But somebody has to pay those taxes before the cargo is allowed to go any further."

"I'm with you so far," said Lindsey.

"Okay, so what these companies do is hire a customs broker to pay the taxes on behalf of the shipping company, which lets the goods pass over the border without having to send cash with the person driving the truck."

"You're right- that does sound boring," Lindsey said through a sly grin.

"Right," Jim agreed. A smile tried to tug at the edges of his lips. "And my job is the worst part. I do the data entry stuff. When the trucker is getting close to the border, in my case it's over the Peace Bridge or the Lewiston-Queenston Bridge, they fax their paperwork into the office and I basically just type in what it says on the papers so Customs knows what's in each load."

"That still sounds like a better job than I've got." She did have a point. "Well, here ya go."

Lindsey gestured to show Jim the rack of shower curtains. Jim, pretending not to have a preference, grabbed the one with the lowest price, a plain white plastic sheet.

"Great, thanks for the help." Jim smiled at her, unsure if she was going to leave him there or if she planned to see him out as she had on Saturday.

Lindsey did leave him at that point. She told him that she still had five or six more aisles to stock and then had to mop the back room and she didn't want to fall behind on her schedule. She smiled and patted his shoulder, telling him, "It sounds like things are going pretty good for you, Jim. I'm glad. I'll see ya later."

When she had gone, Jim sneaked back to the cooler aisle and grabbed a six pack of Guinness. Dissatisfied in how things had gone with Lindsey, he planned to remedy his bruised pride and punctured masculinity with a night of drinking. He paid for the items and walked through the exits, not raising his eyes from the ground immediately in front of him.

How stupid he was. What had he expected to come of this, that Lindsey would tear her clothes off and jump on him right there in the soup aisle? Or maybe she'd be so impressed by his two-dollar purchase she'd ask to move in with him. What an idiot. Dejected, Jim slithered across the parking lot to his car.

He shuffled past the front of the car to the passenger's side. Jim hefted the beer under his left arm, gripping the shower curtain in his hand. His right hand groped around in his front pocket trying to unbind his keys from within. Distracted with the task at hand, Jim almost didn't notice the bright red blotches standing out against the fender's soft metallic blue paint.

"What the f-" Jim mumbled to himself. He bent to examine the dotted and runny patterns formed on the car by the hot stuff of life. Jim glanced to his right and then behind him. He stood upright and performed a slow, full spin to look over the entire parking lot.

The blood covered most of the passenger's side fender. Some of it appeared to have gotten into the engine compartment, spilling into the gap between the car's outer wall and the hood. There were also red spots on the tire and aluminum wheel.

Had he hit someone and not noticed? Impossible. Wasn't it? How often did he take the time to look over his car before getting in? He almost walked right past it just then. And what about Saturday? He wasn't paying attention to his driving while he was running all over town trying to find where Beth had run off to. He could have easily side-swiped a pedestrian and remained oblivious, especially given how clouded his mind had been at the time. Could he really have been driving for two days with blood stains on the outside of his car? How many people would have seen it?

Jim felt sick. His palms were sweating more than normal and he was getting dizzy. What if he'd really hurt someone? It looked like a small amount of blood, not that there was any way to measure it. But that doesn't necessarily mean anything.

He could have struck someone who then bounced off the car and kept bleeding out on the ground. What if he'd killed someone and had no idea? Were the police now on the lookout for an average-looking mid twenty-something year old guy driving a two-door Pontiac? Someone might recognize his car, it's the only one with DNA evidence glued to the side.

Jim gradually lowered himself to the ground. He sat on the pavement in the empty parking space next to his car and placed his keys on the cement beside him. The car would have to be washed. Thoroughly. Does car wash soap remove blood?

Shaking hands wiped sweat from his eyes, fingers rubbed his forehead. He looked up again, about to curse his misfortune when he saw a swollen red pearl rolling along the contour of the car's body. Reaching the top of the wheel well, it hung frozen for half a second before collecting itself and falling free. Jim sat upright as the droplet splashed onto the concrete.

"Holy shit!" He reached forward with his right hand and slid his index finger across the largest section of streaks. It was fresh, still wet. Still hot. Not only that, but the blood only ran downward, not toward the back of the car as it would have if the car had been moving. This must have happened since he'd gone into the store. But who the Hell would bleed all over his car? And why? Maybe someone got into a fight or had an accident. He looked behind him again but didn't see anything unusual. Who cares- he was in the clear. Relief rolled through Jim's body; his tension easing.

"Oh, dammit," Jim exclaimed. Sticking his bare hands into blotches of strange blood was probably not the best idea. He'd have to give his hands a good scrubbing, but after the car was thoroughly washed.

Chapter 15

Now sparkling clean and freshly waxed, Jim's car wheeled across the parking lot and slid into his assigned spot. He stopped at the Spray 'N Wash on Delaware Avenue before going home. Jim had managed to work the coin-operated car wash and do all of his driving without touching his soiled finger to anything. He'd had to hold it in the air to keep from touching the steering wheel and used his middle finger to work the stereo.

When he reached to grab the key from the ignition, Jim's attention was drawn to a movement in the rear-view mirror. The garbage bins were still where he had last seen them, lying horizontal in the middle of the parking lot, next to a bloated mound of trash and spoiled food. Only now, someone was cleaning up the mess.

Jim stepped out of the car. He placed the beer and shower curtain on the ground before walking over to the girl; the very fit, very attractive girl in a satiny green dress. She was facing away from him, hunched over the mess. The young woman turned the containers upright and, using only her index finger and thumb, carefully picked up a plastic bag from the ground and held it at arm's-length before dropping it into one of the bins.

"Excuse me," he called.

"Huh," the girl turned to face him, "Oh, hey Jim."

Oh boy, did she look good. Her light brown hair hung freely, coming to an end just beyond her shoulders. The spaghetti strap dress adhered to her thin frame, nicely complimenting her waist and hips. Her tan, toned legs were on full display and something magical was happening with her breasts. They were lifted and pressed together to form a surprising amount of cleavage. Jim had never seen her all dressed up before. He realized he was staring and forced himself to talk before she noticed.

"Jenna, I- I didn't recognize you at first," he stammered.

"I hope I didn't startle you," she said, keeping focused on the chore of picking up garbage, one ripe parcel at a time.

"Not at all." Jim told her. He waited a few seconds before adding, "You look nice, by the way."

"Oh, thanks. That's sweet of you to say." Jenna forced a polite smile.

"What's the occasion?" Jim asked, thinking that if he was going to make small talk, he was probably going to have to help with the trash.

"I'm stupid," she answered, bending to pick up another plastic bag.

"That's odd, I never dress up when I'm being stupid," Jim tried to joke, but it fell flat. "I'd probably run out of nice clothes."

Jenna eyed him and offered another small grin, but it was clear she wasn't in a playful mood.

"Here, let me get that." Jim gestured for her to step back and snatched up the bags and loose pieces of garbage indiscriminately.

Jenna scrunched her nose.

"I gotta give my hands a good scrubbing when I get in anyway. It's a long story," Jim stated without explanation. "So, you were saying?"

"Okay, so I let my mom set me up on a blind date," she stopped to let her eyes meet Jim's questioning glance. "Like I said, I'm stupid. We were supposed to meet for dinner, I forget the name of the restaurant. You know, it's that real fancy place downtown, right near the river. You know where I'm talking about?"

Jim nodded. He collected another handful of scraps and tossed them into one of the bins.

Jenna continued, "So, I got there first. The reservation was in his name, but they let me sit at the table and wait for him. I ended up sitting alone in the middle of the restaurant for over an hour. The dickhead never showed up. If he was going to blow me off, he could have called to let me know. What an asshole."

She sighed. "I mean, I really wouldn't have cared if he wasn't into me. It just would have been nice to know before I went and made an ass of myself."

"Yeah, that's pretty lame," Jim said. As usual, he didn't know how best to respond. "So, I take it you decided to leave eventually?"

"I think the hostess decided for me," she answered. "She came over and quietly asked if the rest of my party was going to arrive soon because if I wasn't going to order anything, they needed to have the table free because they were getting busy."

"At least she was quiet about it," Jim attempted to add a positive spin.

"I guess." Jenna clapped her hands together to shake off what she hoped was only food particles and not mold- or something more disgusting. "She, my mother I mean, is always giving me unsolicited dating advice. 'Go out with this guy or that guy,' she says. Or, 'Maybe you can find a nice guy at church to go out with.' She means well, but things haven't exactly panned out."

"You go to church?" Jim asked, not sure why he was surprised at this.

"Uh huh," Jenna answered. "Every Sunday with my mom. And as I'm sure my mother has noticed, the only guys there are men old enough to be my grandfather."

"You don't want to date an older man?" Jim asked in jest.

"Very funny," she smirked. Jenna straightened the strap over her right shoulder.

"What church do you go to?" Part of Jim was legitimately interested, but a larger part just wanted to keep chatting with the hot chick in the tight dress.

"Mount Calvary," she told him. Her response was met with a blank stare so she elaborated, "It's the small brick building over on First Avenue."

"Oh," Jim tried to draw on his memory, but came up blank.

"It's like three blocks from here," Jenna pointed across the street and beyond a row of homes. "You must have driven past it a hundred times."

"Yeah, I think I know where you mean." Jim squinted. Over the neighboring roofs and through a handful of tree branches, he could just barely make out the tip of a gold cross standing tall over the other buildings. It looked small and plain from that distance but it had a nice shine to it.

"You should come with us some time," Jenna suggested.

Jim grinned, "Maybe I will. And maybe I can find someone's grandma to date."

93

The pair laughed at this as Jim finished collecting the garbage from the ground and dumped the last of it into the receptacle.

"Anyhow, I'm sorry you had a bad night," Jim was trying to sound genuinely compassionate. "If the guy knew what he was missing, he'd never forgive himself for standing you up."

"Thanks. That's sweet of you to say," she said. Jenna turned away so Jim wouldn't see her blush. "And if that wasn't bad enough, I come home to find garbage all over the place and I get to spend twenty minutes cleaning trash off the ground."

"Yeah, I saw-" Jim stopped. He was about to admit to seeing, and leaving, the mess before he went to work that morning.

"You saw what?"

"I saw you out here when I pulled in," Jim recovered. "Any idea who did this?"

Jenna shrugged. "I have no idea. And I can't believe how no one here could be bothered to clean it up. I guess they'd rather deal with the smell than have to lift a finger and help."

"They're a bunch of lazy bums," Jim grinned like a dope.

"Well, except for you," said Jenna. "Thank you for helping me."

"No problem." Jim grabbed the handles to one of the trash cans and began dragging it to the side of the building where they were normally kept. Jenna took the other one and followed behind.

When she placed her bin in its place, Jenna looked to Jim and said, "Do you realize I've been single for over a year now?" It was a statement more than a question.

"Yeah, but that's okay," Jim replied. "There's nothing wrong with being single."

Jenna huffed. "I suppose, but I get lonely. You're lucky. You've been seeing that girl of yours for a while now, what's her name again?"

"Beth," Jim answered. "And I don't know how lucky I am. I don't think it's going to work out."

"No? Why is that?"

"She's got sort of a leg problem."

"A leg problem?" she asked. Jenna gave Jim an inquisitive look and said, "I'm not sure that's a fair reason to break up."

"Well, it's the type of leg problem she has," Jim told her.

"Okay. What kind of leg problem is it?"

"It's kinda like she's only got one."

"Only got one?" Jenna scratched her head. "I don't think I follow."

"It's like she's only got one because she can't seem to keep them closed." Jim held out his hands and slowly brought them together.

"Oh no, that's awful!" Jenna stifled a laugh at Jim's lame joke.

"Right..." Jim trailed off.

"You should say she's got twenty-four-hour legs, since they're always open."

Jim forced a smile and said, "That's clever."

"Sorry, I'm being a jerk. Has she been cheating?" Her sympathetic tone said she could relate.

Jim rolled his shoulders. "Cheating, whoring around, whatever you wanna call it."

"That's too bad," she said with more than a hint of empathy. "I've only seen her in passing but she seemed like such a nice girl."

"Yeah. Evidently she's very nice- to everyone she meets. Or at least everyone with a penis."

Jenna walked with Jim to his car to get the new shower curtain and beer before making their way to the door on his side of the building. She could tell his mood had shifted. Jim was being polite and helpful and maybe flirting a little bit. Since she mentioned Beth, he'd grown quiet. His animated expression had vanished. Without missing another beat, she changed the subject once again.

"Do you think Charles might know something about the spilled batch of garbage? I don't think he's left the house today. His car hasn't moved." Jenna pointed to a maroon-colored Mercury Sable situated several rows down from Jim's Pontiac.

Jim shifted his weight, holding the goods in his right hand. He asked, "You think it's worth it to ask him; check if he knows anything?"

"I don't know," answered Jenna. "I've had about an ass-full of Charles lately. I can't stand him at times. Doesn't it feel like he's always talking down to you?"

"Yeah, sort of," Jim agreed halfheartedly.

Jenna elaborated, "He's one of those guys who thinks that because he wears Dockers and a tie, he can condescend to everyone."

"Yeah, that's Charles."

"I wonder where he gets that attitude from. He can look down his nose at people if he wants, but it makes him no better than anyone else. He's still a loser; a loser who lives in this small town in a tiny shitty apartment, just like me." Jenna didn't notice that her hands had transformed into clenched fists while she was talking.

"And just like me," Jim contributed.

"Oh. No, that's not what I meant, I was-" she started to say when Jim spoke up.

"It's okay," he assured her. "I know what you mean."

"Okay, okay. Sorry, I'm just still in a bad mood I guess."

"It's cool. I know the feeling." Jim smiled at her but he wasn't sure why.

"Alright, I should probably head inside. Thanks again for helping with the trash and thanks for listening to me whine," she said.

"I don't mind," Jim replied. He opened the glass door and stood holding it open with his back pressed into the outer frame. "It's no problem at all."

"Well, I appreciate it," she said. "You still going to check with Charles?"

"I think so," answered Jim. "Just to see if he saw or heard anything."

"Good luck with that. I'm sure you're in for a real treat."

"I'll let you know how it goes," Jim promised.

"You do that." Jenna took a step closer. She leaned into him and gave him one of those awkward one-arm half-hugs before saying, "Have a good night, Jim. I'll see you later."

Jenna released him and strode down the front walkway to the other side of the building; her high heels clicking and clacking against the pavement. Jim stood in place, still holding the door open as he watched her go. She pulled the door open and disappeared inside without looking back. Alone, Jim spoke more to himself than anyone else, "Goodnight."

He turned and walked into the building. Instead of going to the right and taking the stairs up to his door, he veered left and went down the six steps to the basement landing. The floors in the lower level weren't carpeted like they were in the upper hallways. The walls were painted in the basement but they hadn't been touched up in a long time. Bare spots of drywall had started to show through what used to be solid white paint. Jim turned to his right, facing the door to Charles' apartment, and knocked. He placed his beer and shower curtain on the bare cement floor and waited for a response.

No one answered so after a few moments of waiting, he knocked harder. That time, Jim could have sworn he'd heard a voice from within. It was too low in volume to tell whether it was Charles, but who else would be in there? Maybe it was that woman he had been bringing around lately. Could it be that neither of them had anywhere to go all day?

"Hello?" Jim called. "Charles, are you in there?"

Nobody answered and from inside the apartment, it sounded as if something had been thrown or knocked over. It was like something heavy had been dropped on the floor or slammed into a wall.

"Hey, are you alright in there?" Jim shouted and pounded his fist on the door.

"Hey man, what's with all the banging down here?" a voice asked from behind him.

Jim looked up to find Danny standing at the top of the steps. He had on only a pair of frayed sneakers and black jeans. Danny was shirtless and his long black hair reached all the way to his exposed nipples. His torso looked pasty and frail.

"I was trying to get a hold of Charles to see if he knew anything about the trash outside," Jim explained. "But he's not answering and it sounds like something crashed inside his apartment."

"Pff," said Danny, waving a hand in front of his face. "Don't worry about Chucky, he's fine. But wait- what trash?"

"The trash that was left in the middle of the parking lot all day," Jim clarified.

"I didn't see any trash," Danny countered.

"Right."

"Right?" Danny looked confused.

"We cleaned it up." Jim was exasperated. "Me and Jenna, just now."

"Oh, okay." Danny was piecing things together. "So, what do you need Chucky for?"

"I guess nothing, since he's not answering." Jim raised his voice and added, "Even though I know he's in there."

"Hey man, forget Chucky," Danny instructed.

"You're right." Jim started climbing the stairs, carrying his purchases. He passed in front of Danny, who then followed him up.

"Jimmy, I hate to be a bother," Danny paused to allow for Jim's questioning glance. "Do you have any Pepto or something for an upset stomach?"

"I don't think so, sorry. Are you getting sick?"

"Not sure. I ate some raw eggs this morning and now I'm feelin' kinda queasy."

"Why are you eating raw eggs?" Jim asked. "Trying to bulk up?"

Danny chuckled. "Not exactly. I was in a hurry and didn't have time to cook them. Now I'm thinking that was a bad idea, I've been spraying out mud all afternoon."

"Okay. Thanks for that," Jim said, shaking his head.

"Ha- You got it Jimmy."

"But I'm sorry, no. I don't have anything that will help with your, uh..."

"Trouser chili," Danny advised.

"Right, can't help you there. But good luck."

"Thanks Jimmy. Well listen, I'll see you later. I'm going to get inside." Danny slid around the corner, gripping the handrail and following the steps to the floor above.

"Okay man, I'll see ya later."

Jim walked into his apartment, closing up behind him as he always did. He pulled the packaged shower curtain out of the plastic supermarket bag and pitched it toward the bathroom. The Guinness went into the fridge, but only five of them. And then Jim gasped, finally remembering himself. He walked directly to the kitchen sink where he scrubbed his hands with soap and the hottest water he could stand.

Chapter 16

A slimy tongue rolled out between a pair of black lips. A bubble of saliva fell to the floor as the creature examined the small bowl. A wet nose rubbed at the brim and hot breath formed a small cloud against the metallic finish. More than a dozen smears of dribble and snot marked each spot where it had been touched and nudged. The dish had been sitting empty for at least an hour already but that didn't stop Duke from walking over every five minutes to look inside.

It was one of those shiny metal bowls that should have held a small mountain of kibble, the kind with chunks of beef and real gravy- or maybe some delicious morsel left over from breakfast. Nothing was better than people food. After all, he had been extra good lately and he deserved a treat. But every time Duke checked the bowl's contents, he found nothing but crumbs and his own distorted reflection staring back.

How long had it been since he'd last eaten? Days? Weeks? Months? That seemed most likely. He could barely remember what his food even tasted like. Duke was starving and it seemed no matter what he did, no one would give him anything to sate his hunger. Since his owner and his owner's dip-shit son refused to feed him, it was only a matter of time before Duke literally wasted away to nothing.

He groaned and walked from the kitchen to the living room where he stopped right in front of the television. Standing silently, Duke looked first to Albert and then to Adam. He pleaded with his eyes for one of them to get up and refill his dish.

"Move out of the way, dummy," Adam scolded the dog from his recliner. He was dressed like a slob and hadn't shaved in a couple days.

"He's hungry, give him his breakfast." Albert answered on Duke's behalf. He sat in a matching chair a few feet from Adam's. Albert was dressed in tan slacks, a button-down collared shirt, and one of those short-brimmed caps that he always wore. In his hand was a wooden smoking pipe with a fresh wad of tobacco. He generally tried to avoid smoking indoors, instead opting to sit on the balcony and take in some clean air and sun while he puffed away. So far this morning, his sore hips and bad knee had kept him in his seat.

Hanging above him on the wall was an oil painting of Albert and Adam. Both men looked much younger in the picture, by ten years or more. There was a middle-aged woman with soft brown hair as well. They were all wearing formal clothing and had obviously posed for the painting. Each of them had a big warm smile pasted on their face. All three people were either genuinely happy to be together as a family, or they could fake it better than anyone. Albert and the woman sat on chairs facing each other. Adam knelt in front of them and held a six-month-old Duke in his arms.

"He already ate his breakfast," said Adam, stretching his neck to see around the dog.

"Then give him a biscuit," Albert instructed, ready to trade barbs with his son.

"You give him a biscuit." Adam tried to sound argumentative but he couldn't completely hide his smile. He liked giving his dad a few jabs here and there and they both knew it was all in fun.

"Listen you son of a bitch," Albert's voice was stern but light enough for Adam to know he was playing along. "I said you get him a biscuit, so you get him a biscuit!"

"Yeah, yeah," Adam said, waving him off. "I'll get it when I get up. I gotta run downstairs in a minute anyway."

"What's downstairs?" Albert asked, adjusting his taxi-driver hat.

"Laundry," Adam said. "Should be done washing by now, gotta throw it in the dryer."

"Okay. But don't you forget," Albert pointed a finger at his son.

"Fine, but get him outta the way," Adam complained. Then he turned his focus back to the dog and shouted, "Move your ass!"

Duke complied. Sort of. The old German Shepherd circled three times, still in front of the TV set. He eventually came to a stop but was still obscuring the view. The dog sat and stuck his snout between his hind legs to lick his balls.

"Dammit, Duke. Knock it off," Adam scolded.

"Oh, let him be," Albert said

"Oh, so you want to watch him go at himself like that?" Adam looked to his father expectantly. "It's disgusting."

Albert laughed. "You're just jealous that you can't do that."

"Yep. You got it. It's jealousy," Adam rolled his eyes. "I just can't stand that he can lick his balls and I can't."

Albert sat quiet for a moment, looking up to the ceiling and rubbing his chin as though he was deep in thought. Knowing his son was expecting a response, he looked to him and said, "Well, maybe you could. But you'd probably have to pet him first."

The older man erupted with laughter that promptly turned to loud coughing. He slapped his knee and asked, "Ya get it?"

"Got it." Adam was trying to hold in laughter of his own.

"Or maybe you could bribe him with a bone," Albert added, still chuckling.

"Ha ha," Adam said dryly. "You're so funny. Could you get him to move?"

"Maybe he'd let you get to second base with a belly rub," Albert went on.

Adam just sighed.

Albert whistled, "Come here bud. Who's a good boy? You want a biscuit? Of course you do. And you're such a good boy, you should get many biscuits."

The eleven-year-old German Shepherd finished cleaning himself and tramped across the carpet to Albert's feet. Duke didn't move as quickly as he used to. His brown and black fur looked faded with more and more gray hair creeping in. There was a bit of a hunch to his stride, his head hung low and a slobbering tongue dangled from his panting mouth.

Albert leaned forward in his seat to pet the dog. Duke was still a puppy to him. He was a puppy with bad hips and a prescription to treat canine arthritis, but a puppy nonetheless. He ran his hands over Duke's head and looked down at his tired eyes. The old dog turned and stretched out on the floor at his master's feet.

About ten minutes passed. Adam, Albert, and Duke had been watching the morning news. The same types of stories came up so often, the men sometimes wondered if maybe Channel 4 had taken the day off and were airing reruns. First, the anchors discussed plans to improve the Peace Bridge. Then they moved on to a discussion about whether Bass Pro Shop would ever open a store in Buffalo; they didn't sound hopeful. Before going to a commercial break, they teased a story about some sort of protest-turned-riot that had started overnight. The news reader, an attractive brunette in her late twenties, pondered aloud, "How long until the police can get it under control?"

"Alright. Laundry and biscuits," Adam announced. He stood up from his chair and yawned, stretching his hands over his head and arching his back.

Duke's ears perked up. He slowly pulled himself to his feet and followed Adam into the kitchen; his tail gently wagging. As Adam knelt to open the bottom cupboard next to the oven, Duke took the opportunity to check his food dish one more time. It was still empty, but when the dog looked back to Adam, he was presented with a small treat in the shape of a bone. He took it greedily, chewed once, and swallowed. Duke looked back to Adam for another, but the man was already opening the apartment door and stepping over the threshold.

"Alright, Pop. I'll be back in a few," Adam said and pulled the door closed as he moved into the hallway.

The walking surfaces in the corridor were covered by a stained and faded blue carpet. The color had once been a deep, almost purple shade. The flooring in no way matched the walls, which were painted a bright sky blue with baby powder white for the trim. And the hallway didn't just look ugly, it smelled ugly. The stairwell reeked of something like baked garbage. There was always a summertime funk in the basement and hallways, but that morning the stench was extra pungent. Adam's nose crinkled and he frowned, waving a hand in front of his face.

He hiked up his loose-fitting jeans and rolled up the sleeves of his baggy sweatshirt. Adam skipped down the eight steps to the landing, just in front of the entrance to the building. He turned sharply to the left and followed the next six stairs down to the basement level. On his left was the door to one of the building's basement units. To his right was the door that led to the unfinished section. Adam pushed the door open and went in.

The carpet stops once you walk into the basement area. When Adam stepped from the hall and onto the exposed cement floor, his sneaker slipped out from under him. Had he not still been holding the doorknob, he would have fallen right on his ass.

"Whoa!" he exclaimed. Adam was now fully awake and felt his pulse banging through his chest. He grinned and scolded himself. "Watch your step, ya clumsy asshole."

From where he entered the lower level, there was a washing machine and dryer to his right. The units sat along the wall at the front of the building. The walls themselves were just the concrete blocks of the foundation which had been painted white. Above the laundry area was a large window that let in enough sunlight to see the machines, but not much else. Next to the washer and dryer was a large two-bay wash bin and a plastic trash can. Past the garbage pail, was a partition with a door that led to the other half of the basement.

The man stood just inside the doorway. To his left was a darkened narrow hall that went straight back to the rear of the building. Five individual storage units lined the left side of the walkway. Each compartment was constructed of bare plywood and had a number written on the door in black marker, one through five. Along the right side was a fence that stood in front of the boiler and water heater for that side of the building.

A loose chain was wrapped around the handle of the gate with an open padlock hanging at its end. Adam always wondered why the appliances were enclosed by chain link fencing. Maybe the landlord didn't want the residents tampering with the utilities. But if the idea was to keep people from accessing the boiler and water heater, why leave the gate unlocked?

The next step toward the washing machine was just as slippery as the first. Adam wondered if the machine had leaked or overfilled but as he got closer, the floor seemed to get drier. After only a couple of strides, his shoes gripped the cement easily. He bent to place his hand on the ground. The concrete was cool and dry. The lid on the washing machine was closed firmly in place and the handle of the machine was dry as well.

Adam looked back toward the door. There was a small puddle, clearly disturbed from where his foot had lost traction. He could also make out a few glistening footsteps in the basement's limited lighting. The wet spots were in the exact pattern as the bottom of his sneakers. There were no bubbles or suds on the floor and the fluid had a dark, thick look to it.

He kicked the laundry basket out of the way and began transferring his clean wet clothes from the washing machine to the dryer. With the washer empty, Adam collected a few stray items that had fallen to the floor and tossed them in to be dried. Once all the clothing was accounted for, he nudged the dryer door closed and fed a dollar's worth of quarters into the machine. It hummed to life, the heating element warmed up and the drum began to spin inside. With that done, Adam returned to investigate the liquid near the doorway.

It wasn't as though Adam felt an obligation to tidy up, but he did want to make sure the floor was dry. His father would be coming down to do laundry later in the day and he wouldn't have the same quick reflexes if he stepped in something wet and slippery. The last thing Adam needed was to worry about the old man having a nasty fall. Adam would never admit it, but over the years he had grown more protective and concerned with his dad's well-being. If Albert got hurt from falling on a wet floor, in a puddle that Adam neglected, the younger man would be plagued with guilt.

Adam looked around for a cloth or some paper towels. There weren't any to be found and he didn't feel like walking back upstairs to grab some. Laziness dictated that he would search the garbage can first. Maybe there would be something in there he could use to mop up the floor. It might sound gross, but no one ever used the basement for anything but doing laundry, so the trash can only held used dryer sheets, empty detergent containers, and the odd sock that had forever lost its mate.

He was searching through the bin, in up to his shoulder, and so far had not found anything useful. Roughly one third of its contents had already been yanked out and dropped to the ground. Adam's concentration was broken by the sound of something scraping across the floor; a heavy shuffling drawing near.

Adam assumed someone had come downstairs to begin a load of laundry. He called over his shoulder without looking up, "Hi. The washing machine is free. I'm just using the dryer."

Nobody answered and Adam had just about given up trying to find a cloth or paper towels in the trash can. He pulled his arm free and dusted lint off his hands as he asked, "Hey, you don't happen to have some paper towels or something, do you?"

When his question was again met with silence, Adam let out an exaggerated sigh and called out a little louder than was necessary. "Hello?"

The man spun around to find no one standing at the washing machine. His shoulders shrugged. It must have been his imagination. Or maybe it was the wind outside or a rattle in the plumbing overhead. Adam reached back into the trash and pulled out a handful of used dryer sheets. It was better than nothing and preferable to walking back up the stairs and into the apartment just to come back down to wipe up the mess.

When he pressed the wad of sheets into the puddle, the liquid just smeared around on the floor. As he mostly expected, the dryer sheets were useless, not absorbent at all. To make matters worse, the fluid was now all over his hand. It was warm, almost hot, and tacky on his fingers.

"Oh dammit," he muttered. Adam lifted the sticky wet glob from the ground and walked to the laundry area to toss the sheets back into the trash.

A brilliant ray of sunshine poured through the window. As he walked into the light, Adam was stunned by the site of what he held in his hand. He shrieked, dropping the ball of dryer sheets to the floor and automatically drawing his hand back to his torso. Embarrassed and thankful his father wasn't around to hear him squeal like a girl, the man collected himself and considered whether his eyes might have been playing tricks on him.

"What the fu-" he muttered. Adam let his voice trail off, mindful of his language.

Nervous sweat cooled Adam's forehead and armpits. The thick wad of dryer sheets and lint was indeed stained a deep shade of red. It was definitely blood, and fresh based on the temperature. But whose was it? And why was it all over the floor? What on Earth had gone on down there? Maybe if he looked hard enough, an explanation would present itself.

But that explanation would have to wait until a time when his hands were no longer covered in mystery blood. Moving quickly, Adam rushed over to the wash bin and ran the hot water. He scrubbed his hands together to get the blood off the best he could before drying them on the legs of his jeans.

When finished, he walked back to the doorway and flicked the light switch; something he should have done in the first place. A pair of suspended fluorescent lights clicked and popped as they came alive. It took a moment for them to turn on and when they did, the bulbs illuminated the rest of the basement and showed Adam that he wasn't alone down there. The man, previously concealed in the shadows, was standing all the way in the back of the basement and facing the rear wall. Adam's throat sunk into his chest with the realization that this person must have been there the whole time, standing alone in the darkness.

The man, about six feet tall and with a shaved head, slowly turned around. He had on a pair of blue jeans, a white tee shirt, and a gray zip-up hooded sweatshirt that was open in the front. His body wasn't huge, but it was muscular. His shoulders were wide and thick. Several garden hose veins bulged out of his neck. Patches of stubble covered his chin and cheeks. Both sunken bloodshot eyes sat above purple circles.

As the man continued to pivot, the origin of the spilled blood became apparent. A deep oozing gash ran from the middle of his forehead, down a clearly broken nose, and stopped at a split upper lip. Each side of the busted lip had dried and cracked, separating enough to reveal the gap of several missing teeth. The ridges of scabbed skin had started to die and turn black. Red fluid soaked into the man's shirts, several drops fell to the floor, splashing on the dusty cement. An elastic strand of spittle followed closely behind.

Adam knew right away who this guy was. He and his father had been inside watching TV the night Danny and Charles were attacked. Neither Adam nor Albert had actually seen the confrontation or the deranged man who'd initiated it. None of the other tenants could provide a clear description of the perpetrator. As far as anyone knew, he had been scared off, never to be seen again. Adam was frozen, staring, with no doubt in his mind that he was looking at that very maniac who had already tried to harm two people in the building.

Still standing in front of the door, Adam gripped the knob and swung it open. The bleeding man screamed like an animal, pounding his feet on the floor and racing to catch his victim before he could get out. Adam, with one foot in the hallway, could already sense the man upon him. A hand- a claw swung for the back of his neck. Filthy nails dug into skin as the bastard grabbed hold of Adam by the neckline on the back of his shirt.

Refusing to go down easy, Adam threw an elbow behind him but it failed to connect. His right arm flailed uselessly behind him. The other man growled, the sound was low and muffled by gurgles in his throat. Adam was pulled back by his shirt and felt slippery lips and gums press into the side of his neck. Teeth on his assailant's lower jaw scraped and applied pressure but it wasn't enough to break the skin. This bastard was trying to bite him! He *was* biting him; like some kind of toothless stinking vampire. This wasn't just some belligerent asshole looking for a fight. This was a man with a severe mental illness and a violent delirium.

Instinct and panic set in even further. There would be no reasoning with this lunatic. Adam wasn't in danger of just getting beat up, his life was on the line. He kicked his right foot behind him as forcefully as he could. The bottom of his shoe slammed into one of his attacker's legs, clipping the front of his shin. Adam hoped it had been hard enough to break a bone or two, but he wasn't about to stick around and check it out. At the very least, the kick had been enough to make the man lose his balance and fall backwards into the open doorway.

Upon impact, the flimsy hollow core door caved in and folded around the assailant. It was still being held up by its hinges but the door offered no support to the falling man, who collapsed through it and landed on the ground. A resounding thud echoed through the basement when the man's head bounced off the floor. The sound was promptly followed by palms slapping cement. The aggressor, whose hands had come free from Adam's shirt, now struggled to pull himself upright.

Adam, no longer being held by the bleeding shithead, turned to face him. He was relieved to slip away, but the sick man was still between himself and the exit. If Adam was going to get out, he was going to have to go through the wanna-be vampire. Using his left hand to hold the attacker at bay, he balled his right hand and began firing fist after fist into the man's mangled face.

Several punches glanced off the man's head, but most landed solidly against his already-mutilated features. Red pearls jumped up and landed on Adam's shirt. Both hands were spattered with blood and a few drops got enough air to land on his hair and face. Another swing; Adam felt his two outermost knuckles burst when they crashed into the man's skull. Knife-like pain exploded through his broken hand, causing him to flinch for a half of a second.

"Fuck you!" he cried. Ignoring the sharp pangs that rolled from his fingers to his wrist, Adam rocketed another blast into the man's face and taunted, "Come on you piece of shit!"

The bald man didn't even flinch. Every time Adam punched him, he didn't duck or dodge or try to protect himself from the strikes. He just kept trying to grab onto Adam's arm, which was too slick from perspiration and bodily fluid. Failing to catch him, he opened his mouth wide in anticipation of the next blow. Missing his upper teeth, the ghoul couldn't chomp down on Adam's hand. And since the punches were relentless, he still couldn't get to his feet.

Another punch, one that would turn out to be the last in this exchange, found Adam's swollen knuckles smashing into the bleeding man's bottom jaw. The lower lip split to match the upper, but Adam's fist scraped across the grating surface of a jagged tooth. The skin over his knuckles got sliced wide open.

"Shit," Adam exclaimed as bright red liquid filled the open wound.

He shook his hand in hopes that the pain would somehow lose its grasp and fall away. Adam's anger had intensified. He was furious at the invasion of his home and frustrated that he hadn't been able to beat the man into submission. Adam looked down at the bastard, used the door frame to steady himself, and blasted a kick into the center of his chest. At least three ribs crackled like a snapping tree branch and the beast gasped for breath.

"How's that, asshole?" Adam bellowed in triumph. What might have been a grin quickly turned into a frown. Adam's eyes grew wide and he swallowed a heavy gulp, now shocked to find he was unable to reclaim his leg.

Even with no air in his lungs, the man with the ruined face had managed to catch Adam's leg when it connected with his chest. As Adam tried to pull away, the creep yanked him by the ankle and pulled his feet out from under him. Landing hard on his back, Adam could feel a pair of strong hands pulling him by the legs. The crazed dickhead crawled forward and hovered over his shoes. Overcome by a renewed sense of terror, Adam damn near shit his pants and then did the only thing he could think of. He ferociously kicked the man in the face. Over and over, the bottoms of his sneakers crashed into the man's cheeks, nose, and forehead.

Blood poured from the wounds. The split in his lip grew wider. His gums turned purple and several teeth broke inside the man's mouth. Adam was certain he could see bone where a flap of skin on the man's forehead tore away from his skull and flopped back and forth. Flattened nose, busted jaw, cracked facial bones; it felt like ages had passed before the savage abuse had finally become enough to make the man's hands come away from Adam's blood-soaked pants.

Adam scrambled backwards, putting as much distance between himself and the madman as possible. He was still on his back, but now sat only inches from the steps. Flipping over to face the bottom riser, Adam crawled on his hands and knees up the six stairs that led to the front landing and the main door to the building. He felt like a coward for running. The right thing to do would have been to kill that son of a bitch. But enough was enough.

He reached the final step and something pulled the sneaker off of his left foot. Adam looked back to see the monster standing behind him and holding his shoe. He was still coming for him. There was just no fighting this man; or at least there was no stopping him. It seemed impossible, like the injuries didn't even affect him. How could someone take so much punishment and keep going?

In the landing at the top of the steps, Adam had two options. He could run back up to the main floor to find safety, search for a weapon, and call the police from inside the apartment. Or, he could turn and run outside. The apartment might seem like the logical choice, but there were no real weapons inside. Plus, how long would it take for the police to show up? Would this guy be able to force his way inside? Maybe another tenant would arrive home and become the next person to be assaulted, maybe even killed. It was too risky.

Going outside seemed like a lousy option too. Adam wasn't sure how far he could run with his twenty extra pounds and one shoe. The man would still come for him and chase him down outside in the parking lot. If he could make it across the street, perhaps the traffic would create enough of a barrier to keep him protected. Better yet, maybe the bald guy would get hit by a car.

He could try to knock the man out; keep him restrained and wait for the cops to haul his limp body away. Although, this was pure fantasy. If repeatedly kicking the maniac in the face didn't leave him unconscious, Adam had no idea what would. Maybe he would have to kill him after all. Maybe Adam would be killed instead. It wasn't a question. This was ending in death one way or another, either in self-defense or murder.

The decision was made in an instant. There was only one reasonable choice. Adam's priority was to get this sick asshole as far away from his dad as he could. Adam turned and bolted out the front door. The bleeding bald man was close behind.

Chapter 17

Beep, beep, beep. The alarm on the cell phone was going off. Beep, beep, beep. It's time to get up! No one was around to shut it off, so the alarm kept ringing and ringing for at least fifteen minutes. Jim, who had been awake since before the first alarm sounded, shut the water off and stepped out of the shower to hear the cell phone making noise from its place on the living room table.

"Alright, I hear ya." Jim wrapped a blue terrycloth towel around his dripping body and walked briskly out of the bathroom, past the new shower curtain resting on the kitchen table, and out to the coffee table to silence the alarm.

He found himself awake earlier than usual and surprisingly refreshed. When Jim had come inside the previous evening, he fell quickly and easily to sleep. He didn't wake at all during the night and if he had any dreams, he couldn't remember them. It had been a long day of work and running errands, not to mention the emotional thrashing Jim had endured. The drama with Beth and obsessing about the Lindsey situation had left him feeling tense and wistful.

All of these things must have worn him out, but the talk with Jenna seemed to relax him enough to get some of that restorative slumber he'd been missing. She was a sweet young lady and spending a little time with her really put him at ease. Maybe he would join her at church next Sunday, after all.

Jim dressed himself in a familiar ensemble consisting of cargo shorts and a solid black polo shirt. He didn't care much for the low pay at his job but he could definitely appreciate the relaxed dress code. Jim was also pleased to find that the circles beneath his eyes had almost completely gone away. He leaned in toward the mirror, looking up his nostrils for any unruly hairs that needed clipping before combing some gel through his hair and flicking the light off on his way out of the bathroom.

Back in the kitchen, Jim snagged his keys from the table and headed for the door. Sliding his sneakers onto his feet, he could already sense the dew of fresh perspiration rising up his back. He was determined not to let it bother him, he would blast the air conditioning in the car and enjoy a nice, cool drive in to work. It might seem like a simple, common thing but a full night's sleep and a jump start on his morning routine had a strong impact on Jim's outlook. Nothing was going to stop him from making it a good day.

A good day was one thing, but when Jim walked out of the apartment and into the hallway, he saw that Danny must have had a good night. Danny was coming down the steps to the landing in front of Jim's door. He walked behind a girl who was just as pale and thin and obviously shared his fashion sense. Long black hair ran over her shoulders. She was a little shorter than Danny and she wore a pair of tight leather pants and a black tank top that exposed a belly button ring and tattoos over most of her bare skin.

She got close enough for Jim to see that the piercings were not limited to her ears and belly button. Her right eyebrow and bottom lip had rings through them as well. As the girl reached the landing, she looked to Jim, briefly making eye contact before looking back to her feet and continuing past him. Danny was close behind and nodded to Jim in acknowledgment.

"Morning," Jim said, then adding in a softer voice, "Nice."

"Huh?" Danny stopped walking and let the girl get ahead of him. He seemed surprised.

"Nice, man," Jim whispered to Danny, using his eyes to indicate he was talking about the girl. "I'm a big fan of that outfit. Where'd you pick her up?"

Danny frowned. "That's my sister."

"Oh." Jim felt his face getting red in embarrassment. "Sorry, I didn't realize."

Danny shrugged and replied, "It's okay. But she is hot, right?"

"What?" Jim asked, not knowing how to respond.

"You want me to put a word in for you? She's single." Danny asked, not showing any emotion. Jim, still feeling foolish, didn't know what to say.

"Um," was all that came out.

"I mean, did you take a look at that ass? You know you can't resist that," Danny pressed. He stared at Jim, waiting for a response. "Plus, those tits; those are top-notch."

"Look, I didn't..." Jim stammered.

Danny couldn't hold back any longer. His laughter echoed up and down the stairway. "Come on, Jim. I'm just messing with you. Oh boy, that was good. You looked so uncomfortable." He leaned forward, resting his hands on his knees and taking deep breaths between chuckles.

Jim chortled at himself. "Yeah. Sorry about that. I just- I didn't know you had a sister."

"No problem, Jimmy." Danny then added in a louder voice to indicate an introduction was about to take place, "Jimmy, this is my sister Lucy. Lucy, this is my buddy, Jimmy. He lives downstairs from me."

"Hi," Jim offered an impotent wave in the girl's direction. "It's just *Jim*, actually."

The girl, who had reached the bottom landing near the front door, looked back up the steps and said, "Hey." This was the extent of their conversation.

In a lower tone, Danny explained, "She had a fight with her boyfriend and she's been crashing at my place. I've been trying to get her to leave him but I think she's afraid of him. I don't see what she ever saw in that guy in the first place. He's a real piece of shit. It's sort of a long story though. What happened was that a couple of nights ago-"

He was on a roll and Jim knew that Danny would stand there yammering on all day long if he didn't speak up.

"Yeah, that sounds like a tricky situation," Jim interrupted. "I hate to cut you off, but I really have to get to work."

"Sure. No problem, man. I'll catch ya later." He glanced down the steps and then back at Jim to make eye contact. "I mean it though. You're a good guy and based on what you told me about Beth, it sounds like you're available. I'd rather see her with someone like you than some abusive asshole."

"I don't know, man. We'll see. Let's talk about it tonight, okay?"

"Sure thing, buddy. Stop by after work."

Jim walked down the remaining steps and left Danny with his sister as he continued outside towards his car. He forced a polite smile for Lucy on his way out the door and turned briefly to say, "Well, I guess I'll see you guys later."

There weren't too many vehicles on the road that morning and it made for an easy commute.

107

Jim passed a handful of cars here and there, but the roads weren't nearly as jam-packed as they would have been on any other day. He chalked this up to unexpected and unusual good fortune; just something else helping to make this day a great one. He'd slept well, he had loads of energy, and he was avoiding the typical rigors of morning traffic.

Maybe he should buy a lottery ticket. Maybe he *should* ask Danny to put a word in with his sister. Then again, that might be pushing his luck. She wasn't exactly his normal type. A change would be welcomed though, considering his normal type were jobless cheating skanks with personality disorders. Jim spent the rest of the drive daydreaming about how Lucy's ink might look if the canvas was completely uncovered.

The lot behind the office was only about half full. Jim parked roughly fifty yards from the back door of the building. Despite the shorter walk across the parking lot, a glaze of sweat formed on Jim's forehead and his feet already felt clammy in his socks. The sun was bright, the heat was blazing, and a haze of humidity hung in the air as a thin, barely visible fog.

The summer warmth could be tolerated, at least long enough for a smoke. The clock on his cell phone told Jim that he still had a few minutes to kill before logging in for work so he stopped just outside the entrance to the office and lit a cigarette.

"Jimbo!" Paul was there to greet him. "I know you got one of those for me."

"Two days in a row?" Jim handed the man a cigarette. He jested, "You know they sell these at stores, right? You are allowed to buy them."

"Yeah, yeah." Paul waved a hand dismissively. He accepted the smoke eagerly, sparking it with a borrowed lighter, which he handed back to Jim and said, "We're in for a Hell of a day today."

"What makes you say that?" Jim asked as he slid the cigarettes and lighter back into his pocket.

"Karen, Nicole, and Kelly all called off today. Lucas from the overnight shift apparently never showed up last night. I've been getting calls all night and all morning about people either calling in sick or just not coming in to work. I tried calling Lucas to see what happened but he hasn't answered the phone." Paul drew in another lungful of smoke.

"I'm not sure who any of those people are," Jim admitted.

"Really? How can that be?" Paul asked. "You've been here for what, three years, right?"

"Yeah," Jim started. "But you know how it is here. No one really talks to each other. Everyone just sort of keeps to themselves. It's not a real social environment."

"Maybe it's you who's being antisocial," Paul suggested.

"I don't know about that," answered Jim.

"Well anyway, lots of people are out today so we're going to be backed up on work. We've had drivers calling to see why they're being held up at the border." Paul took another puff. "And if that wasn't bad enough, Xavier from the Detroit office has been calling non-stop. Looks like they're having the same issues with the staff there and he wants me to have people here help pick up the slack."

"Well, I'm here early," Jim said with an air of positivity while trying not to sound like too much of an ass-kisser.

"Yep," Paul said, obviously not pleased with this consolation. "Yes you are."

"And I know you'll remember that when time comes for doing reviews and handing out raises," Jim forced a small laugh.

"Alright, alright." Paul replied, quick to change the subject. "On a related note, you got any news about the fish girl?"

"How is that related?" Jim asked.

Paul chuckled at an inside joke that only he understood. Then he added, "Man, she puts a tent in my pants that just won't quit."

Jim moaned and placed both hands across his belly, making pretend Paul's comment made him physically ill.

Frowning, Paul said, "So, back to my question. Is that a *no*, then?"

"That's a *no.*"

Paul grumbled and added, "I figured as much; just wanted to ask."

"I'm not the person to ask about that," Jim told him. The two men simultaneously drew long pulls on their smokes, not saying anything for several moments.

"I saw my bitch ex-wife at the Walmart last night," Paul blurted.

"Oof," Jim winced. "How was that?"

"It was shitty. How do you think it would be?" Paul asked rhetorically.

"You talk to her?"

"Hell no."

"Did she see you?"

"I don't know how she could've missed me." Paul blew out a cloud of smoke. "I was in the back near the car stuff, looking for a new set of floor mats and she just walked by. She looked right at me, we made eye contact. She kept on moving, thankfully."

"Probably just as well," Jim noted.

"Right," Paul agreed. "It's just so weird though."

"What's that?"

"You get married and you think you'll be with this person forever."

"Uh huh," Jim nodded.

"It's odd that one day you've got your tongue in someone's ass, and the next you're pretending you don't even know each other."

Jim shuddered, not wanting to know on which side of that equation Paul would have been.

"Anyhow, I guess we should get a move on. Like I said, it's going to be a busy day." Paul tossed the butt to the ground and picked up his briefcase. "Ready to get started?"

Jim followed Paul inside and made his way to his work station. The desk had only a small pile of invoices on top. *A real busy day, huh?* Jim started to doubt Paul's assessment until his boss walked by and dropped a six-inch tall stack of paperwork on top of the original heap.

"Dammit," Jim complained.

"Sorry, Jim." Paul waved his hand toward him, but kept walking and didn't look back.

The morning passed eventually. The abnormally large workload should have kept Jim focused and busy enough to make the time pass quickly. But it did not. Lunch break couldn't have come soon enough. Jim logged off his computer and stood up from his chair, arching his back and stretching his arms over his head.

He almost couldn't wait until he was outside before lighting a cigarette. Too engrossed in the task of grabbing and lighting a smoke, Jim nearly ran right into a coworker who was coming into the building as he was walking out.

"Oops, sorry Renee." He stepped back to avoid walking through her.

"No problem. I wasn't paying attention. I'm a little off today," she explained, quickly looking down to her feet and then glancing over her shoulder. She had on a pair of long black formal pants and a dark gray sweater with a turtle neck.

"Hey," Jim called before she could go inside. "Why are you so bundled up today? You must be sweating your balls off."

"I don't have balls, Jim," she said, obviously getting the joke but not playing along.

"Right," said Jim, "You haven't got balls because you've sweated them off."

Renee couldn't help but smile. "I don't mean to be rude, but I really have to get to work, I'm just coming in now. It was sort of a rough morning."

"How so?" Jim asked, turning his head to blow a cloud of smoke away from her.

Renee stepped closer to Jim and looked behind her to make sure no one was within earshot. "I was assaulted today."

"Assaulted?" Jim shrieked louder and with far less grace than he'd intended.

"Shh, keep your voice down," Renee insisted. "I don't exactly want it broadcast."

"Right. Sorry about that," Jim apologized. Almost in a whisper, he asked, "Are you alright? What happened?"

"It was right outside my building. Some junkie asshole just ran at me and started swinging and scratching at me."

The young woman pulled the collar away from her skin to reveal a series of bandages over her neck and shoulders.

"Holy shit," exclaimed Jim. "I guess that explains the long sleeves."

"That's not all of it either." Renee then rolled up her sleeves to show that both forearms were marred by scratches and scrapes. Most were very shallow, leaving little more than a red spot on the skin. Several were much deeper though; the flesh still open and weeping.

Images from a few days earlier flashed across Jim's mind. He remembered the police at his building, Danny and Charles explaining how someone had attacked them, the trash cans being tipped over and left in a mess. Hadn't Lindsey mentioned something about bums fighting and tearing apart the dumpsters outside the store?

"Then what happened? To the guy I mean, how'd you get away?" Jim asked. "You did get away, right?"

"Well, obviously I got away," said Renee. She continued; her voice taking on a bitter tone, "I just tried to cover up and call for help. I didn't know if he was trying to rob me or rape me or what he

110

wanted. It was broad daylight, right outside the front door to my building."

Jim was surprised she wasn't crying but he didn't say as much. He wasn't sure why he picked up on that or why he expected her to be in tears, but it struck him as odd that she looked mostly okay with what had happened. Obviously she wasn't all smiles or making jokes, but aside from the physical wounds, she looked to be unshaken.

"So, you fought him off?" he asked, taking a final puff and tossing the cigarette butt toward the street.

"No, I just froze. I slumped down and sort of tucked my knees into my chest and covered my face with my arms. I must have been screaming though because the next thing I noticed was Mrs. Dawsey, she lives next door, and she had come over." Renee rubbed her temples and ran fingers over her head. "I've never felt so helpless. Looking back now, I'm more embarrassed than anything. I didn't even fight back."

"Mrs. Dawsey fought him off?"

"No. Well, not really. Mrs. Dawsey is like ninety years old. She was outside in the garden and heard me yelling, so she came over and sprayed him with a hose."

"A hose? Did she think he was going to melt?" Jim's mild attempt at humor fell flat.

"I'm not sure what she expected, but it worked. Maybe he was afraid she would call the police or someone else would step in, but as soon as she sprayed him, he backed right off. He growled at her and then ran away."

"Growled?"

"Growled."

"Jeez. How bizarre." Jim commented. "I'm glad you're okay. Did you go to the hospital? Get checked out?"

"No, he didn't really hurt me. I'm okay."

"Are you sure about that?" Jim asked. "Your neck and arms look pretty messed up."

"I'm sure. It looks worse than it is. It actually doesn't hurt at all. The real bad thing was he kept coughing and spitting up on me when he was standing over me. It was so gross."

"Okay, as long as you're alright. I assume you at least called the police." It was a question more than a statement.

"I did," said Renee. "But they wouldn't send a cop out. They asked if the man was still around. I told them he wasn't and since there was no longer an immediate threat, they were too busy for someone to come to me. They asked me to come to the station and file a report for the assault."

"So did you do that?"

"No."

Jim just looked at her, questioning with his eyes.

"What good would it do?" Renee paused to look behind her again. Confident no one was there, she continued. "I'm fine and the guy got away. I mean, it's not like the police are going to track him down. They couldn't even be bothered to send somebody to my apartment."

"Okay, I guess that's a fair point," Jim said. "But you gotta be careful. Do you live in a rough neighborhood?"

"Not particularly," she replied. "I didn't think so anyway. I'm in Allentown, near the bars and stuff down there, but it usually seems safe enough."

"Well, I'm glad you're okay," Jim reiterated.

"Thanks," Renee said. "Sorry to rush off, but I should get in."

"No problem. I'll see ya later." Jim held the door open for Renee to go in.

With no plans for lunch and no appetite for food, Jim walked around the corner to the back of the building. Facing the rear parking area, he lit another cigarette and slumped to let his upper back rest against the brick wall. His lungs pulled in a fresh load of smoke, he held it for just a second, and exhaled deeply, looking up to watch the smoke dissipate as it floated toward the sky.

It was probably going to be a short break. Sigler Global Logistics offered paid lunches, which was nice. At most of his previous jobs, Jim would have had to punch out for lunch. Technically, he could take forty-five minutes, but with nowhere to go and not wanting to eat, there wasn't much point in just doing nothing for almost an hour. Jim recalled the growing collection of invoices on his desk and that helped form his decision to return early.

The cigarette butt fell to the ground and Jim snuffed it out with the bottom of his sneaker. He drew his wrist across his forehead, whisking away beads of sweat and then drying his hands on his shorts. Jim pulled himself off the wall and began to head back inside the office. As he reached the corner of the building, someone called to him.

"Jim!"

The voice was strained, yet familiar. He turned around to see Paul about halfway between the building and the first row of parked cars. The man was staggering, fighting to keep himself upright and his feet moving.

"Jim, I need help," he begged as he dropped to his knees. Paul pressed his palms to the pavement and tried once more to stand.

"Paul?" Jim took a few tentative steps in his boss' direction. "Shit, man. What happened?"

"Help me get inside," Paul yelled. "He's coming back."

Quickening to a jog, Jim called back and asked, "What? Who's coming back?"

"Just help me inside," the man pleaded. "I need help. Please, Jim."

Jim was sprinting at this point. Paul had fallen flat to the concrete. His arms and legs hadn't quit altogether but he could no longer move on his own accord.

"What happened to you?" Jim demanded as he reached the man on the ground. Kneeling, he grabbed the man by his shoulders and tried to pull him up.

"Shit!" Jim gasped as he got a closer look at Paul. The front of his white shirt was torn open and a deep laceration ran from the bottom of his throat to just above his belly button. Paul's sunglasses were smashed to bits with most of the broken pieces scattered on the ground. Five or six sections of jagged tinted glass were lodged inside the wound.

"Jim," he cried, "Please help me get away."

"Get away from who?" Jim asked but felt he may have already discovered the answer. He saw a glimpse of something, a form, a body moving between the aisles of parked cars. The body was

112

moving fast. Horrifyingly fast.

"I need an ambulance," Paul whimpered. He paused to choke out a couple coughs before adding, "I have to get in and call for help, call the cops."

"Okay, okay." Jim had managed to pull the older man to his feet. He wrapped Paul's right arm around his head and shoulders. Paul leaned heavily against Jim, relying on him to support most of his weight.

"Can you walk?" Jim asked, but didn't hear the answer. Jim was looking further into the parking lot, watching as the distant form of a running person grew closer. He was looking toward the sun. The bright light and glare made it impossible for Jim to see who was coming for them. He couldn't tell if this person was dangerous, if they had a weapon, or even if it was a man or a woman.

"He grabbed me at my car," Paul muttered. A thin current of red ran out of his mouth and down his chin. Blood speckled the cement at his shoes.

"What?" Jim wasn't listening; too focused on the entity approaching and trying to move his boss closer to the entrance of the office.

"He grabbed me at my car. Came from nowhere. I don't know." Paul was rambling and his knees buckled, making him rely completely on Jim for support. "Inside. Just get me inside. I need to get away."

"Alright. Let's move then, Paul." Jim half walked, half dragged Paul's weakened body. "Work with me, man. You can do this."

Jim took another look behind him. The form moving between the cars now looked like it was farther away. Had the person been scared off? The darkened outline of a body seemed to have shrunken into the distance.

"I think we're okay," said Jim. "The guy's leaving."

"Leaving?" Paul asked. His eyes fought to stay open as blood pooled beneath him.

"It looks like it. He's further away from us," Jim paused and squinted his eyes to see where the person had gone. The person was definitely farther away than he had been at first. To be accurate, this specific person was farther away.

"Never mind," Jim said. After surveying the lot again, he found that there were in fact several forms moving at a high speed. They darted around and in between the parked cars. "We have to go. Right now."

Paul was no longer cooperating. He slumped down, landing hard on his knees and yanking Jim to the ground with him. Jim planted his feet on the pavement and pressed with all of his strength. Ignoring the red splatter spreading from Paul's chest and onto his sleeve, Jim held the man up by the arms and shoulders, trying to haul him toward the building. Paul had gone completely limp and Jim was making no progress.

Multiple pairs of feet stomped across the lot. The footsteps were louder, faster, and getting very close. Jim eased Paul to the ground and turned to face the people coming in his direction. A torrent of adrenaline roared through his veins. He squeezed his hands into fists and sucked in a breath of air, promptly trying to ready himself for a fight. Sweat pumped out of his palms, brow, and pits. His unblinking, fixed eyes locked on those sprinting toward him.

There were four of them, three men and one woman. They moved too swiftly for Jim to catch much detail. The woman and two of the men looked to be in their late twenties or early thirties. The other man was older, late sixties maybe. Each of them had sunken eyes, tatters in their clothing, and fresh blood dripping out of their mouths. All four snarled like animals and descended upon Paul's motionless form. And they all ignored Jim, like he wasn't even there.

The oldest of the group rammed his bare fingers into the gash on Paul's torso. Both hands forced their way under the skin, down to the knuckles. Paul's scream was piercing and prolonged. His maulers remained undeterred, resolute in their mission to consume the dying man.

The younger three tore at his shirt and skin, scraping nails into flesh before leaning in and biting, chewing, swallowing. The elder man pulled both hands free from the hole in Paul's chest. He clutched glossy grayed meat and stuffed the blood-soaked sinewy matter into his mouth. A good portion didn't make it in and instead fell to the ground with a sickening wet splat.

"Hey!" Jim shouted at them. The intensity of that single syllable ripped at his vocal cords. None of them reacted so Jim cried louder through his raw throat, "Hey! Come on, you shitheads."

The woman looked up, her eyes piercing Jim's; her face soaked in red. She had a flap of loose skin stuck between her teeth. It rolled out of her mouth and hung down over her chin. She growled at Jim. The sound was that of a lion or some other horrible beast letting him know exactly who was in charge. The bitch bared her teeth at him, still emitting a guttural rumble.

That was enough for Jim. He took a step backwards and held his hands palms-out in front of him, trying to appear as non-threatening as possible. The woman's gaze was still fixed on Jim, who had now put ten feet between himself and the cannibals. Feeling it was as safe as it was going to be, Jim turned and raced back to the building.

He pulled the door closed behind him, fumbling with the metal latch to engage the lock. In the vestibule, Jim looked out through the glass door and tried to see if the people had chased him to the building. They didn't appear to have done so but the door faced away from the parking lot, so it was impossible to see where they had gone, or if they had moved at all.

Jim pulled his cell from his pocket and dialed 9-1-1. He pressed the phone to his ear and listened for an answer. Not only was nobody on the other end, there was no sound at all; no ringing, no absent humming. He held the phone out to where he could see it. The screen indicated the call had been dropped. Pressing the button to redial, Jim kept his eyes on the display, which indicated the phone was dialing and then connecting.

The receiver blasted a series of tones into Jim's ear and then a recorded voice stated, "All circuits are currently busy. Please try your call again later."

"Come on, for fuck's sake," he said aloud. Frustration and panic rising, Jim slid the phone back into his pocket. He opened the next set of doors, which separated the vestibule from the main office space on the first floor. Looking from the rear of the building toward the front, he called, "Hey, I need some help. Someone call the pol-."

His voice cut off in his throat. He walked in to find the office awash in madness.

Chapter 18

A stack of papers flew overhead and crashed into the ceiling tiles. The bundle broke apart and hundreds of sheets slithered in slow motion down to the thin carpet of the office floor. A thrown stapler crossed the room, missing its intended target and crashing into the back of a man's head. Skin ripped open and spewed blood into hair-sprayed locks and a yellow cotton collar.

Everyone was up from their seats, fighting each other as they raced for the exits. Men shoved and punched one another. Women pulled each other's pony tails and blouses, forcing their coworkers to fall behind so that they could escape. With someone behind you, the monsters would take them first and you'd have enough time to get away. Hopefully. Somebody cursed Jim, pushing past him to get to the back door. A number of bodies banged into his chest and shoulders as they ran by. Most didn't acknowledge him. They certainly didn't try to help him get out.

Two women screamed. They each covered their mouths with one shaking hand and pointed with the other. Jim followed their gaze. Looking up, he found Renee standing on top of a desk. Eyes wild with red sap dripping from her lips; she held lengths of something pink and slimy in each clenched fist. The neck of her sweater had been stretched out and torn. Loose wool tinsel fell from each arm. Renee's gently tanned skin was spotted with pearls of red. She jumped from her spot on the desktop, landing on one of the frightened women and dragging her to the ground.

Jim couldn't see what Renee did next but felt confident he could guess. The other woman, the one who hadn't been pounced on, made no effort to mount any sort of rescue. Instead, she backed away; shock rolling over her flushed features. She stared for a moment before spinning and bolting for the front exit.

It was obvious by this point that Renee wasn't the only one acting up. A younger guy, who Jim had never seen before, ran across the front lobby. The unplugged cord of his phone headset dragged on the floor behind him as he ran to the front desk and dove over it to attack the receptionist. She was frozen, too afraid to get away or defend herself. The couple hit the ground hard and Jim didn't see either one of them getting up.

Jim stepped further into the office, down the center aisle between the two main rows of cubicles. His movements were slow, measured. He was trying to observe, trying to make sense of what he saw. The growling, screaming, and crying faded to barely a hum of white noise. Jim kept going, heading toward the reception area at the front of the building. Too scared to intervene and not skilled enough to be of any help, Jim's aim was just to see. He had to watch what was happening. There was an overwhelming need to confirm what he witnessed in the parking lot, if only to make sure he hadn't lost his mind.

Most of the desk chairs had been toppled. But one work station, located three spaces from the end of the row on Jim's right side, had a chair still upright and pulled in all the way under the desk. Given the current circumstances, this struck Jim as being out of place. He knelt down and looked under the desk. A young blonde woman, thin and maybe twenty-two years old, was huddled on the floor. She used the chair, desk frame, and cubicle wall for cover. This was someone Jim had definitely seen a bunch of times around the office yet somehow managed never to talk to or to learn her name.

Tears smeared her makeup and a gash had been opened up on her forehead. The girl looked up so that her eyes met Jim's. She raised an index finger to her lips, pleading in silence for Jim not to reveal her hiding spot. Jim obliged, he stood back up without making a sound and kept walking to the front lobby.

He reached the front desk and placed his hands on top, next to the phone and tray of Sigler Global Logistics business cards. Jim could see the shirt on the back of the younger man heaving up and down, little by little. Leaning in further for a clearer view, he watched as the former customer service representative chewed a hole through the neck of the unmoving mass that used to be the receptionist. The woman's eyes were wide open and staring straight forward. Her head rattled a bit as the man on top of her leaned back, using his teeth to tear more skin free from her body.

Something bumped against Jim's leg. He looked down but there was nothing there. Jim continued watching the lunatic devour the dead woman and then again felt something brush against the same spot on his right leg. He patted the spot over his shorts and felt a pulsing coming from inside the pocket. His phone was vibrating. Someone was calling. With his eyes still fixed on the man in the headset, Jim reached for the phone, which slipped out of his fingers and dropped to the ground.

He bent to retrieve the still-vibrating device from the floor. Realizing this was not the best time for a chat, he jammed the phone back into his pocket. He rose to see the man in the headset was now standing up as well, looking at him from the other side of the reception desk.

"Hey," Jim said softly. He hoped for, but didn't expect, to receive a coherent response. As he'd done in the parking lot moments earlier, Jim held both hands palms-out toward the man in a futile effort to reason with the beast.

The man's face was streaked with blood and sweat. Short dark hair was matted against his scalp. The headset had fallen down to rest around the back of his neck. His mouth opened to reveal a set of teeth stained red. Sounds came out but no words, just a sort of angry groan. The ghoul threw his arms forward, reaching for Jim but coming up short thanks to the desk that stood between them.

Jim stepped back, sure to keep a safe distance. Glad for the small head start, he turned to make a run for it. Most people had already made their way outside, so the path to the back door was clear of obstacles and panicked coworkers. Jim sprinted down the aisle, back in the direction from which he had come- past the overturned chairs, past the woman hiding under her desk, and around gore-soaked office equipment.

As he went, Jim could hear the man behind him climb over the desk and land on the floor, snarling and growling with each jerking movement. The former customer service worker gave chase; his adrenaline-fueled body quickly making up ground. Jim chanced a look over his shoulder to see the man approaching fast. He had never seen a human being move with such speed. He was going to catch up. The man was going to catch Jim.

A shrill and deafening scream rang out, followed immediately by the sound of something heavy being slammed to the ground. Jim reached the door that led to the rear vestibule and stopped to see what had happened. The blonde woman was scrambling out from under the desk and the man in the headset was on the floor, pushing a chair off of his chest.

"Thanks," Jim called to her.

"Run," she called back. "Keep running."

The blonde woman pumped her arms and streaked down the hall towards Jim. She grabbed him by the arm and tried to drag him from his spot. Jim didn't need any encouragement, but where were they going to run to? Outside, sure. They had to get out of immediate danger, but then what? He pushed through the door, now dragging the blonde girl instead of the other way around. They moved through the vestibule and out into the hot afternoon sun. Things weren't much better outdoors.

Everyone who was able to escape the office had done so. Fleeing people poured from all of the exits, moving like a river around parked cars, trees, and the bodies of people who had fallen and may or may not be getting back up. Those who had gotten into their cars were driving over curbs, cutting across lawns, and ignoring all traffic signals. They were all trying to put as much distance between themselves and the office as possible, as quickly as possible.

Jim caught a glimpse of two men running next to each other for a couple of paces before one of them turned and attacked the other. The man who was being attacked tried to put up a fight, but it was brief and ineffective. He died right after. There was almost no way to tell the people fleeing and afraid for their lives from the people who were actually doing the attacking. Everyone looked like a threat, like one of the monsters.

Two cars had collided head-on in the center of Broad Street. The owners were nowhere to be found, they just abandoned the smashed, still-running cars. A beige sedan was pulled over to the shoulder of the road. A man was locked inside, having some sort of fit. It was an older gentleman, screaming and flailing his limbs about. Droplets of blood streaked the inside of the windows with each thrust. No one was coming to his aid; too afraid he might be one of *them.*

Jim, with the blonde woman in tow, pushed through a small group of people who remained gathered around the back door to the office. She was falling a couple steps behind, still crying and breathing heavily.

"Let's go," Jim yelled at her. "Keep moving your feet."

With his right hand around the girl's wrist, he pulled harder, forcing her to keep pace as he tried to clear a path with his left arm. Most people were jumpy and moved easily out of the way, but two or three of them had turned around and looked to be running back toward the building. With this, he felt the woman come to a complete stop.

"What is it?" Jim asked, looking back to her.

"Maybe we should..." her words trailed off, but her eyes darted back to the building. "Maybe we should go back in."

"No," he answered firmly. "Let's get to my car, we can get outta here."

Jim tried to pull her forward, but she resisted further. She planted her feet in the ground and tried to reclaim her arm. People still ran by them in all directions. None of them seemed to notice the stationary pair in the hustling crowd. And no one was stopping; not to ask if they needed help, not to offer them a ride, not for anything.

"Listen. You want to go back inside?"

"Yes," she shouted.

"For what?" Jim tried to reason with her. He softened his grip and looked her in the eye. "It isn't exactly safe in there, is it? We have to keep go-"

Jim got cut off. One of the people running by wasn't fleeing. He was hunting. A man in gym shorts and a hoodie snatched the young woman, pulling her away from Jim and completely out of his grasp. The woman screamed, a sound that could barely be heard over the commotion of the crowd, and then they both disappeared into the sea of people.

"Shit!" Jim cried.

He tried to follow her, tried to get her back. Jim pushed past bodies, ducking low and searching between legs and moving feet in an effort to locate the blonde woman. He hadn't even seen the man who grabbed her, at least not his face or anything to distinguish him from the group. Jim didn't see where she had been dragged to but he did find something she'd left behind. A tuft of blood-spattered blonde hair clung to a loose glob of skin on the concrete. He knew then that she was gone. Even if he found her body, Jim knew it wouldn't really be her.

There was no reason to investigate any further. Jim started running. He went as quick as he could go. His shoes pounded against the cement, grinding bits of gravel between the pavement and the souls of his sneakers. The smoker's lungs ached. Sweat trickled down his face, burning as drops splashed into his eyes. Both arms felt numb. They moved and swung, but weakly. Jim pushed harder to move faster past the rear side of the rows of buildings and separate himself from the pedestrians near the office. He sprinted for the parking area.

Jim ran past immobile cars and across the lot to where he had parked the Pontiac that morning. Here and there, he could see people running from car to car in groups of twos and threes. They looked through windows, searching for occupants and moving on when they found the vehicle to be vacant. One such group had gathered around a black Jeep that was eight or nine spots down from Jim's car. They forced themselves inside, despite the driver's resistance. Jim couldn't tell whether they were carjacking or cannibalizing.

Guilt washed over him and cowardice stained him yellow. Jim felt like a piece of shit for thinking it, but he was glad those men were going after the person in the SUV. It meant they weren't coming for him. Not yet, anyway. Whoever it was that was either being forced from their vehicle or being eaten alive, it was someone else that Jim couldn't help.

Jim pulled the keys out of his pocket with quivering hands and tried to unlock the driver's side door. The trembling was so severe, he had to hold the key ring in his right hand and guide the key into the keyhole with his left. He jumped inside and wasted no time in locking the doors, pressing the power lock button several times to be sure, and then sticking the key into the ignition to start the car. The engine came alive and so did the radio. With a shot, Jim's thumb mashed the power button to silence the speakers.

In his shorts pocket, the phone vibrated again. Simultaneously shifting into reverse and backing out of the spot, Jim grabbed the phone and held it up to read the screen. The caller ID showed that it was Beth calling. He pressed the button to ignore the call and dropped the phone into the cup holder in the center console. The car shifted into drive and Jim pulled forward in the direction of the exit from the parking lot, which would bring him right past the rear of the office building.

Inside the holder, a handful of change jingled as the phone started to shake again. Jim sighed and picked it back up, still rolling forward in the car. It wasn't Beth this time. The screen indicated there was an incoming call from a number he didn't recognize. The full number was displayed, but it was just the digits, no name was saved in his phone.

"Hello?" he answered the call.

"Jim?" It was a girl's voice.

"Yes?"

"Jim, it's Lindsey."

"Lindsey?" Jim paused for a moment, looking to see if anyone had gotten close to the car. "I hate to be rude, but this really isn't a good time."

"I know," she answered. "Where are you?"

"At work. Or, leaving work I mean. I'm in my car."

"Are you okay?" she asked.

"Yeah, I'm-" Jim stopped mid-sentence.

A heavyset middle-aged man in a red-soaked tee shirt and jeans jumped in front of the coupe. He was waving his hands in front of him and pounded his fist on the hood. With the windows up and the phone to his ear, Jim couldn't make out what he was saying. The man, sopping with blood, ran around to the passenger's side of the car and reached for the handle. Finding it locked, the man slammed his fists into the window- and not just once. He was trying to break in.

"Get outta here, asshole," Jim loudly scolded the man and tried to drive ahead.

As the car pulled forward, the man smashed his forearm into the glass. He did this over and over for as long as he could keep pace with the car as it sped through the parking lot. With the fourth or fifth blow, the skin on his arm opened up, spraying red fluid onto the window and down the side of the door. The glass held strong, refusing to break or crack. Ignoring the odd pothole, Jim punched the gas, speeding ahead toward the street.

"Dickhead," Jim muttered, then remembered he was still holding the phone and went back to talking to Lindsey. "Oh, sorry about that. Not you. You're not the dickhead. Sorry. It's just sort of crazy over here."

"I know," said Lindsey. "It's happening here too."

Jim cussed but didn't offer much else in the way of a reply.

"Are you alright?" she asked again.

"Yeah, I'm fine I think," he answered. "What about you? Are you okay? Where are you?"

"I'm at Bennett's," she answered.

"Where?"

"The store- I'm at work," she cried.

"Is it safe in there? Are you locked in?"

"I'm in the break room. I locked myself inside. I think it's safe for now, but I don't know how long it'll stay that way." Her words were pushed out in a hurry and punctuated by gasps as she tried to catch her breath.

"Okay," Jim said. He tried to stretch out his response, looking for something to say. He had just pulled out of the parking lot and around the smashed-up cars on Broad Street.

"Can you come get me?" Lindsey asked.

"What?"

"I know it's a lot to ask and I wouldn't have called you unless I was desperate. I don't know what else to do."

Jim swerved to avoid what looked like a small pile of dead bodies in the middle of the road. He cleared his throat and began to speak but was interrupted.

"Please, Jim." There was a strain in her voice. She hated having to ask for help. With a

whimper, Lindsey begged, "Please don't let me die."

"Alright," he said. "But what about, uh, your boyfriend- what's his name? Have you gotten in touch with him? Doesn't he work with you?"

"He left me," she uttered.

"What?" Somewhere far behind Jim, a car blasted its horn but the car itself could not be located. Red fluid on the windows turned horizontal as he accelerated.

"He left me here," she repeated into the receiver. "He took my keys and he left in my car."

"Okay." Jim took a breath. "I'll come get you, but I don't know where we're going to go."

"I just need to go home. Can you take me to my apartment?"

"Sure," said Jim. "I'll take you home. How secure is the room you're in right now?"

"I don't know. Why?"

"It may take me a little bit to get there. I need to make a stop on my way," Jim told her.

"A stop for what?" she demanded.

"I think I need to get a gun."

"Do you have a gun?" she asked.

"No. But there are guns at my aunt and uncle's place. Remember my uncle used to take me and my cousins hunting?"

"Okay. Just try to be quick," she urged.

"As fast as I can," Jim assured her as he passed the on-ramp for the Youngmann Expressway. That route would have cut down on travel time, as long as cars were still moving and there hadn't been any accidents. But if the Expressway was jammed up, it would be impossible to get off. Jim feared he'd be stranded in miles of stalled traffic. "I'm gonna stick to side streets to be safe, but I won't take too long. I promise."

"Okay." Lindsey exhaled a breath of the tiniest relief. "Thanks Jim. I can't tell you how much I appreciate this. I don't know what I'd do if... if not for you. Promise me you'll be safe."

"Sure," Jim answered. Trying to sound collected, "I'll be fine. Is this your phone? Can I call you at this number when I get there?"

"Yes. Call me when you get here. You don't have to come inside, but let me know if it's clear for me to run out."

"I'll be as fast as I can. Be careful and I'll talk to you soon." Jim ended the call without saying goodbye.

The phone was tossed onto the passenger's seat, where it began to vibrate again just moments later. It was another call from Beth. Jim picked up the device, pressed the ignore button, and put it back down. He wouldn't pick it back up until he was in front of the supermarket.

With the windows up and his hands wrapped tightly around the wheel, Jim's car roared down the street. Rushing through intersections and forgetting speed limits, Jim drove into the suburbs. He was headed for the home where his aunt, uncle, and cousins lived. This particular house was a demure two-story dwelling with redwood siding and a one car garage attached on the left.

Chapter 19

"I can honestly say I've never seen anything like it. We are live in downtown Buffalo right now and as you can see, things have gotten completely out of control. We lost contact with our ground crew and street reporters after the Channel Four news van was overrun and turned on its side. You can see this in the upper left-hand corner of your screen." The woman paused for a moment to let the camera zoom out from a close-up shot of four people converging on a bystander.

The view expanded. Hundreds, maybe thousands of running, fighting, panicked, and deranged people blurred into an indiscernible pulsating blob. As the news anchor had stated, you could in fact see a full size white van that had been pushed over. The circular red logo with the numeral 4 in white lettering was now obscured by spilled blood and severed limbs. Dozens of maniacs crawled over and climbed inside the vehicle. You could see patches of flashing red and blue lights here and there; the glow barely visible in the sea of bodies.

At the far left side of the screen, a pair of white and blue Buffalo Police cars screeched to a stop at the edge of the crowd. The overhead lights flashed, headlamps blinked an alternating strobe, the horns sounded. Using an amplified loudspeaker, one of the drivers shouted for the combatants to back up and disperse. The officers couldn't even open their doors. Moonstruck marauders pounced, engulfing both vehicles without hesitation. Windows busted and shattered inward. Bloodthirsty cannibals fought each other to see who would get to the uniformed meals first.

The woman continued. "Obviously it has become too dangerous for us to have anyone directly on site. The footage you're watching now is being provided by our Channel Four news chopper, which usually brings us our traffic updates. It has been redirected to cover the riots taking place in the city. We are being told that traffic into Buffalo is virtually non-existent at this time, while cars heading out of the city have been slowed to a crawl. On the Canadian side of the Peace Bridge, American travelers are being turned around and sent back. There has been no official word, but from all accounts, the Canadian Border Patrol is only allowing Canadian citizens to enter the country."

Albert sat up, pressing down on the footrest at the front of the recliner. Already clutching the remote control, he mashed his thumb into one of the buttons. Green bars appeared on the television screen, increasing in number as the volume grew louder.

"It goes without saying that anyone on the roads should make every effort to avoid the downtown area. The mayor's office has issued a statement recommending that no one drive within city limits. But of course, walking doesn't seem like a safe alternative. If you can, the best thing to do would be to stay inside. Keep your doors locked and secure all basement and ground floor windows."

Albert looked to the sliding glass door at the front of his living room. Did this count as a first-floor door? Technically he was on the first floor, but the first floor was several feet above the ground. The glass door was half open with just the screen pulled across to let some air inside. And what about the main entrances to the building? Should he look for a way to secure them? Was there a way to keep them from being opened? There had to be, but what if one of the other tenants came home? It wouldn't be very neighborly to keep them locked outside with whatever else might be out there.

Maybe he was over-thinking it. He lived more than nine miles from where the action was taking place. There was no one running around and carrying on like that in his neighborhood. Actually, things were so calm and quiet where Albert lived that the police must have been bored to tears most of the time. If this violent foolishness spread to the suburbs, the cops would be ready. And

Albert still thought that was a pretty unlikely scenario. Mostly. His confidence wavered as he studied the news broadcast.

The TV screen shifted, rotating between a series of shots taken moments earlier. They were sure to cut away just in time to avoid showing the precise moment where an unsuspecting victim took his or her last breath. They wouldn't televise the transition from living to deceased. But they would jump right to another scene taking place seconds before someone else would invariably be slaughtered by one or more disease-addled monstrosities. It was okay to show savage beatings and brutal attacks, just so long as the victims were still alive while they were being eaten.

The news reader went on. "According to representatives from Sisters of Charity Hospital and Kenmore Mercy Hospital, they are both beyond capacity due to a growing number of patients arriving on a constant basis. Some are being brought in by ambulance but most are being driven in by relatives or just coming in on foot. Most of the injuries are from bites and scratches, not gunshots or stab wounds, as earlier reports had indicated."

Orange letters scrolled across the screen to spell out the words, *Unrest in Buffalo*, which then shrunk into a small emblem in the bottom right corner of the display next to the Channel 4 logo.

The woman on TV reiterated, "Yes, Bites. If you've been watching our broadcast of the crisis downtown, you might have observed that people are biting and clawing at each other. Sadly, the death toll has been on the rise. We have confirmation that most of the victims, once attacked, have not been able to make their way to safety."

The camera pulled back from a green and gold sign reading, *Shea's Buffalo*, to reveal an enormous masonry building with polished tan stone at the front. A canopy was suspended beyond the marquee and above the row of glass entry doors. Light bulbs lined the canopy and sign. The lights were off and many of the bulbs were broken. Beneath the canopy's cover, a woman clung to the metal rafters in a desperate attempt to avoid the circling herd of animals below.

You couldn't make out her features, the camera was too far from the heart of the action. It was definitely an adult woman in a yellow dress, but it was impossible to see any more detail than that. The mob was so vicious and so dense that if she fell, the woman would be ripped apart before hitting the sidewalk.

A man in his late thirties with an athletic build, wearing black jeans and an orange tee-shirt, became visible on the left side of the display. He was sprinting and cutting a path for himself through the thick mass. The man approached the woman, leaping and rising above the crowd. His left hand reached over his head and into the canopy's support structure. A vascular fist wrapped its digits around a handful of yellow fabric. The woman, whose identity would forever be unknown, was pulled from her perch. She plummeted for an instant before disappearing into the ravenous assembly.

"Cut it," the anchorwoman commanded. "Cut the feed!"

She was not being shown on the screen, but was evidently shouting to whichever producer was overseeing the live footage.

"God damn it," she exclaimed. Her voice muffled; the woman obviously covering her microphone and trying to keep her voice from making it on air. She apologized for the previous footage as the shot changed to an overhead view. "We're very sorry for the images transmitted just now. We at Channel Four are dedicated to bringing you the latest news and keeping you up to date on the events unfolding in downtown Buffalo this afternoon. Unfortunately, some of the content in today's broadcast may be explicit and unsuitable for our younger viewers."

122

On the television, the view remained fixed on the squirming assemblage. The reporter, again covering her mic, called to another member of the news staff, "Can we go back?"

After receiving an inaudible answer, she explained, "That man, the one with the orange shirt, didn't we see him earlier? I thought I saw him maybe a half hour ago. He was bit by someone, on the shoulder I think."

Albert slid to the edge of his chair. He clutched his cane as if it were a club and he'd need to use it to bludgeon the intruders that were no-doubt heading for his front door. The man glanced down at the floor to discover he'd dropped his pipe at some point. The unsmoked tobacco spilled out onto the carpet. Mesmerized by what he saw on the television, he hadn't noticed at first and when he did, he didn't bother picking it up.

The anchor went on, "What you're seeing now is video taken about thirty minutes ago. You may recognize this man from the vile attack that just took place outside of the Performing Arts Center."

On the screen, a thirty-something year old man in dark jeans and an orange shirt sat on a bench near a bus stop. He was reading a copy of Art Voice when a child less than half his age jumped onto the bench next to him. The kid was wearing a white and red-streaked baseball uniform; the hat pulled down to cover sunken, sinister eyes. Without faltering, the Little-Leaguer sprang forward and sank his teeth into the man's right shoulder.

The man in orange had a strong build and was about seventy-five pounds heavier than the child. In an act of defensive instinct, the man grabbed the kid by the front of his shirt and easily shook him off. The child ran for the man, but was thwarted by a solid fist to the chest. The child fell to the ground and gasped for breath as the older man ran off screen.

"There's no doubt about it. That is absolutely the same man we just saw attack that woman under the canopy," the female news anchor explained. "He was an earlier victim who was bitten and then returned to the melee as one of the attackers."

Duke stirred from his place on the floor, cracking joints as he laboriously pulled himself onto all fours. He whimpered but it wasn't his usual call for food and he didn't want to go for a walk. The dog dragged himself from the dining area to the right of Albert's chair. Small clumps of brown and gray fur fell to the carpet as he made his way.

"You keep it down over there," Albert instructed Duke, not taking his eyes off the television. "I'm trying to hear this."

"The commissioner of the Erie County Health Department has chosen not to have a press conference and has declined an on-air interview, but the Health Department has released a statement," said the woman on the news. "According to officials at the commissioner's office, the people you see acting aggressively and perpetrating these acts of violence could possibly be afflicted with some sort of mass delirium. They were not able to narrow down a potential cause, but further speculated it could be an environmental factor or the result of a disease transmitted via contact with blood or saliva."

While she spoke, the view on the screen was that of a camera located well above ground; details of the carnage obscured.

"The statement went on to recommend everyone keep a safe distance from strangers and loved ones alike. Should you encounter a friend or family member acting irregularly or if you notice someone has a new wound, have that person immediately quarantined in a safe place where they cannot harm themselves or others. Be on the lookout for bites and scratch marks."

"Quarantine?" Albert asked the TV. He pressed his glasses further up the bridge of his nose.

As if the news reader was in the room with him, she answered. "We understand that you'll want to seek treatment for anyone with injuries, but as Channel Four reported earlier this hour, local hospitals are currently beyond capacity. We will provide updates as they become available and let the viewers know when each hospital is able to accept additional patients. Make sure you stay tuned in to Channel Four for all the latest news on the unrest in Buffalo."

The German Shepherd moved past his master, tail upright and pushing a growl from the back of his throat. Duke lunged at the sliding door, barking furiously; angry gnashing teeth leaving behind trails of saliva against the screen.

"Knock it off, ya bastard," Albert yelled.

Duke didn't knock it off. His barks became louder, more intense. All signs of his advanced age had vanished; eyes wide and piercing, the hair along the back of his neck stood upright. He jumped into the screen, clawing and trying to break through. The flimsy aluminum frame rattled from the force. The mesh along the bottom ripped and separated from the metal base as the dog tried forcing himself through the barrier.

"That's enough," Albert stated authoritatively.

The German Shepherd stopped jumping and barking. He looked to his master for a moment before refocusing his gaze through the screen and into the parking lot. Duke kept growling and snarling, but it was more subdued, controlled. He knew better than to challenge his owner.

Clop, clop, clop. The smacking of sneaker soles on cement was just loud enough to hear over the dog's complaints. The fearful cussing was too great in volume to be ignored. Albert followed Duke's stare through the door and his eyes nearly refused to process what they witnessed.

Adam pushed through the pair of glass doors at the front of the building. The one to his left swung hard, all the way open. Brick veneer chipped and crumbled as the heavy metal pull handle crashed into the outer wall of the tenement. Steel self-threading screws pulled loose at the jamb. A clarion blast of metal on masonry let everyone in the building know someone was passing through the threshold.

The younger man rushed across the parking lot. He was heading toward a red Grand Marquis parked right in front of the sidewalk.

"Shit, shit, shit," he cried as he arduously tried to free a ball of keys from the right pocket of his pants. The key ring emerged and came loose, falling to the ground in front of Adam's right foot. He knelt and a shaking, sweating hand shot toward the cement to retrieve it. The ring held an apartment key, two car keys, a plain plastic bottle opener, and a black key fob with three buttons.

A second pair of menacing footsteps joined the commotion. Albert watched from the front door as a massive bald man emerged from the building and headed right for his son. A dark red comet trail dotted the path from the exit to the red luxury sedan.

Adam's pudgy thumb mashed the bottom button on the key fob. When the trunk lid popped, the keys fell back to the pavement. The three steps to the back of the red sedan were passed in an instant and the younger man flung open the trunk. He chanced a look back at the hairless beast that was fast-approaching.

His attacker, complete with crushed nose, ripped-open face, and blood-red complexion, was right on his tail. There was only twenty or so feet between the men. Adam buried his head in the trunk of the car. He brushed aside a snow brush and set of jumper cables to get a grip on a black L-shaped tire iron. There were flecks of rust along the handle and elbow, but it was metal, solid and heavy. It

124

would do just fine. He wrapped his bleeding fingers around the iron, ignoring the torrid pain that radiated from his busted knuckles to halfway up his forearm.

Timing his strike by sound alone, Adam swung out like a backhand with a tennis racket into the growing shadow to his right. He caught the bald man across the mouth. Broken teeth clattered to the ground in a puddle of grumous blood. The plague-carrying aggressor spun from the wallop, slipping off balance and landing hard, chest first on the ground. The animal screamed, but not in pain. It was the sound of pure rage.

"Come on, you fuck!" Adam screamed at his tormentor; eyes wide and challenging. Quivering with ferocity, he held the tire iron with both hands like a baseball bat and waited for the other man to make his next move. He didn't have to wait long.

The assailant squirmed and pushed himself up from the ground. He got to his knees with a strand of saliva and blood connecting the man's fragmented lips to the cement. An expanding flap of loose forehead skin pulled back to show exposed skull and slimy pink flesh. His clothes, his skin, the pavement at his feet; it looked as if a cloud of red rain poured down on him alone.

Keeping low to the ground, the bald man positioned himself into a crouch and sprung toward Adam. Arms outstretched to aim talons of twisted fingers for his prey's face and throat. Both feet left the ground and the man was airborne.

Adam was ready. He drew back and swung for the fences. The outer elbow of the tire iron punched through the man's left temple. The frontal and temporal bones of the skull collapsed inward. Smashed shards dug into gray matter, eviscerating a fist-sized section of the temporal lobe. The hippocampus and thalamus were rendered a useless gelatin. The orbital cavity was demolished. Increased pressure inside the cranium caused the left eye to burst forth from its socket, still attached to the head by rectus muscles. Red fluid sprayed a hefty streak up Adam's shirt and speckled his face.

The bald menace was dead before his limbs finished bouncing against the concrete, but Adam was still poised and ready for the man to keep coming. He held the iron in one hand over his head, ready to bring it down like a hammer. But there was no need. Adam's breathing slowed and his hand lowered to his side, his eyes still fixed on the fresh corpse in front of him.

"He's done."

A speechless Adam looked up to find his father standing fifteen feet away, in the middle of the parking lot. The older man leaned on his cane. His glasses hung from the collar of his shirt. Duke stood next to him, sniffing the air and shifting his gaze from Adam to the body and back.

"He's done," Albert repeated. "You did good."

Adam couldn't answer. The metal tool slipped from his fingers and clamored to the ground.

"Are you hurt?" Albert asked.

His son stared back, not sure if he understood the question.

"Are you okay? Have you been bitten?" Albert's voice remained level. His speech didn't rise in volume and his tone did not reveal his concern.

"I," Adam started. He lifted his hands to show the open, pulsing wounds. The younger man looked down his front and examined the blood soaking into his clothing and drying against his skin.

"I don't know," Adam finally answered. He thought for a minute and asked, "Bitten?"

"Yes," Albert said firmly. "Did he bite you or did you get his blood on you?"

Adam studied his shirt, his pants, his sneakers, the cuts on his hands and arms. He used his wrist to whisk away sweat and red from his cheeks and brow. He almost laughed as he blurted, "His blood is all over me! It's everywhere. I can taste it."

"Okay," Albert said softly, shifting his weight from his right foot to his left and relying on the cane for stability. "You're going to be okay."

"What?" Adam asked. "What are you talking about?"

"You're going to be okay." Albert's voice boomed as he was willing his statement to be fact.

"Alright?" Adam replied. It was more of a question than a statement. He was having a hard time reading the expression on his father's face.

"Go on inside." Albert turned a half step and nodded toward the front door.

"But what about-" Adam tried to speak but got immediately cut off.

"Don't worry about him," Albert said, referring to the deceased. "It's all on the news, something's happening that makes folks go crazy."

Adam just stared at the older man.

"Trust me. Leave him here. You need to get inside." Albert motioned toward the building. "Go on ahead, I'll be right behind you."

The elder man was making a point to keep a safe distance between himself and his son. If Adam noticed, he didn't object. The younger man wiped his palms on what little clean fabric remained on his shirt and took a few slow steps toward the building's entrance. Albert waited for him to reach the door before moving from his place in the lot. Before entering, Adam looked to his father. He waited, holding the door open for the man and his dog.

"Go down to the basement," Albert instructed.

"The basement?" Adam was perplexed by the request.

"Yes, the basement. I'll meet you down there."

"But, wh-"

"Don't argue with me." Albert didn't wait for Adam to get his question out.

Adam shrugged and went inside, letting the door slam on its damaged hinges. Albert watched his son descend the stairs before calling to Duke, who had inched his way closer to the dead beast lying in a heap under the hot sun. The aging pair slogged toward the front door.

Chapter 20

The pair of them might have slept all day. It wasn't as if either one of them had any place they needed to be. Neither had an employer that might be wondering where they were or why they hadn't turned up for work. There wouldn't be any concerned friends trying to get in touch. No obligations. No responsibilities. No future.

Heavy footsteps on creaky wood stairs got Jeremy stirring. A slammed door caused his eyelids to twitch. A man's bellowing voice from outside the window made Jeremy groan and roll to his side. He clutched the stained sheet, pulling it over his shoulder and yanking it off of his slumbering companion in the process.

The shouting man was instructing someone to, "Get your stupid ass in the car now, or I'm leaving without you." Whoever was with him must have complied. Two vehicle doors were pulled closed and after what seemed like thirty seconds of turning over, the poorly-tuned engine fired up.

Despite his resistance, Jeremy was becoming lucid. Well, he was waking up. *Lucid* might not be a fair way to describe him. In any case, he was conscious. But it was still way too early. Was it even noon yet? What gives? Why all the noise at this ungodly hour? Didn't his neighbors understand that the building was a shared space and there may be some people who didn't want to hear them banging around and making a ruckus so early in the day? After all, some people needed to sleep. Sometimes his neighbors could be so inconsiderate.

Jeremy's silent complaints were interrupted by another aural intrusion, a woman's shrill screaming. This was not the routine sound of a rude neighbor. The screeching was rooted in genuine terror. Jeremy's eyes opened wide and fixed on the cracked plaster ceiling overhead. Wrinkles appeared across his forehead as the unemployed stoner tried to figure out who was screaming and what had them so frightened.

It was definitely coming from inside the building. Absolutely. Or it could have been coming from outside. Maybe. No doubt about it. The scream was certainly coming from one or the other, indoors or out. It sort of sounded like the panicked complaint came from above him. So that means it had to be inside the same building, didn't it? Possibly. The scared woman could have been outside still, just overhead somehow. She could have been outside one of the windows on the upper floors. But why the hell would someone be climbing around outside their window? They wouldn't. She must be on the roof. That made more sense, but not the *most* sense. She was on the roof of an adjacent building. That had to be the answer.

So, which building was it? Now it was becoming a game. Jeremy rolled to the edge of the bed, which consisted of a ratty second-hand mattress placed directly on the vinyl floor covering in the center of his studio apartment; no frame, no box spring, no headboard.

His bony knees slid off the edge, falling about four inches to the floor. Wearing only moderately soiled boxer shorts, he pressed bare feet against the tile and pulled himself to a wobbly, yet upright position. Brushing dust off his knees, Jeremy searched the floor of the apartment for something to wear amongst the heaps of laundry, empty beer cans, and plastic food containers. He knelt to retrieve the jeans he had worn the previous day. The denim unraveled, dropping a half-eaten cheeseburger to the ground. Jeremy absently kicked the bun as he pulled on the pants and stepped toward the apartment's lone window.

Leaning over an ancient radiator, he pressed his face to the glass and looked outside. The sun's rays were hot on his pale and shirtless torso. A blinding glare forced him to squint. He held his right hand over his brow, trying to block enough light to search for the roof-bound lady in distress. So far, the only thing he could make out was a blue minivan pulling quickly away from the curb just outside the tenement. It didn't stop for the red light at the end of the street.

There wasn't too much else to see outside. Nobody was around and there wasn't any traffic. Across the street, the roofs of the buildings had cracked and missing shingles. One had a bright blue tarp covering a hole. But of course, none had any people standing on them.

"Huh," Jeremy muttered to himself.

He was about to put the whole ordeal out of his mind when another scream sounded from what had to be the apartment directly upstairs. This one was much lower in volume. The tone held less urgency than the first and was accompanied by the thud of something falling hard to the floor.

"Hey, keep it down up there," Jeremy shouted at the ceiling. After a moment of silence, he added, "Dicks."

Back to the pile of linens and trash, Jeremy snatched up a plain yellow tee shirt that smelled of vinegar and feet. He buried his nostrils in the cotton and inhaled deeply, assessing. Jeremy shrugged his shoulders and then pulled the shirt on over his head.

Both hands plunged into his pockets. The left clutched a ball of lint, three pennies, and a thimble's-worth of loose tobacco spilled from a cigarette pack. The right hand wrapped fingers around a small glass vial. Jeremy pulled the container out of his pants and up to his face. A faint dusting of cocaine lined the inside of the tube. He pulled the cork stopper off with his teeth and turned the tiny bottle upside down over the index knuckle of his left hand. Tapping the bottom of the vial with his fingers, Jeremy watched as nothing dropped free from the glass container.

"Shitty," he complained aloud.

"What's shitty?" a feminine voice asked softly from under the bed sheets. The young woman's face was hidden under a pillow with no cover.

"This is," Jeremy explained, holding up the empty bottle for her to see. "No more blow."

Beth pushed the pillow aside and propped herself up on her elbows, careful to keep the sheet pulled up to her collar bone. "So, what are you going to do about that?" she fairly demanded.

"I'm going to run out and get more, obviously." Jeremy gave her a look to indicate that was the stupidest question he had ever heard.

"And when do you plan to do that?" Beth asked, brushing locks of dark hair out of her eyes. She still made no move to get up.

"When I get to it," he dismissed her with a roll of his eyes. He dropped the small container back into his pocket before adding, "But feel free to run out and score by yourself if it's such an emergency."

"Fine," Beth replied.

She flung the sheet off her nearly naked body, exposing her B-cup breasts and a series of small bruises in the pattern of a bite mark above her left nipple. Jeremy was about to comment on the hickey, to ask if she preferred he take it easy on her next time, but Beth spoke before he got the chance.

"And besides," she continued. Beth put her hands on her tits and squeezed, "I bet I can get a better deal than you can. If you know what I mean."

The young woman stood up on the mattress, wearing only a pair of green thong panties. Ever the enchantress, Beth made no effort to conceal a burp as she dug at her ass to dislodge a wedgie. The seductress turned away from Jeremy and began hunting around the room for her clothes. Despite her crass nature, Jeremy couldn't help but admire the view of her tight butt as she bent to grab a pair of jeans from the mound of laundry.

"Okay, okay," Jeremy relented. "That's not necessary. I'm going now."

"Fine," Beth spat as she stuffed one leg into the tight-fitting pants. "I guess I'll try to clean up around here while you're gone. This place is a shit-hole."

"Right," Jeremy replied, "But if you're going to do that..."

"Yes?" Beth asked, turning to face him.

"You should do it topless," Jeremy said, smiling broadly.

Beth glared at him. The angle of her head highlighted the dark circles below her eyes.

"Right," said Jeremy. "I'll be back in a bit then."

He stepped over the mattress in the living room and sleeping quarters, directly into the kitchen and dining area, which had the same plain white walls and worn-down vinyl flooring. He stopped in front of the refrigerator. It was one of those older, outdated appliances on which the sparkling white exterior had been turned yellow from years of second-hand smoke and a disregard for cleanliness.

The unit only stood chest-high on Jeremy. The freezer was on top. It was barely the size of a small microwave and since it had never been defrosted, an accumulation of ice had essentially eliminated any usable space. The door to the main cavity of the fridge swung open.

Some sort of brown sludge lined the top shelf and a section of the right inner wall. A half loaf of white bread that had turned green and brown with mold sat just out of reach of the viscous goo. There wasn't much else inside; a nearly full bottle of barbecue sauce, an empty water bottle, a jar of grape jelly left behind by the previous tenant, a few odd ketchup packets from Burger King, and some hot sauce packets from Taco Bell.

Jeremy picked up the water bottle to confirm there was nothing inside. He held the opening to his lips and pressed the sides of the plastic bottle together, straining to get a drop into his mouth and having no success. He tried shaking it but his effort was cut short by Beth's complaints.

"I thought you were going?" she called to him.

Jeremy sighed. "I am."

He tossed the empty bottle back into the fridge and slammed the door closed. Pulling his loose-fitting pants back up to his waist, he stepped feet with no socks into a scuffed pair of Nike sneakers and made for the apartment door, which was less than one foot from the left side of the refrigerator.

Beth was still in the center of the apartment, bending down to separate garbage and clothing into separate piles on the floor. Miscellaneous items like keys, the television remote, and lighters were being tossed into a third pile on the mattress. The best part was she was still wearing no shirt and no bra. Jeremy grinned and headed out, pulling the door closed behind him and checking to make sure it had locked.

He was pretty sure he heard Beth call him an asshole once he was gone, but he couldn't be certain. And anyway, she could call him all the mean names she wanted. As long as he could turn back up with a few grams of cocaine and have his filthy way with her, he would be more than satisfied.

"I heard that," he called through the door. There was no reply. She either hadn't heard him or didn't care enough to respond.

Jeremy shook his head and began walking down the stairs from the second floor to the first. After about five or six steps, he slowed to sniff the air in the hallway. It smelled like old baked diapers. Maybe someone had shit themselves in the stairwell. He crinkled his nose and tried to hold his breath until he reached the ground floor.

The main entrance was a heavy solid-core door with a slight warp and tan paint that had mostly chipped off. Jeremy had to pull hard on the knob to get it to open. The remaining paint along the door's edges had grown tacky in the summer's heat and it took a few good tugs to free it from the jamb. There was a notable change in temperature as he left the inner lobby and walked outside. Almost immediately, sweat began to appear on the back of his neck.

He trudged out to the sidewalk and stepped over the curb. Summertime meant no early-morning snow plows, no restricted overnight parking, and no parking tickets for leaving your car in the street between 2am and 5am. This convenience meant that Jeremy could drive home drunk or high and pull right up to the walkway that led to the front door of the building, stagger inside, and pass out with the knowledge that he wouldn't be receiving a parking citation for which he had no money to pay.

The Mazda sat right where he left it. Hopping into the driver's seat, Jeremy started the engine and immediately turned the stereo volume down. It had been turned all the way up and he just couldn't stand the loud music this early in the day. The clock on the dashboard read 11:41am. He rubbed his eyes and spotted a single cigarette lying free on the passenger's side floor. It was probably stale but it was still good enough to smoke and he could really use the nicotine. He leaned over to reach for it when a pair of baleful hands smashed into the passenger's side window.

"Balls!" Jeremy squealed, throwing himself back into the driver's side door.

Fresh blood ran down the glass, flowing briskly from deep gouges in the flesh. The eyes of a woman, maybe sixty years of age, locked on Jeremy. Her lips pulled back into a sneer and biting teeth nipped at the window. Congealing red fluid dotted her features. She drew back for an instant and lunged forward, crushing her nose against the glass as she tried to force her way through and get to the young man in the sedan. More blood and thick, clear sinus juice spewed out of her mangled nostrils.

"Oh shit!" Jeremy cried out; his heart rattling in his rib cage.

Before he could pull in his next deep breath, a second pair of fists thrashed against the driver's side window, just inches from Jeremy's face, which was quickly growing pale as blood drained out. The tweaker jerked back around, the lid to the center console cracked as his weight pressed into it.

The hands of the second attacker were dry, but the rest of his body was covered in bodily fluids. It was a man in his late thirties. His skin was thick and gray and he had one very distinct feature. The lower jaw had been mostly ripped away from the head. It swung in pendulous fashion from a frayed tendon under the left cheek. Black and purple gel pumped out of the hole at the top of his neck. The whites of his eyes were dotted red from ruptured capillaries. The maniac flashed cracked yellow teeth before punching the glass with a solid right hand.

"Oh shit. Oh shit," Jeremy bellowed. Looking back to the passenger's side, he found the window clouded by dull red streaks. Movement in his periphery had instinctively forced the young man to look over his right shoulder.

Two more people were sprinting toward the back end of the car. They were both men, one in

130

his twenties and the other much older. The younger of the pair had on khaki pants and a white button-up shirt that was torn down the right side. Dark stains marred the fabric. His long dark hair was soaked and matted to his scalp. The older man was balding and wore only boxer shorts; a deep and weeping gash in the center of his belly.

A third person, this one a woman, was turning the corner between Jeremy's building and the neighboring dwelling. Her house dress looked tattered, blue linen flailed loosely behind her as she moved. Her hands were out in front of her and they looked to be clutching handfuls of something tan, red, and stringy.

Jeremy was going to be surrounded. Without thinking, he pulled the gear selector into the drive position and his right foot stomped the accelerator to the floor. The engine whined and the transmission moaned. The torque converter spun and finally caught. The car began to move and the right front tire chirped against the pavement.

The Mazda took off down the road, seeming to accelerate faster than ever before. As Jeremy ran the red light at the end of the street, he looked to the rear-view mirror and caught a glimpse of the apartment building as it shrunk into the distance behind him. He considered going back for Beth but promptly convinced himself that she'd be fine locked in the apartment.

Chapter 21

Pulling out of the driveway, Jim kept a nervous eye on the home across the street. The house, a familiar-looking two-story cottage with clapboard siding, a cedar shake roof, and a large flagpole in the front yard, now looked suspiciously still. There was no movement visible beyond the picture window's lace curtain. The front door remained open and while Jim expected to see someone rush out from the darkened entryway, no one did.

Do you recognize this place? You should. Remember way back, when Jim was cruising around and spotted a woman on the roof of her home before going into someone's house and helping himself to their shotgun? Okay, good. You're up to speed.

When he'd driven the length of only one block, Jim looked to the floor on the passenger's side for the fifth time. The gun was still there. Of course it was. It wasn't likely to sprout legs and run off but he had to keep checking. He needed some sort of visual reminder, something tangible to let him know he wasn't dreaming and hadn't gone crazy.

Jim pulled out a third cigarette. He took special care as he removed it from the pack, sure to not let it fall through his quavering fingers like the last two. The first one had dropped into his lap before rolling to the edge of the seat and landing on the floor. Jim then accidentally stepped on it with his heel, crushing it and grinding tobacco bits into the carpet. The second bounced off his wrist and disappeared into the space between the cushion and the center console, never to be seen again.

Now to the task of actually lighting it; this would prove to be more of a challenge. Powerful gusts of wind rushed in through the open window. Every time Jim's thumb spun the striker wheel, the lighter sparked and was immediately blown out. He rolled up the window and tried again. Normally, guiding the flame to the tip of a cigarette required virtually no focus but as Jim glanced down to gauge the distance, he caught a glimpse of the speedometer and his concentration was interrupted.

The needle had just passed the hundred mile per hour marker and was on its way to one-twenty. He was traveling at nearly four times the legal speed limit. Jim wasn't worried about being pulled over and issued a traffic citation, it's just that Witmer Road wasn't exactly designed for racing. Then again, firing up a smoke while driving at top speed would probably turn out to be one of the safest things he would do all day.

To that end, the health risks associated with smoking cigarettes were now much less of an issue. With life expectancy plummeting by the hour, living long enough to develop emphysema would prove to be a rare experience, reserved only for the most fortunate.

Jim pulled in another deep lungful of light menthol smoke as he continued his absent-minded navigation. When you've made a trip to and from a place as often as he had to and from his uncle's house, you learn to make all the proper turns without concentrating on street signs and directions. Before you know it, you've arrived at your destination with barely a memory of the journey itself. And if you're Jim, you remember too late that you meant to take an alternate route to the grocery store.

A body lie in the street; a meaty island in a lake of blood. Jim pumped the brake pedal, slowly advancing toward the motionless heap. Not that he expected the corpse to pop up and come running, but the dead man sure as Hell hadn't killed himself and someone might still be close by. The car crept closer to the deceased man with his back to the sky. You couldn't say he was face-down, that implies the presence of a face. Judging by the exit wound through the back of his ball cap, he would forever be expressionless.

Flies circled. Here and there, one of them would land on eggshell-colored bones that had pushed through skin and flannel to dry in the summer sun. Blood had congealed along the base of the compound fracture. A colony of ants braved the dense puddle to get a few bites of ripped, crusted skin from around the wounds. The insects paid no mind to the approaching vehicle but they weren't the only signs of life nearby.

Across the road and off to the left, a woman in a purple sweater hung by her hands from the roof of a garage. Her bare feet dangled three feet above the ground. She glanced down, judging the distance and imagining a rough landing. On the driveway, inches from the brown metal garage door, lie a rifle with a wooden stock and a leather strap.

A cursory examination of the home revealed why the woman had opted for the roof rather than the front door when making her exit. Halfway out of a second-floor window, raged a shirtless growling man in thick bifocals. He appeared to have gotten himself stuck in the small opening when he'd tried to follow the woman outside.

Instead of being slid open, the window had been demolished, broken through from the inside as the man plunged his upper body through the single-pane barrier. Sparkling bits of shattered glass had been spilled across the low-pitched roof. While trying to make his way out, the spectacled man leaned his belly into the shards along the bottom frame. Sharp edges pierced the skin with each failed attempt to climb through; segments of glass momentarily disappearing into his abdomen. New gaps appeared across his stomach and a thick dark liquid drizzled down the exterior wall. Dozens of purple-colored streams stood out in stark contrast to bright white paint on aluminum siding.

The woman kept holding on as Jim watched from his car. *What is she waiting for*, he wondered. This stalemate couldn't go on for much longer. Her grasp on hot shingles wasn't going to last forever and pulling herself back up wasn't an option. The man upstairs would eventually get all the way through the window. And then what? She wouldn't be able to protect herself, not with that rifle on the ground and out of reach. The woman must have realized this as well. She finally let go but a glimmer of movement between the houses told Jim that she had waited too long.

Jim hit the gas. He steered to the left side of the street, avoiding the rotten obstacle in the middle of the road before coming to an abrupt stop at the end of the woman's driveway. Jim slammed the shifter into park and threw open the door. He wrapped his fingers around the grip of the shotgun and began sprinting toward the woman.

Darting across the back yard and then through the passageway separating the woman's home from the house next door, was an abomination in brown trousers and a denim shirt with a courier bag strapped over one shoulder. His thirteen-year-old legs were short, still waiting for that juvenile growth-spurt, but they pumped like mad and propelled him with preternatural speed. Vulturous cries through a grimace of stained teeth gave only a moment's warning.

The Earth jumped up at her. The woman landed hard on her right leg, forcing the ankle to roll in so the bottom of her foot aimed straight to the left. She gasped and crumpled to the turf, losing her glasses in the process. The woman ignored the pain and pushed herself up off the ground. Kneeling and hunched forward, she reached out for her lost eyewear.

"The gun!" Jim screamed as he ran. He was still twenty yards away, too far from his target for the shotgun to be of any use- not without hitting the woman too.

"Get the gun," he begged.

133

As she pulled her glasses back on, the first thing Susan could see was a young man rushing towards her. He was shouting and, with the hand that wasn't holding a large double-barrel firearm, pointing at her. No, not *at* her. He was pointing *past* her. She looked over her right shoulder and quickly understood. Crawling on all fours, Susan scrambled to retrieve her gun.

Her hand clamped around the weapon's forestock. The woman tucked the rear of the rifle into the crook of her shoulder as she rose to her feet. She stuck her right index finger through the opening of the trigger guard, whirled around to face the assailant, and was smashed back into the ground.

The flesh-hungry adolescent ran through her at full speed and their bodies crashed into the pavement. Skin and bones smacked together; tissue scraped on coarse cement. The woman had the air pounded out of her lungs and fought to catch her breath. Incredibly, she somehow managed to hold onto the rifle; her right hand on the stock, left hand on the boy's collar.

The youth let loose a scream so vicious, so intense, that droplets of blood leaped out of his ravaged throat. Tendons strained. Nostrils flared. Muscles sharply contracting; veins bulging. Capillaries burst. Bright red splotches appeared in the whites of the teenager's unblinking eyes.

He was on top of her with one leg on either side. The kid lunged face-first at her throat; teeth clacking together as they missed their mark. Braids of pink saliva slopped out of his mouth, soaking the woman's sweater and dotting the lenses of her glasses. Rage and frustration grew inside the prepubescent brute. Her neck was out of reach but her arms and shoulders weren't. His talon hands squeezed the arm that restrained him. Claws pierced her skin and opened fresh weeping wounds as bleeding skin clumps gathered under his fingernails.

The woman defended herself in awe-inspiring fashion. Her own anger had spiked and all of her fear was gone. She possessed spectacular strength and reflex for a woman of her age. The flood of adrenaline didn't hurt either. Every time the boy thrust his snarling maw at her face or body, she twisted and dodged to avoid his bite. Unable to use the gun with it pinned against her chest from the weight of the boy, Susan used her free hand to punch him in the face. It wasn't doing any real damage and it wasn't causing any pain but it was enough to faze him, distracting him for seconds at a time.

Neither combatant had any technique, just the unwavering drive for self-preservation. A predator propelled by its nature to feed; his prey driven by a primal instinct for survival. If she was to come out on top, the older woman knew she would have to do more than land a few feeble blows. She wasn't going to beat him up. He, like any other animal gone bad, needed to be put down.

With her left hand holding the boy's shirt, she reached her right hand over his forehead to grab a handful of sweat-drenched hair and pulled as hard as she could. Susan slid her left hand up to his throat and pressed knuckles into his windpipe. A smile formed across the woman's face when she felt the boy's scalp lifting and separating; a muted suction as it pulled away from his skull. Nothing would please her more than to pull his whole damn head right off. That is, if he didn't asphyxiate first.

The kid fought for breath, trying to escape. He squirmed to clear his airway and threatened to free himself from her grasp entirely. She just needed to hang on for another couple of seconds.

Jim was still running. Even if he could afford to stop for long enough to plant his feet and line up a shot, firing from such close range would unquestionably kill them both. But this didn't mean the shotgun was unusable. With both hands on the buttstock, Jim wound up and swung the weapon like a baseball bat. The metal barrels nailed the kid hard on the back of his head.

His small body slumped; his brain rattling in his skull. The boy was still alive but barely conscious. Eager to get out from under her attacker, the woman started to roll the stunned boy off of her. Jim helped by way of placing the bottom of his right foot against his torso and kicking the impaired assailant to the side. The childish menace landed at the edge of the driveway, rolling onto his back. His arms twitched and a knee bent in a lame attempt to right himself and continue the hunt.

Not yet on her feet, the woman scrambled backwards to get away from the dazed hoodlum. She dragged the rifle by the strap as she moved, sure to keep it from getting more than an arm's-length away from her.

"Come on, let's go," Jim instructed the woman as he extended an arm.

She accepted his offered hand, glad for the help. The woman stood and faced the stranger who had come to her aid. Bruises had already formed on her cheeks and forehead. All sorts of goo in a variety of colors stained her sweater and tan slacks, both of which had dozens of small rips and tears. Abrasions covered her hands and a particularly deep-looking cut started on her forearm and disappeared beneath a purple sleeve.

The experience left her more shaken up than she let on. She tried her best to dust herself off and catch her breath. The battered woman knelt to pick small pebbles off of her feet but not before checking her weapon. Loaded, primed, safety off; it was ready for action.

"Listen, we should get moving," Jim told her. He turned to lead her to the car, which still had its engine running in the street. "I need to go, but I can drive you-"

Deafening gunfire sounded from just a couple of feet behind him. He flinched and looked back in time to see the boy drop back to the ground with a bullet hole through the bridge of his nose. An explosion of gore sprinkled brain, bone, and bloodied hair on the side lawn.

"Shit!" Jim exclaimed. "What the Hell?"

"Oh, sorry. Did I startle you?" asked the woman.

"I don't think *startle* is the right word," he answered. "You didn't need to do that. He was down, you could have gotten away without murdering him. I was trying to tell you I can drive if you need to go somewhere. We could have just left."

She paused before replying, as if considering his words. "What's your name?"

"Jim," he told her. His arms relaxed and he held the shotgun at his waist instead of his chest.

"Nice to meet you, Jim," said the woman. She pulled back on the bolt handle to expel the spent casing before shoving it forward and advancing the next round. "I'm Susan."

"Nice to meet you too, Susan," he answered. "So, like I was saying, it's probably not a good idea to stick around."

"Jim, you've got blood on your clothes. And on your arms too."

"Oh, right..." Jim looked down at himself to confirm, wiping his hands and wrists on the sides of his shorts.

"And unless I'm mistaken, there's some on your face as well." She squinted for effect.

Jim absently swabbed his forehead and cheeks with his shirt collar and said, "Ya know, you're not looking so tidy yourself. Where are you going with this?"

"Well, my point is this. That blood isn't yours, is it?"

Jim opened his mouth to respond, but didn't speak in time.

"You've also got that gun," Susan explained. "And something tells me you're pretty comfortable using it. You saw me and you could have kept driving past, but you didn't. You literally ran towards something dangerous, something deadly."

"Well, I-" Jim was cut off.

"So, it seems to me that you are well aware of the difference between *murder* and self defense. Would I be correct in my assumption?" Susan took her glasses in her free hand and wiped away the smears, cleaning the lenses on one of her sweater's few dry spots. She looked straight at Jim the whole time, waiting for an answer. When one didn't arrive, she added, "I bet it was less than an hour ago, wasn't it?"

Jim's shoulders slumped and he looked to his feet. "Yes. That's right."

"Okay then." Susan's stern features softened. "It was a good thing you did for me and I don't want you thinking your efforts were wasted on a bad person, on a murderer."

"Fair enough," Jim told her. "But we're in the clear now, so if there's somewhere you need to go, I can take you."

Susan didn't make a move. "That's very sweet of you but I won't be needing a ride."

"But you can't just stay out here!" Jim exclaimed, motioning to the general surroundings. "I mean- just take a look around."

If the pair of stiffs nearby didn't properly illustrate his point, then the seven or eight visible columns of smoke, the helicopters hovering over the horizon, and the sounds of screams and car alarms might help change her mind.

"I appreciate your concern and I hate to sound rude, but I don't think you should be telling me what I can and cannot do. After all, I'm old enough to be your mother."

"I was gonna say, older sister," Jim responded with a hint of a grin.

"Don't be a smart-ass," Susan replied, though a small smile appeared on her face as well. "I'll be staying here, in my home."

"Okay, if you insist. I just don't think it's a good idea." Jim took a step back and began to move toward his car. "Good luck, Susan."

"Who was it?" Susan asked.

Jim frowned. "Who was who?" He turned back to face her.

"You know who." Her eyes narrowed at him.

He sighed. Jim took a beat before answering. Rubbing his forehead and looking away from her, he answered, "My cousin's girlfriend."

"You killed her."

It was impossible to tell whether she was asking or stating a fact. To Jim, she sounded like a matriarch challenging her child to be honest; knowing the answer, but giving him the opportunity to come clean on his own.

"Yes." One word was all that was needed.

"And how is that any different from this?" As she finished speaking, she made a point to look at the boy's corpse to emphasize her point.

Jim glared at her. "It was different because no one else was there to help me. I tried to get away without hurting her, but she came at me, got a hold of me. I'm not sure I had any choice."

"I didn't have a choice either," she professed.

"He was down!" Jim raised his voice to nearly a shout, pointing at the motionless body at the edge of the lawn to emphasize his meaning. He lowered his pitch and added, "I just thought killing him could have been avoided, that's all."

"No, it couldn't." Susan took a breath and explained, "I could not allow that little bastard to keep on living. They don't stay down and they don't give up. They're fast and they just keep coming for you. It's like the devil himself is taking hold of people. But you know that already."

Jim nodded in agreement.

Susan went on, "Even if we both ran as fast as we could, he would have been on us before we got to your car."

Shooting a glance to the corpse in the road, Jim asked, "Did you do that too?"

"He spotted me on the roof and was heading my way. I think they try to eat people. And if you're lucky enough to get away, you really haven't escaped. If you get bit and live, you eventually start attacking folks too. Trust me, Jim. Killing them is the right thing to do. You can't have mercy for them. They'll certainly have no mercy for you."

"I'll remember that," Jim promised. "And just to be clear, you shot him?"

"Well, we didn't have a fist fight."

Jim rolled his eyes. "So, that's a *yes*?"

"It took a few tries, but yes. I'm not what you'd call a sharpshooter," Susan admitted.

"Did he get run over too? I mean, how did he get so... broken?"

"Beats me," she answered. "He was up and walking around like that."

Jim's eyes widened, "With his arm like that?"

Susan rolled her shoulders. "If I didn't already know better, I'd think I had lost my marbles."

"Since we're on the topic, I don't understand why you're staying here," Jim started. "I know this is your home and everything, but it's too dangerous."

"I have a feeling that everywhere you go is going to be dangerous from now on. It's admirable you want to help but if I tag along, I'll only make it more dangerous for you," she warned.

"Listen, if you're worried that you'll slow me down or-"

Susan held up a hand to cut him off. She gently placed the rifle on the ground and rolled up her sleeves past her elbows. On the inside of her left forearm was a half circle of bleeding teeth marks. Then she pulled on the neckline of her sweater, stretching it far enough to reveal her right shoulder, which had a bite-size gouge of missing skin.

"Oh, I see." Jim hesitated.

He had been too late; someone else he couldn't save. Was she going to turn into one of those crazy people? She seemed okay, but it was only moments earlier that she'd been bit. Should he run? Should he do to her as she had done to the others and put her down?

"Are you sure it's the bite that causes this? Maybe it's something else, like a chemical spill or something," Jim suggested hopefully.

"I'm positive. That little prick was our paperboy. My husband saw him outside earlier this afternoon and went to say hello. That's when he attacked, biting at him, got him in the shoulder and chest. Less than an hour later, my husband transformed into that monster," she pointed to the window over the garage but the man was gone. "And since he got us both, I guess I should say he turned *us* into monsters. That's the other reason I had to kill him."

"I'm sorry," was all Jim could muster.

"You don't need to apologize," Susan assured him.

"But I-"

"Thank you, Jim." She smiled at him. "I'd be dead already if you hadn't come along."

"I'm not convinced you're any better off." A globe of sweat rolled from under his arm and out of the sleeve, just one in a series of droplets that had been raining from his body all day.

"I'll admit it's not ideal," she said, bending to pick up the rifle. "But I'm still breathing, my heart's still pumping. That's more than I can say for the paperboy. At least there's one less of them running around. And after what he did to my husband, I have to admit to feeling a certain satisfaction in knowing that I'm the one who stopped him."

"All's well that ends well," Jim replied without a trace of conviction or humor.

"Yeah, I suppose so." Susan tried to keep a happy expression, but it only came off as defeated.

"So, what will you do? Do you want me to..." Jim's words faded before he finished asking his question. He hiked up the shotgun.

"No, Jim. I certainly do not want you to shoot me," she answered firmly.

"Okay, okay. I just thought I'd ask in case you, ya know, wanted to be put out of your misery."

"I feel like I should thank you for the offer but I'm not sure that type of offer warrants much gratitude," she responded.

"Right- sorry."

"Besides, I'm not sure I'm really in any misery," said Susan.

"You sound surprisingly optimistic, given the circumstances. And what about those bite marks? They must be excruciating," Jim observed.

"It's nothing. I can't even feel it," she told him.

"Really? Because they look pretty painful. And gross."

"Such a charmer," she chuckled. "But no, it doesn't hurt."

"And your ankle?"

"That's fine too." The woman grinned. Her shoulders and arms relaxed.

Standing there and looking as she did, Susan almost seemed happy, which should have been a positive thing. And at any other moment, it would have been. But for Jim, it was unsettling. He needed to wrap up this little chat and put some serious distance between himself and this woman.

"Oh. That's good, then." His reply was short and noncommittal.

"So where are you going from here?" Susan probed.

"I have to pick up a friend from the grocery store."

Susan nodded and Jim elaborated, "She was working there when everyone started going crazy."

"Oh, Lowell's?" Susan asked.

"Bennett's," Jim corrected her.

"Hmm, I like Lowell's better," Susan remarked. "Lower prices."

Jim glowered.

"So," the woman went on, "You think she's still there?"

"She called me while I was driving, said she locked herself in the break room."

"Is this a girlfriend?" Susan inquired.

"No." There was more he wanted to say about that but it didn't seem like the appropriate time to babble on about his personal life.

"You sound disappointed by that," she commented, placing a hand on her hip.

"It's sort of a long story," he said dismissively. "But who knows, my chances may improve with this whole end-of-the-world thing."

"End of the world? Don't you think that may be a little dramatic?"

"I hope so," Jim said earnestly. "So, what are you going to do after this?"

"I'm going to head back inside and hope someone shows up with a cure and some way to fix everything; keep the world from ending."

Jim nodded and Susan added, "I'm no fool though. I don't expect to be saved or anything like that. But as long as I'm here and with my husband, I can't ask for anything more at this point."

"I was going to ask about that." Jim shifted the gun from one hand to the other. "Won't your husband attack you as soon as you open the door?"

"I don't think so." She shook her head gently. "When I was on the roof, I saw some of the others. They didn't fight each other. It's like they can tell whether you've been infected and if you have, they don't go after you."

"While that may seem like good news for you, it's terrible news for me," said Jim, who suddenly felt compelled to check over his shoulder every three to five seconds.

"You'll do fine," Susan assured him. "Keep your gun handy and don't let your guard down. When you pick up your lady friend, get somewhere safe and lie low for a while."

"That's the plan," said Jim. "Those freaks- they can't use firearms, can they?"

Susan shrugged. "I'm not sure. I don't think so. Why do you ask?"

"Your rifle," Jim started, looking down at the weapon. "Do you think you'll need it?"

"I'm keeping it," she told him without hesitation. "I may not be able to use it in a few minutes, but I'd like to stay protected until that time."

"Of course," Jim pushed his words out quickly. "That makes sense."

Everything fell silent for a moment. Susan's features appeared vacant and instead of looking at Jim, she seemed to be staring through him. Her bottom jaw hung open and the only movement on her body was from a yarn of drool trickling out from the edges of her lips.

"Susan?" Jim spoke her name as if trying to wake her from a nap. "Can you hear me?"

The woman didn't say anything. Her form stayed motionless and her gaze remained fixed in Jim's general direction.

"I think I should go now." Jim's fingers tightened around the shotgun.

"Where are you going?" Susan asked as she was starting to come to.

"The supermarket, remember?"

"Oh, there's no need." Susan's broad smile highlighted the glossy quality of her eyes. "I have food in the house. I can make you some lunch. My husband is getting the grill warmed up."

Shit. Was this how it started? Jim kept a watchful eye on the woman as he took a few steps backwards. "Sure, that sounds great. You head into the house and I'll be inside in a minute."

"Take your time, dear." She began to turn and head for the front door. "I'll set another place for you, just come in when you're ready. I hope you remembered to invite your friends."

"Sounds great," Jim replied. He raised the barrel and pointed it at her torso, still backpedaling. He silently prayed he wouldn't have to shoot her. Keeping the gun trained on her was just a protective measure.

Susan let the rifle drop to the ground. She continued walking toward the door, patting her pockets as if searching for keys. As she muttered to herself and reached into empty pockets, the woman didn't notice Jim scrambling to his vehicle. She didn't hear the door slam closed or see the blue coupe drive away. Susan walked up the stoop and gripped the doorknob.

Chapter 22

"Come on, you bastard." Lindsey held the phone in her hands and willed it to ring.

It didn't make a noise but the Bennett's Supermarket staff break room was anything but quiet. A thundery racket sounded from the threshold as something smashed into the door from the other side. This was not the first interruption of its kind that afternoon. Every so often, something heavy and solid threatened to break right through the doorway to invade the relative serenity inside.

Suspended florescent lighting flickered in time with each massive bang. Every firm whack against the door frame sent strong vibrations through the framework and into the ceiling. Tiles rattled overhead to shake loose a fog of mineral fiber. Brown and white snowflakes fell in slow motion to form a thin, even layer across the floor.

"Just work," she pleaded. "Damn it, please work."

Pacing from one side of the room to the other, the young woman used her only available resource to call for help. Or, to try and call for help. Lindsey clutched her cell phone in both hands as she marched the length of the small room. She reached overhead and held the device as close to the ceiling as she could get. Eyes glued to the screen, she watched the reception bars appear, slowly multiply, and then vanish in quick succession. She moaned in defeat as the last reception bar, the tiny one all the way on the left, blinked twice and disappeared. In its place, a pair of words scrolled across the display. They read, *No Service,* but they might as well have said, *You're Fucked.*

"Jim, where are you?" Lindsey spoke aloud as her frustration intensified to match her level of panic. She was careful not to let her voice get louder than a whisper. Just beyond the flimsy wall, was a horde of human-shaped demons that would love to have her for their next meal. She wasn't sure whether they could hear her whimpers over all the commotion. The constant wails of the killing and dying served to remind her that death might come for her at any moment.

Locked in a flyspeck, windowless break room at the back corner of Bennett's Supermarket, the promise of rescue seemed to grow more empty with each passing minute. But how many minutes had it actually been? Ten? Twenty? Lindsey couldn't tell. And had it only been minutes, or should she be estimating in terms of hours? When was Jim going to get there? *Would* he actually get there? It was Jim, after all. Was she wrong to put such faith in him, to trust him with her life? Probably, but it's not like she could call a taxi or take a leisurely stroll down to the bus stop.

Maybe calling him would prove to be a mistake. If not for her fear and desperation, she wouldn't have bothered. Lindsey had first-hand knowledge of Jim's propensity to disappoint those around him. She herself had been let down by him on more than one occasion. But this, this was different. He *had* to come through for her this time, didn't he?

Time and again, he had proven himself to be a slacker, an underachiever, and generally unmotivated, but was he a coward as well? When was the last time Jim had to act in an emergency? How many life-and-death scenarios had Jim faced before today? Probably none. Her confidence waned, but Lindsey was certain of at least one thing. When it came to matters of life and death, he wouldn't abandon her.

As she waited, throngs of horror-stricken people were sprinting from their homes and places of business. All at once, they raced to their loved ones and tried to get out of town as fast as possible. Behind the wheel, urgency would replace caution. Accidents were inevitable and the immense volume of traffic would have roadways clogged. Rather than putting distance between themselves and the danger, folks would be stuck in their cars and able to do nothing but wait for the danger to arrive. And while that may be, Lindsey couldn't picture Jim relaxing in his car, whistling along with the latest pop tune and snapping his fingers to the beat as he waited for the streets to clear up.

Jim was on his way, he had said as much. He wouldn't give a shit about traffic laws or safe driving and if the streets were gridlocked, he'd go over curbs and across lawns if he had to. Lindsey would just have to be patient for a little longer. Soon enough, Jim would show up and whisk her away to some haven of safety and prosperity. But that doesn't sound right either, does it? So where was he? What the Hell was going on?

She shuddered at the myriad answers to that question. Jim told her he needed to stop and get a gun before he came for her. What if things didn't go so well along the way? He could have crashed his car and got stranded, or turned around somewhere and got lost, or carjacked, or killed and eaten. Lindsey supposed the possibilities were endless but they all had two critical common elements; each scenario concluded with a lifeless Jim and no one coming to get her.

Her pacing continued, back and forth along a narrow walkway between a row of lockers and a water cooler next to a refrigerator. After three more laps, she paused to stand over a round pressboard table as she re-tied her ponytail and cleaned the lenses on her glasses. Having given up on trying to call someone else for help, Lindsey stuffed the phone back into her pants pocket and considered her next move.

She could continue to wait for Jim and hope that none of the crazy people broke into the break room in the meantime. They would get in eventually and once they did, there would be nowhere for her to go. Her only other option was to make a run for it.

Lindsey had worked at Bennett's long enough to know the layout of the store and the location of all the exits. There were two fire doors at the rear of the building and one on each of the other walls. If she was fast and quiet, Lindsey could sprint through the aisles and get to one of those exits unscathed. If she ran into any trouble, she could double back and find another way out. And then she could... And then she could do what?

Escaping the building was just the first step in making her way to safety. After that, she'd be outside, alone, unarmed, and exposed. At least, that would be true if she tried to escape at that exact moment. All the activity happening in and around the store couldn't go on forever. It would, at some point, have to die down.

"Okay, you're safe for now," she said, trying to convince herself. She stated her plan out loud in an effort to keep her thoughts straight. "Wait til things settle down out there. Don't go until it's quiet."

As strategies go, this was pretty lousy. Hide in this crappy, cubicle-sized break room and make pretend the cheap-ass, hollow-core partitions would insulate her from the ongoing massacre? What were these walls even made of? Some kind of thin plastic hung on a skeleton of what had to be recycled soda cans. What a dump. And not a single window in this bland Purgatory? That had to be some sort of fire code violation.

Lindsey estimated she could punch right through the discount material used to form the walls. She held up a hand, palm out and placed it against the soft yellow surface, drawing back as soon as it made contact.

"Shit," Lindsey gasped. Another thud against the door; more falling dust, another flicker of the lights. A pair of cracks appeared above the door frame and ran all the way up to the ceiling. A sheen of cold perspiration broke out across the back of her neck as she watched the structure begin to deteriorate before her eyes. Her guts felt like she had chugged a glass of sun-warmed milk that she'd had to chew before swallowing it down.

She was going to have to be ready to defend herself when one of the loons ultimately forced his way in to greet her. Lindsey, aware she should have done this much earlier, began searching for something to use as a weapon.

It wouldn't take long to comb through such a small room. At the end closest to the door, was a wooden coat rack comprised of a five-foot rod bolted to the wall with three metal brackets. A dozen mismatched aprons and light jackets hung from cheap plastic hangers. Two zip-up sweatshirts fell to the floor as Lindsey swatted clothing out of the way and gripped the wood rail with both hands. She yanked hard but couldn't free the pole from the wall. The only detachable items were hangers and those wouldn't be worth a shit when it came to self defense.

Wasting no more time, she grabbed the shirts, aprons, and jackets to see if anything was hidden in the pockets. Beyond the odd bit of change, bunch of keys, or crumpled receipt, they were empty. Lindsey moved on to the lockers that lined the adjacent wall.

There were twenty in total, two rows of ten, one row on top of the other. Lindsey intended to search each of them but seven were secured with locks. With a frantic fluidity, the young woman started at the top left corner and flung the door open. There was nothing inside. She didn't bother to close the cabinet door before moving on to the next. In the second locker, Lindsey found a math text book with a calculator and some loose sheets of paper. The third unit was locked.

She almost skipped right past it, but something inside her nagged at her to try the lock itself. It was a Master Lock, combination style with a circular dial. She grabbed it by the base and pulled down, twisting and wobbling the dial. The lock held firm. Lindsey was not getting inside. Fine- there were still seventeen left to go.

The next locker held a plastic comb and pocket mirror. Locks secured the next two and the one after that contained a baseball cap and July's edition of Car and Driver Magazine. A fake leather purse was in the next. The zipper top was open to expose a handful of makeup applicators and a few dollar bills. The ninth unit was locked and the tenth held a pair of headphones, the noise-reducing, over-the-ear type.

Stepping back to the left side of the lockers, Lindsey swept her hand across the top row, closing all the open doors so she wouldn't bang her head on them as she searched the bottom row. She crouched and continued hunting through the metal cabinets. Lockers eleven and thirteen were locked but number twelve opened to reveal a canvas backpack stuffed inside. She jumped up, throwing the bag on top of the table to her left. Lindsey flipped the sack over and emptied it onto the tabletop.

A pair of socks, a water bottle, gym shorts, a pair of leather gloves with no fingertips, and some medical tape spilled out. Somebody's workout gear? Totally useless. She sifted through the items, checking for anything she might have missed. The medical tape might come in handy. She tucked the white roll into her front left pocket. The rest of the stuff however, would do her no good.

Lindsey cursed and swiped at the pile of junk, knocking it to the floor. She felt a surge of anger rising, but quickly caught herself. What did she expect to find in there? Had she thought maybe one of her coworkers kept a pistol hidden amongst his exercise apparel? Of course not. And more importantly, this was not the time for a temper tantrum.

Kneeling back down to the lower row of lockers, she found the next one, the fourteenth, to be

143

empty. An old, moldy and foul-smelling pair of sneakers sat alone in the next cabinet. Lindsey made a point to close the door to this locker right away, to keep the eye-watering funk inside. She wouldn't be going back in that one, not unless the ghouls outside might be repelled by a cloud of stink.

There was a heavy winter coat in the next locker, one of those parka-style jackets with a fur-lined hood. Who the Hell needed this in August? After this was another locked unit with two empty ones next to it. That brought her to the twentieth, and final locker. With dwindling expectations, Lindsey reached for the handle and opened the small metal door. Inside the storage unit, in the center of the floor, was a single clean plastic spoon.

"Damn it!" she shouted, slamming the door closed. An empty metallic clang filled the room. Near-deafening at first, the vibration seemed to hang in the air, echoing for several seconds before returning to silence.

And then it dawned on her. Lindsey couldn't hear anything. For the first time since she'd locked herself inside the lounge, she couldn't hear any noise at all. She stood frozen for about thirty seconds, checking to see if there was anything for her ears to detect. Nothing.

As quietly as she could, Lindsey slid across the dusty floor and over to the exit. Cupping her hands to form a megaphone around her right ear, she pressed the side of her head up against the door and listened for signs of life or rescue. Or more violence. But instead, there was still nothing.

Was the coast clear? Could it be safe to go out? Maybe, but not as safe as if she'd found some sort of weapon. Lindsey was reminded of that last locker, the one with the spoon. Not that a chintzy plastic utensil would be of any use, but a real utensil might be. A knife could come in handy, specifically a durable knife with a large blade, like the kind they keep at the deli shop.

Lindsey planted her shoulder against the door, ready to slam it shut again if needed. She twisted the tab to unlock it and turned the knob slowly in an effort to remain quiet and undetected. The latch let out a soft click as it passed through the strike plate to indicate the door would now open freely. She huffed a deep breath to prepare herself for whatever she may face on the other side as she cracked the door open and peered out.

To her left was a short hall that led to the restrooms. The frozen foods section was to her right. Directly in front of her was the rear aisle of the shopping center, which ran the entire length of the back wall. Roughly fifty feet down the aisle, past a series of coolers and open-faced refrigerated shelving units, was the sandwich counter. Opposite the rear wall, was a series of narrow aisles that ran to the front of the store. The supermarket looked as if a tornado had gone through and then someone tried cleaning up the rubble with hand grenades. What she saw next made her regret looking.

Lindsey didn't want to go out there anymore. What she wanted to do was close the door again, lock herself back inside and plan to never leave. She could sleep on the floor, using those rotten old sneakers for pillows and the parka for a blanket. Maybe there was some food in the fridge- she hadn't thought to check. And if not, no biggie. She didn't mind starving to death as long as the break room would keep her isolated from the mayhem. Instead of following her instincts and retreating, she opened the door far enough to squeeze through and walked out into the store.

Fifteen or more bone-gnawed corpses lie strewn across the floor. It was difficult to get an accurate count since some of the bodies were now in several pieces. The beasts had attacked indiscriminately; male and female cadavers, old and young. Dead-eyed expressions of terror and pain stared in every direction; features twisted into permanent scowls and silent screams. Few were lucky enough to have their heads and faces intact. All had too many broken bones to count and most had glossy red innards spilled out on the floor next to them.

Wherever there was exposed skin, there was missing flesh. Generous portions of skin and muscle had been torn from arms, necks, legs, shoulders, and faces. Fingers, sometimes entire hands, were missing. The body closest to the break room was already swelling to unnatural proportions as the flesh broke down and decayed. Skin turned gray, joints stiffened. Blood and spoiled groceries covered every surface in sight.

Someone had turned off the store's music system. *Thank God for that,* Lindsey thought to herself. If she were forced to take this all in while listening to smooth Jazz, it would have been more than her brain could take. It was still quiet and she couldn't make out any movement; another small and temporary bit of good fortune.

But she wouldn't be counting her blessings for long. Lindsey took three short steps down the rear aisle. Now that she was in the shopping area, there was nothing protecting her nostrils from the profane aroma of pissed pants, decomposition, and the spilled contents of intestines ripped open with claws and teeth. Her stomach pushed out a dry heave but Lindsey otherwise managed to keep her visceral reactions under control.

She needed to pick up the pace. A few quick steps around an overturned shopping cart brought her to the back end of the first row of shelves. Trying to be stealthy, she edged her way to the far side and looked down the aisle toward the cash registers. There was more blood and broken food containers but there weren't any people, dead or alive. She scurried past the opening and ducked behind the shelving unit at the back end of the next aisle to repeat the process; careful to remain unseen but not wanting to waste any more time.

She peered down the next aisle and it looked identical to the last. Planting her left foot to push off and make a quick dash to the next row of shelves, Lindsey felt something squish between her sneaker and the tile floor. Using the corner of a Corn Flakes box from the shelf above her, she scraped the offending substance from the bottom of her shoe. A flattened slab of skin met the floor with a wet slap. If she hadn't looked closely, she could have convinced herself it was a slice of salami or bologna. But Oscar Mayer products don't usually come with hair and a mole.

Before she could make her next move, a flurry of footsteps sounded from the front of the supermarket, followed by glass breaking and boxes falling to the ground. As she suspected, Lindsey wasn't alone in the store. No more screwing around. She had to get to the deli counter, find herself a knife or some other kind of weapon, and get out of there.

From where she stood, there were three corpses, a wheeled freezer chest for ice cream, and a pond of crimson fluid between Lindsey and the sandwich shop. It was only about thirty feet. If she went quickly, and could avoid falling as she crossed the mammoth puddle of blood, she could get to the cooking station before anyone could reach her. Without further hesitation, she took off.

Stepping over the mangled legs of the first body, Lindsey ran at full speed, splashing through the red lake. Thick droplets jumped up, soaking into her tan khakis with each footfall. She shoved the ice cream chest out of the way and rounded the corner at the deli stand to duck below the grill.

A stainless steel counter stood next to the grill. It had three drawers built in below the metallic work surface. Still on her knees to keep from being seen, Lindsey pulled open the bottom drawer. It was full of latex gloves and rolls of receipt paper. The middle drawer held an assortment of large spoons and ladles next to a stack of paper plates. Of course it was the top drawer, the last one she opened. There it was, a serrated slicing knife with a ten-inch blade and thick onyx handle. There were other knives too, most of them small with dull blades. Only the big one was worth taking.

Weapon in hand, Lindsey stood up and began walking back the way she had come. With some means of defense and a commotion erupting at the front of the store, taking the rear exit on the far end of the building seemed like the best option. Rounding the edge of the service counter to get back to the store's rear aisle, the young woman stopped, frozen in place. She gulped, unaware she was now holding her breath. Lindsey looked up to find herself standing face to face with a living obscenity.

The boy stood in her way, obstructing her path to the emergency exit. His nose was obviously broken. Its tip pointed to the side while the left nostril was pinched off, pinned against his upper cheek. Fully dilated pupils blocked out almost all the brown of his irises. Faint blue veins became visible through a pale complexion. His bottom lip was split open down the center and formed a spout from which blood and saliva spilled onto his neck and chest.

Scraps of pink flesh stuck to his baseball cap. Black slacks were shredded in front, letting bloody, bony knees poke through the openings. His green polo shirt was torn at the right shoulder. Dark brown stains had dried in the fibers of the fabric, forming a rigid crust on the sleeves and collar. A metal fork stuck out of his chest, just below the collar bone. Red spatter covered most of his name tag but Lindsey could still make out the word. *Lance.*

The infected teen reached for her, grabbing her by the front of her shirt. He growled and lurched forward, mouth open. Before he could bite into her, Lindsey swung the knife at his face. The blade slid in and ripped open a new hole below his right eye; a flash of bone visible for an instant. Reddish fluid dumped out of the new wound but it didn't slow the boy down. He lunged again. Teeth clattered together just shy of Lindsey's chin.

Lindsey plunged the blade into the boy's abdomen. Lance lost his grip on her shirt but didn't seem to be affected by the wound. Lindsey twisted the blade inside before pulling it free. It came out with a slurping sound and a spritz of red liquid. She jumped back to avoid being sprayed and in doing so, put more than two feet between herself and her attacker.

Still clutching the knife, the young woman turned and darted back toward the frozen food and bloating corpses, well aware that Lance would give chase. Halfway to the break room, she heard the clamor of something falling hard to the floor, followed immediately by what sounded like a head of cabbage being torn apart. Still moving, Lindsey chanced a look over her shoulder and found that Lance had slipped in the burgundy pool near the mobile freezer chest. His limbs flopped around in the blood and within seconds he was back on his feet.

As he stood, Lindsey immediately determined what had made that horrible noise; the sound of biting into an apple. Lance's right elbow was bent the wrong way, so that the joint pointed inward toward his torso.

How was he not writhing in pain and screaming in agony? How was he up and running again? Lindsey wasn't about to stop and ask him. She ran the last few steps to the entrance to the break room, grabbing the door as she went inside and slamming it closed. But something was in the way, blocking the door from closing. It was Lance's foot. In some bizarre violation of medical science and physics, he had caught up to her.

Lindsey threw her shoulder into the door, gripping the knob and trying to form a human wedge between the floor and the door. A bleeding left arm jutted in through the doorway and swiped at her hair and neck. She dodged the blows and thrust the full weight of her body into the door, trying to break her attacker's arm or leg in the process.

He had several stab wounds and a broken elbow. The aggressor wasn't going to be incapacitated by a few nudges from a thin plastic door. Pain didn't affect him and Lindsey wasn't strong enough to keep him out. She couldn't hurt him, couldn't outrun him, and in that contemptibly small employee lounge, there would be no place for her to hide. Lance reached in once more, wrapping his fingers around Lindsey's wrist. He pulled her hand away from the knob and pressed his way head-first into the break room.

Chapter 23

At just over four feet in length, the bottom of the device could not be easily reached. The young man had to lean all the way forward and use one of those lighters that normal people keep for when they're lighting a charcoal grill or a fireplace, the type with an extra-long metal neck. He pulled the small plastic trigger and directed orange flame into the center of a scorch-marked fire bowl jutting out from the top of a bulbous water chamber. A sprinkling of marijuana glowed red and turned to ash. Fluid sloshed and bubbled as swirls of smoke collected and rose up through a clear glass tube.

Challenging himself to hold the THC in his lungs for as long as he could, Danny stood the bong upright on the floor and counted off the seconds in his mind. His eyes went to the ceiling and he remained motionless. Twenty-seven seconds. Twenty-eight seconds. Something stirred in the next room but he ignored it. Thirty-one seconds. Thirty-two. His head felt lighter than air and a burning sensation spread from the center of his chest to his entire abdomen. Thirty-six. Danny lurched sideways, covering his mouth to block errant globs of spittle as he coughed out a much smaller cloud than he would have expected.

"Woo!" He cried out in satisfaction and sat back waiting for the drug to do its thing.

Danny was seated on the floor of his living room next to a ratty old bean bag chair. He rested his back against the front of a sagging leather couch with his legs straight out in front of him. There was a television on the far wall with the display showing a paused video game. The character on the screen was frozen mid-throw, ready to toss a grenade at a group of Nazi combatants.

He was about to continue playing and, without getting up, searched the room for the controller. Danny saw it resting about eight feet away, right in front of the console. With this, most of his interest in the game was lost. He'd have to stand, or at least crawl to the other side of the room, untangle the cord, and walk all the way back to his original position before the action could resume. It was just too much effort and he simply could not be bothered.

And besides, the game was silly and its whole premise was flawed. Was the intelligent American consumer expected to believe that a single person was capable of winning the second World War all by himself? Had a lone soldier traveled through Europe, killing Nazis one at a time until he reached the Fuhrer? Was that what had happened? That's not very strategic. Where was all his backup? The US government would certainly know better than to send just one guy. How could he possibly carry all those weapons and all that ammunition without any help? And what if he got lost or sprained his ankle? Then what?

"Yeah, then what?" Danny said aloud in an otherwise empty room. Then, through an intensifying haze of intoxication, he had another thought.

Was this even based on World War Two? It was never explicitly stated anywhere in the game. But it had to be, right? After all, the enemy fighters were all wearing Swastikas on their uniforms. Or did the game's programmers think that Nazis were somehow going to be a problem again? Was the world headed for another conflict with antisemitic Germans? Danny supposed there was no way to know for sure. The one thing of which he was positive, was that he wouldn't be purchasing another gaming system until they came out with one that could be controlled with thoughts and played via brainpower alone. With the controller beyond his immediate grasp, it may as well have been on Mars.

Danny needed a way to pass the time that didn't require too much movement. This didn't leave him with many options but he did know one way to amuse himself for at least a couple of minutes. Wedged between the bean bag and sofa was the glossy pearl-colored body of a Gibson ES-175. Danny pulled the guitar out by its neck and plopped it down in his lap. A thick black cord connected the instrument to a small speaker resting in the center of the floor.

The would-be musician tightened the tuning keys and twisted the volume knob. With no pick in sight, Danny used his pasty fingers to pluck the strings. Secretly wishing he'd have taken at least a single lesson, Danny went on strumming. He played no song in particular and filled the small apartment with amplified tone-deaf rubbish. What he lacked in talent, he more than made up for with enthusiasm. He bobbed his head, letting his long black hair drape over his closed eyes as he imagined himself on stage at Madison Square Garden, playing for thousands of adoring fans.

As his daydream developed, taking on a new level of clarity, Danny saw that the stands were filled with large breasted women in varying states of undress. A collection of bras and panties surrounded his feet, having been thrown on stage by his lustful female audience. *They must be taking their clothes off now to save some time after the show*, he thought. Through a series of knowing glances, the band members secretly agreed to make this fantasy concert a brief show. The after-party could get started early that night.

Danny's headbanging went on with no concern for harmony or rhythm. Or the neighbors. He played even louder. His fingers wildly manipulated guitar strings and he swung his hair around until someone's shouting brought the tune to an end.

"This stinks," Lucy asserted with enough volume to be heard over the noise.

"Huh?" Danny placed the guitar across his thighs and looked to his sister, who stood at the edge of the room in the entryway to the kitchen. She had on a pair of tight dark jeans and leather vest with no shirt underneath. Her attire showed off a lot of ink and skin. A full-colored array of flowers, snakes, and fiery skulls covered her exposed midsection, disappearing up her shirt and below the line of her pants. Danny frowned but didn't comment.

"It stinks," she repeated, not looking up from the cell phone in her hand.

"That's not very supportive," he replied. "You'll never be in the band with that sour attitude."

"What are you talking about? What band?" Lucy put the phone in her back pocket and continued, "And I'm not talking about the music. Don't get me wrong, that's terrible too, but I meant it actually reeks in here."

Turning away from her, Danny asked, "Since when do you mind the smell of pot? Usually you're drawn right to it. You want some, by the way?" He motioned to the novelty-sized smoking apparatus.

"No, you idiot. I mean, yes I do want some pot," Lucy was getting annoyed. "The kitchen garbage. It smells like shit. How is it not making your eyes burn?"

Danny's gaze followed Lucy's pointed finger to the bin, the lid of which was held open by the hefty pile of trash. "If it bugs you, take the bag out. You know where it goes."

"Why should I have to take it out?" she demanded. "It's your garbage."

"But *you're* the one who's bothered by it," Danny countered. With a satisfied grin, he added, "I'm perfectly content with my trash staying where I put it. If you find it offensive, I'll grant you permission to get rid of it."

"What a marvelous person you are," she spat sarcastically.

"I like to think so," Danny answered through a yawn, stretching both hands over his head and arching his back.

Exasperated, the young woman threw her hands down at her sides. "Well?" Her voice developed a sharp tone.

"Well what?"

"I'm going to stand here and repeat myself until you get off your lazy ass and take the garbage out." Lucy crossed her arms over her chest and stared at her prone sibling in the next room.

"Whining and complaining until you get your way- is that how the modern, empowered woman gets ahead nowadays?" Danny meant to sound playful but his sister wasn't in the mood for his jokes. Her eyes burned holes through his dumb smiling face. Five long seconds of silence passed before Lucy put her plan into action.

"Daniel!" she announced, cupping her hands around her mouth to form a megaphone. "Your kitchen stinks like ass. Stop being a slob and take out the garbage."

 When about ten seconds had passed with neither person speaking, Danny made a great show of yawning and then turning to face his sister. He wore a mask of fake surprise, as though he hadn't noticed her standing there until that very moment.

He raised his eyebrows and asked, "I'm sorry Lucy, did you say something?"

The next sound coming from Lucy could only be described as primal frustration. Mashing her teeth together, Lucy punctuated her moaning screechy vocal discharge by bringing her fists up to her forehead and then flinging her fingers outward in an exploding hands gesture.

"Alright, alright," Danny said with a labored breath. With some effort, he pulled himself off the floor, not minding where the guitar happened to fall in the process. "But first-"

He hoisted the bong from its resting place and spun the lighter around his index finger, as if he were a Wild West gunslinger twirling a six-shooter after a successful duel. With practiced precision, he grabbed the handle and snapped the trigger on the long Bic. Danny held the flame over the cannabis and the young stoner fiercely drew in another bong load. It was like he was about to embark on a long, arduous assignment and weed smoke provided him with the fuel necessary to complete the task that lie before him. Now that he'd adequately prepared himself, Danny rounded the edge of the sofa and passed by Lucy as he trudged into the kitchen to tend to the waste can.

"Thank you so much," Lucy patronized her brother as he walked by with his shoulders slumped. "Look at you being a big boy and doing chores. While you're at it, feel free to do some general tidying up. This place is gross."

Danny rolled his eyes and lifted the lid to the bin. The acrid odor of week-old chicken wings, pustular tomatoes, and fuzzy green mayonnaise pierced his nostrils.

"Don't press your luck," he warned. "I'm doing this as a favor to you. I personally don't mind leaving everything right where it is."

With a flare of exaggeration, Danny sniffed in the acerbic scent. A wrinkled nose and watering tear ducts betrayed his words. He wasn't fooling anyone.

"You sure about that, pissy-eyes?" Lucy challenged.

"Positive," came Danny's defiant response. "But, explain something to me. Why is it that you're the one who wants the garbage out, but I'm the one who has to do it?"

"Because it's your apartment, your mess, and your trash," came Lucy's smug reply. "And besides, I'm a guest here."

"*Leech* is more like it," he mumbled, lifting the overstuffed bag from the plastic contained.

"Excuse me?" Lucy snapped accusingly, fixing him with a look that told him he'd better mind his tone.

Tying the drawstring into an airtight knot, Danny looked to his sister and asked, "So how long do you plan to be a guest here, exactly?"

"Are you going to kick me out?"

"No, nothing like that." Danny kept talking as he crouched in front of the sink and opened the lower cupboard where he kept the box of trash bags. "I sorta thought you and Darryl would've worked things out by now."

Lucy's voice softened. "So did I. But he hasn't been answering my calls the last two days. Do you think he could be seeing someone else?"

"Probably." Danny kicked the cupboard door closed and placed a new bag into the trash can.

"Don't be a dick." Lucy looked insulted.

"Well, you're a pain in the ass," Danny explained as he closed the lid. "I mean, you did just throw a tantrum about taking the garbage out."

"Ugh, I don't know why I talk to you." She turned to walk out of the room, heading toward the back of the apartment.

"Because of my witty insight," he told her. Danny once again considered her appearance as she walked away. Observing that her pants were so tight they forced her to walk like a stiff-legged robot, he called to her, "You going to get dressed then?"

"Dressed for what?" she shouted back.

"Dressed to not look like a streetwalker. Unless that's part of your plan to replace Darryl, in which case, it should work fine."

Lucy stopped and turned back to face him; her face reddening with anger.

Though it was meant as a joke, Danny's statement had missed its mark. Smiling through a thinning cloud of pot smoke, he tried again. "I'm sorry. That was out of line. Obviously the guilt of staying here rent-free has driven you to working the streets so you can contribute financially. It's good of you to take responsibility and earn your own way."

"Screw you, Danny." Lucy shot back, "You think you have any right doling out fashion advice? You look like an idiot with those scrawny arms and your cut-off tee shirts."

Danny held his hand to his heart in mock-hurt. "Please. This is a great look," he argued.

"It is if you're homeless," she remarked as she stepped into the bathroom. And with that, the feuding had ceased.

Changing the topic, the poorly-dressed man-child asked, "Hey, you gonna be in there long?"

"I doubt it. Why?"

151

"I'll need to use the latrine," Danny patted his tummy. "I got a sloppy stew a' brewin'.'"

"You are so disgusting," Lucy told him, as though she'd never been more repulsed. Then she tacked on, "If you ever find yourself wondering why you're single and no girls are interested in dating you, this is why."

Danny waved a dismissive hand. "You're crazy. Women find me charming and irresistible. And not to mention handsome."

"And delusional," she jabbed. Before closing the bathroom door, the young lady pointed to a space behind her brother and asked, "Don't you have something to do right now?"

"I'm going, I'm going," he told her, turning his attention back to the garbage bin.

Moments later, Danny carried the bulging sack of refuse down the stairs and through the lobby. He pushed through the glass doors and immediately felt the sun's rays soaking into the pale skin of his bare arms. He whistled the Star Wars theme and between verses, caught a whiff of old vegetables and fetid meat. Danny wouldn't tell her as much, but Lucy was right. The garbage had gotten pretty stinky. Hopefully the stench wouldn't linger in the kitchen for too long. He could always open a window, or turn on a fan, or spray some Febreze. But how many errands was he expected to perform in a single day?

Danny turned the corner to the side of the building to find the big green trash bins lined up against the wall. He huffed quietly, all four containers were filled to the brim with black, clear, and white plastic bags. With a shrug, the young man tossed his own garbage on top of the smallest pile. It shifted, expelled a puff of tainted air, and then fell to the ground. Not wanting to handle the muck for any longer than was required, and with no desire to risk slopping any leaking sludge onto himself, he left it where it was. Heading back to the front walkway, he muttered, "Close enough."

The reefer enthusiast was halfway back to the entrance when he stopped, thinking he heard someone say his name. Danny listened for a second but didn't hear anything further. He started moving again when the voice shrieked once more.

"Danny!"

The long-haired youth looked up to see a young woman leaning over the railing of her second-floor balcony. "Hey Jenna. What's happening?"

"What are you doing outside?"

Danny, senses numb from inebriation, failed to detect the concern in her words. Squinting, he held a hand over his brow to block out the sunlight. "Well, Lucy's still staying at my place and she was carrying on about the trash in the kitchen. *It stinks, get it out of here*, she whined. I tried telling her if she's got a problem with the smell, then-"

"That's not what I'm talking about." Jenna sounded like a parent scolding a child. She put one foot back inside her apartment, looked to be listening for something, and then stepped back out. "Haven't you been watching the news?"

With a snicker, Danny pretended to straighten an invisible bow tie and answered sarcastically, "Oh but of course. I've been checking in on the stock ticker and minding my investments."

"Damn it, this is serious." She tightened her ponytail and went on, "You remember that guy who came after you and Charles the other night?"

It was about then that Danny noticed the baseball bat in the corner behind her, leaning against the siding. "Yeah," he replied cautiously.

"According to the news, there's more people like him- crazy people. They're all over the place and attacking anyone they come across. They're-" Jenna's words got caught in her throat as she struggled to accept what she said. "They're eating each other. It's from some type of brain infection or something. They weren't very clear but the police are saying that everyone should stay inside and keep their doors locked."

Danny waved a hand at her. "Come on Jenna, you know how they love to sensationalize their stories. The news is always blowing things out of proportion."

The young woman stood fully upright and pointed to an area along the right side of the parking lot. "Oh yeah, then where do you suppose that came from?"

From a distance, a slowly sobering Danny looked to the spot indicated. A Grand Marquis was parked with the engine off. Its trunk was open but no one was around. Less than three feet from the bumper, was a thick red puddle. A large tire iron rested several inches from the burgundy pond. At the edge of the liquid, the side closest to the building, was a long streak leading toward the adjacent lawn.

"Isn't that Adam's car?" Danny asked, looking back to his neighbor.

"Yeah, or Albert's. I'm not sure. I've seen both of them drive it." Jenna nervously shifted her weight from one foot to the other.

"Maybe a nosebleed?" he offered.

"I wouldn't count on it," she answered; no hint of humor in her voice.

"So what happened?"

Jenna let out a long breath and rubbed her forehead. "I can't say for sure. I heard a commotion and came out to look. I saw Adam and Albert walking inside. There was a huge bald guy lying in the middle of the blood. I thought he was just knocked out, but... but then Albert came back outside."

"And then what?" Maintaining the parent-child dynamic, Danny could have passed for a small boy begging his mother to finish a bedtime story.

She swallowed hard and brushed her fingers through her hair, tucking a few stray strands behind her ear. "The bald guy was dead. Albert dragged him around the side of the building. It took forever with his bad leg and all. I don't think he saw me watching him, which is fine by me. Last thing I needed was for him to ask me to help."

"So, what did you do?" Danny questioned. "Call the police?"

"I tried," Jenna told him, "But I couldn't get through."

"Couldn't get through?" he asked, repeating her words.

"No, I kept getting that 'All circuits are currently busy' message. 'Please hang up and try your call again later.' I tried for about fifteen minutes before I gave up. That's when I turned on the news."

"So, what do you think we should do?"

"First, I think you should get inside. Come upstairs and we'll talk about it up here." Jenna made a waving gesture to illustrate the importance of her words.

"Wait just a second. Are you telling me there's a body somewhere over there in the grass?" Danny asked, eyes wide with excited curiosity. "I gotta check this out."

"Danny, no!"

153

"Just hold on, I'll only be a second." He started to move back to the place where he'd thrown his garbage.

"Come inside," pleaded Jenna. "Danny, it isn't safe out there."

"I'm hardly worried about a corpse," came his reply.

"That's not what I'm talking about. On the news, they said anyone can be afflicted with the virus or whatever it is. Anyone you see outside can be one of them," Jenna warned; the volume of her voice lowering considerably.

"I don't see anyone out here."

"Are you high?" Jenna didn't realize just how accurate she was in that assumption. "There's someone right across the street."

Danny looked to confirm she was telling the truth. A pudgy boy, about seventeen years of age and wearing a tie-dye shirt, wandered along the sidewalk. Following a few steps behind, was a taller kid of roughly the same age. He was rail-thin and wore no shirt.

"Okay, there's people outside. So?"

"So? How are you not getting this?" Her voice got louder than she'd intended. Lowering it again, she continued, "You need to get inside and lock up. Right now."

Jenna watched the pair of teens across the street. They had stopped moving after her last outburst. The boys were now looking in her direction and walking toward the roadway.

"Them?" Danny pointed, "I'm not worried about them. They look harmless."

"Maybe you should look again," Jenna suggested. "As you make you way inside."

The teens had crossed the four lanes of traffic and were stepping onto the curb. From their vantage point, neither Jenna nor Danny could see the boys' wounds at first. As they approached, a long and jagged incision became visible on the skinny kid's right side, running from his ribs to just past his belly button. His companion's tie-dye shirt was not tie-dyed after all. He wore a plain white shirt with a tremendous number of stains from both grass and blood.

"Danny get in here now!" Jenna was practically screaming at him.

"I'll be in soon," he answered coolly. Danny combed back his long black hair.

When the pair of bloodied youths were about forty feet from Danny, they broke into a sprint; the tall skinny one pulling well ahead of his partner. The young woman on her balcony saw this and cursed loudly as she ran into her apartment.

The pale stoner crouched slightly and held both arms out in front of him. Having never been in a fight, Danny did his best impression of what he thought a boxer might look like. He sort of looked like Popeye, minus the muscles and sailor's cap. And the anchor tattoos. And the can of spinach in his pocket. Okay, so he looked nothing like Popeye. Aside from the penchant for pipes and goofy speech mannerisms, the two didn't have all that much in common.

True, he had no combat experience. But there was no reason this triviality should affect his confidence. Danny balled his fists. He aimed his knuckles at his onrushing foes and announced, "It's clobberin' time!"

The long-haired man took two decisive steps toward his attackers and readied himself to throw the first real punch of his life. It would be at an odd angle and he'd have to time it just right. The first

154

lunatic was nearly a foot taller than Danny and he was coming upon him quickly. The novice warrior wound back and snapped forward like a pitcher unleashing a fastball. His right hand cut through the humid breeze; a solid fist of clammy white knuckles rocketing toward the boy's jaw. The punch was sent far too early, with too much weight behind it, and with no face to wallop.

Danny stumbled; his body's own momentum pulling him forward and threatening to yank him to the ground. He planted his left hand on the pavement and managed to keep himself upright. The skinny thug failed to anticipate this sudden change in position and ran a number of steps past his target. It was a mistake that might buy Danny a few seconds to regroup. He scrambled to ready himself so he could try again and hopefully land a strike, but he wouldn't have time. The brute was already coming back fast. The underfed monster was little more than a foot away and his fat friend was closing in.

A brittle crack broke through the air. The stoned fighter thrust both hands forward to push the savage back and give himself a little space. Before his palms could make contact, the shirtless barbarian twisted and crumpled to the ground.

"What the f-" Danny murmured.

"Get out of the way!" Jenna yelled from her balcony, hoisting an all-black Savage Arms model 64 FXP.

Danny looked back, stunned to see her looking through the scope of a small rifle held up to her shoulder. His surprise left him gawking at her instead of heeding her command. Another sharp crack split the air. A small cloud of dust and broken pavement jumped up from the ground about a yard away from Danny's left foot.

"Sorry," called the shooter.

She squeezed off two more shots at the fat monstrosity, who was still charging right for Danny. The first bullet hit him in the stomach and didn't seem to affect him. In fact, the only way to tell he'd been shot was by the fresh blossom of dark fluid forming a new stain on his shirt. The second round blasted into the center of his chest and the heavy beast dropped to his knees. Two quick gasps escaped his lips before he collapsed face-first onto the paved lot.

Adrenaline eclipsed the effects of the drugs. The pale man in his stylish cut-off tee shirt was now completely sober. He praised the efforts of his trigger-happy savior. "Nice one!"

"So do you believe me now?" Jenna lowered the rifle and called down, "Didn't I tell you?"

"Take it easy. No one likes a braggart." Danny began moving toward the entrance to the building. "Hey, where'd you get a gun?"

With a nearly imperceptible smile, Jenna withdrew a small magazine from in front of the trigger guard and counted the number of remaining bullets. "My dad got it for me when I was little. It's a twenty-two caliber. No kick-back so I was able to handle it. We used to go target shooting on weekends when he didn't have to work."

"Nice," Danny commented. "Looks like it came in handy today."

"When I moved out of my parents' house, my mom made me bring it with me." She grinned thoughtfully. "I thought she was crazy. I told her I'd never need to keep a gun in the apartment but she insisted."

"See," Danny took on a mock-condescending tone. "Now aren't you glad you listened to your mother?"

"Hey, it wasn't me down there with those things. Aren't *you* glad I listened?" she asked. "Now get your stupid ass inside."

Chapter 24

Erie Avenue was coming up quickly. Too quickly. The anti-lock brakes protested, churning and grinding as Jim pressed hard on the pedal and cranked the steering wheel all the way to the left. At this irresponsibly fast rate of speed, a last-second stomp on the brakes wasn't enough to keep the car from sliding out of control. The front wheels cut hard but the blue coupe carried on in its original direction, gliding sideways through the intersection as if he'd tried stopping on a plane of ice. Inertia spun the ass end of the car in a wild arc, leaving the driver unable to straighten the wheel.

Screeching tires produced a cloud of smoke from beneath the vehicle as it drifted farther to the right. Both passenger's side tires skittered into the dirt shoulder before the car slowed enough for Jim to regain control and straighten his steering. Rubber fought to grip pavement. Violent torque kicked up dozens of roadside pebbles to ping against the undercarriage and fenders. A heavy foot punched the gas pedal, propelling the vehicle through a haze of still-rising dust and leaving behind a pair of smoldering skid marks.

Jim tried to keep his focus on the task of driving. Looking ahead through the windshield, he reached across the interior and felt around with his right hand. His slapdash maneuvering had jostled the car's contents and as a result, the shotgun slipped to the far edge of the passenger's seat where it got lodged between the cushion and door panel.

The supermarket was still a few minutes away but Jim wanted to keep the gun within reach, just in case he needed it in the meantime. Car thieves and cannibals were not likely to pause their attack to let their victim retrieve a misplaced firearm. They can be really rude that way. Jim only swerved once before his fingers located the wooden stock. He grabbed the weapon and positioned it so the trigger rested only inches away from the gear shifter. His hand then went to his pockets to make sure the shells hadn't spilled out. For the most part, they hadn't.

Good. Jim's false sense of security had been restored. He pressed the accelerator down to the floorboard. The throttle opened wide and the tailpipe belched out a fresh cloud of exhaust. The screaming engine could be heard from several blocks away. The transmission downshifted and the driver's back slammed into its seat cushion as the car rushed ahead. Jim's metaphorical finish line was now within sight.

Bennett's Supermarket was less than a mile away and home was just a few more miles after that. But was that the plan, to go home? If it was, would Lindsey go with him? Where else would she go? What if she had already gone somewhere? Was she even still alive? If not, that would pretty much settle the debate about what to do next.

Don't get ahead of yourself, Jim thought. *There's a lot you need to do before you can think about going home.*

He was approaching a disabled minivan that had stalled in the road approximately two-hundred feet in front of him. The vehicle was turned sideways to obstruct a full traffic lane and it was surrounded by a small flesh-hungry horde. Jim prayed the van's driver and passengers were able to get away before the freaks showed up but as he neared the scene, it became clear they hadn't been so lucky.

The passenger's side door was wide open and a slumped-over torso was still belted into the seat. Bones barely held to withering flesh as two humanoid monsters used their teeth and claws to pull away skin and muscle. Blood had been sprayed all over the interior, enough to block the view through most of the windows. The tinted glass on the tailgate was smashed in. Through the opening, Jim could make out the movement of multiple bodies climbing over seats and jockeying for position.

Erie Avenue only has one lane in each direction. As there were no cars heading towards him, Jim steered onto the opposite side of the street to avoid hitting the van. He kept a watchful eye on the vehicle as he passed by. Along the driver's side, another pair of murderous creatures hunched over a shredded carcass; hands and teeth pulling madly at a mass of guts and bones.

The Pontiac zoomed past the cannibals and gore-filled van without incident. Jim had thought about pulling over and wasting the ghouls with a few blasts from the shotgun but he couldn't afford any further delays. And from the looks of it, there was no one left to save. His efforts and ammunition would be to no one's benefit.

He was coming up to Division Street, which was one-way only and not the direction he needed to go. Jim wasn't about to waste more time driving several blocks out of his way just so he could turn around and approach the store while facing the appropriate direction. The coupe whizzed past the shitty, rundown muffler shop on the corner and Jim made another sharp left turn. He managed to negotiate this intersection without losing control of the car. The entrance to the supermarket was now only a hundred feet away.

A bright yellow Volkswagen sped at Jim head-on. The driver swerved hard to his right and blared the horn but, gave Jim plenty of room to get around. It was streaked in fluids of various colors and the Beetle was riddled with dents and scrapes that probably hadn't been there an hour earlier.

Another tire-squealing left turn and Jim was in the parking lot of Bennett's Supermarket. There were more cars there than he'd expected to see. Some were still running. Others looked like they'd never run again. Shoppers and clerks still rushed through the exits; each trying to be faster than their raving stalkers, or at least faster than the nearest employee or customer.

With a quick reaction time and a few slick maneuvers, Jim was able to avoid hitting the stopped vehicles and groups of pedestrians. He wheeled the Pontiac around the first row of parked cars and stopped halfway between a shopping cart receptacle and the fire lane in front of the building. The windows rolled up. The ignition turned off. The seat belt unfastened.

His heart was in his throat again. Jim's palms were runny with sweat. He reminded himself to breathe as his right hand absently grabbed for the shotgun. A wet and shaking thumb pressed the top lever and the twin barrels dropped down. Two fresh shells beamed up at him, ready for action. Fingers tapped the outside of his front pocket. The rest of the shells were still there. Lightheaded, dizzy, and more afraid than he'd ever been, Jim snapped the barrels closed and opened the car door.

No sooner had the door closed behind him than Jim found he was already under attack. A fiend in a ripped yellow tee shirt came charging at him. The ghoul's skin was greasy and pale. Blood dripped down his face from a receding hairline. Oozing bite marks covered his bare arms. Broken and twisted fingers reached for his victim as he closed the distance.

There was no time to think. Jim wouldn't have a chance to plant his feet and secure the weapon at his shoulder. He gracelessly leveled the shotgun in front of himself and squeezed the trigger. The top barrel belched out an invisible mist of lead pellets. Screams of passersby were barely audible to his ringing ears. The force of the shot kicked the gun backwards into the center of his chest, sure to leave an oval-shaped bruise.

The shot connected. It hit him in the leg, not the head or face like Jim would have preferred, but it was enough to put the creep on the ground. The skin that used to hold the knee cap in place was nothing but frayed slices of tissue and hair. The patella itself; a shattered porcelain saucer painted red. That filthy bastard squirmed and flopped on the concrete, still trying to get to his prey.

For his part, Jim wasn't startled by this. He knew well enough by now that a wound, even a substantial one from a shotgun blast, wasn't necessarily enough to keep these shitheads at bay. Jim hated the idea of leaving one of these creatures alive. They were a scourge that must be exterminated. A gunshot from point blank range would make for a fitting send-off but this one was already down, essentially neutralized. And since there wasn't an infinite supply of ammunition, Jim decided not to waste another shell.

He made a move to walk around the body and head into the store. As he did this, the monster reached out and grabbed for his leg. Jim was too quick for him. He lifted his left foot off the ground and stomped down, pinning the beast's hand to the cement. Knuckles popped under Jim's full body weight. Phalanges snapped like bleeding pretzel rods as he swiveled his heel. The loon bellowed a hateful moan as the flesh of his hand was churned against hot pavement.

Nothing else stood between Jim and the building's automatic doors, which thankfully still seemed to be working. He ran the remaining distance to the entrance. Sprinting with the gun raised and held out in front of him made for clumsy, uneven strides. The added weight of ammo-filled pockets didn't help either. His shorts were in a losing battle against gravity. The rescue attempt was not off to a smooth start.

Still outside, he pressed his back to the front wall, just inches from the doorway. Pulling in a mouthful of air, Jim held the gun under his armpit to free both hands for a moment. The dark fabric of his polo shirt felt cool and heavy with perspiration. Sucking in his gut, he hiked up his shorts and tightened his black leather belt. Jim dried both palms against the side of his shirt before planting a firm grip on his weapon; left hand on the forend, right hand ready to pull the trigger.

He kicked away from the wall and launched himself into the lobby. Sprinting through the bottle return area and dodging overturned carts, Jim crossed the threshold into the supermarket to find himself accosted once more. Trying to be stealthy, he ducked behind a wooden pallet holding a four-foot stack of soda cans. But it wasn't quick enough. He'd already been spotted by a big man with a raging infection.

About fifteen feet from Jim's cola barrier, halfway between the front of the building and the cash registers, was a large bottled water display. More than a hundred cases were piled on top of each other to form a chest-high pyramid of hydration. Running past the stacked cases, was a very large, very angry supermarket employee. And it wasn't the small paycheck and lousy working conditions that had got him so heated.

The monster's name was Todd, or at least that's what it said on his name tag. Todd was bigger than Jim, standing over six feet tall and built like a college cornerback; a cornerback with a smooth tan and too much hair gel. Thick, vascular arms hung from wide shoulders. Forearm muscles twisted and flexed with each movement. Specks of blood dotted a chiseled jawline. Jim would have hated him even if Todd wasn't about to try to kill him. Handsome cocksucker.

Todd was much more intact than most of the other miscreants. His Bennett's Supermarket uniform was still mostly clean. His baseball cap was missing, but you can't expect him to cover up that slick hairdo with a ratty old hat. You'd miss it if you weren't looking for it but the good-looking brute was missing the tip of his right middle finger. That was all it took, a small open wound; more than enough for the virus to get in.

Jim wasn't keen enough to make this observation. About the severed digit, that is. But he knew

159

well enough there was something peculiar about the clerk, something dangerous. The berserk expression and loud growling probably gave it away. That, and the trailing ribbon of drool.

There was no time for Jim to find a place to hide, he'd already been spotted. The pretty-boy prick was in front of him, a couple yards beyond the twelve-ounce soft drinks. *Make a run for it.* The thought darted across his mind but Jim knew he wouldn't be able to outrun the savage named Todd. Why hadn't he taken better care of himself and stayed in shape? Jeez, go for a jog every once in a while, Jim. You know where the gym is.

He needed to go left, deeper into the store, where he assumed the employee lounge would be located. Even if he could move faster than the contagious clerk, Jim knew he would give chase. The last thing he wanted to do was find Lindsey's hiding place with a horde of these bastards nipping at his heels. There was no way around it. It was time to kill Todd.

With his weapon held tight, your shotgun-wielding protagonist swung the barrel over the cases of soda and fired at his advancing enemy. So, Jim isn't what you'd call a marksman. Even using a shotgun, where accuracy is all but guaranteed, his shooting leaves something to be desired. Some of the pellets definitely connected. Todd's shirt twisted slightly; its fabric tearing at the left side of his abdomen. Most of the shot, however, took out the top rung of the bottle pyramid. Plastic cases burst open, spraying Todd and dousing him with more water than blood.

"Balls!" Jim's foe was still up. Instead of running for cover, Jim stood his ground and was shocked to observe that his opponent was no longer moving in his direction.

Thrashing his arms, Todd shrieked and clawed at his skin. He yanked the fabric on his shirt like he was trying to rip it off. The beast howled and stepped back to avoid the growing puddle on the floor. Todd's venomous gaze fixed on the streams of water that flowed from damaged bottles. His screaming was more than just rageful and demented. It almost sounded like he had a trace of fear in his voice.

Jim pressed the top lever on the shotgun and a smoldering pair of spent plastic shells fell to the floor. He grabbed two more from his pocket and loaded them into the barrels as he leveled the shotgun and aimed for where Todd had been standing. But he was no longer there. The beast seemed to have forgotten all about Jim. Instead of continuing the hunt, Todd was wailing and flinging his arms around as he backed away from the pool of spilled water.

It was time to move again. Jim began walking further into the store, stopping briefly to hike up his shorts once more. He made his way down the first aisle behind the cash registers; gun at the ready as he went. With racks of soup cans to his right and shelves of Minute Rice to his left, Jim could get to the back of the building reasonably undetected.

At the end of the aisle, Jim found he had arrived at the sandwich shop. Between himself and the deli counter was an overturned freezer chest filled with ice cream novelties. Inches away, was a large pool of blood which looked to have been recently disturbed. A pair of red footsteps led away from the puddle to Jim's left and toward the back corner of the store near the restrooms. Jim knew right away that he'd find Lindsey at the end of this gory trail.

From somewhere close by, the sound of shuffling and what might have been voices could be heard. He was getting close. His stride hastened to a jog, just steady enough to keep the shotgun even at his shoulder.

Right by the bathrooms, Jim spotted an artificial wall made out of flimsy partitions. At the end closest to the back of the building was a door slightly ajar with a sign that read, *Employees Only.* This had to be the break room. And the red footprints went right up to the doorway.

160

"Lindsey?" he called. No one answered but the scuffling continued. What he originally thought to be voices sounded more like the grunts of a wounded animal.

Creeping toward the room's entrance, Jim tried desperately not to make another sound. His index finger slid onto the trigger. He wiped beads of sweat from his forehead with his left hand, drying it on the front of his shirt before gripping tight to the gun's forestock. Pulling in a deep breath and holding it, he stepped through the doorway ready to destroy whatever he might find.

But he wasn't prepared for what he saw. The first thing that came into view was a pair of legs wearing tan khakis and white sneakers. They were sprawled out on the floor. The legs definitely belonged to Lindsey and they weren't moving. A demon in a green uniform was on top of her, pinning her torso to the ground and leaning in toward her neck. Jim's heart might have stopped for a moment. He could feel the blood drain from his face. It was the realization of what he feared most. He was too late.

Chapter 25

There were four twenties, seven tens, four fives, a lonely fifty which had been torn in half and taped back together, and sixteen singles. Two hundred thirty-six dollars. The cash had been divided into five neat stacks and placed beside a few pens and a yellow legal pad.

Lucy had changed into a loose-fitting black tee shirt and tied her hair back with a white bandanna. She sat at the kitchen table sipping from a mug of coffee and scratching notes to herself on the pad of paper. How could she only have two hundred thirty-six dollars? While she'd been staying with her brother, Lucy had gone out of her way to save every dime she could. With no car payment, no lavish purchases, and no nights out with friends, she would have expected to have saved nearly five hundred by now. Maybe some of the bills had been overlooked or misplaced.

Some of the notes must have gotten separated from the rest. They were probably lost and mixed in with the clutter inside her purse. The young woman glanced down to the black leather sack at her feet. It was open; the top completely unzipped. There wasn't any cash staring back at her.

From the next room, Lucy could hear the knob rattle and the front door creak open. She saw Danny walk in but didn't say anything. He strolled past her to the other side of the kitchen and poured himself a glass of water from the sink. Danny slurped it down, spilling a little and breathing loudly between gulps.

"You gonna close the door?" Lucy called after him, keeping her eyes on the money piled in front of her.

Danny finished his water. As he poured himself a second glass, he said, "No. Jenna's going to come by, she'll be over in a sec."

"Jenna?" Lucy raised her eyebrows, spinning a pen between her fingers as she turned to face her brother. "Who's Jenna? Don't tell me you've got a girlfriend."

"Be serious." Danny chuckled as he placed his glass back in the sink. With both hands, the pale stoner made a sweeping gesture from his head to his waist. "You know this is in high demand. I couldn't possibly limit myself to a single lady."

"Oh please." Lucy rolled her eyes and told him, "I've got a pretty good hunch that you're currently at zero ladies and the only way that's going to change is if you bump into one between your bong and the refrigerator. Probably not much chance of that happening."

"Yeah, yeah," Danny waved her off and started walking toward the living room.

"Well?" Lucy asked firmly.

"Well what?"

"Are you going to tell me who this girl is?"

"Girl?"

"You stoned idiot!" Lucy yelled. "You said Jenna was coming over. Who is Jenna?"

"She's a chick who lives in the building, over on that side." Danny pointed at the wall opposite the kitchen sink. "I was talking to her when I was outside. She's all worked up about something she saw on the news and said she wants to come over and talk about it."

"Alright." Lucy wasn't really listening anymore. After making another notation on the scratch pad, she reached a hand into her pocket and pulled out a wad of money. Three crumpled bills were unfolded, counted, and added to a pile on the tabletop. "Two thirty-nine."

"What are you doing?" Danny asked, changing direction and heading for the kitchen table.

Lucy sighed. "Since you're in such a hurry for me to move out, I'm trying to figure out how much money I need to save before I can get my own place."

"Cool. So how much do you have?" Danny reached for one of the stacks, as if he was going to count it for her.

"Hey!" Lucy shouted. Swatting his hand away, "Keep your dick-beaters off my money."

"Jeez, take it easy." Danny backed away from the table, holding his hands up to show he hadn't taken any. "Just curious. How much is there?"

"Not enough," she answered through a groan.

"And why is it spread out all over the table?"

Lucy straightened the piles as she explained, "I'm trying to work out a budget. I have one pile for groceries, one for rent, another for the electric bill-"

"Don't forget the gas bill," Danny blurted as he balled his hands into fists, lifted his right foot off the floor, and pushed out a big squealing fart.

"You're so gross," Lucy replied in disgust. She had to shout to be heard over Danny, who was laughing like a madman and fanning the air to waft the gas in her direction.

"Whoo!" he cried, waving a hand in front of his face. "Uh oh, that one had some punch to it."

"Get out of here!" Lucy commanded, trying to sound mad but unable to hide the hint of a grin.

"Oh come on," Danny pretended she'd hurt his feelings. "Just look at you- ya get a couple of bucks in your pocket and suddenly you're too good to enjoy a good fart?"

Despite the funk in the air, she was able to breathe and let out a few giggles. Lucy threw the pen at her brother. "You stink like a hundred hobos."

"And you thought the trash smelled bad," Danny joked. He bent to retrieve the Bic and tossed it back to her. "I bet you're going to miss all this when you move out."

"Um, hello?"

Danny and Lucy looked to the open doorway and found Jenna standing just outside the apartment. She had the rifle slung over her shoulder and held a baseball bat in her left hand. Her hair was in a tight ponytail and she had on sneakers, jeans, and a long-sleeve denim shirt buttoned all the way up.

"Come on in," Danny invited. Gesturing toward the kitchen table, he said, "Jenna, this is my sister Lucy. Lucy, Jenna."

Introductions ignored, Jenna walked in. She closed and locked the door behind her with the deadbolt and the chain lock. She gave a slight tug on the chain and pulled hard on the doorknob. Satisfied the door was secure, she addressed the so-called man of the house. "Danny, you shouldn't leave the door open. Make sure you keep it locked from now on."

163

Then she caught herself. Jenna was being rude; a trait which under normal circumstances, she would avoid at any cost. Stepping toward the young woman seated at the table, Jenna held her hand out to shake and said, "I'm sorry, that sounded really impolite. It's nice to meet you, Lucy."

Lucy stood up to greet her but stiffened when she caught sight of the rifle. "Why do you have a gun?" she asked sharply. Incredulous, Lucy turned to her brother, "Why does she have a gun?"

Jenna glanced down to her extended hand and let it fall to her side. She walked to the opposite end of the kitchen where she stood with her back to the refrigerator. Jenna set the bat down, propping it up against the front of the oven. Making sure to keep the barrel pointed at the floor, she slid the rifle off her shoulder and held it with both hands.

"That wasn't a rhetorical question," Lucy stated flatly. "And what's with the bat?"

"Danny, didn't you tell her?" Jenna asked; her tone thick with disbelief.

"Tell me what?" Lucy demanded. She was now standing beside her chair.

"How could you not tell her?" Jenna called to Danny. Scolding, "What's the matter with you?"

"Take it easy, everyone. No need to flip out." Danny shrugged his shoulders. He leaned against the kitchen counter and brushed back a handful of long black hair. "Lucy, I forgot to tell you. There's zombies now."

Lucy rolled her eyes and replied, "Very funny, dickhead. You want to tell me what's *really* going on?"

"Zombies," Danny repeated.

Jenna cringed at the word but the others didn't notice. Without realizing it, she had moved her hand down the stock of the gun. Her index finger lightly tapped the safety button.

"Right," Lucy answered sardonically. She turned to their guest and asked, "Can *you* tell me what's happening?"

Before the young woman could respond, Danny persisted. "I'm telling you the truth. It's zombies. Jenna said they've been talking about it on the news and we just saw some outside. She shot two of them!" His speech was pressured but he sounded excited; no trace of panic or concern in his words.

"Zombies?" Lucy's question was clearly directed at Jenna. She wasn't ready to buy into her brother's story just yet.

"The news didn't use the word *zombie*," Jenna corrected. She now held the rifle like a cane, with her hand on the buttstock and the barrel resting on the kitchen floor. Facing Lucy, she clarified, "They're not sure what it is, maybe a virus- they don't know yet. But something is affecting people, making them crazy and violent."

"That's Zombies!" Danny exclaimed, waving his arms in the air. "Plus, you told me they were eating people!"

"Okay, I'll play along," Lucy huffed, brushing the cash aside and taking a seat on top of the table. "Dead people- sorry, *undead* people are digging out of their graves and looking for brains to eat. I think we're safe, no sign of any brains in this place."

"The news didn't say they were zombies, Danny." Jenna's voice grew firm with irritation. Why wasn't he taking this seriously? "They aren't corpses. They're very much alive and have some type of infection that's making them act like that. And as you witnessed, you don't have to shoot them in the head to kill them."

"I'm not saying they're old school zombies, like in Night of the Living Dead," Danny argued. "They're more like the people in 28 Days Later. They got some kind of virus that makes them all pissed off and try to kill you. That still qualifies as zombies in my opinion."

"Call them whatever you want. That's not really the point, Danny." Jenna was almost yelling. "I thought I could count on you to help make this place safe."

"Well, that wasn't very bright," Lucy interjected.

"It is safe," Danny argued. "We're off the ground, the door is locked, nobody's gonna get in here."

"And what about the front doors?" Jenna asked.

"Huh?"

"Downstairs," she snapped. "The main entrance to the building."

"Well, I-" Danny stammered.

"And the other people in the building?"

"Um..."

"Do you have anything you can use to defend yourself in here?"

"I... do not," Danny admitted.

"I didn't think so. Here, take this." Jenna nodded to the baseball bat. "Hopefully none of us will need to actually use these weapons. Again, I mean."

"*Right*," Lucy answered with a manufactured smile. As if humoring a child, "With a bit of luck, we won't have to hurt anyone while we're hiding away from all the zombies outside."

"You know- if they were shamblers, then we'd probably be okay." Danny raised his eyebrows and pointed an index finger to Jenna, like a professor might do when explaining a math equation to a room of eager young pupils.

"Shamblers?" Jenna eyed him cautiously.

Danny replied, "Yeah. Ya know... Shamblers."

"Hey dummy," Lucy called. She crossed her legs, placing her right heel on the edge of the table and resting both hands on her knee. "You do realize that just repeating the same word doesn't actually explain what you're talking about, right?"

"You guys know what I'm talking about. It's the zombies that are all decayed; real slow moving 'n shit." Danny held both arms straight out in front of him and began a stiff-legged march across the room. Moaning as he went, "Brains!"

"You stupid ass," Lucy grumbled. "You're doing Frankenstein."

Danny, still holding his arms up, "Doctor Frankenstein, or Frankenstein's Monster?"

"The monster, obviously. And he's not a zombie."

Letting his hands drop, Danny answered his sister. "Well, that depends on how you look at it."

"Can we *please* stop dicking around?" It was definitely more of a command; not so much a request. Jenna slammed the barrel of the rifle on the floor to punctuate her statement.

"Alright, alright," Danny whined. "I'm listening. What do you want me to do?"

Jenna and Danny kept bickering. Jenna raised her voice; her words sharp and demanding. Danny's tone sounded defensive at times, confused at others. Lucy had grown bored and was no longer paying attention. She could only listen to this bullshit for so long. There were more important things to worry about, like re-counting her money and figuring out a way to get more. Plus, she could really use a smoke.

Lucy slid down from the tabletop, grabbing her purse from the floor and tossing it where she'd been sitting. She collected her cash and slipped it inside, zipping the bag closed after retrieving a pack of cigarettes. Only five left.

Interrupting her brother, who was still locked in a debate with his neighbor, Lucy asked, "Danny, do you have a lighter I can borrow?"

The pale stoner patted his pockets and found them both to be empty. "Oh- there should be one in my office." He motioned to the living room in the direction of the bong and the bean bag chair.

"Thanks," she said over her shoulder, already making a move toward the smoking equipment.

"Um, where are you going?" Jenna called after her.

"Outside. Well, on the balcony," Lucy answered, not stopping or turning around. "Danny doesn't let me smoke in the apartment. For some reason pot is okay, but cigarettes are a no-no."

"You can't do that," Jenna said flatly.

"Do what?" Lucy found the lighter, a white plastic Bic, next to the controller for a video game system.

"You can't go outside," Jenna clarified. She straightened, holding the rifle tight with both hands like a sentry at a guard post. "Not even on the balcony."

"Aw shucks, lady," Lucy answered with a snap of her fingers; her tone smarmy with a hint of false reverence. "I sure do appreciate you looking out for my well-being, but you can relax. I heard a pack of werewolves did away with all the zombies."

"Really?" Danny asked from the kitchen. "Jenna, you didn't say anything about werewolves."

"So stupid." Lucy shook her head and walked to the front of the living room, where she pulled the blinds aside and pushed open the heavy sliding glass door.

She hadn't been out of the apartment all day and it was always dark inside. Danny liked to keep the windows covered and the blinds closed. That way, there wouldn't be any glare on the television and no one could look inside and see him doing drugs. Lucy liked to remind him that no one gave a rat's ass about what he was doing and even if they did, it's not like anyone could actually see into his second-floor apartment.

Lucy stepped outside and onto the balcony. It was tough to see at first but it looked like there were three prone figures lying on the ground, two near the center of the parking lot and one on the far side, near the visitors' parking area. Oh boy. She was really losing it. Stress about money and relationships combined with Jenna's story about zombies had Lucy seeing things. Danny's ever-present cloud of marijuana smoke probably wasn't helping matters. *Stop being stupid,* Lucy told herself. *It's probably just dark spots and uneven pavement.*

She held a hand to her brow, shielding her eyes and giving them a chance to adjust to the bright afternoon sun. As Lucy's vision corrected, she came to realize that the dark shadowy thing near the visitors' parking area was actually a large puddle of dark reddish fluid. And on the near side of the parking lot, she could now see that what she thought and hoped were clumps of gravel and patchy cement were in fact two motionless bodies.

A cool sweat broke out on her neck and thighs. Lucy's breath caught in her throat. An unlit cigarette fell from fingers paralyzed by fear and disbelief. It landed on the balcony's outdoor carpet where it bounced once and rolled toward the edge. The lighter soon followed, landing on the floor with a soft but audible thump. Lucy noticed but she didn't dare look down to retrieve it. Her eyes, now adjusted and focused, remained fixed on the pair of young corpses.

They were male. Young boys actually, probably sixteen or seventeen years old. One was scrawny and shirtless. Through tanned pinkish skin, you could count his ribs. The ribs that were intact, that is. Several had been broken, shattered so badly you couldn't tell where one ended and the next began. The other kid was shorter and quite a bit heavier. He had on a tattered red and white shirt, though it had been only white when he'd gotten dressed that morning.

The skinny one was face-down on the ground. His hefty pal on the other hand, seemed to be looking right at Lucy. With eyes wide open, he wore an enduring grimace; his features painted an expression of inexorable rage. Neither of the boys moved but a now-frozen Lucy worried they would spring up at any moment and come running for her.

"Those are the zombies we were talking about."

Lucy jumped in place, jarred by the unexpected voice and feeling as if her guts were being squeezed by a giant invisible hand. Thankfully, her heart didn't stop beating and her underpants stayed clean.

"Wha- what?" she muttered, unable to form a proper sentence and refusing to look away from the pair of youthful cadavers.

"Right there," Danny said. He had managed to sneak up behind his sister and was pointing at the corpses. "They were coming right for me and Jenna shot them from her balcony."

Lucy took a breath and swallowed hard. Finally able to look away, she pushed past her brother and hurried back inside.

"Wait, where ya going?" Danny asked.

She didn't answer. Lucy walked past him and made her way toward the kitchen table. Danny followed her in, closing and latching the sliding glass door thanks to a firm reminder from Jenna, who had been monitoring everything from the next room. After he pulled the blinds closed over the door, Danny watched his sister grab her purse and empty its contents onto the table.

Grabbing her cell phone from the spilled clutter, Lucy pressed a series of commands on the display and hit the send button to place a call. She only held the device to her ear for a second before hanging up and redialing. After two failed attempts to connect, Lucy slammed the phone down on the tabletop and blurted, "Shit!"

"What's the matter?" Danny asked from the living room. "Who're you trying to call?"

"The police!" she shrieked. "I'm trying to call the police but the God damned phone won't work, it's like the line is dead."

"The lines are down," Jenna told her. "At least, I think they're down. Or they might be overloaded from too many people calling. I must have tried calling the cops a dozen times before I

167

gave up and came over."

At the sound of her words, Lucy marched up to Jenna and cried, "Are they real?"

Jenna tensed and stood up straight. She tried to step back and give herself some space, but her ass bumped into the refrigerator door. "Are they real?" Jenna repeated Lucy's question. Her inflection indicated she'd need some clarification.

"The people out there! Are they real? Did you really shoot those people?" Lucy's voice was growing in volume; her tone accusatory.

"Yes." Jenna spoke softly and hoped that her calmness was infectious. "They're real and yes, I shot them."

"Why?" Lucy snapped. She pulled off her bandanna and ran fingers through her hair, leaving it a glossy black rat's nest. "How could you shoot someone? How could you *kill* those people?"

"I had to." Jenna made certain to avoid sounding defensive. The girl in front of her was unraveling and this was no good. Everyone needed to keep their head straight and not flip out. "They were going to harm your brother if I didn't."

"Oh my God," Lucy said; her voice barely above a whisper. Heavy and hard, reality crashed into her like a tidal wave, leaving her awash in dread. This girl, a girl that she'd never met before, stood in front of her, clutching a gun, and admitting she'd just murdered someone. Lucy took a big step back and away from her.

It was getting harder to breathe and the apartment felt like it was a hundred degrees. The sweats were back and with them came a fresh torrent of nausea. Lucy bent at the waist, resting her palms on her kneecaps and closed her eyes. She repeated, "Oh my God."

Now that there was a couple of feet between them, Jenna was able to relax a little. She let her shoulders drop and exhaled deeply. "I'm sorry Lucy. I know this is a lot to take in but I swear, I didn't have a choice. They were coming to attack your brother, I did it to keep him safe."

"Keep him safe from what?" Lucy's tone had lost some of its edge. She stood back up, dried her hands on the front of her shirt and said, "They're just kids!"

"Lucy, I know they look like they're just kids but they're not. They were dangerous and they would have killed him. Or worse."

"Worse?"

"If they had gotten to him, and if he somehow escaped, I'm almost positive he would have gotten infected with their disease or whatever it is."

"I'm not sure that's worse than being killed," Danny interposed. He stood at the border of the two rooms; his feet on the seam where crappy carpet met cracked tile.

Lucy and Jenna looked to Danny and asked in unison, "What?"

Shrugging, the young man answered, "I'm just sayin' that if it's up to me, I'd rather be a zombie than be dead."

"That's ridiculous," Lucy replied.

"Oh, I don't know about that," said Danny. "If you're dead, you're dead. But if you're a zombie, it could just be temporary. Maybe someone will come up with a cure."

"And who is going to do that?" Lucy huffed. "And how? And why would they bother? From the looks of things outside, these so-called zombies don't live long enough for a cure to do them any good."

"That's true," Danny agreed. "But I bet some of the fat-cat pharmaceutical companies are working on a cure right now. They could round up all the zombies that survive long enough to be cured and sell them the antidote at a thousand dollars a pill. People would pay it too- what choice would they have?"

"Antidote?" Lucy asked.

"Yeah." Danny scratched his head and added, "Or medicine, or whatever you want to call it."

"But doesn't everyone become violent? How are you going to administer a treatment to someone who's trying to kill you?" Lucy hated to play along with her brother's absurd hypothetical fantasies but it was helping her to get a better grip on the situation.

"I don't know, I'm not a scientist!" Danny put up his hands defensively. "Or a doctor."

"No doubt about that," Lucy shot back, half joking and half annoyed. "Don't worry, nobody is going to mistake you for either one of those things."

"Well anyhow, I'm just saying that if I somehow become a zombie, at least there's a chance I could get cured," Danny reiterated. "And besides, I don't think anyone would want to kill me if I got infected. I wouldn't freak out and try to hurt anyone."

"Well, if you get infected, you're on your own," Lucy explained. "You ain't staying here, so good luck."

"But it's my apartment," Danny argued. "Why should I leave?"

"You guys!" Jenna shouted to disrupt the bickering. She'd listened to just about enough of their bullshit. Danny needed to start taking things seriously and Lucy had to keep herself from having a panic attack. "If we're smart about this, if we make sure everything's locked up and we don't draw too much attention to ourselves, then we won't have to worry about anyone getting killed or turning into a zombie. But there are a few things we need to do and the sooner, the better."

"Okay, okay," Danny said. He almost forgot that Jenna was in the room. "I trust your judgment and it sounds like you know the most about what's going on."

"Thanks Danny, I appreciate that."

"But before we do anything," Danny continued. "Just so we're all clear, you do agree that they're zombies, right?"

Chapter 26

The left shoulder, just below the clavicle. That's where the blade first went in. It was tough at first, clumsy and imprecise. The tip got caught on the shirt's coarse green fabric, then again when it punctured the skin and fibrous tissue. The blade would have popped out the other side if the scapula bone hadn't been there to stop it. The trauma should have been debilitating; the pain unendurable. But the beast seemed unimpaired.

The second slice went across the belly. Viscera churned and blood spilled freely from the yawning gash. The deep laceration and ruinous intestinal injury should have brought him down. Hypovolemic shock should have followed. And though he'd been abused and butchered, the barbarian refused to be stopped.

He was bigger, faster, taller, and stronger than his prey. A supreme predator, he'd chased down and cornered his victim. There was no way out. She was trapped in a small room and he stood between her and the only exit. Advancing quickly, he snatched her by the shirt collar and lurched forward. He pounced, mouth open and teeth-first. Lindsey could do nothing but close her eyes and pray it was over quickly.

Her feet slipped forward; sneakers losing grip on the dusty floor. Faded tiles jumped up to meet her, forcing the air from her lungs as she landed hard on her back. Her attacker, still clutching her shirt and baring his teeth, followed her down. The bastard landed on top of her. His weight kept Lindsey's arms pinned between her chest and his torso. She couldn't move. She couldn't escape. Lindsey could only close her eyes and scream. Loud and shrill, her last breath was one of panic and helplessness.

The room went silent. And then... Well, and then nothing happened. The assault was over and Lindsey was still alive. At least, she felt like she was still alive. She was fairly certain that if she had died, she would have felt something right before the moment of death; the sensation of teeth digging into her skin, flesh being ripped from her bones, something.

But she felt nothing. Nothing but the weight of a human body on top of her, that is. It took a moment but Lindsey noticed there were several more things she could sense. The first was an intense pressure in her right hand. The palm was slick with perspiration; knuckles sore and tense. Her forearm detected something wet, hot and sticky. Lindsey could feel her pulse thumping through her fingers, which were wrapped very tightly around an object of some sort.

The knife! Lindsey had forgotten she'd been holding it. It was still in her hand when Lance grabbed and lunged at her. When he landed on top of Lindsey, the tip of the blade tore through his shirt, punched through the sternum, and punctured his heart. He was gone the second they hit the floor.

Lindsey gasped when she finally opened her eyes. Another pair stared back at her from only an inch away. Sunken and bloodshot, the dead man's eyes were glossy with a tinge of yellow. They were fixed on her and for a moment, Lindsey was frozen. Afraid to move, she was convinced the moment she did, Lance would wake up and finish what he'd started.

But he wasn't going to. Short of bloating and decay, Lance wasn't going to be doing much of anything. Lindsey was safe for now but she'd have to start moving if she wanted to stay that way. The young woman wriggled her arms loose and tried to sit up. Maneuvering beneath the dead weight was more difficult than she'd expected.

Rolling onto her right side, she placed her right hand on the floor for balance and shoved the corpse aside with her left. The body rolled onto its back. Its head bounced against the floor tiles once before it came to rest; wide eyes with an empty gaze to the ceiling.

Free to get up and move, Lindsey pulled herself into a sitting position and took a few seconds to catch her breath. She then remembered the door to the lounge was still open. If she was going to take a couple minutes to rest, she'd better make sure no one would be popping in to join her. With a groan, Lindsey moved into a crouch and began to stand. She looked to the doorway and found herself staring down the twin barrels of a twenty-gauge shotgun.

It wasn't the scariest thing she had seen that afternoon. It didn't even crack the top ten. But the shock was still enough to make her jump back and nearly trip over the cadaver. Instinct made her duck away from the barrels and put her hands in front of her face, but she kept herself from screaming.

"Whoa, whoa. Lindsey it's okay. It's just me." The man lowered the gun to his side. He held his free hand palm-out as if to say, *everything is okay. You're safe now.*

"Jim?" Lindsey blinked hard. The pounding in her chest began to slow.

"Are you okay?"

"Oh my God- Jim!" she cried. "You're not dead! And you're here!"

Lindsey moved toward him; arms open for a hug. Jim flinched and took a half step back to remain out of reach.

Lindsey stopped and frowned. "What is it?"

Jim wanted nothing more than to pull her in close and never let go. Under normal circumstances, Jim would have jumped at any opportunity to make contact with her, even if it was just a friendly embrace. Pathetic, right?

The world around them had come undone and she called Jim to come get her, to rescue her. Through all the chaos and walking death, he'd managed to find her. Now under these less-than-normal circumstances, her affection should have meant that much more. Challenging as it may have been, Jim had to avoid her touch.

"Um... You're sort of-" Jim pointed to her shirt. "It's all over you."

That's when Lindsey caught sight of the blood. She really should've seen it sooner; it being literally right in front of her face. Her glasses had somehow managed to survive the ordeal but the lenses had so many red speckles they could've passed for pink stained glass. It was all over her. You'd think her hands and forearms had been dipped in red paint. The front of her shirt looked as if someone had doused her with a bucket of marinara sauce.

"Oh. Right," she said. "I should get cleaned up. Can you close that door please?"

Jim did as he was told, dutifully closing and locking the door. He leaned his back against it just to be certain no one would be coming through.

Lindsey turned around and looked down at the limp form on the ground. The blade was still buried in its chest with the handle protruding from the wound like a tiny onyx flagpole. She was going to have to take the knife with her. Hopefully it would slide out just as easily as it had gone in. She knelt next to the body and grabbed the knife by the handle.

"What are you doing?"

"What do you mean?" Lindsey replied without looking up. She freed the blade with a gentle

171

tug. Razor-sharp stainless steel slurped and belched on its way out.

"With the knife," Jim clarified.

"I'm going to need a weapon," she answered. Lindsey then used Lance's shirt to wipe down the blade and handle. "There's nothing else in here I can use. I already checked all the lockers."

"I do have a gun," he reminded her.

Seeing her hunched over the motionless creature made Jim uneasy. He gripped the shotgun a little tighter, keeping the barrel aimed in Lance's general direction.

"But what if we get separated?" Lindsey asked. The knife was as clean as it was going to get without some dish soap and a scouring pad. She tossed it on the plastic tabletop and asked, "Were you able to get another gun or any other weapons?"

"This was the only gun left in the case," Jim told her.

"At your uncle's house?"

"Yeah."

"I thought that there were like six or seven there, rifles and shotguns. What happened?" Lindsey stepped over the cadaver and walked to where the coat rack was mounted on the wall.

"I don't know. They were gone. I was lucky to find this one."

"How are you on ammo?" Lindsey asked. She found an apron that didn't look too badly soiled and did her best to clean herself off. A good deal of blood soaked into the canvas. Some had already started to dry. It streaked along her skin, sticking to her fingertips and congealing in the lines across the palms of her hands.

Jim thought for a second. "I've got a full box of twenty-five and then a handful of loose rounds."

"Better than nothing."

"I suppose."

"But I'll hang on to the knife," Lindsey told him. "Just to be safe. Hopefully I won't need it and hopefully you won't need the gun either."

Jim stifled a dry chuckle. "That's awfully optimistic."

"Is it bad out?" she asked, suspecting she already knew the answer.

"Yeah, it's pretty bad out." He sighed and shook his head. "It's like everyone has gone crazy. I mean, they're not just attacking each other, they're *eating* each other."

"I know, I saw that," Lindsey said softly.

"And they don't stop," he continued, recalling some recent advice from a strange old woman. "They don't seem to get scared of anything and they don't get hurt. They just keep coming."

"That's what happened with Lance," Lindsey explained.

Jim motioned to the body on the floor, "Maybe we shouldn't get too close to him. Are you sure he's dead?"

"Pretty sure," Lindsey answered flatly. "He looks dead to me."

172

"Right." Jim kept his eyes on Lance, still expecting him to jump to his feet at any moment.

"I'm going to try to get cleaned up and then we should get out of here," Lindsey told him. "Is your car out front?"

"Yep, right near the front doors."

"Good."

Lindsey began to take her shirt off. She had on a thin black tank top underneath. Careful not to touch her face, she pulled the gore-soaked polo over her head and tossed it to the other side of the room. She then yanked a second apron off its hanger to use as a towel. She marched past the row of lockers and over to the water cooler.

Now that the action had died down and Lindsey had taken a moment to collect herself, her emotions were beginning to catch up to her. She was still alive but no closer to safety than she had been an hour ago. At least she wasn't alone any more. Jim had made it, but had anyone else? Her parents? Her two brothers? Any of her friends? She sniffled, looked down and avoided eye contact with Jim.

She wanted a shower. She wanted to scrub herself with soap and hot water until her skin was raw, to rinse the sticky red goo from the ends of her blonde hair. She wanted a place to be safe and alone, a place where gallons of water could stream over her, washing away her tears until she was clean once more.

But the dingy little break room at the back of Bennett's Supermarket didn't have a shower. It didn't even have a sink. There was no soap or hand sanitizer either as far as she could tell. Until Lindsey could get home, the water cooler would have to do.

It was one of those chest-high models with a big plastic jug on top. The bottle was half full, more than enough to rinse her hands off. There was a single nozzle on the front of the machine with a blue plastic tab on top. Lindsey knelt down and rinsed her hands under the spout. Ice-cold water ran over her wrists and fingers, then onto the front of the dispenser and onto the floor. The water cooler didn't have a proper drain, just a shallow tray with a plastic grate to catch overflow. A growing puddle of pink fluid formed on the floor.

"Is your cell phone still working?" Lindsey dried herself off and dropped the apron on the ground to let it soak up some of the spilled liquid.

"I think so, why?" Jim reached into his pocket for the device. The screen came on but the reception bars were gone. In their place was an icon of a triangle with an exclamation point inside. "It seems to work, but no service. Do you think the lines are down?"

"No, that sounds about right. It's impossible to get a signal in here. I just want to call my parents and see if they're okay," Lindsey said. She pulled her glasses off and rinsed them under the spout on the water cooler. "What about on your way here? After we talked, were you still able to use your phone?"

"I think so." Jim put the device back in his pocket and resumed a two-handed grip on the shotgun. "Beth called a couple times but I couldn't answer."

"Beth? Is that your girlfriend?" Lindsey used the front of her tank top to dry her lenses.

"Um, sort of," Jim said.

"Is she okay?"

173

"I don't know. I think so."

"Alright." Lindsey put her glasses back on and straightened her shirt. "Do you have somewhere we can go?"

Jim scratched his chin and thought for a moment. "I was planning to go home but now I'm thinking maybe we should try to get out of town, put some distance between ourselves and everything that's happening here."

"Yeah," Lindsey agreed. "That sounds good to me."

Jim worked the top lever on the gun, causing the barrels to open so he could make sure there were two fresh rounds inside. Satisfied, he snapped the barrels closed and said, "I'm good to go whenever you're ready."

"Just a sec." Lindsey wiped away the last bit of moisture from her hands on the front of her pants. She walked up to Jim, kissed him on the cheek and wrapped her arms around him. She squeezed him tightly and said, "Thank you for coming for me."

"Of course," Jim said, hugging her with one arm so he didn't drop the gun.

Lindsey rested her head against his chest for a moment before releasing him and said, "I'm so happy you're not dead."

Jim grinned. "Yeah, me too."

"Okay," Lindsey straightened and composed herself. "Let's get out of here."

Chapter 27

"Hey, my game!"

"Shut up, Danny." Lucy stood next to Jenna in the center of the living room. Remote control in hand, she flipped from channel to channel, ignoring anything that didn't look like a newscast. "We're trying to find out if there've been any new reports."

Her brother, after searching the apartment for anything the group could use to defend themselves, began to experience what he described as a *nervous tummy* and excused himself to the bathroom. After dropping a batch of diarrhea, he washed his hands and opened the window to let the room air out.

Danny emerged from the restroom to find that his television had been commandeered. The game, in which his character was about to set a new high score and navigate to the next checkpoint, had been replaced by a rotating display of commercials, old sitcoms, and local news anchors.

"I was about to level-up," he wailed.

"Danny!" Lucy shot him a cross look. "Not now."

Jenna, yet to relinquish possession of her rifle, turned to him and said, "We put it on pause."

"Thanks, pretty lady!" Danny flashed her a big toothy smile.

"Hey Stonehenge," Lucy called to her brother. "What were you able to find?"

"Huh?"

"Before you destroyed the toilet bowl, you were going to look for weapons. Remember?"

"Give me two seconds," Danny replied, already turning and heading for the bedroom.

Jenna and Lucy stayed in the living room while Danny rummaged through the bedroom closet, kitchen cabinets, and hallway closet. The young women landed on the Fox News Channel, which was showing a live broadcast of a press conference. It was a military briefing that was being held in The White House. The girls watched as a man in a suit with gray hair and glasses spoke directly to the camera, already mid-sentence.

"...a state of emergency throughout the country. The President has declared the continental United States under martial law as of three PM Eastern Standard Time. All military reservists are ordered to report to their assigned armory for activation and deployment. In an effort to stop the spread of this contagion, our nation's borders with Canada and Mexico will be closed. All air traffic, both domestic and international, will be suspended." The man paused to take a drink of water. Cameras flashed off screen and reporters could be heard shouting questions in the background.

The man at the podium set his drink down and rubbed his chin. He looked past the cameras to survey the crowd in front of him. Without addressing any of them directly, he continued. "A nationwide curfew will go into effect tonight, from nine o'clock PM until seven o'clock AM. Anyone caught outdoors while the curfew is in effect will be assumed hostile and subject to detention without trial or representation. This also applies to any individuals found looting or conducting unauthorized militia activity. Military personnel are authorized to use deadly force when dealing with..."

"Is that the Secretary of Defense?" Lucy asked.

Jenna shrugged. "I'm not sure."

About three minutes had passed since Danny left the room and he was now ready to rejoin the ladies in front of the television. He rushed into the living room and dropped an armload of gear onto the carpeted floor.

"Okay," Jenna said, "Let's see what we've got."

There was a golf club, a machete, two large kitchen knives with wooden handles and dull blades, a pair of chemistry set safety goggles, and a broom.

Lucy eyed the pile of equipment and asked, "Why do you have a machete?"

"I got it for when I go camping," Danny told her.

"When's the last time you went camping?"

"I'm an avid camper," he told her.

"Yeah right," Lucy rolled her eyes.

"This is good, Danny." Jenna picked the machete up off the floor. It was all black except for the edge of the blade, which had been machine-sharpened and had a shimmering silver surface. "This and the golf club might really come in handy."

"Really, Danny? A broom?" Lucy groaned. "What's your plan, to sweep the zombies into a dustpan?"

"No," Danny replied smartly. He snatched the broom by the handle and began unscrewing it from the head. "See? The part with the bristles comes off. You could use it as a club. And besides, I don't have a dustpan."

"I think I'll take the golf club," she said. "Probably better to have metal than wood. And that broom looks like it's about ninety years old. I bet it breaks the first time you swing it at one of those creeps."

Danny smirked. "That's why I brought it, so you could use it. I'll be taking the machete. That is, unless you want it." He turned to Jenna to confirm.

"It's all yours," she told him. "I'll stick with the gun."

"Smart," Danny said. He kicked the broom, which was now in two pieces, into the corner of the room along with the goggles. Then he picked up the knives and walked out of the room. He called over his shoulder, "I'll leave these on the kitchen table in case anyone needs them."

Lucy held the golf club in her hands. It was light but solid, weighing less than two pounds. She had never played a real game of golf, but she recognized the club as a putter. Not a real putter like they use in the PGA, it was the kind you use at a miniature golf course. It was cheaply-made and scuffed along the shaft and handle. The grip and head were covered with a thick red plastic. She called to her brother in the next room, "Hey Danny, did you steal this from Putt Putt?"

"No," he shouted from inside the bathroom. "I got it from Adventure Landing."

His guts were churning again, this time threatening to push things up and out. It was probably just nerves but in the interest of playing it safe, Danny popped open the medicine cabinet. He chewed on a Tums and washed it down with a Pepto chaser. As he turned to leave, Danny found a dark blue bandanna hanging over the doorknob. Moments later, he walked back into the kitchen wearing it tied around his noggin like a Rambo-style headband.

"You look ridiculous," Lucy told him.

"I look awesome and ready for action," he corrected her. "This is how a man dresses when he's about to kick some ass."

"Hey guys, can you come in here please?" Jenna was still in front of the television but the news had been replaced with static. "Something's wrong with the TV."

Danny strolled into the room to assess the situation. He checked the power to the cable box. It was plugged in and the indicator light was still on. Then he reached behind the set to make sure none of the wires had come loose. The cord connecting the cable receiver to the television was still firmly in place. Everything looked like it was set up correctly.

"The cable must be out," Danny said. "I have an antenna in the closet. We can at least tune in to the local stations if they're still broadcasting."

"That's good, Danny," said Jenna. "When we get back, we should get that set up. We should also look around to see what else we have lying around, batteries, flashlights, stuff like that is probably going to come in handy."

"I should have some double-A's in the kitchen somewhere," Danny told her. "And I think there's a flashlight or two, maybe in the bedroom closet. I'll have to check, but I-"

"Get back from where?" Lucy interrupted. She held the grip of the golf club and let the head thud against the floor like a judge striking his gavel. "If there's still people running around biting each other, I'm not going outside."

"Not outside," Jenna answered. She still kept one eye on the TV set, half expecting the signal to return and not wanting to miss it if it did. The static had disappeared, replaced by a black screen with white letters that read, *No Signal*, in the middle of the display. "I meant, when we get back from securing the front doors and checking on the neighbors."

"Right," Danny agreed.

"Right," Lucy parroted with much less enthusiasm. She walked to the far side of the living room and flopped onto the sofa. She set the golf club down across her lap and put her face in her hands.

"Okay," Jenna began. "Here's what I think we should do: Since we're already over here, we should check to see who's home on this side of the building. When we know that everyone's safe and accounted for, we'll figure out a way to keep the front door closed. Then, we can do the same on my side of the building."

Lucy didn't say anything. She didn't even look up. Danny put his hand in the air, giving it a slight wave and stretching toward the ceiling.

"Danny?" Jenna eyed him curiously. "What is it?"

"I have a question," he told her.

"Okay, well you don't have to raise your hand."

"Sweet," he nodded. "How are we going to keep the doors closed? They don't latch and there's no locks."

"We'll probably have to chain them shut, or maybe use some rope or something like that to tie around the handles."

Danny moved to raise his hand again but caught himself. "Where are we going to get ropes or chains?"

"I'm hoping we can find something in the basement," Jenna answered. "But I guess we could even use belts and things like that if we had to."

Lucy stirred on the couch. "What about the windows?"

"We're two stories up," Danny reminded her. "I don't think anyone is getting in through the windows, there's no way to get up here."

"I know that," Lucy shook her head. "What about the first floor? And there are windows that lead into the basement."

"The basement windows are small and narrow," Jenna tried to assure her. "It'd be tough for someone to get inside that way."

"But not impossible," Lucy replied. Her breathing had become heavy. She could feel her pulse grow faster. Lucy's skin had a thin layer of cold sweat across her whole body. "What are we going to do if *they* get in?"

"They're not going to get in," Jenna said; an unexpected air of confidence in her voice.

Lucy stood up, letting the club fall to the floor at her feet. Nearly shouting, "You don't know that! How can you be so sure?"

"Lucy, relax." Danny tried to keep his tone neutral. "You're freaking out. Just take it easy."

"It's okay, Danny. We're all freaked out by what's going on." Once again, Jenna was keeping order, doing what she could to keep everyone calm and focused. "Lucy, we'll do what we can to keep the building sealed up tight. If anyone's home on the first floor, we'll ask them to keep their windows closed and barricaded. We'll use furniture if we have to and we can do the same in the basement if it looks like someone could get in."

She paused to let Danny or Lucy get a word in, but neither spoke. "It's not ideal, but I'd say we're luckier than most right now. We're inside, we've got food and weapons and doors that lock. And most importantly, we're together."

"Okay," Lucy said quietly. She fell back onto the sofa, rubbing tears from her eyes and brushing her hair back from her face. "Okay, you're right. I'm sorry."

Danny, who'd been standing at the edge of the room, just feet from the main door, cleared his throat and pushed out a small cough in an obvious call for attention. Lucy and Jenna both looked over at him to find that once again, he had his right hand held over his head. His expression was that of a schoolboy begging the teacher to let him use the restroom.

"Yes, Danny?" Jenna said. "What is it?"

"About the thing you said," he shifted in place. "The thing about food..."

"What about it?"

"Well," he frowned as he started walking toward the refrigerator. "I don't know if you've had a chance to check out the fridge and cupboards, but I'm afraid I've been neglecting my grocery shopping duties as of late."

Danny flung the door open, revealing shelves that were mostly bare except for an extensive collection of condiments and a handful of take-out containers that probably should have been tossed in the garbage weeks earlier.

"See what I mean?" He closed the fridge and made his way to the row of cabinets over the counter top.

"Alright, alright." Jenna held up her hands to stop him. "I believe you. And it's alright. I actually just stocked up a couple days ago. I should have enough food to keep us going for at least a few days."

"Nice." Danny grinned at her. "You're the best, Jenna. You go to Bennett's?"

"Huh?"

"Bennett's Supermarket," he repeated. "Is that where you shop?"

"No," she said. "I shop at Lowell's."

"Lowell's Food Emporium?" Danny continued, "Why not Bennett's?"

"Why would I drive across town to go to Bennett's when Lowell's is like two blocks away?"

"Bennett's carries RC Cola," Danny told her. "Lowell's only has Coke, Pepsi, and their own generic stuff. Gross. Plus, there's more good-lookin' chicks working at Bennett's."

Jenna groaned as she knelt to tighten the laces on her sneakers. "Believe it or not, Danny, that's not a factor for me when deciding where to buy my groceries."

"You mean the hot chicks?" Danny asked. "Or the RC Cola?"

"Neither," Jenna snapped as she stood up. "Er, both. Or whatever. Listen Danny, if you're done screwing around, we should get moving. We've got a lot to do and I'd like to make sure it's all done quickly so we can be back inside before it gets dark."

Lucy interjected immediately. "I thought you said we weren't going outside," she complained.

Jenna looked back to Lucy. She was on her feet again, now holding the golf club with both hands in front of her body.

"I know, I meant we should be back inside the apartment," Jenna said soothingly. She tried to sound genuine but her patience was wearing thin and the heat was getting to her. As she spoke, Jenna rolled up the sleeves of her denim shirt. "We're not leaving and if all goes right, we won't need to go outside either. We'll check the other apartments and make sure the doors will stay closed. Then, we're back here for the night."

This didn't seem to make Lucy feel any better. She let the club fall to the floor again. Her features distorted, "So that's the plan?"

Thoughtfully, Danny looked at Jenna and then to Lucy. He stood up straight, took a deep breath and opened his mouth as if to speak. And then said nothing. He dropped his shoulders and exhaled, long and audibly.

"That wasn't rhetorical," Lucy said bluntly. This is who she was counting on? Her survival rested in the hands of her half-stoned slacker brother and a girl she'd never met before and looked like she was barely out of high school? "We're just going to seal ourselves inside and what? Wait for things to blow over? And hope someone comes along to rescue us?"

"Yeah." Jenna shrugged and repeated, "Yeah, that's pretty much it."

179

"Oh, that's just perfect," Lucy told her with over-the-top sarcasm. She could feel herself tensing again; thoughts beginning to race, nerves forcing her to squeeze her hands into fists. Clench, release. Clench, release. "We'll just hang out and hope for the best. Genius plan."

"Hey, if you've got a better one, I'm all ears." Jenna had been cordial and held her tongue for as long as she could. Who did this bitch think she was? If she was just going to whine and complain and second-guess everyone, she could learn to fend for herself, by herself. "Otherwise, we need to stay put. Someone will be along eventually."

"Who?" Lucy demanded, throwing her hands up in exasperation. "And when? How long do you think we'll last in here while we're waiting to be rescued?"

Jenna was ready to scream. She was tired. It was hot as Hell in the apartment. Her skin was slimy and sticky. Her clothing clung to her like Saran Wrap over warm meat. She'd had about enough of this petty arguing with someone who was happy to pick knits instead of offering anything helpful. Jenna clenched her jaw, sucking a deep breath through her teeth. She was ready to unload her frustration, but it was Danny who spoke first.

"Actually, I think that's a good plan."

Lucy locked eyes with her brother, not sure if she heard him correctly. "What?"

"We're not exactly waiting around, hoping to be rescued or however you put it." Danny, with a look of vacant wonderment, swung the machete in front of him, listening to the whoosh of sharpened metal whizzing through the air. He kept doing this as he talked. "So, there's two things to think about here. You were just-"

"Can you stop?" Lucy pointed to the long blade in Danny's hand and shouted, "Stop swinging that thing around. You're going to hit someone."

"Alright," Danny replied, rolling his eyes. He placed the machete on the kitchen table and went on, "So anyway, you were just saying you didn't want to go outside, that's thing number one. And that's good. We shouldn't go outside. Not now anyway. We don't necessarily have anywhere to go, and even if we did, we don't know what places are safe."

Jenna nodded her agreement.

Lucy did the same. "And thing two?"

"We're not just sitting around." Danny laced his fingers and cracked his knuckles; joints popping loud enough to echo off the kitchen wall. "We're securing the building. We're going to make sure we know who's inside and make sure everyone's okay. We're sticking together and we're going to look out for each other to make sure we all stay safe."

"Right," Jenna chimed in. Stepping into the kitchen, she moved past Danny and set the rifle down on the tabletop. Then she flipped the gun over and pulled a black lever in front of the trigger.

Danny continued, "And when we're done, we'll stay in here. Together. And I'll get the antenna set up so we can watch for any news. We'll know what's happening and when the cops or National Guard or whoever gets things under control."

"Good," Jenna said, not looking up from the gun. "We should grab a radio too, in case the TV channels go offline."

Danny watched over her shoulder. She had to wobble it a little, but after a few seconds, a small black box slid out of the wood part of the gun.

"Whoa, what is that?" Danny asked

"The magazine," Jenna told him. She could tell by the blank expression on his face that he didn't understand. "It's where the bullets go."

"Pfff, I know," Danny said. "Everybody knows that. Everybody who plays first-person shooters, anyway."

"It's not the same, Danny." Reaching into her pocket as she spoke, Jenna pulled out a small fistful of bullets and spread them out on the table in front of her. One at a time, she fed the rounds into a slot on top of the magazine. "Playing video games does not make you a gun expert, so just keep that in mind and be careful."

"Oh my God!" Danny exclaimed. "Are those the bullets? Look how tiny they are- they're so cute!"

"Danny!" Jenna spouted sharply. She gave the bandanna-clad stoner a stern look to let him know she wasn't screwing around. "I need you to take this seriously."

"I know, I know," Danny answered with a comforting smile. "I'm all business from this point on. Don't you worry about that."

"Oh- and one more thing," Jenna began, "We'll need to take turns keeping watch. We should take shifts keeping watch through the windows so we'll know right away if anyone's coming."

Lucy shifted in place, trying to stop herself from pacing.

"What is it?" Jenna asked.

"The three of us," she turned to her brother, "Are we going to stay here, in your apartment?"

"I guess so," he answered. Then, turning to Jenna for confirmation, "Does that work for you?"

"Yes, that's fine with me," she replied.

"Jenna, I usually sleep on the sofa. Lucy's been using the bed since she's been staying here," Danny explained. He motioned to the couch and said, "But you can take it for tonight. It doesn't fold out, but it's still pretty comfy. I can crash on the loveseat."

"We can't all sleep at the same time," Jenna reminded him. "At least one of us should be up to make sure no one's trying to get in. And about that, I don't suppose you've got any coffee?"

"Um..." Danny scratched his head and didn't really answer the question.

"That's okay," Jenna said. "I have some. I'll run back to my place in a bit and bring some over. I'll grab some extra food and stuff while I'm at it."

"Good times," Danny grinned. "It'll be like a slumber party. But ya know, with zombies."

"I guess," Jenna replied dismissively. "Are you guys ready to get moving?"

"Danny, Jenna," Lucy said softly.

"Yes, Lucy?" Jenna asked as she turned to face her.

"What's up?" Danny asked, bending to retrieve his weapon.

"Are we going to be okay?" The question was just above a whisper. Her words had lost their hard edge. She liked to think of herself as a tough, kick-ass kind of woman but now she felt and sounded like a scared little girl. She didn't lift her gaze from the carpet under her toes. "I mean, what

181

are we going to do if one of them gets in?"

"That's not going to happen," Danny told her, trying to sound confident. "Once we get the doors locked and make sure there's no way into the basement, nobody's getting in."

Lucy was listening but she wasn't convinced. "Yeah, but what if-"

"We'll deal with it," Jenna said abruptly. She held up the rifle and added, "That's why I've got this. That's why we've all got a weapon. We'll defend ourselves."

"We're all going to be fine." Danny walked across the living room and over to his sister. He picked up the golf club and handed it to her. "Here, hang on to this. But I bet you won't even need it. We'll make sure no one gets in here. You're going to be okay. I promise."

Lucy looked up from the floor. She took the offered club and was about to thank him when he called over to Jenna.

"We don't all need to go downstairs, do we?"

Puzzled, Jenna asked, "What do you mean?"

"I think Lucy should stay here," he said.

"I don't think we should split up," Jenna contended. "It's better if we stick together, that way no one gets lost."

"No one's gonna get lost," Danny argued. "You said we should have someone on lookout, so maybe she should stay here and keep an eye out. We won't be able to monitor what's happening outside when we're going up and down the steps."

Jenna had something more to add to the discussion but Danny wasn't hearing it.

"Hold on just a sec." He turned and walked out of the kitchen and into the bedroom, where he closed and latched the window. Danny pulled the curtains over the glass, leaving just enough space so a person could peer out without being visible to someone who might be trying to look in.

That done, he marched through the hall and back to the kitchen. He did the same with the window over the sink and then hurried to the sliding glass door at the front of the living room. Jenna and Lucy watched him as he grabbed the metal frame to make certain the doorway was sealed. Danny locked the door and closed the vertical blinds. The room went mostly dark.

"Alright," Danny said. "This place is closed up as tight as it's going to get."

"Okay?" Jenna turned on a lamp in the corner of the living room.

"Lucy, we need you to stay here and be our lookout." He said this without hesitation. Danny looked to Jenna for confirmation. His sister obviously didn't want to leave the apartment and he wasn't about to make her. Sure, Jenna made a good point about everyone sticking together but Lucy would be safer staying put.

"That's right." Jenna had finished reloading. She slammed the magazine into the rifle so it rested flush with the wood stock. "I think that's a good idea."

"Okay," Lucy replied. Her mood was immediately lifted. "I can do that."

"We won't be gone long," Jenna told her.

"Wait," Lucy said, moving from her place in front of the sofa and walking toward her brother.

"What's up?" he asked.

"Thank you," she whispered. "Please be careful."

"We'll be fine," Danny answered. "Don't worry. Just stay inside and watch for any activity outside. We'll be back in no time."

Lucy couldn't remember the last time she hugged her brother. Maybe never. She wanted to now. It felt like she might not have a chance to ever again. No, that was ridiculous and she was getting herself worked into a panic again. She had to keep her composure. Lucy gave Danny a slap on the shoulder and said, "Okay, then I'll see you soon. Both of you."

"I'll keep him safe," Jenna told her. "Promise."

"Thank you." Lucy forced a grin and then turned away from them, heading to the kitchen sink so she could watch out the window.

"Ready?" Danny asked.

"Yep," Jenna answered with confidence. She checked the rifle and switched the safety off. With her free hand, Jenna gripped the doorknob and said, "We'll go on three."

Danny nodded; his grip tightening on the handle of the machete.

"One. Two," Jenna counted off slowly. "Three!"

With that, she twisted the knob and flung the door open.

Chapter 28

Jim unlocked the door and turned the knob. He pressed his right foot forward just far enough so the toe of his sneaker kept the door from closing again. Both hands squeezing the shotgun, Jim looked over his shoulder to Lindsey. "You ready?"

Lindsey stood just a few feet behind him. Her knees were bent; her posture rigid. She had her hair pulled back into a ponytail. After scrubbing the dirt and dust from the soles of her shoes, she'd re-tied the laces in double knots. The last thing she needed was for the damn things to come undone in the middle of the store. What if she lost a shoe? Or worse- what if she tripped over a loose lace? She'd be done for. If Lindsey wanted to survive, everything had to go perfectly.

She held a large knife in her right hand, keeping the blade several inches in front of her abdomen. The other hand was balled into a fist, but not the kind of fist you'd throw at someone. It was the kind of fist you make when you're pumping your arms and running as fast as you can. Lindsey stared straight ahead with her eyes glued to the doorway.

"Hey," Jim whispered, trying to get her attention while keeping his voice low. "Are you ready?"

Lindsey nodded her confirmation without breaking her gaze.

"You remember the plan?" Jim asked.

"Stay right behind you, don't make too much noise," Lindsey replied.

"Right," said Jim. "We'll take the most direct route to the front of the store and get out as fast as possible. Watch your back and try not to be heard or seen."

"Got it," she answered, careful to keep her voice down. "But what if one of them sees us?"

"Run like Hell and I'll meet you at the car."

"Okay," Lindsey replied. "So, should I take the keys then?"

"Funny," said Jim. He took a deep breath and opened the door, leading them out into the back of the supermarket.

The store had grown quiet but the signs of chaos were all around them. From bright crimson-painted milk cartons in the dairy case to deep burgundy streaks across the floor, nearly every shade of red was accounted for. And it was on just about every surface. A pink film had dried on the sneeze guard at the deli counter and the Mr. Cooley's Ice Cream cooler had been overturned and came to rest in the center of a rosy pond.

Many of the shelves were left bare but it wasn't from looting, there hadn't been a chance for that yet. The flailing limbs of fleeing shoppers could account for the damaged and tipped-over display cases. Countless boxes of rice, cereal, and pasta had been knocked from the racks and lie scattered about the floor. Eight or ten boxes of Cheerios had been broken open and left to spill tiny O's all over the dingy tiles. Jim and Lindsey were careful not to step on any of them as they crept down the long aisle toward the front of the store.

Every few steps, Lindsey would turn around and check behind her to make sure she wasn't being followed. Jim did the same, except he was mainly checking to make sure she was still behind him. So far, so good but neither was willing to test their luck.

As they reached the end of the aisle, the cash registers came into view. So did the bodies. There were at least four, from what Jim could tell. Two of them were cashiers, both young women. One of the clerks was slumped over the grocery conveyor belt, face-down on top of a loaf of bread and two cans of peas. The other was on the ground between the check-out station and a rack of dopey tabloid magazines.

The other two bodies were those of shoppers, a gray-haired man in a white polo shirt and tan slacks, and a teenage boy in a blue tee shirt and khaki shorts. The man was lying face-up with his legs under a table topped with snack cakes. The boy had somehow become wedged between a small cooler filled with sodas and the shelving unit stocked with candy and gum.

All four of them were drenched in blood; their bodies ravaged, covered in bite marks. Hefty chunks of flesh had been torn away from their arms, necks, and faces. All four had eyes wide open and faces frozen in a grimace of terror and agony. Jim cringed at the sight. He turned to face Lindsey and held a hand up, gesturing for her to stop moving.

"Hang on a sec," Jim whispered.

Lindsey nodded and Jim stepped out from the end of the aisle to have a look around. The front of the store looked much like the back. Boxes, cans, and bottles were strewn about. Shopping carts were either tipped over or abandon half-filled with groceries. Blood slicks dried to a crust on the floors, cash registers, and end caps.

Letting the shotgun lead the way, Jim slowly made his way closer to the check-out stations. The exit was now within view, just beyond the stacked cases of soda cans and bottled water. If not for the potato chip display and a poster advertising a sale on fruit, he should have been able to see his car parked just outside the vestibule. Squinting, Jim could make out a small patch of blue through the glass. He breathed a small sigh of relief. If they could just make it to the car, everything was going to be okay.

But they were going to have to be quick about it. A tingling in his ear told Jim that he and Lindsey were not alone in the supermarket. It came as a hurried throaty breathing at first. Then came squishing, chomping, and slurping. Someone was eating and despite being in a grocery store, Jim knew that the meal in question had not been taken off the shelves. Somewhere several rows down, some poor soul's body was being consumed.

Jim glanced back to where Lindsey stood, still ducked behind the nearest row of groceries. Her back was to him and she appeared to be watching the opening at the far end of the aisle. Jim tried waving to get her attention but she didn't seem to notice.

"Psst," he called quietly. "Lindsey!"

She spun around, swinging the knife out in front of her as she moved. Her eyes met Jim's as he began waving his hand toward himself, beckoning her to join him. Lindsey cautiously peeked around the corner of the aisle, sure to check both ways before stepping out. As she began walking to meet him, he raised an index finger to his lips.

"Shh," Jim said almost silently. He pointed to his right, to something unseen further down the row of cash registers.

Lindsey tried to follow but she couldn't see what he was trying to point out. She furrowed her brow and looked back to Jim with a shrug. Jim held a hand up for her to stop moving. He cocked his head to the side as if trying to hear something obscure or at a low volume. But the noise was gone. The chewing sound had stopped and the only thing his ears could detect was the shitty soft jazz music still playing on the store's overhead speakers.

That could only mean one thing. The snacking ghoul must have heard them and stopped eating so he could figure out what had interrupted his meal. Jim's eyes grew wider at the realization that he and Lindsey were now the hunted. The expression on his face sent fresh chills down Lindsey's spine. The muscles in her thighs twitched from anxiety and anticipation. Her hands began to tremble in front of her. She tried to stay calm, forcing herself to remain still. But before the blade stopped shaking in her clenched fist, it was time to move again.

Jim waved for her to come closer to him. His movements were hurried this time, almost panicked. As soon as Lindsey started to move, he raised his weapon and aimed in the general direction from which the chewing sounds had originated.

Lindsey scurried across the floor and closed the distance between herself and Jim in about two seconds. When she got there, she reached up and tapped him on the back between the shoulder blades. The touch was intended to let him know that she had reached him but in that simple action, Lindsey was struck with a sudden wave of comfort. She was safe, protected. Her thumping heartbeat began to slow and her breathing returned to normal. Something told her that they were going to be okay. But her sense of security would soon be revoked.

Jim began leading them toward the exit, careful to avoid the check-out line with the dead cashier. He led with his right foot, making as wide of a stance as he could reach, and then sliding his left foot over to meet it. Jim did a quick visual sweep of the area and everywhere he looked, the shotgun followed. After a few more steps, he and Lindsey had reached the bagging area. The exit was now less than twenty feet away.

When he took his next step and planted his right foot back on the floor, a slight sloshing sound could be detected. Cool liquid seeped into Jim's shoes and socks. The broken water bottles; a wide, shallow puddle had formed across the floor at the front of the supermarket. He knew it was there and he knew what it was, but Jim couldn't help himself. Out of pure, stupid instinct, he looked down at his feet. Lindsey had noticed as well.

"Water bottles," Jim explained softly.

Understanding there was no time for otherwise-harmless distractions, Jim and Lindsey looked up and re-focused their gaze down the long row of registers before them. And this time, there was someone gazing back, peering over the top of the counter from three aisles over.

He had long hair knotted with congealed blood which dripped coppery stains onto his white tee shirt and denim jacket. An equally long beard was matted to his chin and neck. Infected eyes stared through red-dotted frames on wire-rimmed sunglasses, which had somehow managed to stay on his head. A thick yarn of clear and red fluid slid out of his mouth. The behemoth reached two gore-covered hands onto the ledge and pulled himself upright. He groaned a throaty growl and began to pull himself over the check-out station.

"Oh shit, oh shit, oh shit," Jim said aloud; his words inaudible over the sound of Lindsey's screaming. He raised the barrel of the shotgun and said to himself, "Okay, here we go."

The beast jumped over the check-out station and landed on the next conveyor belt in line, only two more to go before he'd reach his next two victims. It was more of a running motion than it was jumping. One long stride after the next and within seconds, he had reached the next row in front of Jim and Lindsey. Without slowing or stopping, he leaped again. And then came an eruption.

A flurry of metal pellets from the shotgun blast left the infected bastard a shredded mess of splintered skin and torn denim. A few strands of raw flesh were all that kept his head attached to his shoulders. The round of buckshot also tore through the candy rack, sending gum and mints into the air. A few new holes formed in the back of the shirt worn by the slumped-over cashier. Her body jiggled ever-so slightly, but otherwise remained in place.

As candy wrappers and register tape floated back toward the ground, the gunshot's echo faded to silence. Jim and Lindsey's ears adjusted and the notes of soft jazz returned. But this wasn't the only sound they could hear. Footsteps. A dozen or more could be heard running in their direction from further back in the store. Hidden amongst the grocery aisles, neither Jim nor Lindsey could see the runners, but they knew the only types of people that would be rushing toward the sound of a gun being shot: The Infected.

Jim turned back to check on Lindsey. She was still behind him, crouched down with her back pressed against the neighboring check-out stand. One hand was up over her head as if to shield herself from potential debris.

"You okay?" Jim asked.

She looked up at him and asked, "Time to run?"

"Time to run," he confirmed.

Without a moment's hesitation, Lindsey jumped to her feet and they both ran for the door. Their feet splashed through spilled water as they sprinted side-by-side past the beverage display cases. The footsteps behind them grew louder as they approached the exit. Lindsey sped up and got a few paces ahead of Jim. She reached the doorway first and turned back to wait for him to catch up.

Years of smoking and an aversion to exercise made it tough for Jim to keep up. A glimmer of foolish hopefulness had him pause not only to catch his breath, but to see if it might be innocent bystanders looking for help, rather than a group of cannibals rushing toward him. This hope was quickly extinguished when he chanced a glance over his shoulder to see two forms appear from behind the grocery aisles.

There was a woman in green scrubs and a man in a blue hat, black tee shirt, and dark athletic shorts. They were too far away and moving too quickly for Jim to make out much detail but the bright red splotches across their hands, chests, and mouths made their intentions clear. As the two fiends reached the front end of the supermarket, they stopped running. Both of the ghouls looked at the floor in front of them before making a sharp right. They began to sprint again, still heading for Jim and Lindsey but they were going the long way, around the back side of the registers.

"Jim!" Lindsey called from the doorway as three more blood-soaked freaks emerged from the ends of the shopping aisle. "Come on!"

He didn't need to be told twice. Jim ran to meet her and the pair rushed through the threshold, out of the supermarket and into the hot afternoon sun. The gray-skinned ghoul in the yellow shirt who had attacked Jim in front of the store had since bled out. His bloated and run-ripened corpse lie unmoving just feet from the car.

Jim stepped over the body and opened the car door, punching the unlock button so Lindsey could get in on the passenger's side. She climbed in and slammed the door closed. Before he could do the same, Jim was spotted by the first of the maniacs who'd followed him out of the store. It was the man in the tee shirt and gym shorts. Jim swung the gun around and took a shot at the beast. The bastard staggered but Jim didn't wait to see if the shot was enough to put him down.

Hopping into the car, Jim handed the shotgun to Lindsey before closing and locking the door. He started the engine and put the car in gear. As he lifted his foot off the brake pedal, Jim jumped in his seat at the sound of hands thumping against the car's trunk lid and windows. The rear-view mirror showed nothing but thrashing arms and the grimaces of the damned. They swarmed the Pontiac, threatening to break through the glass.

"Oh shit!" Jim exclaimed.

"Let's go!" Lindsey shrieked.

Jim stomped his foot down on the accelerator, leaving the small horde in a cloud of dust and exhaust fumes. Some of them tried to give chase but it was no use. In mere seconds, the blue coupe was out of reach and out of sight. Jim jerked the wheel hard to the left, turning the wrong way down Division Street and speeding away from Bennett's Supermarket for the very last time.

Chapter 29

"Go!"

Jenna, poised to shoot, let the barrel of her rifle lead the way. Danny followed closely, machete at the ready. The pair rushed through the threshold and into the hallway. They were ready for action, ready to kill if need be. Adrenaline flooded their veins, muscles tensed; pulses racing. Neighbors and friends turned warriors, nothing would stand between them and their mission to protect their building, their homes, and each other. They set out with unwavering resolve to do just that. Anything standing in their way would be destroyed.

And then it was quiet again. The hallway was empty. No signs of life. No infected brutes coming to get them. No fearful residents desperate for shelter. There was no movement of any sort, apart from the door swinging closed behind them. They could hear footsteps on the other side of the wall as Lucy came over to lock the deadbolt and then walked away, presumably back to her post at the kitchen window.

"I have to admit," Danny said, "I'm a little disappointed. That was very anticlimactic."

"Don't get too comfortable," Jenna told him, making her way across the hall to knock on the door opposite Danny's. "We're just getting started, but let's hope it stays this quiet."

"I think we'll be fine," Danny replied casually.

Jenna knocked again when no one answered the door, harder and louder this time.

"Maybe people are afraid to come to the door," Danny offered. "If they know what's going on, they might think it's a zombie trying to get in."

"I don't think zombies- err, infected people are polite enough to knock," Jenna said. "Plus, there's a peephole. They can see it's not one of them."

"No, but what they will see is a chick with a gun and a dude with a small sword," he explained. "That might make someone nervous."

"That's a good point." Jenna pressed her ear to the door and listened for movement inside.

"And besides," Danny began, "That's Larry's place. He's out of town."

Jenna groaned a breath of frustration. "If you knew that he's out of town, why'd you let me keep pounding on the door?"

Danny shrugged.

"Fine," Jenna huffed. "Let's keep moving. Do you know if anyone else is away?"

"Well," Danny's eyes drifted to the ceiling, something they always did when he was straining to remember things. "Jim hasn't been back since he left for work this morning."

"Have you spoken to him?" There was a sense of urgency in her words.

"Um. Well, no. I haven't heard from him."

"Shit. That's not good," Jenna commented. She looked as if she might have something else to add but then she just repeated, "Shit."

189

"The apartment across from Jim's is empty," Danny told her. "So, I guess that just leaves Charles on this side of the building. But I don't know about him, I haven't seen him too much in the last few days."

"Okay, we'll check it out." Jenna started heading down the steps. "His car is in the parking lot, so unless he left with his girlfriend or something, he's probably home."

Danny followed her down the stairs. With no one home on the first floor, they kept going until they reached the ground level at the main entrance to the building. Jenna continued heading for the basement but Danny paused to look out the front door. The tenement cast a long shadow in the late afternoon sun, across the parking lot and to the sidewalk.

Everything was still. The space outside would have appeared normal if not for the absence of traffic. That, and the two dead bodies laid across the pavement. Thankfully, Danny didn't see any people out walking around. For now, the coast remained clear.

"You coming?" Jenna called up to him.

"Yep, sorry." Danny scurried down the stairs to join her in the basement landing.

"I knocked but no one answered," she told him, gesturing to Charles' door. "I guess he is out after all. Looks like you, me, and Lucy have this side of the building to ourselves."

"And Jim," Danny reminded her.

Jenna looked him in the eye; a solemn expression on her face. "Danny," she said.

"Yes?"

"I know you and Jim are friends and all," Jenna continued. "But if he's not here, he may not be coming back."

Danny waved a dismissive hand in the air. "He'll be fine. Jim knows how to take care of himself."

"I hope you're right," Jenna said as she opened the door to her right. This door, opposite from Charles' door, led into the unfinished portion of the basement which held the laundry machines, water heaters, boilers, and the guts of the utility systems. Before going in, she asked, "Have you talked to him since this morning?"

"I have not," Danny admitted.

"Okay, we'll try calling him when we get back upstairs." Jenna started to move through the doorway and motioned for Danny to come with her. "Coming?"

He nodded but before they could get too far, the sound of a heavy thud made them stop in their tracks. They looked at one another, keeping silent and hoping that whatever had made the noise would reveal itself.

"What was that?" Danny whispered.

Jenna shrugged her shoulders. "It sounded like it came from in there," she pointed back across the narrow hall to the door to Charles' apartment.

"I'll check it out," Danny said. He walked back over to the door, getting as close to it as possible without touching it and listened for more. After a few moments of silence, he gently rapped his knuckles against the wood finish. Keeping a hushed tone, he asked, "Anyone home?"

When nobody answered, Danny reached for the doorknob to see if it was unlocked. He looked back to Jenna for approval. She was frantically shaking her head but Danny forged ahead anyway. He was surprised to find that the old rusty metal knob turned. It wasn't locked. To Jenna's dismay, Danny gave the door a little shove and let it swing the rest of the way open.

The scene inside and the stench pouring out were enough to make both of them wretch. A fetor of rot hung heavy in the air and there was blood everywhere. Dark red splotches covered the walls, the carpet, and the furniture. It streaked across every visible surface and concentrated in a syrupy pool in front of the sofa. At the center of the burgundy puddle lie a broken heap of bones and decaying flesh. Glistening globs of uneaten skin and organs were strewn throughout the kitchen and living room amid the gore-soaked remnants of ripped clothing and demolished furniture.

There were holes in the walls, broken dishes, and a smashed table. Even the ceiling had been sprayed with blood. The carpet was so badly stained, it was impossible to tell its original color. The apartment had transformed into a slaughterhouse and in the middle of the kitchen, under its only source of illumination, stood the butcher himself. Charles had his eyes fixed on his next two victims.

From head to toe, the man was drenched. Red and pink fluid had congealed to form a brown crust over his skin and clothing. His shirt was torn at the collar from where his prey had ineffectively tried to defend herself.

Chest heaving and fists trembling, Charles drew his upper lip back into a sneer. He pushed out a growl through clenched teeth; bits of red spittle leaping out and dribbling down the front of his tattered shirt. With a frenzied look in his eyes, Charles took off like a shot aimed right at Danny.

He almost forgot he was holding a weapon. After only a brief pause, Danny wound up like he was swinging a tennis racket rather than a machete. The blade connected just inside the shoulder. It split through skin and shattered the man's left clavicle, shredding fat and muscle along the way. A torrent of fresh blood poured out of the open wound, a much brighter shade of red than the fluid which had already dried on his skin and clothing.

More snarling. More incomprehensible groans. To Danny's extreme displeasure, the injuries inflicted were not enough to stop Charles. It didn't even seem to slow him down. Danny spun to his right to avoid being run over by the larger man, who was still in pursuit. As Charles closed in, Danny held the machete straight out in front of him. He locked both hands around the handle and as Charles took his next step toward him, Danny lunged forward, driving the tip of the blade into his belly.

Sharpened steel slid through cotton fabric and pale skin but it didn't run him all the way through. Charles flailed his arms as he tried to grab onto Danny. Danny leaned back to stay out of reach. Charles then grabbed onto the blade itself, slicing his fingers along the razor-fine edge. More blood spurted out, spilling onto the machete and then to the floor.

Crack! Crack! Charles' arms fell limp and his body stayed suspended for a beat. A small cloud of red mist materialized. Two holes appeared on his face, one in the center of his forehead, and one on his right cheek. Matching trails of red fluid rolled out. Charles fell backwards, away from the blade stuck in his gut, and landed flat on his back.

Danny, shocked, looked to the doorway of the apartment. Jenna still had the gun pointed at the large dead man on the floor. It was the second time that day she'd saved Danny's life.

"Th- thank you," he stammered.

"Are you okay?" she asked.

"Um. Yeah." Danny sounded unsure as he took quick stock of himself. He hadn't been harmed, not really. The only discomfort he felt was in his hands and he realized the pain was coming from how tightly he held onto the machete handle. "Yeah, I think I'm alright."

No sooner had the words escaped his mouth than a wave of nausea rolled over him. Danny bent forward and heaved. He pushed out a thick mouthful of yellow and orange vomit, most of which landed on the corpse in front of him.

"Whoa," Jenna lowered the gun and rushed over to Danny. "Come on, let's get out of here. We'll get you some air and a place to sit down."

"No, no," Danny waved her off. "I'm okay, let's keep moving."

"Are you sure? We can take a break, it's okay."

"I'm sure," Danny told her. "I'm good, just maybe a little embarrassed. Ya know, because of the vomit."

"Don't worry about it," said Jenna. She smiled and gave him a friendly slap on the shoulder. "I mean, it's not like it could smell worse in here, right?"

Danny nodded. "Yeah, I guess that's true." He finally relaxed his hands and wrists, letting his arms fall to his sides.

"Okay, we'll keep going," Jenna said. "But if you need to stop or get some water or whatever, just let me know."

"Will do," Danny forced a smile and nodded. "And Jenna?"

"Yeah?"

"Thank you," he said. "I mean it, I'm glad you're here."

"No problem," Jenna answered casually. "You'd do the same for me."

"If I could," Danny replied. "But I'm not sure I'd be as good at it as you are. That's twice now you've had to save my ass."

Jenna shook her head. "I wouldn't be able to do this on my own. As much as I'm protecting you, you're doing the same for me and your sister."

"Yeah, I guess so."

"So," Jenna began, "You ready to move? I'd prefer not to spend any more time in here than we absolutely need to."

"Sure." Danny cleared his throat and spit a wad of orange-colored phlegm on the floor. "Shouldn't we see if there's anyone else in here first?"

Jenna took a quick look around without moving deeper into the apartment. She was looking for signs of life but saw only images of death. Charles, covered in blood with a pair of .22 caliber bullets still rattling around in his skull, was strangely not the most troubling sight. That honor belonged to the other corpse in the room. Although, to call it a dead body would be generous and a little misleading. The remains were little more than a hollow hull of torn skin flaps strung over a pitted red skeleton.

It had obviously been a woman, presumably Charles' girlfriend. The face, what was left of it, had on a pair of pink retro-style glasses with cat's eye frames and rhinestones. Pale skin appeared where patches of hair had been ripped from the scalp. In the dim light, the hair looked to be dark brown or black, but it very well could have been blonde beneath all the blood and soot.

"No, there's no one else here. If there was, we'd have seen 'em by now," Jenna pointed to

Charles, "Especially if it was anyone like him."

"Fair enough." Danny said, "Okay, let's go."

Jenna took two steps backwards, moving out of the apartment and into the hallway. Danny followed her out. He pulled the door closed behind him and met Jenna in the hall. She gave him a nod and pushed through the next doorway, which led to the unfinished section of the basement. The thin blue carpet came to a tattered end on the other side of the threshold, leaving only bare cement.

The unfinished portion of the basement was divided into two sections, each with a no-frills, minimalist decor. Jenna and Danny had entered on the side that had, at one time, been used as a workspace for the building's maintenance man. Straight ahead, about twelve feet from where they stood, was a partition with a doorway that led to the other half of the basement, the side with the coin-operated washer and dryer. Danny began to move past her but Jenna put a hand up to stop him.

"Hold on a sec," she said. "Let's take a quick look around first."

To their left, along the block wall at the front of the building, was a large plastic drain tub and a wooden chest of drawers. Junk was scattered everywhere. Between the doorway and the tub, was an assortment of loose papers, cardboard boxes, an overturned garbage pail, empty beer cans, and bottles of various cleaning agents whose labels had long ago worn off. Every item was coated with a layer of dust and grime that seemed to grow thicker before their eyes. The funk of a neglected sump pump hung heavy in the humid air.

Opposite the drain tub was a narrow path that led to the rear of the basement. Along the left side of the walkway was a row of five padlocked storage closets. On the right side was the water tank and heating unit for that side of the building. In an apparent bid to keep tenants from meddling with the utility systems, the property owner had used chain link fencing and lumber to construct a cage around the boiler and water heater.

"I'm going to check out the other side," Danny told her as he walked over to the doorway that led to the laundry area.

"Alright," Jenna replied. She had placed the rifle on the floor and was opening the top drawer in the chest. "Just don't go too far."

"No problem." Danny rested his free hand on the doorknob and before opening it, he turned back to her and asked, "What are you looking for?"

"A chain or rope or something," she answered without looking up. Jenna closed the top drawer, pulling open the next one down and rummaging through its contents. "Anything I can use to tie the handles together on the front doors. I want to make sure no one can get in unless we let them in."

"Yeah, I was going to ask you about that," Danny started. "Those doors open out. I can see how zombies might try to push through to get in, but do you think they'll figure out they have to pull the handles to get them open?"

"They might. I think we'd be safer to assume they can," said Jenna, sighing as she slammed the second drawer closed and moved to the next one below it. "And I'm not just worried about them."

"You want to keep *everyone* out?"

"Maybe not everyone," she explained. "If someone is in danger and needs help, then sure, we'll let them in. But there may be some people who aren't infected that may be looking to take advantage of all the chaos."

"Looters?" Danny asked.

"Looters," Jenna confirmed.

"Alright, I'll see if I can find anything over here then." Danny opened the door and let it close behind him as he disappeared on the other side of the wall.

"Useless," Jenna mumbled to no one. There was nothing but junk inside these drawers; half-empty bottle of Elmer's glue, an old calculator with a crack in the display, a landline phone without its cord, a paintbrush caked with enough white paint to turn the bristles into a useless solid lump.

She closed the third drawer, leaving only one more to search. If nothing useful turned up, she'd have to come up with a different plan. Maybe she could wedge something into the hinges at the front doors, or maybe try to find some way to just barricade them, block them off altogether. That might be a good way to keep people from coming in, but what if they needed to get out?

Jenna knelt on the cement floor and yanked open the bottom drawer. At first it looked like more of the same; a flashlight with no batteries, a rusted pair of scissors, a roll of masking tape. She shuffled the items around inside the bin and saw a thick orange wire. Brushing aside a hair comb and an old TV remote, Jenna grabbed the wire and began pulling it from the rest of the clutter. What she found in her hands was a fifty-foot extension cord. Naturally, the end had been clipped and the plug part was missing. It wouldn't actually be able to power anything but it should be long enough and durable enough to tie a pair of door handles together.

She held one end of the cord in her right hand and wrapped it between her palm and elbow, using her arm as a spool. Satisfied with her find, Jenna stood up and grabbed her gun from the floor. Taking one last look around and deciding there was nothing else worth taking, Jenna took one step toward the partition door to see how Danny was making out. But instead of joining him on the other side, it was Danny who was coming back to meet her.

He stepped through the doorway, still clutching his weapon and also holding an unopened package of coaxial cable. The young man once again wore a panicked expression. Even in the dim light of the basement, Danny looked pale and it seemed as if he was going to be sick again.

"What is it?" she asked.

"Coaxial cable," he said as he lifted up the package. "The label says it's thirty feet. I found it in a pile of junk in the next room, figured it might work for the doors."

"I can see that," Jenna replied. "I meant, what's wrong?"

"Well," Danny began. "You remember how you said you saw Adam and Albert walking into the building after Adam got attacked by one of the crazies?"

"Yeah?" Jenna shifted nervously in place. Whatever Danny was about to say was almost certainly going to be bad news.

"And you said you didn't know what happened to them next?" he asked.

"That's right."

"Well, I found Adam." Danny tilted his head to the side and back to indicate that the subject of their conversation was on the other side of the wall.

"Okay," Jenna replied with caution in her voice.

"But he's not looking too good."

"Is he..." She let her words trail off and paused for a moment before finishing her question. "Is he dead?"

194

Danny shook his head.

"Infected?" Jenna asked.

"It appears that way." Danny reached to open the door again and said, "Come on, I'll show you."

"Wait!" Jenna cried. "Is he in there?"

"He is, but it's okay," Danny assured her. "He's not dangerous."

"Not dangerous?" Jenna asked. "How can that be?"

"Trust me," Danny said. "It'll be easier if you see for yourself."

"Okay," Jenna agreed reluctantly. "But you're going first. And if you're messing with me, I'm going to kick your ass."

She followed him through the doorway and into the other side of the basement. There, Jenna saw him immediately. It was definitely Adam, or at least it had been Adam. His clothes, blue jeans and a baggy sweatshirt, were coated in dried blood that formed a brown crust against the fabric. An array of cuts and deep gouges covered his hands and face.

Adam was inside the cage that housed the water heater and boiler unit. The gate was closed and locked. A thick heavy-duty steel chain was wrapped around Adam's waist and cinched in tight like a belt. His restraints were secured with a padlock behind his back. From there, another length of chain had been tied around a three-inch metal pipe that ran from the boiler up to the ceiling.

"What's wrong with him?" Jenna asked, not taking her eyes off the trapped ghoul.

Adam stared back through half-lidded eyes. His feet shuffled and he staggered forward as far as the chains would allow. His arms swung loosely at his sides. Adam wasn't lunging or trying to grab at them. He didn't growl or scream like the infected people they had previously encountered. He made a few grunts here and there but it was little more than heavy breathing. Every few moments, Adam would snap his jaw closed and bite at the air. Otherwise, his mouth hung open and leaked a steady stream of saliva across his belly.

"What do you mean?" asked Danny.

"I mean there's something wrong with him," Jenna insisted. "He doesn't seem right."

"He's infected," Danny answered plainly.

"Yeah, I know that," she replied. Waving her hand for emphasis, Jenna added, "I mean, just look at him. Why isn't he lashing out and trying to kill us?"

"There, there," Danny said as if trying to comfort her. "I'm sure he'd kill us if he could. Don't you worry about that."

"Very funny. You know what I mean." Jenna clarified, "It's like he's all worn out."

Danny turned to face her, finally relaxing enough to lower his blade. "What time was it when you last saw Adam and Albert?"

"Not sure," she shrugged. "It was early. Sometime this morning, why?"

"I bet Albert put him down here right when they came inside," Danny explained. "If that's the case, then he's been down here for hours. He's had plenty of time to tire himself out."

"I suppose so," Jenna said. "But he's the only one I've seen who looks like this, so sedated and slowed down."

"Right. But the other ones, the ones we've seen so far, were probably infected more recently," Danny wondered out loud. "The other ones move so fast, it's like they've got a rush of adrenaline or something. That adrenaline has to run out at some point."

"That makes sense," Jenna concurred. "But what about Charles? He must have gotten infected days ago and he still moved pretty quickly."

"Yeah, but just think about it. When you have an adrenaline rush, it eventually fades and goes away. But then you can still go on to have another adrenaline rush when you've had a chance to recover. When he first got infected, he probably freaked out and burned off all of his energy. Then he gets some rest and has something to eat," Danny paused to make a face of disgust when he said the word *eat*, and then went on to complete his thought. "Then his energy levels are back up and he's got a fresh load of adrenaline."

"Ya know," Jenna started. She turned to look him in the eye. With a grin, she said, "That's pretty smart, Danny. You're not as dumb as people think you are."

"Thanks!" Danny smiled back. Then he frowned and asked, "Wait, who thinks I'm dumb?"

"Take it easy," she said. "I'm only joking."

"Yeah, of course. I know that," he told her, masking a pained expression with another toothy smile. "I am a genius, after all."

"Okay, Einstein." Jenna gave Danny a playful nudge with her elbow. "I think we have to go check on Albert."

"What about him?" Danny asked, pointing to Adam.

"I don't think he's getting out of there," Jenna replied. "We're probably okay to leave him for now. The reporters on the news kept saying that anyone who's been infected should be quarantined until further notice. He should be fine as long as he stays locked up."

"I don't suppose you're still looking for chains?"

"I was, but I can make do with this." Jenna held up the extension cord.

"There's a couple good chains in there." Danny shot a glance to the utilities cage. A playful look on his face let her know he was only joking.

"If you want to go in there to get them, knock yourself out," Jenna said. "But even if I had the keys for those locks, there's no way I'm getting that close to him or anyone else who's infected."

"I bet Albert's got the keys," Danny offered.

"I bet you're right," she replied. "But like I said, I'm not getting any closer than this."

"Probably for the best."

"Alright," Jenna said; her expression growing dour once again. "Let's go see how Albert's holding up."

Chapter 30

The car roared down Division Street, driving hard against the grain of one-way traffic. A black Ford Ranger with a smashed-in headlamp came bearing down on the Pontiac. Its grille was bent inward with bits of red flesh and hair clinging to the molded plastic. The truck swerved to the right, avoiding the blue coupe but clipping the curb in the process. It bounced from side to side for a few seconds before the driver regained control of the pickup.

After about a hundred feet, the Pontiac reached the crossway where Division Street meets Robinson Street. Broken glass, strips of leather, and shards of metal were scattered all over the pavement. A bright red stain streaked through the intersection. The trail was just over fifteen feet in length and led right to where eight rabid cannibals surrounded an overturned motorcycle. The Suzuki sport bike lie on its side with a pair of bent wheels and a pillar of smoke rising from the engine. If the rider survived the fall, he didn't survive what came next.

Jim steered to the right toward Robinson Street. He immediately cut the wheel back to the left to avoid hitting the ghouls in the middle of the roadway. Too focused on the rider's half-eaten body, most of them didn't even notice. Lindsey watched in horror, briefly catching eyes with one of the savages as the car raced by. A shorter, pudgy-faced fiend gazed at her through the window. His lips pulled into a sneer and he bared bone-gnawing teeth.

"Oh God," said Lindsey as she turned to look away from the murder scene. She folded her arms over her stomach and lurched forward in her seat, trying to quell a rising torrent of nausea and panic. Lindsey could only lean so far because the shotgun was between her legs with the muzzle on the floor and the buttstock up in front of her chest.

"What is it?" Jim asked; his voice loud and hurried. He straightened out the car and pressed down firmly on the gas pedal. The engine whirred and the coupe accelerated hard as they headed southbound on Twin Cities Memorial Highway.

About a block down, a stalled Nissan sedan was turned sideways in the right lane. Its front bumper hung over the curb while the rear bumper stuck out far enough to block part of the next lane. Jim eased off the gas and pulled the Pontiac all the way to the left, just far enough to avoid hitting the disabled car.

The body of the sedan shook and bounced on a worn-out suspension. Someone was obviously inside. A struggle of some kind was taking place but there was so much blood splattered against the inside of the windows that it was impossible to see into the car. A hand pressed against the window, smearing blood and slapping the glass before falling away once more.

Lindsey stared as they passed by. She craned her neck to see and then turned around in her seat to watch through the back window. Inside the Nissan, something else brushed against the rear driver's side window, followed by another spray of blood. Then the jostling stopped. Lindsey groaned again. She turned back around and slumped into her seat.

"What is it?" Jim asked again.

"Nothing. It's nothing," she told him after taking a second to collect herself. Lindsey tried to sound calm and keep her voice even. She was having a hard time but there was no way she was going to let herself break down. After all, Jim was going through the same thing and he wasn't whining about it. There was no way she was going to fall apart on him, not after all he'd done for her. Lindsey swallowed hard, took a breath and added, "I'm okay."

"Alright," Jim replied without looking at her. His tone felt dismissive and detached, even to himself. Lindsey either didn't notice or didn't care.

She watched the road for a few moments before letting her gaze drop. Scanning the inside of the car, Lindsey searched for somewhere she could focus her attention, rather than having to watch everything that was happening outside. Her eyes traced the dashboard, the radio controls, and the gauge cluster. Lindsey couldn't see the speedometer and she figured that was probably for the best. The Pontiac was really moving now and the last thing she needed was to concern herself with how fast Jim was driving.

It was getting hot inside the car. The windows were still rolled up. The vent fan was on but it was set to the lowest speed and seemed to be churning out warm air. Lindsey reached for the button to lower her window and it was only then she realized she was still holding the knife from the deli counter at Bennett's Supermarket.

She held it up in front of her, slowly turning it over and examining the sharp edge and dull finish of the stainless steel. It somehow felt strange in her hand, in a way it hadn't when they were still inside the supermarket. It was an odd sensation, a dirty sensation. She'd *killed* a person with that knife. Lindsey wasn't just holding a tangible reminder of a taken life, she was literally holding the murder weapon. This thought turned her stomach more than anything she'd seen that day.

So maybe *murder* wasn't the right word. She wasn't a murderer, but she was a killer and an internal debate over semantics would do little to soothe her conscience. Lindsey knew, on a logical and rational level, that she had done what she needed to do. It was self-preservation. She was attacked and had to defend herself. Someone was definitely going to die. Lindsey just took appropriate measures to make sure it wasn't going to be her. Oh, and if only things were that simple.

In about a month, Lance would have been starting his senior year in high school. He worked at Bennett's part time, mostly on the weekends, and he'd been there for a little over a year. His father would drop him off before each shift, and then his mother would come pick him up when he clocked out. Lance was saving up for a car so he could eventually drive himself. Every so often, Lindsey would overhear him giving his coworkers an update on how much he had saved and how much he had left to go. He was on track to have his own ride before school was back in session. He was a good kid overall, a little shy, but friendly and hardworking. And Lindsey had killed him.

She recalled the wild, rageful look in his eyes and watching them lose focus as they were slowly drained of life. Lindsey sniffled. Her face felt puffy and hot. It was getting to be too much and staring at the knife in her hands was only making matters worse.

Turning it so the blade pointed down, Lindsey wedged the knife between her seat and the center console. She pressed it down far enough so that only the handle stuck out. It was within reach if she needed it, but out of the way in the meantime. That done, she finally hit the button to lower the window a couple of inches.

The slight breeze felt cool against Jim's arms and neck. He somehow hadn't noticed the rising temperature inside the car until his underarms were damp with perspiration. His hands and forehead were drenched as well. Jim dried his palms one at a time against the front of his black polo shirt and then pulled his collar up to dry his face.

"You want me to turn on the air conditioning?" he asked.

"No, I'm good with just having the window open," Lindsey answered. "But I mean, you can turn it on if you want. I'm okay either way."

"Okay. I need you to do me a favor," Jim started to say as he reached a hand into his pocket. He grabbed two shells, handed them to Lindsey and asked, "Can you load these into the gun?"

"Yeah, sure." Lindsey took the rounds and placed them in her lap. She took hold of the firearm, lifting it up and examining the receiver.

"It's right here," Jim told her, pointing to the top lever above the grip. "You just gotta-"

"I know," Lindsey snapped. "I can do it."

"Alright, alright," Jim murmured as he placed his hand back on the steering wheel.

Lindsey sighed and rubbed her eyes. "I'm sorry. That sounded shitty."

"It's okay," he told her. "It's stressful, I get it."

She opened her mouth to speak but then closed it without saying a word. Lindsey returned her attention to the weapon in front of her. She thumbed the top lever and pressed down on the grip to open the top end of the barrels.

"Oh!" she cried, startled as the shotgun's extractors kicked out the plastic shells inside. The spent rounds popped out of the barrels, bouncing off the inside of the window and landing somewhere on the floor or under the seat. Lindsey huffed and replaced the shells, closing the barrels and engaging the safety. Then, leaning to her left, Lindsey lifted the weapon over her right hip and laid it to rest between her leg and the car door. That settled, Lindsey peered through the windshield to examine the road ahead and asked, "Okay, so what now?"

"Well..." Jim started to say. Having no real plan to speak of, he let his voice trail off.

Assuming there wasn't more to come, Lindsey asked, "Is there somewhere we can go?"

"I uh," he began to say, lifting his foot off the gas pedal as the car drifted past the Dollar General on the corner of Schenck Street. Confirming the coast was clear, he punched it again and accelerated through the intersection before completing his sentence. "I actually hadn't thought this through. I think we should probably try to stay off the road, maybe find some place to hide out until things blow over."

"Did you have a particular place in mind?" Her tone bordered on accusatory and she again caught herself immediately. "Sorry, I just- I just don't know what to do."

"It's okay," Jim assured her. He dragged his wrist across his forehead to whisk away beads of sweat before letting his right hand drop onto the gear shifter. "We'll figure it out."

"Okay," she said softly.

Lindsey reached out and put her hand over Jim's, giving it a squeeze and weaving her fingers between his. Instantly feeling his tense up beneath hers, she removed her hand and placed it back in her lap. Hoping to avoid an awkward moment, Lindsey asked, "So, if I hadn't called and you didn't have to come get me, where would you have gone?"

"I probably would have just gone home," he answered. "Get inside, lock up, and wait it out."

"I don't know about that," Lindsey told him. "What if it doesn't just blow over? What if it's days or weeks or even longer before it all stops? Do you have enough food and supplies to last that long holed up in your apartment?"

Jim thought back to his bare cupboards and nearly-empty refrigerator. How long could they last on a stick of old butter and a few ounces of sliced peaches? Even that film-covered purple meat wouldn't keep them going for more than a couple days. He groaned and admitted, "Probably not."

The car continued to speed down the road. To the right was a chain link fence which had long been overtaken by bright green ivy, an aging barrier between Pine Woods Park and the four-lane thoroughfare. At irregular intervals, the vines receded to show rusted steel wires and a seconds-long glimpse at the park beyond. At the first such break in the thick vegetation, Lindsey caught a brief view of an expansive lawn and a row of benches next to a paved walking trail. It was gone too quickly to be certain, but Lindsey could have sworn she saw someone standing beside one of the benches.

She felt like she should say something but quickly decided not to. Lindsey wasn't positive she'd actually seen a person. And even if she had, so what? Who would be out for a stroll in the park at a time like this? They'd have to be completely oblivious to the danger that now seemed inescapable. More likely, it was someone who was already sick and in need of medical attention that neither she nor Jim could provide.

"Oh!" she exclaimed after another moment of quiet. Lindsey held up her hand and an outstretched index finger for emphasis. "The hospital."

"Huh?" Jim asked, not understanding. "What's the matter, are you hurt?"

"No," she said. "I mean, let's go to the hospital. If we keep going straight, we'll pass right by DeGraff Memorial."

"Okay..."

"It's gotta be safe at the hospital," Lindsey explained. "Just think about it. It's a secure building with security guards and surveillance cameras. And there's a cafeteria so there would be food inside, and beds, and doctors and..."

She was talking quickly but it made perfect sense.

"Of course!" Jim proclaimed. "Ugh, I can't believe I didn't think of that. Nice one, Lindsey!"

She smiled at him and gave his forearm a squeeze. He smiled back and without thinking, he began to raise his hand to meet hers. Lindsey had already pulled back and let her hands rest on her knees. Now that he'd hesitated, Jim thought it better to just let her be. Hoping Lindsey hadn't noticed, he gripped the steering wheel and drove toward their newly-defined destination.

Lindsey continued watching out the window, hoping for another opening in the fence so she could catch another glimpse of the park. The vegetation became thinner as the car approached the intersection at Christiana Street. It wasn't a perfect view, but the ivy was thin enough to let Lindsey see through to the other side. There was another large field with a backstop for an overgrown baseball diamond on one end and an unpainted basketball court on the other.

At the edge of the pavement, just behind the nearest basketball hoop, was a small group of about five or six people. They were huddled up tight and formed a small circle facing one another. All of them were either kneeling or down on all fours and appeared to be digging at the ground with their hands. Lindsey leaned toward the window for a better view, holding a hand between the glass and her brow to block out the glare.

"Oh God," she murmured. Her guts began to churn and bubble. It was just like the scene back at the motorcycle crash.

"What is it?" Jim asked without taking his eyes off the road.

"It's just-" she stammered. "Just more of ...them. They're everywhere."

"Oh." He thought for a second and said, "We're alright though. And we're going to be fine. Just keep an eye out and be careful."

"I hope so," Lindsey said with a sigh.

"Just try to relax," Jim told her. "We're only a few blocks from the hospital."

She nodded but didn't say anything. Lindsey let her gaze drop to her lap and she made a point to avoid looking out the window. Nothing good was out there. She slumped back in her seat and tried to get comfortable. Lindsey leaned to her left and then to her right, shimmying from side to side before realizing that she'd been sitting on something. She pressed her feet into the floor and arched her back to lift her butt off the cushion. Reaching behind her, Lindsey felt around and searched for the cumbersome object.

"Is this yours?" she asked, holding a cell phone and raising it up for Jim to see.

"Oh," he said. "Yeah, thanks."

"You've got three missed calls," Lindsey told him as she worked the on-screen controls. "One from Beth, one from Danny, and one from a private number."

"Did anyone leave a message?"

"Doesn't look like it," she replied. "Where should I put this?"

"Um," Jim thought for a moment. "Doesn't matter, wherever there's room."

"Okay," said Lindsey. She placed the phone in the car's cup holder between the center console and the gear shifter. "I'll leave it here in case you need it."

"Okay, thanks." Jim forced another smile. "I'll have to call them back once we get inside."

"I'll have to make a few calls too." Lindsey reached into her pants pocket and pulled out her own cellular phone. "As soon as we get in, I want to call my parents and let them know I'm okay."

"And you should be able to do that in just a couple of minutes," Jim assured her.

The hospital was about two-hundred yards in front of them. They could see the parking lot come into view on the right side of the street. Eager to arrive as quickly as possible, especially now that they actually had a specific destination, Jim pressed down harder on the gas pedal. The street was mostly clear up ahead and neither Jim nor Lindsey wanted to be out and about for any longer than was absolutely necessary.

"Almost there," Jim observed.

"It looks like there's quite a few cars in the lot too," Lindsey commented. "That's gotta be a good sign, right?"

"I hope so," he answered. "At least we know it's not abandoned."

Jim steered the car to the far side of the right lane, out of the way of a conversion van that was stopped in the left lane. The passenger's side doors were open and no signs of life could be seen inside as the Pontiac passed by. Lindsey breathed a sigh of relief, thankful for being spared another ghastly view like they had seen when they passed the stalled Nissan. Jim eased the car onto Tremont Street and pulled into the parking lot.

He turned down a row of cars, looking for a place to park. Jim thought back to Lindsey's observation and said, "You were right about the parking lot, I don't see a single open spot."

"Maybe we should pull up near the entrance," she suggested. "So we can get inside quick and not have to walk across the entire lot."

"Yeah," Jim agreed. He reached the end of the row and made a right to circle back toward the entrance. "But I don't think we're supposed to park up near the building. Do you think they'll care if I park in the fire lane?"

"I kinda feel like the parking situation is pretty low on their list of priorities right now," Lindsey told him, trying to keep the mood light. "I'll tell ya what- if you get a ticket, I'll pay for it."

"I'll hold you to it," Jim teased.

As the car pulled around and cruised toward the main doorway, Jim was still scanning the parking spaces for a vacant slot when Lindsey jerked forward in her seat and cried out. "Shit!"

"What?" Jim asked, unable to hide the sudden spike of panic in his voice. He put the car in park and tried to follow her gaze.

"Over there!" she shouted, pointing across the dashboard toward the building's entrance. "In the building."

Out the driver's side window, Jim finally found what had her so horrified. The hospital lobby was in a state of total anarchy. Bodies littered the floor. Blood and gristle clung to the glass doors. Brutes chased the injured and dying through the entry hall and down the corridor. Through glass walls at the front of the building, Jim could see a man maneuvering through the chaos and hurrying toward the exit. He pushed through the doors and ran out onto the walkway. A pair of ghouls tried to follow him but they were unable to negotiate the push-bar to unlatch the door.

The man, dressed in black trousers with a white shirt and black tie, was now sprinting toward the car. He had dark hair with graying edges and thick rivulets of blood streaming down his face from a deep wound on the left side of his forehead. He pumped his arms for momentum; his left hand balled into a fist with a polished, glimmering revolver in his right.

"What do we do?" Jim stammered. "What do we do?"

"Go!" Lindsey shrieked.

"But wha-" Jim stuttered. He hesitated. His hand was on the gear shifter but he hadn't put the car back in gear.

The man reached the vehicle and without saying a word, he grabbed the driver's side door handle. He pulled on it but the door was locked. Eyes wide, the man peered through the window. His jaw dropped, as if he was just now discovering there were people inside.

"Jim, go! He's got a gun!" Lindsey screeched.

The bloodied man glanced over his shoulder. Several ghouls had gathered at the hospital exits and were pressing their hands and faces against the glass barrier. Some pounded their fists against the windows and others seemed like they were trying to chew their way through.

Up close, Jim could make out the details of the man's wounds. What he'd first thought were simply cuts and scrapes were actually bite marks. Every patch of exposed skin had been bitten. His hands, arms, neck, and face; all littered with tooth-sized puncture holes oozing the man's fleeting lifeblood. Even a patch of his scalp, just above the right ear, had been bitten and torn away. A sleek pink hue glistened and wept.

Back at the hospital, one of the freaks must have accidentally pushed against, or fallen into, the push-bar. With the weight of a dozen bodies pressed against it, the door was flung open and a small horde of frenzied ghouls poured from the exit, which was only about thirty yards away. Some shambled lazily, as if they could care less whether the man got away. Others sprinted like their lives depended on catching their prey before it could escape.

Jim found himself overtaken by a sudden moral dilemma. This man was certainly doomed. He would have definitely contracted the infection that would turn him into a bloodthirsty maniac. But how long did he have before the transformation took place? It hadn't happened yet. For now, he was still a regular person; a regular person that was about to suffer an agonizing death at the hands of a rabid predators. Jim wanted to help the man, but it seems the man thought he could help himself.

"Open the door," he demanded.

"Jim, do not let him in here," Lindsey objected in a hurried and forceful tone.

"Obviously," Jim replied.

"Open," the man began. He took a step back so he had a full arm's length between himself and the driver's window. The man raised his right hand and pointed the revolver at Jim's face before adding, "The door."

"Jim," Lindsey whispered. "Lean back."

"Whoa, just take it easy," Jim said as he reached for the gear shifter and hoped the man didn't notice. But of course, he did.

"Don't even think about it," he barked. "Touch it and I'll blow your brains out."

"Alright," said Jim in his most pathetic and servile tone. He lifted both hands to show his willingness to comply.

"Jim, lean back," Lindsey told him. Jim ignored her.

"Good," said the man brandishing his revolver. He tapped the stubby chrome barrel twice against the window and said, "Now open the door."

"Jim!" Lindsey shouted. "Lean back."

A pair of twenty-gauge barrels swung over the dashboard and hovered in front of Jim's chest. Lindsey leaned forward in her seat and pressed the muzzle to the glass of the driver's side window. Her finger rested on the trigger with the gun aimed squarely at the man outside.

"Back up," she commanded; her voice cracking mid-syllable. "Or so help me God, I will blast a hole right through your chest.

The man didn't say a word. There was no objection, no begging. He made no further demands. His only response came as a long sigh of resignation. The handgun fell away from the window and the man seemed to deflate. Both arms dropped to his sides as the man did as he was told and backed away from the Pontiac. Lindsey kept the shotgun trained on the man as he turned around to face the hospital and the dozens of ghouls rushing from its exits.

"Should I roll the window down?" Jim asked, keeping his voice low.

"No," she told him without lowering the weapon. "Let's just get out of here."

Jim nodded in agreement but he couldn't keep himself from watching the man outside the car. He was still there and the freaks were only a few feet away. The revolver came back into view as the man took a step toward the onrushing cannibals. He raised the gun in his right hand and drew back the hammer to advance the next round. With the gun cocked, the man began waving it around. He was speaking but Jim and Lindsey couldn't hear his words.

The man gave one final glance over his shoulder to the car and its occupants before turning his back to the approaching crowd. He slid the stubby chrome barrel into his mouth and squeezed his eyes shut, wincing in anticipation. The man sucked in a deep breath and held it; every fiber of muscle tensing, his chest burning, stomach twisting end over end. And then he pulled the trigger.

Chapter 31

"Oh shit!" Jim cried out. Wads of brain and shattered skull rained down on the car's hood and roof; the final thoughts of a panicked man clinging to blue paint and window glass.

"Oh my God, oh my God." Screams erupted from the passenger seat as filthy hands clawed doors, fenders, and bumpers. Lindsey shrieked again, "Get us out of here!"

But they were already moving. The Pontiac was in gear; a foot stomping the gas pedal. The car tore out of the parking lot. Jim turned back onto Tremont Street, still accelerating. Tires screeched, the coupe slid sideways and the traction control mechanism moaned in protest. Jim lifted his foot from the accelerator to correct their trajectory and to avoid clipping the curb on the left side of the street. It only took a second for him to straighten the wheels and then he punched it again.

Some of the freaks gave chase but they couldn't keep up. Sure, the fresh fast ones could be quick on their feet but even the newly-infected were no match for a speeding car. The dickheads sprinted to the edge of the parking lot and in the briefest of moments, their prey was out of sight. Jim and Lindsey were in the clear. For now.

Without braking or slowing, Jim cut the wheel hard to the right and turned back onto Twin Cities Memorial Highway. Lindsey unfastened her safety belt and turned around in her seat so she could see out the back window, just to make sure none of the brutes were still in pursuit or worse- on the car itself.

But there were none. By now, Lindsey could barely distinguish the ghouls from the parked cars in the hospital lot. The infected herd was well behind them. So was the massive brick building, which up until two minutes earlier, she thought would be their safe haven. How stupid must she have been to think that they'd be safe in a hospital of all places.

Only the most pathetic of morons would think they could stroll up to a hospital and find refuge at a time like this. They were in the midst of the world's newest and most unpredictable disease- one that turns its victims into tweaked-out cannibals, and these two simpletons think there's a warm bed and hot meal waiting for them at the hospital? Idiots. Lindsey's ill-begotten optimism had died even before their encounter with the gun-wielding stranger in the parking lot. So what now? They had no plan. No direction. Nothing to do but watch their would-be sanctuary shrink in the distance.

"Hang on," Jim told her.

"Huh?" Lindsey asked. But without warning, she was tossed hard to the side as Jim weaved the car between a pile of orange construction cones and a fallen Vespa. Her left hip and shoulder slammed into the door with a solid thump.

"Geez," Lindsey groaned, righting herself in her seat and reaching for the lap belt.

"Sorry," Jim said without looking over. "You alright?"

"I'm fine," she told him, rubbing her shoulder and straightening her shirt.

The Pontiac continued to rumble down Twin Cities Memorial Highway. They were on an incline, heading south. In a few hundred feet, they would reach the first of two bridges as they crossed over the Erie Canal. If they continued straight for another three quarters of a mile, they'd reach the second bridge to take them over Ellicott Creek.

"That's strange," Lindsey murmured. It was more of a thought and she hadn't necessarily meant to say it aloud.

"There's quite a bit that's strange today," Jim quipped.

"There's a boat out on the water," Lindsey commented. She pressed her face to the window and held up a hand to block the glare of the setting sun. "It's a little fishing boat and it looks like there's no one on board."

"Maybe it came loose from a dock and just sort of floated away," Jim suggested. "The owner might not have noticed with everything else going on today. If the owner's still alive, that is."

"Yeah," she agreed halfheartedly. "Actually, I don't see anyone down there. Ya know, none of those infected people or whatever. I guess they can't all be everywhere, but it just looks so peaceful down there along the canal. It's like none of this has even happened."

"Maybe they can't swim," Jim told her.

"Yeah, maybe," she replied. Lindsey kept her gaze fixed on the small watercraft, watching it gently rock from side to side as the soft current carried it upstream.

"Shit," Jim blurted after a moment of silence. He pointed ahead through the windshield.

They were past the canal now. At the base of the bridge was a Mr. Cooley's Ice Cream truck, which was actually a re-purposed postal delivery vehicle that had been painted white and emblazoned with a picture of the creepiest clown you've ever seen. The truck had been tipped over. It lie on its driver's side in the left lane with its front end in the grassy median.

There would be enough room to drive around it but it was going to be a tight fit. From his current vantage point, Jim couldn't get a clear view of what might be lurking on the other side of Mr. Cooley's capsized clown-mobile. He took his foot off the gas, letting the car lose some momentum before applying the brakes and steering the coupe to the far edge of the right lane.

As they got closer, what Jim had first thought to be a shadow began to glisten in the fading sunlight. A dark reddish hue appeared and several small mounds began to take form. About twenty mostly-crushed ice cream cones lie scattered across the burgundy puddle, along with torn wrappers from frozen novelties and clumps of sprinkles bound together in balls of congealed blood.

The ice cream truck's side window, the one that slides open for bratty kids to get their treats, was smashed in. All of the broken glass seemed to have landed inside the vehicle. The rear door was halfway open. As the Pontiac crept by, Jim tried to look into the truck but it was too dark to tell if anyone was still inside.

"You want to stop for some ice cream?" Jim teased.

Lindsey frowned. "What?"

"Ya know-" Jim stammered upon realizing his joke had fallen flat. "Because it's an ice cream truck. Sorry, I'm just kidding, trying to lighten the mood."

She let out a long breath and said, "Alright, yeah- sorry. I guess I'm not really up for joking around at the moment."

"Yeah," he replied, somewhat dejected. "Okay."

The Pontiac rolled past the overturned truck. On the other side, Jim and Lindsey both expected to find some sort of beast hiding and poised to jump out at them. When no such beast appeared, Lindsey shifted in her seat and reached for her pockets. Her knee bumped the shotgun in the process and the weapon rattled against the car door. Jim glanced over but didn't comment.

Lindsey's hands shot out and grabbed the buttstock, steadying the firearm and double-checking the safety before gently placing it against the edge of the seat cushion. She then reached back into her pocket and pulled out her cell phone. The screen was smudged with what she hoped was only sweat. Lindsey punched a few keys on the display and held the device up to her ear.

Jim was concerned the vehicle's driver might still be hanging around nearby. He kept watch over the toppled truck as they drove past but the ice cream man wasn't on site. Or if he was, not *all* of him was there. What he found instead was a small carcass at the center of a ten-foot wide puddle of blood. The body was too mutilated to tell what it was for certain. The damned thing looked like it had been turned inside out. Glossy pink and white flesh bound loosely to what seemed to be one half of a rib cage. If the thing had previously possessed a head or limbs, they were long gone.

"Jesus," Jim muttered quietly to himself.

"Huh?" Lindsey asked; her phone still pressed to her ear.

"Nothing. Never mind," Jim replied. Then, waiting for her to hang up the phone, Jim asked, "Who's that? Did you get a hold of someone?"

"Voice mail," she said flatly. "But it never rang. My service has been in and out, so I have no idea when the call actually came in."

"Right," Jim started. "So the apartment's out. And the hospital's out. Any suggestions?"

Lindsey dropped the phone in her lap and pressed her hands to her face, rubbing her forehead and combing fingers over her scalp. "I don't know," she admitted after a moment's hesitation.

"What about your place?" Jim asked. "Is it near here?"

"Um- not really," she said. Thinking for a second, she added, "We shouldn't go there anyway."

"Oh," Jim replied. He gave her a quick glance and looked away again. There was something in the way she said it, something that made him think she was holding something back. The expression on Jim's face and the tone of his voice both told of his desire for more of an explanation, but he wouldn't come out and say it.

"I mean, ya know," Lindsey's words rushed out. "There's no food there either. I usually eat out. I'm terrible when it comes to grocery shopping."

"But you work in a grocery store," Jim observed; a slight tilt to his head like a dog hearing a new sound.

"Yeah," she said. "The cobbler's son is barefoot."

"Huh?"

"It's one of those old sayings," Lindsey explained. "It's like, 'The architect's house is crooked,' or 'The mechanic's car leaks oil.' Ya know, it's an idiom."

Jim's eyes narrowed to slits. "Right."

"Plus, it's all the way back across town," Lindsey went on. "I mean, you don't want to turn around and head back that way, do you?"

"No," Jim answered. "I guess not. But then where *should* we go?"

"What if we just took off?" Lindsey asked. She ran her fingers over her forehead and tucked a few loose strands behind her ears. "We could leave town, er, at least until everything calms down, until it's safe again."

"Okay," Jim said cautiously. "But where would we go? I'm up for getting out of town and finding some place quiet, some place less populated, but we need an actual destination. I don't want to end up getting stranded somewhere."

"Yeah..." Lindsey sat back in her seat and thought for a moment. Then, she snapped her fingers and exclaimed, "Oh, I've got it! My family still has that hunting cabin in Allegany, right by the state park. We could go there."

"Allegany?" Jim asked. "I'm not so sure about that."

"It's perfect," Lindsey insisted. "It's in the middle of the woods so there's never any people around. There's guns in case we need them. And it'll be stocked with food."

"Okay," said Jim. "But how would we even get in? I mean, do you have a key? And how do you know it will be stocked with food? Why would your dad keep loads of food there? I thought he only goes there a couple weeks a year."

"He does," Lindsey told him. "But when my dad goes there with his friends, it's more about drinking beer and hanging out, and less about the actual hunting. Sometimes he'll go down there for a whole week and never even fire a shot. Every fall, just before hunting season, he stocks up on food and booze to make sure he's got something to eat in case he doesn't get a deer."

"The food part sounds good," Jim commented. "And so does the beer. But what about-"

Lindsey cut him off, "There's a spare key inside a fake rock on the front porch."

"Oh."

"It's our best option," Lindsey asserted. She pivoted in her seat, turning to face him. "What do you think?"

Jim looked back at her, just for an instant before moving his eyes back to the road. "It sounds like a good plan," he told her.

"You don't sound so sure," Lindsey observed.

"No, I am." Jim tried to sound convincing. "It's just a long way to go. It's going to take a while to get there."

"Exactly," said Lindsey. "It's about eighty miles from here. But isn't that the point? To get out of the area and put some distance between us and all this craziness. And it won't take us that long to get there. I bet we make it before dark."

"Eighty miles," Jim repeated, glancing down at the fuel gauge.

"How much gas do we have?" Lindsey asked.

"About three quarters of a tank."

"That's enough to make it eighty miles," Lindsey said; a hint of wary optimism in her voice. "Isn't it?"

"Um, yeah. I think so," Jim replied. "I hope so. Well, I suppose we'll find out."

"I'm sure it'll be fine," Lindsey assured him.

"But what if there's traffic, or if we get lost, or if we run out of gas?" Jim was beginning to sound flustered. "And what if-"

"Relax," Lindsey interjected. "If there's traffic, we'll find another way to get there. If we get low on gas, we'll stop and fill up."

"I don't know about that," Jim argued. "I mean, everywhere you look, people are killing and eating each other. I don't want to get caught out in the open. It's not like they're going to stand back and wait while I fill up the tank."

"They're not here now," she said. "Jim, look around. I don't see any of them here. It's like we're driving away from the danger and the chaos. The farther we go, the fewer there seem to be. And there's less and less... bodies."

"That's a fair point," Jim admitted. "I don't think we've seen any since we left the hospital."

"That's what I'm talking about. And besides, if worse comes to worst, we still have this," Lindsey told him, giving the shotgun a tap. "But I bet we won't even need it. By the time we get to the cabin, everything is gonna be fine. You just have to trust me, okay?"

Jim took a deep breath and stole a few seconds to collect his thoughts. She was right- what other choice did they have? Going home seemed like a shitty plan and apparently they couldn't go to her place. He briefly considered suggesting a hotel- a place to sleep and a place with a kitchen or restaurant attached to it. But after the hospital incident, they'd have to be idiots to try another large public building like that. From where he sat, leaving town seemed to be the most attractive option. Jim wiped a few beads of sweat from under his eyes and said, "Okay."

"So does that mean you're in?"

"Yeah, ya know what," Jim paused for effect and then declared, "Yeah, I'm in."

"Awesome!" Lindsey blurted, falling back in her seat and breathing a big sigh of relief. "And ya know, I always used to think about leaving town and running away with you."

"Oh yeah?" Jim couldn't hide a growing smile. He reached over to place his hand on Lindsey's.

"Used to," she reiterated.

"Oh." Jim sheepishly withdrew his hand and placed it back on the steering wheel. "So, what's the quickest way to the cabin, then?"

"Just stay on Twin Cities until we get to the Youngmann Expressway," Lindsey told him. "We take that to the Thruway and then keep going south."

"I can count on you for directions from there?" Jim asked.

"Yep," she confirmed. "I told you, I know where we're going."

"Alright, good." Jim eased off the gas and pumped the brakes. He pulled onto the shoulder of the road and put the car in park.

"Whoa, what are you doing?" Lindsey asked. "Why are we stopping?"

"I've got to make a phone call," he said.

"A phone call?" Lindsey demanded. "Now?"

"I have to call my parents," Jim explained. "To let them know I'm alright, so they don't have to worry."

"And we have to stop for that?" Lindsey pressed. "I thought you wanted to keep moving?"

"It won't take long," he told her as he lifted his cell phone out of the cup holder. "I just want to let them know I'm okay in case they've heard about what's going on up here. Since there's no one around right now, I think this is as good a time as any."

"What are you going to tell them?" she asked.

"I'll tell them I'm with you," Jim said; a sideways grin forming across his face. "They like you."

"Thanks, but that's not what I meant." Lindsey instinctively looked away so he wouldn't see her blush. "Are you going to tell them where we're going?"

"Not yet," Jim answered. "I'll tell them after we get there. They'll be worried if they know I'm on the road."

"Okay," she said. "I get it. And I don't mean to sound pushy, but please try to be quick. I want to get there while it's still light out."

Lindsey leaned forward for a better view. There was nothing in the road between them and the bridge over Ellicott Creek. No cars and no bodies- alive or otherwise. Through her window, there wasn't much to see besides tall grass and weeds on the other side of the guard rail. She turned back in her seat to look behind them, nothing there either. Lindsey completed a full rotation in the passenger's seat, scanning all directions.

She craned her neck to see around Jim and through his window, using her hand to shield her eyes from the setting sun. There was a small grassy median and then another pair of empty lanes. Beyond the opposite shoulder was a steep drop-off into a ditch and then a row of trees about fifty yards in the distance. Everything appeared still. All was quiet. Maybe they really had driven out of harm's way. Maybe they had escaped.

"Hey mom, dad. It's me-" Jim's voice caught somewhere deep in his chest as he spoke into the receiver. He forced a cough and continued. "It's Jim. You must be out or busy or something. It's just about dinner time, so I must have just missed you. No biggie, I just thought I'd call and check in, see how everything's going down there. I've been sorta keeping an eye on the weather forecast and it's supposed to be pretty hot down there this week. So, ya know, try and take it easy if you're going to be out in the sun."

Jim took in a deep breath, holding the phone away from his face so the sound of him sucking air wouldn't be audible on the other line. Biting his quivering lip, Jim went on as casually as he could muster. "So anyway, I don't know if you've been keeping up with the news from up here, but if you have, you might have seen some, well, strange reports coming out of the Buffalo area. Apparently, there's been some sort of infection going around that's making people act strangely. Well- er, the news is saying it makes people violent but it's really not a big deal. You know how the news is. They tend to blow everything out of proportion and make every little thing seem like it's the end of the world.

"Either way, I just wanted to let you know everything is okay." Jim cleared a scratching in his throat and continued, "And actually, now I'm wondering if it was even worth mentioning. I'm fine here and I'd hate to get you worried over nothing."

Jim took the phone in his left hand, holding it away from his head once more. His right hand came up to cradle his face. His eyes clamped shut. He rubbed his forehead and, turning away from Lindsey so she wouldn't see, pressed his thumb and middle finger on opposite sides of the bridge of his nose and whisked away a budding tear.

Still facing his window, Jim lifted the phone back to his ear and said, "I wanted to mention too, I was thinking that maybe I could come down for a visit soon. Getting some time off work shouldn't be a problem, so if that works for you, I'd really like to see you both. I know I say that a lot, about coming down to visit, and I'm sorry- I know it's been a while."

Something cracked on the line and Jim heard some sort of popping sound in his ear, followed by a static buzzing. He checked the phone's display to make sure he still had a connection. The call was still active, so Jim went on, "Oh, sorry about that- I think the call is starting to break up."

Jim realized he'd been sitting parked out in the open for a couple of minutes now. He checked his mirrors, looked out both side windows, through the windshield and down the road. Still no movement. No obvious danger, but that wasn't going to last.

"Like I said, I'm sorry I haven't been around in a while. I've kinda been feeling like I've been letting you down an awful lot lately. Er, maybe not just lately. I know we haven't really talked about the school thing in a while but you know, I think you're right. I've sort of screwed around for long enough and it's probably about time I got my shit together. I do wish I would have done better, continued on in college, gotten a good job, actually made something of myself.

"And I know that's not all of it. I know I've let you down and I've been difficult at times. The more I think about it, the more I realize how lousy and selfish and lazy I've been. I've caused fights and stress and I know I haven't always been the best person to be around.

"And no matter what bullshit I've pulled, you've only been patient and understanding and supportive. You've both been great parents and though I don't always show it, I'm lucky to have you. I still want to be someone you're proud of and I'm going to try. I'm just sorry it's taken me so long to get it together and..."

His words tailed off as Jim lost focus for a second. He had the sniffles now and his eyes had grown misty. "Okay, sorry about that- I'm sort of rambling at this point. But I should get going now. I've got my cell phone on me, so you can give me a call back when you get in, or I can call you again later and tell you about the next crazy story they cook up for the news. Oh- and you'll never guess who I ran into. I'll tell you about it later. I love you both and I'll talk to you soon."

Jim ended the call. He let the phone drop back into the cup holder. Looking straight ahead, he grabbed the steering wheel and reached for the gear shifter to put the Pontiac back in drive. Lindsey reached out to catch his hand before he could do so.

"Whoa," she said; a solemn look on her face. "Are you okay? What was that about?"

"Oh uh, yeah. Sorry about that," Jim told her. "I wasn't sure if they would have heard about what's going on up here. And I didn't want them to worry about it if they did."

"Yeah, I get that much," Lindsey said. "But what was up with all that other stuff, about being a bad son and everything?"

"Were you eavesdropping on my private call?" Jim tried to joke with a half smile and an expression of feigned surprise. His bloodshot eyes and ghostly pallor betrayed any sense of humor he'd hoped to convey.

"Yeah, um, sorry about that," she replied. "But it's not like I could excuse myself to another room."

Lindsey reached across the car and squeezed his shoulder. "It's okay though. You don't have to tell me if you don't want to. Seriously."

"No, it's fine," Jim insisted. He finally shifted the car out of park, keeping his foot on the brake for a moment longer. "But if we're going to make it to Allegany before dark, then maybe we should talk about it while we're on the move."

"Right," Lindsey agreed. She reached over her shoulder for the safety belt before realizing it was already in place.

Jim hit the gas and the car lurched forward. Still on a downward slope away from the first bridge, the Pontiac picked up speed quickly. The road ahead remained clear and Jim would want to cover as much ground as possible, lest they become stranded at nightfall.

They were coming up on the intersection where Twin Cities meets Fillmore Avenue. There was no power to the traffic lights- not that he would have stopped anyway. Jim gave a hurried look in each direction. Satisfied no cars were heading his way, he stepped down harder on the accelerator. The car soared through the intersection as they raced ahead.

"So, I guess I was thinking," Jim said finally after a minute of quiet. "That with everything going on, I just wanted to get that off my chest. In case, ya know, something happens and I don't make it. I mean, maybe everything will be fine and if it is, I don't want them to worry. But then again, if I don't get another chance, I just- well, you know."

"I get it," Lindsey told him. "I've been trying to reach my family all day. I probably left ten messages like that when I was back at Bennett's."

"Do you mind if I smoke?" Jim asked. So far, he'd made a point to avoid smoking in front of her. He wasn't sure if Lindsey would find it off-putting or gross or otherwise offensive, so he'd been holding out for as long as possible. She must have seen a stray butt floating around the car somewhere or noticed some tobacco dust sprinkled on the floor mats, so Jim's smoking was no secret. And given the circumstances, he figured he'd earned himself a cigarette break.

"I don't mind," she answered.

Jim hadn't really waited for a reply. He was already fumbling around in the center console trying to find his pack and lighter.

"I'll get it," she told him, resting a hand on his. "Just focus on driving."

Lindsey lifted the lid on the console and rooted around inside until she found a pack of cigarettes. It took a few moments but she eventually found a lighter amidst the old pens, owner's manual, and insurance documents. She took a cigarette from the packet and brought it to her lips. Holding the lighter to the tip, Lindsey puffed just enough to get it going and held it out for Jim to take it. "Here ya go," she said.

"Thanks," Jim took the smoke and drew in a heavy lungful. "You want one?"

"No, I'm good," she replied. "I haven't had a cigarette since we were seventeen."

"Oh," Jim took another puff. He rolled the window down farther to make sure all the smoke would roll out of the car. "That seems like forever ago."

"Yeah," Lindsey agreed. Her gaze dropped to the floor as she searched her mind for a proper reply. Finding none, she looked back to Jim expectantly and simply said, "So..."

"So," Jim echoed.

He drew another long puff from his cigarette to mask his reluctance. Turning his head to the left and leaning closer to the open window than was necessary, Jim pushed the smoke out of his lungs. A purposeful exhalation; he tried his best to make sure every last wisp of smoke escaped the car's interior. Despite this effort, a slim ribbon of gray fog slid along the inside of the glass, curling around itself and passing through the back seat before it settled along the dashboard in front of Lindsey. She didn't seem to notice or care.

"Okay, so maybe I'm not up to speed," Lindsey told him. "You said all that stuff about school and work but last I heard, you were heading to university on a scholarship to study actuarial science. That's impressive. I mean- boring, but impressive."

Jim shrugged and took a drag off his smoke. "It would have been more impressive had I finished."

Lindsey's eyes narrowed and her head tilted ever so slightly. "What do you mean? You didn't get your degree?"

"I did ultimately get a degree," he explained. "But I quit for a while. I made a big show of how smart and independent I was, and how I always knew better than everyone, so I moved out and declared that I'd be putting myself through college."

"Yep," Lindsey frowned. "I remember that."

"Well as it turns out, I didn't know what I was doing. I didn't have any money and I didn't have the credit to get a student loan." Jim took another puff and added, "Being too stupid and too stubborn to ask for help, I just quit."

"But you went back?"

"Sort of," Jim answered. "Eventually I went back to community college and got a useless associate's degree in Communications."

"Still, that's better than nothing," Lindsey commented. "People who stop going to college almost never go back."

"Yeah," Jim scoffed. "And a world of good it's done for me."

"What do you mean by that?" Lindsey asked. "I thought you had a decent job?"

"I basically do data entry," Jim told her rather abruptly. "I take stacks of paper off a fax machine and whatever's written on the paper, I type it into a computer system. There are people there who have important jobs, who manage deals and make important decisions, but that's not me. My job is simple, mindless, repetitive entry level hog shit that comes with a pay scale marginally better than minimum wage."

Jim waited for Lindsey to say something but when she didn't, he continued. "I didn't need a degree to get this job. And I certainly didn't need the decade's worth of student loan debt that comes along with it."

"Everybody has student loans to deal with," Lindsey observed.

"Fair enough," Jim acknowledged; his eyes still fixed on the road. "It just seems like a waste."

"Oh come," Lindsey objected. "It can't be that bad. You live on your own, so I mean, you must make enough money to support yourself, right? So far I don't see a problem."

"You don't see a problem?" Jim took a final drag from his cigarette and flicked the butt out the window. "Just look at me. I work all day at a lousy dead-end job and then I get in my beat-up twelve-year-old car and drive home to my small, crappy, lonely one-bedroom apartment. I've got no savings, no health insurance, hardly any food in the fridge. I can barely make my rent every month. I haven't had a vacation in like seven years. When you're scraping by paycheck to paycheck, taking a week off to go away somewhere- even just to go see my parents, seems virtually impossible.

"Ya know, I got the flu last winter. My throat was raw from coughing and my fever hovered around a hundred and four for a whole week. I was so stiff and sore I could barely walk. But I still went to work every day. Apart from having no insurance, I literally cannot afford to miss a single day of work. If I have an accident or get hurt or if my car breaks down, I'm screwed. It's been like this for years now and I haven't seen any sign of things improving. And it's my fault. In a lot of ways, that's the worst part about it."

Lindsey opened her mouth to speak but said nothing. The car's interior fell silent save for the churning of the engine and road noise as the Pontiac cruised onward. They were on an incline again, approaching the bridge over Ellicott Creek.

Jim took a breath and let out a long sigh. "I'm Sorry. Things just haven't been great lately. And not to mention the, well, you know." He raised both hands and gestured in all directions toward the world outside the car.

"It's okay," she assured him. Lindsey reached across the console. She placed her left hand just above Jim's knee and gave his leg a slight squeeze. "I'm not sure what you think you're missing out on or what you think you should be doing. As far as I can tell, you're doing fine."

A beam of warmth dashed up his spine to the back of his neck. Jim was suddenly very aware of himself. He forced a chuckle and said, "Oh come on now, you're just trying to flatter me in case you need me to save your life again."

"Uh oh, you figured me out," Lindsey said in jest with a sly grin. "But I mean it. You're doing fine. And you're still young, there's plenty of time to figure things out."

"Is there?" Jim asked. The playful tone in his voice had gone.

"Of course," she replied. "I mean, you're only twenty-four."

"That's not what I meant," he explained. "Everything we've seen today makes me think that I might have a lot less time than I'd previously thought. And also, I'm twenty-five."

"Twenty-five!" Lindsey's eyes opened wide in mock surprise. She joked, "My mistake then. I didn't realize just how elderly you'd become. Your best years are certainly behind you, old man."

"Okay, okay," Jim waved her off. "But you know what I mean. I did sort of think that things would just improve or work themselves out, or that I'd always have the time to figure things out and sort my life out. Now, I'm not so sure. And after what happened at the office today, I don't think I'll even have my crappy job anymore."

"I wouldn't be so sure." Lindsey made a broad sweeping motion with both hands, gesturing toward their general surroundings. "Everything seems to have died down. We haven't seen any of those things since we crossed over the canal. It might already be starting to blow over. I bet things are back to normal in no time."

"I'll feel a lot better about it once we get to the cabin. Especially if we make it there without any issues along the way," Jim told her. "I know things were pretty grim for you back at the supermarket, but I haven't told you about what happened at work or about all the things I've seen since I left the office. Trust me, it's going to be a long time before things are back to normal."

"I know," Lindsey agreed. "I'm just trying to stay positive and- oh, hey!"

214

Jim's head jerked to the side to see what was wrong. "What? What is it?"

"When you stopped going to school," she began. "You were living in that tiny apartment downtown? The one above the carpet store?"

"Oh," Jim thought back to that decrepit shit-hole he'd moved into six months after graduating high school. It was even smaller and more rundown than his current place of residence. "Yeah, that's the one. Why do you ask?"

"We were still in contact back then," Lindsey stated.

"Back when we were still friends?"

"You know what I mean," she told him. "So, we were still talking when you stopped going to school?"

Jim nodded.

"How come you never said anything?" asked Lindsey; her expression one of genuine hurt.

"Remember what I was saying about being stubborn and foolish?" Jim asked rhetorically.

"You could have told me," she insisted.

"Yeah, I probably should have," Jim admitted. "It's one of about a million regrets I have from back then."

"A million, huh?" Lindsey joked. "I'm sure it's not that many. It's probably more like half a million. Three-quarters of a million, tops."

"Ha ha," Jim replied as the coupe crossed over the waterway several yards below. "Anyway, I'm sorry for not telling you. And as long as we're on the subject, I probably owe you an apology for a lot more than just the school thing."

"Huh?" Lindsey looked over at him. The puzzled look on her face went unnoticed by Jim so she asked, "What are you talking about?"

"Well," Jim began, wavering somewhat. He considered reaching for another cigarette but quickly decided against it. "I've been thinking a lot lately, er, ever since I ran into you at the store the other day, about all the stuff that happened with me and you-"

"Jim, don't," she interrupted. "It's fine, really. We don't need to get into it."

"Okay, but-"

Lindsey cut him off again, "Seriously, it's okay."

"I just wanted to tell you," Jim blurted, but he couldn't get much more out before Lindsey interjected once more.

"Jim-" Lindsey objected.

"Shit!" he exclaimed.

"Shit?" she asked.

"Yeah. Shit," Jim confirmed. The car was heading back down the other side of the bridge away from the creek. He was staring ahead through the windshield; eyes locked on something in the distance. Without breaking his gaze, Jim spoke softly. "Alright, Lindsey. Don't freak out."

215

Chapter 32

"Gdzie są te pieprzone ziemniaki?" Albert asked aloud as he searched the contents of the refrigerator. He would do this from time to time; muttering to himself in his native language. It was a habit generally reserved for times of immense stress. And if there was ever a time that qualified as stressful, this was it.

A casserole pan filled with hunter's stew was cooking in the oven. Albert had spent a large portion of the afternoon slicing up cabbage, kielbasa, and mushrooms, taking a break every so often to check the television for news updates. The TV was still on in the next room, though it had been mostly silent for the past hour with the broadcast signal dropping in and out. When the station would come through to the set, it was just more of the same from news anchors and public officials. "Stay inside, lock your doors, blah, blah, blah."

He didn't have much of an appetite, but it was his favorite dish and preparing the evening meal was a convenient way to distract him from the day's events. The only recipe he'd been able to commit to memory would make enough to feed four people. It was too many servings but he reasoned that when someone found him, they might want to stay for a snack.

The stew wouldn't be ready for another thirty minutes and Albert thought he'd make some mashed potatoes with mushroom gravy for a side. Since he was having his favorite food, he thought it would be nice for Duke to have his favorite as well. Duke was typically only allowed to have people food on special occasions. Albert supposed that this was as special an occasion as any and he wanted to make sure Duke would eat. As it was, Duke's dish remained full and untouched as it had all afternoon, ever since Adam had left and not returned.

Albert closed the fridge, wheezing and leaning heavily on his cane as he did so. He looked to Duke, who was lying on his belly in the center of the kitchen. Albert spoke again, this time in English. "Sorry buddy, we're out of potatoes."

Duke lifted his head to look at his master, then to the oven before coming to rest again and placing his chin on the cool tile floor.

"Okay, okay," Albert told him. "You can have some stew but we've got to clean up first."

The old man hobbled his way from the fridge past the oven and over to the counter where he'd done most of the food preparation. It was covered by a dusting of black pepper, some stray bits of carrot, and a few pieces of garlic peel. Albert used a napkin to dust the scraps onto a plate to be transported to the trash, balancing the cane in one hand and the refuse in the other. He then wiped down the counter top with a damp rag, which was also tossed into the garbage can. With his work space cleaned of debris, it was time to prepare one final ingredient.

From the overhead cupboard, Albert grabbed an over-sized bowl and a large metal spoon. Then, using the counter's edge for leverage, he stooped down and opened the cabinet below the kitchen sink. It was difficult to see inside. His body blocked the light from the ceiling lamp and there was no means of illumination from within. Albert reached in and began to fish around in the dark.

He'd be able to identify the item by touch alone. Albert just needed to feel around until it presented itself. The older man pushed aside a slender metal container- Lysol, that's not it. A stout plastic bottle- dish soap; not it either. Ajax, Windex, and Febreze; these and several others were all swatted away until his fingers landed on the lid of a small cardboard box sitting all the way in the back of the cabinet. Albert grabbed the package and held it up in front of his face to make sure he'd found the right one. It was roughly the same size and shape of a box of Minute Rice, but this carton had a yellow label with white letters that read, *Rat Assassin*.

Albert placed the box on the countertop above him and used the ledge to pull himself up off the floor, kicking the cabinet door closed in the process. The old man then shuffled back to his freshly-cleaned work space. There, he tore open the top of the Rat Assassin package and poured out a handful of tiny green pellets. Albert used the bowl and spoon as a makeshift mortar and pestle, pulverizing the pellets until they formed a fine green powder.

Once all the solid pieces were turned to dust, Albert poured in another handful of pellets and repeated the process. He did this a few more times until the yellow box was nearly empty. Then he took another large bowl from the cupboard and grabbed Duke's food dish from the floor, placing them both on the counter next to the powdered concoction. All that was left to do was wait for the oven timer to go off. Twelve minutes to go.

"Come on, pup," Albert said to Duke as he moved from the kitchen into the living room. "Let's check the television."

Duke obediently followed his master into the next room, walking a few tight circles before lying down in front of Adam's empty recliner. Albert flopped down in his own chair and snatched the remote control from the armrest as he settled in. Before he had a chance to change the channel, Albert was interrupted by a knock at the door and the sound of muffled voices from the other side.

Chapter 33

"Don't freak out," Jim repeated. "But we've got some company up ahead."

"Telling me not to freak out is probably the best way to get me to freak out," Lindsey advised.

"Um, right." Jim gave a slight shake of his head. "Fair point."

Lindsey followed his gaze, tracing the lines over the steering wheel, along the dashboard and through the windshield. On the opposite side of the street sat an abandoned Toyota with its hood up and both front doors open. Beyond the stalled sedan, there was a pedestrian bridge just ahead of Luksin Drive and even further down, she could see the light blue water tower standing tall over the edge of the horizon. But Jim was talking about something else. And now Lindsey saw what it was.

"There's not too many of them," he said. "Probably won't be an issue."

There was a small crowd of seven or eight people in the middle of the street about a hundred yards in front of them. Another five or six were close by, wandering across the median and along the side of the road. The group appeared to be moving in the Pontiac's direction but didn't seem to be in much of a hurry. They walked in a slow and meandering sort of fashion. None were sprinting and animated like the monsters Lindsey had seen earlier.

"Do you think they're..." she began to ask.

"Yep," Jim answered before she could finish her question.

"Are you sure?" she pressed. "They're not, ya know, running or freaking out like they were back at Bennett's."

"I'm sure," Jim answered flatly. "Why else would they be out here?"

Lindsey cocked her head slightly. "Um, but we're out here," she contended.

"We can stop to confirm if you'd like," Jim told her. He meant for it to sound like a joke, but his tone carried a harder edge than he'd intended.

Lindsey frowned and didn't reply.

"You know what I mean," Jim told her. "At this point, I think we need to assume everyone's infected until we prove otherwise. And as a general rule, people who aren't infected shouldn't be hanging out in the middle of the road."

"Alright. Fair enough," she relented.

"They should also be less, um, bloody," Jim added, now that they were close enough to make out some detail.

There were thirteen in total, eight men and five women- or at least that's what Jim had surmised based on their stature, build, and hair length. Apart from that, there wasn't much in the way of identifying characteristics, especially in the clothing department. They all looked like they'd just been pulled from a pit of mud and excrement. Dark red stains and crusted brown muck caked every garment; their original colors a distant memory.

"Can we go around them?" Lindsey rubbed both hands palms-down against the front of her pants as she slid further back in her seat.

"I'm gonna try," Jim answered, taking a peek at the speedometer. The needle hovered just below sixty miles per hour. He lifted his foot off the gas pedal and the car began to slow. "But if not, we can go through them."

"*Through* them?" Lindsey asked in disbelief.

"Yeah," Jim confirmed. "I mean, you know, probably. If we have to."

"Probably?"

"Relax," he told her with an air of false confidence. "I'm sure it'll be fine"

"Oh God," Lindsey groaned.

"Don't let the faded paint and missing mirror fool you. This is a pretty tough ride." As Jim spoke, he reached his hand over the radio and air vents. He let his fingertips caress a short length of the dashboard, leaving a pair of lines in the thin layer of dust. Self-conscious, Jim withdrew his hand and put it back on the wheel.

"I'll take your word for it," she commented. "I'd rather not have to find out first-hand, so let's just try to go around them."

"I'm tellin' you, we could go right through them," he teased. "It'd be no problem."

Lindsey opened her mouth to argue but stopped when she saw the mischievous grin on Jim's face. Exasperated, she replied, "Let's make that Plan B."

"Plan B," Jim concurred. "But you're really taking all the fun out of this zombie apocalypse."

"Zombies?" Lindsey asked.

"I'm not sure what else to call them," Jim explained. His foot remained off the gas pedal, letting the car coast forward as he steered into the middle of the roadway and drove directly over the dotted white line. The small crowd ahead was least concentrated in the center portion of the street.

"Yeah," Lindsey nodded. "But *zombies*?"

"I know- that sounds sort of silly," Jim admitted. "But what *should* I call them? I mean, just look at them."

He pointed to the right side of the car, directing her attention to the nearest member of the ghastly gang. Lindsey watched through the window as they passed by the tattered, shambling mess which, based on the uniform and name tag, had once been a fast food worker. He still wore that crappy hat with the ridiculous picture of a smiling hot dog.

"Okay," said Lindsey. "On second thought, *zombie* sounds about right."

Jim hit the switches for the power windows to make sure they were both rolled all the way up. He applied the brakes, cutting the speed from forty to twenty miles per hour as he prepared to maneuver around the loitering ghouls.

Had it been up to Jim, he would have just punched it- put the pedal to the metal and plow his way through. He'd floor it all the way down Twin Cities Boulevard and the entire length of the Thruway until they arrived at the cabin. And when they did arrive, he'd burn the last few drops of gasoline doing doughnuts on the front lawn.

But Lindsey wanted him to play it safe and Jim wanted to weasel his way back into her life, so the decision was made. The coupe came to a stop in front of the moldy cretins. There were four of them in the car's immediate path with a small gap between bodies toward the right side of the car. Jim steered into the opening and pulled forward. The creeps adjusted and began to converge on the idling auto, albeit slowly.

The savages standing along the curb and by the center guardrail began to move. Depraved automatons, corrupted by disease and fueled by blood-lust, closed in and circled the car. Blistered, broken hands pounded body panels and swiped at windows. A film of pink and brown smudges only partly obscured the faces of the damned. Longing, hateful expressions dulled by exhaustion and exposure pressed against the glass.

Lindsey sank into her seat. She slumped her shoulders and lowered her head, trying to get below the bottom edge of the window. Her eyes fixed on the floor in front of her. Lindsey raised her hands to her head, resting her fingertips against her temples to shield her periphery.

The Pontiac moved at a snail's pace, slowly carving out room for itself through the stinking herd. In all the mirrors and through all the windows, Jim could see only snarling grimaces, gnashing teeth, and trails of red-speckled saliva. Ghouls had surrounded the crawling coupe with some even standing before the front bumper. Jim gave a quick tap of the gas. The engine growled and the car jumped forward. It was enough to push the beasts back a couple of feet but they quickly closed the distance once again.

More fists landed heavy blows against the roof and trunk lid. The thundering sound grew louder and was soon accompanied by the sharp crack of bone and skin against window glass. Brutes leaned across the hood, reaching for the windscreen but grabbing only air.

Jim tapped the accelerator once more. He held it down a little longer this time. The dickheads in front of the coupe got pushed back a bit further and a couple of them were nearly knocked to the ground. They staggered backwards for a few steps before collecting themselves and returning to their posts in front of the car.

"Damn it," Jim grumbled.

Lindsey rocked forward in her seat and moved the shotgun so it was situated between the door and her right leg. She rested her elbows on her knees and closed her eyes. Her back heaved from heavy breaths as she pulled herself into a sort of upright fetal position. Lindsey slid her hands to the back of her head and laced her fingers. She was trying to block it out; trying not to hear the banging and cracking of more than a dozen rabid loons trying to reach her.

So far, no luck. Each time the vehicle jerked forward, the pricks just seemed to grow angrier. The commotion somehow grew louder; the discord more intense. Every blow shook the car. An unending barrage of fists and elbows tested the Pontiac's creaking suspension. Bang!

"Shit!" they cried in unison.

Lindsey and Jim both jumped at the sharp sound of splintering glass. Lindsey instinctively recoiled, turning her back to the passenger's side door. Cowering, she braced herself for a shower of broken glass and waited for the demons to snatch her up. But then came no glass. No hands. Lindsey opened her eyes and looked up to Jim.

"It's okay," he told her. Jim motioned toward the back seat behind her. The quarter window on the passenger's side had been damaged but not breached. An intricate asymmetrical spiderweb of cracks made for an obstructed and distorted view through the glass.

220

"They didn't get through," he assured her. But the strikes kept coming. The ghouls continued to dole out punishment and that window had probably absorbed as much as it could take.

"How long do you think it'll hold?" asked Lindsey.

Jim responded with a half shrug, "Hard to say."

"Alright. We need to get outta here," she said.

"I'm working on it." Jim gave another two-second jab to the gas pedal. Once again, the creeps staggered back a few steps before quickly retaking their place along the front bumper.

"It's not really working though, is it?" Lindsey replied. Her question was rhetorical, but not acerbic.

"We're making progress," Jim noted. "I mean, do you have a better idea?"

"Well, no," she answered, settling back into her seat. "But you did."

Jim raised an eyebrow. "I did what?"

"You had a better idea," Lindsey clarified.

A vacant and glazed-over expression stared back at her.

"Oh for God's sake," she blurted. "Plan B!"

"Plan B?" Jim repeated, trying to hide a grin of satisfaction.

"Plan B," Lindsey confirmed.

"Nice." Jim placed both hands firmly on the steering wheel. "You got your seat belt on?"

She did. Lindsey straightened herself and pressed her back into the seat cushion. She cinched the belt in tight across her waist and pulled it snug over her shoulder. She slid the shotgun out of the way and grabbed onto the inside door handle with her right hand. Lindsey's eyes darted about, looking for something to hold onto with her left.

"Okay, here we go."

There were four of those cocksuckers standing right in front of the car. Jim did one more quick tap on the gas pedal, just enough to push them back and give himself a little room. The ghouls stumbled backwards, leaving about a yard between themselves and the Pontiac's chipped black and silver grille. But now, Jim wouldn't wait for them to fill the gap as he gradually inched his way forward.

He stepped down hard on the gas pedal, pressing it to the floor. The engine whirred and the tires dug in. Three of the four asswipes were pushed aside. They spun sideways before falling to the ground to be left behind with the rest of the plague-carrying freaks. The fourth, however, would not be dismissed so easily.

An infected woman was clipped in the shins by the front license plate. She lost her footing and fell forward onto the hood of the car. She was thirty-five or forty years old and wore a white tank top under a pink bathrobe. She was probably wearing slippers when she left the house, but those were long gone. A torrent of blood ran down from beyond her scraggly hairline and a pair of bite-shaped wounds could be seen poking out from under a terrycloth sleeve, still weeping and oozing a viscous fluid.

Her apparent injuries weren't enough to slow her down. The irascible hag had her fingers curled over the top edge of the hood and she held on tight. Her free hand swiped at the windshield, leaving brown smudges and red streaks whenever she managed to make contact.

"Bitch!" Jim wailed.

He jerked the wheel hard to the left and then to the right. The witch slid across the hood from side to side, but it wasn't enough to shake her loose. She was still there, still holding on and trying to reach the passengers inside.

"Jim, do something!" Lindsey shrieked.

"I'm on it," he told her. "I've got an idea."

Jim kept accelerating for another few seconds. He let the car get to about forty miles per hour and then he turned to Lindsey and said, "Hang on."

She was still holding onto the inside door handle. Lindsey lifted her left hand and held it a few inches from the dashboard, bracing herself for impact as Jim slammed on the brakes. The car's sudden deceleration caused the tires to screech for an instant before the anti-lock brakes engaged. Gears churned beneath their feet and the front end pulled hard to the right.

The shotgun jostled against the door. The lid for the glove box rattled. Pens, lighters, and unused air fresheners shook loudly in the center console. Whatever junk was rolling around in the trunk slid forward and whacked the rear side of the back seat. Jim and Lindsey both lurched forward as they tried to restrain themselves. And when the car finally came to a stop, they looked up through the windscreen to find that their stowaway was no longer on board.

Wriggling and thrashing, the gore-stained shrew slid off the hood of the car. Her furious shrieking came to an abrupt end as she hit the ground hard. The haggard bitch rolled several times as she tumbled down the shallow ditch to the center median.

"Nice!" Lindsey exclaimed.

"Awesome," Jim added, echoing her sentiment. "But we're not out of the woods yet."

Another group of freaks waited for them just up the road. They were about two hundred feet away, past the point where Twin Cities Highway crosses Luksin Drive. Jim kept the accelerator pinned; no gentle approach this time. No more screwing around.

"Better move your asses," Jim murmured aloud. "Pieces of shit."

"Are you sure about this?" Lindsey asked.

"Don't worry," he told her with a comforting grin. Jim gave the wheel two gentle taps with the palm of his hand. "This car, virtually indestructible."

Through the intersection and under the pedestrian bridge, the Pontiac charged ahead. Cords twisted beneath the skin of his forearm as Jim squeezed hard on the steering wheel. The whir of the engine grew louder. The air became hotter, heavier. Nobody said anything. Nobody moved. Lindsey's fingernails dug into the plastic handrail. Jim held his breath in anticipation of impact. And here they were.

Bang! A hollow metallic thud boomed through the coupe. And then another. And another. Limbs twisted. Bones snapped; a symphony of nausea echoing through fenders and bumpers. Bodies flew through the air- up and over the speeding automobile. Metal crunched and glass splintered. A bright red slick of fresh blood doused the windshield and a long crack appeared on the passenger's side window. Hands, feet, and lost shoes bounced off the hood and roof before crashing back to Earth somewhere in a cloud of exhaust.

222

When the Pontiac collided with the small herd, five of those bastards had been unlucky enough to be in its immediate path. Those who'd been standing along the curb tried to converge but it was a paltry and pathetic attempt. Most of them had depleted their adrenaline and ATP hours earlier. They were low on oxygen and low on blood. What little energy remained was being used to digest their coworkers and neighbors. They could stand upright. They could walk and move around. But they had absolutely no chance of catching a speeding four-wheeled target. Most of them, anyway.

There was one, however, standing by his lonesome a few yards to the rear of the pack with both feet on the curbside rumble strip. This asshole looked like he'd already been run over. A horseshoe crown of stringy brown hair lie in matted clumps against his scalp. His grimy shirt was damp from blood and saliva; his trousers from piss. Tall and lanky, he must have been well over six feet tall. And unlike his colleagues, this angular ogre still had a little juice left in the tank.

Pupils dilated. His heart rate elevated. Arterial pressure began to rise. Adrenal glands wrung out like a pair of filthy sponges secreting their hormones into the bloodstream. Spittle, blood, and a half-chewed eyelid spat from his mouth as the beast growled and began sprinting toward the onrushing vehicle.

Over the shoulder marker and across the first traffic lane. He moved as fast as he could- faster than he'd ever been able prior to the infection. Legs pumping, muscles twitching; the fiend covered the distance in almost no time at all. The son of a bitch was quick but it wouldn't be enough. He was going to fall short. He'd miss his mark. So without a speck of hesitation, in a move dictated by instinct and desperation, the beast did the only thing he could. He jumped.

Both spindly legs kicked off the ground. With all of his might, the brute launched himself skyward. He soared for over eight feet, closing the distance in the air. Outstretched arms grabbed for the car; a last-ditch effort to prevent its escape. But gravity intervened and the pavement was rushing toward him.

Just before landing, the open palms of his gore-stained claws touched rubber for only the briefest of moments. Inertia carried his disease-ridden body a few feet further. Mouth open and teeth snapping, the ghoul skittered across the cement, getting closer to the car. And closer to the passenger's side wheel well.

The bastard slid under the front bumper, where he became wedged beneath the air dam. Steel pipes and plastic molding pinned him to the ground. The street was unforgiving; the car unyielding, still moving and still accelerating. The would-be predator was pushed into the road. The grating surface shredded his shirt and chest. Skin and muscle liquefied; a bright red blood slick trailing behind. Exposed ribs chipped, cracked, and broke free.

Flailing and twisting, the ogre struggled to free himself. He tried to catch hold of something, anything for leverage. Reaching up with his left arm- which, despite having lost a good deal of skin, still had enough intact muscle tissue and tendons to move, the brute grabbed onto the first thing it felt, the wheel itself.

A fresh geyser erupted. Blood filled the wheel well as whirling alloy spokes wrenched fingers free from the hand. A red liquid smoke billowed from beneath the car. Bones and ligaments, flesh and fingernails ground into paste by the spinning wheel and churning gears. The entire hand was gone and in an instant, so was the arm; torn away at the shoulder by apathetic steel and unrelenting torque.

The shattered demon wasn't fighting anymore. Its blood and lungs coated a quarter-mile stretch of highway and the lanky beast had perished. Its body, however, remained in its place beneath the Pontiac. The one-armed corpse was dragged another fifty feet or so until enough of his body had been

223

scraped off to the point where it could shake loose from under the car's front bumper.

Crack! A squishing thud reverberated through the suspension as the wheel slammed into the cadaver. Pink and rubbery red chunks flew in all directions. The right side of the car lifted several inches as the wheel climbed up and onto the body. The tires were still driving but they found no purchase on loose skin and glossy bone.

"Shit!" Jim blurted as the coupe swung hard to the right.

He spun the steering wheel all the way to the left to try and correct their trajectory. But it was too far. When the tires finally regained traction, the car jerked and spun back the other way. It continued to move, sliding into the left lane of traffic.

Lindsey shrieked as red ribbons splattered against her window. She flinched and ducked, leaning back and away from the glass, expecting it to break. Her hand tightened its grip around the door handle and all she could manage to do was cry out, "Jim!"

"Hang on," he told her. Jim struggled to regain control of the vehicle. He turned the wheel back once more, again over-correcting.

The Pontiac was now drifting sideways with the driver's side in the lead, but it was losing speed and momentum. Jim tried again to straighten the car. He turned the wheel and stomped the brake pedal. The wheels locked up, leaving behind four skid marks- three black and one red. With a cough from the engine and a groan from rickety shock absorbers, the car finally came to rest.

Jim's heart was pounding in his chest and there was a sharp pain in his right leg. The top part of his thigh felt like it was being squished in a vice. He looked down to find Lindsey's hand locked onto the leg of his shorts. Her fingers were wrapped tightly around a ball of fabric with her fingernails digging through and pinching his skin.

"Oh. Sorry," she said when she noticed Jim staring down at his lap. Lindsey released the fistful of cotton and explained, "I was trying to find something to hold on to."

"No problem," Jim told her. Smoothing over his bunched-up shorts, he said, "Another couple of inches and that could have been a pretty dangerous maneuver."

"Heh," she scoffed playfully. "Not much to worry about there. I think you're safe, even if I were aiming for-"

"Yeah, Yeah." Jim smirked.

Lindsey began to speak again but was interrupted by something banging on the outside of the car. Jim and Lindsey both turned to look over their shoulders. An infected woman bared her teeth and glared at them through the back window.

She was one of the slow-moving zombies who had apparently survived a partial impact with the Pontiac. Blades of grass and clumps of dirt clung to her ratty blouse. The right side of her face was bright red and badly swollen. Her mouth was open and she looked like she was growling or screaming but no sound came out. The rotten bitch took another swipe at the trunk lid and then began shambling along the driver's side of the car, slowly making her way to the front.

"We should keep moving," Lindsey stated flatly; the hint of amusement now gone from her voice.

"Yeah," Jim agreed. His foot lifted off the brake pedal and the Pontiac began to roll forward. He pressed a button on the steering column to activate the wiper spray. The wipers came on but they just sort of mixed the blue washing liquid with the congealing blood, spreading a thin purple glaze across the glass. It took about a half-gallon of washer fluid and a few dozen passes of the wipers before the windshield was clear enough to see through.

Jim accelerated slowly, half expecting to find that a tire had gone flat. He paid great attention to how the steering felt, whether the car would pull to one side, or if the ride seemed uneven. And to his surprise, it all seemed okay.

"Ha ha!" he proclaimed. Jim patted the top of the steering wheel like he was rewarding an obedient puppy. "What did I tell you- indestructible."

"Oh?" Lindsey asked. Her eyes motioned toward the front of the car.

He followed her lead and looked through the windscreen. Near its front edge, just above the front bumper, Jim could see the crease of a substantial dent in the hood.

"Ah shit," he grumbled.

He'd have said quite a bit more than that had he been able to see the rest of the car's exterior. The bumper was riddled with cracks and small holes. The fenders had a bunch of new scratches and the entire passenger's side looked as if someone had tossed a can of red paint on it. But as far as he could tell, the damage was mostly cosmetic.

"So, the car might not be much to look at," Jim told her. "But it seems to be driving okay."

"Good," Lindsey replied. "You still trust it to get us to Allegany?"

"Absolutely." Jim answered. His artificial confidence had returned. "I think we can probably make up some time too, once we get on the Thruway."

"That's good. The sooner we get there, the better." Lindsey forced a cautious smile. "And hopefully we can get there without any more... um, incidents."

Convinced it was safe to drive like normal again, Jim hit the gas. He eased up on the accelerator when the coupe got to about sixty miles per hour. The car whizzed past a long row of trees and under the pedestrian bridge. It was only another mile or so before they'd reach the ramp onto the Youngmann Expressway.

"Hey, would you mind handing me a cigarette?" Jim asked.

"Sure," Lindsey replied. She opened the center console and pulled out the pack. Then she said, "Oh, I've got something else for you too."

"Huh?" Jim looked over just in time to see the back of her hand swat him in the chest.

"Hey," he complained. "What was that for?"

"That's for almost putting us in a ditch," she stated. Lindsey tried to sound firm, like a nanny scolding some pesky kid who refused to clean up his toys. But Jim could see through it. A whimsical glimmer in her eye and a smile just below the surface told him she was joking with him. Mostly joking, anyway.

Jim opened his mouth to object but caught himself before speaking. He simply asked, "So what about that smoke?"

Lindsey lit it for him, same as she had done earlier. She handed it over without saying a word. Jim immediately pulled in a deep lungful and breathed out a long audible exhale. And for the next several minutes, they rode in silence. Here and there, a flap of wet skin would dislodge itself from the tire treads to jump up and land on a body panel or the passenger's side window with a sloppy wet pop.

The car was otherwise soundless.

No screaming, no shouting about where to go, no lunatics pounding on the hood. Just quiet. It was the perfect atmosphere for two young travelers to think and reflect, to remember, to second-guess their every move. To wonder how their loved ones had fared thus far, contemplating where they might have been when everything turned to shit. Their friends and relatives- were they alright? Had they been at home where they could lie low and protect themselves? Or was everybody dead?

Alive or otherwise, there was no way to know. And worse, there wasn't a fucking thing they could do about it. They could invest as much worry as they liked, but it wouldn't change the fact that both Jim and Lindsey were helpless to do anything but obsess about all the things they couldn't know. And with no distractions, nothing to stifle their anxiety, they would do just that.

The angst was consuming. Jim could feel sweat on his chest and belly as a gurgling, sour sensation formed in the center of his bowels. He found himself hoping to run into another zombie horde, just to take his mind off of things. Lindsey was having a similar experience; too much quiet and a rising panic. She needed somewhere to focus her nervous energies- something, anything to serve as a distraction.

Lindsey leaned forward in her seat and asked, "You ever think about trying to quit?"

"Huh?" Jim asked. "You mean quit smoking?"

"Yeah."

"Maybe," he replied with a shrug. "But I think we've got more pressing matters than a little second-hand smoke. Ya know, like not getting eaten."

Lindsey clucked her tongue. "Weren't you just saying something about learning to listen to people who might know better than you?" she asked; an inquisitorial expression on her face.

"I think I was saying I'm not good at it," he told her, sure to avoid eye contact as he spoke.

"You were also saying that you need to work on it," Lindsey reminded him.

"Alright, alright," Jim rolled his eyes.

Frowning, he took one last drag off his cigarette and then rolled the window down further. He groaned audibly as he exhaled. Jim stuck his hand outside the car and flicked away the half-smoked cigarette. He rolled the window halfway up and looked to Lindsey, casting her a snarky glance as if to say, *I hope you're satisfied.*

"I was only teasing," Lindsey told him. "You didn't have to toss it."

"No, it's okay," Jim told her; his features softening. "I do tend to smoke more when I'm stressed out or nervous about something. Shit, I'm surprised I haven't been smoking two at a time all day today. But it is sorta nice to have someone keep me in check like that."

"That's me. I'm a huge nag," she joked. "Any time you need a good scolding, you know who to ask."

"Good to know," Jim remarked. "But I knew you way back when you used to be fun. Like, you remember when we used to skip school and go to Darien Lake?"

"I remember getting grounded for a month when my mom found out about it," Lindsey replied. "Oh my God, she was so pissed. And if I remember correctly, that's not the only time you talked me into doing something stupid."

"Oh yeah? Like what?" he asked. Jim steered the Pontiac around an empty police cruiser that had been parked and abandoned in the right lane.

"Let's see," Lindsey said thoughtfully. "There was that time we sneaked out in the middle of the night and went swimming in your neighbor's pool."

"That's true," Jim agreed. "The dumb part was doing it right next door. We should have gone a few blocks down so the homeowners wouldn't recognize us when they woke up."

"So they'd call the cops instead of calling your parents?" Lindsey asked. "And what about the time we got kicked out of Watkins Glen for climbing down into the ravine?"

Jim couldn't help but laugh. "That's what I'm talking about. Sure, it was stupid, but it was fun. And funny."

Lindsey smiled. "Yeah, I guess it was pretty funny."

"Do you remember the park ranger's reaction?" Jim asked. "He was so pissed."

"It was part anger, part confusion," she said. "He was like, 'What the Hell are these two assholes doing?' Do you remember what you said to him?"

"I think I told him it was your idea," Jim told her, searching his memory. He pulled the car into the right lane to avoid a stalled Ford pickup truck that was halfway onto the grassy median. Its rear bumper hung over a portion of the left lane and both of its doors were left open.

"You did!" Lindsey blurted. "I was so mad at you. I couldn't believe you blamed me!"

Jim's head cocked slightly and he replied, "As I recall, it *was* your idea."

"That's besides the point," she chuckled. "You didn't have to tell him that."

"Ha! What was I supposed to do?"

Lindsey shrugged and said, "I don't know, maybe do the chivalrous thing and take the blame. Or you could have just not said anything at all."

"I thought he might go easier on us if he thought it was your idea," Jim told her.

"Why would that matter?" Lindsey asked.

"Well, think about it this way," Jim began. "The guy sees a young couple doing something foolish and dangerous and quasi-illegal. If he thinks that I pressured you into it or talked you into doing something you didn't want to do, then that doesn't look very good. In that scenario, I come off as some sort of predatory weirdo who's putting some poor girl in harm's way."

"Okay," Lindsey nodded.

"But on the other hand," Jim continued. "If he thinks that it was your suggestion and I went along with it because I'm just some dopey guy who got talked into it because he's trying to impress his hot girlfriend, well then that doesn't seem quite as bad. It's just some innocent fun that happened to violate the rules of the park."

"Alright, that makes sense. Sorta," she commented. "But he still kicked us out."

"He threatened to have us arrested," Jim reminded her. "But instead, he only asked us to leave. And that's thanks to me and my quick thinking."

"Thank goodness for your brilliant mind," Lindsey said sarcastically. "But at any point while we were being accosted by park authorities, did it occur to you that maybe you should clue me in to your genius plan?"

"Oh," Jim thought out loud for a moment, "Right. I guess I probably should have told you. But you know what else I was thinking about that-"

"Jim!" Lindsey cut him off.

"What is it?"

"Um," was all she could muster. No further explanation would be necessary. Lindsey was leaning all the way forward in her seat. She reached over the dashboard and pointed ahead through the windshield.

Chapter 34

"...okay, so call me back when you get this." Lucy sniffled as she hung up the phone. That was the third voice mail she'd left for her mother. Lucy had left the same number of messages for her father. Neither had picked up. Neither had called back. A spot of moisture appeared in the corner of her eye. She dabbed it away with her sleeve, sucking in a big breath of air and willing an end to the waterworks before they really got going.

Lucy uncrossed her legs and let herself fall backwards into the couch cushions. A glance to the far end of the sofa let her know the golf club was still where she'd left it, leaning upright against the armrest. Still holding her cell phone, she checked the screen for any missed calls or unopened messages. But of course, there were none.

Now there was nothing to do but wait for Danny to return and hope her parents called back. Lucy needed a way to distract herself. She needed something to keep her from completely freaking out. And she really needed a cigarette. Maybe she could neglect her lookout duties for a couple of minutes while she took a smoke break.

Lookout- yeah right. Danny and his friend had obviously assigned her the lookout position because they felt sorry for her. That, and they were probably afraid she would freeze up and make a mistake. Or maybe they expected her to break down and become totally useless while they were sealing the doors and checking on the neighbors.

As she walked from the living room to the kitchen, fear and concern morphed into anger and resentment. Sad little Lucy needs to be hidden away from anything that might scare her. She can stay locked up in the apartment while Danny and Jenna are off playing hero. How had they become the stalwart defenders of the tenement? Danny only seemed so confident because years of constant pot smoking had numbed him to the point where he couldn't intellectually grasp how real the danger was, and how quickly it was closing in on them.

And Jenna- well, Lucy didn't quite know what to make of her. All that rifle-toting, kick-ass, tough-as-nails bullshit seemed forced and inauthentic. Lucy rolled her eyes as she stooped to dig through her purse and fish out a cigarette.

Then again, maybe she should be grateful Jenna was around. If not for Jenna, Lucy would be stuck riding this out alone with her brother. Now Danny had someone to motivate him; someone to give him a kick in the ass so he would put down the bong and actually be productive. It's a shame he hadn't spent more time with her over the past few years.

Lucy found her pack at the bottom of her purse. She took out a cigarette and held it between her lips as she strode through the living room to the glass door at the front of the apartment. Leaving the blinds closed, Lucy slid the door open just far enough to squeeze through. She stepped out onto the balcony and lit up.

It would be getting dark soon and the streetlights had come on. This was a good sign. It reminded her that the electricity was still working. Of course she would have noticed if the power had gone out but the thought hadn't crossed her mind until now. She didn't know how the power grid worked or whether the pandemic would cause a service interruption. She also hadn't charged her phone in a while and wasn't sure if Danny kept any candles or flashlight batteries on hand. But everything was working for now. Hopefully it would stay that way.

She blew out a cloud of blue-gray smoke and decided to try calling her folks one more time. Because even though they hadn't answered three minutes ago, ten minutes ago, or sixteen minutes ago, they were *definitely* going to answer this time. Lucy shook her head and decided against making a fourth call in under twenty minutes. If she called and got voice mail again, which she would, it would only leave her feeling more worried.

Lucy stared at the phone screen. She had to do something to keep her mind from wandering. She wanted to talk to someone familiar to make sure she hadn't lost her mind and to find out if there was anyone out there that was still okay. But who? It was a terrible time to realize your social circle barely extended beyond your immediate family. Only one name came to mind, Darryl.

Darryl, the cheating, lying, chronically underemployed loser ex-boyfriend who'd booted Lucy out of his apartment. What a dickhead. Phoning him might work as a distraction, but not a nice one. Lucy could already feel an anger rising; teeth clenching and fists forming around her cell phone and cigarette lighter.

If he answered, it would mean he's okay. Lucy couldn't make up her mind about whether that would be a good thing or a bad thing. She supposed if he did answer, it would give her one last chance to tell him what a prick he was. If he didn't, then Lucy could assume he'd either been killed or turned into one of those infected assholes. She almost chuckled at the thought. Darryl was already an asshole, making the leap to violence and cannibalism didn't seem too far off.

"Screw it," Lucy murmured as she continued scrolling through her contact list.

Her cigarette break was nearly over and it was almost time to go back inside. Lucy took one more puff and tossed the smoldering butt over the railing. Just as she was about to head back inside, Lucy caught sight of something in the parking lot and nearly screamed at what she saw. There was a man down there and he was looking right at her. Had she bothered to look up from her cell phone a little sooner, she might have spotted the sadistic stooge before he was able to get so close.

Now that she had seen him, there were two things that immediately stood out about the man. The first was how well he was dressed, like he might have been on his way to a wedding. He wore a light blue suit with a pearl-colored tie tucked under a white vest. He even had a bright yellow boutonniere fastened to his lapel. How fancy.

The second thing Lucy noticed about him was the blood; lots and lots of blood. His hands and face were painted in it, particularly around his mouth and lower jaw. A red-brown crust covered his sleeves and the front of his vest. His trousers were torn above the left knee. Dark fluid from an open wound caused the fabric to cling to his thigh. He moved slowly, barely lifting his feet from the ground as he shuffled forward.

He wasn't screaming or running around or freaking out like she had seen them do on TV. In all of the news footage, people who'd been infected were much quicker. Those with even the most grievous of injuries were running, jumping, and attacking with astounding speed. Lucy first thought the man might just be injured and not necessarily infected. But his burbling growl and vacant expression quickly disabused her of this notion.

Maybe this is what happened to them when they got tired. Or maybe they started weak and slow and then became faster and more aggressive as the infection grew inside them. For whatever it was, Lucy was grateful. He was slow and he was by himself. For now.

She turned and reached for the door. Lucy had to get inside, but then what? Scamper into the apartment and pretend she hadn't seen anything? Or perhaps more importantly, to pretend nothing had seen her? That wouldn't make for a very good lookout.

A chill spread across her shoulder blades and gooseflesh appeared on her forearms. Was that from the fear or the cold? *Could* she be cold? What was the temperature outside? It was the middle of summer, so how cold could it possibly be? Wouldn't she have noticed a precipitous drop in temperature? And when had the air become so thick? Had it been made denser somehow? But how, exactly, would that have happened? It felt like it does after a heavy rainstorm, when the air is heavy and wet. But that's not what was happening here. There was no rain; no thick invisible fog. Lucy was beginning to lose control.

Keep it together, she told herself. *Breath in, breath out.* Although it's probably not normal to have to tell yourself how to inhale and exhale. No, definitely not normal. Breathing is an activity which shouldn't require a tremendous amount of concentration.

Lucy was struck by a sudden spell of dizziness. She grabbed onto the rusted metal railing with both hands and fought to maintain her balance. A tightness formed in her arms and calf muscles as she used every bit of her remaining strength to keep herself from falling to the floor.

Down on the ground, the man in the suit had made it more than halfway across the parking lot. He nearly tripped over the skinny teen corpse bloating on the pavement but easily regained his footing and continued toward the building.

A fresh layer of sweat appeared on the back of Lucy's neck and under her arms. She wanted to call for help, to run inside and lock herself away from all of this. The violence, the gore, the anxiety and panic; it was all too much. Lucy now knew she was going to die.

Of course, it's not like she had previously thought she was going to live forever. Obviously, Lucy had always understood on an intellectual level that all things would one day perish. Her own demise, however, was a concept so distant and foreign that it almost wasn't real. That was something that changed in a hurry.

Death was no longer an obscure destination in the unspecified future. It wasn't waiting for Lucy to slowly approach over the course of the next few decades. Death, it seemed, had grown impatient. It was coming to get her. And now, it had arrived.

A new surge of adrenaline had Lucy's pulse racing. Everything seemed to slow down as her senses became sharper and more attuned to the low light and relative quiet. Lucy could see every wrinkle and frayed stitch on the man's suit. She heard every faint footstep and the sound of individual leaves scraping the cement as the wind gently pushed them along.

A stinging sensation formed in her fingertips and her chest began to ache. Lucy's vision started to narrow, growing darker at the corners of her eyes. She realized she was holding her breath and had been for several moments; an observation she found both odd and terrifying because she could still hear someone's heavy breathing.

The next breath she took would be through a scream. Lucy looked down and to her left. On the ground, at the edge of the grass near the corner of the building, stood another man. He was a stocky guy with broad shoulders and a substantial belly with a receding hairline and dressed in a black button-down shirt and tan trousers. The man looked up at her and flashed a terrible smile of clenched teeth. Spittle dripped out of his mouth with each heaving breath; his chest rising and falling in time.

The man tried leaping at her but fell short and ran into the exterior wall of the tenement. With a roar of anger, he kicked and scratched at the brick veneer, scraping off some skin and fingernails in the process. Dozens of bright red rivulets appeared on the siding as the barbarian howled and pressed on, trying to gain purchase on the wall and pull himself up.

And then someone else came to join them, another fast one. He appeared from around the side of the building and followed suit, wailing away and grabbing at the wall in a failed attempt to reach Lucy, his intended victim. Then there was another. And another. They were appearing too quickly to count but more than a dozen insane men and women had gathered on the ground below her.

Lucy turned away and reached for the door handle but became distracted once more as she caught a glimpse of something moving in the street. Yet another person; an older woman with glasses wearing tan pants and a plain purple sweater. She was moving much slower than all the rest but she had come close enough for Lucy to see that she too was drenched in blood.

It was time to get inside, time to warn the others. Lucy spun around, grabbed the handle to the sliding glass door and flung it open. Before she could make it in, she heard something small hit the floor and bounce a couple times before coming to rest at the edge of the balcony, just below the bottom rung of the railing. It was her lighter. She should have just left it. She should have gone inside, locked the door, and prayed for a miracle. But without thinking, she turned back and crouched down to retrieve her Bic. That's when Lucy witnessed the absolute worst thing she'd ever seen.

Sure, the videos on the news were pretty bad. The cadavers scattered across the parking lot were an awful sight to behold. The group of disease-ridden freaks trying to claw their way to the second story balcony were downright horrifying. But what she saw now was nothing short of nightmarish.

Down the road at the nearest intersection, about a thousand feet away, was a throng of people walking down the center of the street and moving in her direction. There must have been more than a hundred of them and many were beginning to run, sprinting past some of their slower comrades. The fast ones would arrive in seconds. Within minutes, the entire building would be surrounded.

Chapter 35

"Should we leave the light on?" Jenna asked.

"For Adam?" Danny shrugged, "What's he got to look at down here?"

"Not for him," Jenna clarified. She slid the spool of extension cord up and over her right shoulder as she spoke. "In case someone else comes down here, so they won't be so startled when they find him."

Danny nodded his agreement and followed Jenna away from the chain-link cage, leaving infected Adam to drool on himself in private. He pursued them with his eyes; an action that went unnoticed as the pair drifted out of sight. Adam could hear them as they walked through the side door and began climbing the stairs to the first floor.

A moment later they arrived in the small entryway, a grimy foyer that always inexplicably smelled like the underside of a dock. Jenna turned the corner and began traversing the next set of steps, the steps that would lead her to Albert's apartment. Danny, who had been right behind her, paused in the hallway before continuing on. It might have been his imagination, but he could have sworn he'd just seen something race past the front door.

Each entrance was equipped with a pair of modern-looking porch lights which were mounted to the exterior wall with one on either side of the doorway. They might have been the building's newest and fanciest features; so much so that they looked a little out of place next to the rusted aluminum door frames, clouded glass, and stained siding. The sconces were made of brushed nickel and came with a frosted cylindrical shade to create a soft white glow.

Anyone wanting to take a good look at the elegant light fixtures would have to do so during daylight hours. They were more decorative than they were functional. Even though the sun had just started to go down, you basically needed to have your face pressed up against the glass to be able to see who or what was approaching the front door. So when Danny saw something, or thought he saw something, there was no way to be sure without further investigation.

"Psst," he called. "Jenna, hold up a sec."

She paused halfway up the staircase and cast a glance over her shoulder. "What is it?"

"I think I saw something," he told her. Danny knelt to place the package of coaxial cable on the floor.

Jenna, now turning back and descending the stairs, gave Danny an expectant look. "What do you mean?"

"I'm not sure, something outside." Danny pointed to the doorway with his machete. He took another step closer, trying to observe the darkened walkway and parking lot in front of the building. "I guess I may have imagined- oh shit!"

Danny's words cut off. Something else streaked past the door and this time there was no mistaking. It was a person; a person running at top speed, sprinting past the entrance and covering the length of the parking lot in under two seconds. Danny hadn't even seen where he'd come from. It was like this dude had just appeared out of nowhere.

"Danny, get away from the door," Jenna instructed. She then jumped the last four steps to the floor of the lobby, careful not to drop her rifle in the process.

Ignoring her request, Danny moved closer to the doorway. Slowly and with caution, he placed one hand on the push bar and applied enough pressure to open the door about six inches. Just as he did this, another person sprinted past the entrance.

"Where are they going?" Danny wondered out loud.

"Who cares?" Jenna replied.

Danny didn't say as much but for an instant, he let himself believe that something or someone might have the freaks on the run. Maybe the military had finally shown up; a highly-trained and heavily-armed squad bent on ridding the world of their foul infestation. Maybe the zombies had been confronted by soldiers and tanks and were running for their lives.

It was a foolish and hopelessly optimistic thought. And if they weren't running *from* something, which the infected were not known to do, then they must be rushing *toward* something. This was obviously the more likely scenario. But maybe, hopefully, they were on their way to somewhere far away from his home.

"Come on," Jenna called; her tone somewhere between a whisper and a shout. "Get away from there."

Dutifully, Danny did the opposite. Making as little noise as possible, he opened the glass door a little wider, just far enough for him to squeeze through. Machete-first, Danny stepped out of the building and onto the cement block walkway in front of the tenement. Looking to his left, the direction the ghouls had been heading, Danny hoped to determine what it was they were after.

No more than sixty feet from where he stood, several dozen infected lunatics bit and clawed at the exterior wall. They were all there together; men, women, children, people of all shapes, sizes, colors, and backgrounds. And they all had the same goal, to hunt, destroy, and consume.

Danny did his best to observe without being noticed. Some of the zombies were just like Adam. Visible injuries and gore-stained clothing helped them blend in with the crowd but they were unmistakably different. They moved slower, almost off-balance. If one of the slow-movers managed to make it to the front of the pack and get to the building itself, they didn't scrape and claw like the rest. They lazily reached their hands up and just sort of swatted at the wall.

The eyes of a sprinter burned with remarkable intensity; a vicious and primal anger that overtook not just the expression on their face, but their entire soul. Their bumbling, slow-moving counterparts lacked that ferocity.

The staggering dimwits appeared wobbly and uncoordinated. They seemed to have to work much harder just to stay upright. The slow ones couldn't sneak up on you. They couldn't chase you down. As long as you stayed conscious and mobile, they couldn't harm you. They were much more manageable. At least, that's how it seemed to Danny.

Unfortunately for him and his crew, the slow-pokes outside the building were vastly outnumbered by their faster-moving colleagues. In this particular horde, more than two-thirds were sprinters. As he studied the churning mass, Danny concluded the toe-dragging, foot-shuffling snails were probably the minority in the zombie population as a whole. Bad times.

Danny took another step closer to the group. He couldn't tell whether they were all working together as a unified force, or if the fiends were actually competing with one another to see who'd get the next kill. His chances of finding any answers were slim and the poor lighting conditions weren't helping matters.

However, the darkness couldn't hide everything. A growing field of red could be seen glistening on the side of the building as ghouls shredded fingers and knuckles against the coarse brick veneer; a puddle of tacky blood forming at their feet. Skin flecks and scraps of torn clothing clung to the building's outer wall.

The beasts were also exchanging injuries with one another. There were split lips, crushed noses, busted jaws, and broken bones. Most of the damage was inflicted by the sprinters. They shoved the others aside and pushed their way to the front of the pack. Fists and elbows swung wildly. More strikes connected with the torsos and faces of other zombies, both fast and slow alike. Yet they all pressed on, each unfazed by the wounds they received and unaware of the wounds they levied.

They were obviously trying to get in, trying to get to something, but what? They weren't going for the door or windows- not yet, anyway. It took a moment for Danny to make sense of it, but then it struck him. Nearly all of the savages were looking up. They weren't trying to penetrate the wall, they were trying to climb it. Needless to say, they weren't making any real progress. But it wouldn't be long before one of them found their way to the entrance.

Had a person, presumably someone fleeing the mob, climbed onto one of the balconies? There was no way anyone could get onto the roof, but what about one of the windows? He didn't see any that were open or broken. Maybe the ghouls had caught sight of someone through a window. Or maybe they had just been drawn to the light coming from within.

Following their gaze, Danny scanned the front of the building and hoped to find whatever it was those punks were after. His eyes traced the edge of the wall, moving upward past Jim's balcony and then to his own. He caught a brief glance of someone in a black tee shirt scampering into the apartment. Lucy. While on lookout, she must have somehow been spotted by the barbarians. But what was she doing out on the balcony?

Danny resisted an urge to call out to her to make sure she was alright. It would have been impossible, but he found himself terrified that one of those infected assholes had in fact climbed up the wall and gotten inside. Or worse- what if they had already been inside? What if he and Jenna had somehow missed one that had now gotten into his apartment?

Moisture formed under his arms. Maybe it had already been there. Danny hadn't noticed until a swollen bead of perspiration rolled out from under his sleeve, past his elbow and onto his right wrist. His hand squeezed tighter on the machete's handle, ignoring the sweat and the cool wet line it had drawn on his arm. Danny's attention was somewhere else.

He could hear footsteps, soft and muffled by distance and grass. Another body was on its way to join the band of cannibals. How did they know where to go? The commotion must be drawing them in from all over the place. Or- the muscles in Danny's neck tensed as he wondered- did they have a heightened sense of hearing?

The footsteps were growing louder, moving closer. They had reached paved ground.

Maybe the zombies somehow developed a way to use echolocation like bat sonar, using sound waves to locate their food. Worse yet- maybe it had nothing to do with regular sensory input. What if they were communicating not with language or visual cues, but through telepathy. Danny shook his head and thought, *stop being ridiculous.*

They were heavy now; each step smacking cement and echoing down alleys. The footsteps demanded attention as their impact vibrated the ground. Their sound rang through the air, heralded by perking ears and chilling sweats.

"Danny!" The shrieking cry of a warning sent too late.

He knew what was coming and he understood what would be necessary. Eyes closed. Lungs inhaled. Danny lifted his right hand up from his waist and across his chest; the machete momentarily hovering over his left shoulder. He flexed every muscle in his left leg, planting it like the trunk of a tree in the Earth. His right leg kicked out and pulled back. Letting his heel lead the way, Danny flung his right foot past the left and then stomped it into the ground. He let the rest of his body pivot to the right, using its own momentum to spin. Hips twisted, then torso, abs and chest, and then his right elbow. Triceps contracted dramatically as he spun, extending his arm and swinging the blade with all the power he could muster.

The footsteps were no more. Their driving force had been nullified. Everything became silent.

Danny opened his eyes and exhaled. There was still no sound, as if all the world's noises were played through a stereo and the speakers had been unplugged. The wind, nearby traffic, and distant screams had all been muted. Pandemonium, both inside the building and out, failed to register on any audible scale. Once deafening, the tumult of bodies below his balcony had become reticent. Behind the glass door, a terror-stricken Jenna let loose a wordless, soundless scream.

Dots formed at his feet and without sound, they lacked context. Above them, his arm was still outstretched; his hand still grasping the handle of his weapon. A shining red rivulet traced a crooked line across the top side of the blade. On the opposite end of the machete, the razor-sharp edge was lodged deeply in an open, fatal neck wound.

236

Chapter 36

They were passing through the Young Street intersection, still traveling down Twin Cities Highway. The first of two on-ramps for the Youngmann Expressway was about fifty yards in front of them. This would take them west and would ultimately bring them closer to the City of Buffalo, the opposite of where they were trying to go.

If they wanted to go east on the Youngmann Expressway- which they did if they wanted to get to Allegany, they would need to continue down Twin Cities Highway for another eight hundred feet, drive under an overpass, and take the next ramp on their right. This would lead them to the New York State Thruway. From there, they would need to head south toward Allegany. Under normal circumstances, the trip would take about two hours.

Of course, Jim and Lindsey weren't the only people who'd had the bright idea to flee from the city and suburbs, so a little traffic along the way was to be expected. What was not expected, however, was total gridlock. All movement on the Youngmann Expressway had seized. Both on-ramps and all six lanes of traffic were completely clogged with hundreds of stationary vehicles.

Cars, trucks, vans; there were too many to count. A succession of stopped vehicles stretched for miles down the road. A number of motorists had tried to split the lanes and cut between two rows of traffic. Others had pulled onto the side of the road and tried to make up some ground along the shoulder. None of them, no matter the strategy, had gotten very far.

Several, in fact, had managed to get themselves wedged between a pair of cars or pinned against the guardrail. It was too tight to even open their doors, so many drivers, along with any passengers they might have on board, were left trapped inside their vehicles.

Some dickhead in a white conversion van had gone up the west-bound ramp and tried to bypass a row of nine cars by driving along the side of the road. He got about halfway up the ramp before he ran out of space. Instead of stopping, the jackass cut to the left and tried to make room for himself to get by. The van smashed into a Kia and a Toyota as the hysterical driver made a desperate attempt to reach the highway. Pushing a couple of lightweight compact cars out of the way wasn't any trouble for the six-thousand-pound van but after bullying his way across two lanes of traffic, the dip-shit van driver clipped the back end of a Tahoe and that's as far as he got.

The van driver wasn't the only one who'd attempted this maneuver. All types of vehicles were all over the road. No attention was paid to traffic signals, signs, or the lines painted on the cement. Plenty of cars were left straddling lanes or turned sideways. A handful of sport utility vehicles had been stuck in the ditch along the side of the highway after their drivers had tried to put their four-wheel-drive capabilities to the test.

It didn't take long for most of these people to realize they wouldn't be going anywhere any time soon. At least, they wouldn't be driving anywhere. Many of them, determined to get out of town one way or another, left the relative security of their cars and attempted to flee on foot. It was the worst thing they could have done.

Healthy uninfected people weren't the only ones traversing the Youngmann Expressway. Crashing cars, honking horns, and the general commotion of the roadway might as well have been a giant dinner bell calling out to every mad cannibal in town. It was feeding time and anyone stupid enough to get out of their vehicle had essentially volunteered to be an appetizer.

Pedestrians were ripped open and eaten alive. Terrified onlookers watched from inside their cars with the doors locked, unable to do anything but hope the ghouls would have their fill, lest they come for them next. Shredded skin, half-chewed organs, and buckets of blood doused the pavement. Jim and Lindsey observed the chaos from the street below; distance sparing them the intimate details of the carnage unfolding above.

You're screwed, a voice seemed to shout inside Jim's head. He kept the car in its lane and eased to a stop just ahead of the first ramp. Taking the Youngmann Expressway was obviously not an option. Traffic on the Thruway was bound to be just as bad, if not worse. Turning around wasn't an option either. He knew what was waiting for them back near the supermarket and hospital. Yep, Jim thought to himself, you're screwed.

"Shit." Jim took one long drag from his cigarette and then flicked the butt out the window. "Lindsey, I'm sorry. I- I am really, very sorry."

"About the smoke?" she asked. "It's fine. I'm just busting your balls, Jim."

"No!" The word rushed out faster than he'd intended. Jim turned to face Lindsey and her gaze met his. He spoke, resolute and unblinking. "I've owed you an apology for a long time. And in case I don't get another chance to tell you, I'm telling you now. I'm sorry."

She stared back at him. Lindsey didn't say anything until Jim's eyes returned to the road. When she did speak, her tone was cautious and uneven. "Okay, so we obviously aren't talking about the cigarettes anymore..."

"The cigarettes, the groceries you bought for me, the TV I borrowed and never returned, the birthday party I ruined, that stupid winter formal dance you wanted to go to... Everything." Jim sighed. He'd lost his nerve to look at her when he spoke but he kept going. "The lies, the manipulating, taking you for granted time after time. Of all my many regrets, the one that weighs heaviest is how I treated you. I can't even count the number of apologies I owe you. And I know it won't make things right or undo any of the shitty things I've done, but I needed to tell you."

He stopped and turned to face her once again, waiting just long enough to regain eye contact before saying, "I'm sorry."

Lindsey reached up and placed a hand on his shoulder. She gave it a little squeeze, smiled, and said simply, "Thank you."

He seemed to relax; a great weight lifted from his shoulders. "Jeez, that wasn't as bad as I expected," he told her.

Jim reached is hand up to meet hers. He placed his palm over her fingers and gently caressed. Lindsey stiffened slightly and began to pull away. Of course she did. Could Jim really think his bumbling quasi-romantic moves would work at a time like this? What an idiot. His *moves* never worked and the last thing Lindsey needed now was for Jim to try pawing at her with his sweaty stumpy digits. She let her hand fall to the top of her knee. Then, her head tilted almost imperceptibly.

"Wait," she said. "What do you mean? About not being as bad as you expected?"

"I know it's been a while since we've, ya know, hung out or spent any time together, but it's been on my mind an awful lot." Jim looked down at the steering wheel and continued speaking. "In my mind, I ran through all the ways this might have played out. I mostly just assumed you'd want to yell and scream at me; curse me out and tell me what a piece of shit I am."

238

"Come on, Jim," Lindsey replied. "You've known me for what, eight years? Nine years? When have you ever seen me curse someone out?"

"I've heard you curse before," Jim pointed out. "And I suppose I would have deserved it. That is, if you didn't just dismiss me immediately. After all the bullshit, I didn't think you'd even want to speak to me. I thought about calling you a few times but I could only muster up the nerve to call once. It was probably about a year ago. I called but you didn't answer."

"I know," Lindsey told him.

"Yeah," Jim went on. "I didn't feel right leaving a message, so I just hung up."

"You should've left a message," she told him. "I remember you calling. And I remember deciding not to pick up. I assumed you were calling to ask for money or because you needed some kind of favor, or... whatever. If you left a message, I would have known it was something else."

Jim forced a chuckle, "I'll be sure to do that next time I've got a huge apology to unload."

Lindsey didn't share his sense of humor. She just looked back at him and waited to see if he had anything else to add.

He cleared his throat and continued. "Like I said, I've been wanting to tell you that for a long time. So, um, I guess that's it."

"It's alright," Lindsey replied. "I appreciate that, Jim. And if it makes you feel any better, it hasn't really bothered me in a while."

"No?"

"Well, I mean, it's been sort of a long time," she said.

"Right," Jim agreed. "I feel sort of silly now, having said it out loud."

"No, don't feel silly," Lindsey told him. "I guess I've just sort of moved on. I don't really think about it anymore."

"I think about it all the time," Jim confessed.

"Oh." She looked surprised to hear that.

"Especially since running into you at the supermarket," he added. "Every day I think about it- how I wish I would've been better. I wish I had-"

"Jim," Lindsey interrupted. "I don't mean to be rude, but can we continue this discussion on the road?"

She motioned toward the roadway above them and said, "We gotta move."

Twenty or more bloodthirsty miscreants were making their way down the ramp at full speed. Dozens more followed closely behind. Sprinting ghouls stomped through piles of sun-dried innards and splashed puddles of spilled transmission fluid as they blitzed headlong through the assembly of parked cars.

In the brief instant it took for Jim to look up and identify the incoming threat, the freaks had already closed half the distance between the top of the ramp and the blue coupe. He and Lindsey were still a safe distance away, but that would change in a matter of seconds.

"That's probably a good idea," Jim answered as he punched the gas pedal.

The Pontiac jerked forward and started to pull ahead, accelerating toward the pair of overpasses

239

which lie just over a hundred feet away. Each overpass held three of the six lanes that made up the Youngmann Expressway, suspending them about thirty feet above Twin Cities Memorial Highway.

In another eight hundred feet, Twin Cities would come to an end and split into two smaller streets. To the left of the fork was Eggert Road. To the right was Colvin Boulevard, Jim's street. His apartment building was only a few blocks away, but could they actually get there? Was the path clear, or would this be another flimsy, half-assed plan that would fall flat on its stupid face as soon as the ill-conceived notion was stated aloud? From this distance, it was impossible to say. Jim couldn't see far enough in either direction. And once he picked a route, it might be impossible to turn back.

As Jim was looking down the road, Lindsey was looking up. She watched overhead as they approached the two overpasses. A handful of creeps were running from left to right across the bridge, racing toward the ramp in pursuit of anything that moved. With a row of cars obstructing her view, Lindsey could only make out the tops of their heads as they weaved a path through the labyrinth of stalled vehicles.

The closer the Pontiac got to the first overpass, the slower the ghouls seemed to move. At first, Lindsey thought they were simply running out of steam, fatigued and sluggish with a belly full of other peoples' guts. But then they came to a stop all at once. They all turned around and began running in the opposite direction, back toward the middle of the bridge.

Nothing seemed to be scaring them off or chasing them away. Plus, the ghouls weren't exactly known for retreating. Lindsey looked farther down the highway, using her hand to shield her eyes from the lowering sun. All that lie ahead were more deserted cars and scattered corpses. So, what were they after? What could have caused these bastards to all reverse course at the same time?

Several pairs of shoulders came into view. Then she could see their chests, their abdomens and waists became visible. They moved to the edge of the road, bumping into each other as they crowded the near-side guardrail. First there were five of them. Then came a sixth and a seventh. The fiends congregated at the edge of the bridge, peering over the railing; streamers of glimmering saliva trailing from their open mouths. Their plan, if you wanted to call it that, snapped sharply into focus as the Pontiac moved to within thirty feet of the first overpass.

"Jim look out!" Lindsey shrieked. She pointed through the windshield to where the first blood junkie was pulling himself up and over the railing.

Head-first, with arms outstretched and fingers curling into bright red talons, all seven of the infected pricks scampered over the guardrail and leaped for the speeding blue coupe thirty feet below. The first two jumpers had been too eager. They'd gone too soon and missed their mark. The first one made a sort of half-flip in the air before landing on the top of his head; his skull collapsing in on itself as his neck compressed to leave his chin flush with the clavicle.

The second managed to use his hands to break his fall. Sort of. The ulna and radius, the bones between your elbow and wrist, snapped in both arms. Their blood-soaked jagged ends punched through skin, ejecting a mist of red fog as the beast flattened his face on the concrete. While both brutes had failed to connect with the car, they did land directly in its path.

"Shit!" Jim whined, jerking the steering wheel hard to the left.

A third body dropped down from the overpass. It crashed to the ground, landing only a foot from the passenger's side door. The impact caused its skin to burst open like a water balloon filled with blood and gristle.

"Oh jeez," Lindsey cried, flinching away from the window. Without thinking, she grabbed for the stock of the shotgun; eyes locked on the crumpled cannibal, waiting for him to spring up and punch through the glass. Her grip loosened after a moment. The pulverized fiend wasn't getting up. He wasn't doing much of anything except bleeding out on the cement.

"Easy," Jim cautioned as they rolled beneath the gap that separated the two elevated roadways.

Behind them, the sound of four soft wet slaps could be heard as the remaining topside ghouls leaped from the bridge and departed the Earth. Jim watched in the rear-view mirror to see if any would rise. Six of the seven lie in motionless heaps; twisted, battered bags of skin leaking an array of viscous fluids. There was only one who moved. The freak managed to lift an arm that looked to have grown a second elbow. Its hand swiped in the air at nothing and then flopped back to the ground. It remained as immobile as the cement that had broken its fall and sent him to Hell.

Jim's attention stayed focused on the dead and dying savages that now littered the street behind him. As the car passed below the second overpass, he looked from the rear-view to the driver's side mirror and then to where the passenger's side mirror should have been. He grumbled in annoyance as he recalled how the mirror had been torn off earlier that day.

"So which way?" Lindsey asked, drawing Jim's attention to what lie in front of the car rather than behind. They had arrived at the fork where Twin Cities Highway came to an end.

"We'll go to the right," Jim answered. "Down Colvin Boulevard."

"Oh," she replied. "But if we take Eggert Road, we can still get out of town. There's got to be another way onto the Thruway."

"Sure, but who's to say it'll be in any better shape than this?" Jim argued. He ineffectually waved a hand in the general direction of the highway to their rear.

"Alright, so then we won't take the Thruway," Lindsey countered. "We can just stay on Eggert. It'll eventually bring us to Harlem Road and then to Seneca Street. We'll just keep heading south until we get to Allegany."

Jim eased the car to a stop in the center of the three-way intersection. He opened his mouth to object but Lindsey cut him off.

"I know what you're going to say," she told him. "And yes, it's going to take a little longer to get down there. But once we get out of the suburbs, it's mostly just farm country and open roads. I bet no one else is taking that route to get out of town."

"But *should* we be trying to get out of town?" Jim asked. "I mean, how do we know it's any better in Allegany than it is here?"

"It's our safest option," Lindsey asserted.

"Based on what?" Jim demanded. He looked away from her to do a quick check of the mirrors and to take a few breaths to try and calm himself. "Look, I'm not trying to be a dick, but you said the same thing about the hospital. And then you said we needed to get to the Thruway. And then-"

"It doesn't need to be the Thruway," she blurted. "We just need to get out of this area. There are other ways to do that."

"Listen," Jim began, "I'm happy to go wherever you want. Going to your cabin sounds great, but it also sounds like a pretty big gamble and I'm asking you to convince me it's the right thing to do."

"Of course it's the right thing to do! Just take a look around." Lindsey waved both hands in a wide circulation motion and added, "You want to stay here and see just how bad things are gonna get?"

241

"No, I don't," he answered softly.

"Neither do I," she agreed. "The cabin is right at the edge of the state park, totally isolated. I almost never see any other people down there, especially at this time of the year. We'll probably be miles away from the closest infected person. It's our best shot at getting through this."

"Sure," Jim said as he looked down at the fuel gauge in front of him. "But that's assuming we can actually get there."

"How are we on gas?" Lindsey asked.

"About half a tank," he told her.

"That should be enough to get us there," she said.

"It would be, unless we get turned around again and have to find another detour." Even as he challenged her, Jim couldn't help but wonder what the sleeping arrangements would be if they did spend a night at the cabin. "I mean, who knows what's going on between here and Allegany. It sounds great- it really does. But the most remote and well-stocked cabin in the world isn't going to do us any good if we're stuck by the side of the road because we ran out of gas."

"That's still better than staying here," Lindsey persisted. "We'll be better off once we're out of town. Even if we don't make it to the cabin, we can find another place, a place where all this craziness isn't happening. I'd rather find a hotel or go to a stranger's house somewhere farther south where we know it's safe."

"But do we?" Jim asked.

Lindsey stared at him from across the car. "Do we what?"

"Do we know it's actually safer somewhere else?" he pressed.

A look of confusion and frustration appeared on Lindsey's face. She once again gestured to the world beyond the coupe, "What are you talking about? Any place has got to be better than here."

"I don't know why I didn't think about this earlier," Jim admitted. "But what makes us think the cannibal outbreak is limited to the Greater Buffalo Area?"

Lindsey's mouth hung open. She paused for a moment and collected her thoughts.

"It's got to be," she finally said; hints of denial betraying her words. "What, you think this is happening everywhere? That's ridiculous. It- it just can't be. It doesn't make any sense."

"If I'd told you a week ago that people were about to start going nuts, killing and eating each other, what would you have said?" Jim inquired.

Lindsey sighed. Her eyes dropped to the floor and she muttered, "That you were being ridiculous and it didn't make any sense."

"Right," Jim told her.

"I also would have told you that you need to get out more, and to stop reading so many crappy horror and sci-fi novels written by authors no one's ever heard of."

"Fair enough," he agreed. "But do you see my point?"

"Yeah, although I'm not sure that changes things," she contended. "If this is happening all over, it's still a good idea to get away from places where there's a lot of people."

"They'll spread out," Jim contested. "If it's happening everywhere, the zombies- er, infected

242

people will eventually make their way to the rural communities as well. Before we risk getting stuck in the middle of nowhere, why don't we see if we can find out what we're really dealing with."

"I still can't get a signal." Lindsey held up her cell phone for emphasis. The words, *No Service*, appeared along the top of the screen where the reception bars should have been.

"Try the radio," Jim suggested. He grabbed the steering wheel and lifted his foot from the brake pedal. "See if you can get a signal, something with the news on."

"Okay," she answered, reaching for the knob to turn on the stereo. Lindsey felt the vehicle begin to roll forward and asked, "Um, where are we going?"

"We gotta move," he told her. Jim pointed through his window at a strip mall across the street, on the other side of Eggert Road. Roughly fifteen people could be seen making their way across the parking lot. They were moving toward the car and it wouldn't be long before they arrived. Jim steered to the right and pulled the Pontiac onto Colvin Boulevard. "I know where we can go until we figure this out."

"Where is that?" Lindsey asked, hurriedly working the radio's scan button. She waited just long enough to land on the next station, hear only static pour through the speakers, and then pressed it again. The digital display shuffled to the next channel and the process was repeated.

"My apartment's just a few blocks from here," said Jim.

Lindsey looked up from the radio dials and asked, "You mean the apartment with no food in it? That's where you're taking us?"

"The apartment with *some* food in it," Jim clarified. "Yes, that apartment. It's also where my friends are, and other tenants as well. I'm sure there's food somewhere in the building."

"That's probably what they're thinking too." Lindsey glanced toward a pair of ghouls loitering by the side of the road. The brutes both started to move, slowly marching toward the car as it passed them by.

"Things may not be so bleak," he replied, forcing a tone of encouragement. "I mean, I'm sure Danny's home- that's my buddy who lives upstairs from me. And I'm sure there are other people there too. Whoever's there, they probably have a plan on what to do to stay safe. For all we know, they might all be doing just fine."

"Somehow I doubt that," Lindsey huffed.

"Worst case, we'll run in, grab some canned peaches or whatever food I actually have in the kitchen, throw it in the car and keep moving," Jim said. "We'll check in with anyone who might be home. We can still try to get out of town if we have to, but if things are looking up, we may decide to stay. I'm sure they've been following the story on TV and keeping up on things."

"I wouldn't count on that," Lindsey remarked. She pressed the scan button again, and again failed to land on an active broadcast. "If the radio's not working, I wouldn't hold out much hope for the TV."

"If not the TV, then maybe the internet will be working," Jim offered.

"The internet?" she repeated in a tone that sounded very much like an accusation. "If the God-damned radio and phones don't work, what the Hell makes you think the internet's going to be on?"

"I don't know," he responded defensively, sinking into his seat a little. Jim shrugged and said, "It's different signals, different towers and services or whatever. Just because one's down, it doesn't

243

mean that everything's down."

Lindsey scoffed and crossed her arms.

"I'm just trying to stay positive," Jim continued. "There's gotta be some form of communication still working- you think the whole world's gone offline in a matter of hours?"

"No, I don't think that," Lindsey said flatly. "But that seems to be the case here, which is why we need to leave."

Not to be deterred, Jim pressed on. "Back at the building, maybe some of the other tenants will have heard something. I mean, they *must* have heard something by now. And who knows- they might even have some good news to share."

"Good news doesn't exist anymore," she said; a sharp rejection of Jim's manufactured optimism. "It died several hours ago along with our friends and people we worked with and God knows how many others. And you want to stay here? For what- you in a hurry to join them?"

"Of course not," Jim blurted, not quite sure if her question was meant as rhetorical. "But setting out for an eighty-mile road trip with everybody going nuts and trying to kill everything that moves- that's not exactly the best way to keep ourselves safe."

"I just can't stay here," she argued; her voice growing louder. "I can't stay in this town."

"Why not?" Jim's frustration was intensifying. "Just tell me why-"

"Because I killed someone, Jim!" Lindsey shook her hands as if to amplify her statement.

"So did I!" he shouted with the same intensity. "But that doesn't mean-"

"It's not the same," Lindsey interrupted. Her eyes began to swell as she was obviously trying to keep from crying. "I killed someone I knew, someone I worked with and was friends with. It's all I can think about and I can't stand to be here."

She paused, took a breath and rubbed tears from her eyes before continuing, "I just need to get as far away from here as I can and if you don't want to go, then just let me out. I'll hitchhike or steal a car or whatever I need to do to get out of here."

"Lindsey, I just-"

"Please," she cut him off, grabbing him by the forearm.

Jim stiffened. It wasn't the surprise of her touch or the force of her fingers gripping his flesh. What startled Jim was a lot more subtle. He knew what would come next. And he knew he was completely powerless. Lindsey was going to fight him. She was going to argue against his plan in favor of another one of her lousy dead-end strategies.

He was almost home. They were only a few short blocks away from his apartment, a couple hundred yards from somewhere safe, somewhere familiar and comfortable. But Jim knew she wasn't going to allow it. Lindsey would keep insisting that they forge ahead and get out of town. And Jim wouldn't say no to her. He didn't want to say no to her. He wanted to do whatever she asked, give her whatever she wanted. Jim was a useless, spineless chump who had somehow become more afraid of disappointing an ex-girlfriend- someone who'd expressed no interest until she needed rescuing- than he was of a road to nowhere crawling with raging, violent psychopaths. How much weight had he lost since his backbone vanished?

Lindsey loosened her grasp. She stroked his arm where four white spots had formed beneath her nails, rubbing the area until the color returned. Jim could feel the stinging sensation dissipate. He could also feel her staring at him. He let the car coast for a few more yards before bringing it to a stop in front of a two-story home.

Jim put the car in park. He kept his hand on the gear shifter, ready to move in a hurry should the need arise. Lindsey rested her hand on top of his. She felt the warmth of his skin and the tension in his bones.

"Jim, please," she began, pausing for a breath. Lindsey's eyes had grown misty. They looked glossy and bloodshot. Her complexion had gone pale and most of her ponytail had come undone. Shimmering blonde locks hung over her shoulders and down to her chest. Stealing a moment to maintain her composure, Lindsey finished her thought by saying, "I can't stay here."

And that's why Jim couldn't say no. Lindsey wasn't some stubborn overly-confident narcissist who always needed to have her own way at all costs- far from it. She was a sweet, considerate young lady who'd never been anything but kind and generous and giving. And she was breaking.

Of course she couldn't stay. There was nothing left to stay for. Her boyfriend had seemingly abandoned her- a fact that Jim had not yet had the balls to bring up. She'd been attacked, almost ripped to pieces. Lindsey had to kill a person, a coworker and friend, plunging a knife into his heart and staining her clothes with his blood just so she could make it out alive.

Everything had turned to shit. The neighborhood where she'd grown up, the place where she worked every day, and everything she had ever known had been torn apart and drenched in blood. Moreover, there was no way he was letting her try some dumb shit like hitchhiking or trying to steal a car. How long would she last wandering around on foot through a lawless cannibal wasteland? It was a ridiculous plan.

"Alright," he finally said. "We'll keep moving."

Jim put the car in gear and pulled into the nearest driveway to turn around and head back toward Eggert Road, trying not to think of himself as a pushover along the way. He was doing what was right for Lindsey, not being manipulated by her. He was taking her away from everything bad that had happened. He was rescuing her. This was the right thing to do. He silently predicted that in time, Lindsey would recognize all that he'd done for her. She'd thank him for it. She'd *love* him for it. And he'd love her too. They would arrive at a place and time where it would all be good again, where this day's agony was long-forgotten. Jim just needed to get them there.

245

Chapter 37

Soft and stretchy. It was loose-fitting and cute, and not too revealing. She loved the color, a faded maroon, but what really attracted her to the shirt was the T-strap back. It allowed her to show off her narrow figure and fresh tan in something a little more respectable than a bikini top or strapless shirt. Plus, unlike a tube top, she didn't have to adjust and readjust the garment every three minutes just to keep herself from popping out. The bottom hem was cut in a slight angle and hung about an inch past the waistline of a white tennis skirt.

She was beautiful. Her skin was like that of a porcelain doll, smooth and creamy, flawless. Wavy dark brown hair flowed just past her shoulders and the young woman styled it to her right with a loosely-defined part. Round almond eyes looked straight ahead; a hint of pain and mounting despair. Dimples shown at the edges of her lips, just below the cheek bones. They grew in definition when she smiled, a feature that would not be seen again.

The young woman reached out, desperately grasping not for the steel blade lodged in her neck, but for the man who'd put it there. Blood raced out of the wound. An artery had been violated. Her neck, chest, and favorite new shirt were now drenched in red. The heart was still beating; her body literally squeezing out its own blood. But her pulse would quickly become a thing of the past.

It wasn't the first time she had bled that day. There was a trickle from her right nostril, a weeping scrape across her left leg, and a bite-shaped laceration just above the elbow on her left arm. It wasn't really her anymore. Her friendly spirit and warm personality were gone, replaced by something grim, something evil. All that remained was her shell; a breathing malignant husk. The fun-loving girl next door had died hours ago. Now her body would do the same, taking its virulent demons with it.

As meager and short-lived as it was, Danny did feel some relief. Looking into the eyes of the dying girl with his hand still gripping the machete handle, he knew that what he'd done was okay. Don't misunderstand- it wasn't great or fun or nearly as bad-ass as he might have envisioned. But it was the right thing to do. Unfortunately, cold logic does little to assuage one's guilt, especially when it comes to taking a life.

Coppery fluid squirted across the flat edge of the blade, turning it red as the blood moved closer to Danny's fingers. He knew it was poison, knew he couldn't let it touch him lest he share the same fate as the once-stunning young woman before him. Despite how well he understood the danger quickly rolling toward him, Danny stood paralyzed, unable to release himself and unable to free his weapon from the body of the first person he'd killed.

The girl did it for him; one last act of kindness. She collapsed to the ground and in doing so, freed the blade from her neck. There was a final twitch accompanied by a muffled gurgle and then she was gone. Completely. And with her went the silence.

The footsteps were back, lots of them. Danny spun to look behind him; sheets of blood dripping from the machete as it sliced through air. It looked like his second kill was already on its way. A sprinter was closing in on him with a group of ghastly companions not far behind.

Danny readied himself. He drew back his weapon and prepared to strike. His heart hammered in his chest. Throughout his body, muscles tensed and fluttered. All of his senses were on fire. The sound of running feet and snarling creeps became overwhelming, in a way that made him question how he'd been able to block it out. And then there was the screaming.

"Danny!" Punctuated by a crack from the rifle, Jenna cried out for him to come back, to retreat to safety and shelter.

Three yards away, the quickest of the horde fell to the ground with a new hole in his head and bloodied brain matter on the sidewalk beneath him. Then fell another, and another. Jenna stood in the doorway with one foot inside and one foot out. She leaned into the door, propping it open as she leveled the rifle and fired another round. A fourth sprinting body fell to the ground. At such close range, it was easy to keep her shots on point but she couldn't do this forever. Only six bullets remained in the magazine and there wasn't much chance the hellions would take a break to let her reload.

"Danny- now!" Jenna shouted a second plea, but Danny was already running toward the entrance.

He darted past her and into the relative safety of the building's lobby. Jenna wasted no time in closing the door, pulling it shut as soon as Danny crossed the threshold. If she'd waited any longer, it wouldn't have been just Danny coming inside. Zombies instantly crashed into the glass barrier. Five of them charged in close together and more lined up behind them to form a wall of flesh that was already six or seven bodies deep.

Jenna dropped her gun and grabbed the door handles. She pulled as hard as she could, planting her feet in the filthy carpet and leaning back to use her body weight as leverage to keep the doors closed. Fortunately for her and Danny, the monsters failed to understand the intricate workings of an outward-swinging door. If they planned to get inside, they'd need to pull the door handles rather than push against them.

"Grab the cord," Jenna called to Danny.

She was still holding the doors shut and refused to let go in case the ghouls did somehow figure out how to get in. Just inches from her face, a crowd of infected people pressed against the doors. So many had gathered and they applied so much pressure, the ones at the front of the pack were being crushed against the front of the building. Faces and arms squished against the glass, which had become cloudy with blood and saliva.

Danny did as he was instructed, dropping his machete and swooping down to grab the extension cord from the floor. Without further direction, he began working to secure the doorway. Danny ducked in front of Jenna, getting as close to the door and as low to the ground as possible. For the first few passes, Danny wrapped the rubbery orange rope around the outer edges of the aluminum door handles. He pulled the cord tight and began alternating between making a crisscross pattern from one handle to the next, and tying the cord around the inside of the handles.

"How you doin' down there?" Jenna's words were choppy and forced as she struggled to keep a strong grip on the smooth aluminum bar.

"Almost there," Danny said without looking up. "But we might have a problem."

"Good, just what we need," Jenna remarked. "More problems."

"I can't tie it," Danny said. He held the remaining strand next to the portion he'd started with and explained, "This rubbery plastic material, it's impossible to tie it down and keep it in place. You know how you'd tie a shoelace? This cord won't do that. It's too firm and won't bend far enough to make a knot."

Jenna looked away from the would-be cannibals and down at Danny. Then she looked at the job he'd done on the handles. "We might be okay."

247

"You sure about that?"

"I think so," Jenna said cautiously. "They're pushing against the doors. I don't think they'll figure out they've got to pull them. And even if they do, the cord should hold. For a while, anyway."

Danny nodded and pulled himself to his feet, snatching up the roll of coaxial cable in the process. He held it in one hand and picked up the machete with the other. The blade was streaked with blood and there were several small puddles on the floor where it had been sitting. This gave Danny pause and he could feel himself tensing up again.

It wasn't the blood itself. And it certainly wasn't his concern for the carpet. The flooring was so shitty and old that nobody was going to notice a few new stains. It was the memory. With all the excitement, Danny had momentarily forgotten what had just happened; forgotten what he'd done. He could ignore it for now. He'd be alone with his thoughts soon enough. In the meantime, he needed to stay focused. They weren't in the clear quite yet and there was still work to do.

Danny stood back, machete at the ready in case the freaks got inside. Though, if he would have taken the time to thoroughly examine the situation, he might not have bothered. If all those pricks managed to bust down the doors and get in, he and Jenna would be doomed regardless of how well he could swing that machete. For that matter, Jenna's gun wouldn't be of much help either.

"I'm going to let go," Jenna said. Casting a glance over her shoulder to Danny, "You ready in case something happens?"

Danny nodded.

"Good." Jenna slowly loosened her grip on the aluminum handles. Half expecting the doors to fly open as soon as she let go, she let her hands hover an inch away from the metal rods. The beasts outside failed to adjust their tactics, so the doors remained firmly closed.

"Good?" Danny asked.

"Yeah," said Jenna as she picked up her rifle. "I think we're good for now, but we should keep an eye on it, make sure it's not coming loose."

"Did you notice that some of them out there are slow too?" Danny asked, not sure if she'd had the same opportunity to study them.

"More like Adam, you mean?"

"Yeah," Danny confirmed. "I mean, there's obviously a lot of fast ones, but there are some foot-draggers too. The fast ones had to shove them out of the way."

"I didn't exactly have a chance to stand around watching them," Jenna answered; a hint of annoyance creeping into her voice. "After all, one of us had to make sure the other wasn't going to be eaten alive. And make sure they wouldn't get into the building."

"Hey," Danny said defensively. "I helped get the doors locked up."

"My point is," Jenna began, "We can't be stupid about this. What were you thinking going out there?"

"I just thought..." Danny let his words trail off, taking a second to gather himself before going on. "Maybe it would help if we knew more about them, figure out how they work so we can find a way to defeat them and keep them out."

"We keep them out by getting the doors sealed off, not by wandering outside and waiting to be killed." Jenna's tone was harsh, harsher than she'd intended. She paused for a moment and took a big

248

breath, cradling the gun under one arm so she could tighten her ponytail. "Okay. So, what were you able to find out?"

"Well," Danny began, now avoiding eye contact. He looked down at the massive blade in his hand. The coating of blood had started to dry. "Mostly that we've got fast ones and slow ones. So, we obviously knew about the slow ones when we found Adam but there's a lot more of them out there. I guess I wasn't sure if the slowdown was something unique to Adam. And um, ya know, it isn't."

"So, fast ones and slow ones, but no smart ones." Jenna gave him a wry grin and a playful eye.

"Right," Danny said flatly.

"Hey," said Jenna. She waited until he looked up at her before saying, "I'm talking about them. They can't figure out how to get through doors that pull to open. That knowledge might come in handy."

"Yeah, I guess so." Danny forced a smile.

"I agree with you," Jenna told him.

"What about?"

"About studying them. You're right and that's a good idea," she explained. "But first and foremost, we have to be smart about it and stay safe. As long as we're in here and they're out there, we should be good. There will be time to figure out how they work, but we can't put ourselves in danger in the process."

Danny nodded his agreement and once more looked down at his blood-streaked weapon.

Jenna followed his gaze. "It's okay. Or at least it's going to be okay. You did what you had to."

He shrugged.

"I've had to shoot seven of them," Jenna reminded him. "You're a good guy, Danny. It's not murder when you're protecting yourself and the people you care about."

She was trying to comfort him, remind him that he'd acted in self-defense. He wasn't a murderer. If Danny hadn't taken her out, the girl and her friends would have slaughtered him. Instead of standing here to talk things through, he'd be little more than a pile of bones and a red smear on the pavement. Of course Jenna was right. She was right about a lot of things, especially about going outside in the first place.

He didn't have to do that. Danny put himself in harm's way. And it wasn't just himself. Going outside, drawing attention to himself while he stood just a few feet from the entrance to the building, that was risking the lives of everyone inside. If they'd gotten inside, Jenna, Lucy, and Albert would all be in immediate danger. Not to mention Jim and his other neighbors who weren't home when everything turned to shit. If they beat the odds and somehow managed to get back here, they'd arrive to find their homes overrun.

"So," Jenna said. She nodded to the spool of cable Danny was holding. "We should get the other doors sealed off before they realize there's another way in."

"Right."

He followed her down the stairs and back into the basement. They hurried past Adam, who hadn't moved much since they'd last seen him, and made their way to the other side of the building. Adam moaned something indecipherable as they went by. Jenna and Danny pretended not to notice. Secretly, they both knew that they'd have to make a decision about what to do with him, but neither was in a hurry to broach that topic.

Securing the second pair of doors proved easier than the first. By the time the group outside realized Jenna and Danny had moved to the other side, they had nearly completed their task of tying off the handles. Another crowd soon gathered on the other side of the glass. Once more, they pushed rather than pulled and there was little threat of them getting inside.

The zombie-slaying neighbors didn't hang around in the lobby for too long. The loons were stuck outside but they hadn't given up yet. The longer they saw people inside, the longer they'd persist. Danny and Jenna stood at the bottom of the steps, just outside the doorway to the basement. Taking advantage of the temporary calm, Jenna reloaded her gun. She ejected the magazine and reached into her pocket to pull out a handful of small bullets.

"Is it safe keeping them in your pockets like that?" Danny asked as he dragged the wide flat edge of the machete across the inner part of the wooden door frame, trying to scrape the blood off.

"It's fine," she answered. Jenna fed four rounds into the magazine and stuffed the extras back into her pocket before adding, "Plus, I think *safe* is sort of a relative term at this point."

"Alright, so what now?"

"Well," Jenna thought back to what they'd been doing before the savages had interrupted. "We still need to check on Albert. Maybe he'll have some answers about Adam and what he plans to do about it."

"Okay, but can we be quick about it?" Danny asked. "I'd like to get back upstairs to check on Lucy and see how she's holding up."

"Sure," said Jenna. "I'm sure she's okay, but I'm anxious to get back too. We'll be in and out."

"Thanks Jenna," he said. Danny's face had a look of genuine appreciation. "Thank you for, well, you know."

"You're welcome," she answered. "Don't worry about it. Let's just get this done and get back."

"Sure thing," he replied. "You lead the way."

And Jenna did just that. She and Danny crossed through the basement once more, past the disease-ravaged Adam, and up the stairs to see his father. Surely Albert would have an update, an insight, and a plan worth sharing.

Chapter 38

"I sorta think maybe we should've turned at some point," Jim grumbled.

They'd been driving for the better part of an hour and per Lindsey's instructions, they'd stayed on Eggert Road. Their plan, if you could call it a plan, was to just keep driving south until Buffalo was well behind them. To be fair, this was the farthest they had gotten so far- and by quite a large margin, but this was hardly the serene country setting with expansive farmland and long straightaway roads that Lindsey had described earlier.

"We're fine," Lindsey said with all the confidence she could summon. "We're making progress."

Not fast enough, Jim thought. The sun was low in the sky and would soon fall below the edge of the horizon. Shadows of trees grew thick and long, reaching out to cast darkness over the streets. Before long, what little sunlight remained would be gone altogether.

They were yet to see so much as an open field, let alone rows of crops and pastures for grazing livestock. Rather than acres of tillable soil, it was block after block of masonry apartment buildings, duplexes with brown lawns, and strip malls with cell phone shops and liquor stores that looked like they'd been in rough shape before the cannibal plague had kicked off. Sure, the zombies were likely to blame for the crashed cars and pools of blood, but they probably weren't responsible for the graffiti, litter, and stolen shopping carts. If the ghouls were breaking glass, they were smashing windows, not tossing liquor bottles in a parking lot.

Despite their hopes and expectations, Jim and Lindsey discovered that this part of town had not been spared. The beasts were here and their handiwork could not be ignored. Corpses lie in mangled heaps on sidewalks, street corners, porches and alleyways. For the most part, the cadavers had been decent enough to stay out of the way of traffic.

There was little consistency to the state of the bodies. In some cases, only a skeleton remained; picked clean and discarded by the side of the road. Others were much more intact; withering flesh and raw muscle bound tightly to bones to maintain a vaguely-human form. The bodies were left out in the open to foul the air as they slowly turned to sludge.

"Hey Jim," Lindsey said.

"Mhmm?" Jim murmured.

"There's something up with the bodies," she told him. "Why do you think that some were completely eaten and others weren't?"

"Huh?" Jim gave her a sidelong glance. "Oh- yeah. I don't know. That's strange I guess."

"Yeah," Lindsey said, deflating a bit. She was trying to avoid the silence again, trying to block out her own screaming thoughts. It took a moment for Jim to catch on and come to her aid.

"I suppose I could venture a theory," he announced. "But it might be um, ya know, sorta gross."

"I think I can handle it," she assured him.

"Right," Jim agreed. "I think the, um... zombies? Have we agreed on *zombies* yet?"

Lindsey shrugged. "If you say zombies, I'll know what you mean."

"So," Jim continued. "I think the zombies would eat the whole thing if they could, except for the parts they can't chew. As for the bodies only partially eaten, I think those are from zombies that got distracted halfway through and found someone else to chase after."

"Makes sense," she commented. "You think they'd want to savor their meals; finish what they started before moving on to something else."

"They're pretty selfish that way," he quipped.

"Very inconsiderate." Lindsey smirked and let a dry chuckle escape. She realized she was almost smiling, and it made her feel guilty.

"Speaking of which," Jim began. "Are you getting hungry?"

"Oh sure," she replied sardonically. "All this zombie talk has really got my mouth watering."

She was relaxing and starting to joke around again. This was a great relief for Jim. It meant he was doing his job, helping to make things better for her. He was keeping his promise to protect her, and that didn't just mean keeping her free from physical harm. Jim would also have to ward off the agony and despair that would soon set in.

He lifted his foot off the accelerator as he approached the next intersection. The car slowed just enough to let him see if anything was coming in either direction before he sped through. Some of the traffic lights were still working. Some of them were on but malfunctioning, showing all reds or all greens, and some flashed yellow on all sides. This one was just off.

"I don't have much of an appetite either," Jim told her. "But if we see someplace safe where we can grab some food, we probably should. Ya know, just to be on the safe side."

"Ooh yeah," Lindsey agreed enthusiastically. "I could go for a steak. Or maybe a meatball sub. You think there's somewhere close where we could get both?"

"I think I'd aim a little lower," he advised with a skeptical glance.

"I'm just kidding, Jim," she reminded him.

"Yeah, I know. I'm just trying to figure out where we are," he explained. Jim had been slowly inching his way to the edge of his seat. He was leaning forward and getting as close to the windshield as possible without actually lifting his ass off the cushion. He made wide, sweeping turns with his head, peering down each side-street and alley. "It just seems like there should have been a more direct route out of town. Maybe we missed a turn somewhere."

They were coming up to another intersection with no power to the traffic light. The big metal lamp hung ineffectually at the center of two converging roadways. Jim looked farther down the road and saw there was a bridge situated just beyond the crossway. Lindsey must have noticed it at the same time. She stirred in her seat.

Her eyes grew bright as she leaned forward and announced, "Oh- I know where we are!" In her exclamation, Lindsey had unwittingly revealed that, until this point, she actually didn't know where they were, or if they were even heading in the right direction.

Jim picked up on this. But instead of offering admonishment, he simply asked, "So where are we then? Are we going the right way?"

"We're coming up to the Kensington Expressway," she told him. "Or, I guess to be more specific, we're about to go *over* the Kensington Expressway."

"Does the Kensington Expressway connect with the Thruway?" asked Jim.

"Um," Lindsey paused to consider this, straining her memory for some clue that might remind her of the last time she'd traveled more than thirty minutes from home. "I think so."

"You think so?" Jim pressed. His head tilted like a dog's does when it sees a ghost in your living room. "Should we be getting *onto* the Kensington Expressway?"

"Uh," Lindsey muttered. Her eyes rolled up, as if the answer might be scribbled on the car's fading and smoke-stained headliner.

"Maybe we'll have a look first," Jim said. He pulled the Pontiac through the intersection and brought it to a stop in the middle of the short bridge. Jim slid the gear selector all the way forward to put the car in park and grabbed for the door handle.

"Jim don't!" cried Lindsey. She reached across the seat to try and stop him, but it was no use. Jim was already out of the car.

"It's fine," he called back to her through the open door. "There's no one around. I'm just having a quick look."

She growled in annoyance. Taking hold of the shotgun, Lindsey held it out in front of her and shouted, "At least take this with you."

Jim wasn't listening. It wasn't that he was ignoring her, it was just going to be a quick trip to the ledge and then back to the car. He could only see a few people nearby and all they were doing was decomposing; their bodies turning into a purplish ooze that seeped into the cracks in the cement. There were no zombies around- none that were still alive anyway.

Quickly crossing the second traffic lane, Jim took a wide step to avoid putting his foot in a puddle of what he hoped was water, and not motor oil or zombie piss. He then stepped over the curb and onto a narrow walkway that separated the street from a rusted chain-link fence. The metal barrier came up to Jim's waist. It must have been meant to keep people from accidentally falling off the walkway, and not to prevent people from climbing up and throwing themselves off. He peered over and looked down at the Expressway about twenty feet below.

Jim jumped a little when he heard the sound of a car door opening behind him. He turned back to see Lindsey pulling herself out of the coupe.

"What are you doing?" he asked.

She carried the shotgun, holding it with one hand around the grip just behind the trigger guard. The other hand supported the weapon's foregrip. Lindsey kept the barrel aimed at the ground as she moved briskly across the street to meet Jim.

"What are you doing?" he repeated in a much quieter tone. "Why didn't you wait in the car?"

She wrinkled her nose and told him, "You shouldn't be out here unarmed."

"I'm fine. I'm just having a quick look," he explained. "And besides, I meant to leave the gun with you, in case you needed it. I mean, what if they spotted us?"

"I wouldn't need it if I'm in the car," Lindsey contended. "I could just shut the door and lock it. That's a luxury you won't have while you're out here sightseeing."

"Yeah, I suppose," Jim yielded.

"Speaking of which," Lindsey began to say as she walked up to the chain-link barrier. She stood next to Jim and asked, "How's it lookin' out here?"

"Well," Jim paused for a breath. He gestured to the six-lane highway below them and said, "Not very good."

It was a sight that seemed all too familiar- endless rows of abandoned vehicles. The Kensington Expressway stretched straight out for nearly a mile before curving to the left and disappearing behind another bridge and a dense tree line. There were a few hints of movement down there, but they were facing east after dusk and it was too dark to make out any significant detail.

"It looks like the Youngmann Expressway from earlier," Lindsey commented.

"Maybe it's something in the name," Jim replied, trying to sound lighthearted. "Any road with 'Expressway' in the title gets ripped apart."

"Possibly," she agreed without much conviction. "But then again, we've seen plenty of streets, avenues, and boulevards that were pretty well torn to shit."

"So, there's probably no hope for the Thruway then?" Jim asked somewhat rhetorically.

"Probably not," she replied. Lindsey gave Jim a tap on the elbow. She held the gun out in front of her and offered it to him, saying, "Hey, would you please take this already? You know I'm no good with these things."

"Um sure," he said after a moment's hesitation. Jim took hold of the shotgun with his left hand and let the barrel drop to the pavement. "But are you sure? I know you can shoot and I know you don't want to think about it, but you might have to use it at some point."

Lindsey shrugged and asked, "Why would I need to use it if you're here?"

"You know," Jim stammered. "In case I'm not around, if we get separated or something."

"Well, we'll just have to make sure that you and I stay together then." Lindsey looked up to catch his eyes. She seemed to move closer to him- maybe just a couple of inches, but Jim couldn't tell for certain.

"Yeah," Jim smiled at her. "I think that's a good plan."

"I think so too," said Lindsey.

She definitely moved closer to him that time. Her elbow brushed up against his forearm. Lindsey flinched but didn't move away. In fact, the nearer she got, the more she seemed at ease. She let her arms drop to her sides and in doing so, let her hand graze his. Lindsey coolly looked down as if checking to see what she'd touched.

Jim followed her lead, looking down at their arms; the backs of their hands pressed together. He turned slightly, just enough to face her a little more clearly without being too obvious. And now it was Lindsey's turn to follow his lead. She took a step closer, no longer watching the dead highway below them, but facing him straight on.

Her fingers skimmed across his knuckles. Had that been intentional? It must have been. Jim rolled his wrist and opened his hand. His fingertips swept over hers. Her digits fanned out. He reached for her and she accepted him in. They squeezed each other's hand, interlocking their fingers and holding on tight.

Now was the time. Jim wasn't going to get a more obvious sign than this. And if he didn't seize his chance right then, in that very moment, he might not ever get another. He wriggled his hand free. The expression on Lindsey's face was one of confusion; of shyness or embarrassment. She began to speak, to apologize for having been out of line or too forward or for making Jim feel uncomfortable. But her confusion faded quickly.

Jim wasn't pulling away, he was pulling her closer. He placed his right hand over her left hip and drew her near. Lindsey's right hand first went to Jim's chest. With one long slow drag, she moved it over his shoulder and down his back. She grabbed onto his shirt and pulled herself toward him. Lindsey choked back a nervous breath before looking up expectantly. Their eyes closed. They both leaned in. And then the roar of gunfire pierced the air.

Chapter 39

An empty cigarette pack lie on the ground. Someone had given it a squeeze before tossing it away. Littering slob. The box, which was not as crush-proof as the label would have you believe, sat just over three feet from a balding car tire.

Situated on South Transit Street between Gaffney Road and Willow Street in Lockport, is a small dry-cleaning shop in a one-story building with fake brick walls. A young man, alone in his car, had backed into a parking space so his rear bumper was nearly pressed against the outermost wall of the store. That way, nothing could sneak up on him. Anyone or anything that might be coming for him would have to approach him head-on.

More importantly, he was sitting directly across the street from the Kwik Fill gas station and convenience store. He could see everything that was happening inside. More accurately, he could see that nothing was happening. The lights were on and the door was propped open, but he'd been watching the store for thirty minutes and hadn't seen anyone go in or come out.

The driver's window slid down and a cloud of smoke rolled out; the only sign of life in what was fast becoming a ghost town. Every so often, another vehicle would zoom by, but they were few and far between and no one was stopping to chat. Without a peep, the driver sat behind the wheel and watched them race by. Most of them headed south, presumably on their way to the highway or to Route 31 to get out of the city.

A half hour was long enough. If anyone was coming to close up the store, to check for damages, or to take inventory of what was lost, they would have done it by now. If he waited too long, someone might beat him to the punch. By rights, this young man had earned first dibs on the free goods. After all, he had already gone to the trouble of making sure the coast was clear. He put in the time to stake the place out. This was his score. He turned the key to start the engine and double-checked to make sure the doors were locked.

The sun was on its way down, but there was still enough reddish-orange light in the sky to make the headlights unnecessary. This pleased the driver. Turning on the headlamps could draw unwanted attention. In this particular case, any attention would be unwanted. As the rundown Mazda began to creep across the street, a smoldering butt was tossed out the window and fell to the ground, landing just inches from the empty box.

Roughly five minutes later, Jeremy stepped out of the Kwik Fill carrying two plastic bags in each hand. Unable to open the cash register or figure out how to use the gas pumps without swiping a credit card, he would be leaving with no cash and the quarter tank of gas with which he'd arrived.

With no one inside the store to stop him, the tweaker had strolled in and helped himself to all the wares he'd need to ride out the apocalypse. This included cigarettes, lots of cigarettes. He took more than just his personal brand of choice. He filled an entire shopping bag with smokes of all sorts; filtered, unfiltered, menthol, non-menthol, 100's, shorts, blunt wraps, and cigarillos. It was like he hated his lungs.

The other bags held a couple two-liter bottles of soda, eight packages of Pop-Tarts, four bags of potato chips, four bags of corn chips, five boxes of Swedish Fish, six sleeves of Reese's Peanut Butter Cups, two bags of Andy Capp's Cheddar Fries, and a single bag of Chex Mix.

Halfway between the fuel pumps and the building's entrance, the Mazda sat parked and still running. Jeremy had popped the trunk open before entering the store so he wouldn't have to waste much time loading his groceries. He dropped the bags inside. Junk food and cigarette packs spilled out amongst the mess of dirty shirts, CD cases, and an empty bottle of washer fluid.

Slamming the lid closed, Jeremy felt a surge of panic run the length of his spine. He had made a grave miscalculation. How could he have been so foolish? What on Earth had he been thinking? A horrible tragedy would befall him, lest he act immediately to rectify his mistake. If he didn't make things right, he would never forgive himself.

He sprinted back into the store, knocking bags of potato chips and pretzels to the floor as he ran down the aisles toward the rear of the building. Heart pounding, palms sweating; Jeremy reached the built-in coolers and began searching. Past the milk and orange juice, between the sodas and energy drinks, he found what he was looking for. Flinging the door open and crouching down, the mischievous shopper started grabbing as many forty-ounce bottles of malt liquor as he could carry. He laughed in disbelief. How could he leave without taking any free alcohol?

It required a couple of trips to and from the car, but the fiend managed to get all twenty-seven bottles off the shelves and into the Mazda. Twenty-six went in the trunk with the other goodies, and one went on the front passenger's seat. It was too large to fit inside the cup holder, so Jeremy strapped it down using the seat belt.

When he had left his apartment earlier that day, the scrawny stoner did not plan to return. It was too dangerous with all of those infected lunatics hanging around. Some of them had come after him, trying to get in his car. They were violent and irrational. Most of them were covered in blood, and not necessarily their own.

He drove around for most of the afternoon and early evening, looking for a safe place to park and chill out for a bit. Along the way, he turned the rap music off and tuned in to a news station on the radio. He thought it might be difficult to find a station with live people talking about the day's events since more than half of the channels were off the air. As it turned out, every station that remained active had live news coverage. Even the stations that bragged about playing all music with no talk had someone behind a microphone taking calls and reading the most up-to-date reports.

A rotating cast of police officials, politicians, and doctors told the listeners what to do, where to go, and how to stay safe. They each speculated as to the cause of the hostile and erratic behavior. Theories varied depending on who was speaking. The police suggested it was the result of a dangerous new street drug that had been mishandled and cut with an unknown agent. Politicians largely agreed that it was the work of terrorists with chemical or biological weapons, but they couldn't agree on who those terrorists were.

Doctors, nurses, and other people in the healthcare industry presented the possibility that an infection was to blame. They were on the right track, but had still been unable to pin down the exact cause or source. One representative from the Centers for Disease Control and Prevention argued it was a new strain of the influenza virus, citing the prevalent use of vaccines and influenza's astounding ability to mutate and pass between species. Researchers from the World Health Organization were quick to agree that a mutated virus was at work, but were convinced that Ebola was at the root of the problem, rather than the flu.

Not a single note of rap music played in the Mazda for the rest of the day. Instead, talk radio thumped out of the subwoofer in Jeremy's trunk. The people on the radio used big words and sometimes it was tough to really follow the discussion, but his ear was glued to the speaker.

His route was little more than a series of large circles around the city. Along the way, he witnessed people fighting in the streets, others breaking into houses, and some just running down the sidewalk. With all that he had seen firsthand and everything he had heard on the radio, one thing became overwhelmingly apparent. The sickness or infection or whatever it was, was not limited to his neighborhood.

The same type of thing was happening to people all over. The original plan was to drive somewhere safe and wait for things to blow over. From the sounds of it, this was not a viable option. The skinny alcoholic briefly considered living out of his car. After all, it wasn't much smaller than his apartment. But this wasn't a great idea either.

Jeremy couldn't just cruise around forever with no real destination. Fuel was starting to run low and he'd be too exposed in his little Mazda, especially if he ran out of gas and got stranded somewhere. Besides the cramped space, he had no way to charge his cell phone. Plus, what would he do when he needed to use the bathroom? He could use an empty cup or bottle for number one, but what about number two? After careful consideration, Jeremy decided to head home.

He didn't have far to go. Jeremy would be at his apartment in under ten minutes. That gave him a short time to figure out how he would make his apartment secure and how he was going to get all of his stolen food inside without being seen. There was something else he would try to discern as he traveled home. Something played in the back of his mind, making him feel as if he'd neglected something, but he couldn't figure it out. What could he have forgotten? Was it important? Probably not. If it was something important, it wouldn't have slipped his mind.

Only slightly inebriated, Jeremy pulled up in front of a three-story tenement and put the Mazda in park. He took the last sip of his first bottle before replacing the cap and tossing it onto the back seat. It was a good thing he was home. If he had to drive any farther, he would have needed to pull over to get a second bottle out of the trunk. Putting the car in park and beginning to climb out, Jeremy suddenly remembered what it was that he'd forgotten.

"Beth!" he said aloud.

She was bound to be pissed off that he'd been gone all day. She'd probably be more annoyed that he wasn't going to be bringing home any cocaine like he promised. But he wasn't coming home empty-handed. The trunk was filled with adult beverages and an array of salty, high-fat junk food. Maybe he could convince her to help lug it all inside.

The door flew open and the young hooligan pulled himself out of the sedan. It was at that point he remembered to check his surroundings; something that should have been done before the engine was off and before the doors were unlocked. But Jeremy's good luck just kept coming. No ghouls in sight. This didn't mean there weren't any around, it just meant that from where he stood, he couldn't see any.

With daylight gone, he had only the yellow illumination of a single street lamp to guide him up the walkway to the front stoop. The other lamps along the roadside were inoperable. The limited reach of the bulb's dim glow would turn out to be enough. If there were creeps waiting at the edges of the shadows, Jeremy would still have enough time and distance from them to make it inside.

The darkened streets were more of an indication of neglect than of a power outage. For as long as he had lived there, the lights had never come on. Jeremy let himself in the front door and confirmed that the electric service hadn't been interrupted. There was an overhead lamp the size of a basketball hanging by a chain from the ceiling. A frosted globe, whose glass shell had turned from white to yellow to nearly brown over the years, covered a pair of sixty-watt bulbs.

Jeremy walked into the front hallway and pulled the door closed behind him. The building's interior, while filthy as usual, didn't show any signs of disorder. A small trash can in the corner, which was intended to be used for junk mail but was actually used for empty soda cans and fast food wrappers, was overfilling with garbage. Someone's dirty sock lie on the floor in front of the stairway. The carpet was stained and worn and the drywall was dotted with small holes and bad patchwork, but all of these things had been that way since before everyone started losing their minds.

Maybe the building was safe. After all, it had been less than a day since the city went to Hell. Those crazy cannibal bastards couldn't have gotten into every building yet.

Hustling up the stairs, Jeremy felt confident there was nothing to fear now that he was inside. His feet landed hard on each step; floorboards creaking and moaning as scuffed Nike's stomped their way to the second story. By the time he arrived at the second-floor landing, Jeremy's cocksure attitude was replaced with anxiety and panic.

The door to his apartment was wide open. It had clearly been forced open and the frame was busted apart. Aside from a single sliver at the top of the jamb, the inner part of the doorway was completely separated from the wall. Large splinters littered the floor and a handful of finishing nails stood halfway out of the drywall. There was no light coming from within and Jeremy couldn't hear anyone moving around inside.

"Hello?" he called softly, rapping his knuckle against the wall. Feeling silly for knocking at his own apartment, he called a little louder, "Beth? Are you in here?"

Nobody answered. This was good news and bad news. No answer meant no Beth. On the other hand, it also meant there were no boogeymen waiting to come after him. Jeremy cautiously walked inside the apartment; eyes darting frantically into darkness as he searched for the light switch.

An overturned lamp came to life in the far corner of the main room. The space wasn't much more of a mess than when he'd left. Beth apparently hadn't followed through on her promise to clean up. The trash hadn't been picked up and the mound of laundry hadn't been washed. Jeremy was accustomed to a certain level of clutter and filth. If not for the day's events, finding the door kicked in and the lamp knocked over would have led him to believe he'd been robbed. The burglar would have been the world's most disappointed criminal once he found nothing of value worth stealing.

Jeremy gasped at the sight. Without a doubt, something horrific had taken place in his home during his absence. The glaring evidence lie in plain view in the center of the apartment. His mattress had acquired a new stain. A thick burgundy pool covered most of the top pad and it had soaked all the way through to the floor. At the edges of the puddle, the blood had begun to dry, leaving a brown crust that wrapped around the edge of the mattress. Several red streaks dotted the floor and the counter tops in the kitchen.

Where was the body? Could someone lose that much blood and survive? Could they have been injured so badly and still been able to escape? There had to be a corpse somewhere. Or worse- another one of those infected assholes could be loose somewhere in the building. And with the door wide open, there would be nothing standing between Jeremy and them.

He ran back to the door and tried to pull it closed. The bottom of the door rested on the ground. The lower and middle hinges had been ripped out of the frame. Jeremy pulled, but the force on the door just tore more wood from the wall. He tried getting behind the door, grabbing the knob and lifting as he pushed. It was no use. He was just going to end up yanking the door the rest of the way off the frame and making a ton of noise in the process.

His earlier assessment had been wrong. He was not safe in his apartment, and probably not anywhere in the building. Jeremy made up his mind right away. He was going to leave and keep searching for somewhere else to stay. It was a good thing he hadn't carried all of his groceries in, he might have just left them and ran for the exit. He thought about grabbing some clothing, but decided against it. Jeremy didn't want to be inside for a minute longer than was absolutely necessary.

Taking a final glance around the apartment on his way out, Jeremy didn't spot anything amongst the blood and mess that he'd need to take with him. He walked to the refrigerator and checked inside. Still empty. It seemed Beth hadn't bothered to go shopping before getting murdered. And corpses are notoriously unreliable when it comes to running errands. However, that isn't to say she didn't leave anything behind for Jeremy, who found her purse resting on the center of the stove.

Inside, he found keys, about thirty dollars in cash, a nail file, some lipstick, a half empty pack of cigarettes, and a pair of sunglasses with scratched lenses. Jeremy dropped each item to the floor. Except the money and smokes, those he stuffed into his pockets as he made his way toward the exit.

There was no sense in checking the other units. That would mean wandering alone and unarmed through the building. And what for? To check on the welfare of his neighbors? He didn't know most of them and the ones he knew, he didn't like. It's not like they were going to invite him inside and offer him a safe place to stay. They probably wouldn't even come to the door.

He also didn't want anyone to notice he was leaving. What if they wanted to come with him? Absolutely not. Jeremy wasn't about to go out of his way for any of them. They were on their own. Maybe they'll keep this in mind next time they want to complain about the noise or accuse him of leaving empty beer cans in the hallway.

Convinced he was doing the right thing, Jeremy was down the stairs and out the door in no time. Things were still quiet outside, but that could change at any moment. Moving quickly, he held the key out in front of him as he approached the Mazda, sliding it into the hole and twisting. With a pop, the trunk lid flew open and the slender alcoholic grabbed himself two bottles of malt liquor. You didn't think he was going anywhere without a drink in his hand, did you? Don't be foolish.

Locking himself inside, Jeremy fired up the engine and put the car in gear. He turned up the volume on the radio, but it played only static. Another station had gone off the air. That's okay, he'd heard enough talk radio for one day.

As he was searching for a new CD to put on, something caught his eye through the windshield. Maybe a hundred feet away, he saw what looked like a young girl with dark hair in a mini skirt and tank top strolling down the street. Maybe it was Beth. Nope, this girl was too short to be Beth. And her tits were too big. Nice.

The girl walked at a relaxed pace and was heading in his direction. She was awfully casual about being out by herself at night, especially under the circumstances. And especially for being so young. She couldn't have been older than sixteen or seventeen.

Jeremy switched on the headlights to get a better look and to let her know she wasn't alone. His policy of traveling solo could be amended if it meant he was picking up an attractive young woman. Who was he to turn away a lady in distress?

He eased his foot off the brake pedal and the sedan rolled forward. The girl had to have seen him by now, she was looking right at the car but didn't seem to react. Jeremy thought he should honk the horn, but he didn't want to scare her. He also didn't want to risk being heard by the freaks. Rolling down his window and stepping on the gas, Jeremy closed the distance between himself and the girl in the skirt. When she was less than twenty feet from the car, he called out to her.

"Hey!" he blurted. "Do you need a ride somewhere? You shouldn't be out here alone, don't you know what's hap-"

Jeremy had definitely gotten her attention, and he regretted it immediately. Now that she was so close, it became clear that she was one of *them,* one of the infected. The girl peered into the car and looked at the man behind the wheel. As she did so, the right side of her face became visible.

Her cheek and bottom lip had been hacked off. A row of blood red teeth were fully exposed. Colorless fluid left a glossy trail over her chin and chest, soaking the neckline of her shirt. Splashes of pink and brown stains marred her clothing. This young girl had fallen victim to the monsters; now a mindless stooge to spread their plague. And from the looks of it, she was pissed off about it.

A sewer grate of a mouth opened unnaturally wide to reveal a bleeding stump of a tongue. Screeching, the girl ran at the car, targeting the open window and the would-be meal sitting in the driver's seat.

"Oh shit!" cried Jeremy as he feverishly worked the crank to close the window.

He jumped back from the glass as the girl made contact with the car. She was moving so fast, the impact rocked the suspension and shook loose a clump of rusted metal. The quickly-sobering driver stomped on the gas pedal and the Mazda raced down the street, leaving the girl in a cloud of burnt oil smoke and exhaust.

As for Jeremy, he'd learned his lesson. That would be the last time he tried to help anyone. His days as a Good Samaritan were behind him, as was his home town. He drove to South Transit Street and headed south. That's where he had seen all those other people going. Maybe they knew something he didn't. Maybe there was somewhere safe they could all go. Maybe, but probably not.

Chapter 40

A whimper escaped her lips. Lindsey grabbed Jim's shirt and shrank into him. He held her close, shielding her as if his sweat-damp polo shirt might somehow stop a bullet. His mind flooded with panic and confusion. Jim first thought that he'd somehow caused the shotgun to go off, even though he hadn't touched the trigger. He also hadn't felt anything; no kickback from the weapon, no holes blasted into his legs and feet.

Another shot rang out.

"Get down," Jim barked in a harsh whisper. He pulled Lindsey into a crouching position and told her, "Get to the car, keep away from the ledge."

She looked up at him; her eyes saying she understood but was too frightened to speak or move.

"It's alright. I'm right here with you," Jim said softly.

Still holding the shotgun in his left hand, Jim made sure to keep the barrel pointed out and away. He draped his right arm over Lindsey's shoulders and then moved in a half-circle around her to put himself between her and the bridge's ledge. They both faced the Pontiac on the other side of the street. The car was still running and its doors remained open.

They flinched in unison as a third shot erupted. It sounded more like the blast of a shotgun than the sharp crack of a rifle or pistol, but neither Jim nor Lindsey could tell for certain. The noise echoed off the nearby buildings, making it difficult to place the shooter's location.

"Who's shooting?" Lindsey asked. "Where are they?"

"No idea," Jim told her in a hushed voice. He scanned the length of the bridge but there was no sign of movement in either direction. "Just stay low and get to the car."

Lindsey gulped a mouthful of air and began to crouch-walk toward the Pontiac. Jim stayed right behind her, looking over his shoulder as he moved. They only made it about halfway there before hearing the next gunshot. And a voice.

"Come on you sons 'a bitches!"

Lindsey looked back at Jim. Her expression was one of bewilderment and annoyance. Jim held an index finger up to his lips.

"Here I am, shitheads!" the voice called again. It was definitely a male and probably an adult, but his voice alone didn't offer any further detail. Another shot rang out, followed by the chime of shattered glass hitting cement. The man shouted again, "Come get some!"

The gunfire still wasn't much of a clue, but the shouts and crashing glass told Jim and Lindsey exactly where the man was. He was on the roadway below them. Jim motioned to the side of the bridge opposite from where they'd been standing.

"We're okay," he told her. "I don't think he can even see us up here. He's got to be shooting at zombies."

The two wary travelers crept silently to the passenger's side of the car. Lindsey kept going, moving toward the open door to get back inside. She stopped short when she saw that Jim was not doing the same. He was sneaking up to the railing at the side of the bridge.

"What are you doing?" she asked, making a point to keep her voice down.

"I'm just checking things out," Jim whispered. "I'll be there in a sec."

Lindsey huffed, "I wanna see."

Despite Jim waving her off, she crouched down and shuffled over to join him by the railing. They looked out over the edge and down at the highway of death beneath them. There, they found a man faintly illuminated by one of the few working street lamps. He was standing on the roof of a two-door sport utility vehicle.

The man wore a long-sleeve shirt under a camouflage vest. His camouflage pants were tucked into a pair of shiny black boots that laced halfway up his shins. Just as Jim had suspected, the man wielded a pump-action shotgun. The gun was all black with a short stock and an extended magazine protruding from the bottom of the receiver. Four fresh corpses lie on the street, all easily within the weapon's reach.

"Well? Anyone else?" he bellowed in no particular direction. The man spun on his heel, holding the firearm in one hand and aiming it skyward. He was now facing away from the overpass where Jim and Lindsey had been hiding.

"Whoo-wee!" exclaimed the man as two freaks emerged from the darkness about twenty yards in front of him. They were running at full speed and the camo-clad gunner welcomed their arrival. "I got a surprise for you boys. And it goes... Boom!"

On cue, the man pulled the trigger. A deluge of steel pellets exploded from the barrel as a thunderous bang reverberated off of buildings and automobiles. Tiny metal balls ripped through skin and ribs. One of the brutes fell to the ground with a gaping red crater in the center of its chest.

The man drew back on the gun's forend and then slammed it forward again, ejecting the spent cartridge and loading a new round. The second savage was now within ten yards of the shooter. Jittery with anticipation, he fired again. From the jaw-up, the demon's head evaporated in a cloud of red mist with craggy chunks of brain and bone. Some stubborn skin flaps held tight to what remained of the back portion of his skull and just for a second, the bastard's legs kept going. The headless horror took two more steps before collapsing into a mutilated heap.

"That's what I'm talkin' about," the man shouted. He threw a fist in the air and continued to taunt his downed opponents. "Ya'll think you're gonna get me? Well, come on then!"

"Alright, it's time to go," Jim said to Lindsey.

"Wait," she said. "What if he sees the car?"

"It's fine," he answered confidently. "He's more interested in the zombies."

"But do you think he might be with the military or the police?" Lindsey asked. "Or the National Guard or something?"

Jim peered over the ledge once more to assess the man. He considered for a few seconds before answering, "No. He's alone and he's being reckless. He's carrying on like some drunken frat boy at a football game. Not a cop or a soldier. He's just some asshole with a Jeep and a gun."

Lindsey shrugged and nodded.

With that settled, it was time to get in the car and start moving again. Jim escorted Lindsey all the way back to the passenger's side of the coupe. Once she was in her seat, he returned the shotgun to its previous spot beside her before walking around to the driver's side. Moments later, the bridge, the gridlocked highway, and the lone zombie hunter were all well behind them.

After driving for only a couple of minutes, their surroundings felt a lot less dense. Houses and other buildings were fewer in number and spread farther apart. Jim began to think they had finally reached the outskirts of the city as they approached what first seemed to be a large open field. Perhaps it was land to be used for growing corn or wheat, or maybe it was a large pasture for livestock. When it turned out to be a cemetery, Jim huffed and quietly cursed himself for his foolish optimism.

Chapter 41

"Go away," a gruff voice sounded through the door.

Shrugging, Danny began to do as he was told. He turned around to head back down the stairs when he was stopped by a firm hand to the chest.

"Where are you going?" Jenna demanded.

"You heard the man," Danny replied. "He wants to be left alone."

"We're not leaving yet." Jenna pushed past Danny and knocked again. She called, "Albert, are you alright? It's me, Jenna."

"I'm fine," the voice shouted.

"Can we come in?" Jenna tried to smile as she spoke, to make her voice sound friendly and inviting. After a few seconds of silence, Danny tried his hand.

"Hey Albert, it's me- er, it's Danny," he said. "You know, from the other side of the building."

"The dope-smoking kid?" Albert's voice boomed through the wall.

Danny frowned. He looked to Jenna and asked, "How does he know?"

"Everybody knows," she replied. Then she turned to face the door and said, "Albert, let us in. We're not going anywhere until we know you're alright."

Danny and Jenna heard what sounded like a series of curse words followed by the sound of footsteps and the lock being disengaged. The door flew open and Albert appeared in front of them.

"I don't need a damn babysitter," he scolded.

"I know, I know," Jenna said. "We're checking on everybody in the building just to make sure everyone's okay."

Danny and Jenna both expected him to slam the door in their faces or yell at them and tell them to leave. Instead, Albert just huffed and turned around. He left the door open behind him as he walked into the kitchen. That seemed like the closest thing to an invitation they were going to get, so they followed him into the apartment.

Jenna made sure the door was firmly closed and locked once they were inside. She checked the safety on the rifle before setting it down, leaning it upright against the wall just to the right of the entrance. With some encouragement, in the form of an elbow to the ribs, Danny followed suit. He placed the machete, which was now mostly blood-free, on the floor next to the gun.

Albert stood at the stove with his back to them. He switched off one of the burners and used a wooden spoon to stir the contents of a large pot. The broth had reached a boil and steam billowed out over the rim. Albert then opened the oven door, took a peek inside, and closed it again.

Duke, who had been watching Jenna and Danny come in, finally pulled himself to his feet. He began walking over to greet them but stopped halfway so he could tend to a nagging itch. The old German Shepherd sat down and leaned forward, bringing his right back leg up to scratch himself on the neck. With each repetition, a toenail snagged his collar and four metal tags jingled beneath his chin.

Once satisfied, Duke stood himself up on aging hips and made his way over to the visitors.

"Hey bud," Danny said as he knelt down to pet the dog. He rubbed his neck and stroked the fur on top of his head. Then patted his side and said, "Look at you- who's a good boy. You are, aren't ya. Whoozagoodboy!"

Jenna had been standing quietly at the edge of the room and trying to remain polite. She made an exaggerated show of sniffing the air and wafting it up to her nose. "It smells pretty good in here. What'cha cooking, Albert?"

"Let's cut the shit," Albert snapped; his words punctuated by the sound of a wooden utensil being slammed onto a Formica counter top. He finally turned around to face them, pivoting slowly and leaning on his cane for balance. "I know you didn't come here to swap recipes, so why don't you tell me what you want."

If Jenna was surprised or upset by his reaction, she didn't let it show. At least, she tried not to let it show. She didn't flinch. Her posture was rigid. She kept her torso straight and her shoulders back. But if you looked closely, you'd see she was clenching her jaw. Jenna cleared her throat to buy herself another couple of seconds before she'd have to answer.

"Zombies!" Danny blurted out, still crouched and petting the dog.

"Zombies?" Albert rolled his eyes as he adjusted his stance against the cane. "Is that what you've decided to call them?"

It was a serious topic, which warranted serious discussion. Danny wanted to give the older man his full, undivided and un-stoned attention. He gave Duke one last pat on the head and began to ramble. "I know it sounds crazy but it's true. I didn't believe it at first either, but we've seen them right outside. Jenna even killed a bunch and, well, I sorta killed one too. I recently started watching the news and they're talking about it on there too, like it's everywhere, zombies all over the place and-"

Albert had heard enough. He held up a hand to interrupt and demanded, "You think I don't know what's going on out there? I'm very aware of the situation. You kids said you wanted to check and make sure everyone's okay. You've seen me, I'm fine. So if you're satisfied with that, I think it's time you both left." Albert lifted his cane and pointed it at the doorway.

"Fine," Jenna spat, turning abruptly to pick up her rifle and reach for the doorknob.

"Hey Albert, we weren't trying to get you upset," Danny told him. He held his hands up with his palms out and added, "Just take it easy, we're only trying to help where we can."

Albert lowered the walking stick. His shoulders dropped as he let out a deep breath. He looked away from them, first down to the floor and then to the stove to double-check that he'd turned off all the burners. Still avoiding eye contact, the aging man walked stiffly and slowly to the kitchen table and sat down. Jenna finally let go of the doorknob and watched intently as Albert settled into his seat.

"You're good kids," he said. "It's good what you're doing, checking in on folks."

"Thanks," Danny and Jenna said in unison.

"I saw them," Albert continued, "I know they're right outside. And you know what else I know?"

The question hung there for a moment. Danny shrugged and Jenna gave the old man an inquisitive glance. They weren't quite sure what he was asking.

"There's nothing we can do about it," Albert finally said. He let go of the cane and let it rest against the edge of the table.

Jenna began to argue but Albert interrupted and explained further.

"I know you kids mean well but-" Albert forced a chuckle. "I say *kids*, but what are you, twenty-four, twenty-five?"

"Twenty-six," Danny answered.

"Twenty-five," Jenna said. She appeared a little less tense and returned the gun to its previous place on the floor.

"And do you know how old I am?" Albert asked.

"Ninety-one!" Danny called out his answer like a contestant on a game show.

"Ninety-one?" Albert repeated, half insulted and half amused. "Hell, do I look *that* old?"

"Of course not," Jenna shot Danny a cross look. "I don't know, I'd say fifty-five? Sixty?"

"You're being polite," Albert told her. "I'm seventy-four."

"Okay?" Jenna wasn't sure where this was headed. "That's not old. You're barely past retirement age."

"I was reading an article the other day, in the news," Danny cast a knowing glance in Jenna's direction. "And it said that medicine and technology have developed to the point where people can expect to live a super-long time. They said that there's people alive now who will live to be two-hundred years old."

"Rubbish," Albert said dismissively.

"Actually, he's right," Jenna said. "Though, I think the number was a hundred and fifty, not two-hundred. But still, that's a long ways away."

"If that's true, they must have been talking about young people, people born in the last ten years or so," Albert stated. "I bet they didn't say that elderly people with bad knees and an inflamed prostate could suddenly expect to make it another seventy years. And let me ask you something. When did you read this article?"

"About a month ago," Danny answered.

"A month ago?" Albert repeated. "Before people started getting sick, before everyone lost their minds and started attacking each other."

"Right," said Danny. "They may not have considered the zombie factor."

Jenna was relieved that Danny had seemingly managed to get Albert to relax. Danny had a way of making people feel comfortable. He was non-threatening and unassuming. People liked that about him. It's a shame he never harnessed that potential. If he ever decided to work with people, he could probably be quite successful. She let the men chat, thankful for the quiet time; a reprieve from all the chaos that waited for them on the other side of the wall.

She found that she'd tuned out from their conversation. It didn't matter what they were talking about, it only mattered that they were both at ease for the moment. Jenna looked at Duke, who seemed to notice he was getting some attention. He lifted his chin from the kitchen floor and with a little effort, he stood up and walked to the other side of the room.

He seemed to be asking for something, probably something to eat. Duke stopped, turned around, and sat. The old German Shepherd's mouth hung open slightly and he began panting. He looked to Jenna, then glanced up to the counter top above him, and then back to Jenna. Duke didn't bark or whine like some dogs do. His begging was much more subtle. But subtle or not, he knew there was food up there and it was past his regular dinner time.

Jenna scanned the counter top to see if there was anything up there for him. If there was a food dish or something like that, she'd offer to feed him so Albert wouldn't have to get up. There were only a few items, including Albert's pipe, a small cardboard box, and a bowl filled with dog food. She stepped over to the counter and patted Duke on the head.

"That's what I'm saying," Danny said. He and Albert were still talking about medicine and the things Danny had seen in online articles and videos. "They've got these labs where they figured out how to grow organs inside of pigs and transplant them into humans."

"So, you're telling me if I need a new kidney, they'll put a pig's kidney in me?" Albert asked in disbelief. "I don't think people can use pig parts."

"No, it's not pig parts," Danny clarified. "It's human cells and human organs that are grown inside of pigs."

"So is the pig's body using the human kidney?" Albert asked. "Or does it grow an extra human kidney in addition to its own set of kidneys?"

"I'm not sure," Danny admitted. "They weren't very clear about that."

"Wouldn't it be bad for the pig?" Albert pressed. "If the pig needs those organs to live, wouldn't it mean the pig would be killed once someone needs that kidney?"

"I don't know, man. I'm not a scientist," Danny said.

Albert gave a sarcastic chuckle. "You aren't?"

Danny laughed along with the older man and said, "But besides, we kill loads of pigs anyway, for bacon and such. We could take the kidneys out before they get to the bacon factory."

"Sorry to interrupt," Jenna said as she reached for the bowl of dog food on the counter. "But I wanted to see if it was okay to feed-"

Her words broke off mid-sentence. Jenna had seen the box minutes earlier. She'd even read the label, *Rat Assassin*. Rat poison. It struck her as odd, but she didn't give it much thought at first. She had never seen a rat in her own apartment but she lived on the top floor. Did that make a difference? Maybe rats could only climb so many steps. Maybe there was an infestation in the building and she had been lucky enough to avoid it. Maybe there were hundreds of rats living inside the walls and she just never noticed. And maybe the rats had found food in other places, like Albert's apartment, so they didn't need to search for food in her apartment.

All that talk about being old and wanting to be left alone, now it made sense. Jenna should have known something was up, but she didn't piece things together until that moment when she walked over and found what was in the second bowl on the counter. It had failed to register at first, but now she understood. Albert was giving up.

The conversation stopped. Albert's face was in his hands. Danny noticed the mood had shifted but he didn't know why. He looked over at Jenna. She seemed to be studying one of the items on the counter top. Danny tried to follow her line of sight.

"Hey Albert, what's in the pipe?" he asked.

Albert didn't answer.

"Relax Danny, it's not pot," Jenna told him. Then she turned her attention to Albert and asked, "What's going on here? What's with the rat poison?"

"Rat poison?" Danny echoed. "You gotta be careful with that, Albert. You don't want to get any of that in your food."

Albert lowered his hands from his face and looked up at the younger man. The pair had been talking to each other for several minutes, but this was the first time Danny had truly looked at Albert. And when he did, what he saw was the tired stare of a man defeated; a man with nothing more to give.

"Albert." Jenna was raising her voice and held up the Rat Assassin box for emphasis. "You wanna tell me what's going on here."

"No," Albert said flatly. "I appreciate you coming by but I think it's time you both leave."

Danny was finally getting up to speed. "Whoa, Albert. That's no good man. What are you thinking?"

"Like I said," Albert began, "I think you should go. You're good kids and I don't want you to be around for this."

"You're not seriously going to eat rat poison, are you?" Danny was having a hard time getting his head around the idea. "Just because of a few zombies? We're all gonna be fine. The cops or military or whoever is going to have this under control in no time. It's not the end of the world."

"Isn't it?" asked the older man. "Where are the cops? The military? When's the last time you heard a siren go by outside? Nobody is coming. There's no one left to help. And even if there was, why would they come here?"

"It's not over," Jenna interjected. "The whole government can't be gone already and the police wouldn't just abandon us. They can't let everything fall apart just because there's a new disease. Just be patient. Someone will come. Isn't that what they've been saying on the news?"

Jenna and Danny glanced into the living room to check the television. The news broadcast had been replaced by the multicolored stripes of a test pattern.

"Well, what about the other channels?" Jenna suggested. "Or the radio? There's got to be something on the radio."

"There's nothing," Albert said sharply.

"Even if that's true, so what?" Jenna argued. "Just because the TV signal is out, it doesn't mean there's no one left out there. Help could still be on the way."

"But it doesn't seem very likely, does it?" Albert was growing agitated again.

"Yeah, it's not a great sign," Danny admitted. He looked to Jenna for confirmation and added, "But we're inside, we're safe in here, and we're not alone. Someone has got to come along at some point, either with a cure or a way to get rid of the zombies."

"A cure?" Albert scoffed. "And what are we supposed to do until then? Sit around and hope we don't get murdered or starve to death while we wait?"

"We always pull through," Jenna said with fabricated enthusiasm. "Just think about all the other times we've had disasters, hurricanes and earthquakes and stuff like that. There's always someone to come in and help out. It takes time, but we always bounce back."

269

"This is hardly the same thing," Albert replied. "We're not talking about the weather. The rain eventually stops, the wind eventually dies down, and the ground eventually stops shaking. That's when help arrives- when it's safe for people to come in and help. There's no telling when that's going to happen, if it ever happens at all."

Jenna tried to speak but Albert cut her off.

"And there's something you're forgetting," he continued. "Hurricanes and earthquakes, those things happen in a relatively small area. What's happening now, it could be the whole country. It could be the whole world. And it's not going to stop when the weather happens to change."

"I know it looks bad right now," was all Danny could say before he too was interrupted.

"Do you know what it was like before I came here?" Albert asked. "Back in Poland, I mean. We were going through one of the worst food shortages the country had ever seen. There were riots and fighting, it wasn't safe to go outside half the time. People were ready to kill each other just so they could get something to eat."

"Is that why you came here?" Danny asked.

Albert nodded. "Lots of people were dying, taken by violence or starvation, and some just got sick and couldn't afford to get medicine. Hospitals were useless, over-crowded and out of resources. The whole place was a mess. Now, think about how much worse it would have been if everyone had lost their wits and started eating each other."

Jenna opened her mouth to speak, but Albert pressed on. "The big difference now is that we can't just run away from all the bad stuff. We can't simply pack up and move to somewhere better. And even if we could, look at me. I can barely get around as it is. How long do you think I'd last in a world like this, with everybody gone mad and acting like some kind of cannibal gang?"

"But you don't have to worry about getting around as long as you stay here," Jenna told him. "You can't just give up- none of us can just give up. People need you and want you here. What about your friends and family?"

There it was. It was the topic they'd all been ignoring the entire time. Family. Jenna had intended to avoid the subject for as long as possible but she couldn't find another way to get through to him. As soon as she'd said the word, everyone in the room knew they'd have to talk about Adam.

"How'd you get over here?" Albert asked.

"I'm sorry?" Jenna wasn't sure how to answer.

"We just walked," said Danny. "We all live in the same building."

"I know that," Albert replied. Looking at Danny, he said, "But you live on the other side of the building, don't you?"

The younger man nodded.

"So how did you make it from your side of the building to this side?" Albert inquired. "There's a crowd of those crazy folks surrounding the building, so I know you didn't go outside and come in the front door over here."

"We crossed over in the basement," Jenna explained. She realized Albert must have known that already and she understood where the discussion was headed. "We know, Albert. We saw Adam."

"I think that should answer your question," he told her. "About why I'm giving up. When I left Poland, I left all of my friends and most of my family behind. My wife died years ago and the only family I have left is caged up downstairs like an animal. My family is gone."

"Adam's not gone," Jenna said. "You did the right thing keeping him quarantined. That's what they said on the news, to quarantine anyone who seems sick or has symptoms. You're keeping him safe by putting him down there and you're keeping all of us safe too."

"I didn't do it for him," the older man said softly. "I know what they said on the news, so when I found him, I locked him up just like they said."

"Right," Jenna stated. "They must know something about a cure or a treatment or something if they're telling people to quarantine anyone who might be infected. Why else would they do that?"

"You wanna know why?" The question seemed rhetorical but Albert paused for a response anyway. "Because the only other thing you can do for them is kill them, so they tell you to set up a quarantine. I put him down there because I was hopeful at first. But the reason he's still there is because I'm a coward."

"I'm not sure I follow," Danny admitted.

"There is no cure and nobody is coming to save us." Albert took a breath and straightened himself in his chair. "A better man, a better father, would put him out of his misery. I can't stand the thought of him chained up like that, out of his mind and sick the way he is. But I just can't bring myself to..."

He let his words trail off, but Jenna and Danny knew what he meant. They also knew that neither of them could say with any level of certainty that he was wrong. As much as they wished for an answer, some glimmer of hope and optimism, they had to admit that Albert was probably right.

"As for a cure or waiting for the military to swoop in and save the day, I wouldn't hold your breath." The old man grabbed his cane and began pulling himself to his feet. He continued speaking as he walked back to the counter where he'd left his pipe. "And let's say there is someone left, someone in charge of the government or military- don't forget, they're dealing with an unknown and highly contagious disease. Do you know how they deal with deadly new diseases? With fire. They incinerate contaminated material and infected bodies. If there is still an army and they do find this place, I bet they burn it to the ground. That's what I'd do. It's the smart thing to do. It's the only way to keep this kind of disease from spreading."

"I don't know about that," Danny responded. "I think they said on TV that you can only get it from somebody's blood, or if they bite you. Setting fire to everything seems like it might be overkill. Plus, we'd get their attention and let them know we're here. They wouldn't burn down the building if they knew there were uninfected people inside."

"You hope they wouldn't," said Albert as he picked up his pipe. "But under the circumstances, they may not want to risk it. For all they know, you could still be carrying the disease. The virus could be on your clothing or in your hair, just waiting for a chance to get inside your body. There's no way to know for sure. You could end up spreading it around and starting this whole thing over again. I don't think that's a risk they'd be willing to take."

"You could come stay with us," Jenna suggested; a rising sense of urgency in her voice. "We'll all stick together and help each other through this."

"That's very generous of you but I'll have to decline," the old man told her.

"We're crashing at my place," Danny explained. "You can take the bed, I always crash on the couch anyway."

271

"I'm not going anywhere," Albert said firmly. "I wish you both luck, but I'm fine here."

Jenna started to argue, "But Albert-"

"That's enough," he said, raising his voice a bit. "You have my answer so I think it's about time you got back home."

"Back home to do what?" Jenna demanded. "Sit around in Danny's apartment while you kill yourself with rat poison?"

"It's not up to you," Albert replied, fishing in his pocket for the book of matches that had to be in there somewhere. "It's up to me and I've made up my mind."

"And what about Duke?" Jenna asked.

"What about him?"

"What's going to happen to him once you're gone?" Jenna was reaching for anything that might change his mind. "He's not exactly going to be okay on his own. You think he's going to feed himself, take care of himself?"

"Don't worry about him," Albert instructed. It wasn't deliberate, but a quick glance at Duke's food bowl betrayed his intentions.

Danny missed it, but Jenna didn't and she spoke up immediately. "Oh no. Absolutely not."

"Come on Albert," Danny chimed in. "Think about what you're saying. You can't do this."

"Like I said before," Albert looked right at Danny as he spoke. "I've already made up my mind."

"Damn it, Albert!" Jenna shouted. She was trying to mask her sadness with anger and not doing a good job of it. "You've got to listen-"

"No, you listen," Albert yelled over her. "You've said your piece, now it's time to leave."

"But-"

"That's enough." The older man was still yelling. He aimed a finger toward the door and added, "I'm not going to ask again- get the Hell out of here."

"Fine." Her voice was now barely above a whisper. The veneer of strength and rage had worn thin and disappeared. Jenna blinked away tears and said, "Okay. If that's really what you want, we'll go. Danny, grab the gun for me."

Puzzled, Danny said, "Alright, but don't you want to hang on to it?"

Jenna didn't answer. She stormed across the kitchen floor to where Duke was sitting. She took the dog by the collar and led him to the door. Duke followed obediently. He was still panting and his over-sized tongue hung out of his mouth. The German Shepherd looked up at Albert as they walked by but it was only for a second. He followed alongside Jenna as they marched toward the exit.

"We're taking the dog," she announced. Jenna looked to Danny and added, "If he tries to stop us, shoot him. He's so fucking eager to die anyway."

Jenna then turned her attention back to Albert. "You can do whatever you want but we're not going to let you do anything to him. When you come to your senses, and I hope you do, you'll know where to find us."

With that, Jenna opened the door and let herself out. The young woman walked into the hallway and began to head down the stairs. She could already feel the tears welling in her eyes by the time she reached the third step. It was something she didn't want Danny or Albert to see but she wasn't so shy around Duke. Jenna couldn't hold back the tears any longer and she let them fall freely as she led the dog down the stairwell.

Things just kept getting worse and there seemed to be no end in sight. But when Jenna reached the first-floor lobby, she realized there might actually be an end in sight after all. And it might be coming a lot sooner than she had hoped.

The ghouls outside hadn't left. There were more of them now, and they all wanted to get through the doorway. The crowd was so densely packed that Jenna could see only streaks of blood and bodies pressed up against the glass.

At least one of them had died. His body had been crushed under the weight of the others as the group tried to forge ahead. The corpse remained upright, pinned against the translucent barrier. Next to him, more savages were also stuck and unable to move between the building's outer wall and the writhing wall of flesh behind them.

Both doors leaned inward slightly. The cheap aluminum frames weren't meant to withstand that type of pressure. On either side of the entrance, the uppermost hinges were pulling away from the door jamb. The bolts meant to hold them in place were losing their threading as the fixtures were pressed farther and farther in the wrong direction. The extension cord they'd used to secure the door handles was still in place but it wouldn't do them any good if the doors themselves came down.

Jenna bolted down the steps and into the basement with Duke in tow. Once downstairs, she found that Adam had returned from his waking stupor. He wailed from inside his cage, twisting his body and fighting against his steel bonds. Pipes rattled and the boiler itself shook loudly every time he lurched forward. Duke let out a growl and showed his teeth to his former companion.

"Shh," Jenna said softly. She patted him on the back and then ushered him into the next section of the basement, eager to get back to Danny's apartment.

Back in Albert's living room, Danny collected the weapons like he was asked and made his way through the threshold. He turned back to face the old man, stunned that he hadn't tried to stop them. Albert hadn't even moved from where he'd been standing.

"Albert," Danny began to say something but he couldn't find the words. There wasn't anything he could say that would change his mind, so he just said, "I guess I'll see ya."

"Good luck to you kids," Albert replied. There was a warmth in his tone that hadn't been there at any point in their conversation thus far.

It was a strange sentiment. Good luck. An encouraging farewell from a man who opted for suicide rather than fighting. Danny found no comfort or inspiration in those words.

He wanted to argue with the old man, to convince him to come with him and Jenna. Danny even considered forcing him, dragging him back to his apartment. He could lock Albert in the bedroom, away from any sharp objects and toxic chemicals. It wouldn't be much of a life for him, but wasn't that better than no life at all? Danny wasn't sure, so he didn't say any of that. He didn't say anything at all. He simply reached in to grab the door and pulled it closed.

Chapter 42

"What?" Lindsey asked without looking up from her cell phone. She had been fiddling with the device since they'd left the bridge. "Did you say something?"

"Huh?" Jim asked, rubbing his eyes. "Oh, nothing. Never mind. Any luck getting a signal?"

"It's in and out," she explained. "The bars show up for a few seconds and then they blink out again. I tried making a few calls and checking voice mail, but the signal drops before I can connect."

"That's bad news," Jim observed.

"It must be something with the cell towers," Lindsey hypothesized. "But there's a landline at the cabin. We can take turns using it. I'm sure there's lots of calls we'll want to make once we get there."

"I'm not sure who I'd call besides my parents," Jim said as the Pontiac raced below a red light at an empty intersection. "And maybe my friend Danny who lives upstairs from me. Hopefully they're all okay over there. Actually, I'm kind of nervous to find out."

"I know what you mean." Lindsey held her phone up to the window and examined the screen, hoping the change in position might somehow encourage functionality. "I'm already scared that I might try to call someone and they won't pick up. I'm automatically going to assume the worst. And I've got at least ten calls to make."

"At least ten?" Jim teased, "Someone's popular."

"That's not that many," she replied. "I want to get a hold of my family and make sure everyone's okay. And I want to check on a couple friends and coworkers- Kelly and Amy and Chad, to see who was able to get out of the store when everything went bad."

It was out of her mouth before she even realized what she was saying. Lindsey didn't mean anything by it. She tried to gloss over it- tried to let it slide by, in hopes it might go unnoticed. However, she did know that it was bound to come up at some point. And here it was. Chad.

"Oh," was all Jim could think to say.

He had been making a point to avoid the topic altogether. Of course he had. Why the Hell would he want to talk about Lindsey's boyfriend? But that didn't mean he hadn't been thinking about it. Did the title of *boyfriend* still apply? There probably hadn't been an official breakup. But then again, what qualifies as an official breakup during a zombie outbreak? If a guy, particularly an underachieving and unreliable slob of a guy, abandons his too-hot-for-him girlfriend and leaves her to die alone in a supermarket, doesn't that make him the ex-boyfriend by default?

"Oh?" Lindsey repeated. She'd obviously detected Jim's skepticism. "What's the matter with that?"

"Nothing," he said. "I'm just sorta surprised to hear that. The Chad part, I mean. I didn't think you'd want to talk to him, given the circumstances."

"What circumstances?" she asked sharply.

"The circumstances that left you alone at the store while he took off in your car." The rising tension triggered a craving for nicotine. Jim thought about reaching for a cigarette but stopped himself. He continued, "I didn't think you'd want to talk to him after that."

"It's not that I want to talk to him," said Lindsey. "I just, I don't know. I need to know whether he's still alive."

There was a fair chance Chad might have expired. When Lindsey first called earlier that day, a small part of Jim hoped she was calling to say that Chad had been killed. Not his proudest moment; it was shitty and selfish and he knew that. It was something he'd never admit to, especially not to Lindsey. But since then, since he'd had several hours to think about it, Jim began to hope that Chad was still alive. Lindsey might feel guilty if Chad had died. If he was still alive, however, she'd be free to resent him forever.

"I'm sure he's fine," Jim told her. "After all, he had a head start in getting clear of any danger. Instead of you wondering what happened to him, maybe he should be wondering if you're okay- if that's something that would even concern him."

"Hey!" Lindsey snapped. "You're making some awfully bold assumptions. It's obvious you don't like him, but you weren't there. You can criticize all you want, but you don't know what you would have done if you were in his position."

"Don't I?" Jim asked. "Because that's where you're mistaken. Who was it that came back for you?"

Lindsey opened her mouth to answer but quickly realized the question was rhetorical.

"And who left you behind? Who left you alone to be killed or to get infected or to be eaten alive?" Jim was almost yelling at this point. He took a breath to compose himself and added, "I don't mean to sound shitty, but seriously, consider everything you know about Chad and then ask yourself, do you really think he would come back?"

Lindsey looked down at her lap and didn't say anything.

"Was your car in the parking lot when we left the supermarket?" Jim asked.

"I don't think so," she answered, shaking her head.

"Shouldn't it have been there?" he pressed. "I mean, if he was coming back?"

Lindsey shrugged. "Yeah, I guess so."

"Why did he leave in the first place?" Jim asked. "Why on Earth would he have gone anywhere without you?"

"Alright Jim, I got it," she said. "You made your point."

"My point is that I'm not going to leave you," he told her.

"I guess," she stammered, "I guess I just need to know for sure. I need to know if I spent years with someone who could leave me for dead. Or, if I'm angry at someone who's lost their life. You know what I'm talking about. I mean, don't you want to know if um, uh, what's her name-"

"Beth," Jim reminded her.

"Right," Lindsey nodded. "I'm sure you want to know if Beth is okay."

"Honestly," he hesitated. "I know this is going to sound terrible, but I haven't really thought about it."

"I see," she answered.

"I should explain," Jim said. "She's been cheating."

"Oh?" Lindsey raised an eyebrow.

"Not that cheating necessarily warrants being killed," he added.

"How chivalrous," she chided with a smirk.

Jim ignored the ribbing and said, "I just sorta figured that the other guy, or guys, that have been banging her can look out for her well-being."

"I suppose that's fair," Lindsey replied.

"Yeah," Jim agreed without enthusiasm.

"Yeah," Lindsey echoed as she sat back in her seat and once again lifted her cell phone to check for a signal.

The streetlights were now gone entirely. They either had no power or simply didn't exist on this stretch of Eggert Road, Jim couldn't tell for sure. The houses were gone now too, replaced on his right by an open field of overgrown weeds. There was a field to his left as well, but that one was well-groomed and sat between the road and a large commercial-style building with a flat roof. It looked like it might be a school or an office building but again, Jim couldn't tell for certain.

"Does this look right to you?" he asked.

"I think so," Lindsey answered. She pressed her face to the window glass. "It's too dark to really see anything. Oh wait- we're coming up to something."

Jim switched on the high-beams and immediately hit the brakes. About fifty feet ahead of the car, a small group of five or six people sprinted across the street. In the glow of the headlamps, streaks of blood could be seen on shredded articles of clothing. Open, pulsing wounds shown a glossy purple sheen in the artificial light. Dangling flaps of skin bobbed loosely from arms, hands, and foreheads. With teeth bared and neck muscles churning, the tribe of terror moved at top speed past the curb, across a small patch of grass, and disappeared behind a cluster of trees.

"Do you think they saw us?" asked Lindsey, gripping Jim's arm in her left hand and grabbing the neck of the shotgun with her right.

"Doesn't look like it," Jim answered. He switched off the high-beams and began to pull forward. "Or if they did, they saw something else they liked better."

"That's good I guess." Lindsey relaxed somewhat and let her hands drop to her lap.

"Good for us, anyway," Jim agreed. He leaned forward in his seat and turned the brights on once more. They were approaching something, something that reignited his hours-long angst. "More houses!"

The car passed by a speed limit sign- thirty miles per hour. The street was bordered on both sides by long rows of single-family Cape Cod style homes. Jim let out an exaggerated groan and whined, "I thought we'd at least be out of the city by now. Shit."

"What's the problem?" Lindsey asked. "This isn't exactly the *city*. It's a part of the suburbs, well outside the city itself. We're still getting closer and the road has been fairly clear so far. We're still moving in the right direction."

"We might not be moving at all before long," he replied.

276

Lindsey glanced at him; a puzzled expression on her face.

"We'll need gas," he told her.

"Are we running out?" she asked.

"Not yet, but we will. We've got at least another hour of driving, probably more, and we're never going to make it on," Jim paused to look down at the fuel gauge. "About a quarter tank."

"It's okay." Lindsey took Jim's hand and laced her fingers through his. "We've still got time, we'll figure it out. We just have to keep moving and we're going to be fine."

There was something about her touch, something that somehow pulled all the tension out of him. It wasn't the first time he had noticed it, but with each instance of physical contact, Jim felt more at ease. Despite all the evidence to the contrary, maybe she was right. Maybe they were going to be fine. But, ya know, probably not.

"Okay," he said finally. "Then we'll keep going."

And they did. With renewed vigor, Jim and Lindsey kept moving. They kept driving, pressing forward and heading toward their ultimate destination. Freedom and safety lie ahead somewhere in the distance and nothing was going to stand in their way. Except maybe an empty gas tank. Or bad directions. Or possibly an angry horde of rabid cannibals.

Alright, so obviously it wasn't going to be easy. But it hadn't been easy so far and they'd managed to hold up relatively well. They were certainly doing better than most of the people they'd come across. And as far as Jim was concerned, he would do whatever it took to make sure they stayed on top. They would follow this road wherever it took them and as far as it would go. Which, as luck would have it, was for only about another four-hundred feet. And as you may have guessed, Allegany was more than four-hundred feet away.

Jim deflated as the coupe reached the top of a T in the road. Left or right, east or west; lousy options when you need to go south. He looked over at Lindsey and said, "Well, now what?"

"Let's go..." she trailed off, looking right and then left as she examined her options. "Let's go right, I guess."

"You guess?"

"Definitely right," Lindsey said with a tone of false confidence, a tone in which Jim was well-versed. He'd faked enough certainty to know when someone else was doing the same. But in the spirit of politeness, and not having a better idea of his own, he agreed without questioning.

"Right it is," he proclaimed, turning the wheel in the corresponding direction.

They drove the length of another block, weaving around a few stalled cars and a small stack of smoldering bodies. Four corpses were piled on top of each other and set ablaze in the middle of the road. The flames had long since gone out and the firebug was nowhere to be found. This must have been an effort to contain the virus- at least, that's what Jim and Lindsey found themselves hoping. The alternative motives for such an act were too gruesome to ponder.

Jim drove to the next intersection where a suspended traffic signal flashed its yellow bulb. Proceed with caution. *No shit,* though Jim. On the other hand, maybe they didn't need to proceed anywhere. He could take a left turn, which would have them going south again, but it was another short, narrow side street. He'd have to make another quick turn and then another. There was still at least sixty miles between their present location and their destination in Allegany. Navigating through a congested maze of city blocks was no way to cover that type of ground.

"Why aren't we moving?" asked Lindsey after they'd been sitting motionless for nearly a minute. "I didn't think we were acknowledging traffic lights."

"We're not," Jim told her. "Er, not really. But I was thinking, should we keep moving? I mean, at least for now, maybe we should stop, take some time and get some rest, pick this up in the morning when we've got some light and a better sense of direction."

"Alright," she replied with a long sigh, pushing out her frustration and disappointment. "And where would we stay? I don't know this area at all, so I don't know any place that's safe besides right here in the car. And if we're going to stay in the car, we might as well keep going. That's the only way we've stayed safe so far. Who knows who or what might sneak up on us if we're stopped for too long. And then what about-"

Jim put his hand up to cut her off. "I'm not suggesting we sleep in the car. I know that would leave us exposed. But maybe there's somewhere safe, somewhere that looks like it's still intact and unaffected by everything that's going on."

"Where then?" Lindsey asked, but right as she did, she had her answer. She noticed Jim was facing her, but looking past her.

To the right, beyond the sidewalk, was a set of cement stairs that led to a pair of wide glass doors. On the left side of the stairway stood a four-foot statue of a person, though it was too dark to see who the figure was meant to depict. On the opposite side of the stairway was a letter board sign which read, *Welcome Rev. Steve L Parrish.*

Above the main entrance, an array of stained glass reached up to the top of an arched roof; each pane a varying shade of greens, blues, and yellows. The outer walls of the one-story building were constructed of red and tan bricks. And towering over the structure, posted at the highest peak of the roof, was a tall silver cross.

"You want us to stay in a church?" Lindsey asked.

"It seems sort of appropriate," Jim replied. "I mean, if you gotta be somewhere for the end of the world, where better than a church?"

"It's not the end of the world," she asserted. "And look how big that place is. We'd have no way of knowing who's inside- or who might follow us in."

"There's no one inside," Jim said with an air of undue certainty.

"You have no way of knowing that," Lindsey contested.

"Just look at it," he pressed. "It's the only building in the neighborhood that hasn't been ravaged. No broken windows, the doors look secure. There's no zombies banging on the walls trying to get in."

"Speaking of getting in, how would *we* get in?" Lindsey scanned the front of the building. "I can't imagine they'd have left the doors unlocked."

"Yeah, probably not," he agreed. "I guess we'd have to break in."

"So, what's to say someone else won't do the same?"

Jim shrugged and said, "They might, but it might be someone like us, someone just looking for shelter and some place safe to go."

"And if not?" Lindsey asked. "Look, my objection isn't based on faith or religion or anything like that. But there's no way to know who's lurking around out here, and there's no way for us to keep the place secure once we get inside."

"We've still got the shotgun," he reminded her. Although, Jim had to admit to himself that the idea of wielding a gun as he broke into a church was a less-than-savory prospect.

"Plus, that wouldn't solve our food problem," said Lindsey.

"It might. Churches like this usually have a kitchen inside, for when they have social events and stuff like that. And when-" Jim stopped mid-sentence as something raced across the street a few yards in front of the car. He could only discern that it was human before the figure disappeared between two buildings, once again hidden in the darkness.

Two more quickly followed the same path across the street. They too vanished amongst the shadows. The ghouls, which is what they must have been, weren't exactly moving toward the church but they were close enough to foil Jim's confidence in his plan. They reminded him of cockroaches- if you saw one- or three, you could safely assume there were plenty more close by. Trying to break into a church without being detected would be dicey enough. Attempting to do so within sight of a few amped-up cannibals felt like an impossibility.

"On second thought," he continued, "Maybe we should keep moving. But we need to get gas. There's no way we're going to make it the rest of the way to Allegany on a quarter tank."

"Alright, then we'll stop for gas," Lindsey answered, sinking back into her seat.

"Right," Jim muttered as he pressed down on the gas pedal. If they couldn't safely sneak into a church, how the Hell were they going to stand around at a fuel pump and wait for the tank to fill up?

As the car accelerated, so did the churning in his stomach. It was like he had to vomit and shit simultaneously, but his guts couldn't agree on which would come first. Instead of coming to some sort of intestinal compromise, they might just push a hole through his abdominal wall and spew their hot lumpy contents into his lap.

Jim took a few deep breaths and tried to ignore the discomfort. Hopefully they'd have at least a few miles before they found a fueling station and it should give his tummy enough time to settle.

"Oh, we can stop up here!" Lindsey announced with excitement after they'd traveled only a few short blocks. She pointed ahead to a Sunoco station on the right side of the road.

Jim's stomach rolled over again. A cool sheen of sweat formed on the back of his neck. Hot moisture from his palms loosened his grip on the wheel. There would be no time to calm his frazzled nerves after all. He yearned for something that could alleviate his burgeoning dread. A shot of whiskey, a tall mug of frosty beer; he'd swallow a tumbler of laudanum if he knew where to find one. Jim brought the car to a stop in the middle of the street, adjacent to the entrance to the gas station.

"What's up?" Lindsey asked. "Why aren't we pulling in?"

"Just making sure it looks safe," he answered.

There were four double-sided pumps under a large canopy set only a few yards back from the sidewalk. A convenience store was about ten feet beyond that. The lights under the canopy were all on, but the lights inside the store were either all off or no longer worked.

The aftermath of a car crash sat to the left of the pumps, about twenty feet from the edge of the fuel canopy. An old Mercury sedan had collided with the passenger's side of a minivan. The driver's door to the sedan hung open to reveal where blood and shattered glass had been spilled all over the seats, dashboard, and ground between the two vehicles. Both the van and sedan were still and quiet. Their occupants must have fled on foot hours ago.

"Can you see inside the store?" Jim asked. "Does it look like anyone's in there?"

Lindsey pressed her face to the glass and said, "I can't really make anything out. Not from this distance. Why don't we pull through and take a closer look? If we see anyone, we can just take off, keep moving until we find the next one."

The next one, Jim thought. *Who knows when that's going to be.*

"Alright." He cut the wheel to the right and made a slow wide turn into the lot and up toward the front of the building.

As the pair got a little closer, they could see that the inside of the store wasn't totally dark. The main overhead lights were out, but the faint glow of auxiliary lamps mounted on the far wall made it somewhat possible to see in. Lindsey peered through the large windows that made up most of the building's front wall.

There were several large cracks in the glass. The frame of the front door was bent in such a manner as to prevent it from closing all the way. Scattered amongst the banners and placards promising good deals on Pepsi, Tostitos, and Snickers, was a spattering of gore. Chunks of crusty flesh and severed skin clung to both sides of the windows, each with a thick stream of congealing blood trailing down to the ground.

"How's your appetite?" Jim asked, trying to break his own tension with a joke.

"Oh, my mouth is watering," Lindsey answered in kind. "We probably should see if there's anything worth taking though. As long as we're here."

Jim completed a full loop around the parking lot and pulled up next to the gas pump closest to the building's entrance. The Pontiac's fuel door was situated on the passenger's side, so when Jim opened his door, he would be facing the convenience store. He climbed out of his seat and walked to the other side of the car.

Every step felt heavy and slow. Each time his foot landed, Jim could have sworn it clapped like a gunshot. He tried to scan his surroundings, but every image turned fuzzy; every small bit of light forming trails in his vision. By the time he reached the passenger door, his legs were shaking so badly that he had to grip the roof of the car to keep himself from stumbling.

Lindsey opened her door and pulled herself out, shotgun in hand. She offered the weapon to Jim and said, "I thought you'd probably want this while you're standing around out here."

"Thanks," he replied and accepted the gun from her.

"Jeez Jim, are you feeling okay?" asked Lindsey. "You're all pale, I mean- more pale than usual."

"I'm alright," he told her, wiping the sweat from his eyes with his one free hand.

"Are you getting sick?" she pressed.

"No, it's nothing like that." Jim looked over his shoulder to make sure nothing was about to sneak up on them. "I don't know, just sort of nervous I guess."

"Why now?" she asked. "Why all of a sudden? You seemed like you were doing okay before."

"I was okay when we first decided to leave town. We had a plan, a destination. We knew where we were going." Jim combed fingers through his hair and continued, "But now that it's dark and it's getting late and we're lost-"

"We're not lost," Lindsey interjected. She said it softly, careful to not sound confrontational. "We still have a plan and a destination. It's just taking a little longer than expected. But we'll get there. I promise."

Jim nodded and sucked in a deep breath.

"You gonna be okay?" she asked him.

"Yeah," Jim forced a smile. "Yeah, I'm okay."

Lindsey pulled him in for a hug. She wrapped her arms around his stiff torso and held him for a moment. Jim returned the hug with his left arm; his right still holding the shotgun. Pulling away, Lindsey gave him a peck on the cheek and said, "You've been doing great, Jim. Just hang in for a little longer and I promise everything's going to be fine."

She turned away and leaned into the car but didn't get inside. When she stood up again, Lindsey was holding the over-sized kitchen knife she had taken from the supermarket. She closed the car door and began making her way toward the entrance to the building.

"Where are you going?" Jim called after her.

"I'm going to look for food," Lindsey answered. "Remember?"

"Yeah, but I thought we'd go in together," Jim explained. "In case someone's in there. In case something happens."

"It'll be quicker this way," she told him, still walking toward the main door to the shop.

"Well, at least take the gun," he insisted.

"I'm okay. I've got this," she said, waving the blade in the air. "I'll be real quick- in and out."

"Alright," Jim sighed. "But Lindsey-"

"Yeah?" She stopped and turned to look back at him.

"The keys are in the ignition," he explained. "If anything happens, get back to the car and lock yourself inside."

Lindsey nodded her understanding.

"And if I'm not here- if something happens to me, just go. Get yourself out of here," he instructed.

"Okay," she replied. Lindsey glanced one way down the road and then the other. No movement, no sound. She took another step toward the entrance but Jim called to her once more.

"Just be careful, okay?" he implored. "Please."

She stopped moving and turned back to meet his eyes. In a firm, confident tone, Lindsey said, "I will."

Passably satisfied, Jim nodded and returned to the task at hand. He stepped forward to gingerly lean the gun against the car door. As he did this, Jim got his first good look at the state of his beloved automobile. The streaks of blood, the cracks in the windshield, the scraped paint, the dents in the hood, bumper, and fenders; the damage seemed to be magnified under the bright lights of the canopy.

"That's just perfect," he groaned. Jim picked up the gun and indelicately set in on the car's roof. *What's one more scratch,* he thought as he opened the fuel door and uncorked the gas cap.

Still moaning to himself about his car, his predicament, and his general inadequacies, Jim took the nozzle from its cradle and slid it into the coupe's filler neck. He squeezed the lever and groaned a little louder when he felt nothing happen. Jim looked back at the front face of the pump assembly and pressed the button for regular gas. Then he tried the button for mid-grade gas and then premium gas, squeezing the lever each time and getting no results.

He really should have known better. It had been years since he'd been to a gas station that trusted you to pump before you paid. Those might not even exist anymore. They were all prepay nowadays. And from the looks of the darkened, desolate store, no cashiers were hanging around to handle cash and program your fuel purchase.

That didn't necessarily mean that Jim was out of luck. These modern fueling stations gave motorists the option to pay at the pump. But would it still work? With radio broadcasts failing and cell phone service that was spotty at best, did that mean all communication services were out? Would the gas pump still have the connectivity required to authorize a credit card payment?

Of course he had to try. Jim reached both hands into his over-sized cargo pockets. A handful of loose shotgun shells were floating around in the right pocket but he easily found and retrieved his wallet from the opposite side. He removed his credit card and quickly slid it in and out of the card reader mounted to the front of the fuel pump. The LCD screen above it came to life and read, *Authorizing Payment,* in flat gray text. A thin wheel spun below it to give the impression that something was happening.

"Come on you son of a bitch," Jim mumbled. "Let's go."

Inside the convenience store, Lindsey held her knife at arm's-length in front of her as she moved slowly down the first main aisle. The back-up lighting on the far wall only illuminated a two-foot area around each lamp. It was enough to show where the emergency exits were located, but was basically useless for anyone trying to navigate through the store.

The store appeared to be empty so she let herself relax a little. Lindsey couldn't see much of anything more than a yard away but she figured that anyone lurking around in here probably would have charged her as soon as she'd passed through the doorway. Considering this in hindsight, she wished she'd have been a little more cautious when entering. Maybe she should have taken the shotgun with her, after all. But so far, so good.

Her next step landed on something thin and brittle that let out a crunch beneath her foot. Lindsey's heart skipped a beat at the sound, scared the noise might draw some unwanted attention. She crouched down to find a flattened heap of potato chips next to a torn-open wrapper.

Standing up, Lindsey used her free hand to pull her cell phone from her pocket. She switched on the screen and used it as a makeshift flashlight. Aiming the device at the shelves, Lindsey scanned their contents in hopes of finding something worth consuming. This first aisle was mainly filled with junk foods like chips, popcorn, and fried pork skins.

She turned around to check the shelves behind her and in doing so, found that the signal bars on her cell phone had returned. Situated next to them was a familiar icon. It was two small circles with a line connecting them at the bottom, apparently designed to resemble the spool of an audio tape or recording device. She had received a new voice mail.

Lindsey pressed the phone to her ear as she continued searching the row of shelves. It was mostly junk on this side too- mints, candy bars, gumdrops. Some of these would do in a pinch, but she decided to check the rest of the store before settling for sugary candy. Maybe there would be some fresh fruit or maybe they had one of those crappy spinning oven things with hot pizza inside. Not that

282

it would still be hot, but at least it would resemble real food.

Still moving down the aisle and still listening to her voice message, Lindsey took another step and felt her right foot clip something on the floor. She stumbled, more from surprise than anything else, but managed to keep herself upright. This particular hindrance was sturdier than the mound of potato chips and she could hear it slide a short distance across the tile floor.

Lindsey leaned down and aimed the screen of her phone in the general direction of the obstruction. Starting at her feet and working her way out, she waved the device back and forth in search of what she'd accidentally kicked and nearly tripped over.

The floor was littered with candy wrappers, crushed pretzels, and scattered trail mix. None of that was large enough to get her attention. She kept searching and in only a few short seconds, she found the offending object: a bare, severed human foot.

The skin was badly bruised and appeared gangrenous. Thick purple splotches covered most of the appendage. Droplets of rubbery blood clung to coarse dark toe hair. At the top, where an ankle should have been, was a jumble of loose skin that had been ripped in irregular patterns. Strands of muscle and tendon were left strewn over the top ridge of the wound.

Lindsey gasped at the horrible sight and did her best to keep from screaming. She was alone and exposed once again. Only this time, she was in the dark and in an unfamiliar place. Something terrible had happened here, just like everywhere else she'd gone. Why had she come here alone? Why on Earth hadn't she waited for Jim?

The panic was rising. A realization dawned on her and not for the first time that day- that she was not invincible. She was vulnerable. A brutal, agonizing death could be in store for her just as it had been for so many others. Her heart hammered in her chest. Her breathing became hurried and strained. A wave of dizziness washed over her, leaving a sour nausea in its wake.

A trembling possessed her hands. Lindsey was hyperventilating and needed to get control of herself. She closed her eyes and took one long deep breath in through her mouth, slowly exhaling through her nose. But the sound of heavy raspy breathing continued and was growing in volume.

She opened her eyes slowly and let her vision try to adjust to the low lighting. With her shaking hand, Lindsey lifted her cell phone and held it in front of her. The screen's faint glow illuminated a thick trail of clear and red saliva. A fat glob rolled over swollen lips and hit the tile floor with an audible splash. The next sound was that of teeth and snapping jaws, followed by the shuffling of feet over a trash-strewn floor.

Lindsey choked back another scream and took a step backwards. The ghoul was less than two feet away and with jerky, labored movements, it was slowly closing the short distance. The darkness kept her from making out much detail, but Lindsey had seen more than enough to know it was time to get out. Spinning on her heels, Lindsey turned and began to run but had the wind knocked out of her lungs after only two steps.

She'd collided with something heavy and solid, something that was biting absently in the air and reaching for her arm. The impact sent her knife and cell phone clattering to the floor. Gasping for breath, she ducked below the monster's groping hand. With blossoming dread, she desperately searched the area near her feet for her fallen weapon. Just as her fingertips brushed against its plastic handle, clammy fingers found the back of her head and clutched a handful of blonde hair. This time, Lindsey wasn't able to stifle her scream.

Chapter 43

"Where's Danny?" Lucy asked. Her words, when shouted like they were, sounded more like an accusation than a question. The young woman watched through the peephole, searching for a sign that her brother was okay. That nagging, stomach-churning sense of dread and anxiety- the one she felt every time she called her parents and got no answer, returned when she saw that only one person stood on the other side of the convex lens.

"He's coming. Can you let me in please?" By contrast, Jenna's voice was pleading and apologetic. Her tone instilled little confidence and Lucy wasn't moved to acquiesce.

"Where the Hell is he?" Lucy screamed this time. She pounded a fist on the door, "Where's my brother?"

"I told you. He's coming, alright?" Jenna looked over her shoulder. She was still alone in the stairwell. "Just please let me come inside."

He's coming? What the Hell was that supposed to mean? Why had they gotten separated? Had something happened to him? Jenna's strange and vague response had only raised more questions and did nothing to ease Lucy's concerns.

"Coming from where?" Lucy demanded. She did what she could to sound strong and assertive, though a trembling in her voice betrayed her rising panic.

"He was talking to Albert, he's in his apartment," Jenna said, raising her voice to make sure she could be heard through the wall.

"So why aren't you with him?" Lucy asked. "You just left him there?"

"No, er..." Jenna stammered. "He's fine. I can explain if you would just let me in."

"I'm not opening this door until I see Danny, and I-"

Crack! Lucy's words were cut off by an intense bang.

A loud metallic pop rang out from somewhere downstairs and caused both women to jump in alarm. It almost sounded like someone set off a firecracker in the lobby. Lucy, who flinched and ducked slightly, was glad that Jenna couldn't see how startled she'd been. She promptly composed herself and asked, "What was that?"

"There's a group of them outside," Jenna told her. "They're trying to break through the doors."

"Did they?" Lucy couldn't disguise the fear in her voice. "Did they get in?"

"Quiet," Jenna commanded. She turned to look down the stairway and listened for the sound of charging footsteps. Upon hearing none, Jenna said, "No. They're not inside. Not yet."

"Not yet?" Lucy echoed. "Are they going to get in?"

"Look," Jenna snapped, speaking directly into the peephole with more than a hint of urgency in her words. She couldn't make out anything through the dark round glass, but she knew Lucy was watching her from the other side. "I'm not having this conversation, not like this- not shouting through the wall. I'm happy to explain everything to you but you're going to have to open the door."

"Not until I-"

Another interruption, "What are you doing out here in the hall?"

Jenna turned to find Danny climbing the steps and coming up to meet her. She detected a slight tremble in his hands, which were both in front of him and carrying her gun. The machete was tucked through his belt like how a pirate might carry a sword.

"I thought you'd be inside," he commented.

"Your sister wouldn't open the door," Jenna explained, trying to sound calm and diplomatic since Lucy was probably still listening. "She said she wasn't going to let me in until she knew you were okay."

Danny's eyes narrowed. "Why wouldn't I be okay?"

Jenna just stared back at him and waited for Danny to connect the dots.

"Oh right- the zombies," he blurted; his eyes lighting in satisfaction with having solved the riddle. "Yeah, that makes sense. I'm okay though."

"Danny, is that you?" Lucy called through the door.

"Yep, it's me. Can you let us in please?"

Lucy finally complied. She unlocked the deadbolt and with a quick turn of the knob, the door opened. Duke immediately pushed past her. Pulling free from Jenna's grip on his leash, he trotted into the apartment and made himself at home. The old German Shepherd went straight into the kitchen, instinctively looking for a bowl of kibble. He sniffed the floor and around the legs of the table. There were so many unfamiliar scents in this place, strange food and something that reminded him of when he'd been sprayed by a skunk.

"Thank God you're okay," Lucy proclaimed. Stepping through the doorway and into the hall, she wrapped both arms around her brother.

Danny was still holding the rifle, so instead of hugging her back, he awkwardly shifted his arms to make sure the barrel was pointed away from her. Even with one ear pressed against her brother's chest, Lucy could hear the groans and growls echoing up the stairwell. Out here, the anthem of the plagued was too loud to ignore.

"We should get inside," Jenna said.

Lucy let go of her brother. She turned around and walked back through the doorway with the others following closely behind. Once they were all inside the apartment, Danny handed the rifle to Jenna. She took it into the kitchen and leaned it upright in the corner, making a point to check the safety before letting go.

Danny pulled the machete free from his belt, holding it in one hand as he pushed the door closed and engaged the deadbolt. He gave a quick tug on the knob just to make sure the entrance was secure before stepping into the kitchen and dropping the blade onto the table.

"How have you been holding up, Lucy?" Danny asked as he made his way into the living room. Then, after briefly considering, he added, "Ya know, relatively speaking."

"Alright I guess." Halfway into the living room, Lucy sighed as she flopped down onto the beanbag chair. "Relatively speaking."

"That's good," Danny replied. "Have you heard from mom and dad?"

Lucy's eyes went wide with optimism. "No, did you? Did they call you?"

"I'm afraid not," he admitted.

"Oh." Lucy slid further into her seat. "I tried calling but kept getting voice mail. I was kinda hoping that maybe they were out to dinner or something like that and just missed the calls."

Jenna joined them in the living room. She stood against the wall, about three feet from the main entrance and said, "There might be an issue with the cell phone service."

Lucy didn't reply.

"We'll keep trying," Danny told her, trying his best to sound reassuring as he walked toward the sliding glass door that led to the balcony. He stood at the edge of the doorway with the blinds pulled open in front of him.

Looking out over the parking lot, Danny could see nothing but bodies; the pavement invisible beneath a roiling blanket of lost humanity. There were hundreds, maybe a thousand ferocious, flesh-hungry barbarians eager to destroy everything in their path with no regard for their own corporeal shells. These bastards would gladly take a beating, have their bones broken and skin ripped apart, for just one fresh human morsel.

He looked down the block and across the street at the nearby structures, places of business and peoples' homes. They had windows smashed and doors kicked in. Some had lights on inside but most didn't. No movement could be detected, no signs of life. Each building had been picked clean by those savages. That's what this infection did. It destroyed everything, sparing nothing and no one.

And that's what they'll do here, Danny realized. The zombies below, they weren't going to give up and move on. They certainly weren't going to forget about the people hiding in the tenement. In fact, the opposite seemed to be true. More sprinters arrived every few minutes. They pushed past the shambling foot-draggers and fought for their place at the head of the pack. The fast ones were knocking each other over and climbing on top of one another.

At first it seemed like they were somehow getting taller, as preposterous as it sounds. While the low light made for a challenge, Danny was eventually able to see what was happening. It was similar to what he and Jenna had seen in the lobbies. Individual bodies were pinned against the doors and walls, unable to move under the weight of a thousand others pressed against them. This must be happening on the pavement as well; one of them is knocked to the ground and the brute behind him takes his place, right on top of him.

While some of the slow-movers would tire out and fall to the ground on their own, the quicker pricks weren't kind enough or patient enough to wait for it to happen organically. They clawed, pulled, and shoved at each other, forging a path for themselves and upending anyone in their way. As this process was repeated, more and more bodies would stack up on one another to form a growing mound of immobilized carcasses.

The other ghouls could then use them as a stepladder as they climbed higher and higher up the walls of the building, bringing themselves closer to the next point of entry. As Danny watched through the glass door, the first zombie of the group had gotten high enough off the ground to make it onto the balcony below his own. It was a thin male zombie that still had use of his adrenal glands and appeared to be mostly intact.

He tumbled over the railing head-first. A dull thud shook the wall as he landed hard on his ass. The son of a bitch jumped to his feet, knocking over a plastic lawn chair and small glass table. Reaching overhead, the infected man grabbed for the floor of Danny's balcony. He failed to get a grip on his first try but it wasn't time to give up just yet. On his second attempt, the freak lost his footing and fell backwards over the railing, landing somewhere amongst the ghouls on the ground.

This seemed to inspire confidence in the rest of the group, especially those closest to the building. The crowd appeared more energized, more determined to reach their target. Two more were already inches away from reaching the top of the railing to the first-floor balcony.

"Jenna, I think we're going to need that gun," Danny said.

"Why?" Jenna asked as she moved closer to where he was standing. "What's happening?"

"They're climbing on each other," Danny told her. "One of them already got onto Jim's balcony. I was thinking we should be ready to take them out in case they get up here."

"Jim? Is he the one who lives downstairs?" Lucy asked. She was still sitting on the beanbag chair, but had swiveled around to face the front of the room.

Danny nodded.

"He's not home though," Jenna said. "Is he?"

"Nope," Danny told her. "He didn't answer the door and his car's been gone all day."

"For his sake, I hope he's a long way from here by now," Jenna added. She stood at the opposite end of the doorway from Danny, holding the blinds to one side so she could see out.

"Were you able to lock the doors downstairs?" Lucy asked. "Or block them off somehow?"

"We were able to tie them closed," Jenna explained. "We found some cables in the basement and wrapped them around the handles so the doors can't be pulled open."

"Okay, good." Lucy slouched in her seat and appeared to relax momentarily. She quickly sat upright again, growing rigid as she spoke. "And it's holding up okay? There's no way they can be pulled apart?"

"The zombies were pushing instead of pulling," Danny said. "The cords will probably be fine, so long as the doors themselves hold up."

"And are they holding up?" Lucy asked.

"Yeah," Danny answered. "Well, mostly."

Lucy and Jenna both glared at him expectantly.

"When I was coming back upstairs," Danny began, "It looked like the door frames were bending in a little bit, starting to pull away from the wall. The glass parts looked okay, but there's definitely some damage to the metal part near the hinges."

"Shit!" Lucy exclaimed. "I thought you said-"

"Relax," Danny cut her off. "The doorways are still sealed off. I think they'll need a lot more weight pushing against the doors to actually knock them down."

"But what if they do?" Lucy demanded. "What if they do get in- then what?"

"Even if they get through the doors downstairs, which isn't going to happen, they still can't get in here," Danny said. He motioned to the main door to the apartment, "They won't be able to knock that one down."

"And how do you know that?" Lucy asked. She stood up from the chair and began pacing the

287

living room floor.

"There's got to be a thousand of them out there, right?" Danny paused but no one said anything. "So even with all of them pushing against the doors, they haven't been able to get in. But let's say they do somehow manage to get inside, how many do you think would fit in that little hallway out there? Ten? Maybe fifteen? It's going to take more than the weight of fifteen bodies to push through this door."

"He's probably right," Jenna chimed in.

"Right," spat Lucy. "But that's still a pretty shitty spot to be in. With those things surrounding the building, filling the hallways and stairwell, there's nowhere for us to go. You realize we're trapped in here. We're as good as dead."

"Take it easy," Jenna told her. "That's the worst-case scenario. And even then, as long as they're out there and we're in here, we're safe. Eventually, they'll have to move on."

"You sure about that?" asked Danny.

"Pretty sure," said Jenna. "I know it seems like they've been out there a long time, but they will eventually get bored or distracted. We'll just have to wait them out."

"Alright, alright," Lucy relented. She stopped pacing and flopped down onto the sofa. "Maybe we'll get lucky and someone will drive by and catch their attention, lead them away."

"I haven't seen any cars go by in a while," Danny told her. "But you're right, that would probably do the trick. They could at least draw some of them away. Or run some of them over."

"That reminds me," Jenna said, turning to Danny. "If Jim is still alive, he's better off not coming home. Even if he made it back here, he wouldn't be able to get in. Maybe you should try calling him again, let him know it's not safe to come here."

"Sure," Danny agreed as he reached into his pocket for his cell phone.

"But before you do that," Lucy said. "Could one of you please tell me why there's a dog in the apartment?"

Chapter 44

Jim was out by the gas pump when he heard the shriek. He dropped his wallet and snatched the shotgun from the roof of his car as he sprinted for the building. The door flung open and Jim burst into the store with the gun raised in front of him.

"Lindsey?" he cried.

The sound of scuffling feet and shaking display racks led him right to her. She was on her back in the center aisle, besieged by a duo of the damned. One of the zombies was on its knees and leaning over her. Lindsey had her hands pressed into his shoulders, keeping the savage at arms-length so his snapping teeth couldn't reach her skin. The other was down by her feet, getting kicked in the knees and hips every time it tried to get closer.

"Jim!" she hollered. "I'm here."

"Stay down," he commanded, taking a few steps toward her. Jim aimed the shotgun at the bastard grappling with Lindsey's ankles and said, "Keep your feet down!"

She gave the brute one final kick to the groin before lying her legs flat against the ground. The fiend stumbled backwards but didn't go down. Before the creep could take his next step, Jim squeezed the trigger. The barrel roared as it sprayed a few hundred pellets into the zombie's chest. The broken-hearted hellion collapsed into a mangled heap, sprinkled with chunks of nougat and candy wrappers. Jim was on to the second infected prick while the first was still twitching.

He grabbed the beast by the back of his collar and gave it a yank. Jim kept pulling until the dickhead was completely off of Lindsey. The freak's feet came out from under him and his rump hit the floor. Now free from the monster's grip, Lindsey scurried away, moving farther down the aisle and deeper into the darkness.

The ghoul reached over his shoulder and behind his neck, trying to get a hold of Jim. Once he was confident that Lindsey was out of harm's way, Jim released the zombie's collar and pressed the shotgun barrel to the back of his head.

"Lindsey, where are you?" he called into the shadows. Jim could hear her moving about, but it was impossible to tell where she had gone.

"Right here," she answered through a wheeze, struggling to catch her breath and to keep her heart from exploding in her chest. Her voice came from behind him and to his left. Jim still couldn't see her but she was definitely not in the line of fire.

"Plug your ears," he said mere seconds before pulling the trigger and sending a hailstorm of brain and skull fragments all over the snack aisle. The absent-minded ghoul fell flat on his back. A pool of red fluid poured out from the gaping hole at the top of his throat.

"You good?" Jim called out.

"I'm okay," Lindsey answered. "Don't shoot, it's me- I'm coming over."

"I'm out," he said. Jim switched the top lever to eject the spent shells from the shotgun and reached into his cargo pocket for two more. He slid them into the chamber and slammed the barrel closed just as Lindsey came up beside him.

"Hey," Jim said to her. "Are you alright? You didn't get-"

Without speaking, Lindsey threw her arms around him and squeezed as tight as she could. Jim returned the hug with his left arm while his right hand held the gun at his side. They held each other for several moments without saying a word. Lindsey's chest heaved against his, struggling to regain her breath and holding on to Jim as though he was the only thing keeping her tethered to the Earth.

Jim softly rubbed her back and let his fingers roll down her spine. After a few more seconds, Lindsey loosened her embrace. She leaned back but didn't let go; her belly and hips still pressed against his. Her hands moved from his back, over his sides and up to his shoulders. She tilted her head back and even though it was too dark to see, she knew Jim was looking right into her eyes. Lindsey grabbed him tighter, pulled him in closer. She leaned forward and pressed her lips against his.

A flash of confusion left Jim thinking that she had probably just bumped into him by accident. But she didn't pull away. Her grasp on his shoulders tightened. Jim could feel the muscles in her back relax as he returned the kiss. He began to melt, overtaken by a combination of relief and excitement. Their tongues met and Jim's hand found the back of her head; his fingers stroking her silky blonde hair.

He took her by the waist; his fingertips gripping the small of her back. Lindsey stroked the back of his head and combed fingers through his hair. Now they were both breathing heavily. It felt like they were teenagers again, hiding behind the theater after a movie had finished, sneaking away to make out before one of their parents showed up to drive them home.

Jim pulled her in closer, their hips pressed firmly together. His free hand slid the rest of the way down her back and onto her ass. Jim began to crouch so he could place the gun on the floor. That way, he'd have use of both hands. Lindsey stopped him with a hand to his chest before he got that far.

"We should get out of here," she said.

"Yeah," Jim agreed. "That's probably a good idea."

"I mean, not that this isn't terribly romantic," she added with a smirk that was hidden by the darkness. "Nothing gets a girl in the mood like being attacked by cannibals."

"I thought that would turn you on," Jim joked. "But seriously, please be more careful. We really shouldn't go wandering off by ourselves if we can help it."

"I know, I know," Lindsey sighed. "I thought the store was empty and I let my guard down. And then I got distracted and..."

"Got distracted?" Jim echoed. "By what?"

"I was using my ph-" Whack!

A thump ripped through the shadows, cutting her off before she could explain any further. Jim and Lindsey both jumped at the sudden interruption. It first sounded like something inside the store had toppled over, a display case or cooler- something heavy and solid. But the strikes continued and the two nighttime travelers soon realized that someone was trying to break in through the front door. Lacking the wit to negotiate a door that needed to be pulled rather than pushed, a fresh adrenaline-fueled flesh junkie pounded blood-encrusted fists against the outside of the store's main entrance.

"The gunshots must have drawn them here," Jim said. He took the shotgun in both hands and moved toward the front of the store. "Shit, we really gotta go."

"They're already here," Lindsey blurted, reiterating the obvious. "What are we going to do?"

"There's only one out there," Jim told her as he approached the doorway.

On the other side of the glass stood a thick-necked ghoul in a torn flannel shirt. The ogre let out a predatory scream as it caught sight of Jim. His mouth opened to reveal that most of his upper teeth were missing, as was his right ear. Pulsing streams of red fluid leaked from his mouth and the side of his head. The infected aggressor smashed both hands against the door, leaving wet pink smears across the translucent barrier.

"Stay back and get ready to run to the car," Jim shouted to Lindsey as he raised the shotgun and pressed the barrel to the glass.

He didn't wait for a response before pulling the trigger and vaporizing some gray matter. Blood, brains, and shattered glass exploded into the parking lot, forming a crystal-covered streak across the pavement. The headless horror crumpled to the ground in a lifeless twitching mound of meat.

Jim slammed his shoulder into the metal door frame and called over his shoulder, "Now- Let's go!"

The stubborn skin sack blocked the door so it would only open about a foot and a half but it was enough for Jim to squeeze through. Fallen chunks of glass crunched beneath his sneakers as he stepped outside. Gun raised, Jim moved to the side so Lindsey could make her way through the doorway.

Zombies were coming from all directions, from the side street to Jim's right, from between the duplexes across the street, from the alleyway off to the left side of the store. Some staggered, clumsy and slow, while others moved with astonishing speed. Onrushing zombies had already crossed the street and were closing in.

"Get in the car!" Jim screamed, spinning to his left and pulling the trigger again. The shotgun sprayed buckshot at another sprinting zombie who'd gotten within twenty feet of his beheaded companion.

Lindsey bolted past the pair of corpses and raced toward the Pontiac. Jim was close behind, pausing only long enough to eject the last two rounds from the shotgun. He had caught up to Lindsey by the time the plastic casings hit the ground. Still moving as he loaded the next two shells, Jim swung the barrel to his right and aimed it in the direction of heavy footsteps slapping concrete. He fired again, hitting another rabid freak and tearing a hole from his chest to his pelvis.

The boom of the gun- so close, unexpected. Lindsey couldn't help but yelp in surprise. Jim, thinking she'd been attacked, spun back to his left, ready to keep firing. He kept searching with the nose of the shotgun until it found two gore-soaked goons coming from between a pair of gas pumps and threatening to intercept Lindsey before she made it to the car. Another gunshot rang out.

Steel pellets hit one would-be assailant in the chest, dropping him. The other one got clipped in the shoulder. His right arm slumped and flailed around as the brute continued his pursuit. With one less hand pumping for momentum, the son of a bitch lost a step and slowed down just enough to give Jim time to adjust his grip on his weapon.

When the infected attacker took another four steps, Jim swung the shotgun like a baseball bat. The twin steel barrels cut through the air and connected with an audible crack of splitting skin and snapping bone. A growl escaped the ghoul's battered lips as the left side of its jaw caved in. The impact of the blow twisted the zombie's head to the side and it began to collapse; a stream of blood trailing as it fell to the ground. Jim left the prick sprawled out on the oil-stained cement and hustled to escort Lindsey the rest of the way to the car.

She shut herself inside and waved to Jim through the window, urging him to get in quickly. Lindsey screamed from inside the coupe, "Jim, let's go!"

While the dozens of approaching zombies might disagree, she was right. It was time to go. Jim worked the top lever of the firearm, ejecting the two spent cartridges. He didn't bother reloading this time. He was close enough to the car to get in without firing another shot. The door flung open and he tossed the weapon onto the back seat before climbing in and pulling the door shut. Jim started the engine and slammed the gear shifter into drive.

Before it even began to move, the Pontiac was surrounded by six infected combatants. The engine revved and the coupe lurched forward, pulling away from the fuel pumps and leaving the shitheads in a cloud of gray exhaust. Jim cut the wheel and drove toward the parking lot's exit where three more plague-carriers were waiting for him.

"Hang on," he said just before punching the gas pedal. The car jumped forward and drove through the small horde, leaving behind a twisted and mangled mess of broken bodies strewn across the driveway.

Jim pulled out of the parking lot and turned left, driving back toward the church they had passed earlier. He watched in the rear-view mirror as some of the gas station fiends gave chase. In under a minute, there was sufficient distance between the car and the ghouls to render them harmless. Once more, Jim and Lindsey were on the move; back on the road, running low on both fuel and options.

"Were you able to fill up before, um... before my incident in the store?" asked Lindsey after they'd traveled six or seven blocks.

"Uh," Jim stammered, avoiding eye contact. "Not exactly."

"Oh," she said. "Sorry about that, by the way. How much were you able to get?"

"Um..." he replied with a telling glance to the gauge cluster.

"Jim?"

He paused for a moment, taking a deep breath before answering. "None."

"None?" she asked. "What do you mean?"

"I couldn't get the pump to work," he explained. Jim brought the car to a stop and put it in park. "It was prepay. I tried using a credit card, but it wouldn't go through."

"Did it get declined?" Lindsey pressed.

"No, it wasn't declined," Jim answered. His tone was a little more defensive than he'd meant. "The screen just kept saying, 'Processing,' like it couldn't make a connection. But I guess that makes sense, given there's no cell service."

"There is some cell service," she corrected him. "I mean, here and there. It sorta comes and goes I guess."

"I guess I haven't really been paying attention for a while," he responded.

"Yeah, me neither. But I was using my phone as a makeshift flashlight inside the store. When the screen came on, it said I had a voicemail." Lindsey patted her pockets, remembering too late that she'd dropped her cell phone. She hadn't gone back to collect it after getting attacked in the convenience store. Lindsey cursed silently and continued, "That's how I got distracted. I was listening to the message when they snuck up on me."

"Oh," Jim replied. He wanted to ask who had called but thought that maybe he shouldn't. Maybe he didn't want to find out. If it was important for him to know, she would tell him. Until then, it would remain a nervous curiosity.

"So," Lindsey began after another moment of awkward silence. "How much gas does that leave us with?"

"Just under a quarter tank."

"Shit," she huffed.

"Yeah," he agreed.

"Maybe we'll find another gas station," Lindsey suggested with forced optimism. "Maybe one that's not prepay, or one with the card reader working."

Jim shook his head. "Too risky. What if we run out of gas before that happens?"

"Yeah, that's a good point." She dropped her face in her hands and rubbed her temples with the tips of her fingers. "Alright, so what are we going to do?"

Jim gripped the steering wheel with both hands. He stretched, arching his back and pressing his shoulder blades into the seat cushion. Drawing in a long breath, he braced himself for an argument and said, "I've got enough gas to get us back to my place."

Lindsey lifted her face from her hands and looked over at him. Before she had a chance to speak, Jim continued to plead his case. "It's the only place I know I can get into- and one of the few places we've got enough gas to get to. The apartment is up off the ground, so it'll be real hard for anyone to get in unless we want them in. We can drive back the same way we came, so we know it's safe- as safe as it's going to get. I know it's not what you wanted to hear, but I'm really at a loss. At this point, I don't know where else to go and even if I did, I doubt we'd have enough gas to get there. I mean, maybe we'll find something better along the way, but-"

"Let's do it," she cut in. With a slight shake of her head, Lindsey added, "You're right. And we should've just done that in the first place."

"Oh," Jim said with his eyebrows raised. He'd expected a little more resistance.

"I shouldn't have given you such a hard time about it," she admitted. "I just, ya know..."

"I know. It's okay," he said gently. Jim lifted his hand to take hers but hesitated before making contact. Self-conscious, he let the arm fall back to its position on the center console.

Jim reached for the gear selector and put the car in drive. He waited a few seconds with his foot still on the brake pedal, and then slid the shifter forward to put it in park again. He gave a quick glance to each mirror and peered down the road as far as his headlights could reach. Seeing that the coast was clear for the moment, Jim turned in his seat to face Lindsey and said, "I killed someone too."

"Huh?" Lindsey wore a puzzled expression and said, "Yeah Jim, I know. I was there for some of them- as recent as like two minutes ago."

"Um, right," he stammered. "I meant, I also had to kill someone I knew, someone I had gotten sort of close to."

"Oh. I didn't realize," replied Lindsey. "Who was it?"

"My cousin Mark," Jim told her. "His girlfriend was at Uncle Ted's house when I went to get the shotgun."

"Oh my God," she said with effortless sympathy. "I'm so sorry Jim, I had no idea. Was anyone else there?"

Jim nodded. "My aunt was there and I think my uncle was somewhere in the house but I didn't see him. Someone was upstairs on the second floor but I didn't go up to check."

"Your aunt," she gasped. "Did you...?"

Too afraid of what she might hear, Lindsey let her words trail off before completing her question. Jim shook his head. "No. But it was too late for her anyway."

"Infected?"

"Yeah," he sighed.

"Shit." Lindsey reached over the console and took both of his hands in hers. "I'm so sorry. Why didn't you say anything?"

"I guess I probably felt the same way you did," he explained. "I mean, would you have wanted to talk about Lance just moments later?"

"No, probably not." Lindsey gave Jim a warm smile, touched that he remembered his name. She let go of his hands and began to nudge his arm off the console, telling him, "Scooch."

Jim did as he was instructed and slid over. Lindsey opened the lid to the small storage space and found his half-empty pack of cigarettes. She took one out and felt around for a lighter.

"No thanks," Jim told her, holding a hand up. "I'm okay."

"This one's for me, actually," she said with an expression that asked for permission. "A little something for the nerves."

"I see," he replied. "In that case, I suppose I should probably have one too."

Lindsey lit two cigarettes and passed one to Jim. She opened the window and blew out a big cloud of smoke, settling into her seat and pulling the safety belt over her shoulder.

"Alright. I guess we should get going," Jim said, exhaling a sizable puff of his own.

"Yes we should," Lindsey agreed. She looked over, locking eyes with him and said, "Let's go home."

Chapter 45

Thanks to the gas station fiasco, Jim and Lindsey hadn't made it much farther than the southernmost terminus of Eggert Road. Now they were driving back the way they had come. This of course meant they would once again drive past the church on the corner; the church whose brick exterior, stained glass, and inviting entryway remained totally unscathed.

Approaching it from the opposite angle allowed Jim an unobstructed view of the structure's left, front, and right sides. There were still no fiends lurking about, no broken windows, no smashed-in doorways. More like a fortress than a place of worship, the church seemed to possess a strength; something powerful keeping all things dangerous at a safe distance.

Jim knew that was silly. It was, after all, just a building. But it was the only building in the neighborhood that had been spared by the day's events. And it wasn't just free from damage. The property looked pristine. The massive silver cross mounted to the roof seemed to glow in the light of the moon. The trim along the doorway shimmered, polished and clean. The statue on the lawn appeared milky white and flawless. Even the landscaping, blossoming flowers and meticulously pruned shrubbery, remained without a blemish.

There was still something appealing about this place, something that seemed to draw him in. Jim once again felt tempted to make the case for stopping and going inside. He knew in a way he couldn't articulate that he and Lindsey would be safe here. No harm would come to them in the church, just as no harm had come to the church itself. He also knew that there would be no convincing her. For this reason, and since she had finally agreed to come back to his place with him, Jim kept driving and passed by the church without saying a word.

In no time at all, the traveling couple found themselves turning left and heading north on the carrion causeway known as Eggert Road. The trouble at the gas pump had reignited Jim's fuel-based anxieties. The Pontiac should have plenty of juice to get them back to town, but that wouldn't keep him from nervously checking the fuel gauge every few seconds.

His eagerness to get home continued to outweigh his fear of an empty gas tank. Now that he was familiar with the path, and aggravated at having to traverse it for a second time, Jim smashed the accelerator with little hesitation. He sped past houses, the cemetery, and that strange institutional-style building in a hurry to be done with this doomed road trip. Now that they had finally settled on a legitimate and reachable destination, he could do just that in less than an hour.

Never mind that Jim had suggested this a number of times, only to have his plan dismissed and replaced with some cockamamie scheme to get out of town which only served to waste time, burn fuel, and put their lives in further danger. It had been a rough go, but Jim knew that he and Lindsey had been luckier and more successful than many others. Everywhere he looked, there was something to remind him of his good fortune.

Every mound of rotting flesh, half-eaten corpse, and drying puddle of blood left Jim feeling grateful. Grateful to still be among the living, that is. And now, despite their failed attempt to flee to the safety and seclusion of the Allegany woods, there was finally something to look forward to.

There was still a ways to go and Jim always did a good job of making sure he never felt too comfortable or optimistic about anything. There was still a decent chance they could be killed, eaten, or become infected. The car could break down- when was the last time it had been tuned up? Or they could get a flat tire, there were plenty of toppled street signs and broken glass in the road. And at any moment, without warning, they could find themselves surrounded by an army of cannibal commandos.

Jim wasn't the only one enjoying an unyielding fit of anxiety. Lindsey's mind also filled with thoughts of what potential trouble may lie ahead. She kept a vigilant eye on the path ahead and behind. Twice she could have sworn she'd seen a pair of headlights reflecting off the side-view mirror but when she turned back to look, there was nothing there. She would then go back to watching for ghouls and other perils of the road.

The ride was quiet for the next mile or so. Neither Jim nor Lindsey had much to say and the only sound was that of crackling static from the car's speakers as Lindsey periodically scanned the radio stations trying to find a live broadcast. She'd made it up and down the AM dial and was now starting to scan the FM stations. After two presses of the seek button, Lindsey felt the car begin to slow. She looked up to find that they were back on the bridge over the Kensington Expressway.

"What's the matter?" she asked. "Why are we stopping?"

"I just need to check on something," Jim told her, sliding the gear shifter to park and grabbing for the door handle. "I'll only be a second."

"What do you need to check on?" she demanded. "That idiot from earlier? The one with a shotgun and a death wish?"

Jim was already out of the car and quickly walking toward the ledge. Lindsey unfastened her seat belt and began to follow him out. She flung the door open and reached between the seat and center console. Finding nothing, Lindsey felt around on the floor in front of her and then under the seat and beside it. Then she remembered. The knife was gone. She had left it, along with her cell phone, back at the convenience store.

"Shit," she murmured as she pulled herself out of the car and hustled over to join Jim. "Do you see anything?"

"Um. Sort of," he replied, peering over the metal barrier. "Nothing moving though."

Lindsey slid in next to him and looked down at the roadway below. There were still a few street lamps working. They were probably the same ones that were on earlier but she couldn't be sure. The light was adequate to illuminate more than she cared to see.

Corpses- probably thirty or more, were piled up between two rows of parked cars and the whole scene was awash in blood. Vehicles had been pushed into one another and left with shattered windows and craggy dents. Body panels were dotted with countless puncture holes from multiple shotgun blasts. The gun itself lie on the cement, encased in a purple-red crust between a smashed-up sedan and a minivan with its roof caved in.

"Do you think he made it out?" asked Lindsey.

"Well, the Jeep is gone," he told her. "So that's a good sign."

"That's true," she agreed. "Where would he have gone though?"

"That's a good question," said Jim. "I'm kind of surprised we haven't run into him. Or anyone, for that matter."

"I'm sure we will," Lindsey said, trying to sound comforting. "I mean, if not the Jeep guy, then we're bound to run into somebody at some point."

"I hope so," he replied. Walking back to the car, Jim added, "I hope to God there's more survivors than what we've seen. I mean, we don't know how far this thing has spread."

"It's only been a day." Lindsey made her way around the back of the coupe toward the passenger's side. She climbed in and closed the door. "I mean, it probably first appeared in a hospital or something, right? How far could it have gone from there?"

"Who knows," Jim shrugged. "This infection or disease or whatever it is- it has basically ravaged Western New York in about ten hours or so. It seems to travel pretty quickly and when you consider how many people are in and out of Buffalo on planes and buses and trains, it seems like it could have gotten all over the place by now."

"I don't think so," Lindsey argued. "Once news of this got out, they'd be watching the flights and trains out of here, keeping an eye out for people with symptoms. I'm sure they've got the airports and stuff locked down pretty tight."

"That's good for everywhere else," he observed. "Not so much for everyone left behind, assuming there is anyone left behind. Aside from us, that is."

"It couldn't have gotten everyone," Lindsey contended. As Jim reached for the gear shifter, she grabbed him by the hand and said, "There's more people out there. I'm sure of it."

How could she be so certain? Jim wondered if it had something to do with that voice message she'd received. But true to his spineless nature, he wouldn't ask. He just put the car in gear and continued driving. Jim knew they would learn the full extent of the devastation soon enough.

"Although," he wondered aloud. "How do we know it started here? We've been assuming that it must have started somewhere in Buffalo but how do we know that's what happened? It probably could have started anywhere. And it could therefore be anywhere. Or everywhere."

Lindsey shook her head. "No way. We definitely would have heard about it if it had started somewhere else."

"Yeah. I suppose," said Jim. He was not convinced.

They continued to make decent time on the drive back to town and it was beginning to seem like their cataclysmic commute would soon be over. Jim considered the potential end of civilization and tried to solve the case of Lindsey's secret voice mail, while she watched out the window and occasionally worked the radio controls. The next fifteen minutes seemed to fly by. Before they knew it, the young travelers were back where they had been hours earlier, on Colvin Boulevard.

Kenney Field was approaching on their right and there was a row of duplexes to their left. Apart from the specific buildings and individual landmarks, the landscape here looked no different from anywhere else they had been so far. The state of other vehicles had become a reliable barometer by which the trauma and impact of the outbreak could be measured. There were a few abandoned cars, mostly along the curb with doors left open. A pickup truck had been parked on a lawn where a pair of deep tire grooves in the grass came to an end.

Someone had wrapped the front end of their Buick around a lamp post. Its driver's side headlight lie in shattered pieces in front of it. The car's tan bumper had become detached but remained suspended above the ground, pinned between the car's radiator and the steel beam which had brought it to a sudden and violent stop. Jim tried to sneak a peek inside as they cruised by. The driver's seat was vacant but the passenger's seat remained occupied. The stiffened body of a man sat hunched forward with his face resting on the dashboard.

In addition to the vehicles, there were several other clues to indicate things had gone terribly awry. A lawnmower had been left unattended in the middle of a yard. Front doors were left open. Windows had been smashed. A pond of bright red fluid had formed on one of the driveways in front of a two-family home. Other, smaller puddles of blood were spilled on sidewalks and left to dry in the sun. All of these things had become commonplace in the last few hours but there was one thing that struck Jim as odd.

"There's no one around," he observed out loud. "No one who's alive, I mean. Or infected, from the looks of it."

Lindsey glanced up from the radio to have a look around. "That's gotta be a good sign, right?"

"Could be," Jim said with a bit of hesitation.

"Maybe your neighborhood didn't get hit so hard. Maybe things are starting to die down." Lindsey's tone betrayed a cautious optimism. She sat upright, brushed back a few loose strands of blonde hair, and said, "How far to your place?"

"About a half a mile," he answered.

Lindsey let out a long breath and sat back in her seat. She watched the big open field pass by on her right with nobody else in sight. It was calm. It felt like normal, like everything was going to be okay again. She allowed herself to relax and couldn't help but smile. Lindsey looked over at Jim and said, "You did it."

"Huh?" Jim asked as he hazarded a glance in her direction.

"You got us to safety," she told him. "Just like you said you would."

Jim felt a tug on his right hand. It was Lindsey and she was lifting his hand off of the gear shifter. He lifted and turned his wrist so his palm was facing up. She brushed her fingertips over his skin and slid her fingers between his. Lindsey wrapped her digits over Jim's knuckles and squeezed. Jim squeezed back and she softly rubbed her thumb along the side of his hand.

"Can I ask you a favor?" Lindsey inquired.

"Um, sure," Jim replied.

"Once we get to your place, would it be alright if I took a shower and maybe borrowed some clothes?"

"Of course," he answered. Jim pressed down on the gas pedal. Imagining Lindsey in the shower, in *his* shower, before toweling off and sliding into one of his old tee-shirts and a pair of pajama pants made him even more anxious to get home. Maybe he'd even be able to score himself another grab of her tush before the night was through. "I'm sure I've got some clothes that'll fit you. But ya know, don't expect to look as attractive and stylish in them as I do."

"Oh, I know," she chuckled. "I've seen the way you fill out a hoodie and sweatpants. How could I ever compete with that?"

"Now let me ask you this," Jim began. "Now that you'll know where I live, once this all blows over, do you think you'll want to come back at some point to, ya know, hang out or have more showers or whatever?"

"You are so silky smooth," Lindsey said sarcastically, rolling her eyes. But she wasn't really annoyed. "I'm sure I can find some time for you. You did save my life and all that, so I suppose it's the least I could do."

"You're so gracious," he prodded playfully. Jim let go of the steering wheel so he could scratch an itch on his neck with his left hand. This way, he wouldn't have to let go of Lindsey. He didn't want to let go, and he'd try like Hell to make sure he'd never have to.

"So, this is probably going to sound pretty strange, considering everything that's happening, but this is nice." Lindsey pulled Jim's hand onto her lap. She placed her right hand on top of his and added, "I like this."

A somewhat puzzled Jim looked out the left side window and saw the upper half of a man lying across the threshold to the front entrance of a house. The screen door had been torn from its hinges and the heavy wooden door was wide open. An oozing stream of blood covered the stoop and trickled down the cement steps in front of him. The man didn't move.

"Sure," Jim finally said with a hint of a grin. "What's not to like?"

"You know what I mean," she objected.

"I know, I know." He looked her in the eye and said, "I like this too."

"So, I know it didn't sound like it earlier, but I'm glad we decided to go to your place," Lindsey admitted. "I think we're going to be okay."

Jim paused for a moment to consider. He returned his eyes to the road in front of him, staring straight ahead. "Yeah, I think so too," came his eventual response; the words robotic and unconvincing. Jim knew better than to allow himself to be hopeful. After all, they weren't in the clear quite yet. Even if they do get back to the apartment and manage to get inside, what then? If he had his druthers, Jim knew exactly what would come next.

They'd take turns in the shower and he would offer her a clean pair of pajamas. He'd make dinner for her and she'd thank him with a kiss. And after they'd finished their meal, they'd snuggle up on the couch for some TV before bed.

Jim would offer the bed to Lindsey and say he'll sleep on the sofa- he didn't mind, he slept there most nights anyway. But Lindsey would insist he sleep next to her and Jim would oblige. He'd pull her closer, holding her and protecting her while she slept. She'd ask him not to let go, to stay with her no matter what. And he would.

Lindsey would lie her head on Jim's chest. She would look into his eyes and smile. They'd say how thankful they were to have found one another and how relieved they were to have gotten through such terrible events. Lindsey would say that she could never have done it without him. Jim would caress her skin and comb fingers through her silky hair. He'd tell her she was all that kept him going.

They would make plans for tomorrow. And the next day, and the day after that. They would spend every day together. Life would carry on. Jim and Lindsey would be as one; their affection growing stronger as time marched forward.

"We fit together so perfectly. Like two pieces of a puzzle," she would say. And they would both slide into the calm serenity of a peaceful sleep, wrapped in each other's embrace. Their most beautiful dreams would still fall short of their new life. A life together.

The car had reached the edge of Kenney Field. They'd driven past the now-abandon video store and were coming up to the newly-trashed coffee shop. They were so close. They were almost home.

Chapter 46

"That's Duke," Danny told her, as if that explained everything.

"Okay," Lucy replied. "And why is he here? Doesn't he belong to someone? Won't his owner be looking for him?"

"He's Albert's dog," Danny said. "You know Albert, right?"

Lucy answered with a blank stare.

"Albert," Danny repeated. "Adam's dad."

Lucy shook her head and shrugged her shoulders.

Danny thought for a moment and added, "The old German guy from the other side of the building."

"Polish," Jenna corrected. She pulled out a chair from the kitchen table and took a seat.

"Polish?" Danny asked. "Really? Are you sure?"

"Yeah, I'm sure." Jenna tapped her knee and motioned for Duke to come join her.

"But if he's Polish, then why does he have a *German* Shepherd?" Danny asked.

Jenna rolled her eyes. Duke was now sitting in front of her, panting softly as Jenna stroked the fur on his head and neck. "I guess the pet store was out of Polish shepherds."

Danny chuckled. "A Polish shepherd, do they even make those?"

"Hey!" Lucy snapped. "Can we get back to my question please?"

"Right- sorry," said Danny. "The dog's name is Duke and he belongs to Albert. He asked us to look after him."

"Okay," Lucy replied. "I know it seems like I'm asking a ton of questions, but why did he ask you to do that? I mean, how long is he supposed to stay here? Why can't Albert look after him?"

Danny and Jenna looked to one another and shared a knowing glance. Neither one of them wanted to lie to Lucy but they also didn't want to have to tell her the truth. They silently agreed that it would be best not to mention the infected person in the basement and their elderly suicidal neighbor. This news would only serve to upset Lucy even more than she already had been.

"Hello?" Lucy called from the next room. "Is someone going to fill me in?"

Another moment passed before Danny finally spoke. "Albert's an older guy, he doesn't get around too well. With all the stuff that's going on, he thought it would be better if we took care of Duke for a while."

It was a weak story and Lucy wasn't buying it. She looked first to Danny and then to Jenna for clarification. When it was apparent no further explanation was coming, Lucy said, "It's not like he's going anywhere. If he's just locked up in his apartment, why would he need you to take his dog? It doesn't make sense."

"Alright," Danny began, but he was cut off before he could continue.

"Danny!" Jenna called to him. The loudness of her voice startled Duke. He walked away and sat down on the other side of the kitchen.

"There's no sense lying to her about it," Danny argued. "It won't change anything. Not for us or anyone else."

"You're starting to freak me out." Lucy slid forward to the edge of the couch. "Not that I wasn't thoroughly freaked out to begin with."

"Okay," Danny started. "But I want you to remember we're still safe in here. Nobody's getting in and there's nothing to worry about."

He paused for a moment and considered. "Well, nothing new to worry about."

"Alright," she said. "Just please tell me what's going on."

Danny walked over and sat down next to her on the sofa. He dried his palms on the legs of his jeans and cracked his knuckles before saying, "Albert's son, Adam. He got infected."

"Oh my God!" Lucy recoiled as if Danny had just spat a wad of orange phlegm on the cushion between them. Then, a little embarrassed by her reaction, she forced herself to relax and said, "That's terrible. I'm really sorry for him, but I'm still not sure why we have his dog."

Lucy glanced up thoughtfully. In a different context, she'd look like she was trying to work through a tough math equation in her mind. Then a light of clarity sparked in her eyes and she said, "Oh no! Did Adam kill Albert?"

"No, that's not it," Danny told her, immediately wishing he'd taken a moment before responding. Had he answered in the affirmative, that might have been the end of the conversation. Lucy wasn't likely to keep asking questions and she certainly wasn't going to go over to Albert's apartment to see whether the story checked out.

"Did Albert get infected?" Lucy pressed him. "Did Adam attack him or bite him or something like that?"

"Well, no," Danny said. "Albert was okay. We talked to him for a little bit."

"I still don't follow," Lucy admitted. "What am I missing?"

"Stop pussyfooting around, Danny," Jenna scolded.

"Pussyfooting," Danny giggled. But his grin soon turned into a frown when he caught Jenna glaring at him from across the room. "I'm working on it. Do *you* want to tell her?"

"Fine," Jenna said.

"That was rhetorical," Danny stated. Then he turned to face his sister again. He said, "Adam got attacked by a zombie in the basement."

Before he could explain further, Lucy interrupted. "I thought you said they hadn't gotten in?"

"They're not inside," Danny assured her. "It happened earlier today, before being a zombie became so popular."

He paused so Jenna and Lucy could appreciate his quick wit and charm. Neither seemed impressed, so he continued. "Apparently, Adam led the zombie out of the building and killed him in the parking lot."

"Him?" Lucy asked.

"Um," Danny thought aloud, "Yeah, I'm pretty sure it was a dude."

"Don't call them *him* and *her*," Lucy instructed, wrinkling her nose and making a face like she'd been sucking on a lemon. "It humanizes them."

"But aren't they still human?" Danny countered.

"I'm not sure," said Lucy. "It's like they're something different, more animal than human."

Danny rolled his eyes. "Maybe so, but you'd still refer to an animal as *him* and *her*."

"Yeah, if it's a pet," she argued. "But if I'm talking about some random bird or fish or bug or something, I'm not saying *him* and *her*. I'm saying *it*."

"I don't know about that," Danny rebuffed. "If it's me and I-"

"Enough!" Jenna shouted, tossing her hands up in frustration and annoyance. "Would you please get to the point."

"Right," Danny said; a detectable shift in his tone. "Like I was saying, the zombie chased him outside and that's where Adam killed him- er, I mean, where he killed *it*. But Adam had already gotten infected by that point. I guess he must have gotten bit when they were fighting. Anyway, Albert locked him up downstairs near the boiler, tied chains to him so he couldn't get out."

"Holy shit," Lucy remarked.

"Bad times," Danny concurred.

"So let me get this straight," said Lucy; her eyes narrowing and focused on her brother. "Albert is still alive and he's not infected?"

Danny nodded.

"But there *is* one of those infected things inside the building?" She looked from Danny to Jenna, confused and not sure if she should be more concerned.

"Well yeah," Danny answered. His tone and the way he drew out each syllable gave both Lucy and Jenna the impression he had more to say, yet he said nothing.

"What if he gets out?" Lucy couldn't hide the fear in her voice as she asked the question. "What if he gets up here? What are we going to do?"

"We'll be fine," Jenna told her. "Even if he somehow manages to get loose, he won't be able to get in here. He probably won't even know we're here."

"But what if he does?" Lucy stood up from the sofa and nearly shouted her question. "I know you're both trying to be calm and rational, but just look outside. Obviously, lots of irrational shit is happening. People killing each other, people eating each other, it's not rational. It's one thing to know they're outside, it's another to know there's a fucking cannibal- zombie, whatever you wanna call it, inside our God damn building. So please, just humor me. What is our plan if he gets out?"

"It's not going to happen," Danny told her. "He's not getting out and he's not going to come and find us."

"And you know this how?" She was still standing, but the look of panic in her eyes was slowly being replaced by one of hope and expectation that Danny might actually have something reassuring and helpful to say.

"We um," he shifted in his seat as he searched for the right words. "We could put him down."

"Brilliant," Lucy said, rolling her eyes. "We obviously aren't-"

Danny cut her off. "Humanely, of course. With Jenna's rifle. Or if you'd prefer, we could just sort of incapacitate him so he can't go anywhere."

"Sure," Lucy replied sarcastically. "We'll just *humanely* shoot a sick man in the legs while he's chained to the wall. And how do you think Albert is going to react when he finds out you've maimed his son?"

"I don't think that's going to be an issue," Jenna told her.

"Yeah," Danny agreed. "I think we're in the clear as far as Albert goes. Best not to worry too much about it..."

He let his words trail off. The story didn't get much better from there and Danny knew that further explanation was only going to cause more strife. He hoped that he'd already provided enough information to satisfy his sister's curiosity without giving a full account of his trip to Albert's apartment. As it turns out, he hadn't.

"What makes you say that?" Lucy asked her brother. Then, looking to Jenna, "I don't follow."

Jenna pointed her chin at Danny and said, "You wanna take this one?"

"Um... sure," Danny replied, clearing his throat. He pulled off the headband he'd been wearing and used it to wipe away the sweat from his forehead and cheeks. "Well, like I said, Albert was convinced that no one was gonna come along with a cure for Adam."

"Yeah," Lucy replied with an encouraging nudge. She sat down next to him and said, "Go on."

"In fact, he didn't think any of us would even make it through the night." Danny let out a long breath and looked up to Jenna for confirmation. She nodded with near-imperceptible subtlety.

"So he's planning to kill himself," Danny said. He motioned toward Duke and added, "And he was going to kill the dog too."

"I wasn't about to let him hurt his dog," Jenna stated. "So I took him out of there."

"And he just let you leave with him?" Lucy asked.

"Yeah. He actually seemed relieved," Danny explained. "Didn't try to stop us or anything."

Lucy rubbed her face with both hands. She untied her bandanna and massaged her scalp. After this revelation from Danny and Jenna, she needed a moment to collect her thoughts. Eventually, needing elucidation, she asked, "So he wants to commit suicide? Because his son got infected?"

"That's right," Danny confirmed; his tone and posture far too relaxed for this discussion. "That, and because Albert thinks we're all going to die anyway. He basically said we're screwed. Even if somebody was able to come up with a cure, we'd all be dead long before we ever got a chance to see it. The zombies will get in, or the government will fire-bomb the whole area, or we'll starve to death waiting for help-"

"We got it," Jenna snapped, observing the mask of fear that had overtaken Lucy's visage. She looked to her, hoping to put her mind at ease, "We've got no reason to think any of that is true."

"Fair enough," Danny said. "But Albert was convinced we're all doomed."

"He's giving up- just like that?" Lucy was incensed.

"We tried talking some sense into him, but he wouldn't listen," Jenna told her.

303

"He was being a real downer about it," Danny added.

"So what's his plan?" Lucy pressed. "How's he gonna do it?"

"Rat poison," Jenna answered. "I think he's going to mix it in with his food. He was cooking a huge pot of stew or something and-"

Lucy interjected, "Wait- he's doing it tonight? Like right now?"

"I think so," Danny answered. "Why?"

"I thought he'd at least give it a few days, maybe a week; see how things go." Lucy stood up from the sofa and began fidgeting with her hands. "I didn't know he was doing it now, like right now while we're sitting around chatting about it. You didn't tell me that."

"Sorry, I thought that was implied," Danny said. "Ya know, based on everything we've been talking about."

"Yeah, sorry about that Lucy," Jenna added. "But after all we've said, I'm not sure what made you think he was going to wait."

"You two!" Lucy exclaimed, waving her hands in the air.

"Us?" Danny asked. "What do you mean?"

"We told you he was going to kill himself, but we never said it was something he had planned for some unspecified point in the distant future," Jenna told her somewhat defensively. "I don't know what gave you that impression."

"What gave me that impression," Lucy started, "Is that you two assholes just left him there to do it. You left a man, a suicidal man who just lost his son, alone in his apartment to cook his own last meal. You knew he was about to kill himself and you just left?"

"We didn't just leave him there." Jenna found herself yelling back at Lucy. Then, still aware of the angry horde outside and the need to remain relatively quiet, she said, "We tried reasoning with him. It didn't work."

"We did try to talk him out of it," Danny said. "He wouldn't listen to us."

"You tried reasoning with him?" Lucy asked; her tone somewhere between inquisitive and accusatory. "Tried talking him out of it; he wouldn't listen, so you left?"

"I don't know what more you wanted us to do," Jenna started to say. "Under the circumstances, there wasn't much more we *could* do."

"Right," Lucy scoffed. "You politely asked him to reconsider his suicide plan and he said no. Well, I guess that settles it."

"Don't give me that bullshit," Jenna shouted. "We were trying to make the building safe, make sure nothing could get in. If you think someone should sit there and babysit him to make sure he doesn't do anything stupid, then maybe that's what you should have been doing instead of hiding out here the whole time."

"Fuck you! You know damn well I wasn't just hiding out," Jenna shouted back. "You both said I should stay here and keep an eye out. But had I known someone was in trouble, I would have actually done something to try and help."

"Okay, okay. Let's just chill out for a sec," Danny said, speaking to both women; an impotent attempt to keep things peaceful.

"I don't know what she expected us to do," Jenna replied. "I mean, seriously. What are we supposed to do, physically restrain him?"

"Yes!" Lucy cried, wringing her hands in front of her face. "That's exactly what you're supposed to do! What you're *not* supposed to do is walk away and let a troubled person harm himself, or worse."

"I hear what you're saying, I'm just not sure how we could have done that," Danny told her. "It would have been too dangerous. Under the circumstances, I think you're asking an awful lot."

"I'm just asking that you do the right thing," Lucy exclaimed. She walked past Jenna and into the kitchen, calling over her shoulder, "I don't get how you guys don't see that."

Lucy opened a cupboard. She took out a sixteen-ounce tumbler and placed it on the counter. Then she moved over to the fridge and opened the freezer door. After rummaging around inside for a few seconds, she found a two-hundred milliliter bottle of Seagram's Extra Smooth vodka. Lucy took the booze out and slammed the freezer door closed.

"Hey Lucy," Danny called from the next room. "What's up, what are you doin'?"

"I'm having a drink," she answered, removing the cap from the bottle and tossing it beside the glass. Lucy poured herself about four ounces of straight vodka. She took a small sip, grimacing as she swallowed it down. Lucy hated vodka.

She set down the glass and walked to the opposite end of the kitchen where her purse sat on the floor. Lucy knelt and pulled out a cigarette from the already-open pack. She called to her brother and said, "And I'm having a smoke."

Lucy paused, waited for an objection that never came. "You hear what I said?"

"Yeah," Danny answered. He walked into the room and took a seat at the kitchen table. "Just do me a favor and open the window, okay?"

She nodded as she lit her cigarette. Lucy strode back to the other side of the room, grabbing the glass of vodka as she went. She set it down next to the sink and then reached over the faucet to open the window as her brother had asked.

"Hey guys," Jenna said as she appeared in the doorway. "Are we packing it in for the night?"

"I guess so," Danny answered. "You still wanna stay here tonight?"

"Yeah," she replied; her shoulders relaxing slightly. "I think that would be for the best."

"Sure. We can sort out sleeping arrangements in a bit." Danny lost himself in thought for a moment and then added with a sly grin, "I bet two people could fit in my bed."

"Very funny," she said flatly. Jenna was not amused. "I'm sure I'll be fine on the sofa. In the meantime, do you mind if I turn on the TV and see if there's anything on the news?"

"Sure," Danny said. Then, turning back to his sister, he asked, "What do ya say, Lucy? When you're done smoking, you wanna join us, see if anything has changed?"

Lucy was taking a long drag off her cigarette. She drew in, held for a moment, and then blew out a large cloud of smoke, doing what she could to get as much of it out the window as possible. Most drifted out, but a few wisps curled up and hovered just below the ceiling. Lucy flicked a wad of ash into the sink and picked up her glass, swirling it gently before taking a gulp. She swallowed it quickly, so as not to have to endure the wretched taste for too long.

Danny wasn't sure if she was listening. He sat forward in his seat and said, "Hey Lucy, when you're done with-"

"I heard you," she interrupted.

"Oh," Danny replied. "I wasn't sure, since you didn't say anything."

"You're asking if I want to watch the news with you and Jenna, correct?"

"Yeah, unless you wanted to get some rest or something," Danny said. "I was joking about taking the bed, it's all yours if you want it."

"Can't," Lucy replied, lifting the glass to her lips. Accidentally catching a whiff of the revolting liquid, she lowered the glass without taking a sip.

"Can't?" Danny asked. "Can't watch the news, or can't go to bed?"

"Neither- err uh, both. Whatever," Lucy stammered. She shook her head and took another big puff from her cigarette; this time not bothering to try and get it out the window. A tobacco fog rolled up and spread out, filling half of the tiny kitchen.

"Okay," Danny replied cautiously. "What are you going to do then?"

"Which apartment is Albert's?" Lucy asked her own question instead of answering his.

"Why do you want to know that?" Danny asked; his demeanor suddenly growing firm. He looked to Jenna, as if to say, *What is this about?*

Jenna was still standing in the doorway. She shrugged, waving a hand in front of her face to drive away the wafting smoke.

"I'm going over there," Lucy said flatly. "To stop him from, well, you know."

"Killing himself," Danny finished her thought for her.

"Yes," said Lucy, rolling her eyes once more. "Obviously, from killing himself."

"I don't think that's a good idea," Danny told her. He stood up from the chair and then, unsure what to do with himself, sat back down again.

"Definitely not a good idea," Jenna agreed.

"Yeah, probably not," Lucy added. She swallowed down another mouthful of vodka before taking another long pull from her cigarette. "But I'm doing it anyway."

"Lucy, I really think we all better just stay inside," Danny argued.

"Yeah, sorry Lucy, but I agree with Danny," Jenna said, echoing his sentiment. "None of us should be going anywhere. At least not for a while, until maybe, I don't know, until they start to forget we're in here. Once they lose interest and move on, then maybe we can talk about leaving the apartment but for the time being, we should stay where it's safe."

"That's fine," Lucy told her, keeping an even tone. "You both can stay here and be safe. I'm going to go help Albert and hopefully save his life."

"I'm serious, Lucy." Jenna was beginning to raise her voice. "Don't you think I'd rather be at home, in my own apartment and getting ready to sleep in my own bed? I haven't even been back there because it's too dangerous to risk it."

"Too dangerous?" Lucy was incredulous. "Five minutes ago, you were giving me shit because

306

I was 'hiding out' in the apartment while you and Danny were off playing hero."

"Playing hero?" Danny asked.

"Yes, playing hero," Lucy reiterated. "Making pretend you were helping people, saving people. And all in the face of grave danger. Meanwhile, you had time to go to everyone's door, chat with a neighbor, and find yourself a pet. The one person you came across, the one person who really needed your help, you left him. You left him on his own to kill himself."

Right up until this very moment in the evening, Danny had done whatever he could to minimize the danger in his sister's eyes. He'd been reluctant to tell her just how bad things had become, how close they had been, and how close they remained, to death. It was for her benefit, so she didn't have to worry. At least, he hoped she wouldn't have to worry any more than she already had been. He joked with her, prodded her with mild bickering, and tried to make her feel at home. Danny tried to nourish a sense of normalcy, a feeling that everything would turn out okay. But maybe it wouldn't. Maybe he was lying to her and to himself. Maybe they were all doomed.

"Lucy, I told you we tried to talk some sense into him," Jenna persisted. "But no one else is here, there's no one else to keep the building safe and to-"

"I killed a girl," Danny blurted.

"What did you say?" Lucy asked; a smoldering butt wedged between her fingertips.

Jenna said nothing. She already knew what Danny had done. Her eyes fixed on him nonetheless, and both women waited quietly for him to say more.

"I killed a girl." Danny spoke directly to his sister. "I got distracted for just a second and I almost got killed."

"Oh shit," Lucy exclaimed. "Are you okay? You didn't get bit, did you?"

"No, I'm fine," Danny assured her. "But my point is, it's dangerous. It's very dangerous and until now, I've been sorta downplaying just how bad things have gotten."

Lucy flicked the last bit of ash into the sink and then turned on the faucet, sticking the butt into the stream of water to extinguish the glowing ember. She immediately lit a second cigarette and puffed on it; a long drag of smoke dry and gritty in her throat. Lucy drank from her glass to ease the soreness. She was starting to get used to the disgusting taste.

Danny then told her, "Adam wasn't the only zombie in the building."

That statement caused Lucy to raise her eyebrows.

Danny continued, "Chucky, the guy who lived downstairs from Jim. He didn't answer the door so we checked inside."

"Apparently Charles had gotten infected," Lucy added. "We found him and what was left of his girlfriend in his apartment."

"We had no idea he was down there until we went in," Danny explained.

"What happened?" Lucy blew out a lungful of smoke. This time she leaned over the sink and aimed out the window. "What did you do?"

"Jenna had to shoot him," Danny explained. "I hit him with the machete but it wasn't enough. He kept coming."

"Okay, so are there others?" Lucy looked from Danny to Jenna and then back to Danny.

"We don't think so," Danny answered.

"But we aren't sure," Jenna clarified. "We tried every door and we didn't find anyone else, but that doesn't mean there isn't anyone in there. For all we know, there could still be infected people in the building, waiting for someone to open the wrong door or walk down the wrong hallway."

"And not only that," Danny said. "And I didn't want to mention this because I didn't want to scare you, but to be totally honest, I'm not sure how long those doors are going to last."

"The main doors to the building?" Lucy asked.

Danny nodded. "It was the same on both sides. There's so many of them, so much weight pushing against the doors, I'm worried they'll just break apart and come off the hinges."

"So, until things quiet down out there," Jenna started, pointing through the living room and toward the front of the building. "The best thing we can do is stay put. Nobody should go anywhere alone and nobody should go anywhere unless it's absolutely necessary."

"But you guys don't get it," Lucy said; smoke escaping through her lips and nostrils as she spoke. "This *is* absolutely necessary."

Both Jenna and Danny opened their mouths to object, but Lucy kept going.

"This isn't up for debate," she asserted. "I'm going to go over there and, one way or another, I'm going to stop Albert from killing himself."

"But-" Danny tried to get a word in.

"You were right before," Lucy said to Jenna. "Maybe I was just sort of hiding out and relying on you and Danny to do the heavy lifting, the dangerous work. And maybe it's time for me to do something useful, something that can actually help someone. Maybe I can't fight or take out an infected person-"

"Zombie," Danny interrupted.

"Shut up, Danny." Lucy kept going without missing a beat. "Maybe I can't save someone from a *zombie* but there's got to be something I can do, something that's helpful and important. And besides, it's the right thing to do. And aren't we supposed to do the right thing?"

She paused for a response, even though it was clear her question was rhetorical. Danny sighed and let out a long breath. Jenna seemed to be taking it all in, but didn't say anything.

Lucy went on, "I know there might be some danger involved and I'm not saying it's going to be easy, but that's when things like this matter the most. Morality is a fixed constant. We're not supposed to give up and sit on our hands just because things get hard or shitty or scary and God damn it, I can't just stay here and do nothing when I know that just a few feet away from me, someone is on the verge of taking their own life."

She stopped to take a breath. Lucy took another drag from her smoke, lifted the glass to her lips and said, "So I'm going to finish my cigarette and this horrible drink, grab my golf club, and go out and try to help someone. If you don't want to tell me which apartment he's in, I'll knock on every door until I find him."

"Lucy wait," Danny called to her.

"What?" Lucy asked sharply, expecting another argument.

"Pour one of those for me," he told her. "I'm going with you."

Chapter 47

"Is that it? Is that your building?" Lindsey was leaning all the way forward in her seat. She pointed ahead to a two-story tenement a short distance away.

Jim wasn't sure when, but Lindsey must have let go of his hand at some point, leaving it limply draped over the gear shifter. His other hand dropped from the steering wheel to land on his thigh. The static from the speakers seemed to grow louder, punctuated by cracks and pops at random intervals. The car wasn't moving. Jim's foot was pressing the brake but he didn't remember stopping the vehicle.

"Are you listening?" Lindsey was peering over the dashboard and studying the space beyond the windshield. "Jim?"

"Is that your building?" she repeated, unable to contain the dread in her voice.

He swallowed hard and nodded. They were stopped at the edge of the neighboring property. Between them and the building, stood a battalion of barbarous bastards.

The mob was too large, too thick. There was no way to get through them. No way to get around them. There had to be two hundred freaks gathered in the parking lot, and that was only counting the ones in front of the building. Countless more were sure to be surrounding the rest of the structure, moving along the sides and rear in search of another way in.

Thanks to the dim light and the wall of bodies, it was impossible to see all the way to the front doors. The crowd was especially dense at both entrances. Jim couldn't tell whether they were still closed off, or if the pricks had already gotten inside. If they had, his neighbors were as good as dead. And there was nothing he could do to help them without getting killed himself.

"What are we going to do?" asked Lindsey.

"I- I don't know," was all he could muster.

"Can we at least get out of here before they come for us?" Lindsey pleaded. But the ghouls closest to the car had already begun to take notice. It seemed these were of the sluggish variety. The faster ones, still chock-full of adrenaline and rage, had made their way up to the building and left their slower, shambling brethren to clumsily bump into each other as they flooded the street.

"Yeah, but I don't..." Jim's voice trailed off. He put the car in reverse and was halfway through a two-point turn before any of the staggering zombies got to within arm's reach. He concluded his stammering statement with, "I don't know where to go."

Lindsey opened her mouth to speak but before she could offer a response, the radio came to life. It had been on the whole time but both she and Jim had learned to tune out the static and white noise. The sound of a voice, a real person actually speaking on air, came as a bit of a shock to them.

"...that this is no longer thought to be a containable situation," said a woman's voice. She continued, "In addition to the reports out of Canada and Mexico, we've also gotten word that similar outbreaks of violence have taken place in multiple South American and European nations. The epidemic now appears to be a global event and not just limited to the continental Unites States, as originally believed. Coming up shortly, we are expecting to hear from the White House for an emergency briefing by the Secretary of Defense..."

Global event. Those words echoed and replayed in Jim's mind.

"How are we on gas?" Lindsey asked.

Global event. Jim didn't really hear what she was saying. He looked over at her. "Huh?"

"Gas!" she repeated. "How much gas do we have left?"

"Um," Jim looked down at the fuel gauge as he cruised to the first intersection. The needle was just below the quarter-tank notch. He made a left turn onto Brighton Road and said, "We've got a little bit left, but-"

"Where are we going?" Lindsey cut him off.

"I don't know," he said defensively. "I told you I don't know where to go. I'm just getting away from the horde."

"But why are we going this way?" she challenged.

"Where do you want me to go?" Jim barked. "Back down Colvin for a fourth time? Where we know there's more zombies and more shit? I'm trying to get us away from that."

Lindsey recoiled. Jim's harsh words and aggressive tone stung more than he'd intended but he didn't apologize. She slid forward in her seat and shot back, "Don't shout at me- I'm asking because if we're running out of gas, then *maybe* it would be good to have an actual destination."

"Yeah," he scoffed, hitting the gas pedal harder. "That's a great suggestion, except that it's several hours overdue."

She shook her head and waved her hands in frustration. "Is there enough gas to get us back across town?"

"Yes," Jim answered in a dry and matter-of-fact sort of way.

The car drove into another pocket of reception and the radio came alive once more. This time it was a man's voice speaking, "...that the majority of communities are without internet service and phone service, both cellular and landlines. As previously reported, cable and satellite TV providers are experiencing widespread blackouts. Citizens are urged to stay indoors. Do not attempt to travel or reach loved ones. As resources become available, the National Guard is set to begin establishing emergency centers and rescue stations. More on that as information becomes available."

"A Hell of a lot of good that does now," Jim mumbled under his breath.

"Okay. Turn right at the next intersection," Lindsey instructed.

He shot her a glance, an eyebrow raised in confusion and curiosity.

"I know where we can go," she said. "But you're probably not going to be happy about it. Promise me you're not going to be mad?"

Chapter 48

"Are you sure?" Lucy asked. She turned on the faucet and ran the spent cigarette butt under the stream. She briefly considered lighting a third but decided against it. There was less than a half a pack left in her purse and it might be a while before she'd be able to run down to the convenience store to buy more.

"Yep," Danny answered with enthusiasm, rising from his chair. He marched across the room and opened one of the cupboards to grab himself a glass. Danny, reaching overhead for a tumbler, paused and looked over his shoulder. "What do you say, Jenna? Should I pour a third?"

Jenna shifted weight from her right foot to her left. She pinched the bridge of her nose as if holding back a sneeze. Then, after about ten seconds of consideration and immeasurable consternation, an answer finally came.

"Um, ugh. Sure," she stammered.

"Yeah?" Danny asked for confirmation.

"Ugh, shit," Jenna murmured. "Yeah. Why the Hell not."

"Woo yeah!" Danny wailed. He took two glasses from the shelf and slammed them on the counter top, punctuating the sound with a, "Boom!"

"Okay, okay," Jenna moaned. She strolled across the floor to stand next to the others. "But let's be quick about it, okay? I still think this is a bad idea."

"Don't you worry about bad ideas," Danny advised, flashing one of his trademark dopey grins. "I've been having nothing but bad ideas for well over a decade and look at me- I'm practically king of the world."

"You're an idiot," Lucy replied. "And that's just another reason no women want to date you."

Jenna, not quite sure if it was okay to laugh, held a hand in front of her mouth to hide her smile.

"Oh please," Danny countered. "Women want to date me, they're just intimidated."

Normally, Lucy would take this opportunity to pile on. She'd correct her brother and tell him that women aren't into guys who split their free time between video games and masturbation. Nor are they drawn to guys who exist inside of a near-permanent cloud of marijuana smoke. Ladies are generally repulsed by guys who walk around with days-old body odor and armpit funk thanks to their laissez-faire approach to showering and personal hygiene. Lucy might also mention that women are not turned on by dudes who wear nothing but tattered cut-off jean shorts and sleeveless shirts to show off their milky white skin and arms completely devoid of muscle tone.

Of course, this would compel Danny to point out how Lucy had acquired a vast collection of failed, chaotic and codependent relationships; not to mention the fact that she's needed, on multiple occasions, to move in with her kid brother because she lacks the responsibility and financial literacy to support herself.

Bickering, though playful and joking, would ensue. But there simply wasn't time for that now. If all goes well, they could pick this up again in ten minutes or so, and hopefully have a grateful, aging

Polish immigrant to act as moderator.

So instead, with a hint of sarcasm, Lucy said, "Well Danny, you certainly know what the ladies like."

"You know it," Danny replied, pouring about an ounce of vodka into the pair of glasses in front of him. He handed one to Jenna and kept one for himself. They drained their glasses all at once; the same sour expression on their faces as they dropped the empty tumblers into the sink.

"Okay," Jenna began. "You guys should probably bring more than just the machete and golf club. Ya know, just in case."

"Right," Danny said. "There's lots of sharp stuff in here we can use."

Jenna and Lucy began rummaging through the kitchen drawers and cupboards. Jenna picked up an over-sized metal spatula, felt its weight in her hands, and then dropped it on the counter top. She opted instead for one of several kitchen knives, a chef's knife to be exact, carefully sliding it blade-first between her belt and her jeans.

Lucy did the same, finding a large boning knife amongst the clutter and sliding it under her belt over her left hip. Then, considering it might not be enough, she added a two-prong stainless steel barbecue fork. She slid it under her belt on the opposite side before turning to grab her golf club.

Danny had been standing back, letting the women have their pick of whichever items suited them best. He already had the machete and, in his estimation, this was the ultimate knife. There were a few smaller carving and paring knives left in the drawer, but with over two feet of slicing surface, the machete made these other blades seem paltry and inadequate. He instead decided to check what might be in the hallway closet.

There wasn't much in there but Danny did find a hammer. It was all metal with a thin layer of rubber around the handle and a hint of rust near the head. This would do just fine. It was heavy enough and solid enough to do plenty of damage should the need arise. If a head needed bashing in, this was the ideal tool for the job. It was too heavy and clunky to carry on his belt, so Danny slid the handle into his pants pocket. The hammer stuck out about halfway, but it wasn't going to fall out and it would be easy to reach if he had to act quickly.

The trio was nearly ready for action, although they all privately hoped that this journey to Albert's apartment would be quick and uneventful. Lucy re-tied her bandanna and Danny adjusted his headband. Jenna ejected the magazine from her rifle to make sure it was fully loaded.

"Okay," Lucy finally announced. "Everybody ready?"

Jenna, standing silently near the doorway, nodded in confirmation.

"Wait," Danny said. "Does anyone have a pad of paper or a notebook or something like that?"

"For what?" Lucy asked.

"I was thinking we should maybe write down what's going on," he explained. "Ya know, record everything for posterity, so people know what happened."

"Don't worry about posterity," Lucy told him. "Worry about your posterior."

"Huh?" Danny's eyes glazed over.

"Your ass!" she shouted. "Just watch your ass and let's get this done. Alright?"

"Oh," Danny replied. "Okay, let's head out then."

"Looks clear to me," Jenna said. She took her eye from the peephole and shrugged, adding, "I don't hear anything either. I think we're good."

"Okay, let's roll," Danny instructed, reaching for the doorknob.

The door swung open. Jenna, Danny, and Lucy crept into the hallway, each carrying their weapons of choice. It wasn't totally silent, as Jenna had led them to believe. They could hear the steady rumble of moaning, grunting, and snarling which had essentially morphed into ambient sound by that point. What they were really trying to hear was whether any of the infected goons had managed to get in.

"Make sure you pull the door all the way closed," Danny said in a hushed tone. He was speaking to Lucy, as she was the last one out of the apartment.

"Do you have your keys so we can get back in?" she asked, also whispering.

"That's a good question," he answered, still keeping his voice low. Then, reaching his hand into his pocket to make sure, he stated, "Yep. Got 'em."

"Good," Lucy said as she pulled the door closed. She shook the knob and pressed against it to make sure it wasn't going to open. Then she asked, "And also, do we need to whisper?"

"Shh!" Jenna scolded.

"I guess so," Danny told his sister.

"I want to make sure we can hear if someone's coming," Jenna clarified.

The trio began their procession down the stairwell; old wooden planks squeaking and popping under their feet as they went. Since Jenna was the only one in the group with a firearm, she was leading the way. And since Lucy was the most nervous about going, even though it was her idea, she was last in line. They were all within arm's reach of one another when they started, but when Lucy reached the first-floor landing, she turned back to discover that Danny and Lucy were a dozen or more steps behind her.

"What's the-" Jenna began to shout before catching herself. Then in a loud whisper, she asked, "What's the hold up?"

"The stairs," Lucy told her. "They're creaking."

"They are sorta loud," Danny said as he stepped down to join Jenna in the small hallway. "We were trying to stay quiet so none of the zombies will know where we are."

"I know I told you guys to be quiet," Jenna began. "But we can still move at a normal pace. Or even better, a fast pace. I don't want to be out here all night."

"Neither do I," Lucy agreed, still standing three steps from the landing.

"Alright," said Jenna. "Then let's get to it. And Lucy, I don't mean to freak you out, but at the bottom of these steps, we're going to be in the lobby near the front doors."

Lucy narrowed her eyes. "Okay?"

Jenna went on. "Well, there's a lot of them out there and they're pressed up against the doors. But don't worry, they can't get in. Just ignore them and follow me and Danny down the next set of steps to the basement, okay?"

"You got it," Lucy answered.

So far, Jenna had been carrying the rifle in a relaxed sort of way. She held it with one hand on the forend, the barrel aimed at the floor. The stock was tucked gently under her shoulder and none of her fingers were anywhere close to the trigger. But in the seconds before she led the group down into the lobby, her entire posture changed.

The barrel was now up at eye level, pointing down the hall. Jenna stood with a slight bend to her knees; her back straight and rigid. She held the weapon with both hands and switched the safety off. When she turned, the rifle turned in front of her. Anything she looked at was in the line of fire. Her index finger rested on the trigger housing, ready to squeeze down in an instant.

"The cord's still in place," Jenna commented when she reached ground level. She was referring to the extension cord she and Danny had used to tie the doors closed by wrapping it around the inner handles. It wasn't as snug as it had been when they first tied it, but the bright orange cord was still tight enough to keep the doors from being opened. "But I think we might have a problem."

"Shit. I think you're right," said Danny. He could see it too.

"What is it?" Lucy asked from somewhere behind him.

"The door frame," Danny explained. He pointed toward the entrance and said, "The whole doorway is coming apart."

"It's doing what?" Lucy walked the rest of the way down the stairs. She stepped into the lobby and gasped in horror.

Jenna hadn't been exaggerating when she warned her about what she might see. There was a wall of flesh pressed against the doors. They were being crushed, nearly flattened between the doors and the mass of countless other bodies. Of the ten or so that were directly against the glass, more than half of them had died from the pressure and related injuries. None of them could move, so the only way to tell which ones were still alive was to wait for them to blink or watch for their breath to form condensation against the glass when they exhaled.

As if that wasn't bad enough, Lucy then observed something that made this gruesome sight even more horrifying. The aluminum door frame had been torn away from the wall. It was still holding near the floor, but the top portion had come so far from the wall that Lucy could look up and see the dark cloudless sky above. It was at that moment she knew with absolute certainty that the ghouls outside were going to get in.

"What are we going to do?" Lucy asked.

"Keep going," Jenna told her. "It's still holding for now, so we should be okay."

"Are you sure?" Lucy wanted to argue with her. She wanted to tell Jenna and Danny that she had been wrong. This was a mistake. They should have never left the safety of the apartment. The smartest thing they could do now is turn back, head upstairs and lock themselves in Danny's apartment. Maybe Albert had been right. Maybe none of them would make it through the night.

"Hey, this was your idea," Jenna reminded her. "We're already out here, so let's just get it done."

Lucy didn't say anything. She looked at Danny to gauge his reaction.

Danny returned her gaze and said, "We're good. Let's keep moving."

So they did just that. The three of them walked down the final set of steps and into the lower level. At the bottom of the stairs was a door that would lead into the unfinished portion of the basement. Jenna, who was still leading the way, turned the knob until she felt it click but she didn't open the door just yet. Instead, she put both hands on the rifle and leveled it in front of her before kicking the door open and walking barrel-first into the next room.

The space was quiet and dimly lit. Only a single bare bulb hung overhead to shine a faint illumination over the drain tub and old workbench. The light couldn't reach the back section of the basement, but nothing came charging out of the shadows, so it seemed safe to continue. Jenna motioned for Danny and Lucy to follow. They quickly made their way into the next section of the basement where the laundry machines and utility systems were housed.

There was also an infected person on this side of the basement but the trio knew he wasn't going to be a problem. Danny found himself wondering if the contagion would ultimately kill the host. Instead of trying to find a way out of his chains, Adam might be navigating the early stages of decomposition. Out of curiosity, Danny looked down the short dark walkway toward the cage that held the boiler and water heater. He could make out the shape of something slumped on the floor, but didn't feel compelled to investigate any further.

When they reached the next door, Jenna turned back to address Lucy. "Past this door, we'll be going back up to the ground level and we're going to go past another set of glass doors. Just keep moving, same as last time. We'll go to the right and up the next set of stairs. Albert's is the first door on the left."

"Okay," Lucy whispered.

"We're right behind you," Danny chimed in.

The group forged ahead. They went out of the basement and up the steps that led them to the building's second lobby; a now-familiar sight ready to greet them when they arrived. The doorway was much like the one on the other side of the building, with a few notable differences. These differences, it seemed, were the result of an ever-increasing pressure against shitty, cheap, poorly-maintained, decades-old architecture.

On this side of the building, almost all of the loons that were pinned against the doors had perished. No tiny clouds of breath appeared on the glass above their dry, cracked lips. None of them blinked. Milky eyes stared straight ahead and remained fixed on nothing. From behind their motionless forms, a second and third row of fiends watched in lustful anticipation as three healthy people could be seen approaching.

They too were unable to move from the neck down. Despite their efforts, wriggling shoulders and swinging heads from side to side, none of these brutes could manage to free themselves. This only served to intensify the hatred radiating from the group. Crazed eyes darted about wildly as they bared their teeth and snapped their jaws. They were spellbound, captivated by an insatiable hunger. Most of them had a thick gooey rope of saliva dripping out of their mouths. Drops of spittle and skin flecks sprayed into the air, reflecting briefly under the dull porch light before disappearing.

The door frame had been mostly torn away from the wall. There was now a two-foot gap between the interior wall and the top of the casing. The frame was still firmly in place along the threshold but it had come loose everywhere else, causing the doors to lean into the foyer. Broken bits of drywall lie scattered on the lobby's carpeted floor. The screws that used to hold the hinges in place had snapped, leaving the hinges themselves to dangle ineffectually several inches from where they'd originally been fastened.

Jenna led the others as they scaled the last few risers from the lower level. She kept the rifle raised in front of her, looking down the barrel and keeping a steady aim as she moved. Her right index finger slid off the trigger guard and onto the trigger itself. She was careful not to let it show, but it was

315

at that exact moment when something drastic changed inside of her.

As her sneaker first touched down on the ratty and unwashed carpet of the lobby, she was struck by a crushing reality. As Jenna looked across the short hall at the sea of unhinged cannibals, she knew that the thin layer of glass keeping them out was the only thing keeping her, Danny, and Lucy alive.

If the doorway didn't hold and the beasts got in, every living thing in the building would be eviscerated. Any effort to fight their way through would be beyond futile. Sure, Jenna had a gun, but she might as well have been carrying a teddy bear for all the good it would do. The rifle held only ten rounds and even if she was accurate with each shot, the brutes would be on her before she'd be able to empty the magazine. Jenna and her friends would be overwhelmed in an instant, left with no option but to hope for a quick death.

Danny was the next to see it. He had been carrying the machete up and over his shoulder, ready to swing it down on the head of any zombie that came his way. Now that he'd made the same observation Jenna had, his shoulders dipped and his arms fell to his sides. Needless to say, if a semi-automatic rifle couldn't take down the enemy, then neither would a couple feet of sharpened metal.

Lucy, who'd been following behind her brother, was still halfway down the short stairway and hadn't yet seen the mountain of bodies about to break through the doorway. But she could tell something was up by the way Jenna and Danny had both stopped moving and seemed to deflate simultaneously. That, and the rising volume from the crowd outside was all the evidence she needed to know that something very bad was about to happen.

The delirious battle-cry of the diseased and the damned had reached earsplitting levels. Groaning, growling, and screaming pierced the air outside and echoed through the halls of the tenement like a klaxon alarm sounding to let everyone know their doom had arrived.

Several rows past the entrance, feral humanoid creatures pressed on, pushing through their fallen comrades as they tried to break in. The glass doors, still in their frame, rocked forward, bobbing up and down as they pulled farther from the wall. Drywall cracked. Aluminum bent and twisted. The first floor of the building sounded like the hull of an old metal warship that was under fire and taking on water.

"What's happening?" Lucy asked. She was still holding the golf club in one hand as one might hold a tennis racket. The other hand held the boning knife she'd taken from the apartment. "Why'd you guys stop?"

Danny turned to look back at her. He didn't want to tell her, but he was done trying to keep things from her. And she was going to find out anyway. "The doorway. It's in bad shape."

"How bad is it?" Lucy asked; her eyes widening a bit.

"I'm not sure," he told her. "I kinda think we should turn back."

Lucy nodded once and waited for somebody to say something more. She noticed the half-relaxed, half-defeated posture that Jenna and Danny had assumed and was tempted to follow suit. Suddenly the knife felt thin and frail in her hand. It seemed too flimsy and small to be of any use. Lucy slid it under her belt next to the barbecue fork and tightened both hands around the grip of the golf club.

Danny nudged Jenna from behind. "What do you think?"

"We're almost there," Jenna told him. "But I don't think those doors are going to hold for much longer. We can probably get to Albert's apartment, but if they get in, there's no way we can get past them to get back to your place."

"So we'd be stuck inside," Danny said. It was more of a statement than a question.

"That's *if* we get inside," Jenna reminded him. "There's a chance we might already be too late. If the door is locked, we might be screwed."

Danny took a second to consider. "I suppose we could come back and try again later, maybe once they forget about us and move on. You think we should head back?"

Jenna would have said yes. She would have told him that not only should they get back to his apartment as quickly as possible, but Jenna would have explained to him how stupid it was for them to leave in the first place. This would have been the perfect opportunity to illustrate how she had been right and they had been wrong. She might have even scolded Danny and Lucy for questioning her, for arguing with her. It would have sounded harsh and bitchy and Jenna probably would go on to feel like she owed Danny and Lucy an apology for speaking to them in such a way.

But for better or worse, Jenna wouldn't get to answer. She wouldn't need to say anything. The decision about what they should do would be made for them. And that answer came in the form of a deafening crack. The last few bolts holding the door frame in place finally snapped and gave out. All at once, dozens of bloodthirsty savages poured in through the collapsing doorway.

Chapter 49

When he'd first thought of it, Albert liked the idea of cooking his own last meal. Feasting on his favorite dish from his home country seemed like a fitting and poetic way for his story to end. It would be his choice and he would do it on his own terms. He knew his time was running out and he didn't have the energy or spirit to fight it. So instead, he embraced it. Death was on its way, but that hardly meant he would spend his last few moments fearing the inevitable. Sitting down to a delicious banquet before he took his own life, rather than waiting for it to be taken from him, was the perfect way to look the Grim Reaper in the eye and say, *Fuck you.*

But that was over an hour ago. Cooking your own last meal seems romantic and idyllic, right up until it's time to sit down and eat. His zeal had gone and with it went his appetite. Albert lifted a casserole pan out of the oven and sat it on the counter next to a bowl of brownish-green powder. He took a fork from the drawer and slowly stirred the stew. Albert poked at chunks of kielbasa and mushrooms, making sure they were spread evenly throughout the broth. It had come out perfectly. The food looked great. It smelled delicious. And Albert couldn't imagine taking a single bite.

He dropped the fork. It made a clang as it dinged the side of the pan before sinking down to disappear into the stew. That was the only sound in the apartment. Albert had turned the television off when the signal went out. He considered trying it again to see if any channels were back on the air, but decided against it.

Albert left his food where it was and walked out of the kitchen, leaning heavily on his cane with each step. He pulled back the curtain from in front of the sliding glass door and looked out. Nothing had changed, not that he'd been expecting anything different. He made his way back into the kitchen and looked out the window over the sink. Again, there was nothing new to be seen. Then he started walking to the back of the apartment toward his bedroom. Albert was going to look out the back window, but he stopped himself. He knew what was happening and he knew what he was doing. He was just wasting time, putting off what he'd planned to do.

He was free to procrastinate all he liked, but the fact of the matter was that Albert would not be leaving this place alive. His options, of which there were only two, were simple. He could wait for those things outside to get in and kill him, or he could end things his way like he'd been planning all day. Given the choice, Albert would rather not be torn apart. In his estimation, suicide by rat poison would be the quicker, easier, less painful way to go. Although, he might have reconsidered if he knew what was in store for him in the next half hour.

But for now, his mind was made up. All that was left to decide was when he'd actually do it. He'd have no way of knowing it, but he and Jenna were about to have a shared experience, for this too was a choice that would be determined for him. Just like Jenna's decision to retreat was made by the ghouls knocking down the doors, so too was Albert's decision as to when he should take his own life.

After some deliberation, Albert continued walking toward the back room, but he was stopped in his tracks by a great cacophony that shook the walls and floor. Vibrations from the impact ran through his socks and up his legs. As quickly as he could manage, Albert hobbled back to the front of the living room and once again looked out through the double-pane glass.

They were in. Dozens, probably hundreds of them raced through the entrance and into the building. A bottleneck formed at the front of the tenement. The infected crowd covered the whole parking lot and they were all trying to get in at once. The commotion quickly intensified. Countless pairs of feet could be heard stomping through the halls, up and down stairways, muffled only by snarling and screeching. Seconds later, several loud pops could be heard. It sounded like they were coming from somewhere deeper in the building.

Albert made his way to the apartment's main door and looked through the peephole. All he could see on the other side was a set of grinding teeth behind a pair of blistered lips. It wasn't clear whether they knew he was inside, but they were at his door and that was enough. Death had arrived. Albert's time was up.

He hurried across the kitchen floor. Albert took a large glass from the cupboard next to the window and filled it halfway with water from the tap. Next, he took a spoon from the silverware drawer and began scooping the powdered poison into the glass. The water inside turned murky and brown as he tried to mix in a second spoonful.

Unfortunately, the box of rat poison didn't have human dosage or serving information on its label. Albert thought that two heaping tablespoons might be plenty, but he didn't want to leave anything to chance. If he miscalculated and failed to prepare a lethal dose, there was a chance he would only become very ill or suffer for several hours before he ultimately perished. That was no good. He needed this to work and he needed it to be efficient.

Albert ladled in a third tablespoon. And a fourth. Inside the glass, the fluid became viscous and took on a mud-like consistency. He dumped in a fifth spoonful and stirred it to try and make all the clumps dissolve. Once the glass looked as if no more poison would fit inside, Albert tossed the spoon into the sink. He held the glass in front of him, turning it to examine from all angles.

Before he drank it down, Albert gave one last look to the pan of uneaten hunter's stew. For a moment, he considered leaving a note saying that the stew was fine and he hadn't added any poison to it. But would anyone believe that? They probably wouldn't want to risk it. Plus, he doubted the stew would remain edible for that long. By the time anyone found him here, if anyone found him at all, every last bit of food in the apartment would have gone bad, grown mold and sprouted hairs.

The older man would look through the peephole for the final time before settling in for the permanent night. Albert walked to the doorway; one hand on his cane, the other holding his deadly home-brewed concoction. What he saw on the other side of the door didn't change his mind with regard to the poison. The bloody teeth had moved away from the glass and they presumably belonged to one of the six fiends that had gathered in the hall outside of his apartment.

He made sure the door was locked- not that it mattered all that much anymore, and continued on into the living room. Albert flopped down on his recliner and let the cane fall to the floor by its side. He reached for the TV remote and let his hand hover over it for a moment. Deciding instead to enjoy his last few moments in silence, he left the remote on the arm of the chair. The aging man closed his eyes and silently asked God for His understanding and forgiveness. Albert lifted the glass to his lips, plugged his nose, and began to drink.

The fluid was so thick and lumpy that Albert had to jostle the glass to get it all to pour out. Then, once it was in his mouth, he practically had to chew it in order to swallow. Albert was surprised to find it tasted sweet at first. As he gulped the toxic beverage, the liquid grew bitter and started to burn. After what felt like an eternity, Albert had finally emptied the glass. He sat back in his seat and took a deep breath. It wouldn't be long now.

Only fifteen minutes had passed, but the knowledge that a heavy toxin was about to make him rot from the inside out made every second feel like a year. The drooling, fleshy demons bumping into each other in the hallway just outside his door weren't making matters any easier. Albert did the best he could to relax as he waited for something to happen. And then it finally did.

A bubbling and churning sensation formed deep in his gut. It was sort of like being punched in the stomach, but from the inside. This was accompanied by a tightness in his chest. Albert could feel his heartbeat speeding up for a few seconds and then slowing down, back and forth, up and down. Breathing became difficult and the muscles in his chest felt like they were on fire.

Albert sat up in the chair and gasped for breath. The abrupt movement brought about an instant wave of dizziness and he almost fell out of his seat. Easing himself back into a reclined position, Albert became very aware of a scorching metallic taste at the back of his throat. He tried to swallow it down and ignore it. But this was just the beginning. Albert was starting to bleed to death.

Within moments, his lungs began to fill with fluid, mostly blood. His liver and kidneys began to fail. Dozens of small ulcers formed in his stomach and intestines. Pain devoured his abdomen and a wet, gurgling rattle sounded from inside his chest with every breath. Albert tried to clear his throat but the stinging rawness persisted. He coughed and a hot red puddle landed on his chest.

His heart rate dropped and with it went his blood pressure. Without realizing it, Albert's hands had balled into fists. He squeezed his eyes closed, focusing on breathing, trying to relax. But his body would not cooperate. The muscles in his legs contracted hard, his knees bent and his feet curled. His arms followed in kind, bending at the elbows and locking against his chest; both hands trembling all the while. Both heels dug into the footrest of the recliner, jerking and quivering beyond his control.

Another cough, another tepid splash of blood across his belly. His nose was running now and Albert did his best to control his quaking arms so he could run a sleeve below his nostrils. He opened his eyes to see a bright red streak across the forearm of his shirt. The warm, wet sensation of red tears had Albert dabbing them with the opposite sleeve but it did little to stem the burgundy tide. Before long, he would lose control of his arms altogether, leaving him helpless to do anything more than keep his eyes closed to keep the blood out.

Both legs extended; the quadriceps locked in a contracted state, hamstring fibers stretching and tearing. Severe spasms of the axial muscles forced Albert's back to arch and his spine to bend backwards. He was stuck in this position with his back bowed so drastically, little more than his shoulder blades and heels made contact with the chair. The inexorable torment made that much worse by his inability to clean the blood from his eyes and face. Each wheezing breath sprayed another cloud of red mist into the air.

After several minutes of rampant agony, his parasympathetic nervous system became overwhelmed. With every pain receptor firing at once and his blood pressure fading, Albert finally, mercifully, fell into neurogenic shock. He soon lost consciousness, slipping into what would be a short coma. His organs would shut down and be taken by necrosis. Blood and other bodily fluids would pool inside of his abdomen and seep out through the nearest orifice. Albert would stop breathing and his heart would stop beating.

Then it would all be over. The pain would end. Albert would find his way out. It was torturous, but he'd get to leave on his own terms. His pledge to himself that he'd not leave things to chance, that he'd not be a victim of circumstance, and that he'd look the Devil in the eye and extend his middle finger, would be fulfilled.

Chapter 50

"Your apartment?" Jim was incredulous. He was yelling again and he couldn't stop himself. "You bring this up now? After all this?"

The coupe sat idling at the intersection where Brighton Road met Delaware Avenue. Its right blinker was on. Jim wasn't sure why he'd bothered to use the signal. He didn't remember hitting the switch and he wouldn't have noticed it was on if not for the click-click, click-click sound coming from under the steering column.

Across the street lie the aftermath of a multi-car accident and subsequent bloodbath. The scene was faintly illuminated by the Pontiac's headlamps and an overhead street light. Most of the lampposts along Delaware Avenue remained on; the exceptions being those that had previously malfunctioned due to burned out bulbs and poor maintenance.

A bright yellow convertible, so badly damaged as to render the manufacturer and model unidentifiable, had crashed head-on with a full-size custom Chevy van. The van had its grille pressed in and a large puddle of fluid had leaked out from under the engine bay, but the Chevy was otherwise intact. The massive vehicle had a specialty paint job with a high-gloss finish. It had a polished walnut-colored base with a giant mural of a haggard old wizard, replete with wooden staff, flowing black robe, and long white beard against a background of stars. The scowling old coot blasted a lightning bolt from long wrinkled fingers like he was casting some sort of spell.

It must not have been a spell of protection because it didn't do shit when it came to protecting the van's driver and passengers. There was evidence of multiple brutal deaths. Evidence of magic on the other hand- not so much. Four fleshy heaps of what used to be the van's occupants lie strewn across the sidewalk and intersection. A pair of cannibals crouched over two of them, shoveling mounds of mangled meat into their grinding maws.

Jim switched off the blinker. The ghouls didn't seem to notice the Pontiac, but he thought it best not to encourage them with a bright flashing yellow light. After what seemed to be an absurd length of time with no response, Jim asked, "I thought you said we couldn't go to your apartment?"

"Yeah but-"

"You said there's no food," he pressed. "It's not safe there- it was too risky. What changed?"

"There isn't much food there," Lindsey affirmed. "And I wasn't sure if it would be safe. But it is. At least it should be. It should be fine. And the food situation, we'll figure something out. There's probably enough for a couple days."

"I'm not worried about the food part," Jim clarified. "I'm worried about the part where we're about to use the little bit of gas we've got left to drive to a place you've been arguing against all day. So before we do that, I need to know we can get there and get inside."

"We can." She paused for a moment and then corrected herself, "We should be able to."

Glaring from across the car, Jim gave her a look that said, *Go on.*

"Okay, so, remember back at the gas station? When I said I got a voicemail?"

Jim nodded. Of course he remembered. It had been rolling around in his brain ever since she'd mentioned it. He'd been trying to figure out who called without having to ask.

"It was Chad," said Lindsey.

"Chad!" Jim exclaimed. The shock in his voice was a bit of an exaggeration. His tone shifting to one of ire and disgust; "The same Chad who stole your car? The Chad who abandoned you when your life was in danger, who left you to die alone in the break room at some shit-hole supermarket?"

Lindsey blew out a breath through clenched teeth and said, "Yes, that Chad."

"Fantastic," he spat, retrieving a cigarette from the center console. "So, what did awesome Chad have to say?"

"I didn't get to listen to the whole message," Lindsey explained as she handed him the lighter. "But he said he didn't mean to leave me behind. He said he borrowed my car on his lunch break so he could go to Taco Bell, but that was before everything happened."

"Right. Sure he did," Jim sneered.

"Can I continue?" she snapped.

Jim went to answer but his attention was pulled back to the other side of the street. A third zombie had staggered up to join the first two. It plopped down beside one of the available cadavers and began to feed, leaning in mouth-first and pulling away a glistening glob of chest meat.

"Anyway," Lindsey resumed speaking. "He said he tried to get back to the store but couldn't get through, something about all the traffic- too many cars blocking the road in front of the parking lot and he wasn't able to get in."

"I managed to get there okay," Jim grumbled through a mouthful of smoke.

"I'm just telling you what he said," she argued. "I wasn't there, so I don't know what happened. But he said that since he couldn't get back to the supermarket, he went home. He said that if things calmed down enough, he'd drive back over and try again."

"What a hero," Jim huffed. "I bet the traffic didn't stop him from getting to Taco Bell."

Ignoring the dig, Lindsey continued. "In the meantime, Chad said he'd be at home. But if I was able to get out and make it there, he said things were relatively calm at our apartment and it should be safe there."

"*Our* apartment?" Jim was aghast. "You never mentioned you were living with him!"

"Gee, I wonder why," Lindsey said sarcastically. "Look at how you're reacting. Of course I didn't want to say anything."

"So that's why you said we couldn't go there?" he asked. It was more of an accusation than a question.

"That's part of it," she admitted. "But what I said about not wanting to be here in town, about wanting to get as far away as we could- that was true too. And besides, if I would have told you about Chad and the apartment and everything, would you have wanted to go there?"

"Nope," Jim answered flatly. Taking another drag from his cigarette, he added, "And I'm not too keen on going there now either, to be perfectly honest."

"I'm not either," said Lindsey. "But at least it's some place safe we can go."

"Wait a second," he began. Jim took a final puff of smoke and tossed the butt through the open window. "That voicemail was from what, several hours ago?"

Lindsey shrugged. "Probably. Why?"

"Anything could have happened there since a few hours ago," he explained. "How do we know it's even still safe to go there?"

"I guess we don't," she confessed. "But what else can we do?"

"Well, before we burn the little gas we have left driving over there, why don't you call Chad and see if the coast is clear?" Jim suggested. The whole thing tasted like shit in his mouth and sitting beside Lindsey while she chatted away with Chad wasn't going to make it any better. But at least it would buy him a few seconds to try and come up with an alternative.

"I can't," Lindsey told him. "I dropped my phone back at the gas station and I didn't have a chance to get it before we left."

"Here, use mine." Jim pulled his cell phone from his pocket and handed it to her.

She looked at the screen for a moment and began to dial but hung up after only a few seconds. Lindsey handed the phone back to Jim and said, "No signal. He probably wouldn't have answered anyway. He never answers when he doesn't recognize the number."

"Alright," said Jim as he took back the device. "But we still don't know whether it's actually safe. I mean, what happens if we drive all the way over there only to find it overrun by zombies? Or what if the streets are blocked off or something? What if, for one reason or another, we can't get there? What then?"

"I don't know!" Lindsey blurted. "I guess we'll find out along the way. We have no other choice- unless you'd prefer to keep driving around aimlessly until the car finally runs out of gas. Then we're stuck spending the night locked inside the car. Is that what you want?"

She was obviously trying to make a point, but spending the night inside the coupe still sounded better than shacking up with her and Chad. Jim rolled his shoulders and said, "You jest, but we've never been safer than when we've been inside this car."

Across the street, the three zombies were beginning to stir. Two of them had stopped eating and seemed to be looking at the Pontiac. One of them pulled himself upright and took an uneasy step toward the car. About twenty yards to their left, four more shamblers had made their way out of the shadows and were moving closer to the scene of the crash.

"Listen, can we get moving before they get too close?" Lindsey asked, pointing through the windscreen at the approaching ghouls.

"Yep," Jim answered with a curt sharpness. He cut the wheel to the right and hit the gas. The engine whirred and the car picked up speed. Jim, without making eye contact, told her, "Just tell me which way to go."

He wasn't done. After everything that had happened, there was no way Jim was going to deliver her right back to Chad's grubby arms- not without some resistance. He would come up with something, some other way to keep her protected and to keep her by his side.

They drove down Delaware Avenue for less than a mile before Lindsey said, "Take a left up here."

"Where?" asked Jim. There were multiple streets coming up along the left-hand side of the road. "Is it before the strip mall, or after?"

323

"Doesn't matter," she said. "We just need to get a few blocks over."

Jim gave the wheel a hard turn. Tires squealed as the Pontiac jerked to the left and sped down the side street. A row of homes passed by on their left; the looted strip mall to their right. The next intersection was coming up quickly.

"Which way?" Jim asked.

"Take a right on Military Road," she instructed.

He gave the steering wheel another yank. The car roared down the four-lane thoroughfare and was coming up to a silver Ford SUV. The vehicle was parked at an odd angle by the side of the road and it seemed to be leaning to the left.

It wasn't until he passed by that Jim noticed the front driver's side wheel was missing. It was unclear whether an accident had caused the wheel to come off, or if this was just the result of some sort of shoddy at-home auto repair. In any case, Jim didn't see any bodies, or any parts that looked like they'd recently been removed from a body, so he assumed that whoever was driving must have gotten away safely.

After a few more blocks had gone by, it dawned on him that maybe he shouldn't be in such a hurry. This type of hard driving was just going to make the car run out of gas even quicker. Plus, it would give him less time to devise a plan.

Jim gradually eased off the gas pedal, so as not to make it obvious. The Pontiac stopped accelerating and began to slow. Lindsey, seeing that the road ahead was clear, gave him a questioning glance, but he didn't give her a chance to speak.

"Let's say, hypothetically, that we can't get back to your place," he began.

"Alright." Lindsey thought for a moment and asked, "Where are you going with this?"

"I've got a plan- a plan that's better than risking another trip across town to your apartment." Jim gestured with his right hand toward all the homes passing by on both sides of the car. "We're back in the suburbs. It's fairly quiet here, not a lot of people around from what I can tell."

"Yeah?"

"Well, just look at all these houses," Jim waved his hand over the dashboard again. "I bet most of them are empty. And anyone who's not home probably isn't coming back. Not any time soon, anyway."

"Jeez, Jim. A bit morbid, don't you think?" Lindsey commented.

"You know what I mean," he argued. "We could pick an empty house, get inside and barricade the doors. We'd be off the road and we'd have somewhere safe to stay until someone comes to help or until there's more news or whatever. It'd work."

"Yeah, I don't know." Lindsey shook her head. "How would we even know whether someone was already there?"

"We'd make sure it was empty before going in," Jim told her.

"Alright, but how?" she asked. "I mean, if someone's there, they're going to be pretty pissed off if they find us trying to break into their house. And what if they think we're infected? Jim, what if they have a gun or something?"

"We've got a gun," he pointed out. "Oh, remind me to reload, by the way. I didn't have a chance to do that when we left the gas station."

"So that's your plan?" Lindsey challenged. "Have a gun fight with a homeowner? Shoot your way into a stranger's house?"

"No," Jim answered, shaking his head. "Of course not. If someone's home, we'll move on to the next one."

"Right," she replied. "But back to my original question, how are we going to know if someone's there before we go inside?"

"We'll knock first," he said.

"We'll knock first?" Lindsey asked in disbelief.

"Yeah. We'll knock first," Jim repeated. "Zombies aren't going to knock. That's how they'll know we aren't infected. Or, ya know, we can ring the doorbell if they've got a doorbell."

"So they won't think we're zombies, they'll just think we're looters or home invaders," Lindsey commented. "What would you think if two people showed up at your door in the middle of the night carrying a shotgun?"

"Then we'll just find a house we know is definitely empty." The road went into a long, wide curve as it angled to the left. Jim steered accordingly and kept arguing his case. "It's a good idea. It'd definitely work."

"I don't know. Maybe I guess." Lindsey had stopped paying attention. She was still watching where they were going and making sure she was ready to give directions. Pointing ahead at the upcoming stop sign, she said, "Make a right up here."

Jim pulled up to the intersection and brought the car to a stop. He turned in his seat to face Lindsey and said, "Hey, let's do it. Let's stop driving around and check out one of these houses to see if we can get in. Whichever one you want, it'll be fine. We'll be safe and we'll be together, like we were talking about."

"You said that was your suggestion for if we couldn't get to the apartment," she reminded him. "I'd rather not break into someone's house if we don't have to. Especially when we're so close to where I actually live."

"Is it because of Chad?" Another accusation framed as an inquiry. Jim turned back in his seat so he wouldn't have to look directly at her.

"No, it's not because of Chad," Lindsey shot back. "I mean, not entirely. It's a factor- he is my boyfriend, after all."

Her *boyfriend*. She was still calling him that? After all this?

"But it's not just that," she continued. "It's my home. I know the place and I know I'll feel safe there. Do you know what I mean?"

"Yep." Jim turned to look out the driver's side window. He was trying to keep his cool, trying not to show how this was affecting him. And right now, annoyance was painted all over his face. Still looking in the direction opposite to her, Jim added, "Safe at home and with Chad. Just like that, all is forgiven and forgotten about."

"You're not listening to me," Lindsey contended. "It's my home- it's all my stuff. That's why I'm going there. And as far as Chad, I don't know what to think yet but I should at least let him know I'm alive."

"You don't owe him a damn thing," Jim interjected. "Not after what he did. That piece of shit left you for dead. And if he was at all concerned about you, he wouldn't have kept his fat ass parked at home on the sofa all day."

"You think I'm happy about it?" Lindsey shot back.

Jim opened his mouth to respond, but realized her question was rhetorical and decided to keep quiet.

"I'm actually quite pissed about it," she went on. "But there's not a whole lot I can do about it now. And hey, maybe he'll have a decent explanation. Maybe he won't. Maybe he's a coward and maybe he and I will be over and done with. None of that changes the fact that I need to go home."

Lindsey paused and thought for a moment. It seemed as though she was undecided about what she was going to say next. She looked at Jim and then down at her feet. Without looking up, she added, "And it's not like I'm going to leave you out on your own. It goes without saying you're more than welcome to stay with us."

"Stay with you? After everything, I'm supposed to do what? Crash on your sofa and hang out watching you and idiot Chad play house?" Jim's ire was on the rise once again.

"I'm not going to argue with you about this," Lindsey snapped. She popped open the console between the seats and got herself a cigarette. "This is not the time to discuss this."

"Please," Jim blurted, taking her by the wrist. He wavered and froze up for a few seconds as he looked down at his hand. It felt detached, like he was somehow observing himself behaving in this terrible manner. He released her arm but kept urging her to reconsider. "What about the bridge? The convenience store? What about everything that's happened today? You can't tell me there isn't something going on with us."

Lindsey held up a hand to cut him off but Jim kept going. "Lindsey, please. I need you, more than I ever have. I need you to be with me, to stay with me. I can keep protecting you. I can keep you happy."

"Are you kidding me with this?" Lindsey shouted. The mood in the car shifted to one of an interrogation. She lit her cigarette and blew a puff of smoke out the window. "Everyone we know might be dead and you're worried about what- that I might be dating the wrong guy? Or that I should pick you? I should leave everything behind and be with you, is that it?"

"No, it's just-"

"Am I missing something here?" It was Lindsey's turn to do the cutting off. "Is that the reason you came to get me when I called?"

"N- no, of course not," Jim stammered. It was happening. He was pushing too hard, pushing her away. Just like always. And the girl he loved was pushing right back, about to push him right out of her life altogether.

The girl he loved... That is who she had been, and was now again. Maybe it was a status that had remained unchanged over the years. His affection for her had certainly been neglected, misused, and maybe even rejected. But had it ever truly gone away?

It was a concept that hadn't been fully articulated until now- probably because Jim knew that his love for her, or his attraction to her, or infatuation or whatever you want to call it, would have almost certainly been one-sided. Lindsey would have rejected it- would have rejected him. And she would have been right to do so. But what about now?

326

He should tell her. He wanted to tell her. Jim had the overwhelming feeling that if he didn't speak up now, the chance may never come again.

And you're right, by the way. Jim should have been concerning himself with more pressing matters, of which there were plenty. He still hadn't heard whether his parents were okay. And now that he'd learned the outbreak was not a local phenomenon, their odds of survival were ever-decreasing. Not to mention his friends and coworkers. There would be no returning to work any time soon and probably no home left to return to either.

Everything was gone. He had lost everything in less than ten hours. That was probably why he'd been clinging so tightly to Lindsey and the life he'd been constructing for them in his mind. Pure fantasies- you can count those amongst the things lost as well. He wanted so badly for it to be real, like it might somehow make everything okay again. Jim had to make a move. That was all he could do, speak up now or forever add it to his mountain-size pile of regrets.

"Then what is it?" she demanded. "What am I missing?"

"Lindsey," he began gently, trying to ease the tension between them.

"Yeah?" Lindsey pivoted in her seat to turn and face him. She looked right into his eyes. He had her full attention, though her demeanor was yet to soften.

"I- uh," Jim hesitated.

"Yes?" she said, sliding forward and moving inches closer.

"I..."

"Jim, what is it?" Lindsey asked, her eyes narrowing and intrigue growing.

"I, um," he stammered. Jim cleared his throat and dried his sweating palms against the front of his shorts. "I just get worried, that's all."

What a pussy. Jim, once again, failed to come through. He could drive through Hell, face down zombies, and kill those who threatened him and those around him, but he couldn't tell a pretty girl how much he cared for her. Pathetic.

"Oh." Lindsey's expression fell as she slid back in her seat. She'd obviously expected something a little more substantive. But she'd made the mistake of relying on Jim to deliver it. "I get what you're saying, about Chad and everything. But we're not going to be able to figure it all out tonight. I understand you're worried and I get where you're coming from. I really do, but I need to go home. I have to do this and I know it's uncomfortable for you, but I'd like to have you with me. Okay?"

"Yeah," he replied; his tone quiet and subdued. She was right and he hated it.

"Alright." Lindsey gave him a squeeze on the hand. "Then shall we go?"

Deflated. Defeated and helpless. Jim gave her a nod but kept looking straight ahead to keep his shame out of view. He put the car in gear and began driving to the last place on Earth he wanted to go, a place where he knew she would leave him forever.

For the rest of the drive to the apartment building, the only talking that took place was Lindsey giving directions and Jim acknowledging them. Jim remained flush with embarrassment, ashamed for having broken down the way he had. It was meant to be an honest proclamation of his feelings. What it turned into was begging, whining, and carrying on like some kind of disgraceful idiot. How humiliating. Lindsey had produced a swift rejection, leaving both of them with very little to say.

"It's right up here on the left," she said after another long period of silence. "The one with the porch light on."

"The power's still on. That's a good sign," Jim observed.

A long blacktop driveway ran past the left side of the building to a four-unit garage situated at the rear of the property. The apartment building looked as though someone had taken Jim's tenement and cut it in half down the middle.

It had two full stories above ground and what appeared to be a garden level at the bottom. The structure had the same faded brick siding and there was a big glass door under a small porch cover at the front. A lamp was on in the hallway beyond the front door. The rest of the building looked dark and deserted.

Jim eased the car into the parking lot. He switched off the headlamps but left the engine running. Lindsey pressed her face to the window and watched for signs of movement on the other side of the glass. The nearest street lamp was off, as were most of the lights in the houses nearby.

"Well, here we are," Lindsey said in a tone often reserved for the end of an awkward date that she wished had ended sooner.

"Yep. Here we are," Jim repeated. "So, I obviously wasn't thrilled about coming here at first, but I'm glad you have a safe place to go."

His hands dropped from the steering wheel to land in his lap. This too was Jim's sullen bad-date posture and at first, he wasn't sure why this felt so final, like this was the end of everything. But the answer came to him in a hurry. It was because Lindsey, the girl he'd fallen back in love with, was about to hop out of his car and into the arms of her live-in boyfriend.

"*We* have a safe place to go," she corrected. "Aren't you coming with me?"

"Are you sure that's a good idea?" he asked. "Me, you, Chad; seems like it could be pretty uncomfortable for everyone."

"You're being ridiculous," Lindsey told him. "You can stay with us. It's no big deal."

Jim shrugged. "I don't know about that. I doubt Chad's going to be happy about me showing up and moving in."

"What do you think, he's going to kick you out? It's going to be fine," she insisted. "If anything, he's going to be glad and appreciate you bringing me home safely. And besides, even if he does have a problem with you being here- which he won't, I'd have the final say about who stays and who doesn't. It's more my apartment than it is his."

"How's that?" asked Jim.

"My name is on the lease," Lindsey explained. "I lived here for a while before he moved in."

"Oh really?" Jim scoffed. "How much do you think that matters now? I mean, it's not like you can call the landlord to have the rental agreement enforced."

"Well then what are you going to do?" snapped Lindsey, growing increasingly frustrated.

"Um..."

"Well?" she pressed.

"I could do my house idea." Jim's answer sounded more like a question than a statement.

"Fine," said Lindsey as she reached for the door handle. "You've got a perfectly good place to stay, but you'd rather break into someone's house? Because what- you don't like my boyfriend? Or because you don't like that I even have a boyfriend? You're being really petty right now, Jim."

"Lindsey wait," he said. "That's not it."

She let go of the handle and turned back around to face him. "Then what is it?"

"It's just," Jim paused. He looked to the front of the building and then out through the driver's side window. "Something just doesn't feel right. You're right, I don't like Chad and I don't like that you're with him. But it's something else too. Something is just off about this."

"You're overthinking things," she told him.

"Yeah, maybe," he answered, letting out a deep breath.

"Just give it a chance, okay?" Lindsey slid forward in her seat, moving a few inches closer to him. She took both of his hands in hers, lifted them to her shoulders, and pulled him in for a hug. Whispering into his ear, she told him, "It's okay. I'm not going anywhere."

"Yeah," Jim said softly. Reluctantly at first, he returned the hug. His hands slid across her back as he pulled her in tighter.

After holding each other for a few moments, Jim and Lindsey released their embrace. They returned to scouting the area to make sure it was safe to make their way to the building's entrance. Jim checked the mirrors and scanned the driveway in front of him. His eyes traced along the front of the building, trying to see through one of several darkened windows. Then he turned around to watch through the car's back window to see if anything had been sneaking up behind them.

"Looks all clear to me," he said.

"I think someone's coming," Lindsey told him. She had been watching the front of the building.

Through the front door, they could see a patch of darkness moving across the hallway. The rest of the lights were still off, but someone seemed to be walking toward the entrance. The shadow grew larger and gradually took the form of a person staggering up to the doorway. And there he was. Standing just inside the threshold, still wearing the Bennett's Supermarket staff uniform of black pants and a green polo shirt, was Chad.

"We should go," said Lindsey.

"Why don't I give you a minute to get him up to speed," Jim suggested. "So he knows why I'm here and what's going on."

"Don't be silly," she argued. "I told you he's not going to mind you being here."

"Then why is he just standing there?" Jim asked. "Why hasn't he come out?"

"He probably doesn't know who it is," Lindsey explained. "I doubt he recognizes your car. Don't worry. I promise it's going to be alright. Just relax, okay?"

"Yeah, no problem," he replied. "But you go ahead, I'll catch up in a sec. Explain to Chad what's going on and that'll give me time to gather up the gun and everything."

The shotgun lie across the back seat in the spot where he'd left it when they fled the gas station. Thankfully they hadn't needed it since. And while this suburban neighborhood seemed relatively quiet and safe, it would be a long time before Jim went anywhere without a firearm.

"Okay," Lindsey said as she grabbed the handle and opened the door. "Just don't take too long."

She climbed out of the car and closed the door softly, careful not to make too much noise. Jim watched as she did a light jog across the lawn and up to the front porch. Chad took a half step backwards as she reached the entrance and pulled the front door open to let herself in. Satisfied Lindsey had made it inside without incident, Jim turned around in his seat and reached for the shotgun. It was at that moment when a shrill, blaring scream pierced the night's air.

Gun in hand, Jim was on his feet and sprinting for the building. The silhouette of commotion could be seen from beyond the entryway; frantic limbs twisting and flailing. A heavy thump hit the floor and echoed through the hall. A geyser of blood sprayed the glass. The sole of a shoe kicked up and smeared a thick red streak along the inside of the clear barrier.

"Lindsey!" Jim cried out from mere feet away. He hopped over the steps to the porch landing and kicked in the door.

The walls were covered in blood. A massive puddle formed on the floor. And at the center of it all was Lindsey. She was on her back, eyes open, mouth locked in a permanent silent scream; her beautiful face forever transformed by the grip of abject terror. Lindsey wasn't moving, save for a slight wiggle as a gore-slicked Chad leaned in to take what would have been a second or third mouthful of flesh from her gaping neck.

No. No- fuck. This couldn't be happening. This was just a bad dream, a horrible trauma-induced nightmare. He'd wake up and snap out of it any second now. He had to. He just had to.

"Lindsey!" he screamed again. Jim's vision blurred. Darkness crept in from the edges. He couldn't breathe.

Chad was on all fours and hunched over his dying girlfriend. His greasy hair was matted to his scalp. A dark viscous fluid dripped from his left ear. His pudgy forearms were covered in bite marks and oozing lesions. The sleeves and collar of his shirt were stretched and ripped open to reveal more wounds, torn skin with a pink crust where the flesh had been violated.

"Get off of her!" Jim bellowed.

The Chad-shaped creature looked up to see the business end of a double-barrel shotgun hovering only inches from his nose. His head tilted; the confused expression of a rabid animal studying something novel and unfamiliar. Chad's lip pulled back into a sneer, flashing a row of burgundy-stained teeth. Jim pulled the trigger.

Click.

"Shit."

He pulled the trigger again. Click.

"What the f-" Jim looked down at the gun. He flicked the top lever and the barrels dropped open to reveal a pair of long empty tubes. No shells. He'd never bothered to reload after the gas station incident.

Chad sprung to his feet and propelled himself forward. He found little traction on the sodden red carpet, so instead of leaping onto his intended victim, the beast could only awkwardly rush toward him. Slipping and somewhat off balance, the top of Chad's head slammed into Jim's chest, followed by his left shoulder.

Jim gasped as he was thrown back against the door frame. Chad fell when they collided but he quickly scrambled to his feet and was charging once more. Jim lifted the shotgun with both hands in front of him as he lunged forward to meet his attacker.

The top of the barrels connected with Chad's face, bashing him right in the mouth. An audible pop sounded as one of his front teeth cracked and split against the cold metal. Blood and disease-laced saliva ran down, over the bastard's lips and onto the weapon. Chad swung his hands like claws, trying to grab onto Jim's chest and neck. Jim held him at arm's-length, keeping the shotgun held sideways and blocking that rotten piece of shit from getting any closer.

Chad let out a furious shriek and pressed harder, pinning Jim between himself and the wall. The edge of the door frame dug into the skin between Jim's shoulder blades. That greasy-haired cocksucker tried stepping in closer, but his feet once again failed to find purchase on the carpet, which had grown soggy and saturated with spilled blood.

Jim seized the opportunity, lifting his right foot and kicking Chad's left knee. Both feet slipped out from under him and the prick's hefty frame dropped straight down; his chin catching the shotgun barrels on his way to the floor. A fresh fountain of red sprayed out of his mouth and the severed tip of his tongue flopped to the ground at Jim's feet.

A pair of swollen hands grabbed onto Jim's ankle as Chad tried pulling him to the floor. Jim kicked out, slipping away from the monster's grip and slamming his foot into the side of his head. The ghoul fell back, splashing into a dark red puddle as his ass hit the ground. Thick droplets sprang up and doused the wall behind him.

Chad tried to pull himself upright as Jim rushed forward to deliver another kick- this one straight to the face. The beast howled as he staggered backwards, losing his footing and then tripping over Lindsey's limp body. The cannibal fiend began to fall and before he could recover, Jim stepped up to close the distance. He drew back the shotgun like it was a golf club.

The savage looked up just in time to catch a glimpse of the shotgun barrels racing through the air, right before they connected with his skull. His skin split wide open. Jim could hear the orbital bone snap and then a nauseating squish as the eye itself burst apart.

A wail of agony rang out as Jim pulled back and swung down hard. The next blow flattened Chad's nose, followed by another that broke his jaw. Jim let out a scream of his own as he continued swinging. Every strike was punctuated by a spattering of blood. All sorts of fluids surged out of the growing wounds. And Jim kept on swinging.

He swung until Chad's arms stopped twitching, until his face had been caved in, until everything above the shoulders was mangled and crushed. All that remained was a mutilated pile of shattered bone, stray hair, and red sludge. Jim swung his weapon until it made its way clear through to the floor, until the shock of impact took away the feeling in his arms, until he'd depleted every ounce of his energy. And when it was over, both he and Chad were left utterly decimated.

Jim fell back against the wall and struggled to regain his breath. The gun slipped through his numb fingers as he slid down to the floor. He buried his face in his throbbing hands, unable to lay eyes on what had become of the girl he loved. Jim, a true failure in every sense, sat alone in the silent hallway and wept.

Chapter 51

The piercing timbre of grinding metal; a noise somehow discernible above the ballad of the apocalypse. Drooling marauders, all clamoring to get inside, screamed a song of starvation and hate. The rabid goons numbered well into the hundreds. They could fill every hallway, stairwell, and apartment within the tenement. If only they could get through those doors.

Despite their volume, the skull-ringing snap of ruptured bolts could be plainly heard. The entire door frame dipped and jerked forward just before collapsing into the lobby. A layer of still-twitching corpses landed atop the wreckage of shattered glass and wrenched aluminum. The swarm erupted all at once and the infected insurrectionists stormed in. The cannibal stampede was underway.

Some of them, those closest to the entrance when the doorway finally gave out, lost their balance during the unexpected shift in pressure. Five or six of them were knocked to the ground, unable to withstand the force of the horde surging behind them, and helpless to protect themselves from the herd's trampling feet. They could only lie there and watch as a flurry of footsteps crushed their bones and flattened their organs. The rest of the hellions forged ahead.

Even though the entryway had been breached, the opening was too small for them to all get in at once. However, this fact was of little comfort to the three remaining residents. The ghouls that were still tweaking on adrenaline were the ones who had pushed their way to the front of the line. These were the ones that were faster, stronger, angrier; the ones you can't outrun. And those were the first to enter.

To Jenna, Danny, and Lucy, it hardly seemed real. It felt like they were seeing it all unfold in slow motion from a thousand miles away. They weren't actually there in that dank little lobby, they were in the world's crappiest movie theater watching the world's shittiest film at half speed.

Any minute now, the final credits would role and they'd return to reality. No longer would their home be under siege. The loons trying to eat them would all be gone. Soon enough, they'd be back in the real world; a place where their toughest challenge would be figuring out how they could scrape together enough cash to pay next month's rent. Any minute now.

After all, this type of shit wasn't supposed to happen. Not to them, anyway. That's not to say real tragedy didn't exist. But hardship and sorrow, well, that wasn't for them. That was reserved for other people, the people you hear about in a blurb on the news. There was always someone else to soak up the grief.

It's like hearing about some dude getting mauled by a lion in the Serengeti, or when you see some footage of a flooded town in Columbia. It's tragic and awful, but it's so far away it registers like fiction. It never happens close to home. And it certainly never happens to the invincible youth.

They were supposed to be safe, protected. They were supposed to survive. Nothing could touch them, especially if they stayed inside like they were told. The Grim Reaper wasn't supposed to find them when they were locked away in their homes. Yet here he was. And he hadn't brought a rising tide or a big cat to collect the survivors. That cocksucker brought zombies. Lucy, Danny, and Jenna had no recourse but to run for their lives.

As fast as they could move, they went back down the steps and into the basement. Now Lucy was first in line. With both hands gripping the golf club, she jumped down the short stairway and landed awkwardly on the cement floor. A sharp stinging sensation formed in her ankles but Lucy managed to stay on her feet. She pushed through the door that led to the laundry area, not looking back and trusting that her brother was right behind her.

He was. Danny followed her lead and jumped the length of the stairs. His was also a hard landing. Still holding the machete, Danny used his one free hand to keep himself from slamming into the wall at the bottom of the steps. He made a quick right turn and sprinted into the unfinished portion of the lower level, trying to keep up with Lucy. Behind him, he heard three loud cracks as Jenna fired into the onrushing crowd.

Pop! She aimed for their heads. If the gunshot wasn't fatal, it wasn't going to slow them down. At least, not until they bled out. They'd get to her before that happened, and Jenna would win the race to room temperature. The first shot hit a fiend in the face. His head jerked back and his body fell to the floor. Two beasts tripped and fell over the lifeless lump. Instead of trying to break their fall, they reached out and swiped at Jenna's legs. Neither was close enough to make contact. She fired twice more before turning her back to the horde and racing down the stairs.

Jenna reached the lower landing. She turned right and followed the same route that Lucy and Danny had taken. Danny was standing in front of the washing machine with his machete out in front of him. He was waiting for her to catch up and watching to make sure she was okay.

"You good?" he shouted to her.

"Yeah," she called back. "Go! Go!"

Behind her, a mass of flesh came barreling down the stairs. The diseased freaks had tripped over the carcasses of their fallen cohorts and then rushed toward the stairway too quickly. A dozen or more went careening down, tripping over one another and turning end over end before crashing into the cement floor below. A gore-soaked assembly of creeps formed just outside the laundry room. The loons were off their feet, disorganized and uncoordinated. But they were less than five feet away and they'd be back on their feet in no time.

From the top of the infected mound, one of them rolled off and charged at Jenna. It was male, about five and a half feet tall with an athletic build and a goatee. The creature had on a pair of tattered khaki shorts and a black tee shirt that glistened with hot wet blood. His auburn-colored hair was matted to his scalp and thick streaks of red marred his otherwise pale complexion. He was ahead of the pack and quickly closing the distance between himself and the young lady with the rifle.

Jenna leveled the gun, pointed it at the zombie, and pulled the trigger. She didn't bother aiming. She didn't need to. From this distance, it would be almost impossible to miss. The small rimfire round exploded from the barrel and traveled directly into the face of the monstrosity. Its nose caved in as the bullet smashed through and made its way into the skull where it punctured a series of holes through the brute's rotten brain.

One shot, one kill. As the infected man crumpled to the floor, Jenna considered how much better off she'd be if she had something more substantial than the small caliber rounds. She had already fired four shots, leaving only six in the magazine. Jenna thought, and not for the first time that evening, that with such a limited supply, she really needed something with a little more stopping power. Instead of getting lodged or lost inside of the first ghoul it hit, she needed a bullet that would punch through and keep going into the next creep in line.

But she didn't have time to dwell on this. And if she didn't move her ass, Jenna wouldn't have time for anything else either. More plague-carrying maniacs were on their way. Those that had fallen down the stairs had pulled themselves upright and were wasting no time as they continued their pursuit.

There was no sense shooting at them. Gun or not, Jenna would be dead within seconds if she didn't start running immediately.

So she did just that. The young woman pumped her legs as hard as she could and moved as quickly as she could to the opposite side of the basement. She darted past the laundry machines, drain tubs, and scattered junk to make her way into the next room where Danny and Lucy anxiously waited for her to arrive.

"Let's go!" Danny cried, waving her on.

Lucy stood in the doorway that would lead them to the lower landing on the opposite side of the building. To her credit, Lucy was standing her ground quite well. She pivoted to stand sideways with one foot on either side of the threshold so she could see danger coming from ahead or behind. And if danger did come, she'd be ready. At least, she prayed she'd be ready. Lucy lifted the golf club over her shoulder to resemble a batter about to take a swing.

Danny had his weapon drawn in much the same manner, both hands on the machete's handle and ready to strike. He positioned himself directly in front of Lucy, prepared to act as a human barrier to shield her from the oncoming zombies if need be. Both he and his sister were determined to wait for their friend and make sure they all made it to safety in one piece.

Jenna rushed to meet them. With the mob of freaks drawing near, she called to Danny and Lucy to, "Go! Go! Go!"

Lucy didn't need to be told more than once. She began running up the steps, taking them two or three at a time until she found herself back in the lobby on her own side of the building. Now she was alone, separated from a herd of diseased beasts by the already-damaged doorway. Massive spiderweb cracks had formed in the glass panels. The top portion of the door frame was torn away from the wall and leaning into the building, just like it had been in the other lobby right before it collapsed. The commotion seemed to have caused a frenzy amongst the invaders. It wouldn't be long before they tore through this entrance too.

Danny was still in the lower landing. He stepped aside to make way for Jenna to get by. As soon as she ran past him, he leaned in and pulled the door closed, sealing the savages inside the unfinished section of the basement- or so he'd hoped.

A thunderous boom sounded as five or six creeps moving at top speed collided with the flimsy hollow-core door. Splintering plywood and deafening growls caused Danny to jump back from the doorway as the head of a ghoul busted through the frail barrier. He fell backwards, landing hard on the floor and dropping the machete in the process. Vulnerable and defenseless, Danny felt naked and weak as he lie on the floor without his weapon. The young man rolled to his side and brought his hands up to shield his head from the dust and debris filling the small hallway.

The zombies couldn't figure out how to work a doorknob, but that wouldn't matter. They didn't need to open the door, they'd simply tear right through it. And they would probably do so in less than a minute. They could see Danny through the hole they'd formed and this only made them angrier, hungrier, and more frantic in their pursuit.

"Let's go," a voice called from somewhere above. Danny looked up the stairwell to see Jenna shouting down at him. "Come on, Danny!"

He collected himself, grabbed his machete and pulled himself to his feet. More broken bits of wood and paint chips rained down around him as the zombies smashed into the door again and again. Danny wiped the grime and wood fragments from his face with his one free hand and made a move for the stairs. He'd make it about three steps, just far enough to get his foot over the first riser, before something forced him to stop.

"Shit!" Danny cried. He looked down to see a massive red-streaked hand locking its thick, dirt-covered fingers around his forearm, just below the elbow. One of the ghouls had reached through the hole in the door and grabbed him. The bastard was yanking on his arm, trying to pull Danny's exposed flesh closer to his snapping yellow teeth.

He jerked and tried to free his arm- his right arm, the arm that held his blade. But the zombie pulled too and it was much stronger. The creature yanked again, pulling Danny's entire body against the doorway, jarring him and causing him to drop his weapon once more.

"Danny!" Lucy shrieked from the top of the stairs. She watched, frozen in horror, as her brother tried and failed to free himself from the grip of the beast. A gaping, drooling jaw opened wide as Danny's flesh grew closer and closer.

Jenna could, and would, do more than just watch. She ran halfway down the short stairwell and raised the rifle to her shoulder. It should have been an easy shot, especially from this distance, but when Jenna looked down the barrel and lined it up, she found only Danny in her sights.

"Hey," she shouted. "Duck!"

Danny, who hadn't noticed her approaching, looked up to see the barrel of a gun pointed at him. He tried to drop to the floor and get out of the line of fire, but the piece of shit zombie wouldn't let go. Danny's head and most of his chest were still blocking the shot.

"Move," Jenna commanded. "Get out of the way."

"I'm trying," he called back.

"Damn it, Danny," Jenna cried. "Move your ass."

"Hold on," he pleaded. Danny reached down with his free hand, looking for something-anything he could use to kill the asshole who was trying to eat him.

He felt around near his waist, finding something hard and slender in his pants; a tool used for pounding. With the machete always at the ready, he'd almost forgotten about it altogether. Danny reached into his pocket and grabbed the handle of the hammer. He swung it as hard as he could and aimed for the zombie's nose.

It broke the skin, entered the skull, and became lodged inside for a brief moment. The hand clenching Danny's arm went limp and the zombie fell to the floor. Danny held tightly to the hammer and a sick wet pop sounded as the tool slid free from the hideous caved-in face.

"Are you alright?" Lucy asked. She was still at the top of the steps.

"Yeah, I think so," he answered.

As soon as the beast fell away from the door, two more cannibals stepped up to take his place. Danny stooped to retrieve his machete, still holding the hammer in his left hand. The rabid loons continued to pound on the other side of the door, all buzzing for a mouthful of fresh meat. More filthy, bloody arms reached through the opening.

One of the zombies swiped at him as he tried to reach the stairs. At this point, Danny had no more patience for this bullshit. He lifted the machete and brought the blade down hard on the outstretched arm. A wide gash opened and a fountain of blood erupted from the gaping wound. As he'd expected, this did not deter the beast to whom the arm belonged. So once more, Danny swung the blade and sliced into him harder, deeper. Again and again, Danny swung the machete a fifth time and a sixth; each blow tearing open a new slit in the skin.

Red fluid sprayed across the broken door and pooled on the floor at Danny's feet. The claw of a hand twitched and kept grabbing for him, but with each strike of the blade, the grasping limb became weaker and weaker. As tendons were severed and muscles were torn to shreds, the fingers lost their ability to move. The sharpened steel kept coming. It smashed through one bone and then the next.

Danny kept swinging. The intensity of his rage matched that of the zombies. His arm swung, the machete dropped, the blade cut. It was almost mechanical. He did this over and over until the hand fell away from the arm and landed in a puddle of its own blood on the disgusting basement floor. At last, the zombie finally pulled back; a mangled red mess of chewed-up soft tissue and dangling flaps of skin where its hand used to be.

"Danny, come on," a voice called to him. He looked down at the severed appendage. The front of his shirt was dotted with specks of blood. Danny came out of his murderous daze and began climbing the stairs.

"Come on, let's go!" Jenna shouted again. To her rear, the metal door frame at the main entrance swayed and bobbed as the crowd outside pressed against it. She motioned over her shoulder to the pair of glass doors and said, "We don't have much time."

Danny picked up the pace and ran the rest of the way up. Behind him, the brutes in the basement were back at work trying to smash a bigger hole in the door. The opening was already large enough for one of them to squeeze his upper body through. The creep bent at the waist and put his hands on the ground, trying to pull himself across the threshold and into the tiny hallway.

Jenna stood back and let Danny slide past her. She pointed the weapon down the stairwell, using the rifle's sights to aim for the creature's head. Crack! In an instant, a fresh coat of red paint splattered onto the far wall and the beast stopped moving. He was large enough to fill the hole in the door and stop the others from reaching through. She prayed it would buy them enough time to get upstairs. Moreover, she hoped they'd encounter fewer than five of the brutes between the lobby and the apartment. Otherwise, she'd be out of bullets.

"Everybody okay?" Lucy asked. She'd been keeping one eye on Danny and the other on the horde just outside the glass doors. The left side of the frame was pulled farther from the wall and the barbarians threatened to get in through the gap.

"Yep," Jenna replied; her gaze still focused on the basement doorway.

"Yeah, I'm-" Danny's words cut off for only a split second before he shouted, "Lucy- look out."

Lucy spun around in time to see one of the freaks pulling himself into the lobby between the wall and the detached aluminum door frame. The boyish fiend couldn't have been more than fifteen or sixteen years old. He wore tattered jeans with no shirt and a slew of cuts and bruises across his chest and abdomen. His arms, shoulders, and head were inside the building, but his hips had become stuck where the opening between the wall and door frame grew narrow.

Before the ghoul could wedge his way through, Lucy swung the golf club and smashed it into the side of his face. Its body slumped to the side but only for an instant. The creature jerked itself upright and now, instead of pulling itself forward, it snapped its jaws and reached for Lucy. She swung the club again. This time, blood and saliva poured from its mouth. A couple of broken teeth landed silently on the carpet.

Lucy would not relent. She mimicked her brother's actions from a moment earlier. Again and again, she swung the golf club, striking the beast in the head over and over until it finally fell limp and lifeless. Or, hopefully lifeless. She couldn't tell whether it was dead or simply unconscious, and she wouldn't have a chance to find out. As soon as she was through dealing with the first ghoul, a second and third were pushing their way through and trying to nab her.

She swung for the next in line but instead of cracking a zombie skull, the heel of the golf club collided with the metal door frame. The impact sent a jolt down the shaft and into her arms, causing Lucy to drop the club. It landed on the floor between her and a big male creep with a shaved head. He lurched forward and grabbed for her. Without thinking, Lucy reached to her waist and grabbed the first thing she could find, the barbecue fork. She took it by the handle and thrust it forward into the monster's face.

Both three-inch prongs punched through skin and bone, leaving the fork lodged in the prick's cheek. The ghoul still swung its arms at her, but Lucy refused to let up. She pressed harder on the handle, forcing the utensil deeper into its head until the beast finally stopped moving. Its lifeless body fell in a heap on top of its shirtless comrade; the fork still buried in its face.

"Don't let them get in," Jenna called. She aimed her rifle toward the opening in the wall, but couldn't get a clear shot. Lucy was too close to the action and Jenna didn't want to risk hitting the glass, lest it shatter and make an even bigger entrance for the bastards.

Lucy quickly reached for the knife tucked under her belt, barely bringing it up in time to see a female creep lunging at her through the gap between the wall and the door frame. This one looked to be about thirty years old. She was pale and gaunt and her blonde hair was caked with dirt and various fluids. Lucy swung the knife in an underhand motion, driving the point of the blade into the stomach of the beast standing before her. She knew that once wouldn't be enough, so she kept stabbing its abdomen and chest, avoiding the onslaught of groping hands until the cannibal slut joined the growing number of deceased.

By now, Danny was by her side, doing his best to keep the zombies at bay. Lucy poked them with her kitchen knife and he swung the machete at any weirdo foolish enough to stick an arm or a hand past the threshold. The opening was still only large enough for one or two of them to fit through at a time, but if either of the blade-wielding combatants stepped away from the doorway, they'd all come flooding in.

"They're piling up," Danny shouted between machete blows.

"Yeah," Lucy answered as she plunged the knife into the belly of another ghoul.

He was right. Every time another zombie tried to get in, it was promptly hacked to death and would fall to the ground on top of the last. If enough of them piled up on top of each other, their corpses might jam the opening long enough for Danny, Lucy, and Jenna to make a break for it and try to get upstairs before the bodies could be pushed out of the way.

"The dead ones," said Jenna. "When there's enough of them blocking the hole, we'll go. Wait for me to-"

She wouldn't get a chance to finish. Danny and Lucy were keeping the savages out, but too many of them were pressing against the doorway. Each time Lucy slayed one of them with her knife or Danny cut one down with his machete, another would push its way to the front of the pack and slam its full weight into the doors. Every time this happened, the aluminum frame would bend and sway, lurching farther into the lobby and creating an even bigger opening.

Jenna ran forward and leaned a shoulder into the glass in an effort to keep the doorway from collapsing in. The beasts howled and pounded on the glass as they tried to break through. She turned, pressing her back against the door and digging her heels into the floor for leverage. From this vantage point, she could see straight down the stairs to the basement. Jenna had a clear view of the door at the bottom of the steps. And she could see a pair of fists punching through it.

Danny was saying something to Lucy, but Jenna couldn't make it out over the commotion of screams, snarls, and body parts slamming into the walls. She also couldn't make out the sounds of the lower door being broken apart, but she could see it all the same. Another arm broke through, sending broken shards of plywood scattering across the floor. Then an elbow and a shoulder. And then a head came through, and another.

"Guys," she shouted. No one responded, so she tried again, louder this time. "Guys!"

"Yeah?" Danny answered, holding his arm out and motioning for Lucy to back away from the opening in the wall. He didn't stop fighting. Danny swung the blade down hard against the side of a zombie's throat as he asked, "What is it?"

"We have to go," Jenna yelled. "They're getting in downstairs."

"If we stop, they're going to get in here too," Lucy told her. She saw her golf club on the ground and considered reaching for it, but it was too close to the rabid shitheads trying to get in. She pointed at it and called to her brother, "Hey Danny, could you?"

"Sure," he replied, kicking the golf club away from the door so Lucy could reach it. Without missing a beat, Danny swung hard at an outstretched arm reaching into the lobby. The blade cut through its wrist and if not for a stubborn patch of skin and tendon, it would have cut the hand clean off. The brute flailed its arm wildly, spilling blood and banging its near-severed hand against the ghouls by its side. Danny called over his shoulder to Jenna and asked, "How ya holdin' up?"

"Bad," Jenna told him. She was bent over at the waist; the glass doors weighing heavily against her shoulders. No matter how hard she pushed with her legs, the doorway leaned in farther, getting closer and closer to the floor. She added, "I don't think I can hold it much longer."

"Right," Danny said. "And how's it lookin' down there?"

"Worse," she answered. At the bottom of the steps, two of the creeps were more than halfway through the door. They were destroying it, bashing apart what little remained. Then a third joined them, each fighting to be the first to get to the other side. "They're almost in."

"Shit."

Another hinge, the middle one on the right side, let out a pop as its screws snapped off. The entire door frame lurched forward; the force pushing Jenna away from the entrance. She stumbled, trying but failing to stay on her feet. The rifle slid free from her grasp and skittered across the lobby floor as both of her knees scraped against the dingy carpet.

Without someone pressing against it from the inside, the door frame had only one stubborn hinge fighting to keep it upright. The gap along its top and left side grew larger with each passing second. More infected heads and limbs reached in through the opening. Danny and Lucy did their best to ward them off, but time was running out.

Jenna scrambled on her hands and knees to recover her weapon, which had come to rest just inches from the top of the stairs leading to the basement. She grabbed the rifle from the floor and looked up just in time to see the form of the first creep who'd made it completely through the lower door.

It was another male. Apart from the bruises and streaks of crusted blood, his skin looked pale and gray, as if he'd been locked out overnight in a snowstorm. He had on a pair of black shorts and a white tee shirt with a thin gold chain around his neck. The shirt had some sort of writing or branding across the chest, but with all the red stains and ripped fabric, it was impossible to make out the words. Somewhat disoriented, the brute staggered and took a half step back as he regained his equilibrium. Once he'd steadied himself, the prick looked up and focused his gaze on Jenna. Then, with a primitive scream, he was leaping up the stairwell with his fists clenched and mouth open.

The monstrosity made it halfway up with a single jump; his feet landing heavily on the fourth riser. But he wouldn't make it any farther. His brief hesitation, the split-second he'd wasted composing himself, had been long enough for Jenna to reach her weapon and fire a single shot. The tiny bullet smashed through his sternum and tore into the left ventricle in his heart. Such a small round won't always have an exit wound. Instead, it'll sometimes ricochet off of bones, tearing apart soft tissue until it runs out of momentum. The brute collapsed backwards, dead before he hit the cement floor at the bottom of the stairs, and before the bullet stopped bouncing around inside his chest cavity.

At the lower end of the stairwell, another ghoul nearly tripped over the corpse. This one had on a pair of jeans with no shirt. His chest and abdomen were badly cut. Massive sections of skin and flesh had been torn away- injuries that must have been caused by something larger than a kitchen knife. Not even Danny's machete could have done that kind of damage. The exposed tissue, which looked very much like ground meat that had spoiled, oozed a reddish-purple goo that stained his pants and dripped to the floor with each step. It was amazing that this creature was still alive with so much skin gone and blood lost. But he wouldn't remain that way for much longer.

Crack! Another round exploded from the barrel of the gun. This one caught him on the bridge of his nose, right between the eyes. Again, there was no exit wound but the bastard was dead just the same. And just like the monster before him, there were already others ready to take his place and continue their pursuit.

"Guys," Jenna called. She was still kneeling and had the rifle pointed toward the basement.

"Yeah," Danny answered mid-swing and without looking up. "You alright over there?"

"We have to move," she shouted. "Like, right now- they're about to get in."

As if on cue, a thick burly hand punched through the upper portion of the basement door. The last significant portion of the hollow-core barrier shattered into several pieces, showering the downstairs hallway with more dust and splintered plywood. Two hairy-knuckled hands swatted at the few remaining bits of what used to be the door and the ogre made his way across the threshold.

The bastard had an imposing build; mammoth muscles planted atop a tall frame and wide shoulders. A cluster of protruding blood vessels ran over his meaty hands and well-muscled forearms. He looked like he could have been a bodybuilder before he turned into a raving lunatic. Well, maybe an amateur bodybuilder. His outfit, a short-sleeve twill jumpsuit and plain yellow tee shirt, both smeared with spots of oil, gave the impression he would have made his living as a mechanic prior to his infection.

Now the prick would look to add a few more stains to his uniform, those of blood and saliva. He stepped into the small hallway and immediately spotted Jenna at the top of the stairs. The giant fiend began walking up. He moved slowly, as if each stride took a tremendous amount of energy. The bastard was a lot more sluggish than the newly-infected ones, but he wasn't alone.

With the door completely gone, a flood of cannibals poured into the basement hallway. Most were smaller and faster and they scurried to try and push past their very large leader at the front of the group. The only problem with this was that the musclebound mechanic was so big and had such a wide frame, he nearly blocked the entire path inside the narrow stairwell. Until he reached the top, the others could do little more than wait and fight amongst themselves to see who would be first to slide past the behemoth once an opening presented itself.

"We need to go," Jenna shouted, pulling herself to her feet. "Now- they're coming!"

"Shit!" Danny proclaimed, looking past Jenna to where a line of zombies were making their way up the steps. He turned to his sister and said, "Lucy, we need to get upstairs."

"I know," she answered before clubbing another savage in the head. "Just one second."

Between Lucy with her golf club and Danny with his machete, the siblings had managed to stop the freaks from getting in. The gap between the wall and the broken door frame was much wider than it had been just moments earlier, but each time one of the bastards tried to crawl in, Danny and Lucy were there to put it out of its misery. They'd killed a combined total of eight zombies so far. Their motionless bodies would drop where they'd been slain; eight cadavers in a sloppy pile, enough to clog up the crude opening to the building.

Next up was a young infected woman who'd already received three solid bashes to the head, courtesy of Lucy's putter. The girl zombie must have been about twenty-two years old. A thin layer of what looked like soot covered most of her face and neck. She was curvy with strawberry blonde hair and a set of C cups that threatened to pop right out of her skimpy, two-sizes-too-small tank top. If not for the head wounds, which were growing in number, she could have been quite attractive.

"Bitch!" Lucy cried out as she swung the club once more, slamming it into the side of her head. A sickening thud echoed through the lobby and the infected woman went limp, slumping onto the pile of putrid meat in front of the doorway.

The stack of bodies had become large enough to plug up the hole, at least for a minute or so until the others could push them out of the way. With any luck, it would keep them occupied long enough for the three survivors to get upstairs and lock themselves inside Danny's apartment. Now it was time for them to run.

"Go!" Jenna screamed. The big mechanic was only three steps from the top of the stairs. Had she waited any longer, he would have been able to reach out and grab her. Behind him, a squad of frothing maniacs stirred in anticipation as they tried to squeeze past the sizable brute.

The siblings did as instructed. Danny stepped aside to let his sister start up the stairs ahead of him. She ran, taking them two and three at a time to cover the distance as quickly as she could while still holding the golf club with both hands. She was several strides ahead of Danny as she reached the first-floor landing, making a left and heading up the next set of steps.

Danny was only halfway up the first set of stairs as Lucy rounded the corner and disappeared from his sight. He slowed to look over his shoulder and check on Jenna, only to find that she was right behind him on the second riser. From where he stood, he could see the top of the mechanic zombie's head as it took its first step into the lobby. Danny hopped up to the first-floor landing, just outside of Jim's apartment.

"You good?" he asked Jenna as she stepped up to meet him.

"Yeah," she answered breathlessly. "Let's just-"

Danny couldn't hear the rest of her sentence. Below them in the lobby, the doorway finally gave way to the enormous pressure leaning into it, buckling and collapsing under the weight of untold bodies. Glass shattered. Drywall popped and buckled. Aluminum beams twisted, groaned, and crashed to the floor.

Neither Danny nor Jenna said a word. They just ran. Jenna gave Danny a push on the shoulder, urging him to go first. Since she had the rifle, she should bring up the rear in case any of the fiends got too close.

Carrying only a machete, Danny was able to get up the stairs in no time. With only five more steps to the second-floor landing, he stopped again to check on Jenna when he heard her gasping and sounded like she was struggling with something. He took a step back and looked down the stairway to find that one of the zombies had caught up with her.

It was a girl, maybe seventeen or eighteen years old. She had on a soft white skirt and a pale pink top with a floral pattern embroidered along the left shoulder. The witch had her hair pulled up into a pair of double-braided buns. A layer of wet blood covered her right arm and a deep cut ran along the top of her left eye. The girl was thin and athletic, which might have been why she was able to get so far ahead of the rest of the pack. She had caught up to Jenna, who was now fighting to put some distance between herself and the drooling teenage ghoul.

"Jenna!" Danny cried out in a panic.

The infected teen was in close, snapping her jaws at Jenna's neck and face. Jenna, still holding the rifle, used it to try and fend off the crazed attacker. With one hand on the stock and one hand on the barrel, she pressed the forend into the monster's chest and pushed her away. The diseased bitch staggered back and barely kept herself from falling down the stairs. Just as the wench caught her balance, Jenna swung the weapon at her. The butt of the gun cracked the ghoul on the left side of her face, crunching bone and tearing away a patch of skin.

She didn't so much as wince. The rabid girl leaped forward with her hands out in front of her. Jenna swung again, missing her face but bashing the side of her neck. It was enough to make the savage lose some momentum, but not enough to take her out.

The feminine fiend threw all of her weight into Jenna, knocking them both to the floor. Jenna went down hard on her back with the rifle landing sideways across her chest. The predatory girl scrambled to her feet and pounced on her would-be prey. Jenna once again took hold of the weapon and held it out in front of her to shield her body.

By now, Danny had made his way back down the stairs to find the zombie girl on top of his friend. Jenna had her back pinned to the floor; her exposed skin mere inches from doom. Danny kept moving as he reached the landing at the bottom of the steps. Still running, he kicked his right leg out as hard as he could and drove his foot into the demon's ribs.

The impact sent the zombie girl toppling over, falling off of Jenna and landing on her side. Jenna kicked her feet, pushing herself backwards along the thin carpet to put a couple of feet between herself and the rabid hussy. The infected floozy wasted no time, steadying herself and preparing to bound after her victim once more. But Jenna wasn't going to give her the chance. She sat up, pulling her shoulders off the floor and leveling the rifle. Jenna pulled the trigger.

Danny jumped back in surprise. The now-thoughtless girl zombie slumped to the floor in a heap; lumpy and misshapen, soaked in blood like a stuck animal.

"Holy shit," Danny commented. "Are you alright?"

"Um," Jenna murmured.

"Danny?" a voice called from somewhere above them, followed by footsteps. It was Lucy. She started to come back down the stairs, but not far enough so that Danny could actually see her. "What's going on? I heard a gunshot, are you okay?"

"We're good," Danny answered. "Why don't you head inside, we'll be there in a sec."

"You've got the keys," Lucy shouted down the stairwell. "I'm locked out."

"Locked out," Danny said softly to keep his sister from hearing. "I hope I've got the keys."

"I can still hear you, dipshit," Lucy scolded from the second floor. "And you better have the damned keys."

"Um," Danny stalled while fishing in his pocket. "Yep- got 'em."

"Good, then hurry up and get up here," Lucy commanded. Her footsteps could then be heard moving back up the stairs to the second-floor landing.

"Yeah, yeah," he muttered. Danny turned back to Jenna and extended his free hand to her. "Here, let me help you up."

"I'm- I'm okay," Jenna stuttered. She waved his hand away, "You'd better not touch me. With all the blood and everything."

He might not have noticed if she hadn't said anything. Danny watched as she stood up from the floor. Jenna's shirt and pants both had several dark stains to match the red smears on her arms and neck. Burgundy strands formed a webbing between her fingers. A layer of blood clung to the contours of her hands and in the wrinkled skin of her knuckles.

"We'll get you inside and you can get cleaned up, take a shower if you'd like. I'm sure Lucy's got some clothes you can borrow- unless maybe you think you'd look better in something of mine," Danny offered with a chuckle. "But I should-"

"Danny, lookout!" Jenna interrupted.

Danny stepped back and got himself flat against the wall. Another fast-moving ghoul came racing up the steps; another one that was built like an athlete, but this one was male. He too must have managed to slip past the large man at the front of the pack.

The beast wore a blue track suit with zip-up top and black sleeves over a gray tee shirt. His blond hair was matted to his scalp by a viscous red goo. As he ran past, Danny was able to make out another distinguishing feature, his nose- or rather, the absence of a nose. Between the freak's eyes and mouth where his schnoz should have been, was a shallow hole in the center of what looked like chewed red bubble gum. Rivulets of blood and mucus streamed across its face.

Danny cursed himself for not being prepared. He should have been ready, should have sliced the zombie's throat or jammed his machete through its chest. The last thing he should have done was jump out of the way to give it a clear shot at Jenna. But there was a reason she'd told him to get out of the way. And before he could piece it together for himself, another shot rang out. The track-suit zombie collapsed to the floor with a brand new hole in his head.

"Jeez," he said to Jenna, who hadn't yet lowered her weapon. "Nice shot."

She nodded. "Yeah, thanks."

"There's more coming," Danny told her, not that it should come as any surprise. They could both hear the fevered drone of the crowd and the heavy footsteps of the diseased mechanic leading the way. "We should go."

Danny turned and started to head up the steps, content to leave the pair of newly-deceased bodies in the spots where they'd perished. Four risers up, Danny noticed that Jenna wasn't behind him. He stopped moving and called down to her.

"Aren't you coming?"

She was looking down at the floor, transfixed by the cadavers. Jenna didn't look up. She didn't respond.

"Jenna!" Danny called to her a little louder this time, not hiding the urgency in his tone. "What's the hold up? We need to go, like now."

"I can't," she said softly, without turning to meet his gaze.

"Why not?" Danny fairly demanded. "What's the problem?"

Nobody said anything for what felt like an eternity, although it had only been a few seconds in reality. In that brief moment of silence between them, the horde sounded louder than it ever had. The infected had conquered the building. It belonged to them now. By this point, there were hundreds of them standing between the tenement's only two exits and its three remaining occupants. Before the next minute was up, they would cover every inch of the building's common areas- including the stairways. They were closing in.

"Jenna, we need to move!" Danny shrieked at her; his voice somewhere between a plea and a command. "Let's-"

Jenna interrupted with words too soft and muffled for Danny to understand. She raised her head slightly but still refused to look at him directly. Behind her, a greasy jumpsuit came into view. Danny could see the mechanic climbing the final flight of stairs with a writhing troop of ghouls following closely and trying to sneak past him.

"They got me," Jenna admitted. She still hadn't looked up from the floor.

"Got you? What do you mean?" he asked, pointing to the meat husk in the track suit. Danny's voice cracked and he felt a growing pressure in his chest. "He didn't even get close to you."

"Not him," Jenna clarified. She lifted her left arm and revealed a set of tooth-sized puncture holes on her forearm, about two inches above the wrist. The wounds were barely visible, hidden by a thick layer of tacky blood. But they were there nonetheless, and there was no denying what they were. Jenna raised the gun, using the barrel to point at the school-girl zombie. "She got me."

Danny's mouth hung open. He couldn't speak and he couldn't move. The seething mob was now only a few feet away.

"You need to go," she told him. Jenna finally looked up at him; her eyes revealing an expression of untold dread and infinite sorrow.

"But, I-"

"Now," she snapped. Jenna was trying to sound firm, but the anguish had not left her features. "I'm sorry, Danny."

There was one round left in the rifle and it was for her. Danny watched in petrified awe as Jenna turned the weapon around and placed the barrel under her chin. A final gunshot erupted just as the mass of infected bodies descended upon her lifeless form. Jenna vanished beneath the monsters, and she was gone forever.

Chapter 52

Drip... splat. It sounded like drops of water falling from a leaky faucet. But Jim knew better. He didn't have to see it to know what it was. There was no sink around. No bathtub, no shower. No spigot in need of a plug. And no reason to turn around.

So he didn't. He kept facing forward. Jim stood on the threshold and looked out across the lawn. He wasn't focused on any particular thing. He was just kind of staring into the night. Staring, and listening.

There wasn't a lot to be heard. No traffic. No voices. No televisions or radios. He'd catch the rustling of leaves every so often when the wind picked up. Jim could also hear the faint shuffling of feet being dragged over cement somewhere off in the distance. However, there was one sound that resonated above all the others. Drip... splat.

The average human body contains nearly a gallon and a half of blood. Losing around forty percent is usually enough to be fatal. Jim got to see firsthand what it looks like when that happens. No matter how hard he tried to avoid looking, Jim couldn't help but see blood.

It was hard to believe that so much could come out of only two bodies. Everything was covered. The doors, the walls, everything. A pool on the floor had started to dry. Bubbles on its surface congealed to form hollow crimson spheres. It was even on the ceiling. And every so often, a heavy red droplet would fall and splash into the sodden carpet. Drip... splat.

The drips came fast at first but gradually slowed as time passed. Jim wasn't sure how much time had gone by since he'd collapsed to the floor, but it must have been at least an hour. He'd kept his head down with his face hidden, tucked between bent knees and shielded by his arms. Jim couldn't bring himself to look at the slaughter that lie before him.

He too had gotten hit with his fair share of spatter. Dark stains covered his shirt and shorts. A pink crust formed on the bare parts of his arms and face. Sticky and thick in his hair, he could feel warms globules tugging at his scalp when he moved.

The blood had almost certainly gotten into his eyes. And probably his mouth, or into some scrape or opening in the skin he hadn't noticed before. With each passing minute, Jim grew more and more convinced that it was only a matter of time before he succumbed to the infection. His head spun and his innards churned. Was that part of it? Is that what happened just before he turned into one of those... things? Was he about to become a zombie?

And then what? Would any trace of his personality remain? Would he know on some level what was happening to him? Would he retain some awareness and be forced to witness himself turn into a ravenous monster? Or would his mind, his entire being, be gone forever? He hoped it would be. Jim prayed his consciousness would leave and take his suffering with it. There was no way to know for sure, not yet. He could only sit and cry alone while he waited for the infection to take him away.

But it never did. And eventually, there were no more tears. The well was empty and so was Jim's stomach. A sense of unrelenting agony, the rancid stench of corpses; at a certain point it was too much for his guts to bear. He lurched forward and heaved. There wasn't much to push out, only a mouthful of gastric acid and yellow phlegm.

His feet hadn't been quick enough to avoid it. The thick batch of clear and orange fluid grazed his shin and sneaker before it hit the ground. Spongy clumps clung to his leg hair and a thin vomit broth soaked into his socks. It was going to leave a mark, but what's one more stain? All of his clothes were already ruined and no amount of scrubbing and washing would ever remove the brown and burgundy stains.

Jim coughed and spat out another viscous wad. It landed on the carpet with a plop. The warm layer of fresh puke slid down his leg toward his ankle and he could feel himself starting to gag again. The slimy texture on every surface, the stink of death and regurgitation, the confined space and stagnant air; he couldn't take it for much longer.

After spitting out one last ball of mucus and sludge, Jim leaned forward and pulled himself to his feet. He knelt to retrieve his unloaded shotgun, making a point to keep his eyes fixed on the ground in front of him while he moved. Each footstep landed with a squish and left behind wet red tread marks that matched the bottom of his shoes. The blood seeped into his sneakers. It was tacky and made his toes stick together.

Taking the shotgun by the barrel, Jim swiped it under his armpit and tried to wipe off some of the blood. He faced the wall while he did this, determined to keep his eyes off of Lindsey and to never see what had become of her. If he had to look at her- if he had to see what he had allowed to happen to her, Jim might not have the patience to wait for the virus to take his life.

So instead, he had just watched his feet move while he walked to the exit, which is where he's been standing for the past ten minutes or so. Jim used the inside of the door frame to scrape dried blood from the palms of his hands. He was still looking forward, still unable to face her. Jim had promised to protect her, to keep her safe and take care of her. But just like with everything else he tried to do, he failed.

He should have known better than to promise her anything. Maybe she should have known better than to trust him. But in either case, the blame fell squarely upon Jim. Her fate was in his hands and he let her down in the worst way imaginable. Lindsey was dead and it was his fault. And now he didn't even have the spine to look at her, to face what he had done. Worthless coward.

Jim felt like he should say something, like he should say goodbye or tell her how sorry he was or offer some sort of eulogy. But he couldn't bring himself to do that either. He wouldn't know what to say or even where to begin. Plus, that would mean spending more time here, and Jim had already been here for too long. There was somewhere else he wanted to be, somewhere he *needed* to be.

He still didn't know whether the infection was coming for him. But if it was, Jim wasn't going to keep sitting around waiting for it to happen. He was going to do something. He was going to strike back the only way he could think of. And to do that, he needed to go home.

The sound of shuffling feet had grown louder. To his left, Jim could see three slow-moving ghouls staggering down the road in his direction. There were at least two more behind them but they were all more than sixty feet away and they were too slow to be of any concern.

With a deep breath, Jim stepped through the doorway and onto the stoop. He thought that he should pull the door closed behind him, but immediately reconsidered. There was still a chance he might accidentally catch a glimpse of Lindsey soaked in her own blood; her face wrenched in terror. He decided to leave the door open.

Jim walked across the lawn and got into the Pontiac. Tossing the shotgun in the back seat, he pulled the door closed and started the engine. Jim put the car in reverse and backed out of the driveway, eager to put some distance between himself and this horrible place. Once he was back on

345

more familiar roads, he couldn't help but drive faster and faster.

Eighty-five. Ninety. Ninety-five. The red needle continued to climb until the speedometer read one hundred miles per hour. And it kept going. Jim kept his foot heavy on the gas pedal. Despite some mild objection from the engine, which came in the form of an occasional sputtering or slight hesitation from the transmission, the Pontiac continued to charge ahead.

He took a big drag off his cigarette and exhaled slowly to let the smoke gradually pour from his mouth and then gently drift outside through the car's open window. Jim was on the bridge over the canal. Just like earlier that day, nobody was around. The shoreline looked peaceful and quiet.

This is where he'd stopped to call his parents. It's also the place where he promised Lindsey he'd quit smoking. He meant it when he said it. But now- at this point, why the Hell should he bother? There were dozens of things that would kill him quicker than cigarettes would, and a fair number of those things were now less than a mile away.

The end of Twin Cities Boulevard was coming up quick. Jim flew through the intersection and pulled to the right when the road split off into two directions. He was back on Colvin Boulevard. He was almost home. There would be no hesitation this time. No second-guessing. No passenger to question his decision. And anyone in their right mind would have questioned this decision.

Rage had taken over. His grief and regret were still there, but it was like the volume had been turned down. It felt better this way, it felt *right*. His body seemed to agree. His hands had stopped shaking. The tension in his chest abated as his heart rate returned to normal. He had even stopped sweating. Well, he was sweating a little less. The anger-induced stupor helped put him at ease with what lie ahead and Jim felt okay with how everything would end.

As he took his last puff and tossed the cigarette butt out the window, his mouth felt dry and tasted like ash. His lips were salty and chapped. What he wouldn't give for a nice cold Newcastle Ale or a big frosty mug of root beer, or even a lukewarm sip of water. Jim glanced down at the cup holder. It was empty. He sighed and rolled his eyes. Of course it was empty.

Jim shook his head and tried to ignore the rough texture of his tongue as it brushed the roof of his parched mouth. It wasn't just the thirst that irked him. There was something else, some sort of fleeting memory or elusive concept that was triggered when he thought about having a drink. He just couldn't put his finger on what it was. Maybe it was nothing. Maybe he was going crazy.

"Meh, who cares," Jim said aloud.

A chime sounded from somewhere under the dashboard and a small orange light turned on next to the fuel gauge. The dial was nearly on empty. Not a problem. Jim had seen this light plenty of times and never actually ran out of gas, even when he continued driving for several miles before stopping to fill up the tank. At this point, he didn't have too far to go.

His final stop was approaching quickly. Jim steered around crashed cars and mounds of flesh as he sped past Kenney Field and its collection of corpses. The abandoned video store and the now-derelict coffee shop went by in a shadowy blur. He passed under the darkened traffic light at the Brighton Road intersection. Jim was mere yards away from his ultimate destination.

It was not going to be a warm homecoming. The apartment building was now in sight and there were at least two hundred plague-carrying savages waiting to greet him. Jim had been counting on this. Now that some time had gone by, it seemed less likely that the infection was coming for him. Now it was Jim who was coming for the infected. He was going to take out as many of those motherfuckers as he could until his time was finally up. And he wanted them to know it.

346

Jim pressed a hand into the center of the car's steering wheel and the horn blared. He demanded their full attention. These bastards were going to know exactly who was coming for them. They were going to look him in the eye and see a rage as hot as Hell's fire glaring back. Those at the outer ring of the horde were already turning around and facing his direction.

He pressed down hard on the gas pedal but found it was already pinned to the floor. Jim released the horn and grabbed the steering wheel with both hands. The pale skin over his knuckles turned white as a sheet of paper. He took in a deep breath and it felt like his lungs might explode as he readied himself for the collision.

Then, in an instant before impact, it came to him. *Water.* It was when he was thinking about water. That word made something click inside his brain. It was huge, but also so simple. How stupid he must have been for not seeing it sooner. Renee's story about her neighbor using a garden hose to fend off an attacker, the brutes in the supermarket avoiding the puddles on the floor, the fact that there were never any zombies near the canal; it couldn't have been more obvious.

"Holy shit!" Jim exclaimed. "They're afraid of water!"

Fin

-The End-

Thank you for reading

Late Arrival

By Christopher Ross